TRUE TO THE GAME

OMNIBUS

TRUE TO THE GAME

OMNIBUS

Teri Woods

AMISTAD

An Imprint of HarperCollinsPublishers

TRUE TO THE GAME. Copyright © 1998 by Teri Woods.

TRUE TO THE GAME II. Copyright © 2007 by Teri Woods.

TRUE TO THE GAME III. Copyright © 2008 by Teri Woods.

Foreword copyright © 2026 by Teri Woods.

All rights reserved. No part of this book may be used or reproduced in any manner whatsoever without written permission except in the case of brief quotations embodied in critical articles and reviews. For information, address HarperCollins Publishers, 195 Broadway, New York, NY 10007.

HarperCollins books may be purchased for educational, business, or sales promotional use. For information, please email the Special Markets Department at SPsales@harpercollins.com.

harpercollins.com

Originally published separately as *True to the Game* in the United States of America in 1998 by Teri Woods Publishing LLC, *True to the Game II* in the United States of America in 2007 by Grand Central Publishing, and *True to the Game III* in the United States of America in 2008 by Grand Central Publishing

FIRST AMISTAD PAPERBACK PUBLISHED 2026

Designed by Jason Kayser

Library of Congress Cataloging-in-Publication Data has been applied for.

ISBN 978-0-06-348961-5

Printed in the United States of America

$PrintCode

Contents

Foreword

*T*rue to the Game has represented so many different things for so many different people. For me it represents a piece of time and a journey of relentless survival. What seemed to be a story that no one cared about, or was deemed irrelevant because of the way it was written, became a cult classic, taking on a life of its own, far beyond my imagination. For me to represent a space in time and to share these characters' lives has meant the world to me. But to also represent the thoughts, the struggles, and the realities that the inner city has faced has always been my truth in words.

Having these first three books packaged together for the first time and getting ready to share *True to the Game 4* with you all (soon!!) means so much. To be a voice no matter how small, a reflection of what once was, and to make sure this book turns a new page and a new chapter for the characters that folks have cherished all these years. The pressure is real, and for me the stakes are high. I know some of you know my journey of rejection, selling books on the streets of New York and harassing you on 125th Street to buy my book. Then harassing you when I saw you again to read it. Not only did you read, but you also named your children after my characters, you invited me into your homes, and some of you even gave me a place to stay so I wouldn't sleep in my car. You were everything to me and you always will be. I'll never forget the love and acceptance you showed me. I already know what is going to happen when *True to the Game 4* is released. I already know how busy and how hectic and, for some, how the struggle is real trying to cope and survive, especially in the inner city. But I also know that for a short time, I'll have you back with me, and you will be reading this book from prison cells, buses, and planes traveling to faraway lands. And that for me is everything, it's priceless.

For my first-time readers, I say welcome. For all others, I say you're finally back where you belong, where we once started out of the trunk of my car, and I'm so glad you're back home with me, with this book, exactly where you belong.

Enjoy the journey.

As always, I thank you for your support.

Stay true,
Teri Woods

TRUE
TO THE
GAME
TERI WOODS

This book is dedicated in loving memory of my father, Clinton "Brother" Woods, and to my mom and my stepdad. Thank you for being there. You are always there and you are always right.

Jessica, you are what life is all about. I love you.

—Mommy

Game Anthem

As you struggle to hustle, taking gain after loss, don't get discouraged. Just remember who's boss. Handle your business and always watch your back. Don't sleep on the stickup boys waiting to attack. As you creep through the streets, the crack fiends holler. They've done any- and everything just to give you those dollars. I hope it will last. I hope you make something of it. Time will tell if something good can come from it. But as you count the highs, count the lows, too, and whatever you do, forever remain true. What choice do you have? It's in you by nature. Your only fault is . . .

Being a player.

A Night Out

Harlem, New York. It was the summer of 1988, and it was hot. Too hot. Harlem had to be the hottest place on the planet in the summertime. Exiting off Riverside Drive onto 125th Street, Gena was amazed to see so many people standing outside a nightclub. "Damn, look at that limousine, girl. We need to be with them!" Laughing out loud, she was now suddenly anxious to get farther uptown.

Sahirah looked smug. "We damn sure do."

It was amazing. There was nothing like 125th, a mini Greek playland in the middle of Harlem. Gena had no understanding. It wasn't like Philly. It was larger, and the niggas looked like Eric B. and Rakim, with humungous gold chains and diamond medallions the size of bread plates. If it was meant to represent wealth, that shit did its job. And Gena liked it.

She gazed at the scantily clad girls who wore sexy and revealing clothing. Gena craved to be among them, fucking with niggas and getting her life on. New York was the shit, even though there was no way she could ever live there. The niggas, the cars, and the lifestyle were all too fast for her. The magnitude was large, along with the number of men.

Gena didn't know if it was the rims, the tires, or something else, but even the cars looked different in New York. The dashboards were customized and they had Louis Vuitton and MCM leather seats, not to mention the detailed piping and thousand-dollar sound systems. Everything about New York turned her the fuck on, especially the guys. And to think, this was all so normal for them.

Suddenly, Sahirah did an about-face and shouted, "No! Look at that BMW. Is he the man of life or what?"

Riding by, there he was with a squad of brothers deep in his Beemer. Sahirah couldn't contain herself. Leaning out the window, she yelled, "Hi!" Turning back to Gena, she grabbed her arm. "Girl, don't he look good?"

"Sahirah! Bitch, is you crazy? This is Harlem!" Gena tried to pull the top of her friend's body back into the car. "You can't wave at these people up here!"

"Oh, shit, Gena. He's pullin' over."

"Yeah, but he's all the way on the opposite side of the street."

Against Gena's protests, Sahirah made a U-turn in traffic, causing every moving vehicle to screech to a standstill so that she could meet the guy driving the BMW. She waved and called out to the driver as she double-parked behind them.

He stepped out of the car, fine as wine, and walked toward the girls. "What's up?"

"What's up?" Sahirah repeated.

"What's your name?"

Getting out of the car, she replied, "I'm Sahirah. What's yours?"

"Rasun."

"I see you have Pennsylvania tags. You from Philly?" Sahirah asked.

"Yeah. Tell your girlfriend to get out of the car."

Gena climbed out and chimed, "I'm Gena."

Rasun openly admired what he saw, looking her up and down.

"What's up, Gena? I'm Rasun." He nodded his head toward the

BMW. "That's my homie Quadir in the car. Why don't you go over there and talk to him?"

Gena crossed her arms over her chest. "What does he look like?"

Rasun chuckled. "Go and see."

How convenient, she thought. *Sahirah gets the driver, and I get the passenger.*

When she reached the car, she announced, "Hi. I'm Gena. Your friend told me I should come over here and talk to you."

Quadir studied Gena as though he'd been introduced to a goddess. "My name's Quadir." After another minute, he thought he should say something and stop staring. "So, do you live in New York?"

"No, Philly. What about you?"

"North Philly."

"Oh. I live out West."

"What are you doing up here?"

Gena thought quickly about how to cover her and Sahirah's manhunting designs on this side of the Lincoln Tunnel. "My aunt is sick, and I came up here to spend the day with her." *It's a little white lie*, she told herself. *It can't hurt.* "What about you?"

"Business . . . had to take care of some business," he told her, thinking about the kilos of cocaine in his trunk. "What's a pretty girl like you doing out here in this big city all alone?"

"I'm not alone." Gena's head was reeling from Quadir's blatant adoration, and every square inch of her body sported a blush. "I'm with my girlfriend Sahirah."

"Oh," he said, looking at Sahirah as if to say, *How the hell will she save you?* Shifting back to reality, remembering the kilos of cocaine in the trunk of the Beemer, he said, "We got to go, but I want to see you tomorrow. Will you be in Philly?"

"Yes. Wanna switch numbers?"

"Most definitely."

She said goodbye to Quadir and pocketed his number. Even

though he wasn't driving, he was nice *and* he was dark-skinned; that was a plus. Not to mention the diamond bezel Rolex on his wrist.

Damn, the man is dark as night, and his beard and his mustache are so sexy. She would undoubtedly be trying to see him tomorrow. In that moment, the next day felt like a lifetime away.

Gena and Sahirah partied hard and met many guys that night, but Quadir kept invading her thoughts. Before they got on the turnpike, they went uptown to 145th Street to get a Willie Burger. Gena *loved* Willie Burgers. Nothing could fuck with them in the middle of the night. No lie, like 125th Street, the saga continued. Mad money niggas were everywhere.

She got some gas from the station down the street and was ready to make her journey back home. Crossing the George Washington Bridge, she couldn't help but glance over at New York City's skyline. New York was the most happening town she knew of and she always hated leaving.

When they finally reached exit 6, Gena thought, *Home, sweet home.* It was about 5:30 a.m. when they reached Sahirah's mother's house. Gena parked the rental car and looked at her best friend and the slobber and spit dribbling out of her mouth.

"Sahirah, wake up. We're home." She nudged her leg. Sahirah was out, and Gena realized it would be a struggle to bring her back to life. After Gena spent another few minutes calling out to her friend, Sahirah finally wiped her mouth and opened her eyes.

"Come on, let's go. I'm tired. You've been sleeping. I haven't."

"Oh, did you see the EPMD guy, Erick?"

"How could I have missed him? He almost hit your simple ass when you jumped in front of his Benz! You really have some serious issues to deal with."

"Don't even try it. You got nerve. You're jealous 'cause I got Rasun's number. Don't be mad. Besides, I saw you talking to—what's his name? Quadir. Yeah, him."

Sahirah talked as if Gena had behaved as poorly as she had. "What about this guy? Look at our picture." Sahirah held up a Polaroid for Gena to see. "Now, tell me he isn't all that. I could've sucked his dick right out there on 125th Street."

"I know you could have, *and* I'm sure you will," Gena stated with much sarcasm as she shook her head.

"And that motherfucker in the Range Rover? If it wasn't for you, I would've really got my young life on."

"I'm sure you would have."

"Well, what did you think of him?" Sahirah insisted. "Do you think he was cute, or what?"

"Sahirah! Think the fuck of who? I don't know who you're talking about."

Sahirah paid her no mind. Once they were inside the house, Sahirah started counting the telephone numbers she'd collected over the course of the evening.

"Seven numbers!" she hollered.

Gena couldn't help but gawk at her friend in disbelief. "I'm going to sleep."

Gena and Sahirah had been friends since they were five years old. They'd both grown up down in Richard Allen, the projects that niggas wouldn't dare venture to unless they were from there. When Sahirah was twelve, her family moved out to West Philly to North Fifty-Fourth and Race Street. Even though they didn't go to school together after Sahirah moved, she and Gena had always kept in touch.

When Gena turned seventeen, her uncle Michael got her an apartment on Chancellor Street. He paid all her bills. No one in her family knew. Gena had pleaded with her uncle for years to move her out of the projects. He had really been there for her, and whenever she wanted something, he would help her. He kept her in a rental car and gave her money whenever she asked for it. She was fortunate to have someone in her family who'd made it and could show her the way. Plenty of people her age had no one they could turn to in times of need.

That was one thing Gena could say for herself. Even though she was raised in the projects, she had family who believed in taking care of the kids. Some people didn't have family like that, and Gena understood that. Some parents didn't give a fuck one way or the other. *Do what you gonna do, 'cause you gonna fuck something up anyway.* That was the attitude. Half of Gena's friends had parents who said, "Hey, we got a party to go to," and that's where they were, at the party partying. Or if they weren't at the party, they were too busy getting high.

Then you had the motherfuckers sitting right there in the house not giving a damn whether the kids were in the house, in the street, hungry, or safe. A whole generation sat back and said, "Fuck it. I'm not gonna raise my kids." Hence, the saga began.

Shit was rough as hell in Philly. That's why Gena relished her little trips to other cities. Gena and Sahirah had done their share of city-hopping. Seeing that there were other people out there, not just in West Philly or the projects, was positive reinforcement for them. They went to the Baltimore Harbor and met niggas with boats. They went to D.C. and liked the guys but couldn't take the go-go scene. They traveled to Atlanta and met brothers with pets. From Miami to New York, they'd been there. They constantly received flyers for out-of-town parties in the mail. Gena was into the party scene, and life, for her, had been one big party full of the same faces, places, and circles.

When the Junior Mafia began spreading cocaine throughout the city, money was flowing like water from a faucet, and niggas were givin' it up as if it were leaves on trees. Gena's whole entourage of male companions were young, handsome, and very wealthy drug dealers. Hustlers who loved to come on a set and simply break a nigga off. It was too good to be true—and don't talk about sex. You were definitely getting broke down for dropping down, no questions asked. Gena and Sahirah dropped down, *way down,* for the lifestyle they were living. The only way not to give the sisters their props was if they weren't getting paper. Thoroughbreds of the streets, getting money was what it was all about, and you were supposed to get it any way you could.

Across town, on a little side street, sat a burgundy Cadillac. The driver was eagerly and carefully aware of the surrounding sounds. He'd been sitting in the car for three hours, waiting in anticipation. The movement of a tree branch blowing in the wind grasped his attention. He turned back to the gray screen door across the street; *3601,* he thought to himself. Deciding that would be a good number to play, he reached into his shirt pocket and pulled out a baggie of cocaine. He dumped a tiny pile between his thumb and pointer finger and held his hand up to his nose. After he fed his nostrils, he licked his hand clean. On the seat beside him lay an Uzi semiautomatic. He picked up the gun and removed the clip. Restlessly, he replaced it, already knowing it was loaded. The gray screen door flew open and four guys emerged. They hopped into an MPV, never noticing the burgundy Cadillac following them.

The next morning, Gena woke up to the sound of Sahirah's four siblings acting like they were out of their minds. "What time is it?" she asked as Mrs. Bowden walked by the doorway.

"Oh, good morning, Gena. It's nine thirty, baby. You want some breakfast?"

Hell no, thought Gena. *I want some sleep.* "No, ma'am," she replied. "I have to go. Tell Sahirah to call me." Gena was quickly out of there.

She stopped to get her favorite pancakes on the way to her house. At the intercom, she hollered, "No pork! Do not put pork anywhere near my food. Do you understand? No pork. I don't want to see it."

The poor girl at the window looked as if she had something to say but didn't.

Gena gave her the money and waited for her food and change.

A burgundy Cadillac with black tinted windows sped across the parking lot. Suddenly, and out of nowhere, thunderous gunfire jolted Gena out of her reverie and continued to echo through her body. The bullets sent a screeching sound through her body as the gunman met his target, aiming for four guys in an MPV.

Gena's mind yelled, *Run, duck down, hide, get the fuck away,* settling on nothing until her survival instincts took her through the natural progression of ducking down and getting her ass out of there. She sped away from the takeout window and tried to exit the parking lot when the burgundy Cadillac Deville with gold trim, tinted windows, and spoked rims cut her off.

She slammed on the brakes and missed hitting the driver's door panel by inches. For one long moment, she stared right at the driver. He had an Uzi semiautomatic in his left hand and his right hand on the steering wheel. He glared at her, and their eyes locked. Gena recognized him but did not recall from where. She sat frozen at the stop sign, wondering whether she should speak.

The Cadillac driver pointed the Uzi straight at her head, intending to drop her ass, too, and pulled the trigger. Nothing happened, so he tried the shit again but the clip was empty. The thought went through him, *Yeah, dis is her lucky day.* He tossed the gun on the floor mat and sped away.

Gena sat there shaken and confused. She'd never had a gun pointed at her before. She assumed that her beauty had saved her. Little did the simpleton realize, she'd almost become a statistic.

Her heart was pounding like hailstones on a windowpane. Talking her hands into obedience, she wrapped her shaky fingers around the steering wheel and instructed her right foot to come back to life and ease up on the brake. She carefully moved slowly toward the exit for Fifty-Second Street, looking both ways. She drove in silence, creeping down the street without listening to the radio.

She kept checking the rearview mirror to see if anyone was behind her. She couldn't believe what had happened. Man, was her mind playing tricks on her? Not at all. The burgundy Cadillac was so clear in her mind, and the license plate—MAFIA23—was even clearer.

Reaching her favorite parking spot between the two trees in front of her door, she noticed Jamal's Pathfinder parked down the street. She looked closely at her boyfriend sleeping in his SUV outside her door. She walked over and knocked on the window.

Jamal jumped out of what looked like a very uncomfortable sleeping position. "Where the fuck you been?"

Gena looked at him like she didn't know what he was talking about. "I spent the night over Sahirah's, Jamal."

"Oh, that gold-diggin' bitch with the matching hat and shovel?" Climbing out of the car, he continued. "I thought I told you I didn't want you hanging around her!"

"Jamal, this is a free country and I can do what I—"

The words were lost as her body made its way to the pavement with the force of Jamal's backhand. Then he picked her up and began his accusations.

"You been with another man, bitch! Ain't no way you was sleeping with Sahirah unless you and Sahirah is fucking each other! Shit, I been out this motherfucker all night waiting for you!"

The tears had already begun. "I wasn't with nobody."

"You're a motherfucking liar! Why you got to lie?" The question was stressed with another pop upside her head, causing her to spin around and fall into some bushes.

Deciding it was best to remain in contact with the earth, she pleaded with him, "Jamal, I wasn't doin' nothing."

She looked up and spotted Ms. Gladys watching everything from her third-floor window.

Rising to face him, she said, "Jamal, I'm sorry. I won't hang out with her anymore."

"Where the fuck did you go?"

"I didn't go nowhere."

Slap was the sound that could be heard as he hit her again.

"Gena, don't make me kill you out this motherfucker. Where you been? I said, where the fuck you been all night long?"

Too scared to say she had gone to a party in Harlem, she stared at him.

"I'm getting tired of your shit."

"Jamal, I don't want to fight with you. I'm hungry, and I'm tired."

"That's because your trick ass was out in the street all night."

The accusations gathered like storm clouds in her eyes. "I'm not no trick, Jamal."

Focusing directly on his right eye, she realized any feeling she had for him was gone. She was ready to kick him in his nuts and run for safety, as usual. The nigga was crazy; it was in his eyes. It wouldn't make any difference to her if he walked away and she never saw him again.

Jamal had been in her life for a year and a half. He was possessive, controlling, and an overall nuisance. She'd met him down in North Philly on Twenty-Second and Ridge in a pool hall. He was sweet and nice in the beginning, nothing like now.

The day they met was dreary, and when it started raining, he offered her a ride home. Gena didn't miss any free meals, so when he asked if she wanted something to eat, she immediately accepted his offer.

The next day, he was at her door. She was only wearing a towel and shower cap when she opened it. "Hi! What are you doing here?"

"Get dressed. I'm taking you shopping."

He didn't need to tell her twice. After she got dressed, they visited every boutique and shoe store that came to his mind. This all made Gena very happy. *What luck,* she thought.

When they arrived back at her place, he was more than welcome to come in since that was the only way she could get all her bags inside. Once she finished poring over her purchases, hardly remembering buying any of it, and put everything away, she realized she was happier than she'd ever been but didn't know why.

Jamal rolled a joint, which he referred to as a *spliff,* and lit it as she collapsed onto the sofa.

"I'm so tired. Jamal, why'd you take me shopping and buy all this stuff for me?" She really looked confused about the entire situation; the weed was taking effect. "I mean, you don't even know me."

"That's okay. You're gonna let me get to know you, right?"

"Right." *Anything you say,* she thought, looking totally satisfied at her diminished closet space.

She passed the spliff back to Jamal, after choking half to death, and decided she'd had enough. For no particular reason, she jumped up and shut the mini blinds. Jamal realized she'd become paranoid and was determined he wouldn't miss his shot before she was too far gone. He tried to chill her out, and before she even realized what happened, they were on the floor kissing and Jamal was pulling at her clothes.

"What are you doing?" She realized she should stop him. "Don't you think we should get to know each other? Shouldn't you wear a condom? We don't really know each other all that well."

He silenced her with a kiss, and she realized her struggles were in vain. Before she knew it, he was inside her.

"Doesn't it feel good?" he whispered.

She could only think, *You're fucking a stranger, and you need to get him off you.*

Out of fear he would get mad and take back all he'd bought her, she got into the groove. Before it was all over, he was asking, "Who's pussy is this?"

And she answered, "Yours."

After dinner, Jamal dropped her off. For the third time, she looked over her new clothes, then took a bath and slipped into one of her new nightgowns. No sooner had she sat down to calculate the total of the price tags than the phone rang.

"Hello?"

It was *him*. "What are you doing?"

"Nothing. I just finished taking a bath and I'm wearing the Victoria's Secret nightgown you bought me."

"Gena, I can't sleep."

"Why? What's the matter?"

"Because I can't. I'm coming to get you."

"When? Are you joking me?"

"No, I'm on my way."

Before she could protest, Gena heard the dial tone.

Hmm. Can't sleep without me, she mused. *My shit is the bomb.*

In twenty minutes, Jamal rang her bell. She was dressed, packed, and ready to go. Thereafter, Jamal refused to sleep without her. He wanted her there morning, noon, and night. He took her to school and picked her up. It got to the point where, if she went to the bathroom, he was there, sitting on the edge of the tub. Watching her. My, how things had changed.

Now he was beating on her in the middle of Chancellor Street. Gena wiped the tears from her eyes as Jamal got into his SUV, belittling and demeaning her. Looking at her hands, she saw blood from where she'd fallen into the bushes. She noted the neighbors as she walked to the steps of her house, watching them all standing on their porches and peeping out of windows.

"Nosy motherfuckers. And didn't nobody help me."

Inside her apartment, Gena went straight to her mirror. She

looked horrible. Her face was red, her head was pounding, and she was hungry. Her pale skin, all sore and scratched, throbbed with an achy pain, and the tears returned. She had to break away from Jamal.

It was like he owned her, but what could she do about it? How could she break away from him? Without him, she had nothing. With him, she was miserable with money. She needed a plan. On the one hand, if she tried to stop seeing Jamal, it might cause her more harm than good. On the other hand, eighteen-year-old Gena wanted to have some fun.

After entering her bedroom and turning on the television, she lay down on her bed. She was so tired, she was falling asleep, when she heard the news bulletin. An anchorwoman was standing at the very restaurant she had just left. Behind her sat a navy-blue Swiss cheese MPV in the parking lot. Three people had died at the restaurant on Fifty-Second Street, and one was listed as being in critical condition. If not for an empty clip, she'd have been one of them.

Gena offered a prayer to God, thanking Him for His many blessings.

Recovery

Waking from a peaceful sleep, Gena immediately dialed her neighbor's phone.

"Hi, Markita."

"Hey, baby, I heard what happened. You all right?"

"I've felt better."

"I been calling you and calling you all damn day."

"I was asleep. You got anything over there to eat?"

"Girl, please. It's the first of the month. You want some dinner?"

"Is it dinnertime?"

"It's six thirty, Gena. You slept all day."

Markita brought Gena pork chops smothered in gravy, mashed potatoes, and cabbage.

"Damn, Kita, I don't fuck with no swine. Why you bring me this? You might as well have brought me a plate of shit."

"I can take that food home, sister. You don't have to eat it."

Gena sat there hungry as hell, looking at the food as if it were something a diseased yak left behind. Her mind was telling her one thing, but her stomach had a more urgent message. After a very short debate, her stomach won, and she ate the potatoes and cabbage after removing the pork from the plate. Markita had to tell her to slow down.

"Gena, I want to talk to you about that man of yours, honey. If it's one thing I do know, if he beats you up once, he'll do it again. Gena, you don't need no man like that in your life. You're young and pretty and you could do better for yourself."

Gena listened while she finished eating her food. Markita would have to go 'cause she wasn't about to listen to some shit she already knew. Suddenly, there was a knock at the door.

"Damn, what if that's your loony tunes–ass man?"

Gena headed for the door. "You got my back, right?"

She relaxed when she peeked out the peephole and saw who it was.

"What's up?" Gena said, opening the door for her cousin Gary.

"What's up? Damn, what happened to your face?" He shook his head in disbelief, already knowing Jamal had hit her again.

She told him the story, waiting to hear Gary say he was gonna go hunt his ass down and fuck him up for her. Instead, he reminded her that he had warned her about him when she first started seeing him. He also reminded her that the boy was large.

Gary didn't know what to do. He wasn't trying to fuck with Jamal like that.

"Man, stay the fuck away from him," he said. As an afterthought, he asked, "You want me to tell Gah Git?"

Gena thought of her grandmother Gah Git. After Gena's mother died when she was four, Gah Git had raised her. Gary, Gena, Bria, and Brianna were all first cousins who came up together. Bria and Brianna were two years younger than her, and Gary was a year older. The years had been hard and rough on her grandmother, who had raised four boys and three girls. At one point, there were twelve of them in a three-bedroom project apartment, including three of Gah Git's children and their children.

So she fussed a lot and prayed a lot. But her propensity for sending her grandchildren to the store night and day because she "gotta git" this and "gotta git" that earned her the nickname "Gotta Git," which progressed naturally into "Gah Git."

"Tell Gah Git? Hell no, don't tell her. Please, *whatever you do*, don't tell nobody in the family 'cause they'll run right back to Gah Git and tell her."

"Don't worry, Gena. Shit gonna be all right." Handing her a couple hundred dollars before he left, he advised her, "Just stay away from Jamal. You hear me?"

Markita went outside on the porch while Gena listened to her answering machine.

Hollering outside, Gena announced, "He called!"

"Who called?"

"This guy I met last night."

"See, that's why you got your ass kicked."

"Shut up before I don't let you catch this." Since she started fucking around with Jamal, Gena had developed a habit. She reached the porch and began rolling a spliff.

"Okay, but that's still why you got your ass kicked."

The sun was going down, and the sky was a beautiful orange. Markita and Gena sat out on that porch and smoked the spliff, talking about Jamal and the ass-kicking he'd given her.

"Was the neighbors looking?"

"Girl, the Vietnamese people were watching. Everybody was rooting for you, though, especially when he knocked you into the bushes. Shoot, Tonya said she thought you was gonna kick him and run, like before. Girl, that was some funny shit, the last time y'all was out here."

Gena and Markita sat there laughing and telling jokes about Jamal. Meanwhile, everybody who walked by them asked Gena, with intense sincerity, whether she was all right.

Markita laughed at her. "I told you all these nosy motherfuckers got out their beds this morning to watch you and Tune Time out this motherfucker."

Gena's phone rang and she went inside to answer. "Hello?"

"Hello. Is Gena there?"

Not recognizing the voice, she asked, "Who's calling?"

"This is Quadir."

Gena beamed. "This is she."

"Why didn't you call me back? I left a message on your machine."

"I'm sorry. I was about to. So, what did you do today?"

"I slept all day long. You were the first thing on my mind when I woke up."

"You say the sweetest things. Or do you say that to all the girls?" she prompted.

"No, baby doll. You're the first girl I woke up thinking about."

Oh, she thought, smiling from ear to ear.

Quadir continued. "So, what's up with you for the night?"

"Nothing. I'm gonna take a nice, hot bath and climb into bed."

"I thought we were going to Atlantic City."

While Gena was trying to come up with an answer, not remembering anything being mentioned about A.C. last night, Markita came running into the bedroom like a wildcat with its tail on fire.

"Gena! Jamal just pulled up!"

"Did you lock the door?"

"Yeah."

Quadir asked her, "Who are you talking to?"

"Oh, my neighbor. She fed me dinner tonight."

"I would have fed you."

"Oh, you're so sweet, but I got to go now."

"I'll see you in a few."

"You don't know where I live."

"Yes, I do. Sahirah is here. We're on our way over there." Then he hung up the phone.

Chickens couldn't have made more feathers fly. Gena looked from the phone to the door. The phone had a dial tone and the doorbell was ringing. "I'm not going out there, Markita!"

Her friend's mind searched for solutions. "Hide in the bed or something. I'll answer the door."

She headed for the front door as Gena jumped onto the bed and pulled up the covers.

"Motherfucker ain't gonna hit me," Markita swore as she picked up a Ginsu knife from the kitchen counter on her way.

"Who is it?" Markita stood ready with her trusty Ginsu.

"You know who it is. You seen me pullin' the fuck up when you ran in the house and shut the door."

"Don't be getting smart, okay?"

Ignoring her admonishment, he demanded, "Where's Gena?"

"She's sleeping."

"Well, I want to see her."

"She don't want to see you, and you lucky I wasn't home this morning 'cause I'da came outside and kicked your ass, Mr. Big Man wanna beat on women." Kita was looking out the window at him now.

"Here. Give her these."

Kita looked at the boxes he had in his hands. "Leave them on the porch."

Kita waited a few minutes, and when Jamal was gone, she opened the door, picked up the five boxes, and carried them into the house. Gena found twelve long-stemmed roses in each box containing a different color. Red roses, pink roses, yellow roses, white roses, and white roses with pink edges.

"What the hell this motherfucker buy all these flowers for?" Gena asked.

"I don't know, but you can give me some of them flowers if you don't want them," Markita suggested as she munched on a cracker.

"You can have them."

"Gena, that nigga done brought all these flowers over here feeling guilty. That's how women beaters are. They always say sorry. Shit don't mean nothing and neither do these flowers."

"You want them, you can have them."

Leaving the roses in their boxes, she walked away from them. Thinking about Quadir, she felt her power return.

"Remember the guy I told you I met in New York? He's coming over."

"For what?"

"To see me . . . to be with me. What don't you understand?"

"He's gonna see you all right, and if Norman Bates comes back to this motherfucker, you gonna see. Do you understand that?"

"I'm gonna take a shower. Let me know when they get here."

She was nearly finished when she heard the doorbell and quickly stepped out of the shower and into her robe. Patting herself dry, she looked at her face through the steamed mirror. It wasn't that bad, but the bruises were noticeable. She could hear her company down the hallway in the living room. She hung up her towel and walked down the other end of the hallway to her room.

As she was kneeling over to slip on some panties, Sahirah stormed into her bedroom to let her know Markita went home.

Gena folded her arms over her bare breasts. "Do you know how to knock?"

"You act like I haven't seen you naked. You look different, though. Your breasts are bigger," Sahirah said, looking at her girlfriend's nakedness.

She winked. "Thank you. I've been drinking my milk."

Seeing her friend's reflection in the dresser mirror, Sahirah asked, "What happened to your face?"

"Jamal was outside waiting for me this morning."

"What?" Sahirah listened with her jaw down to her clavicle as

Gena described her day, beginning with the shootout, Jamal's attack, and the three deaths at the fast-food restaurant.

"That motherfucker hasn't been right since he crashed his ass into a wall on that motorcycle."

"Well, I've had enough of Jamal. The next girl can have him."

She turned back to the dresser's mirror, inspecting her face.

Sahirah knew she meant what she said. "Oh, I forgot to tell you. Quadir Richards is the man of life."

"Why is Quadir the man of life?"

Smirking, Sahirah served up her gourmet dish. "My cousin used to mess with his sister, Denise. Girl, sit down and let me tell you. G, the boy is paid. The BMW? It's his. He has a Range Rover, too. Guess what? He's a millionaire. Can you believe this shit?" Sahirah plopped onto the bed next to Gena. "A real-life millionaire drug dealer right here in this house."

Gena was starting to like the sound of this. The hair on the back of her neck was standing up straight.

"Guess what else? He's supposed to be seeing some girl named Cherelle who lives up in Germantown. She wouldn't know what to do with that motherfucker if he came with a pamphlet."

"He got a bitch? Why'd he lie?" Gena tried to sound disinterested.

"No, girl. Are you deaf? He's seeing the girl, he's not *claiming* her. Rasun said he don't have nobody at home. The bitch is none of that but some change, G. I'm telling you, girl, you're in the house. You could take over shit and move that bitch right to the curb. You know what I'm saying?"

Sahirah smiled, knowing Gena had a strong con game. "I'm saying, the kid been bugging out all night over you."

"Word?"

"Word. The nigga is trying to see you. Aren't you glad we went to New York? Isn't this shit blue?"

Gena was all smiles. "Yes, so blue."

"Girl, you hit the jackpot; mark my words. You're taking me shopping for this one, right?"

"I got you covered. Tell him to come here for me?"

Sahirah left for the living room.

In another moment, Quadir entered Gena's bedroom. The man was fine. He had on a pair of blue jeans with a polo shirt and a brand-new pair of sneakers. He had recently been to the barbershop. His beard was groomed, and for some strange reason, he looked much better than he had last night.

"What's up?" He noticed the marks on her face. "What happened?"

She told him the entire story. "I won't be seeing him again."

He was glad to hear that but wasn't too sure if he should be in the house without Ena, his favorite 9mm out in the car. "No one's gonna come in here, are they?"

"No one has keys except for me." She reached up and ran the back of her fingers over his cheek. "I don't even miss him. I'm glad he's gone. I wish I could get away, you know?"

"I've been wanting to get away myself. You gonna go away with me?"

She looked him straight in the eye. "Mm-hmm."

"When can you go?"

"Whenever you're ready. I can go right now."

"Let's go to A.C. first."

First Date

Quadir knew exactly where to go. He drove over to Atlantic City. After he bought everyone back in Philly a pair of Gucci sneakers, they gambled. Sahirah lost every bit of the $550 Rasun had slowly given her. Gena, on the other hand, was doing mighty well, taking the $1,000 Quadir handed her and winning, winning, winning. She ended up with close to $4,000 by the time the night was over at the blackjack table.

Later, they took the escalator up to the third level, where there were several restaurants to choose from. Once they were seated, Quadir told Rasun about his little run-in with Jerrell Jackson. Rasun didn't like anything about the Junior Mafia.

"Quadir, don't mess with him. He wants to be Scarface. Own the fucking world and shit. He's the type that'll stab you in the back. Don't fuck with him, Qua."

"Ock, that'll never happen."

Gena was curious. "Who are you talking about?"

"Man talk," Quadir said. "Nobody you know, anyway."

Sahirah smirked. "I know who you're talking about."

Rasun jumped in, trying to shut her up. "You don't know nothing."

"Yes, I do. You're talking about Jerrell Jackson."

Gena brightened a little. "Oh, yeah, I heard about him. Isn't he supposed to be the leader of the Junior Mafia or something?"

"Yes," Sahirah confirmed.

"Really?" Gena turned to Quadir. "How do you know him?"

"What difference does it make? He isn't the mob."

Sahirah wouldn't stop. "He's the *leader* of the Junior Mafia. They *are* the mob, okay?"

Rasun spoke up. "Well, how do you know him?"

Sahirah warmed up to her gossip. "One night, I was with my girlfriend. She was going out with him a lot. Anyway, he gave us a ride back to her house."

Qua didn't like her anymore, and he didn't believe one word she said. The girl might have been telling the truth, but nine chances out of ten, the bitch was lying through her teeth. He tossed some money on the table and got up. "Let's go. Gena, you know how to drive?"

"Yes."

He handed her the valet stub.

Gently, she pulled Sahirah over to her and hissed through her teeth, "You talk too much!"

The drive home seemed to take forever. Everyone had fallen asleep and Gena had no one to talk to. She reached over and rubbed Quadir's leg.

He opened one eye and squeezed her hand. "You still want to go away?"

Gena wasn't sure she was hearing what he wasn't saying. "Isn't nothing gonna happen to me, is it?"

Warming to her childlike fear, he told her, "Baby doll, I wouldn't let anything happen to you." He winked at her. "I'll protect you from all harm."

Gena pulled up outside Rasun's house and dropped Rasun and Sahirah off. When she and Quadir were alone in the car, he asked, "What time will you be ready to go tomorrow?"

"Ready? Where we going?"

"I don't know. Let's go to the Bahamas."

"Are you serious?"

"Yes, I am."

Gena stared at him. She remembered how anxious Jamal was when they first met. Then she wondered if she should leave town with Quadir. What if something happened to her? What if he was as crazy and deranged as Jamal? She gazed into his eyes and didn't have a clue. He could be a rapist, but she had already made up her mind. If he wanted to take her to the Bahamas, she was going.

She turned onto Chancellor Street and pulled up in front of her door.

"Five o'clock. I'll be back at five," he said.

"I'll be ready," she said, real serious.

"So I'll see you later."

"Later."

Gena sat there looking at him. For some strange reason she couldn't get out of the car. Something was holding her. She didn't know what it was until he reached over and put his hand on the back of her neck.

He pulled her closer to him and kissed her. At first, he lightly touched her lips with his. Then he opened her mouth with his tongue and gently probed. Confusion and heat filled her like nothing she'd ever felt before. Like they were magnets drawn to each other, the kiss was magic.

Our first kiss, Gena thought, back in the safety of her apartment. *Sahirah was right: Quadir Richards is the man of life.*

The next morning, she had much to do! Shopping, hair, nails, packing. And that was only the beginning. The phone ringing pulled her out of her trance.

"Gena, it's Jamal."

"Oh . . . Hi." Ice crept into her veins.

"You all right?"

"I'm okay. How are you?"

"I don't feel good. I have a sore throat and a fever."

"Have you been to the doctor?" she asked him.

"No, I'm not going to no doctor."

"Well, I hope you feel better."

"Are you gonna come over to take care of me?"

She could hear the faint hope in his voice. Thinking to herself, *Hell no, bitch. Die.* With satisfaction, she informed him, "Jamal, I can't. I have to go to the beauty salon and get my hair done."

"Well, what about after you go and get your hair done?"

"After that, I have to go to the mall and pick up a few things, and I have to get my nails done. You know what? I think I'll get my feet done, too. Today's going to be crazy and I won't have time to come over there."

Jamal felt like he was getting the brush-off, and he didn't like it. Not one bit. Everything he had done for her meant nothing. He could die and it wouldn't mean anything to her. "Well, Gena, I can tell when I'm not wanted."

"Jamal, why do you say it like that? I thought we understood it wasn't working when you beat me up."

"Gena, you always gonna be mines. What do you mean when you say it isn't working?"

Is he brain dead? Gena thought to herself. "Jamal, I can't come and see you. I'm confused. I need some time. I want us to just be friends."

"Fuck you. All you bitches are the same. You ain't shit!" Jamal shouted.

With enough serene confidence to make his brain explode, she continued, "See, that's the very reason we're not together."

"Everything's my fault, right? You're the one who wants to be at every party on the East Coast. You're the one who stays out all night with other niggas. Yes, you do. Don't lie, Gena. Tell the truth. For once, be truthful. You and that Sahirah bitch stay out in the street all night chasing behind niggas. I know what you do. You don't fool me."

"Jamal, first of all, let me tell you something, okay? I don't chase behind nobody. I get chased. And I'm not out in no street all hours of the night, either!"

He cut her off and really let her have it. He accused her of everything under the sun, saying incredibly hurtful things. She found a wellspring of understanding within herself that told her it was because he was hurting. If the things he was saying were true, it would cut her real deep, but what he was saying made her mad. Jamal had lost his mind, calling her with a whole bunch of bullshit. She hung up the phone.

That was it, the conversation was over. And when he called back, she turned the ringer off. She wasn't about to listen to any more of his threats and accusations.

Quadir was down in North Philly collecting the money everyone owed him. He went to the house where Gena had dropped off Sahirah and Rasun. Rasun and Sahirah were in a deep sleep when Qua woke them up, knocking at the bedroom door.

"What happened to your hair, Sahirah?" Qua asked her as she brushed past him going into the bathroom.

"Ask your friend!" she spat back at him.

Qua chuckled. "Nasty little thing, ain't she?"

Ra grinned. "Yeah, she's not a happy camper."

Ra gave Sahirah another three hundred dollars, but she continued to pout when Qua told her she would have to catch a cab home.

Quadir and Rasun cut through the park in West Philly to see Ms. Shoog. Ms. Shoog was a little elderly lady he did business with. Shoog was something else. Back in her day she ran a speakeasy and a gambling spot. She even ran the numbers game. Shoog had it all. All the men raved about her. She could have had her pick of any of them but chose none.

By the time she was ready to choose, she had so many kids by so many different men, and the streets had beat up on her so bad, she was considered "not the marrying type." Shoog was a hell of a woman, though. Quadir listened to everything she said. He might not have always followed her instructions, but he listened.

He knocked at her door. One of Shoog's granddaughters let him in. She had so many grandchildren. There must have been at least fifteen people living in the three-story row home on the 2200 block of Bouvier, a narrow, one-way street.

Entering the kitchen, he placed a bag holding a quarter kilo of cocaine on the table.

"I need you to cook this up for me, Ms. Shoog."

"Fool, you always needing something. The only time you come to see Shoog is when you need something." She pointed her finger at him. "I got the family coming over today. I got enough cooking around here to do already."

Shoog could cook her ass off. She used to cook and sell platters when she was running her speakeasy back in the day.

"Those niggas used to pay me to cook their food for them and you gonna pay me to cook this shit for you."

"Don't I always pay you?" For a moment, Quadir worried about the once proud and sassy woman whom he'd come to count on. The heavy burdens she carried from decades of doing for others had slowed her down.

"Come on, baby, what's the matter?" he asked.

She sighed. "Everything."

"What?" He softly touched her shoulders and sat her at her own table. A barely discernible squeeze and a touch to her cheek brought a sad smile.

"It seems like you don't be getting too far out here in life, Quadir.

You do what you got to do to survive out here; you try your damnd-est to see there's some food on the table and clothes for the kids, and it don't get you nowhere. Badass motherfuckers around here now don't listen. I done brought mines into the world. These ain't mines. They killing me, Quadir. Sure as there's a God in the sky, these badass kids is gonna be the death of me. Eight damn kids that ain't mine and here . . . look at this."

Ms. Shoog pulled out a piece of paper from her apron pocket and handed it to Quadir, hoping her scam would work. Ms. Shoog always had a scam.

"What is it?"

"It's a get-the-fuck-out notice. I been paying the mortgage on this house now for twenty-seven years. I only got three more to go, then this house is mine. After all this time, you'd think they couldn't do this." Her face began to crumple.

"How much do you need?" Quadir located the total due on the paper. "Oh damn, Shoog, you had me worried! That's all you need? I got that for you, baby. Calm down."

"Quadir, stop your lying. You hardly pay me when I cook this shit up for you. So your black ass not gonna pay all that!" She looked at Qua as if it were all his fault.

The truth of the matter was that Quadir always paid Shoog what-ever she wanted. The price wasn't always the same, but Shoog got paid. He would even stop by to see how she was doing without asking her to do anything for him. The bottom line was everybody wanted something. Everybody had a story. Qua separated the two. He was always gonna look out for her. It was the right thing to do.

"Cook my shit up, Shoog."

He went outside and returned in a few minutes, handing her a bag of money.

Shoog snickered on the inside but, on the outside, showed a look of gratefulness Quadir had never seen.

"There . . . That'll save your house."

Shoog couldn't believe it; it had worked. It was as if the Lord had blessed somebody else and they had passed it on to her.

She could barely whisper her thanks. "That's gonna be more than enough, Quadir."

Qua was glad to bring hope to someone who deserved it.

"Here, get yourself something and get something for the kids." He pulled out a wad of money from his pocket, peeling back a couple hundred-dollar bills. Qua had money all over him.

"I don't mean to fuss at you, baby," she said, changing everything up. "You're the only one who understands. Oh, Qua, I wish that damn John-John had turned out like you," she said, now standing up and reaching for an empty mayonnaise jar, going about the business she was in.

She took the cocaine and mixed it with baking soda. She poured the combination in the mayonnaise jar and added the right amount of water, cooking batches at a time. Shoog knew what she was doing.

Gena got dressed and called a cab, going straight to LeChevue Beauty Salon in South Philly.

"Hi, Gena," said one of the girls who worked there. Everyone knew her.

She spotted Beverly, her stylist. "What's up, Bev?"

"Yo, G." Bev smiled. "Where you been?"

"Nowhere, trying to get my life on."

"Guess who's pregnant by Rik?" Beverly asked.

"Who?"

"I'm not gonna tell you. I know how you run your mouth."

"Who? I won't tell."

"Veronica."

Gena turned her face up. "He been fucking with her?"

"Girl, she told him she was pregnant and Mr. Tyrik ain't called her back since."

"What?" Gena couldn't believe it.

"I'm telling you; shit is crazy."

Beverly finished the girl who was in the chair and took Gena over to the bowl, talking about everybody under the sun. Gena told her how she had been up at the fast-food place when the three guys died. She didn't say anything about the guy driving the Caddy. Nothing said in a beauty salon is sacred. Everybody knows your business as it is. Gena didn't tell any secrets, but she stuck to gossip.

"Well, I don't fuck with Jamal no more."

"Why?"

"It wasn't working, Bev. I care about him, but I can't see myself being with him."

"Well, damn, you don't seem too sad about it!"

"I'm not. It's for the best."

"Girl, I don't believe you're letting your Jamal go. He treated you really good."

"Money can't buy love."

Bev snickered. "Hell, it can buy mine."

The girl sitting under the next bowl was ear-hustling. "Mine too!"

"Shit, he didn't try to take nothing back, did he?" Beverly asked.

"No, but if he wants his shit back, he can have it," Gena replied.

Bev gasped. "I wouldn't give him nothing back."

"Neither would I, honey. Keep your shit. Don't give that nigga back a damn thing," the girl sitting at the next bowl chimed in.

Gena and Beverly stared at the girl for a few seconds. When Beverly finished washing Gena's hair, they went to her station.

Gena couldn't wait to let go of the good shit. "I met this guy."

"Who?"

"His name is Quadir."

"Quadir? Quadir from North with the BMW?"

"Yeah, you know him?"

"Yeah, he supposed to be fucking with Dawn's sister, Cherelle."

"He give her anything?" Gena inquired.

"I don't think so. He probably got her a pair of sneakers and shit, but he ain't throw shit to her like Jamal threw it to you, 'cause if he did, she would be in here running her mouth about it."

"What she look like?" Gena wanted to know.

"She don't look like nothing. She your average light-skinned bitch." Bev admired Gena's chocolate skin tone.

"She don't look better than me, do she?" Gena asked.

"Hell no. Girl, Quadir ain't no joke. The boy is large as hell. Jamal ain't never seen no money compared to that motherfucker. Girl, Quadir's middle name is Stock and you want to invest."

"Guess what?"

"What?"

"I met him Wednesday in New York. Last night we went to Atlantic City and today he's taking me to the Bahamas."

Beverly put the curling iron down. "Bitch, lies."

"No, I'm dead serious. So Cherelle can forget about him 'cause I'm getting ready to put my thing down."

"I guess he playing Cherelle."

"I guess so."

"Damn, she act like she really in love with him."

"She'll get over it. That's the way love goes," Gena said with extreme confidence.

"So you dropped Jamal when you started fucking with Qua?"

"No, I met Quadir after me and Jamal broke up."

Beverly handed her a mirror so she could view the back of her hair. "Here."

Gena got a pump with a long strand of hair hanging down the side of her face.

"So when are you leaving?"

"In a couple of hours. I have to go shopping, buy some luggage, and I need to get my nails done."

"I know you're happy."

"I am. It's something about him."

"Yeah. The man is rich."

"No, it's not that. It's the way he looks at me, and the way he talks to me, like we're on the same vibe. It seems like he's always been there, watching me."

Gena sat there talking about the man with a gleam in her eyes while Beverly wished it was her.

"I gotta go, Bev. I got to meet Sahirah. We're going shopping."

Gena got bathing suits, fashion accessories, short sets, summer dresses, and luggage.

Then the girls went to Nice New Nail Salon on Lancaster Avenue. Pam was booked but acted like Gena had an appointment and squeezed her in. Sahirah and Gena sat in the salon talking about Quadir and how nice he was, especially compared to Jamal, who was so mean.

"I'll be glad when someone comes along for me," Sahirah said.

"Sahirah, you got to settle down with somebody. That's what you need to do. They a pain in the ass, but it's like a job. Besides, niggas sweat you half to death when you got a man. You stay single too long, then niggas gonna think there's something wrong with you. Everybody gonna do their thing, you dig me?"

Pam nodded in agreement as she buffed Gena's nails.

"It's all about respect. I would've been the lowest bitch on the planet if I'd taken them guys up on their propositions, but since I didn't, I showed loyalty to Jamal when I was with him."

Gena looked at Sahirah to gauge if she was even halfway listening.

"Girl, all them niggas think I'm a saint. You got to prove you're woman enough to be true to your man. That's all you got to do. You're not going to get no respect dealing with a brother on that *wham bam, thank you, here you go, ma'am* tip. You need to know the brother got your best interests at heart."

Pam was finishing up with her manicure. "Gena's speaking nothing but facts, Sahirah."

"Money don't mean he care," Gena added. "You can't run tricks on the big boys. Tricks are for kids. So you chill. Slow down, baby. You moving kinda fast, that's all."

Sahirah sat there looking at her friend, knowing what she was saying was true, but she was having fun and couldn't see herself with one man.

Gena finished getting the last coat of paint on her fingernails. "Oh, guess what!"

"What?"

"Guess who the fuck is pregnant by Rik?"

"Who?"

"Veronica."

"That slut. He went up in her ass raw?" Pam asked with disgust. "What's he on? Rik better check himself. I'm saying, though, don't he fuck with some girl named Lita?"

Gena admired her nails. "Now that you mention it, I think he does."

"It probably ain't his." Sahirah rolled her eyes. "She probably don't know who the father is. The bitch is nothing but a whore." Sahirah bristled with righteousness.

"You don't like the girl 'cause of Troy."

"I don't like the bitch 'cause she always up in your man's face. Watch, I bet the bitch will be fucking Jamal in a minute."

Gena sat on the side of the wall until her nails dried, talking to Sahirah. The girls were like sisters. Sahirah really didn't want Gena to go, but she couldn't tell her to stay. Gena would be all right; Sahirah knew that. She was gonna miss her friend.

"How long you guys gonna be there?"

"A week or two."

"Send me a postcard?"

Gena smiled. "I'll do better than that. I'll bring you back something."

Sahirah helped her outside. A cab pulled over, and an Israeli gentleman stepped out to assist Gena with her bags. Being as though Sahirah had lost her money in Atlantic City, Gena slipped three hundred dollars into the palm of her hand. Sahirah took Gena around her head and gave her a hug. The girls kissed each other's cheeks and then let go.

"All right, I'm out. I'll see you when I get back."

Sahirah waved and went back into the nail salon as the cab pulled away from the curb.

The Getaway

Ms. Shoog was finally finished cooking the cocaine. She was letting it cool now so that it could harden. "Didn't it come back good?" She was smiling at her success, revealing her missing teeth.

"Yeah, Shoog. You doing it," he said.

"Motherfuckers tell you I don't know what I'm doing, you tell 'em they is a lie, you hear me?"

"Yeah, Shoog. I hear you." Qua grabbed two large plastic bags and put the rocks in them. "All right, Shoog, I'm out."

She walked him to the door and talked him into his car.

Rasun looked at the bag. "Shit looks like Shoog didn't beat you this time."

"She beat me for a couple thousand to save her house," Quadir said knowingly. Turning to Ra, he asked him, "Now, you sure you can handle this?"

"Man, give me the bag." Ra snatched the bag out of Qua's lap. "I know what to do with it. I'm gonna cap this shit up tonight and be ready tomorrow."

Quadir had some reservations about Rasun's ambition. "I want you to watch out for Jerrell and those sucker-ass niggas, you hear me?"

"Man, what's the matter with you? That girl got you nervous. You don't have to check me, baby."

"I'm not nervous. I want you to watch yourself."

"It's Gena. She got you all fucked up in the head, nigga. I know she do."

"You don't know nothing."

"Watch, by the time you get back, that girl gonna be wearing your pockets."

Qua was annoyed. "Man, get the fuck out of here!"

"But I'm saying, as fine as she is, she could wear my pockets, too, boss."

"She is all that, isn't she?"

"Sis definitely got it going on." Ra got out of the car with his bag, compliments of Shoog's superb cooking abilities. "Later."

"Later!"

Qua pulled off, drove straight to his hideout, and removed all the money he'd collected earlier out of the trunk. Once he was in the apartment, he went straight to the closet door and unlocked it, exposing a huge safe, where he'd been keeping his money for years. He turned the knob, entering his combination. *Click.*

Qua opened the door. His money was safe and sound. The safe took up every inch of space in the closet, standing taller than him. He had old-school money in the motherfucker. He took the money out of the bag and threw it in the safe, locking it back up.

He then packed two suitcases. He made sure his credit cards were in his wallet. He had everything together: his clothes, his money, everything he could think of. He paced around the room, walking back and forth, making sure there was nothing he'd forgotten. He went back over to the closet and made sure the safe was locked, then grabbed his luggage and stepped.

***

Gena was sitting on the porch when she spotted Quadir's BMW turning onto her block. Her heart started pounding and the thought of how she looked to him entered her mind. He pulled up in front of the door as Gena waved.

"You ready to go?"

"I'm ready," she replied.

Rasun delivered Gena and Quadir to the airport, happy to be in charge and happy to have Qua's BMW. Their flight, though somewhat turbulent, landed without a hitch.

"Damn, my ears are still ringing," she noted, annoyed. "How long will it last?"

"Who knows? For me, I wake up in the middle of the night with my ears ringing, so I can't tell you."

"Oh my God! I thought we were going to die. The plane was rocking and shaking like something was going to happen."

"It was enough to make me buy a boat and sail the fuck home," he said like he meant it.

After two and a half hours on the plane, Gena understood how he felt. But Gena enjoyed flying and always preferred traveling by air.

"Look at those trees! Will those kinds of trees grow in Philly?"

Not a hundred and one questions, he thought to himself. "I don't know, baby, but they grow in California."

"Have you ever been here before?"

"Yeah. Twice before." Looking around, he added, "We gotta get a cab."

They located their baggage, and Qua spotted the taxi stand.

Entering the first available ride, he told the driver, "The Valiant Hotel on Paradise Island, please."

The driver was very nice, making lots of conversation, but didn't seem to know where he was going.

Qua nudged Gena, whispering, "I swear I saw the same damn building twice."

"Maybe you're having déjà vu, from when you were here before twice," she said with an attitude.

"Gena, baby, I'm telling you. He doesn't know where he's going," Quadir said softly.

The driver seemed to have been through this type of distrustful whispering before. "Me doe know, but me fine de way. Me know what to do," he said, pulling out his map.

Qua sighed. "Damn, he don't know where he's at."

"Qua, why don't you give him directions; you been here before."

Quadir paid her no mind. "Man, how you don't know where you're at?"

"Me no from here, mon. Me from Jamaica, mon. Me a Yardley."

Gena collapsed into giggles. "Oh, Lord!"

"Well, don't you see nothing that looks familiar?" Qua asked the driver. "Gena, stop laughing."

"Dot's de bridge, mon," he said, pointing far away.

"Okay, that's the bridge," grumbled Qua. "What about the bridge?"

"De bridge takes you to Paradise Island, star. Relax, star. Me fine de way."

Gena glanced over at Qua, who was shaking his head in frustration. "We're going to get there, Qua."

"I don't know how, baby. With Lost Rasta here behind the wheel, we might not make it."

They looked out of their respective car windows, trying to quell their misgivings. It wasn't anything like Philly. There were no skyscrapers and no city streets. No graffiti and no broken-down row homes. It was beautiful. It was nature at its finest. Gena was so glad she was there.

Finally, they reached the bridge. The view was breathtaking; the sun glinted off the yachts, ocean liners, and small fishing boats—some moving, some idling, all completing the canvas. Quadir paid the driver as a bellboy approached to assist Rasta with the baggage.

"All right, Rasta, man, you learn where you're going, okay? I'm gonna tip you 'cause shit is rough for a brother, but the next time you give me a ride, man," he continued, handing the Jamaican a hundred-dollar bill, "I don't want to ride in circles, okay?"

"Yah, me know," Rasta said.

Qua kept saying, "Me know, me know," as the bellboy took the luggage inside the hotel. Gena was so glad to be there, pointing out this and that. The scenery was extremely tropical. There were Bahamian musicians playing island music beside a massive bar that seemed to have every liquor imaginable. Sliding glass patio doors across the expansive lobby led to the swimming pool. Beyond the pool was nothing but white sand and clear crystal-blue water that only seemed to exist in commercials.

Gena glanced through the patio doors to where there was a party taking place. People were dancing and clapping while a man sang on a platform lit by poles of fire in each corner. Gena didn't have enough energy to join the festivities after all that shopping, hairstyling, and flying. She was exhausted.

Qua walked over to her. "Do you want your own room?"

His suggestion left her in a stupor, being she had planned on sleeping with him. She had expected him to have the same intentions and attempted to hide her surprise at his suggestion of separate rooms.

She quickly gathered her composure. "I hadn't really thought about it."

"Well, how about adjoining rooms? That way if you want privacy to shower or change, you will have it, and if you need me, I'll be right there."

She smiled at him. "Okay."

Gena's smile and eyes made Qua's heart melt. He realized he had to have her.

When he finished registering for the rooms, he located Gena outside. "You ready?"

Was she ready? Oh, was she ready.

"Sure," she said as demurely as she could for a sister who had been picked up in Harlem, then received an ass-kicking once she returned home the next morning.

Quadir had two keys in his hand and held them out for her to choose. "Which room do you want?"

"Room 808," she said as the bellboy led them to their rooms.

He opened their doors for them and carried their things inside. He had nothing to say, but he did manage to smile and say "Thank you" when Qua handed him a twenty-dollar bill.

"Why do you give money away like that?"

"Because he needs it."

Quadir walked over to the balcony. Even though they'd had no reservation, they'd ended up with a spectacular view.

Gena looked out the balcony doors with him for a few minutes, but she was so tired, all she wanted to do was lie down.

Qua was thinking about nothing but a spliff. He'd carried the weed right through customs in a vitamin container in his suitcase. Shit was great. Qua sat on his balcony and looked at the water. This was what it was all about. This was living. Quadir wanted to travel the entire world. He had been in the Philly streets all his life, and that was no way to live. He could base his home in Philly and always deal with the streets, but he didn't want to be out there like that for the rest of his life. It wasn't the way; there was something better for him.

Gena lay on the bed, silently watching Quadir as she thought about her grandmother who had raised her since she was four, when her mother died. Her mother . . . She never thought about her. No one spoke of her mother. Gena never knew why. All she knew was when she was little, her father went to prison and her mother died.

She didn't even remember her mother, not one memory. It didn't seem so bad to her that her mother was dead, and the fact she never had a mother didn't seem to bother her. She loved her mother for bringing her into the world. She loved her for sharing her beauty with her and for her hands, her soft and gentle hands. But at sixty-two, Gah Git had patience and a lot of wisdom. She had taken care of her grandbaby, Gena. Gah Git took care of all her grandbabies. She told them stories about where they came from, she taught them all right from wrong, and she made them all attend Sunday school when they were little. She was a miraculous, God-fearing woman, and very strong. Gena loved her grandmother; she was the only mother she knew.

Quadir walked into her room. He had taken a shower. "Will you put this on my back?" he asked, handing her the lotion. "We can go look around the island tomorrow, if you want to."

"Okay, I want to."

After she lotioned him down, she went into the bathroom, showered, and changed into a baby blue satin pajama set. Then she lay down beside him.

"You want to go swimming tomorrow?" she asked.

"Whatever you want to do," Quadir said, reaching over her and turning off the light. He lay back down and pulled her near. His strength could be felt as he consumed her in his arms, holding her close to him. Gena could feel his breath and hear his heartbeat as she lay next to him. He was divine; she couldn't believe it. He felt so warm, and his hold on her was so relaxing and so comforting. She felt safe.

Gena lay next to Quadir thinking of all she had done and all the places she had been, all the men, every single last twenty-nine of them. Could she say they simply got in the bed and held her? They might have fed her, bought her something, laid her body down, and gave her a couple dollars, but none of them simply held her.

They slept in until the afternoon. When they finally crawled out of bed, Quadir went into his room to change while Gena got herself together. By the time Quadir returned, Gena looked like the girl he met in New York, not the one he had woken up with.

Downstairs it was sunny and bright. People were in the pool, and the musicians were still playing island music. The bar was open, and people were already ordering drinks.

Gena grabbed a pamphlet from the information booth at the front desk. "Oh, look! A boat ride! Can we go?"

"Whatever you want," Quadir said, winking at her.

After enjoying breakfast in the hotel restaurant, they toured the island. Qua wanted to see the nude beach and, of course, the casino. There was lots of water and lots of shops. That basically summed it up for the island, so they went across the bridge into Nassau. There was a man selling conch shells.

"Qua, look!" Gena said that about everything she observed.

They rented mopeds and rode around the island for hours, finally taking a road that led into town. It was full of merchants who had everything you could think of, from jewelry to clothes.

Quadir admired a dress hanging on a mannequin displayed in a window. "Gena, you would look good in that."

"Do you think so?"

"I really do."

He walked into the shop and told the saleslady he wanted to purchase that particular dress.

The woman was blatantly aloof and crisply replied, "That dress is eight thousand four hundred and ninety dollars."

She did an about-face and waited for his reply.

"I don't believe I asked you for the price of the dress. I want the dress in the window. Do you not work here?" he asked politely.

"Yes, of course," she replied.

"Well, if I'm getting ready to spend eight thousand on a dress, wouldn't you wanna get ta steppin' and wrap that shit in a box, 'cause I'm getting tired of the small talk."

Quadir looked around and studied the store. The people were appalled by the saleslady's rude display of behavior, and she couldn't bring herself to move. Meanwhile, another saleslady had attracted Gena to the shoes.

"Qua, I have to have these. They'd go perfectly with that dress. Can I get them, please?"

He got her everything she wanted. Gena was getting used to spending other people's money, and she did it very well.

After dragging him around the island like a rag doll and making him carry all but two of the bags, Qua was tired, hungry, and ready to return to the hotel for a meal and a nap. They caught a cab and traveled back across the bridge to the Valiant Hotel.

"Let's order a movie and eat in," Qua suggested. He felt like lying down.

Once they got upstairs, he took Gena's things to her room and went into his. He wanted to figure out how much money he had spent. He wasn't spending any money tomorrow.

Gena gonna take her trick ass down on the beach and call it a day, he thought to himself as Gena opened the door to his room. Quadir had stacks of money lying beneath him on the floor. Quickly, he bent down and brushed it under the bed.

"Are you busy?" she asked, trying desperately to see what was on the other side of the bed.

"Yeah, I'll be out there in a minute," he said, pushing her out the door and closing it behind her. He picked up the phone and called Rasun.

"As-salaam alaykum."

"Wa alaykum as-salaam. I miss you, man. When you coming home?" Rasun was glad to hear from his hero.

"I just got here. So, what's going on? Everything safe?"

"Yeah, shit is tight. I'm gonna meet the boy, Rock, tomorrow, and everything else has been running smoothly. Marlon Hawkins wants you to call him. I told him you was down in South Philly."

"What else been going on?"

"Nothing. Stop worrying."

"All right, I'm out. As-salaam alaykum."

"Wa alaykum as-salaam."

Gotten and Gone

Back in Philly, the summer heat had driven everyone outside onto the sidewalks, porches, corners, and streets. There were open fire hydrants with bursts of water spraying children. Even elderly people were outside trying to keep cool.

As usual, Rasun was pretending to be Mac Daddy in Quadir's BMW. He drove to Gena's house, figuring he would surprise Sahirah with dinner and a movie. When Sahirah came to the door, she had this stupid "I can't believe you're here without calling first" look on her face.

"What's up?" Rasun asked.

"Nothing, I was getting ready to go out with a friend of mine."

"Out? Where you going?"

"Dinner and a movie," Sahirah said as Rasun's smile faded.

She glanced down at him from Gena's porch steps. For a moment she remembered the night before last. It had been less than a week since she'd slept with him, and she was already disinterested. Besides, Quadir and he were nothing but whores. Sahirah was infuriated at the thought of what was going on and was waiting for Gena's telephone call.

"Why does Quadir have Gena over in the Bahamas somewhere with Cherelle?" she asked angrily. "I heard that bitch is supposed to be waiting for him to get there. How is he playing my girlfriend? Answer that."

"Well, I don't know nothing. I don't have nothing to do with it, and I don't know what you're talking about," Ra said, ready to go then. "Being as though you got company and all, I'll push up on you some other time."

"Mm-hmm, later," she replied as she turned her back to him and closed the door.

Rasun walked over to the BMW, trying to figure out why he recognized the burgundy Mercedes-Benz parked near the front door. Sahirah had some nigga up in Gena's house. He felt bad 'cause he really liked her. As much as he felt like shouting, *Fuck you, bitch*, he kept it inside, knowing she didn't feel the same.

Fuck it, he finally said to himself as he turned the sound system up. *There's nine women to every man out here.*

Rasun drove back to North Philly. "What's up?" he said as he pulled up on the corner of Twenty-Fifth Street.

"Nothing, man. What's up?" Reds asked.

"You got the money?"

"Yeah." Reds pulled a knot of paper out of his pocket, handing it to Rasun. "I'm almost out."

"What you got left?"

"Maybe twenty." Reds spotted some girls walking across the street. "Hey, you in the red shorts! Can I talk to you for a minute, baby? Damn, you got it going on," he hollered loud enough for them to hear.

The girls looked his way and walked toward him, smiling and snickering among themselves.

"Yo, I'll be right back," Ra shouted to Reds, who wasn't paying him any mind with all that ass surrounding him. Actually, he didn't even hear him.

Ra drove off in the Beemer, headed back to his mother's house, and got some more caps for Reds. When he got back, Kenny, Reds, and the whole crew were out on the Ave.

"What's up?" Ra asked.

"Rich Green is what's up," Reds answered.

"Man, fuck Rich Green. I'll lay that nigga down." Ra tapped the nine in his waistband. "I promise you, he don't want none of this."

"Okay, we'll see what happens when the motherfucker comes through sprayin'. Let's see what you do then," Pookey said, knowing something bad was going to happen.

Paying him no mind, Rasun looked around and asked everybody, "What's on for tonight?"

"I don't know. Wanna go to Chances?" Reds asked.

Ra heard him, but he didn't answer. He was thinking about Sahirah. He wished he was out with her, not getting ready to go to Chances with Reds. "Yeah, we can do that."

"I want to go," Kenny said.

Pookey seemed anxious. "Me too."

"I'm going," Dontae added.

"How are all of you gonna go?" Ra sighed. "Everybody can't go. Somebody has to stay out here and hold down the fort. Kenny, you and Pookey stay out here. Where's Wiz?"

"He went to take his moms a platter," Dontae said.

"Why the fuck do I got to stay out here?" Kenny demanded to know.

"Because, man, you gots to stay the fuck out here. That's why," Reds told him.

"Man, fuck you," Kenny said.

Ra didn't like the bickering. "Yo, why you drawin', Kenny? Man, you know why you got to stay out here."

"Why?"

"Because, man, you can keep track of shit. If you're out here, shit will be cool."

Ra had been learning from his mentor. It's what Quadir would have said, assuaging the boy, stroking his ego. Unfortunately, Kenny wasn't trying to hear the shit. He wanted to go to the party, too.

"Where's the gat?" Kenny wanted to know, looking at Reds.

"Man, I got it."

Kenny held out his hand. "Well, give it up."

"What you need the gun for?" Reds asked.

"Man, what you need it for? You're going to a party, right?"

Reds didn't want to give up the gun. "What the fuck you need it for?"

"Man, y'all leaving me out here with Dontae and Pookey. No offense, no defense," Kenny said, looking at them. "So you gonna have to give the gat up."

"Ock, give Kenny the motherfucking nine, will you?" Rasun huffed, having no understanding of why they were always fighting over the guns.

"That's right." Kenny had an ally in Ra. "What am I supposed to do if sucker-ass Rich Green comes back around here?"

Reds wasn't satisfied. "Why I got to give him Ena? This is Quadir's. Why don't you give him yours, Rasun?" He stood tall, waiting for Ra's response.

"We can stop by my moms and get Homicide; let Kenny hold the gun. Damn," huffed Rasun, getting agitated. "You gonna be with me, you don't need a gun."

"Man, fuck that. I need mines."

"We all need our own guns," Pookey said.

"Well, take that shit up with Quadir when he comes back," Ra said, knowing Qua wasn't giving them no guns like that. Mentally, they couldn't handle a gun. Putting a gun in their hands with their intellect was mayhem and mass confusion. Quadir wasn't taking any chances on bucks fucking up his game.

Finally, after bickering and debating, Reds gave it up before climbing into the BMW with Ra.

"We'll be right back," Rasun said as he sped down the Ave.

As they drove away, Reds gave Rasun a lecture, which included one hundred and one reasons why he should've never given Kenny the gun. "Man, Kenny will kill somebody with that gun."

"He isn't gonna kill nobody."

"Yeah, right; you know how he is. Why you trying to put a body on a clean gun? Quadir's gun?"

"He *ain't* gonna kill nobody."

"Well, if Rich Green comes back around that motherfucker, shit is on."

Chances was packed. People were everywhere.

"Mercy me, the freaks do come out at night. They is everywhere." Reds admired all the skimpy outfits and the outlines of what was underneath. "Look what her ass got on. Damn, baby, might as well have worn nothing. Just come outside naked, dammit," he hollered across the street to some half-naked girls.

Rasun waved him off. "Man, leave them hoes the fuck alone and don't call them over here to us."

"No problem. I'm getting ready to go over there as soon as I roll this spliff."

"I wouldn't want to fuck with none of them girls, man."

Reds laughed at his best friend. "You might not want to fuck with them, but you *will* fuck them, so shut the fuck up."

Ra realized Reds was right as they both exited the car. *Everybody* was out that night. All Quadir's people who had individually reached the hundred-kilo mark were there. Rik's boys were on the set, but Rik wasn't with them. The brothers were out. They dealt strictly with Amin, who no one ever saw much. The boy Rik, who put Jerrell Jackson and the boy Blair on their feet, was in the house with a bottle of Dom in his right hand and some girl's titty in his left. She didn't mind, 'cause she was half drunk.

Quadir, Rik, Amin, Blair, Forty, and Winston were all making millions in the drug game. Everyone else was down with one of them. Even though the Mafia controlled the majority, it did not keep the others from getting paper. But it made them targets for being so large. The funny thing about it, though, was everyone knew one another. Everyone recognized who was down with one another. Females might not have known all the players—for the most part, they didn't—but the brothers did.

Rasun spotted Jerrell's Jaguar parked outside. He was probably inside trying to figure out who had more money than him. That seemed to be his main concern in life, having the most drug money.

All of Gena's girlfriends were out. Finally, Rasun saw Sahirah with Winston. *That's whose burgundy Mercedes-Benz that was.* The realization stabbed through his heart like an arrow.

Trying to get past it, Ra decided to mess with Reds, pointing to Veronica across the street. "Yo, Reds, there goes your girl."

"Man, I can't stand that girl. She really tried to play me, and for the phone bill at that."

Veronica stopped and talked to Sahirah's old boyfriend, Troy. He was currently hooked up with Val, Jamal's girlfriend prior to Gena. They had a baby together, and Val loved Jamal but not enough to be faithful. Val was there that night with Troy.

One day, Jamal was downtown and there was a brother in his '98, leaning to the side and riding in his car with his woman like he was the owner of both. Being a psychopath, Jamal kicked both their asses and put them out of his car.

When the cops came, they refused to intervene. As a matter of fact, Val was all beaten up and the other guy needed stitches. But the officers called it a domestic dispute; no bones broken, no harm done. They cleared the scene, and Jamal wouldn't speak to Val anymore, even though she was five months pregnant. Sis wasn't sure whose baby it was, so she followed her heart. Her heart didn't have anything to do with it when that baby was born the spitting image of Jamal. Jamal loved his son. He truly did, but Val played him for another man and there was no way his pride would allow him to take her back.

"Is everybody out here tonight or what?" Reds asked.

"Most definitely," Ra said.

Most of the brothers who were out had a woman at home. The funny thing about it was, even though you might be with a guy and really call him your man, you knew in the back of your mind he wasn't your man. He was his own man first and then anybody's man for the moment. That was the bottom line. The brothers were socially acceptable whoremongers.

Gena's girlfriends all understood this, but it didn't make a difference. If they were spending money, nothing really made a difference. Nothing else mattered.

Inside the club, everyone was partying. No one was standing still except the thick-ass bouncers. Ra paid one of them fifty dollars to let him in with his nine. If you thought about how many brothers had paid them to do the same, the bouncers were making big money.

Everyone was partying and having a good time. Rasun was standing near a table with Rock and his people.

"Yo, get with me tomorrow. Same place, same time. I'll see you brothers on the outside," Rock said, ready to make his exit.

"All right," they said, shaking his hand.

"Yo, you ready to go?" Ra asked.

"Waitin' on you," Reds replied as they headed for the door.

Reds and Ra walked across the street to the car.

"Yo, hold up," Reds told Ra, eyeing a prospective one-night stand. He walked down the street in the opposite direction of the car and approached a group of girls.

Ra spotted Winston sitting in his car, but Sahirah wasn't with him.

Where is she? he wondered as he looked through the crowd of faces. Finally, he spotted her across the street standing in front of the club.

He walked over to her. "What's up?"

"What are you doing here?" she asked.

He wanted to tell her that he felt something for her and wanted to be with her, only her, if only for a minute or for longer than that. He wanted her time.

"So you waiting on Winston or what?" Ra asked as they both looked across the street.

Winston was sitting in his car talking to a group of girls that had flocked around his 300 CE. Sahirah knew the girls. She couldn't stand them. Neither could Gena.

"Yeah. How'd you know that?" she asked.

"His car was sitting outside Gena's door earlier, so I figured it out." He shrugged his shoulders. "It wasn't too difficult."

"Oh, I see."

"I'm getting ready to go. You want to ride with me?" he offered, praying she would accept.

Sahirah didn't know what to do. What if Winston left her for one of the other girls?

"You need to come with me, Sahirah. Don't you know about the guys you hang around? You need to be careful out here."

It was crowded outside the club. Cars were riding back and forth, up and down the street. People were standing all around like they had no place to go, while others were walking around aimlessly.

"You really think I should go with you?"

"You should know what you should do, Sahirah, but if you need me to tell you, then, okay, you need to go with me. Look at him with those girls. That's disrespectful to you, and you know it. How you gonna let him play you like that? I would never disrespect you like that. You should have been stepped off."

Ignoring his concern for her, she didn't want to let her status slip away. Being the one Winston and his Mercedes-Benz went home with would confer royalty onto her, and she wanted to be Queen Sahirah.

"He's not playing me. Why don't you mind your own business?" she spat at him.

"Fuck this, I'm out!"

No sooner had Ra walked away, hoping Sahirah would come after him, than Winston's shiny burgundy Mercedes-Benz 300 CE circled the lot and headed her way.

Sahirah thought for a minute about Rasun. Perhaps she should go with him, to play with Winston's mind. Instead, when Winston pulled up, Sahirah got in.

"Who were you talking to?" she asked.

"Some girls from South Philly. They were trying to get me to give them a ride home."

He attempted to reassure her with a pat on her thigh, but she knew he was lying. Those girls were from down the bottom, not South Philly. At that moment, when he lied to her, she really wished she had gone with Rasun.

"Why do you have to lie to me? I know every whore in the city, and they live nowhere near South Philly. They live down the bottom. I can't believe you got to lie. That means you're trying to hide something." Sahirah had a serious "tell me the deal" look on her face. "What? You fuck with one of them or something?"

Winston continued driving, paying no attention to Sahirah as he turned up his radio. The only thing on his mind was whether he should throw her a couple of dollars now or fuck her first and then throw her a couple of dollars. Either way, he was quickly getting rid of Sahirah.

A Cadillac eased up to a red light beside them. A guy in the passenger seat called out to Winston as the windows rolled down. For a split second, Sahirah recognized Ran, and as she opened her mouth to say hello, he opened fire on Winston. The bullets came crashing through the steel, one hitting Winston in the shoulder. His body slumped forward on the steering wheel. The Cadillac sped away as shattered glass continued to fall to the ground.

Sahirah ducked down and started screaming. "Oh my God! Winston!"

Looking at him slumped over the steering wheel, moaning, she realized he'd been shot. At the same time, she couldn't believe it. She felt funny, kind of dizzy and lightheaded. *Probably from being scared,* she thought.

He remained conscious and could see her, all hunched down, and wondered if his mouth still worked. "You okay?" he asked, but he was more fixated on the bullet that had ripped through him.

He slowly pulled himself away from the steering wheel and lifted Sahirah back up into a sitting position. Her hand passed in front of her eyes on the way back up, and she saw it was covered with blood. She felt her face and looked down at her lap. Putting her hand to her chest, she could feel the ripples of blood-drenched flesh as Winston realized she'd also taken a hit.

"Oh my God, Sahirah! You been shot!"

Sahirah heard him from very far away; there was a more interesting channel to watch inside her head. Everything was flashing in front of her. People and places that she had forgotten had come to life. All the moments in time replayed themselves as fast-moving images in her head. *Oh, there goes me and Gena on the swings.* "Hi, Gena." And Mama. "Mama, I don't want no barrettes. I want ribbons. Ribbons are prettier."

Her eyes closed, and Winston felt panic. "Sahirah! Sahirah! Talk to me!"

She tried to look up at him, whispering, "Help me, Winston, it's burning. Please, somebody help me."

She worried Winston's image was fading, but another, more important, occurrence flowed into her vision. So beautiful, exactly like

Reverend Beaumont had described. God was right there, shining in all His glory, waiting to receive her. He was the only one who knew she was on her way. And He'd come all the way to Broad Street just for His Sahirah.

"Sahirah!" Winston screamed, trying to stop the flow of blood that poured from her body. "Sahirah! Come on, baby! Don't die!" But Sahirah was already gone.

Handle Your Business

From the time they left the club, Rasun's jaw was still set in the mad position. "You see Sahirah sweating all over Winston? I'm saying, I really like that girl, but she don't want to act right."

Reds's observation was astute. "Fuck the bitch."

Rasun put on his "women ain't shit" act. "Man, that's what I wanted to do, but fuck it, I'm not sweating no female."

"I know that's right."

Ra pulled up on Kenny's block and pumped the brakes. "Damn, what the fuck happened out here?"

"Some serious shit by the looks of it," Reds answered.

Ra parked the car, and they both got out and walked up to where police cars were angled to block traffic. A paramedics' van was drawing attention as it made its way through the crowded one-way street.

Ra and Reds stood on the block and watched with the rest of the neighborhood. It was unbelievable. The chaos and mayhem surrounding Kenny's house was some real major shit. The police were everywhere. Ra and Reds watched as the police escorted Kenny from the house and into the back of a nearby paddy wagon. His hands were cuffed behind his back and he was calm.

"Damn, what the fuck did he do?" Reds asked, watching the

paramedics push a covered body on a stretcher into the back of the ambulance.

A distraught young girl was headed their way, and Reds stopped her for a moment. "What happened?"

"Kenny killed his father," she said.

Ra went cold. Grasping the girl's arm, frightening her with his grip, he could only get out one word. "What?"

Trying to back away, she told him, "They said he shot him about six or seven times."

"I told you not to give Kenny's ass no gun. The motherfucker done killed his pops," Reds exclaimed.

Rasun came to himself and let the girl go with an apology in his eyes. Adjusting himself to chase the chill, his quick mind speculated on what they should do next. "What are we going to do?"

Reds really didn't know what the next move should be, but he tried to think. Reds and Rasun sat there on a neighbor's porch steps, trying to put everything into perspective.

Ra was thinking of Qua's reaction. "Man, we should've never gone out. That's what Qua is going to say. We should've stayed out on the Ave."

"I know," Reds said.

"I didn't think he would kill his pops, though."

"What are we gonna do?"

"What is there for us to do?"

"We can go get the money."

"Motherfucker, is you crazy? Five-O all up in the house, man." Ra could see only danger in the suggestion. "I'm not going in the house with Ola running around gathering evidence and shit."

"I know where Kenny keeps everything. I'm going to get the money," Reds said, walking down the sidewalk to the front door. When the cops stopped him, he acted like he belonged. "That's my aunt. Let me by."

He started shouting, and Ms. Davis heard the commotion. She told the police to let him pass. She had fresh tears in her eyes, streams of water down her cheeks, and a look of pain on her face.

Once inside, he asked her what had happened.

"I don't know. It happened so fast. Kenny and his dad were cursing and arguing about him drinking and whatnot. I thought it was going to be okay 'cause Kenny went up to his room and when he came back downstairs, he kissed me on my cheek and said he was going out." Tears tracked the lines in her face, but Reds knew they were not for the dead man.

"Who was drinking?"

She looked at Reds as if to wonder where that stupid question came from. "His father." Wiping tears, she continued. "Anyway, when Kenny went to go outside, his father told him he couldn't go nowhere and then they started arguing again. Then Kenny's dad hit him and . . ." She just sat there. "And Kenny shot him," she said, still not believing it.

She had lost a husband to a son and now a son to the system. She looked so tired, not from the drama her home had been exposed to, but tired of getting whooped on. She had taken many a beating in her day from Kenny's father, and it truly showed.

Reds asked Ms. Davis if he could use the bathroom. "Go ahead, baby," she said.

Reds went straight to Kenny's room, opened the closet door, and located the shoebox. He grabbed it and checked the contents. The money and the caps were there, like always. Kenny must have put the caps back after he shot his dad.

Reds quickly grabbed the shit and put it in his pants pocket. *Kenny fucked up*, he thought. *He shouldn't have killed his pops.* He heaved a great sigh and went back downstairs.

"Ms. Davis, I got to go, but I'll be back to check on you."

"Okay." She was crying again.

"Don't worry, Ms. Davis. Everything will be all right. Qua will handle this."

"I sure hope Quadir gets my son out of jail. Oh, Lord Jesus, please don't let them lock up my child."

Reds could hear Ms. Davis praying to herself as he walked out onto the porch and past all the police officers. He went straight to Rasun and handed him the money and the pack of caps.

"What happened?" Ra asked, stuffing his pockets.

"Man, the shit is fucked up. Ms. Davis said Kenny and his pops was fighting and arguing and Kenny's dad told him he couldn't go outside. When Kenny tried to leave the house, his pops hit him and that's when Kenny killed him."

Rasun stood there looking at his friend. He was trying to understand what Kenny had been thinking. Kenny was an abused child, and his pops was a drunk who went hard on him. Yet, Rasun had never suspected it had gotten to the point where Kenny would take the man's life.

"Ra, listen to me. You should've seen the house; blood was everywhere. Ms. Davis was beat the fuck up and shit. It was chaotic." Reds shook his head in disbelief. "Kenny really killed his pops up in that motherfucker."

Rasun's head went up, his eyes working back and forth. "Ms. Davis was all beat up?"

"Man, you know Mr. Davis beat her ass every night when he got home."

"Damn, Kenny's dad on some bullshit, 'cause he wouldn't been hitting the fuck on me."

"If you was a visitor in that motherfucker, you would get your ass kicked like everybody else. That's why I never went inside when Mr. Davis was home."

"We got to tell Qua."

"He's not gonna like this," Reds observed. "What you think he's gonna do?"

"Pay his bail, get him out of jail." Ra was thinking about how this kind of news could ruin Quadir's vacation and decided it would be best not to burden Quadir until the bail amount had been established.

The next morning, Rasun woke up around eleven thirty. He sent his little brother to the corner store to get a newspaper so that he could read about Kenny.

Reds was sleeping comfortably in Ra's little brother's bed. "Reds, you sleep?" he asked, eventually waking him.

Poor Rafik, they treated him so roughly. When they came in last night, Reds put him right on the floor—didn't even give him his pillow or a blanket.

Rafik walked through the bedroom door and surprised his brother with a rolled-up newspaper in the face.

"Nigga, I'm gonna kick your little ass."

"I'm a kick your ass," Rafik responded, slamming the bedroom door.

As Ra scoured the newspaper, Reds observed, "Man, your little brother is bad. If he was my blood, I would fuck him up." Pausing, he then asked, "Is Kenny in there?"

"Wait a minute." Rasun quickly turned the pages. As he smelled an unpleasant odor, he looked at his friend. "Reds, why you fart in this motherfucker?" He stopped turning pages and uttered, "Oh, shit."

"What?" Reds asked, lying in the bed, trying to figure out why he woke up with a limp dick.

Rasun sat there reading the newspaper article, not believing it.

"What?" he asked again, smelling his hands.

"You're not gonna believe it." Ra was in a state of disbelief.

Reds picked the gun up off the floor and pointed it at Rasun. "Man, what does the motherfucker say?"

"Winston was shot and Sahirah is dead."

Rasun dropped the newspaper, forgetting Kenny and ignoring the fact that Reds had pulled the gun on him like he always did.

Reds promised his dick he'd get back to it.

"What? The boy Winston? Who woulda figured that simple motherfucker would take a hit and live?"

Reds reached for the newspaper Rasun had dropped, picked it up, and started reading it aloud.

"Nineteen-year-old Sahirah Bowden was pronounced dead on arrival at Temple University Hospital this morning at approximately 3:47 a.m. Bowden suffered a fatal gunshot wound to the chest area from a semiautomatic weapon. Bowden was a passenger in a vehicle operated by Winston Trimber, age twenty-six. Trimber suffered a gunshot wound to the left rotator cuff. Police believe Trimber was giving Bowden a ride home from a nightclub when the incident occurred. There are no suspects and no witnesses."

Reds glanced up from the paper. "What the fuck is a rotator cuff?"

"It's your shoulder," Ra answered in a soft voice.

Reds thought to himself for a minute and decided he wanted to know all the parts of the body. "I'm going back to school."

"You need to, if you don't know what a rotator cuff is."

"Fuck you!"

Ra couldn't contain his frustration. "Damn, Sahirah would be alive if she had come with us. I tried to tell her. You know I did, right?"

"Man, you tried to get her to go with you 'cause you liked the girl, and you wanted to fuck her. But she had a choice. Sahirah made the wrong one. It's not your fault. That's the only way I see it. She fucked up. She made the wrong choice, and it cost her, for real. She dissed you, so how could it be your fault?"

Rasun didn't respond.

"Now, Kenny's different," Reds continued. "I told you not to put no gun in the boy's hand. Shit, I was worried he was still upset about that girl. I thought the motherfucker was gonna shoot my ass, and you up there telling me to hand the nigga a gun, knowing I fucked his young jawn."

"Kenny wouldn't shoot you."

"You don't know how Kenny is when he thinks you're not his friend. You don't count no more to him. That's Kenny, man."

"Kenny isn't my fault," Ra argued. "I gave him the gat 'cause he was gonna be out there without us."

"What are you talking about?" They hadn't seen Rasun's mother walk in.

"Nothing, Mom."

"What's a gat and who'd you give one to?" she asked, furrowing her eyebrows.

"Mom, it's nothing, really."

"I hope you didn't give Kenny no gun. He killed his father, you know."

"I know," he admitted.

"That's why you sent your brother to the corner store to get that newspaper. I told you Rafik is only nine. He's not allowed outside by himself, and you keep sending him out there. You better start thinking, Rasun, about what you're doing. You, too, Reds."

"Yes, ma'am," Reds said.

"You boys need jobs. You're *gonna* get a job, Rasun."

"I don't want no job. Mom, please don't make me work for the white man." Rasun begged his mother not to pressure him.

"Dammit, a paycheck is a paycheck. You don't want to work for a white man, then work for a Black man, but you're gonna get a job, Rasun."

She was righteous. Nobody in her house was gonna lay around collecting dirty money, taking chances with her baby son, Rafik. "You, too, Reds. I want both of you to get jobs."

All Reds needed was a hat in his hand. "Yes, ma'am. I been looking for a job, Ms. Clair."

"That's good, Reds, but when you gonna get one?"

"I don't know. I don't think nobody is gonna give me a chance."

Rasun couldn't get over Reds kicking it to his mom.

"Well, Reds, you got to keep trying," she advised. "And take him with you."

"Mom, I been working with Quadir. He's letting me help fix up his apartment building, so I can get my winter clothes."

"Well, Quadir is a good person. I know his mother, but you don't need to be giving people no gats or whatever you said. Shit, I don't even know what you're talking about, but it don't sound right."

Ms. Clair was finally at the bedroom door and closed it behind her, leaving Rasun and Reds looking stupefied.

"Oh, and, Rasun," she said, opening the door back up, "your father said don't think about leaving this house without cleaning up this bedroom."

After she closed the door again, Reds joked, "Don't kill your pops, man. Let's clean up the room."

"Man, my moms be bugging. She been on me about getting a job for the longest."

"I don't know why you don't go to college or something. Look at you, moms and pops still together. You got a nice crib. Your moms talks to you real nice. Your pops does shit for you. You never been in no trouble. You never stole 'cause your dad always gave you money. He used to give me money, too," Reds said, thinking back to when they were little and life was easy. "I'm saying, if I had all the advantages you had, I wouldn't be out here hustling."

"Man, shut the fuck up with your bullshit. See me after you get a high school diploma. I'll be done with college by then," Rasun said.

"You know what? Fuck you and your attitude. All I'm saying is

I wish I could've grown up with you 'cause you got a nice family. I really dig your moms."

Ra thought about what he had, and what Reds never had, which was a mother and a father. Reds was a foster child from the age of five until his aunt adopted him when he was twelve. "Man, I'm fucked up. You're right, 'cause it's my fault about Kenny and Sahirah."

"No, it's not. I didn't mean it. I really didn't. You gave Kenny the gun because Kenny needed the gun out there on the Ave. He wasn't supposed to shoot nobody with the gun, just protect himself. If his pops hadn't beat on him all his life, he wouldn't have killed him. Nothing is your fault, especially Sahirah."

Ra appreciated Reds's effort, but it didn't make him feel any better. "Read about Kenny," he said, handing Reds the paper.

"Okay, it says: 'Twenty-year-old Kenny Davis Jr. shot and killed his father, Kenny Davis Sr., with a nine-millimeter semiautomatic weapon last night. Mr. Davis Sr. was pronounced dead in his home at approximately 1:30 a.m. He suffered seven gunshot wounds to the chest. Mrs. Julia Davis called the police while the argument was in progress. When the police arrived, it was too late. The argument between the father and son had already ended in a fatal shooting,'" finished Reds, shaking his head in disbelief.

"Kenny snapped," Ra added, also shaking his head.

"Yo, they got a picture of Kenny looking crazy as hell. Look at this shit." Reds handed the paper to Rasun.

Rasun didn't like what he saw and handed the newspaper back to him. Kenny didn't look right.

Silence filled the room as Rasun and Reds stared at blank space, neither saying a word. For a moment Rasun remembered Sahirah. She was so pretty, with her dimples and soft brown eyes that projected an innocence Rasun felt the night they were together.

Reds sat next to Ra and took in Kenny killing his pops. Kenny would start tripping when he drank syrup and must've been in the zone when he fired that gun. He imagined Kenny wishing he was still at home, getting ready to meet up with the crew on the Ave so they could hang out and kick it with the ladies. Instead, he was in a jail cell.

Pookey said Kenny had drunk two ounces of yella. Once he slept off his high and woke up to the reality of what he had done, that shit was going to hurt.

The silence was too much to handle, and Reds had to break it. "You can't control God's setup," Reds finally blurted out. "Only God knows why He called for Sahirah and Kenny's dad. Haven't you been to a funeral?"

"Yeah."

"Well, the preacher says God has reasons for everything. I don't have the answers to why, but I do know we got business to take care of. Come on."

Slim Sammy, a neighborhood piper, had just finished wiping down the BMW when Ra and Reds went outside.

Ra snapped on the older man. "Did anybody ask you to fuck with the car?"

Reds said, "Chill."

Slim Sammy wiped down cars every day, so Ra's outburst toward him was unwarranted. It obviously came from him being upset over Kenny.

Reds handed Slim Sammy five dollars and said, "Don't pay him any mind. Here you go."

After they got into the car and placed a brick in the back seat, Reds inserted his Geto Boys tape in the stereo system, and Rasun sped off down the block.

Rasun cut through the north side of the park to West Philly. He made a left on Lancaster Avenue and traveled down the Ave. "Yo, there goes Rock."

Reds glanced around, searching for a gold Mercedes-Benz. "Where at?"

"Don't you see him?" Ra pointed at the car. "He's right over there."

"Oh, I see him now."

Rasun and Reds sat waiting for the light to change when a black four-door Volvo drove into the bank's parking lot and pulled up to Rock's Benz. Reds and Rasun watched in astonishment as the driver pulled out an Uzi. The gunshots came from nowhere as bullets started spraying. Anyone within earshot felt a surge of fear and panic. All movement on Lancaster Avenue froze, except for mothers, who never froze when their kids were in danger and quickly grabbed their babies and ducked behind cars. The gunfire ceased. The only thing left to be heard was the sound of screeching tires making their exit.

Rasun and Reds sat at the light watching everything. Their eyes widened, and both felt so bad for Rock. They didn't know him like that, but he was Quadir's people, which meant he was family.

"Damn!" Reds exclaimed. "Rock never even had a chance to see it coming!"

Everything had happened so fast. Rock was left slumped in his Mercedes-Benz with two bullet wounds to the head and four to the chest.

Ra was still sitting at the light. "What are we going to do?"

Feeling like the bullets had ripped through the metal of the BMW and into his own flesh, he looked around to make sure the drama had ended.

"Let's get the money he had for the brick," Reds said, thinking about the thirty grand that would go to the police if they didn't take it.

"Huh?"

"Man, don't sleep!" Reds could hear the sirens all around. Cops would be there with the quickness because it was a bank. "Come on! Pull up next to the Benz."

People had begun to crowd around the car, awestruck by Rock's brains spilling from his skull.

Ra pulled right up alongside the car, his eyes flicking back and forth at the speed of light as he glanced over trying to get a glimpse of Rock's dead body. Reds jumped out of the car and dashed over to the Benz. The sirens were getting louder and closer as he opened the door. People were looking at him as he reached under the front seat and felt a familiar shape—Rock's gun. He pulled the gun out, stuffing it in his jacket pocket, frightening an elderly woman half to death at the sight of that jumbo stainless steel 9mm.

He felt nothing under the driver's seat. *Where's the money?*

He got out and walked around to the passenger side of the car and opened the door. Reaching under the seat, he smelled success. *Bam!* There it was: a plastic bag filled with money. "Hello," he said, grabbing it.

Once outside the car again, he had to get rid of all the people. "All y'all back the fuck up. Step off, old man. You can't save him. Why you standing there?"

He slammed the door and ran back over to the BMW. "Flee this motherfucker, Ra."

Ra was out before Reds could close the door. He pulled out of the lot and turned right on red. Bam, there was Ola, sirens blaring, red-and-blue flashing lights, on their way to the scene of the crime. Something about those vehicles fucked a brother up.

Reds and Ra sat still as all hell while the police went speeding by them. "Yes, that's what I'm saying," Reds said with a sense of relief, thanking God the cops didn't stop them.

Ra drove on, passing more police cars rushing to get to the murder scene.

Reds removed his baseball cap. "Yo, roll like an ordinary citizen."

Ra was stunned. "I don't believe this shit. Every day someone is getting killed."

"Did you see him?"

"No, I couldn't see shit. Was he alive?"

"Hell no. He was dead. D-e-a-d. Dead like Fred."

"Wait till Quadir finds out," Ra stated, knowing the vacation was over.

"Yeah, we got to call him *now*."

"I was going to call him after I took care of Rock, to let him know everything was all right."

"Well, shit ain't all right, man. I've never been that close to a body before. I mean, his eyes were open and he was staring at me when I took his money out from under the seat. And guess what else? He belched. Real loud, too."

Rasun looked over at his friend with disgust.

"Yo, Ock, this lifestyle ain't healthy for a brother," Reds continued.

Reds was looking in the bag at Rock's money when he noticed his arm. "I got blood on me," he said in a low-pitched voice, like a girl.

Rasun stared at him. "How you do that?"

"I don't know. I must've brushed up against something in the car."

"Was blood all in the car?"

"Man, Rock's brains were all over the car. I'm telling you, the whole side of the boy's head was gone." Reds looked in the plastic bag at all the money. "I want you to know, I'm not taking no more money off dead people, or out their cars, or out their houses, or nothing. It should be a commandment not to take shit from dead people."

Rasun kept staring at his troubled friend. "Thou shalt not steal is a commandment, Reds."

"Man, I'm saying, the boy was looking at me, like he was still breathing and could peep me taking his money." He tried to shake it

off. "You should've seen the way his dead, beady eyeballs were looking at me."

"I got to call Quadir as soon as we get back to the spot."

"Yo, what we gonna do with this money?"

Rasun and Reds took a long look at each other, both feeling the
same.

"Rock died with a tab and owed Quadir, but he's gonna mark it
off as a loss because he dead. We didn't fuck up the rest of the money.
Quadir got ninety thousand dollars waiting for him when he gets
back, and he only been gone three days." Reds wasn't sure if Ra was
feeling him, but he really wanted some of that money. "He don't have
to know nothing about this."

Reds realized the only way he could keep some of the money without worrying was if Rasun agreed with him and never told Quadir.

Ra stole a glance at Reds and realized the man needed a cheering
section. "We could come up with this money."

Reds grabbed Ra's hand. "That's what I'm saying—me and you,
baby."

Ra took his time driving back to North Philly, to the apartment.
Reds grabbed the bags out of the car, and they went inside. Ra went
right to the phone, picked up the receiver, and called Quadir at the
number he'd left. Reds opened the bag of money, stuffing some in his
pocket as Ra concentrated on phoning Qua.

The hotel operator connected the call. As the phone began to
ring, Rasun contemplated what to tell him first. Gena would be upset
to hear about her roadie, so he figured he wouldn't tell Quadir about
Sahirah until he came home. Qua would be upset enough about Rock
and even more distraught to hear about Kenny's arrest.

Ra let the phone ring about six times before he hung up and called
back. The hotel operator answered and reconnected him to the room.
Again, the phone rang and rang.

"Damn, where this nigga at?" he said, slamming down the phone.

Stickin' and Movin'

Quadir admired himself in an oval-shaped mirror hanging on the wall. The island was doing him good. For the first time in a long time his ulcers weren't bothering him, and he slept with his gun on the nightstand instead of under the pillow. His face had no blemishes, and the island sun gave his skin tone a chocolate-bronze glow. He zipped up his pants and buckled his belt.

"Where you think you're going now?" Cherelle asked as she stood in the middle of the hotel room, butt naked and angry, with her hands on her hips.

Quadir wondered why she was even there as he stared at her. She could have stayed in Philly. The only reason she was there was in case things didn't work out with Gena. "Where's your plane ticket?"

"Why? It's on the counter."

Quadir studied her and realized the girl couldn't hold him, let alone handle him. She didn't have the mental capacity. After messing with her for three months, he was bored with her. She exhibited no class or ladylike tendencies, and she was continuously annoying. The more time he spent around Cherelle, the more he wanted to be with Gena, who, on the other hand, went with the flow with a smile and without a hassle. Plus, with Gena, she didn't desire anything in return for what she was offering, and Quadir appreciated that.

Checking out Cherelle's reflection in the mirror as she continued throwing a childlike tantrum, he made the decision to permanently step off from her.

Why did I bring her? he kept asking himself. He couldn't find one reason to fuck with her, and while she stood there making an embarrassing scene, he was silently thinking of making his exit.

He turned and stood face-to-face with Cherelle, trying to figure out what she was talking about.

Quadir dug into his pocket and pulled out a knot of hundreds, peeling off ten of them.

"Is that for me?" She held out her hand.

He tossed the bills onto the bed and whispered in her ear, "Don't go nowhere. I'll be right back."

With that, he was gone. Feeling comfortable she could get back to Philly, he left with no intention of returning.

Back at the Valiant Hotel, Quadir headed upstairs on the elevator. He was running late for their seven thirty dinner reservation, and he still had to get dressed. He showered and changed, knocked at the adjoining door to Gena's room, and made his entrance.

Gena wrenched her eyes away from the mirror to inspect him as he opened the door.

"You look so handsome," she said, taking in his Armani raiment. *Hmm. Linen,* she thought. *Hmm. Eggshell. Hmm, it brings out his ... dick.*

"You look good, too, baby doll," he said, nearing to give her a hug. "You really look good." His hands traveled the outline of her figure, letting Gena know her power over him. Smiling from ear to ear, she whispered, "You ready?"

"I was born ready."

Gena grabbed her purse and glanced in the mirror at her face one last time before they headed out for dinner at sea aboard a cruise ship.

Quadir pulled a wad out of his pocket, then put it back in.

"Come on," he said, closing the door.

They didn't hear the phone ring as they walked down the hall to the elevator.

The night was a dream, and she felt like they belonged on the cover of a magazine. Numerous candles softly glowed, bringing a romantic vibe to the ship. They sat together, enjoying live entertainment while waiting for dinner to be served.

Quadir reached under the table and placed his hand on Gena's leg, prompting her to turn to him. Staring at her, he realized for the first time how beautiful Gena truly was. Her skin had a coppery glow from bathing in the sun all day, and her eyes were a tranquil light brown. He thought of how he was feeling as he moved his hand up her thigh. He was so damn princely, so inviting. How could she stop him?

When his hand got to where it was aiming, his intent was to ever so gently touch what would be her panties, to see if they were lace.

She blushed purple. "You . . . You're . . . Where's your . . ."

She tried not to let him notice how hard she was breathing, but she couldn't do anything about her eyelids, which were now at half-mast with lust. "Oops, I forgot to put some on."

"So," he said, realizing he could have lent her his own breath, which was coming in short pants. "Do you always forget?"

He moved his chair a little closer and continued playing. Gena was looking around, hoping the tablecloth would hide their game from the rest of the patrons. Well, okay, the waiters, too.

"Qua, where are your table manners?" He paid her no mind. "Qua, stop," she pleaded, wet but wanting to be proper.

Of course, he paid her no mind and continued until the waiter served dinner.

After dinner, some of the other patrons started ballroom dancing. However, neither Quadir or Gena could envision joining in.

Quadir took her by the hand and led her to the deck of the ship. "Come on, let's look at the water."

They could see their ship heading into the dock; the nighttime lights brilliantly reflected off the water. It was breathtaking. The island was beautiful, as were the people. It felt good to be away from Philadelphia.

For Gena to be where she was, and to be in the company she was in, was like a dream come true. "I can't believe we're here," she said, squeezing his hand.

"I can't believe I haven't had to answer my pager; no one's been bugging me. I can sleep. My mind hasn't played one trick on me since I've been here," he said, looking out to sea.

"Is it that bad, Qua?"

"You have no idea what it's like, having people run up to you, asking for money all day long."

Gena didn't say anything that would have revealed her jealousy that he probably gave his money freely. "I'm going back inside."

As she returned to the dining room area, Quadir turned to look out at the water. *Women,* he thought. *Bitches, young girls, even old heads, they're all the fuck the same. Confusing as all hell.*

Pushing himself away from the rail, he followed her back to the dining room.

They walked through the dining area and up a flight of stairs, to where the other passengers were waiting to disembark.

Feet back on the ground, they caught a cab to the hotel. The Bahamian musicians were playing on. The hotel lobby was bright, and the patio doors that led to the beach gave them a glimpse of people dancing and partying to the sound of the island music. The pool was lit with torches of varying sizes. There were people in the pool, sitting by the pool, dancing by the pool, and running around the pool. They were a rowdy bunch; a little too rowdy for Qua, which prompted him to lead her toward the beach.

Gena and Quadir sat on the sand smoking a spliff as they watched the moonlight bouncing off the ripples of water. Each ripple formed a tiny wave before crashing on the shore.

"Thanks for taking me on that ship tonight," she said.

"It was nice, wasn't it?"

"Yes."

"I wanted to throw you on the table and fuck the shit out of you," he said, smiling this boyish but devilish grin.

"I could tell when your hand was under the table," she said with one eyebrow in the air.

"I wasn't doin' nothin' to you. If I was, it would feel like this."

He moved gently but swiftly under the front of her dress and eagerly directed his hand to the place he wanted, tickling her leg on the way, until his fingers found the split of silky, moistened flesh surrounded by velvet.

"Qua, what are you doing?" Gena asked, looking around to see if any people were close by.

"I'm doing exactly what you want me to do," he said very politely.

"Qua, stop," she whined.

"You don't really want me to do that."

He paused for a second before he kissed her, his tongue caressing every corner of her mouth from her top lip to her bottom. Qua kissed her like he had never kissed anyone. He took his other hand and held her behind her neck. He was holding her so tight, she couldn't back away. All she could do was submit to him.

"Come on," he said, pulling her up.

"Where are we going?" she asked, realizing she had dropped her joint in the sand. Quadir led her closer to the water. "Qua, where are we going? Swimming?"

"Gena, I don't want to swim." He looked so serious. And he was.

He took her to a secluded spot off a wooded area near the water.

"I need you, Gena," he said, pulling her closer to him.

Gena pushed back. "Quadir, Sahirah told me all about you. You have an entourage of women and everyone is supposed to be trying to see you, or don't you know?"

His hands were memorizing her body, his eyes piercing through to the real Gena.

"I don't want them. I've wanted you ever since the day you were with Jamal on his motorcycle. You had your leather riding gear on. I saw you get off the bike and remove your helmet. You were so beautiful. I never forgot your face. I have searched for you. Everywhere I went, I looked, hoping to see you. Every time I saw Jamal, my heart would start racing until I realized you weren't with him." He was embracing her now, holding on like she might disappear. "Do you understand? When I finally found you in Harlem, there was no way I wanted to let you go. Only, business got in the way. Do you understand?"

Gena had heard every word he had spoken, and she believed him. At that moment Gena melted against him with passion that flowed through their bodies like the clouds billowed through the skies. He unhooked her dress and guided her down to the soft, white island sand and positioned himself on top of her. He kissed her mouth, her ears, her neck, her nipples, enjoying the shudder she didn't expect to feel.

Opening her legs, he gently slid his tongue along her inner thigh, back and forth, over here and over there. Every moment was sheer ecstasy.

Is that Barry White I hear? she thought. "Quadir."

He had found the tiny node that makes a woman a woman and proceeded to lick and suck on her like she was a Tootsie Pop. Gena lay there, gasping, squeezing the pristine white island sand through her hands as an unknown feeling went through her body. *I thought only I knew about that place. I thought it was a secret. I thought men didn't know. I thought . . .*

Suddenly, thinking wasn't important anymore. Bucking and moaning, she could only steer herself to that place, that feeling that could release her from all earthly worries and send her straight into the arms of bliss, where the world disappears for one glorious moment and the soul separates from the body.

"Ah! Oh, Qua!" Her final thrust left her shimmering, every nerve placated, unable to move. For the first time in her eighteen years of existence, a man had brought her the rapture she thought she could only give herself. From this moment, sex would no longer be a one-sided pastime, with Gena expecting only affection and gifts in return. This was more than she had ever felt before.

Qua knew what it was time for. With his large, gentle, firm hands, he moved her under his body until she was face-to-face with him.

"Qua, put it in me," she said, feeling possessed by the devil. She had never wanted a dick inside her so bad before in her life. Jamal never made her feel like this. He only worked for his own pleasure. Jamal could only fuck a woman; this was lovemaking. *Qua was the man of life.*

"Quadir . . ." She moaned as she felt him fitting himself inside her, stroking her intensely.

His dick was so big, she felt as if she had no space left. She was completely full. Each pull of the slow rhythm introduced her to a new thrill, unexpected, and with it a surprise. She was completely relaxed and so into it. Her only purpose was to give her body to him, all of her. She was completely relaxed, and with every stroke and every movement, she breathed with him, wanting more and more.

Quadir wrapped her legs in front of his arms, spreading Gena's body completely apart, lifting her from the smooth white sand while his hardness caressed all the little places that made up her being. She reached up and clamped her hand against his shoulder at arm's length, sliding herself up and down, pulling in breath on the way up, and sighing it out on the way down. He made the gargantuan effort not to discharge a drop while he watched her succumb to his passion.

She commanded him, suddenly, not to move, while her body spasmed. He waited for a moment, his teeth bared in fierce control, until she breathed again and squeezed him with muscles she hadn't realized were so useful.

Qua breathed out and began to move, his movements becoming more urgent. She found her passion mounting again as she watched his need overwhelm him. His arms snaked under her shoulders and then under her buttocks, lifting her as his beautiful Black body moved in and out of her, faster and faster, the veins in his neck bulging in his effort to go where he'd just taken her. The sounds from his throat became louder, louder still, until she felt his pent-up fluid rumble through his body, working its way through his shaft into her waiting recesses.

His body spasmed, and he spoke her name. "Gena."

She'd never known so much passion and power. It was a moment in time women never forget.

Quadir rested his body on hers, not moving. His breathing and pounding heartbeat told her he was still among the living.

In another moment, he was kissing her. Tiny, loving kisses over her eyes, her chin, her temple and, between each kiss, he met her eyes with his.

"Baby, don't speak. Don't move," he said, nestling his head between her arm and her breast. Gena was exactly what he dreamed. He knew she would be. His daydreaming was over. He had the real thing now. All the time he'd spent with other girls, picturing the girl he'd seen on the motorcycle with Jamal, was nothing compared with this.

And it had been worth the wait. He finally got up and helped Gena put on her clothes before he got dressed.

"Do you think anyone saw us?" Her eyes were darting about, worrying about who'd seen her, or worse: who'd heard her! Her hair was all over the place and she had that "*happy I got some*" smile on her face.

"I don't know, but if they did see us, they wanted to join in," Qua said as he grabbed her tiny waist and gave her a hug. "That was the best pussy I've ever had in my life," he said, combing her hair down. The brothers did agree all pussy was not the same.

They reached the lobby, and Qua wanted to check for messages. For the first time since they had been there, the hotel lobby was empty.

So, the Bahamian musicians do sleep, thought Gena. That was how late it was. There were no musicians, no tourists, no children running about, only mere silence as the hotel staff prepared for another day.

"What time is it?" Gena asked.

Qua glanced at his diamond bezel Rolex. "Five twenty-three, baby."

Gena admired all the diamonds sparkling from the lobby's track lights. "I like your watch."

"You do? I'll get you one." He shuffled through the messages. "Rasun has called four times and Reds has called once."

"Call them back when we get in the room," she said as they got on the elevator.

"I will, I will," he said, rubbing on her ass, lifting her dress, and playing with her all over again.

Suddenly, she thrust her entire body against him, pierced him to the wall, and whispered in his ear, "I want to make you happy."

He wanted her to suck his dick.

As the elevator stopped at their floor, Gena couldn't wait to get inside her room. Quadir couldn't wait to get off the elevator, either; he had to get to a phone.

Home

Once they were inside the room, Qua tried to call Rasun. He had no success; the phone rang and rang.

"He's probably sleeping," Gena said. Quadir sat there with the receiver to his ear, waiting ever so patiently for someone to answer the phone. "Baby, hang up the phone and call him in the morning."

He finally took her advice but couldn't get it off his mind. "Don't you think he must've really wanted something if he called four times?"

"Yes, and I'm sure he'll call you in the morning if it's really important."

She sounded convincing, but Quadir had a feeling something wasn't right. He ended up trying again, but there was still no answer.

Gena was undressing for a shower, making sure Quadir was aware of it as she moved around him naked.

"Can I take a shower with you?"

Smirking at her success in getting his mind off the phone call, she told him, "You can do whatever you want."

They had less than five hours of sleep. It was 10:30 a.m. and the sound of the phone woke Gena. "Hello?"

"What's up, Gena? It's Ra. Where's Quadir?" the voice said.

Half asleep, she called out for Quadir, passing him the phone. "It's Rasun."

The minute Quadir heard the name Rasun, he woke right up as she handed him the receiver.

Finding an upright position, he mumbled to Rasun as he awoke from his sleep. "What happened?"

Gena listened to Quadir's end of the conversation, feeling something was wrong by the tone in his voice.

"Kenny did what?" Quadir asked. Pausing, he replied, "With my nine. Why mines? Why you give him mine?"

Gena steadily nudged Qua, wanting to know what he was talking about. He gathered all the facts as quickly as he could.

"Rock's dead?"

Gena heard the name and knew exactly who Quadir was talking about. It was such a small world. The same people Gena knew were the same people Quadir knew.

"He got shot in the head? What about the money?" Quadir asked, waiting to hear it was also fucked up.

Rasun replied, "We got the money and the yayo."

"Yo, what are you two, Tony and Manny up in this motherfucker? Find out what Kenny's bail is and stay by the phone. I'm coming home." He replaced the receiver and turned to Gena. "Baby, come on, we got to get home. Someone killed a friend of mine."

"Who did it?" Gena asked, realizing the vacation was over.

"I don't know who," he said, shaking his head as if he really didn't know. "Guess what? My young boy killed his pops last night."

"Who?"

"Remember Kenny? He was in the back seat of the BMW the night we met."

"Yeah."

"Well, him. His pops was always beating on him and his mom. I guess he snapped."

Gena got dressed and called the airport, switching reservations for an earlier flight. She was unable to get first-class tickets and prayed they wouldn't be seated next to an engine.

The bellboy collected all their luggage and transported it downstairs. The same cabbie who had given them a tour of the island when he was lost was there to pick them up. He placed the luggage in the trunk and opened the door so Quadir and Gena could get in the back seat.

"You know where you're going, boss?" Quadir asked him as he shook his hand.

"Where you go?" Rasta Man asked.

"The airport."

"Oh, the airport, me can find it."

Quadir pulled Gena over to him and whispered, "We're gonna miss the flight." He asked the cabbie, "Do you know where the airport is?"

"Of course me know. Me can fine it, mon. Me just look right here for a minute."

Gena couldn't believe the same driver who found his way from the airport was trying to find his way back there. "He's looking at a map. We'll never get there. I might as well drive."

"Might as well."

"What if we don't make the flight?" she said.

"We have to make the flight."

Finally, they reached the airport. Quadir paid the cabbie and gave him another nice tip. The cabbie got their bags out of the car and sat them on the sidewalk so that they could be checked in.

"Take care, mon, of yourself and your lovely lady. May de spirit of de Lord be blessed upon you both. Mercy shall follow you all de days of your life." He shook Gena's hand and then Quadir's, adding, "Another place and time, sir." Then he walked back to the cab.

Gena felt a slight chill. "God, is he spiritual or what?"

For some reason, the Jamaican taxi driver who drove them around in circles when they first arrived in Nassau and drove them around on their way out had seemed to touch them both in a way neither of them understood.

Once they were safely on board the plane, Qua started chewing his gum and stuffing cotton in his ears like the last time.

"Quadir, you look crazy," Gena said as she glanced toward him. "Everything is going to be all right. Here, give me your hand." She placed it between her legs. "See? You'll be fine."

It's good, but it's not gonna save me, Quadir thought as he closed his eyes and started praying.

Gena sat back and looked out the tiny window. She could no longer see the clouds. It was wonderful to be above the clouds, physically and spiritually. She was on a natural high, thinking about Quadir. He gave her such inspiration. He wasn't like the other guys. He had an aura about him that made you want to get close to him. Like the night she'd met him and wanted to touch his face. There was something regal about him that she could not say no to. So far removed from Jamal. It was different, as if she had no resistance to the man at all. And the way he had taken her last night and put his thing down. Lordy, Gena was fucked up and happy about the entire situation.

She glanced over at Quadir. *Do you like me?* she wondered as she stared at his eyelids, which complemented his completely relaxed face. After a few minutes of thinking to herself about last night and where the two of them now stood, Gena found herself asking the stewardess for a piece of paper.

"Thank you."

"Sure thing," she said, noticing Quadir's hand stuffed between Gena's legs.

Gena covered very nicely, telling her, "His hand was cold," as she picked up his limp wrist. "It's warm now," she added, putting Quadir's hand back on his lap.

The stewardess smiled and went on about her merry way as Gena rummaged in her bag for a pen. She wanted to write a poem for him. She sat there for more than an hour thinking about last night. It was over her head. How could she express it? All the times she had thought she was having sex had been wastes of time. Nothing was like last night.

When he awoke from his catnap, she handed him the piece of paper. Quadir took the poem and turned on his overhead light, reading silently:

The Dream

My eyes are closed, but I see you so clear
I stare in your eyes and the world disappears
Leaving us together, so no one can see
Your body moves closer so you're next to me
Your fingers unbutton and take off my clothes
Your hands moving all over from my head to my toes
Without delay, you start to play
Your brown and warm fingers will find their own way
It's feeling so good and when I touch you back
You're long and you're hard and it makes me wet
I kiss your chest in a rapture sublime
As your fingers play music in three-quarter time
We're caught in a rapture without a doubt
You push my head lower, I open my mouth
Hours pass by, you pick up my face
And the look in your eyes states so simply your case
This pussy is yours and you're gonna take it
If I had said no, you know you would've raped it
You flip it and turn it and throw it around
Until you have me face down on the ground
You've found your position, ass up in the air
You get behind me and force it in there

Pushing whatever is stopping your stroke
You fuck me for hours like you're going for broke
You've totally flipped and you're out of control
Your love is insane and I am your goal
You're ready to nut, not a minute too soon
I hear the alarm and I'm back in my room
I open my eyes and I hear the door shut
I thought I was dreaming, but we really did fuck

Quadir looked at her; he couldn't believe her little poem had made his dick hard. "Come here," he said, pulling her face close enough to kiss her. He folded up the paper and put it in his pocket.

The stewardess walked by, and Quadir asked her how much longer the flight would be. Because of so many cancellations, they'd been able to get a flight straight to Philadelphia. He was so glad. He wanted it to be over. He wanted to be home.

"I had the best time of my life, Quadir," she said, looking into his eyes.

"I did, too. I wish we was still there."

"I know! Remember when you fell off the Jet Ski and almost killed us?" she said, laughing at him.

"Yeah, and remember the wave that snuck up behind you and tumbled your ass to shore?" He was laughing now as hard as she was.

"It was really the best. Especially, you know, last night."

"Yeah, it was all that."

"It was so blue."

He seemed puzzled. "So blue?"

"Yeah, you know, the opposite of having the blues is so blue." She paused for a moment, thinking about the time she'd spent with him, then added, "I wish we didn't have to go home."

He took her hand and squeezed. "But we have to, G. We have to go home."

The Drop-Off

For the rest of the flight, they discussed past relationships. Quadir confessed to seeing Cherelle but explained why the relationship was over. He was twenty-five, no kids, had graduated from college with a bachelor's in psychology, grew up in a fucked-up part of North Philly, and was poor until his pops started running street numbers and robbing banks. His dad opened a little store and, from there, he bought a few properties and basically paid his bills on time and established a solid line of credit.

Quadir was a lot like his father. He wanted to get paid and be legit one day. Quadir grew up without seeing a real Christmas. He had seen plenty of hard times. But his family made sure he got his education. Quadir heard the same speech repeatedly. "You gonna go to school, you hear me? You gonna go and you gonna learn. You know why? Because the white man don't want you to."

Over and over, that was all Quadir heard. If Black people didn't go to school, they would always be left behind. That's how it all started. His father told him the Black children picked cotton and worked the fields while the white children went to school. "Niggas didn't know shit, and they don't know shit today because they was brainwashed four hundred years ago, son." His father would go on and on. "Remember that!"

But what his dad had preached to him all those years made him a very positive individual. The substance Quadir was filled with set him apart from other brothers who were out there, especially those who hadn't even finished high school.

Quadir was an intellectual. He had made it through illegal means, through the drug game. After college and supposedly studying to be a dentist, he often wondered how he got caught up in the game. He never wanted this for himself. He'd had no idea he would turn out to be one of the largest drug dealers in the city, but once he got into the game, there was no turning back.

This was not his destination. He was only supposed to pay for school and become a dentist. Hard times hit at home; Pops was getting old with no retirement fund. The streets were calling, and Quadir answered. Hard times led him to this life, and even with the money, times were still hard with all the death, drug wars, and jealousy. It was a savage game and a vicious circle to be caught in.

The money came so easily, and his lifestyle became so large. To stop, even with the money he had saved, would not afford him the extravagant lifestyle he was accustomed to. But the more money he made, the more consequences he faced. For every action, there was a reaction. He never stopped to look at those consequences, just as the people who used drugs never thought about the consequences of what they were doing.

Quadir was relieved when their flight landed. Rasun was at the airport waiting for him by the baggage area. They exited the airport and went straight to the car. As they drove, Rasun and Quadir were busy talking about all the events that had taken place while he was out of town.

Gena simply wanted to go back to her house and make sure everything was still there. Her neighborhood had its fair share of no-good people, in particular the crackheads who would belittle themselves and do anything for a hit of the pipe. Then there were the drug pushers and lunatics with forties in one hand and guns in the other, trying to prove their manhood. The rest were either the elderly or the harmless, and they made up a very small percentage.

Qua interrupted her thoughts. "Gena, I'm gonna drop you off?"

She really didn't want to be dropped off. She wanted to drop her things off and stay with him. There was a big difference.

When they pulled up on her block, everything looked the same. Trash was all over the place. The Vietnamese people were on the corner barbecuing on the sidewalk as usual. Little kids were playing in the street, and adults were sitting on their porches, being nosy and talking about everyone they could.

Quadir and Gena got out of the car. Rasun got her luggage from the trunk and then hopped into the front seat, tilting the chair backward as he played with the CD player.

Quadir walked her up onto the porch, to her door.

"When are you coming back?" Gena asked, knowing she should've played like it didn't make a difference.

"I don't know. I got a lot to catch up on. I'll call you later, though."

A feeling of frustration suddenly covered Gena like a blanket. "What does that mean, you'll call later?" she asked, unlocking her door.

"It means I'll call later. If I can stop back over here tonight, I will. If I can't, I'll see you tomorrow. Gena, I really don't think you understand what's going on. I got shit to take care of. You can understand that, right?"

"I can understand that, Quadir. It's just that I want to be with you."

"Baby, we *will* be together. Let me go so I can take care of some things."

Gena looked at him as if she couldn't believe he was leaving her. As she opened the door, he pulled her close to him and kissed her. It lasted only a few seconds, but felt like an eternity.

As Quadir let her go, he winked at her and smiled. "I'll call you later."

"Bye." She waved, and he was gone.

Gena listened to her answering machine while she started to unpack her bags. Bria, Sabrina, Shay, Kim, Bridgette, Sheila, Mrs. Bowden, Gah Git, Gary, Tracey, Landa, Barry, Brian, Rome, a bill collector, and, of course, Jamal had all called. Jamal, however, had called at least fifteen times.

Gena called Ms. Bowden. Her message seemed urgent. At first, she couldn't believe what she was hearing. Her heart stopped, and tears welled up in her eyes. Gena sat on the bed in a state of disbelief, finding truth only in Mrs. Bowden's voice. *Why, how, when,* and *where* popped into Gena's mind. Mrs. Bowden calmly told Gena the story as it had been told to her by the police.

"I don't know what I'm gonna do without my child here," Mrs. Bowden said, sounding heartbroken.

Gena couldn't help but feel sorrow. She was so hurt, she couldn't speak. Mrs. Bowden, choking back her grief, told Gena the details of the funeral, which was being held in three days.

Gena hung up the phone and sat in complete silence as tears fell down her cheeks, reminiscing about the years she and Sahirah had spent together. From playing with Barbie dolls and getting sprayed by fire hydrants and graduating from high school to double-dating and sharing their experiences with each other. They had always been best friends. For the rest of the evening, until she fell asleep, Gena thought of Sahirah and wished she could tell her about Quadir. She wanted to call her so bad, but she wouldn't be there. The only things that would be there were priceless memories.

The days to follow were rough. Gena didn't eat, nor did she sleep. Not only was she in mourning for her best friend, but she was also in mourning for Quadir. She hadn't heard from him since he'd dropped her off at home. Now it seemed as if he'd disappeared. *He said he'd call,* she kept telling herself. It was a horrible feeling of anticipation. *Maybe I should call him.* She had no idea where she put his number on the night she'd met him in New York. Reminiscing about the fabulous time in the Bahamas only made it worse.

The phone rang, and she ran to answer, knowing it was Quadir. But the voice on the other end would say only, "Where you been?"

"Who is this?"

"Oh! Now you don't know my voice."

Suddenly, she did recognize Jamal's voice. *Figures he'd be calling.* Damn, she wanted Quadir. Gena was so disappointed, she couldn't hold the simplest of conversations.

"Jamal, what is it? Why are you calling my house this late?"

"Oh, it's like that now?"

"Yeah. It's like that."

"You're a fucking trip. You ain't shit. You lucky I don't come over there and kick your ass."

Her slow simmer erupted, her mouth so tight in anger she could barely speak. "I don't have time for you. You're beneath me," she informed him as she hung up the phone.

A few seconds later, it rang again. "What?"

"Well, damn, bitch! Fuck you, too!" he spat before Gena hung up on him again.

When it rang a third time, she said, "Hello," one more time, praying it wasn't Jamal.

"Yo, what up?" said the girl on the other line.

"Hi, Kim. What's up?"

"Nothing, chilling. What's up with you?"

"Nothing. I just got back from the Bahamas."

"You hear about Sahirah and Winston in that shootout?" Kim asked.

"Yeah, and I'm real fucked up about it."

"I know you are, as tight as y'all was," Kim said.

"Her family is real hurt about it."

"Who was you in the Bahamas with? Jamal?"

"No, I went with Quadir. You know him?"

"Quadir from down North Philly?" Kim paused. "Everybody knows him. I heard he got all the young girls strung."

"What do you mean?"

"What I said. Quadir ain't nothing but a whore. But he's good for a couple dollars, though."

"He is?" Gena responded, not seeing her baby boo like that at all.

"Seriously, though, the nigga is no joke. Everybody's trying to see him."

"Who?"

"Everybody! Everybody's trying to see him. What part of the breakdown don't you understand?"

Gena's heart sank at that moment. No wonder his ass hadn't called back.

After pausing, Kim continued. "So, what . . . you done kicked Jamal to the curb now that you're fucking with Quadir?"

Gena didn't know where she was coming from. "It's not going to work out. Shit is over. I can't explain it."

"Did you have a good time in the Bahamas?"

"It was so blue," Gena said, completely changing her tone of voice.

"How'd you get there?"

"We flew over." Gena was loving it.

"I want to go away."

"So, who are you messing with?" Gena asked, assuming she was gonna say Jamal.

"Who aren't I messing with?" Kim laughed at the question. "Shit, the man I want is nowhere to be found."

"Well, maybe you'll find him."

"I doubt it. The ones you want are never the ones who want you."

Gena thought of Quadir. "So true."

"I don't understand why you and Jamal didn't work out."

"Well, damn, why, is you trying to?"

"I'm saying, Gena, Jamal gave you the world. He did everything. Shit, all those women Quadir got, I would've stayed right there with Jamal."

"All what women?" Gena felt her heart sinking fast.

"All the women he got. The man's a millionaire. Qua's shit is blue."

Gena felt like she had to defend herself. "Well, he took me to the Bahamas."

"You in there. I'm not saying you're not. All I'm saying is a nigga like Quadir will be in the Bahamas next week with somebody else. At least with Jamal, you had a motherfucker who came home every night and gave you whatever you wanted. You must not want a brother who's gonna treat you right."

Gena had had just about enough of the Jamal cheering section. Kim had fucked up her night with the bullshit about Quadir. *Why am I telling this bitch my business?* Gena thought. It wasn't like her and Kim rolled on a regular. Usually, she would call about a party or the 411. It was time to check her.

"Damn, you got the motherfucker on three-way? You act like he's the man. If you want him, go be the fuck with him, but don't try to tell me how to run mines."

Kim had heard what she was waiting for. "Gena, you don't have to be getting smart."

"Bitch, you called my house with this bullshit. My best friend has been *killed*. Leave me alone, Kim. I got to go."

Kim wasn't trying to start nothing, being as though Gena wasn't the one to have to fight over a man. She merely wanted to know what was up with Jamal. Kim tried to cover up the shit as best she could. "You going to the funeral?"

"Yeah, I'll be there."

"Gena, look, I hope shit goes the way you want between you and Quadir, and I'm sorry about Sahirah, okay?"

"I can't tell. Instead of calling me with some concern, you calling me about Jamal."

"Look, I got to go. There's someone at my door."

"Mm-hmm," Gena said, happy to slam the phone down, hoping Jamal kicked her ass, too.

The next day, it was afternoon by the time Gena awoke. Sahirah's funeral was at sundown. The entire day was ruined from the time it began, greeted by Mother Nature's gift. *Why must it be this way?*

It was her best friend's funeral and she had nothing to wear. Quadir still hadn't called. *What could be worse?* It had been three long, drenching days without hearing from him, and Gena was a mess, thinking about the inevitable. *He played me. He was only after one thing, and now that he got it, he's gone.*

The ringing of the phone could be heard in every room of the apartment, and Gena picked up the nearest receiver. Because she expected trouble, she addressed it. "Jamal, don't you call this motherfucker no more!" Slamming down the phone made her feel even better. Jamal didn't get a chance to say anything. The phone rang again. "What?"

"What you fronting for? Some nigga in the house?" he asked.

"Jamal, leave me the fuck alone. I don't feel like you today!"

"Damn! I called to see if you wanted to use the Cadillac to go to Sahirah's funeral, or if you wanted me to go with you."

"Jamal, please. You couldn't stand Sahirah. How are you going to go to her funeral?"

"Why's there so much negativity with you? You don't sound happy."

"I would be if you'd leave me the fuck alone."

"See, every time you try to be nice to people, they don't appreciate it," Jamal said.

"You're missing the point. I hope she haunts your Black ass."

"Haunt shit," Jamal said. "What, you trying to root me now?"

"Goodbye," Gena said, hanging up the phone, leaving Jamal convinced she had done something to him.

Immediately, she called her grandmother. Gah Git had a house full of grandchildren and was attempting to brush Gena off the phone when Gena told her about Sahirah. Gah Git was sorry to hear about her friend. She knew the streets weren't any place to be. She had raised six children in the streets. Now she was trying to raise her grandchildren *out of the streets.*

Gah Git was sorry to hear Gena was going to her best friend's funeral.

"Don't wear nothing bright like yellow or orange and don't wear nothing too short."

"I won't. I'm so nervous about this funeral."

"Well, baby, the good Lord has reasons for everything. Wasn't no one closer to her than you. Maybe God's trying to tell you something. Gena, you know these things. You live to die."

Gena stared at her phone. "What?"

"I said you live to die. When you're born into this world, the only thing you're promised is that one day you're going to die, so you're supposed to do the best you can. You're never coming back once you're gone. If you're good, then your soul will rest in peace. If you raise hell, like you do half the time, well, then you're gonna have problems."

"Gah Git, stop!"

"Stop nothing. But I'm glad you're home, baby."

"Me, too, but, Gah Git, it was so beautiful there. I could've stayed there forever."

"Well, at least he didn't kill your ass and hide you in some bushes."

"Gah Git."

"Well, what do you call it when you meet a man one day and is off on some fancy getaway to the Bahamas? Did you sleep with him?"

"I got to go," Gena said, getting ready to hang up the phone.

"Have you heard from him since you been back?"

Gena didn't want to answer the question. If she told the truth, Gah Git would disapprove. Then she'd preach the same, long, drawn-out sermon about being a lady, not a whore. She even had some old Ray Charles song 'bout every time she went to a nightclub, the whole band knew her name, which she used as a metaphor.

"Yes, I've heard from him." Gena felt her heart sink as she lied to her grandmother. "Gah Git, I have to go."

"Well, don't get mad with me. You comin' down later? I'm cooking, so you might as well come and get some dinner. Besides, I want to see you for running off like that."

"Gah Git, I'm grown. I can run where I want to run."

"Baby, you can't never run from home. Believe that."

"I'm not a baby."

"Yes, you are. You're my baby, so run your ass over here after the funeral, get some dinner, and stop being so fussy."

Gena hung up the phone and went over to her dresser. She felt twisted inside, confused about Quadir, depressed and saddened about Sahirah, and mad that Jamal wouldn't stop calling her. She pulled out a knot of money from her dresser drawer. She had won eighteen hundred dollars in the Bahamas, and Qua had thrown her other money here and there that she never spent, even though she told him that she had.

"It's gone," she'd say with a serious look on her face.

Why hasn't he called? she thought to herself, searching her dresser drawers for his phone number. She looked in all the places she might've placed it. Hell, it had been more than a week and with all the weed she had smoked since then, figuring out where she'd put his number was highly unlikely. "Damn, where could it be?"

She searched around the room to no avail before finally taking a shower and getting dressed. Still searching for Quadir's number, she rummaged through the kitchen. She wanted to call him so badly, she didn't know what to do.

Why hasn't he called? Maybe he isn't going to call, she thought to herself. *Maybe Gah Git was right. Maybe I shouldn't have gone to the Bahamas with him. Maybe Kim was right. Maybe I should've stayed with Jamal. Not!*

Back to Business

Quadir rolled over from his sleeping position, sat upright, and planted his feet on the floor. He looked around his bedroom. The new burgundy carpet he'd laid recently set it off. Everything was new and very contemporary. Turning on the sixty-inch-screen TV, he turned to music videos. He threw the remote on the bed and promptly picked up his weed tray.

Things were really starting to happen for Quadir. He was getting a lot of money. He had a squad of youngsters who covered the street corners, had old heads who backed him, and he went through 150 kilos of cocaine, if not more, every week. One month he went through 1,200 kilos; that was the best month. Not only were things really going well, but he also had women. He had more women than any man he knew. He had so many women, you'd think he was the only man on Earth. They would do anything he wanted. *Anything.* He lived his life in the fast lane: fast women, fast money, fast cars, and the beeper always needed fresh batteries. Things were falling into place.

Another year and Quadir would be straight. *One more year,* he thought to himself. He lay there with his boxer shorts on, holding his crotch with one hand, smoking with the other.

Picking up his watch from the nightstand, he noted it was twelve thirty in the afternoon. *I really slept in*, he thought to himself, getting up and walking into the living room.

Another wide-screen TV sat catty-cornered against a far wall; a round, aquamarine-colored sectional leather sofa, a large circle-shaped glass table, and custom-made peach-colored carpet with an aquamarine border going around the wall was his latest interior design. There was a dining room, but Qua had transformed the space into a playroom, where he placed a pool table and, though he never imbibed, a fully stocked marble bar, all beautifully set off by beveled mirrored walls and Hollywood ceilings. Qua was a man of good taste, and he kept his apartment immaculate.

It wasn't the only apartment he had, either. Quadir had a room at his mom's house, another house where he let Rasun stay, and yet another apartment far from the city where he could discreetly take his female companions. But no one knew about it. Not even Rasun. He never allowed anyone to know about the place, the only one where he felt like he could relax and get any good sleep.

The old heads had left no stone unturned when it came to Quadir knowing what was out there. The larger Qua became, the more isolated he became. He trusted no one, and realized everyone was out to get him, or at least a piece of him. It was really fucked up, and he'd learned to be extra careful.

Rock wasn't careful. His funeral was today. Qua couldn't believe the Junior Mafia had taken his boy out; didn't want to believe it. Quadir understood killing Rock meant they wanted a war, and by no means should the boy's death go unavenged.

Easing onto his leather sofa, he played back all the conversations he'd gathered from the streets. Rock's death was nothing more than the Junior Mafia sending him an indirect message. Rik knew what he was talking about when he said the Junior Mafia was trying to weaken him. Rock was flipping keys and getting Gs, and since Quadir supplied him as well as a handful of others, Quadir was vulnerable through the people underneath him. He had to be certain of everyone he dealt with.

The worst nightmare was getting snitched on. All he needed was an indictment behind someone else's bullshit. He didn't want to deal with that any more than his peoples getting killed for buying coke from him instead of the Junior Mafia. He thought about Rock's funeral. He wouldn't be there. He'd been asked to be a pallbearer but demurred. Qua wasn't sure why he wasn't going. He felt bad about Rock dying, but going to the funeral wouldn't make much of a difference. Rock was gone, and Quadir would remember him the way he had been.

Besides, the hoes would be clocking a nigga at a funeral. It was fucked up to say, but it was true. Yeah, they might've shed a tear or two, but they were hoping to get a number and meet up with a nigga later. On top of that, the Feds would be there taking their pictures and videotaping.

Qua dialed a number from his pager and carried his portable phone into the bathroom while he showered and dressed. He made himself a turkey and cheese sandwich, then returned to the couch and waited for the phone to ring.

"Hello," he said, answering the phone on the first ring. "Nothing… Taking it easy, man," he said. The man on the other end controlled the conversation the same way Quadir did with his people. "Next week? Same place? I'll be there."

He called Rasun at his mom's house and told him to meet up with him on the Ave later.

Then he dialed Amar. "As-salaam alaykum," Amar said, answering the phone.

"Wa alaykum as-salaam," Quadir replied. "You just the brother I wanted to talk to. What's going on, player?"

"Nothing, man. Getting ready to go to this funeral," Amar replied.

"You going to the funeral?" Qua asked, thinking of Rock.

"Man, I got two funerals to go to. This girl I used to fuck with and Rock's."

Quadir realized he was talking about Sahirah. She sure did get around. He thought about asking Amar whether he knew Gena but decided against it.

"You going to Rock's funeral?" Amar asked.

"No, you know I don't go to funerals."

Amar said, "I gotta be there. I'm a pallbearer."

"What?" A moment elapsed as Qua thought about refusing to be a pallbearer himself. "So, what's happening otherwise?"

"I'm ready to see you. I want to go to Fifteenth Street."

"You on Hundredth?"

"Yeah, I'm there."

Qua said, "One hour."

"Everything the same?"

"You know it."

"As-salaam alaykum."

"Wa alaykum as-salaam," Quadir replied, and then disconnected the call.

Three minutes later he was out the door. He climbed into a 1987 Cutlass Oldsmobile and went straight to the 4-U Self Storage. Inside his unit was some furniture and a safe identical to the one in his apartment, only this one contained 523 kilos of cocaine. He grabbed fifteen bricks and put them in a duffel bag. He then placed another brick in a shopping bag, to take to Ms. Shoog's house.

He jumped back into the car and drove to a supermarket, parking at the rear of the lot, then rolled a spliff and set the CD player. He sat patiently, as if waiting for someone in the store to finish their shopping, until, finally, Amar pulled into the parking lot. He parked next to Qua. Both got out and shook hands as brothers do.

Amar said, "What's up, man?"

"You look good, player."

"Yeah, man, you know me. I got to be right for my man."

Quadir and Amar talked for a few minutes. Amar assured Quadir there was one hundred thousand dollars in the trunk of the squatter. In return, Quadir assured Amar there were fifteen kilos of cocaine in the duffel bag on the back seat.

Quadir watched Amar get into the Oldsmobile, while he got in the squatter Amar had been driving. He dropped the money off at his apartment and put it in the safe. He then headed down to North Philly to see Ms. Shoog.

Qua pulled onto the narrow one-way street and parked in front of Shoog's house. He grabbed the bag out of the back seat. The moment he opened the car door, he could hear Ms. Shoog hollering down the street.

"And don't come back in this motherfucker until you learn how to act." She was cursing some man out for the entire block to hear. "You dumbass motherfucker, you. I don't know why I even let you in here. You not fit to be in no house!"

"Who was that?" he asked her, walking up the sidewalk to her door.

"Some nigga my granddaughter brought in here," Shoog replied. "His ass damn sure look like what the cat drug in. Don't make no sense. He gonna stand up there and tell me to go to hell. He lucky I didn't break his goddamn neck," she said, taking a breath.

"Come on, get your ass back in the house. Titties hanging out and shit. How you playin', Shoog? See, you got all the neighbors looking. Come on," Qua said, walking her back inside.

Kids were all over the place, and as soon as they saw Quadir, they ran over to him to get a dollar. The house was always junky, but today it seemed as if there was an abundance of junkiness, cluttering up any space the house may have once had. You could easily tell that too many people were occupying the three-bedroom row home.

Where do all these motherfuckers sleep? Qua thought to himself, looking all around. "Shoog, why the house so hot?"

"All these lazy-ass niggas in here. Shit, you can hardly breathe in this motherfucker. I wish they'd come and get they kids and take them the hell on somewhere, and buy my fan them heathens done broke today. They got my blood pressure up so high, Lord, I'm surprised I haven't dropped dead."

She took the bag out of his hand and broke up the coke. "There's no way in a cat's ass you gonna get me in this hot-ass kitchen cooking all this shit today. I'll cook some but I'm not cooking it all. You hear me, Quadir?"

"Yeah, I hear you."

As he sat next to the kitchen window talking to Shoog, he felt a cool breeze kissing his face. He talked to Ms. Shoog about everything. She had her ways, but she wasn't nobody's fool; most old people weren't. They had been here long enough to know how not to play the fool. Shoog was full of wisdom. It was one thing to hear her; it was another to listen.

When she was done, Quadir handed her five hundred dollars and stepped.

"When you gonna get my fan?" she asked.

"Tomorrow."

"Nigga, you know you is a lie. Besides, I'm going to get me an air conditioner, right now."

"You better before your ass drops dead in this motherfucker," hollered Quadir.

He got in Amar's squatter after Shoog cursed him out and headed down to the Ave. Everybody was out. It was the crew. Qua was happy to see his bucks out there. He shook hands with everybody, got right in the middle of the conversations with them, and started kicking it.

"Yo, look at that girl," Pookey said, pointing his finger.

On the opposite side of the street, approximately twenty feet from where they stood, a girl had pulled her pants down, exposing herself. She bent her knees slightly and started peeing between two parked cars in broad daylight.

Ra chuckled. "She really don't give a fuck."

Reds shook his head. "She got to be high."

"I told y'all pipers were inheriting the earth," Pookey said.

Wiz spotted three girls walking down the opposite side of the street. "Hey, baby in the blue."

Pookey turned his face up. "Why are you messing with them girls?"

"Yo, I like fat girls, too; don't get that shit twisted. I'm not one to discriminate. Skinny, fat, tall, short, light, dark—it don't make a difference, man," Wiz replied.

The girls walked over to Wiz and engaged him in conversation. The rest of them looked at the girls real mean with "don't even think about it" expressions on their faces.

The girl in blue said, "I got a boyfriend."

"So, I got a girlfriend," Wiz informed her nonchalantly.

"Well, why are you trying to talk to me?"

"Because. Can't we be friends?"

"No, I don't think so," the girl said as if she'd checked Wiz out and was completely turned off.

"Well, fuck you, then."

"Man, leave them girls alone. Excuse him," Qua said as the girls walked by him.

"Fuck you, too," the girl said, walking away.

"Only if you promise to diet."

At that, everyone, even Quadir, had to laugh.

Quadir walked over to his jeep, which Ra had parked up the

block. Rasun followed right behind him. They decided Reds and Wiz would go back up the way and help cap the package. Quadir handed Ra the keys to Amar's squatter and left.

Across town in West Philly, Sahirah Bowden was being laid to rest. Outside, it looked like a car show. On the inside, Gena saw the girlfriends she and Sahirah had traveled with. The church wasn't packed, but it wasn't empty, either. A lot of brothers were there. Bridgette said she'd seen brothers come through for the viewing. It was nice that everyone came to say goodbye to Sahirah, and even though they didn't stay through the funeral, they did come out to pay their last respects.

She was so young and looked so pretty in a soft, pink cashmere sweater with a matching skirt. Gena couldn't see her shoes because the bottom half of the casket was closed and covered with flowers.

The preacher's bellowing voice echoed over the body of her friend, which lay peacefully beneath his pulpit, the congregation agreeing with him readily. Mrs. Bowden had lost control. The funeral nurse rocked her throughout the sermon.

Gena sat with her head hanging low, feeling the loss of her best friend like an empty pit at the bottom of her spirit. Who would she laugh with? Who would she share with? Who would be her friend? As the preacher delivered the eulogy, a tear fell for every word he spoke. Why did the words *beloved friend* make her fill up with even more emotion? What about Mr. and Mrs. Bowden? They lost a child! How were they gonna deal with that?

She glanced up and looked around the church. There was a huge crucifix suspended on the wall where the preacher was standing. Large blocks of ornate stained-glass windows allowed the last bit of sunlight to shine through as the service proceeded. Each of the faces of the people sitting in row after row of the beautiful Gothic church were as tormented and distraught as the next.

"Dear God," she prayed, "take my friend, Sahirah, in your arms. Love her, protect her, give her peace." Gena surveyed those gathered to bid farewell to the beautiful young girl they all knew, stopping at a familiar face.

All prayers and reasoning power flew from her. She couldn't believe it. *Sacrilege!* He was sitting there two rows in front of her on the right side of the church. He even had the gall to acknowledge he saw her. *Oh my God,* she thought, feeling it was appropriate to express the Lord's name. The first word that came to her mind would surely be unseemly in this church setting.

Jamal was there, sitting with Kim. Kim, who just the night before last had preached to Gena about how she shouldn't break up with him. *That bitch,* Gena thought to herself. She felt a little funny inside, seeing Jamal with Kim. That miserable man. She couldn't believe how he had called and offered to bring her, then had the nerve to show up with Kim. She saw right through him. Jealousy that Jamal was there with someone else was one thing; the aching betrayal that was setting in made her furious.

Don't nobody need to lie to me. Why didn't she say she was interested in Jamal? Why didn't he say, well, maybe I'll see you there anyway, or maybe I'll bring Kim?

He wasn't paying any respect; he was there to hurt Gena. She faced the altar and concentrated on her friend.

The service lasted more than an hour. Sahirah would be buried the following morning at ten. After today, Gena didn't know if she could take it anymore. She had shed all the tears she wanted to and put the memories of Sahirah inside her heart, where they would be forever cherished. Her only consolation was that Gena knew she'd had a friend in Sahirah, and she hoped and prayed to one day see her friend again. The firm belief Sahirah would always be with her, plus the memories they shared together, helped Gena get through the service.

As the congregation made its way down the aisle and outside the church, Gena sat still and waited for Jamal and Kim to exit the building. She wanted to watch them leave to be sure they were together. As they walked down the aisle, Jamal was a few steps behind Kim, all smiles.

What the fuck is he smiling about? Gena thought to herself as they stopped at her pew.

"Hi, Gena," Kim said.

Gena coldly acknowledged them both, silently rolling her eyes at them. "Didn't take you long, Jamal."

"What do you care for? Don't you want Quadir?" he asked.

"I don't want him. I *am* his." Gena glared at Kim as if she could rip the bitch apart. "I'm through with him. He's all yours," she spat at her before staring Jamal down, waiting for him to say one single word out his pathetic, sorry face. "If you'll excuse me, I have better things to do."

All of Jamal's feelings were crushed. He couldn't believe it. She really wasn't upset he was with Kim. His plan had failed. At that moment he got the picture it was over. "Fucking bitch," he rasped.

"Jamal, you're in a church," Kim reminded him.

"God understands. He made all of you, didn't He?" Jamal asked, looking at Kim, waiting for her to say he was right.

"Come on, Jamal," she said, leading him out of the church.

Outside, Gena saw all her girlfriends. Girls from the beauty salons, girls who worked at the mall, girls she hung out with in the park, girls who were close to both her and Sahirah.

"Yo, G. What's up?" Bridgette said.

"Guess what? Jamal is here with Kim."

Bridgette took the bait. "You should've known. I never trusted that motherfucker. Bitch ain't nothing but a whore. And she don't be bullshittin' when it comes to your man, neither."

"I didn't know the bitch rolled like that." Gena knew Bridgette was just as slimy as Kim.

"*Please*, she fucked Adrienne's man and then called her on the phone and told her. She said she felt bad about it, and as a friend, she had to tell Adrienne about her man. Now, you know the bitch is crazy 'cause the day she rings my phone with some shit about my man is gonna be the day she gets her ass kicked."

"I'm not fighting over no Jamal," Gena replied, even though she wanted to.

Bridgette glanced across the street. "Look. Isn't that Quadir?"

Gena's heart raced, her mind scrambled, and her eyes darted. "Where? I don't see him."

Quadir was in his black Range Rover with the black tinted windows, which Gena had never seen. So she turned her back, not wanting to be seen trying to see something she didn't.

Bridgette said, "Yo, the kid is so large it's ridiculous."

Andrea walked over to where Gena and Bridgette were standing. "Yo, what's up? I'm so sorry about Sahirah," she said, giving Gena a hug.

Gena returned her embrace. "I'm really torn up about it."

Bridgette was still staring at Quadir's ride. "Yo, I wonder what he's doing out here."

"Who?" Andrea wanted to know.

"That kid Quadir, from down North Philly."

"Oh God. Is he out here? Where?" Andrea pulled out a pocket mirror. "Girl, the motherfucker's a millionaire." You would've thought she had a winning lotto ticket in the palm of her hand.

Gena stood there feeling two disappointments, one after the other. She felt so fucked up inside. What if he was there to see another girl? What could be worse, besides her girlfriends standing there getting their panties wet over a Range Rover?

Qua pulled the jeep over and parked. Gena stood there with her back turned to him, hearing about his every move from the Channel Zero news reporters.

"He's walking over here," Bridgette said.

Andrea looked at the sky, happy to be near the church. "The Lord is truly among us."

Gena was so nervous; she wanted to turn around so bad to see exactly where he was.

He stepped up from behind, put his hands up to her eyes, and bent in toward her ear. "Guess who."

"I hope it's who I want it to be," she said, pushing back against him.

"Who do you want it to be?" he asked with his hands still covering her eyes.

"I want it to be Quadir."

Andrea and Bridgette looked at each other in disbelief. Gena wanted to pull him over to the side and tell him how much she'd missed him, kiss him a thousand times, and ask him why he hadn't called, but instead she carried on cool and casual with the conversation.

"I thought you didn't come near funerals," she said after he let her go.

"I don't, but I knew you'd be here."

Gena looked him up and down as if she had a serious attitude about something.

"Come here," he said as he snatched her arm and pulled her over to the side. "What's your problem?"

"Nothing."

"Yes, it is. You want to tell me about it?"

"Okay. For starters, you acted like you didn't want to see me anymore when you dropped me off. You never called, and you left like it wasn't nothing to you. Then I come home to find my best friend had been murdered. You have no idea how I've been feeling. I thought we had something, but I don't know where you're coming from. I thought I did, but I was wrong."

"You got the pager number," he said, cutting her off. "Why didn't you call me?"

"Because I couldn't find it. Besides, you said you were coming back."

"Baby, I was taking care of my business, that's all. If I was fucked up and broke, you wouldn't want to talk to me."

"That's not true. I would, too," she said.

"No, you wouldn't. Don't no woman want no broke-ass man."

That is true, Gena thought to herself as she cracked a smile. "Money isn't supposed to matter."

"Yeah, well, tell that to those miners standing over there." Qua used his head to point at Gena's girlfriends. Gena started laughing. "Yo, I couldn't stop thinking about you. I missed you."

"I missed you, too."

Gena went to grab him, but he grabbed her first and pulled her close so he could kiss her.

The anchorwomen down the street acted like they were on CNN's payroll. The news bulletin read: *Gena got it going on! Don't you wish it could be you!* And they wanted more news. Bridgette started walking over to them, and Quadir let Gena go. Gena saw Jamal turning the corner and speeding away as if the police were after him, looking right at her.

"Hi, Quadir," Bridgette said in an "I'm cheap, you can fuck me" voice.

"Hi," he said, looking at her. "Do I know you from somewhere?"

"No, I don't think so," said Kim's twin.

"Do you know Black?" Gena asked, putting an end to the madness.

"Yeah, that's my man. That's where I recognize you from, Black. Where's he at?" Qua said.

Bridgette gritted her teeth at Gena. "Oh, he's downtown."

"Well, tell him to get at me."

"I will." Turning to Gena, she asked her if she needed a ride home.

"No, I'm okay." She turned to Quadir. "I'm okay, right?"

"You're better than okay. You're with me now. Come on."

"Where are we going?" she asked as he led her to his jeep.

"Anywhere you want to go, within city limits," he replied, opening the door for her.

"I got something for you," she said.

"What is it?" he asked. Gena scrambled through her MCM bag, pulled out a folded piece of paper, and handed it to him. Quadir unfolded the paper and began reading:

Come Back
Where did you come from?
Where did you go? Will you come back?
Or don't you know? Or will you get scared and
keep running away? Forgetting feelings
that won't go away?

You can't shake it, or fake it, these feelings inside.
If you'd just stop running, I'd be by your side.

Forever your lady, forever my man,
For the rest of my life, or until the world's end,
I'll love you, you'll see that you can't hide,
And these feelings are memories
of moments lost in time.

The sooner you realize, the better I'll be,
And my love will always be here, for you, from me,

G.

"Come here," he said. Pulling her next to him, their lips touched as he kissed her deeply.

Gena was smiling. She thrived off mad affection. "Did you see

Bridgette? Isn't she a trip? She had no idea I was seeing you. No one did, except for Sahirah, and then I talked to Kim."

Quadir sat there, blocking Gena out for a moment. He thought of the bright side of Sahirah's untimely death. Ra told him that Sahirah knew about Cherelle being in the Bahamas with him and was waiting to tell Gena. *We should remember Sahirah as a big mouth,* he thought to himself as he tuned back in to Gena.

"Bridgette's really a trip. She had to come over there and try to get in your face."

"I dug her. I realized I knew her from somewhere," Qua said.

"You know her from Black, or you might know her from the boy Rich Green."

Rich Green, Qua thought to himself. He didn't like the guy. Rich Green was out to make a name for himself as a member of the Junior Mafia. He was the one who had beef with Qua's young bucks.

"She fucks with Rich Green, too?"

"Yeah, but that's supposed to be on the DL."

"I know Rich Green. Does Black know about them?"

"I don't know. Tell him."

Qua and Gena kicked names around for a long time. It seemed that for every brother Quadir named, Gena had one of her girlfriends to match with him.

"Do you know who Black's woman is?"

"Bridgette," Gena said, looking at him.

"No. Her name is Pam," Quadir retorted. "And she's set for the rest of her life. If you ask me, Black's running game on your girlfriend. She's so busy thinking she's being sneaky and getting over when, in reality, she's getting played." He paused. "The sad part about it is that if Bridgette isn't careful, she'll probably wind up like your girlfriend, Sahirah. That's why you're on probation."

"Why am I on probation? I haven't done anything."

"Gena, I've been watching you for a long time. I heard your name before. I saw your face, and trust me, baby, the two go together well."

"Well, what did you hear about me?"

"I got the dirt on you. I had to dig deep. And you're not so trustworthy, are you?"

"Yes, I am."

"No, you're not."

Gena hated when people talked about her. "You don't know what you're talking about."

Quadir laughed. "I know at least two brothers you messed with while you were supposed to be with Jamal."

"What are you talking about?"

"You said your conscience was bothering you and you couldn't see them anymore because of Jamal. You came off like a saint. That's why you're on probation."

"Who?"

"I'm not saying."

"That's because you're lying. It's not true." She was so fucking convincing she should've been on television . . . until he blurted out a name.

"Dion. Remember Dion?"

Gena couldn't believe the boy was coming at her with the dumbass shit. Damn, she thought, no one knew about that one.

"That's different. I didn't care about him and I didn't do anything with him. I never cheat."

"If you didn't care about him, then why'd you take his money?"

"He was throwing it at me."

Qua made a funny face. "Damn, I wish a motherfucker would throw money at me."

"How do you know about him?"

"Aha! Don't choo wanna know. I don't think so, baby doll."

Gena, headstrong, refused to be caught and continued sticking to a story she thought she had sewn up. "Well, at the time, Jamal wasn't spending any time with me, but I never cheated on him," she said, as if there was absolutely nothing wrong with that.

"How could the man spend time with you if he was busy making money to keep you happy? Meanwhile, you're out foolin' around," Qua said. "You should be ashamed of yourself. That's why you're on probation."

This one is different, Gena thought. He had inquired into her past, knew shit he wasn't supposed to, and then threatened her with probation. What exactly is probation? Does it mean no money or something? What part of the game is this?

Gena couldn't figure him out. Most male creatures were simple as fuck. Quadir, however, was in a class all by himself. He didn't want to simply play. He wanted to win.

During the following months, she stayed on probation. Qua played a lot of mind games. He even paid a friend of his to push up on her. The guy pulled along Gena in a candy apple red convertible Saab in the Starling Mall parking lot. He offered her dinner, then gave her some roses he already had in the back seat, which she gave right back. He talked real nice, giving her all kinds of compliments, but to no avail. Gena wouldn't give him the time of day.

Quadir really gave her a hard way at first; then he started to ease up. Things happened like they were meant to. Gena stayed right up underneath Qua. She was even with him when he took care of business. She realized it was no place for her, and so did he.

They did everything together. By the time Christmas came, she was staying at the apartment where he usually entertained his women. Gena felt so at home, particularly after she burned all the evidence that indicated he had a life before she came along. Gena cooked, cleaned, and even did laundry between trips to Bloomingdale's and Ann Taylor.

She had a ball hurting the feelings of every female who called for him. "Bitch, please, I'm his woman; you're a fuck. He doesn't care about you. Quadir, tell her you don't want to fuck with her." She would always pass him the phone, demanding her position be confirmed. He would do it, too.

Gena had put her thing down, real hard. Her power and wiles were so strong that, for once, they kept Quadir interested. He liked coming home to her at night, and he loved her jealousy. She made such a fuss over every little thing that Qua soon realized he'd have to be a man about his extracurricular activities and keep them hidden from Gena.

Being Muslim, Quadir didn't celebrate Christmas. But he promised that every other year they could celebrate with gifts. One day before the holiday, he hid a box in the house and made her look for it. Finally, she found it in the kitchen closet, a big box with gold wrapping paper and a red bow.

"Not my to-the-floor fur, Qua?" She kissed him before she even opened it.

"How'd you know?" he asked.

Gena paid him no mind, too busy ripping at the paper. "How'd I know," she muttered, sounding as if that was the stupidest question ever asked. Gena thought she would die. It was the coat she had been requesting for months. A mink, to the floor, the most beautiful thing she'd ever seen.

Everything was going so well. The past six months had brought them close, real close. The best part of the whole relationship was they were on the same level with each other. Though they were both the biggest flirts in the world, it was clearly understood there was no messing around. Quadir already knew it would be stupid of him to think there wouldn't be guys trying to see Gena; she looked too good. The brothers would always try their luck. Gena handled it, though; she was never loose. She always maintained her composure and represented Quadir, which was a lot of representation. Qua had always been a flirt, except his flirting was different from hers.

Three days after Christmas a baby girl was born at 4:30 p.m. She weighed six pounds and fifteen ounces. She was a beautiful baby with locks of black hair and beautiful brown skin. Cherelle, the baby's mother, was in the Germantown hospital alone. She couldn't believe she'd given birth all by herself. She'd paged Quadir and told him that she was in labor. He didn't call back. Even though she wasn't sure the baby was his, she played the entire nine months as if she were. She was so glad she finally knew who the father was once she saw her daughter. She hadn't been too sure, but when she came out, Cherelle took one look at her and knew she would be called Quanda.

Qua knew his flirting was going to get him into trouble. That was even his New Year's resolution: No hoes in 1989.

Gena's resolution was much simpler: to save money. Something she'd never been able to do. Gena spent money as if it were falling out of the sky like rain. She didn't save one dime. It was 1989. She would be turning nineteen in March, and she didn't even have a bank account. Jewelry, clothes, shoes, even a fur, and no bank account.

If Qua left her today or tomorrow, if he went to jail, or if *anything* happened to him, she'd have nothing.

Surprise

1989

The months passed quickly. Ever since Sahirah's funeral, Quadir and Gena stayed together, and everyone knew it. He let her drive the Range Rover while he drove the BMW.

He bought her a house in Montgomery County. It had four bedrooms, a pool in the backyard, and a huge front lawn that required landscaping. There was a total of eight chandeliers throughout the house. The vestibule, bathrooms, and kitchen were all complete with coordinating marble.

The basement was Quadir's. No women allowed, only his boys. It had a pool table, a bar, and a sixty-inch-screen TV. He had a sound system throughout the basement that could shake the entire neighborhood. The living room had eggshell carpet, off-white furniture, and contemporary marble. A large curio sat cornered against the wall, where Gena had placed thousands of dollars' worth of crystal. Where the furniture came from Qua didn't care. He did care she had spent thirty-two thousand dollars on the room.

The family room had butter-soft navy blue leather furniture and a custom-made light blue carpet with dark blue trim. In the middle of the far wall was a fireplace. Another big-screen TV sat catty-cornered in the family room next to a stereo system twice the size of the one in the basement. There were sliding glass doors that led out to the backyard and the pool.

The kitchen had been remodeled and had everything from a dishwasher to a food processor. The dining room floor was black marble with a black-mirrored dining room table in its center that seated twelve. A matching breakfront sat against beveled mirrors adjacent to a gray stone wall.

Their bedroom had rich, dark green carpet. A huge king-size bed connected to an elaborate wall unit that stretched across the entire wall and sat facing the door.

The closets were filled with shoes and clothes. Gena and Quadir had so many clothes, both rarely wore the same thing twice.

There were two extra rooms. One Gena had converted into an office, complete with a maple desk, computer, and fireproof file cabinets. In front of the desk sat two bone-colored leather chairs. She had a bookshelf the size of the wall built for the room and went out to bookstores and purchased hundreds of books to occupy the shelves.

The other bedroom was really like a storage area, even though it was intended as a guest room. Though the family rarely visited, Gah Git called every day.

Quadir stayed gone, as if he was lost and couldn't find the house. Gena didn't understand it. He would stay out all night, usually not returning home until the wee hours of the morning.

Even though he was never there, he wasn't going anywhere, either. She felt secure, and she felt happy. But Gena unknowingly had allowed herself to be isolated. Quadir had conveniently and successfully excused it as a safety precaution. None of her girlfriends were allowed in the house. That was first and foremost. Only a few family members had visited. Not only did Gena believe this was right, but she also protected her home and protected Quadir by any and all means. She never took anyone there. No one except family had their home number. She could only be paged. Traveling in certain parts of the city, even talking to certain individuals, was a no-no. And, for the love of money, it was a small price to pay. It was nothing. She had no worries, but she was left alone.

One rainy day, Quadir stayed in. It was a treat to have him home. The two cuddled on the sofa with a blanket and popcorn and watched daytime TV. That's when a commercial came on. The "make each day count" speech, and "why waste another moment?" grabbed her. She turned to Quadir and asked if she could go to college, really wanting to.

"What do you want to study?" he asked.

"You know, I hadn't thought about it. But I like the idea of business management, and it would give me something to do, Quadir. You're not here a lot, and there's nothing left in the malls. I have everything," she said, throwing her hands out in the air, really wondering what he expected her to do.

Quadir was excited for her. He wished he had it in him to go back and finish dental school while she was in college. "Maybe I'll go, too."

"For real, I can go? You're going to come, Quadir," she said, moving over to him, hugging his neck, and giving him kisses in a circle motion over his face.

"Well, I can't do it now. But when things lighten up, I'm going back. I always wanted to be a dentist," he said, trying to get her off his neck.

"I want you to be a dentist, Quadir. I think you would be a great dentist. I really do." She meant every word.

"I love you, Gena."

"I love you back, Quadir."

Gena started college three weeks later and was doing quite well. She occupied most of her days with classes and her nights with studying.

One day, hearing the BMW in the driveway, she peered out the bedroom window to see Quadir pull into the double-door garage. She flew down the stairs and met him as he walked through the door.

"Hey, baby. You all right?"

Her voice was rather cold. "I'm fine."

"What are you going to do today?"

"I want to go shopping and pay my credit card bill," she said, following behind him.

Quadir knew that meant money.

"What are you doing?" she asked.

"Nothing. I got to be somewhere in an hour." He took off his clothes and left them in the middle of the floor for her to pick up.

"It's ten thirty in the morning. Where have you been?" All she needed to complete the picture was a little steam coming out of her ears.

"I been in the street."

"What the fuck is the street? What kind of answer is that? You're always in the street. You never have any time to spend with me. You're never here anymore because you're always in the street."

She stared him down, waiting for an answer.

"Gena, you know what I'm in the street doing. Hustling. Making money. You know, that green-colored paper you love to spend so much of? Look at it, Gena, ten thousand for a dining room. Where's the chairs, Gena?"

"You know they'll be delivered next week."

"Yeah, for an additional eight thousand. Ten thousand and no chairs, and the bedroom, fifteen thousand dollars, Gena. Not to mention a living room no one can go into because it's white. That was thirty thousand right there. Our living room is someone's house.

"Your fucking wardrobe and jewelry are twenty working motherfuckers' salaries per year, and you got a problem with me 'cause I'm in the streets. Don't you think I want to come home? But what the fuck! When I do, I get to hear a bunch of bullshit. I can't even get my dick sucked because you're too busy using your mouth to ask me stupid questions like, Where have I been all night?"

He stopped to catch his breath, and she stood there looking at him. *He needs some pussy*, she thought to herself. He acted as if she were the one with the problem and not him.

Finally, he calmed down and gave in a little. "I got a surprise for you. Meet me here at six."

He handed her a piece of paper with an address on it. From there, nothing more was said about the hours he was keeping. Quadir went into the kitchen. As usual, Gena had made his breakfast and set his plate in the microwave.

When he was done eating, she followed him upstairs to ask him for some money. She felt bad after hearing his speech about all the money she had spent. If he started hollering again, she was going to tell him to forget it and walk away.

As she walked into the room, he was on the phone saying, "You what?" When he looked up and saw her, he hung up the phone.

"Who was that?"

"Nobody," he said with a stupid-looking smile on his face.

"Quadir, please."

"It was Ra."

He was lying; she could tell. His beeper went off, and he picked it up immediately and turned it to the vibrate mode, but he didn't call back the number. It vibrated again, but Gena couldn't hear it.

"I need some money."

"What's new?"

"Quadir, is there someone else?"

"No, Gena. Why would you ask me a question like that? Do you got someone else?"

"Of course not. You don't spend any time with me. I come into rooms and you hang up on people. What's that?"

"Gena, that *is not* true. We go to Atlantic City almost every week and we go out to dinner at least four or five times a week. Hell, you'd starve a nigga to death, so we got to go."

"Sometimes I really think you don't love me."

"Come here."

Gena's fingers busily removed his clothes. Qua kissed her mouth and kissed nipples that reached for his lips in the hope of deep pleasure. He touched her with his wonderful, knowing fingers, becoming more excited with every moan that escaped her lips.

She made him hold still while she worked her knees to the floor. She took him into her mouth and sucked, up and down, on the fleshy instrument God had provided him. Clenching his teeth to prevent himself from exploding too soon, Quadir picked her up with great strength and pinned her up against a wall. She was so wet and so hot. He hadn't seen her this passionate in months, and he was taking every advantage he could of her.

He knew she was an undercover freak and would do the mailman if he wasn't on his job. He turned her around so her back was to him and she faced the wall and, in a standing position, put his thing down. As she felt herself climaxing, she told him to come with her and he did. Releasing, as she basked in the heady state of shimmering pleasure, he whispered, "I love you."

Following her into the bathroom, he stood above her as she was sitting on the toilet. She looked up, seeing his dick pointed straight at her ear. "I've missed you, too," she said as he lifted her onto the bathroom counter.

Wanting every inch of him inside her, she spread her legs open and let him in. He held her thighs so tight as he attempted to push his body and soul into her, all the while whispering in her ear, "It's all about you, Gena. All about you."

Holding on to the counter's edge, she felt his body shudder, giving up the demon, releasing what seemed like all his life force.

How could she doubt him after a shot like that? *He is in the street. He'll never cheat. He loves me,* Gena thought.

Finally able to move, Qua helped her off the counter, reentered the bedroom, and turned on the CD player.

After they showered and dressed, Quadir went downstairs. She knew he was going to the safe. She didn't know the combination; he wouldn't tell her. In a few minutes, he returned and placed three stacks of money on the bed.

"You gonna meet me at six, right?"

"Yeah. How much is there?"

She couldn't take her eyes off the piles of bills in front of her. What bag would she use to carry all that cash?

"Seven or eight thousand."

Quadir was ready to go. "I'm taking the jeep. I'll see you later." She was holding out a piece of paper, which he pocketed and then kissed her goodbye.

He got as far as the jeep before curiosity got him.

Lying Still
I'm lying still and I sense you're there,
Your fingers all over, touching everywhere.
I feel your strength, I feel you inside.
You're taking me someplace insanities hide.
On top of me now, you feel big and strong.
You're making me open, and you're taking control.
The deeper you're able, the deeper you'll go,
'cause you have the power, and I can't say no.
Giving me all and everything that you've got,
I feel you inside me, so warm and so hot.
I'm lying still now; I'm sweating and wet.
It's four thirty a.m. And you're not home yet.
Where are you, what are you doing, and who are you doing
    it with?

Qua turned the key in the ignition and went to work. Happy.

***

Gena called Tracey to see if she wanted to go with her to the mall. She and Tracey had become good friends since Sahirah's passing. The girls talked for a few minutes before Gena left to pick her up.

They went to the Gallery Mall in Center City, something Gena did every day and never got bored with. The established department stores were connected underground. There were many shops in a spacious wonderland. It was like a shopping amusement park, and it felt amazing to be able to buy whatever she wanted.

She picked out a lounging robe for Gah Git and paid for a belt Tracey was admiring. Quadir now had a dozen more pairs of Polo boxers, and Gena got a couple of bottles of perfume for herself and her cousin Brianna. Her only choice was to buy a fragrance she didn't already have.

After leaving the mall, Gena went to Gah Git's house. She was so happy to see her grandmother and fell right into her arms. Of course, Gah Git was always glad to see Gena.

"How's my baby? Come on in here and sit down. Where's Qua? How's he doing?" Gah Git was asking questions so fast, Gena hardly had a chance to answer.

"Quadir is fine. He's at his store."

"How are you, Tracey?" Gah Git said, finally acknowledging her.

"I'm fine. How are you?"

"Oh, I'm pretty good. My leg hasn't been bothering me, praise the Lord."

"Gah Git!" Gena hollered her name so loud, she startled her grandmother. Gena remembered the packages and headed for the door. "I got you something from the mall. It's in the car."

"What's the matter with her? Child scared me half to death." Pausing, she waited a few seconds and then asked Tracey, "Gena know about the party?"

"No, she's worried Quadir has forgotten her birthday," Tracey said.

Gena came running back in. "Here you go, Gah Git."

Gah Git's face lit up at the contents of the bag. "Oh, Gena, baby, thank you! It's so nice. I can't wait to wear it tonight. You hungry?"

"No."

"What about you, Tracey?"

"No, thanks."

They both turned their heads to the clatter on the porch and the opening screen door.

Bria and Brianna, Gena's twin cousins, came bursting into the house. They were drop-dead gorgeous, wore their long hair in wraps like Gena, and were identical except for a mole on Bria's right earlobe. Plus, she had larger feet. Gena couldn't stand Bria, and Bria couldn't stand Gena.

"Brianna, I got you something."

Taking the bag Gena handed her, Brianna exclaimed, "I been wanting this for so long. Thanks, Gena. Do you think you can loan me twenty dollars?"

"What you trying to do?"

"Nothing. I only need twenty dollars. Come on, please?"

Gena handed her a twenty-dollar bill. "Here."

Bria was mumbling something under her breath. She couldn't stand it when Gena came around. Everybody acted like she was some goddess.

With the presence of her archenemy now full-faced, Gena decided to leave. She dropped Tracey at home and then found Quadir engaged in a craps game on the corner of the Ave. After Quadir lost a couple of thousand right quick, Gena followed him to his new store. It was a nice corner storefront property. Quadir sat and told her his plan of opening a beauty salon. Gena worried for a minute but soon realized her man was all about her.

"This is for us. This beauty salon is for you. I want you to decorate it and run things for me. Run the business, our business. So, you down or what?"

"You know I am, baby. I love you, Quadir," she said, kissing her man.

"Come on, let's go celebrate our new beauty salon. It's your birthday, right?"

"Where will we go?" she asked, happy he hadn't forgotten her.

"I don't know. Let's get dressed and go to dinner."

Once they got home, Quadir stood there looking at Gena. She was as beautiful as the night he'd met her on 125th Street in Harlem.

"Something the matter?"

"Trying to figure out if I should give you your birthday gift now or wait until tomorrow."

"I was beginning to think you'd forgotten."

"Forget and have to hear that shit forever? Besides, I know how nice you perform when I remember holidays, birthdays, the day we met, the day we first did it. You know, all your reasons to get a gift."

"Qua, please, you're exaggerating. Now, where is it?" She looked a little possessed as he stood there picking the dirt from under his fingernails. "Quadir, don't mess with me."

"Pretend you're coming through the front door."

She went into the vestibule that connected to the hallway, which spread throughout the rooms of the first floor. On the marble table, placed on the marble floor near the doorway sat a framed five-by-ten professional picture of them, a candy dish, and a crystal vase with red and white roses in it. Quadir would buy her two dozen roses every week, which she placed in the same crystal vase. Gracing the upper corner of the picture was a 24k gold-and-diamond bracelet designed with 1 carat diamond charms, giving it a total weight of 12 carats.

Gena delicately removed the charm bracelet from the picture, adoring it like it was the Holy Grail. She attempted to place the bracelet around her wrist. "It's the most beautiful thing I've ever seen. I love it. It's so blue."

He fastened the clasp for her. "Here, let me help you."

"So blue," she said, marveling at the radiant colors that were bouncing off the chandelier.

"I got you something else upstairs."

"Kiss me." Letting him go was so hard to do. Pulling away from her, he held her hand and walked her upstairs.

It didn't take her any time to open the boxes and find a black Versace pantsuit, a pair of gator boots, and a black Chanel bag with thick gold Cs on the side.

Both of them dressed in black Versace and black gator boots, then arrived at the Malibu Dining Room. Quadir informed the hostess their reservation was for Richards. She grabbed two menus and escorted them away from the dining room, downstairs to the lower level.

The entire lower floor was quiet. As the hostess opened two large double doors, everyone stood simultaneously and yelled, "Surprise!"

They'd only been waiting for about forty-five minutes. For the first five minutes, Gena was inundated with people in her face wishing her "Happy birthday! Happy birthday!" All her girlfriends were there, as if they'd really miss a free meal. All she could do was stand beside her man and take it all in.

"How much did this cost?" she whispered in his ear.

"I don't know. I haven't gotten the bill yet."

She spotted Gah Git, her cousins Bria and Brianna and Gary, all ready to eat. All Qua's friends were there, which meant all the players were in the house. Everybody was determined to make this a good one. As Gena's girlfriends began standing around her, Quadir drifted off to find Rik.

"Come look at the bracelet this bitch got on!" Andrea exclaimed, dragging Bridgette over to see it. After a glimpse, she was as astonished as Andrea.

Looking across the room, Gena spotted Quadir and Forty surrounded by some girls but didn't pay it any attention. Rik and his wife, Lita, walked over to where Gena and her girlfriends were standing.

"What's up, Rik?" Veronica said as the hair on Lita's back stood straight up.

Lord, thought Gena, *they gonna tear this motherfucker up tonight on my birthday!*

"How you doing, Veronica?" he said.

Lita spoke up. "Why are you talking to her? Do you know her?"

Gena sighed. *Lord, here it comes.*

Rik tried to do damage control. "Lita, all the girl said was hi."

"Whatever. Happy birthday, Gena." She leaned forward, kissed Gena on both her cheeks, and said, "I hope you like it."

Then Lita walked away. Gena would've never walked away. Rik looked better than he'd ever looked in his entire life. Or maybe it was the diamonds blinding everyone, since Rik wasn't the most handsome man in the world. Yeah, it must've been the rays of light emanating from his body.

They all stared unbelieving as Veronica turned her venom on him and whispered in his ear, "What happened? I still want my abortion money, or your bitch is gonna find out how her man spends his spare time."

"See, that's why I got nothing for you. And even if you did tell Lita, she'd kick your ass and still stay with me."

Rik stood his ground with Veronica, leaving everyone else standing still, trying to figure out what the hell she'd whispered in his ear.

Unfazed, he turned to Gena. "Happy birthday, G." He kissed her cheek and handed her a small, ribboned box.

"Thank you."

"No problem," he told her, rolling his eyes at Veronica before returning to Lita's side.

Everyone nearby was eager to see what was in the box, reaching their hands out as she opened it. She glowed as she felt their envy.

"It's so nice. A diamond initial pin. G for Gena."

"That is nice," Andrea said.

"It sure is," Bridgette added.

"Let me go thank Lita and show Gah Git." Gena was playing the perfect hostess. "Excuse me."

Gah Git was overwhelmed. "Oh, Gena! Look at you. Look at that!" Her eyes roamed all over her fine granddaughter, taking in the bracelet, the pin, and Gena's beauty. "That Quadir is a good man. You take care of him, you hear me, girl?"

"Gah Git, I *am* taking care of that man. Until the day I die, I'm gonna take care of him." Hugging her grandmother, she asked, "Where are the twins?"

Looking about for the girls, Gah Git noticed a bit of commotion across the room. "What's going on?"

"I don't know. I can't see."

Across the floor, Rik and Quadir were wrestling with the girl Quadir and Forty had been talking to earlier. Before Gena could get a glimpse of the entire picture, the staff ushered the girl out of the dining area.

"What's happening?"

Gena touched her grandmother's shoulder and told her, "I don't know, but I'll find out."

Approaching Quadir, she asked, "What's going on?"

"Nothing."

Why the hell does he always say "nothing," when it's perfectly clear something is going on? "Q, aren't you gonna tell me what happened?"

Rik jumped in, asking her how she liked the pin.

"I love it, Rik. Look, Quadir, did you see the pin Rik and Lita got for me?"

"Let me see."

She showed him the pin and let him kiss her, waited a moment longer, then asked, "So, are you gonna tell me who that girl was?"

"That bitch followed me here and was questioning Quadir about me. Qua told her that I didn't want to fuck with her like that and she got mad."

Quadir broke in, glad that Rik had lied for him. "She's a stalker," he added, laughing weakly. "Rik, I don't know how you do it."

Rik finished the lie. "You're not gonna tell Lita, are you?"

As the men lied to Gena, others were observing the girl through the window.

"Look, that girl is staring at Quadir," Tina observed.

Gail noticed as well. "Look, Bev. Look out the window."

Beverly took a good look. "Damn, she looks like she's about to cry. Don't she?"

Once the girl realized she'd been recognized, she hurried away.

Beverly shook her head. "Bitches are so desperate."

"She straight played herself," Tina said.

Gail asked, "Did you see them haul her ass out of here?"

Tina shook her head. "So embarrassing."

Bev was savoring the gossip. "Wait till I get back in the hair salon. She's the one who's supposed to have the baby by Quadir, but don't say nothing."

Tina and Gail gave each other a knowing glance.

"We won't," Tina said.

Gena was across the room greeting everyone. She finally saw her cousins Bria and Brianna. Quadir was busy introducing his friends to Gena's friends, trying to hook everybody up. Gena couldn't believe the number of people surrounding her.

"Tonight's the night," Rik whispered.

Qua grinned. "Rich Green?"

"Yes."

Quadir was thoughtful. "You know Jerrell isn't gonna like this."

"Let him bring the noise. He started this shit. He's been fucking up my pockets for the longest. Enough is enough. He pushing every motherfucker not to buy coke from me. You know how many bricks I can't get rid of because of him?"

"You? What about me?"

Quinny Day showed up at their table. "Yo, this was really nice, man. I can't stay for dessert, but I wanted to let you know this was smooth, Ock."

"Where you got to go, Quinny?" Rik was feeling a heavy weight of frustration after seeing Quinny's happy face.

"Nowhere. I got to meet this girl. She's going back to Connecticut and I'm saying goodbye to her tonight, if you catch my drift."

"I hear you, player," Quadir said.

Rik spoke up. "When you gonna have my money, Quint?" He'd given Quinny two keys three weeks ago and was starting to wonder when he was going to get paid.

"Nigga, I got you. Don't sweat that shit, baby. Be cool. I got you."

Tyrik shook his head, watching Quinny mingle away in the crowd. Quinny Day never had his money. If he weren't Lita's cousin, he'd have him knocked off.

"Why do I continue to even ask that motherfucker for my money? Do you know what he owes me? Lita's motherfucking relatives are a trip."

"Rik, I want to get out of this shit," Quadir said.

"Out of what?" Rik had no idea what his mentor could be talking about.

"The game. This shit is too much for me. I want to sit at home instead of hustling out here in these streets."

"I know that's right. Motherfuckers are passing out time like it's government cheese."

Qua turned to face him. "I don't know what I'm going to do.

Cherelle calls the house and she follows me around. The bitch is a fatal attraction."

"You played it real cool, though. You didn't even blink when you seen her walking over to you."

"Shit, I wanted to run my ass the fuck out of this motherfucker, but Gena's nosy-ass girlfriends would've had something to say."

"Those are some bitch-ass girlfriends she got. How do you take it? I done fucked almost all of them."

Qua's eyebrows went up at the revelation, and Rik warmed to his subject. "The only one I was really fucking with was that Veronica bitch, and she tried to baby trap me, man."

"Yeah, right. I heard."

"I admit I was sweating the girl back in the day, but sis wouldn't give me no play. Then I got a little paper, became the man, and who do you suppose was on my dick?"

"Veronica."

"I been playin' that bitch ever since."

The brothers clinked their glasses and drank. On the table sat two bottles of Dom and one bottle of Remy XO.

Gena took advantage of a lull in her own conversation to look around. The Malibu Dining Room was fabulous. The only thing missing was Sahirah. Her pretty face, her small frame, and her warm smile. If only she was there with her. She was the one who pulled over Rasun that day in Harlem. If it hadn't been for her, Gena wouldn't be standing there, portraying the perfect queen of the crack stars.

"Sahirah," she mouthed. *I miss you so much*, she thought. Not a day would pass without Sahirah being in her thoughts. She held her glass up, and there was Sahirah with her. *A toast for old times*, Gena thought. She toasted to the memory of her best friend.

"Hey, Gena. Happy birthday," Black said, trying to figure out what she was staring at.

"Hi. Where's Pam?"

"Home with the kids. Where's Q?"

"See him? He's over there, at that table in the corner," she said, pointing.

As soon as he'd left, she heard someone singing, "It's your birthday. Happy birthday. It's your birthday."

"Charlie Tuna, you're so crazy."

"Yo, Gena. You think you can hook me up?"

"Hook you up how?"

"I'm trying to see your girlfriend."

"Who?"

He suddenly noticed her wrist. "Goddamn! That motherfucker is all that."

"Isn't it?"

"You playin' with this piece right here. This is some real high-powered shit. Damn, let me step the fuck back!"

She stood there laughing and smiling as Charlie gassed her head up. Finally getting back to the point of why he stepped to Gena, he asked, "Are you gonna hook me up or not?"

"Hook you up with who?"

"Baby, it don't matter. Give me a quiet one. Y'all women got too much mouth these days, always yappin'. Give me one that don't talk."

"What? We're not supposed to talk?"

"Yeah. When somebody says something to you."

Charlie spotted a girl who attracted him. "Hook me up with her?"

Gena smiled. Charlie had chosen Bev from LeChevue and she never shut up.

"Beverly." Gena took her girlfriend's hand and made an introduction.

She left them there to talk as she walked over to where Quadir was sitting. Coming up behind him, Gena put her arms around him, bent down, and started licking his ear. "I'm ready to go home," she whispered.

They began to say goodbye to everybody who'd come out to get a free lobster-and-champagne meal. Qua told her, "I'll be back. I'm going to take care of the bill so we can go home."

Gena turned to see Andrea watching her slink into her to-the-floor mink.

"You leaving?"

"Yeah, we're going on home."

"You've had a happy birthday, and the shit ain't until tomorrow."

"Yes, this is true." She jingled her bracelet for Andrea. "Qua really surprised me. First, the bracelet, the outfit, and, to top it off, dinner with all our friends. This was enough."

"You're so lucky."

"I'm blessed."

Rik was hanging up the payphone outside the dining room. "Yo, check it out." He pulled Quadir over to him. "Rich Green is no longer a member of the life force as it exists on this earth."

"Dead?"

"Through the heart and through the head. Nigga said since he fucked his baby mom, he shot him in the dick, too."

"Damn."

"Quadir, don't look so sad, 'cause the nigga was plotting. Always riding around the same corners, all damn day and night. Trust me, the boy Rich had a list. Junie was locked up with my brother and told him everybody was on the list. Shit, the nigga's list was so long, by the time the Junior Mafia finished, it wouldn't be nobody left."

Quadir said goodbye to Rik and shook hands with a few other brothers before finding Gena. Getting into the car, Gena looked at her man. "I can't believe you did all of this for me."

"Gena, tonight was nothing compared with what I have in store for us. This is only the beginning."

The Cheddar Will Be Better

Qua sat in the living room of his secret hideout and placed the counting machine on the table. Pulling up a chair, he organized all the money in the safe. He plugged the counting machine into a socket, sat back, and watched it do its job. Two hours later, the total was looking him in the face.

Got to be a mistake, he thought. But there was no mistake. He was speechless. The machine totaled his money at $17.2 million. "I'm a millionaire," he said to the fish in the tank. He'd had an idea but had never counted the money in the safe. He wanted to jump, shout, knock himself out!

Then he sat down and began counting it again. The total was the same. He ran his hands through the bills, stuffing them into his pockets, his shirt, his baseball cap, his jeans—all hundred-dollar bills.

In front of the mirror, seeing all these green pieces of paper falling out of his clothing, he thought to himself, *All this money. Drug money! There's a lot of paper in the ghetto.*

Quadir sat back and looked at all the stacks of money surrounding him. The years of hustling had paid off. People spent their entire lives working to retire and still didn't have shit. Quadir, on the other hand, had hustled for five years and could retire at the age of twenty-five as a millionaire, never working an honest day in his life.

He sat down on the sofa in the sea of money scattered around him. It made him nervous. For the first time, he saw his wealth, and, for the first time, he saw what he really was: a drug dealer. He understood it was wrong. All he did for the hustle was a constant reminder of his own greed. He was down to his last two hundred kilos of cocaine, and he didn't want to purchase any more. For $3,800 a kilo, who wouldn't? But with seventeen million staring you down, why? He was not thinking of finances. He was thinking about the Junior Mafia. It was merely a matter of time before he was a direct target. Things were getting complicated in the streets. The police were downright dirty. They would stick you up, set you up, and give you a case.

The brothers were just as bad. Everybody had a gun. Everybody. Even little kids had guns. Your life meant nothing. It was all about money, who had it and who didn't. Not only had Quadir beat the odds, but he had also lived to talk about it, without owing any debts or favors. That was a task, considering most of Quadir's friends were dead or in jail.

He thought of Tony Santero and the cartel. He thought of Barranquilla, Colombia, and Carlos Escobar. He'd met Tony's uncle, Carlos Escobar, only once. Carlos was so captivating, even with his intense dislike for the United States. Quadir totally enjoyed his conversation. The man had everything he wanted and desired at his fingertips.

Tony's mother was an Escobar. She married a Santero and had three sons. Two of the sons and her husband were killed in a boating accident on the Panama Canal in 1968, when Tony was a little boy. She and her only son then moved in with her brother, Carlos. Carlos raised Tony like his own son. He turned over some of the family affairs to Tony, who took on the responsibility of serving the United States. Through governmental and diplomatic contacts, Tony was free to serve countries. Carlos had two brothers and three sons, all of whom controlled and shared the Colombian drug profits.

After Quadir understood the trade game, he understood who had the power. It was *not* the brothers. The brothers got caught up, too, but not solely them. It seemed like everyone was getting high. The upper class, not only the poor, contributed and depended on it. He thought of the sisters who were out there using and selling their bodies for a gusto, the brothers and sisters who were robbing their own mothers and grandmothers. He thought of his financial destiny: matches torn in two. He thought of the seventeen million dollars. Shit was too good to be true.

How could he stop? How could he tell Tony? What would he say? What would he do? For three weeks, Quadir continued business as usual, dropping his price down to ten thousand dollars a kilo. Everybody and their mothers were trying to see Rasun and Reds, who had basically taken over the Ave. Quadir couldn't figure it out. It seemed like out of nowhere, not only were they selling his shit, but also buying shit from him and doing their own thing.

Rik and Forty were tearing up the drug game down Richard Allen. After the death of Rock, Rik and Quadir paid out two hundred thousand dollars to have five members of the Junior Mafia assassinated. Within the past three weeks, there had been twelve drug-related murders in the city, all of which directly involved the Junior Mafia.

Quadir was tired of the small circuit. He was tired of the drug game. He wanted to not have to walk or drive so fast. He didn't want to look over his shoulder or peek around corners. He was ready to take his money and sit back, enjoy life.

Finally, Qua paged Tony and sat back and waited. An hour later, Tony Santero was telling him that he would be there in three more weeks.

"That's what I was calling to speak to you about."

"Is there something wrong, Quadir?"

"It's like this. I'm not going to re-up."

"What? What the hell do you mean—retire?"

"What I said, Tony. I'm done, man. I'm finished. I can't take it anymore. This shit is really starting to get to me. It's like, every day and every night, I got people chasing me down. Gimme this and gimme that. And then there's the Junior Mafia. They been knocking off my family."

"Well, kill them back," Tony said, not understanding.

"Everyone is going for self. Things are changing. They're losing honor. Everybody's snitching now, and then there's Gena. I'm not spending any time with her. I want to retire alive."

"Yeah. Yeah, I know. That's one nice-looking girl you got there. She's *real* nice, man. You know I'd love to fuck her."

"Yeah, but you can't, so why feel it?"

"See, that's the problem with you Black guys. You don't like to share, do you?"

"I'll share some pussy with you, Tony. Just not that pussy."

"Well, are you sure that's what you want to do?"

"Yeah, I'm positive."

"Well, how can I say this? Um, you can't do nothing, man; you can't lie to me. But if you're really stopping and you want out, then fine, okay. Give me five million dollars and you're free to go." Five million rolled off his tongue with the Colombian accent; then his voice grew stern. "And remember, you're retired. I find out you're lying to me, you'd be betraying me and my family. I'll know what you're doing."

"Tony, on my life, you took care of me and you helped me. I'd never cross you. Why not two?"

"No, for you, four million, Quadir, and no less."

"Three."

"Four."

"Three and a quarter."

"Three and a half and that's it."

"Okay, three and a half it is."

"Take it to the Princess docked at the harbor. Give it to my cousin Sancho; take his number."

Breathing easier, Qua thanked him.

"Keep in touch, Q, and remember what I said. You're retired."

Quadir separated out three and a half million dollars, put the rest back in the bags, and locked it in the safe.

Gena was glad to be out of chemistry class and drove straight home. She marveled at the sight of Qua's keys on the vestibule table. "Quadir, are you here?"

"Yeah!"

"Where are you?"

"Down here!"

"What's up?"

"Come here, baby, we got to talk."

She joined him in the playroom, wondering what was up, and walked into his arms.

"I've been thinking lately, Gena. I haven't been home a lot. I've been so busy taking care of business, I haven't been taking care of you."

True enough, Gena thought, taking a seat. *So, he's finally fessin' up about the bitch Cherelle.*

"I talked with Tony today. I told him that I was done. Finished. Out of the game. The coke I got, I'm going to get rid of, and then that's it."

Gena couldn't speak, her mind racing to compute the implications of his retirement from the game. *Did I push him too far? Did I demand too much? Will they let him retire? Where will all the shopping money come from if he stops?* She kept her cool and listened to him.

He slipped a small baby blue box out of his pocket. He opened it and showed her the contents. "Will you marry me, Gena?"

He took the ring out of the holder and slipped it on her finger.

She gasped. "I've never seen a diamond this big before!"

"It's ten carats."

Gena was in shock. She couldn't believe he was coming at her with marriage.

"Gena, you haven't answered my question. Do you want me to get on one knee?"

"Qua, please." She smirked. "You'd get on one knee?"

He bent his knee to the floor before her. "Janel Louise Scott, will you marry me?"

"Quadir, please get up. You're going to make me cry."

"Not until you answer me; not until you say you'll marry me. You're all that matters to me, and I want you to be my wife."

His face told her this was not fun and games; he was serious. "Yes, Quadir Montell Richards, I will marry you."

She got down on her knees with him and put her arms around him.

The ringing phone broke the happy moment. He smiled, watching her run upstairs as he picked up the phone.

"Hello?"

"I need some money for your daughter, Quadir," a female voice said.

"Look, don't ever call my home again," he said as he slammed the phone down. It immediately rang again.

"Hello."

"Don't fucking tell me not to call there, motherfucker. You got a child that you don't do shit for."

"Look, Cherelle, if you need something for the baby, I'll send it to you. I'll call Rasun and he can bring you whatever you need."

"No, bitch, you bring it. Rasun didn't fuck for this baby, you did."

"Who you think you're playing with?"

"Who am I talking to? Ain't nobody else on the goddamn phone."

"I told you, if you need something, then page me. I'll see to it that you get it."

He hung up and the phone rang again.

"Bitch, stop calling my motherfucking house."

"Yo, Qua. Man, it's me, Rik."

"Oh. What up?"

"Damn, my brother, havin' problems today?"

"Yeah, Cherelle. She's fucking with me again. She's been calling here."

"How did she get the number?"

"I don't know. I don't know what to do."

"Now, calm down, partner. You'll be all right."

"What am I gonna do, Rik?"

"Get a motherfucking blood test. You the only one who thinks the baby is yours."

Qua hadn't heard Gena return. "Quadir, I'm gonna take a shower. Want to join me?"

"No, baby, I'm on the phone."

"Who's that? Gena?" Rik asked.

"Who else is going to be up in my house?"

Rik started laughing at him. "All these hoes runnin' around talking about it's Qua's baby, shit, you might got the Virgin Mary up in that motherfucker. How the fuck am I supposed to know?"

Gena was still trying to entice Qua. "Okay, if you don't wanna shower with me, you're gonna miss out," she said, dropping her robe in front of him on the way to the bathroom.

When she was gone, he turned back to the phone. "Rik, I asked Gena to marry me."

"What, Qua? You getting married, man?"

"Yeah. I'm gonna have a big wedding."

"Well, what's up? I'm waiting."

"Oh, yeah, and I want you to be my best man."

"That's because you know I'm the best nigga out here."

Qua let out a heavy sigh. "You gonna be my best man or what?"

"Oh, nigga, stop bitchin'. You know I got your back. However, there is a problem."

"What?"

"You selling keys for five thousand is the motherfucking problem, man."

"I'm not selling them for no five. I'm selling them for ten."

"What's the fucking difference? How is you playin' with this ten shit?"

"Look, me and Gena are about to go to Atlantic City. When I get back, I'm gonna come and see you. I got something for you."

"When are you coming back?"

"I'll be back later on tonight and then we'll talk."

"Pick me and Lita up some Gucci sneakers while you down there."

They gave each other the salaams and hung up the phone.

While Quadir and Gena were walking on the Atlantic City boardwalk waiting for their dinner reservation, the Junior Mafia was having a meeting in the southwest part of the city. Jerrell was pacing a trail in his peach carpet, talking on the phone.

"I don't understand why no one is buying weight! And no one knows why?" he asked as he stared around the room, using his eyes to demand an explanation.

Finally, someone spoke up. "No one is buying. For the past three days, no one has called or needed anything, or nothing."

"Khyree, I figured that out, since none of y'all motherfuckers got my money."

Jordan looked at Jerrell. "No one is buying weight."

Jerrell looked at all of them as if they were thieves. "Well," he finally asked, "who owes us money?"

"No one from this end owes anything," Khyree responded.

"The caps are moving, but the bricks are sitting there," Mont added.

"Well, do something about it!" Jerrell shouted.

Khyree shrugged. "What do we do?"

"Figure it the fuck out. Somebody got it. They're getting coke from somewhere. It's not like motherfuckers stopped getting high."

Ran arrived, gave and received acknowledgment of his presence, as Jerrell continued.

"Ran, where the fuck are Reece and Derrick?" Jerrell did not like anyone to miss his shareholder meetings. He felt they were important. They brought everyone in the Junior Mafia together.

The meetings were short but informative, or at least Jerrell thought so. After everyone left, Jerrell paged Reece, then Derrick. He was really starting to worry, not so much about them, but about the five bricks and three million dollars they were carrying.

After a few minutes of pacing, with Ran right behind him, Jerrell spoke again. "I really don't like this shit. Somebody who gets rid of ten kilos every day ain't moved a motherfucking thing all week."

"Who?"

"Khyree," he said, walking out of the room.

Ran followed him. "Well, why not?"

"I don't know."

Mark picked up the ringing phone. "Yo, man, where you at?"

It was Skip. "I'm at the hospital. You not gonna believe this shit. The cops brought Reece and Derrick here. I saw them pull them from the back of a fucking paddy wagon. The cops are everywhere. I got to get out of this lobby and get back in the room with my girl."

"Yo, Skip, hold up. Jerrell wants you."

Taking the phone, Jerrell inquired of Skip, "What the fuck is going on?"

"The cops brought Derrick and Reece in here. Man, get somebody down here. My girl went into delivery. I'm saying, it fucked me up, Ock. I don't think Reece is gonna make it. Call Reece's girl and get her ass down here. I got to go."

The news spread through the city like wildfire. Jerrell's right-hand man, Reece, was dead. Derrick was listed in critical condition, however, and would be arrested upon his recovery. Reece and Derrick had led a high-speed chase through the city, fatally shot a police officer, and wounded another. They got away, then crashed into a wall on Lincoln Drive. The police didn't call for an ambulance. They threw the bodies in the back of a paddy wagon, hoping they'd die. The Volvo they were driving was taken into evidence. The police reportedly found two guns, five kilos of cocaine, and one million dollars.

Tonight's the Night

Things changed, and they changed fast. Quadir met with Rik and decided to hand him the rest of his cocaine supply in exchange for a quarter-million dollars. He arranged for Reds and Rasun to do business directly with Rik. Amar and the other brothers he dealt with were free to do as they pleased. Rik's price was better than Quadir's, so the money stayed in the family.

Then there was Gena, who was becoming unbearable to deal with. She knew something was going on, but she didn't know what it was. Quadir wondered if the gossip about Cherelle having his daughter was in the street. He figured it was; that was why she'd asked him. She came right out one night after dinner and asked whether he had a daughter by the girl, and he told her no. That was all she wanted to hear and left it alone.

Why hadn't he said yes? He wished he could've freed his conscience. Instead, he went out and bought her a baby blue Mercedes-Benz 300 CE with a license plate that read: MY CE.

Cherelle, on the other hand, continued to dare him. *Fuck me, suck me, and give me loot or if you don't, I'm gonna tell.* Quadir was tired of dealing with her and couldn't take much more. He was gonna tell Gena. The only problem was what Gena would do.

The worst thing he did was get Gena the car. She didn't know how to act now and was gone all the time. He had to get her a pager shortly thereafter, to keep up. Every time he paged her, she was at the mall or on her car phone, never home.

A few weeks later he called her in the afternoon. "Hey, baby. What are you doing?"

"Oh, nothing, shopping. Meet me at the party 'cause I'm not coming home to get dressed. Got to go. Quadir, I need another cellular battery."

And with that, Gena was out spending drug money, keeping the economy alive. Nine thousand here, another eight thousand there. She just shopped. Anything more than ten thousand had to have Quadir's approval and his credit card, but don't think it couldn't be obtained.

Gena picked up both Lita and Tracey and headed to Black's party. She'd already told Quadir to catch a ride with Rik so she could hang out with the girls.

Lita couldn't get over the 10 carat diamond engagement ring. Quadir had really outdone himself. Tyrik had told her it was ten, but hearing about it and seeing it were two different things. She herself had a 4 carat diamond, and once Rik told her about Gena's ring, Lita told him to upgrade her shit and make it snappy.

"Do you see all this attention we're getting just from this car?" Tracey asked.

Lita smirked. "No, but do you see these motherfuckers staring with no understanding?"

"Mm-hmm." Gena already understood the attention her man got in the street. What she didn't understand was why he lied about it and kept her in the dark.

Tracey decided to whine. "Quadir's so good to you. I hope that I find a man who buys me shit like this."

"This is Quadir's conscience. He feels sorry. He realizes he's fucked up and it's only a matter of time. He buys me shit to make himself feel better. That's why he went out and got this car, to try to make up for some shit he can't even confess."

"Make what up?" Tracey asked.

"Cherelle and her baby."

Lita gasped. "When did you find out?"

"I found out four days ago. Why didn't you tell me?"

"Bitch, Rik was gonna kill me. I got a home, too. Don't think I didn't want to tell you—and I was going to. It's just that if you and Quadir broke up because of something I said, Tyrik and Quadir would blame me. Besides, Gena, did that motherfucker get you ten carats, or what? Did he ask you to marry him? Please. Fuck Cherelle and her baby. That nigga don't want that broke bitch. Rik said the bitch ain't nothin' but a whore and Quadir can't stand her. Rik fucked her, too. Don't feel bad. Mm-hmm, Rik said they both fucked her. I think they did the jawn together."

Gena stared at Lita. She hated the way she knew everything and could hold it inside. Gena's motto was "Tell me, 'cause I'm telling it all."

In Gena's mind, the fact that Quadir wouldn't tell her could only mean he was still fucking with Cherelle. Gena feared losing him, the house, the ring, the Mercedes-Benz, and all. A baby was a bond, and Gena didn't have that with him. She was jealous. What-ifs popped into her mind. Quadir telling her that he was leaving her—Gena couldn't take that. She'd probably faint or beg him not to leave. She didn't want him to be with Cherelle, and she didn't want Cherelle to have any money, either, but she realized Cherelle existed before her. *And* Cherelle had a baby.

The other side of her mind said fuck it. *He wants the bitch, then he can have the bitch.* That was tough, because not only would she give up her man, but also her lifestyle. Gena wasn't about to lose Quadir. She would fight for him to the end. There was no way she was gonna give up all the shit that made her life happy. He was hers. He'd asked her to marry him.

Tracey seemed confused. "Quadir had a baby with someone else?"

Gena rolled her eyes at her. "Who do you think we're talking about?"

"Quadir got a baby by Cherelle?"

For some reason, Tracey kept asking the question over and over.

"That little tramp had the nerve to name it Quanda." Gena was seething. "Quadir must be out of his mind, or stupid, if he thinks I don't know what the fuck's going on."

"I seen her, too, the other day. She did have a baby with her," Tracey fessed up.

Gena panicked. "Did you see it?"

"No, I didn't see the baby." Tracey passed the spliff to Lita. "I wonder do it look like him."

Lita snickered. "Shit, it ought to look like him, as much money as he gives the bitch."

They had reached the club, and Gena smoothly pulled up to the entrance to take a look.

"Damn, look at all those people waiting to get in!" Lita exclaimed as Gena drove on to find a parking spot.

"Well, everybody's going to come to Black's party. You know how it is."

"I hope we can get in," Tracey said.

Gena parked the car. "We will."

The girls turned the corner and walked down the street. People were everywhere. "Is this the club Sahirah was at?" Gena asked.

Lita responded, "No, she was at Chances."

"Rasun!" Gena called out, spotting him walking down the street with Reds. "What's up?"

"Nothing, baby. Just came to do my thang, you know what I'm

saying? I'm trying to meet one of your girlfriends. What's up with that?"

Gena pointed at Tracey. "Here, meet Tracey."

"Damn, baby, you looking mighty good tonight."

After seeing that Tracey wasn't interested, Gena asked, "Where's Quadir?"

Rasun shrugged. "I don't know. I haven't seen him."

"Him and Rik are probably inside," Lita suggested.

"Come on," Rasun said as he ushered everyone to the door. "They wit' me, boss," he told the bouncer, who stood aside, admitting them without hesitation.

Once inside, Rasun asked the women, "You all right now?"

"Yeah, where you going?"

"I'm gonna mingle and jingle," he said, looking at Tracey as if she didn't know what she was missing.

Gena and Lita went looking for Quadir and Rik while Tracey talked to some guy she recognized from junior high.

Gena led the way through the crowd, bumping into someone she knew every step of the way. "Damn, everybody in here or what?"

Lita giggled. "Yeah. It looks like the crew is in the house."

"Hey, Gena baby." Quinny Day gave her a hug. "Hey, Lita baby," he said, doing the same thing to her. "Goodness gracious, the Lord truly blessed us all when He put y'all on the face of the earth. God bless America!"

Lita smiled. "Quinny Day, what's up?"

"Nothing, baby. Just kicking it."

"You seen Quadir and Rik?"

"Yeah, they're downstairs, all the way in the back at a table. Gena, do Qua know you're dressed like that?"

"Like what?" she said, looking down at herself.

"You're gonna hurt something, baby. You're out to hurt something up in this motherfucker, and I got to get away from you, 'cause it's not gonna be me."

"Quinny Day, shut up!" she told him as she moved toward the stairs to go find Qua.

Everybody was in the house. Downstairs, Amin was sitting in a corner with a couple of bottles of champagne on his table, surrounded by at least five girls.

"Damn," Lita said. "You see how he's playing?"

"I see how Quadir's playing." Gena noted that Qua was talking to some girl. "Who's that?"

"I don't know, but whoever it is, don't you start nothing in here tonight, you hear?"

Qua looked up, sensing Gena, and noticed she didn't look too happy.

"Rik," he said, nudging his friend.

Rik spotted the girls, and he turned to Black and started talking. Qua was getting frustrated with Cherelle. It was the same old thing.

"I'm your baby's mother and you don't do shit for me or your baby. I need some money."

"Look, I'll call you," Quadir said, walking away from her and heading for Gena.

"Who's that?" Gena asked, looking at Cherelle standing behind Quadir.

Quadir had no idea the girl was right behind him. *Where's Tyrik? Why doesn't someone usher her away? Why does Gena look like that?* Quadir felt extremely uncomfortable as Gena stared at him and Cherelle.

"Gena, this is Cherelle. Cherelle, this is my wife."

"I'm his daughter's mother," Cherelle said, correcting Quadir.

"Oh, shit!" Lita exclaimed. "Rik, break it up before something gets started."

"Bitch, everywhere I am, you want to be," Gena said to Cherelle. "I know who you are. Quadir told me all about you."

"Whatever," Cherelle said, throwing up her hand like Gena didn't know what she was talking about.

"So, what you want? He don't got nothing for you. How many times has the motherfucker told you to stop calling our house?"

Then Gena punched Cherelle in the face, grabbing her hair with her left and throwing nothing but rights. By the time Quadir and Rik stepped in, Gena had handled her business.

Even after they'd separated the shit and the music had stopped, you could still hear Gena. "Bitch, please. You one of them mother-fuckers who needs their ass whooped every day. Fuck with Quadir if you want to, bitch, and see what the fuck happens." She spoke it all in one breath, ready to throw down again over the bullshit.

As the music returned and Cherelle was escorted away as usual, Quadir started to explain. The problem was that Gena didn't care. She would beat up Cherelle every day if she had to. Quadir knew he should've told her. Not only did he not tell her, but he'd also lied about the girl and the baby.

Quadir led her to a table, fixed her hair, and then poured her some champagne while attempting to explain. "I send the paper to her through Rasun. Don't think I deal with her, Gena. I can't stand the girl," he said, shaking his head and trying to figure out why Gena had to bring her Richard Allen bullshit to Black's party.

He knew that shit was gonna happen sooner or later, though, and he was so glad Gena beat her up, he didn't know what to do. Cherelle made him sick, always taxing him. And wouldn't even let him see the little baby half the time.

"Quadir, I don't care. I can handle the truth. I can't handle lies. You put me on the spot. I should be able to handle a situation be-cause you hipped me to it, not because I heard the shit through the grapevine. I can't believe you left me in the dark like that. I'm really mad at you. You should've gotten me a Rolls Royce for this shit. It would've gotten you out of the doghouse a lot sooner than a CE."

"Gena . . ." Bridgette walked over to the table. "I'm so glad you didn't tear this motherfucker up."

Rik shook his head. "I don't know what y'all gonna do with her simple ass."

Black was clearly irritated. "Put the bitch in the river."

Rik nodded in agreement. "I tried to tell him."

"Well, I'll be at Saks tomorrow getting over all this," Gena said, kissing Quadir so everybody would see they were happy and nothing had changed.

Black wanted Rik and Quadir to come with him to the bar. There were too many girls crowding Lita and Gena. The guys understood. Everyone would be talking about that ass whoopin' for days to come.

Before he got up to go with his friends, Gena leaned over and whispered in Quadir's ear. "Is there anything else I should know about?" she asked calmly.

There's so much stuff you should know about, I wouldn't know where to begin, he thought to himself.

"No, and if there was, I'd tell you," he said ever so sincerely. He got up to leave, and Gena watched him as he walked across the floor.

"Damn, I love that motherfucker."

"We know—there's no doubt." Lita's sarcastic charm couldn't let that pass by.

Bridgette sighed. "Well, everybody thought the house was coming down."

"Shit, Gena *did* tear it down," Lita said. "I'm glad Gena beat that bitch up, 'cause if she hadn't, it would've been a whole different story."

"Yeah. She dealt with the situation rather well, didn't she?" Bridgette said.

"Better than me, 'cause I would've killed the bitch." Lita stared at Bridgette as if to say, *Now try your luck with Rik.*

Gena left the table and followed Quadir.

Qua poured her a glass of Dom and walked her to a table, with Rik and Black opposite them, ordering another bottle of champagne.

"It's crowded in here, Qua."

"Too crowded for me," he said.

"So, that's Cherelle," she said.

"Yeah, that's her."

"Well, she's better-looking than I thought."

"She don't look good to me, and I don't want to talk about her no more."

She wanted to have a good time and decided, as the saying goes, there was no need crying over spilled milk. She kissed her man gently on the lips and went back to the table with Lita and Tracey.

A hush rustled through the club a minute or so later when Pam came in. Her entrance was remarkable. Pam was sharp. She knew exactly what to do with Black's money. She wore it well.

"Where's Bridgette, 'cause she can get her ass kicked next up in this motherfucker," Lita whispered, nodding Pam's way so that Gena could see what she was talking about. "Mm-hmm. She's another one who's gonna end up getting hurt for fucking with somebody's man. Shit, Bridgette gots to be crazy. Ain't no dick worth having to deal with Pam. I don't know how Black even finds bitches crazy enough to fuck with him, 'cause Pam don't be bullshitting."

"Oh, yeah, Pam rolls on motherfuckers about her man," Gena agreed.

"Shit, the motherfuckers been together since eighth grade."

"Where's Tracey?"

Lita pointed. "She's over there talking to Muhammad."

"Oh, maybe I found her a friend."

Lita was glad she didn't have to worry about Tracey fucking with Rik. "She looks like she needs one."

The guys returned to the table with bottles of champagne. Black pulled out a spliff and started smoking it.

Pam looked at him. "Black," she said, "you're not supposed to do that."

"Who paid here, Pam? Huh? Who?"

"You did, Black."

"Okay, then," he said, passing it to Qua.

"Sit your Happy Birthday ass down, nigga," Rik said. "Didn't nobody ask you who paid."

Everybody was having a good time, when Blair walked over to the table. He greeted everyone and gave his best wishes to Black.

"This is my wife, Blair," Quadir said. "This is Gena."

"Oh! It's nice to meet you. Do you like your car?"

"I love my car. How do you know about my car?"

"He sold it to me," Qua told her.

"I suggested he get that particular car. Do you like it?"

"Definitely," she cooed. "It's so blue."

"I like that color." He didn't get it, but it didn't matter.

Just then Andrea walked up to the table, as if she belonged.

"Girl, what are you wearing?" Gena asked her.

"Looks like nothing to me," Qua whispered.

"Nigga, you better stop looking," Gena said with an evil glow.

"Do you like?" Andrea inquired.

"Do you?" Gena hissed, nudging Lita under the table.

Gena wanted Andrea and her see-through dress away from her man, far the fuck away. You could see, but you couldn't see. It was one of those dresses that would make you stare until you did see something.

"Thank God it's dim in here," Andrea said.

"How could a person come out lookin' like that?" Lita asked, challenging the girl.

Oh, shit, Gena thought. *Here goes Lita.*

Qua was looking, everybody was looking, and Andrea played it off, all the while deeply knowing they were all jealous of her. She was body, and those bitches, especially Lita, were jealous. Of course, Rik's slobbering on himself didn't help.

From out of nowhere, Kim walked up to the table. "Andrea," she said, hugging her.

Lita was keeping her eyes on Rik the entire time. "Oh, no. They got to go away from here."

Kim glanced at Gena. "So, Gena, what's up? How you been?"

"Oh, I'm fine," she said, expressing how fine she was with her left hand.

"I heard about you, Quadir. You naughty, naughty boy," she said, hitting his hand as if that was punishment.

This bitch is crazy, Lita thought, looking at Gena, silently asking her if she wanted to roll on 'em.

To ease the tension Rik was feeling from these unwelcome travelers of the night, he decided to speak up. "Does anyone have the time?"

Everyone looked at him as if he were crazy. "Oh, I have a Rolex. I forgot."

Kim looked around. "Damn, Black, where's the food?"

"It's over there," Black replied. Kim and Andrea walked off, and Black was glad they'd gone over there before something was said and Pam came out her shit.

"That's Forty, right?" Tracey whispered, starstruck.

"Yeah, that's Forty in the blue," Lita said. Pausing, she added, "I heard he got Richard Allen locked."

"I heard he got a nice shot," Gena whispered as she sipped her champagne.

"Mm-hmm, I heard about that shit." Lita looked at him, wondering if his dick was as big as everyone made it out to be.

"I heard Forty eats the shit out of some pussy, too," Gena whispered, knowing the rumors had to be true.

"Would you fuck him?" Lita asked as the girls looked Forty up and down.

Gena snickered as Quadir wrapped his arm around her. "No."

I damn sure would, Tracey thought.

Oh, shit. There goes Jamal, Gena noted. It had been such a long time since she'd seen him at Sahirah's funeral. That was the last time, with bitch-ass Kim on his hip.

Gena turned away and pretended she hadn't even noticed him. She didn't fool Qua, though. He observed everything.

Just then, Brother Ramier came by with greetings. "As-salaam alaykum."

"Wa alaykum as-salaam," Quadir said as the brother greeted Rik and Black.

"How you doing, Bridgette?" he asked.

"Hi, how you doing, Ramier?"

Gena could tell something was up. Bridgette had too many skeletons in her closet for there not to be something going on. Rich Green, Charlie, Kevin, Coleone, Winston, Amar, Rock, Black, all the big boys, their brothers and cousins. The list went on and on.

Rasun and Reds came downstairs.

Rasun asked, "Black, where did you get the girl in the see-through dress to do your party?"

Reds chuckled. "I want her at my party."

"I didn't get no naked lady," Black said as if the young boys were bugging.

"They talking about that whore, Andrea," Lita said.

Gena started laughing. "She came like that, Rasun."

"Well, damn! I thought she was getting paid to wear that."

"My bucks, they've grown up, haven't they, y'all?" Qua said.

Everybody toasted to Qua's squad of young boys.

"Damn, I really thought you paid a motherfucker to dress up like that," Rasun said.

Reds smiled. "Maybe soon all of them will dress like that."

Ra said, "I hope so."

Ramier looked at Bridgette, remembering the night he and two of his boys had done her in a hotel room. "If you pay 'em enough, they'll do anything you want."

Sis was a serious gun. He couldn't take his eyes off her.

"Qua, come on. Let's go upstairs," Rik said. Black and Rik got up from the table.

"Q, you coming or what?" asked Black.

"Gena, stay here. I'll be right back," Qua said.

"Why do they always say stay here?" Gena asked Lita.

"They don't want you to follow them 'cause they don't want to get caught."

"I'm tired. What time is it?" Gena looked at her Rolex, answering her own question.

"What time is it?" Pam asked.

"It's four o'clock," she said, looking at her cousins standing over by the bar. "I'll be right back."

She left the table and walked straight over to Bria and Brianna.

"What are you two doing here? How did you get in? You're only sixteen."

"We came with this guy," Brianna replied.

"Bria, I don't know why you're standing there with an attitude. You should be at home. I can tell on you, you know," Gena reminded her.

"You gonna tell anyway, 'cause that's how you roll. So what difference does it make?" she said, staring Gena in the eyes.

"Have you been drinking, Bria? Oh my God. Both of you have been drinking. You need to go home now."

"Why? You go home," Bria said as she walked away, looking for her ride.

"She got so much to say for someone who never says anything to me at all. She lucky I don't hurt her in here."

"Gena, don't pay Bria no mind."

"Brianna, what are you doing in here? You're not supposed to be in no club. If Gah Git knew . . ." Gena didn't even want to think of what would happen to them. "I bet she knows you're not in the house and is worried half to death."

Suddenly, Gena thought she was in a Western film in the middle of a cattle stampede. Her heart stopped as the sound of gunfire unleashed itself above. People were scrambling, trying to find safety. *Bap, bap, bap, bap, bap, bap, bap, bap, bap.* Screaming could be heard above and below, and a mad rush for the lower level caused people to trample over one another and fall down the stairs.

Gena grabbed Brianna's arm and took her behind the bar.

"Stay down!" she said as the girls huddled together for safety. The gunfire was ongoing, and Gena could distinguish the sounds of several different guns. It was true-blue pandemonium. The music had suddenly stopped, and Gena realized the quiet before the storm was the result of the DJ's panic in separating the plug from its outlet while scrabbling under his turntables in a move focused completely on survival.

The lower level was now filled with all those who'd been upstairs. A last shot was fired and then silence reigned. Slowly, almost as one, the members of Black's birthday party began lifting their heads and looking about, but nobody moved from their spot, as if doing so would violate the certainty the silence inspired. Through the silence, Gena heard her own certainty calling to her.

"Gena! Gena! Gena!" It was her man. He was covered with blood, but he was alive, and that was all that mattered.

"Quadir!" Gena popped up from behind the counter.

"Baby, come on! We got to get out of here!"

"I'm so glad you're okay, baby. I was worried. I was so scared! Qua, look at you. You didn't get shot, did you?"

Qua noticed she was shaking like a seizure was imminent.

"Gena, calm down." He suddenly noticed something wrong with the picture, as though anything could be worse. "What are you doing here, Brianna?"

"I don't know, but this isn't where I'm trying to be," she said with a personable attitude.

"Qua, what happened?" Gena was still rooted to the spot as Pam and Lita ran over to them.

Lita's expression changed rapidly from hope to loss and back to hope again.

"Q, where's Rik?"

Quadir stopped, turned to her, and took Lita by the shoulders. "Lita, Rik got hit. He's upstairs. Lita, I can't stay. You got to help Rik, baby. You got to stay with Rik and don't tell the police shit. Black got hit, too."

"What?" Pam pushed her way to the stairs.

"Oh my God!" Gena said. "Qua, what's going on?"

"Gena, baby, I don't know."

"Is it safe to go outside?"

"Baby, I don't know. Where's the Benz?"

"On Market Street, two blocks down, right on the corner of Fifty-Eighth."

"This is what I want you to do. Wait for me upstairs. Wait for me!" he said as they reached the top of the stairs. She handed him the keys. "Gena, stay inside."

"I will. Qua, please be careful, baby."

Pam and Lita were frantically searching for Black and Rik among the bodies lying under tables or slumped in booths. Gena, surveying the carnage, couldn't believe what her eyes told her was the truth: there were five to ten people lying dead in pools of blood; others were hit and injured. Gena, unable to move, looked from one face to another, hoping to see Black or Rik.

Pam's breath froze in her throat and she stopped dead in her tracks after spotting the suit and shoes and recognizing the jewelry. She screamed, "Oh my God! No! No! Baby, please, no! Not Black!"

Gena was nauseated as Pam stood there looking at Black's flesh covered in blood. But through the blood, the parts of his body no one ever saw, the organs whose job it was to keep Black walking, talking, smiling, reproducing, thinking, and functioning under the covering of skin that protected them, were now outside his body. The skin that had been blown apart by the force of an infrared Glock .45 covered the walls. It looked as if the protective covering keeping everything together had been shredded. He was gone; Black was gone.

Gena heard another voice call out, "Oh my God, Rik!" Lita was shouting, "Please! Where you at, man! Come on, Rik! Answer me!" at the top of her lungs.

Gena saw a chair moving, hope filling her and replacing the horror. "Lita! Over there!" She pointed toward the corner. It was him. It was Rik, under a table.

"Lita, don't move him. Wait for the ambulance. Don't move him."

Lita found her way to him. "Okay. Okay. Rik, baby, can you hear me?" She gently covered his hand with hers, continuing to murmur gently.

Pam was in shock, unaware of anything going on around her. People were trying to get out of there, giving thanks to God it wasn't them on the floor. As they glanced at the bodies and the blood, no one stopped to acknowledge the others who were looking for loved ones or friends, and grieving over what they found.

"Here's Qua," Brianna said, hanging out the doorway.

Gena looked at her friend. "Lita, I got to go."

Lita didn't respond at first. She took a deep breath, ordering herself to function. "Okay, Gena."

Gena asked, "Can you help Pam?"

"Pam? Pam who? My man might die, Gena. Shit, can she help me, 'cause Black is gone and I don't want to lose mines! Please don't leave me, Tyrik!" She held his hand and started crying. "Where the fuck are the paramedics?" she hollered.

Gena grabbed her friend's shoulder, trying to calm her down before she left. "We'll page you."

Brianna and Gena ran outside and over to the Benz, where Quadir had the doors open, ready to speed away.

"Black is dead."

At that moment, Quadir went cold. He couldn't think.

Dead? Black? He couldn't believe it. He didn't want to believe it.

"What happened, Qua?"

"I don't know. It happened so fast. They started shooting at us! Damn, why Black and Rik?" he hollered as he pounded his fist on the steering wheel.

Together, Rik and Qua were standing on the wall directly across from the bar where Black was. A red light bounced off the mirrors on both sides of the wall. Rik watched the light as he told Quadir to look at it. The mirror told the ending before the action even began. The light ended at Black.

As soon as they called to him, the bullets rang out. Within seconds, a bullet pierced Rik in the chest, causing him to spin and take a hit in the back before falling on top of Quadir. Quadir reached on the side of Rik for his gun. Tyrik used all his strength to grab his friend's arm.

"Don't go up, Qua. If both of us die, who's gonna make it?" he asked as they stared each other in the eyes.

"You ain't gonna die. Stop fuckin' with me, baby." Quadir looked at his friend, who was half on the floor, half on him. "Don't die on me, Rik."

Quadir wondered whether his friend was gonna make it. He was shot bad. Checking the rearview mirror, his train of thought was completely interrupted. "What's Brianna doing here? Brianna, what do you call yourself doing? You're sixteen! You're not supposed to be out in no place like that! See what could've happened to you?"

Gena had never heard Quadir use such force in his voice.

"I know," she sniffed. "I came with this guy, that's all."

Qua was ready to wring someone's neck. "Who's the guy?"

"His name is Charlie."

Please don't let it be Quick Pockets Charlie, he thought to himself. "Brianna, you stay out of those kinds of places until you're old enough to be in those kinds of places, you understand? When you turn twenty-one, then you can go where you want. Until then, you need to keep yourself in the house where it's safe, so you can get to be twenty-one."

"Don't worry. I will."

Just then a car pulled up along the opposite side of the street and stopped in front of Gah Git's house. A few seconds later, Bria hopped out and ran up to the door.

"What are you doing, Bria?" Quadir hollered, glad it wasn't Quick Pockets Charlie she was with.

"Shh," she said, turning around to see Quadir, Gena, and Brianna.

"Gena, I'ma kill 'em. Let me catch you out again, Bria," Qua fussed, waiting for the two girls to get in the door.

He pulled the Benz off Gah Git's block and went to a gas station. He drove on the sidewalk right up to the payphone so he wouldn't have to get out of the car. He dialed Rik's pager, and within a few minutes, Lita returned the call. She was frantic, and Qua soothed her and told her that he'd be right there. He slid back into the driver's seat and sped away.

Lita was waiting for them in the hospital lobby. "Come on," she said. "They got him back here." She led them to a waiting room.

"Where's Black?"

"Black died, Qua. They was putting him in a body bag when the paramedics took Rik out."

"Where's Pam?"

"I don't know, but she . . . she was standing there until the paramedics took her."

"They took Pam?"

"Yeah, they took her, too. I haven't seen Pam since we left the club. They let me ride in the ambulance with Rik." Lita started crying. "Qua, they was sticking him with all kinds of shit."

Quadir held her as Gena looked on, feeling horrible because they could do nothing.

"Lita, come on." Gena put her arms around her friend. "It's gonna be okay. Rik is gonna be fine. Rik is strong and big. He'll pull through this."

"He was bleeding so bad, Gena. What if he don't?"

"You can't think like that. You gotta be strong, baby. You got to be strong for him."

"You call his mother?" Quadir asked.

"No. Not yet."

"Well, somebody has to call his family."

"You can call them," Lita said, knowing once they got to the hospital, they'd take over.

Qua left to find a phone and called Rik's mom. Within forty-five minutes, his entire family had arrived. Gena curled up on a couch and fell asleep. Quadir consoled Rik's mother while she spoke to the Lord and told the hospital staff about her precious baby, how good he was, how the Lord couldn't take him, and begged the doctor to save her baby.

Seven hours later, a doctor walked into the waiting room and called out, "Mrs. Smith?"

Tyrik's mom was up like a shot. "Yes, Doctor?"

"He's gonna be fine. We removed two bullets, and we moved him into ICU. He lost a lot of blood, but he's stable."

"So, he's okay?"

"Yes. In several weeks he'll be as good as new. I see no sign of any complications with surgery. The bullets were easy to remove and there was no damage to any of his organs, so he should be fine. We'll be keeping a close eye on him for the next couple of days, but I'm sure he'll pull through."

Lita stepped forward. "When can I see him, Doctor?"

"Well, we should let his mother see him and then we should let him rest. He's heavily sedated. But tomorrow you can see him."

"Okay, okay," Lita said, upset she couldn't see her man.

"Oh, thank you." Rik's mother grabbed the doctor's arm. "Thank you, God, for saving my baby."

"You're welcome," he said, liking this woman for recognizing him.

"Lita, come on," Qua said. "We're gonna take you home."

Quadir said nothing, just drove thinking about him and Rik lying together on the floor in the club. He was so grateful Tyrik was still alive. But thoughts of Black cut deep. He'd grown up with the man. It seemed like everybody he'd come up with was dying or in jail. He pulled up alongside Lita's Cadillac.

"Thanks," she said.

"We'll follow you home," Qua insisted.

After leaving Lita's mother's house, Quadir and Gena drove home. The ride seemed longer than before. Quadir's mind was racing, replaying the minutes and seconds before the gunfire began over and over. People who'd looked at him real weird or the guy who'd bumped into him. He was the guy shooting, too. The entire night was a setup. The guys standing on the wall with gators on, no women around, not partying or getting down. He saw all their faces when the infrared light came on.

Gena realized the shit was out of control. Her man wasn't safe and neither was she. Both were touchable, both were accessible, and both could have anything waiting for them when they reached home.

She looked over at Qua; her man was in the zone. Her presence didn't surround him as it usually did. So she simply let him sit. Sometimes it's better to simply let a person be. No conversation, no radio.

As they pulled into the driveway of their lovely home, he finally asked, "Gena, what's it all for?"

"I don't know. I don't ever want to lose you. Nothing is worth losing you for. Nothing."

"You'd give all of this up?"

"To be with you? *Please*. In a wink of an eye."

The Way Players Play

Jerrell Jackson was riding through Mt. Airy in his brand-new black Jaguar. MAFIA65, read the license plate. He had blown up, and in such a short period of time. He was making enemies, but for some reason, he didn't fear them or care.

He checked the time. *Forty-five minutes late*, he thought, thanks to some girl he ran across at the bus stop needing a ride. He gave her a ride, too. Went inside the house, talked to the girl for a few minutes, had his way with her, then stepped off into the sunlight. It didn't matter, though. Girls would sit around and wait for him all day if they knew he wanted to see them. And they did want to see him. Be it for the money, be it for his car, be it for who he really was. For whatever reason, they were trying hard to see the boy. Jerrell had a magnificent home up in Monticello County, complete with marble floors and waterfalls.

Jerrell pulled into the long, narrow driveway of perfectly land-scaped grounds. Everybody was there. He could tell by all the foreign vehicles sitting in his driveway.

"Yo, I'm here," he said, coming through the door.

"What's up?" Khyree said.

They were surrounding a pizza that had been delivered. Everybody shook hands, as usual, and Jerrell sat himself down and grabbed his slice.

"What's up?" Ran asked.

"Man, I don't know. You tell me."

"Everything's rolling smooth."

"Money's right," Sam added.

"People are buying weight," Ran informed him.

Khyree took a bite of pizza. "Everything's fine."

Jerrell finished the mouthful he had and told them about Quadir's retirement. "He was trying to get rid of the last little bit of stuff he had. That's why wasn't no coke moving, remember? The motherfucker was selling keys for ten Gs."

Ran asked, "Quadir ain't quitting, is he?"

"That's what the word is on the street." Jerrell took another bite. "Now . . ." he said, standing up. "If Qua has stopped, that means you-know-who is going to take his place," he said, pointing at Ran.

"Rik!" Ran shouted, as if he'd scored points for the right answer.

"Exactly, which means Rik now has his plus Quadir's piece of the pie."

"Rik's supposed to be real upset about Black," Khyree said. "He told Lita that we was behind it, so now she talkin' 'bout don't call for a while. She'll bring Khy to my mom's house. Man, I don't know what Rik's calling himself doing with my son, you know?"

"Wait a minute. What did he tell Lita?" Ran asked.

"He told her that we was behind Black's party and Black gettin' killed," Khyree responded.

"Like he know something don't nobody else do." Ran laughed. "What else he say?"

"That's it. I doubt he'd tell Lita anything he was gonna do, with her having my son, you know," Khyree said.

"Man, he would tell her. The question is, would she tell you?" Jerrell asked.

Khyree glared at him.

Jerrell scanned the room like a general commanding an invasion. "Let's kidnap Forty."

Jerrell waited for the response.

"Kidnap! Why do you want to kidnap him?" Khyree asked.

"Who's running this shit?" Jerrell glared at him. He hated the way Khyree always had something to say behind him.

Khyree, as well as the others, sat in silence, trying to figure out what Jerrell was talking about. There was no need to ask, 'cause if he wanted you to know, he'd let you know.

It was Christmas Eve. Club Phoenix was packed. Everyone was dressed to impress and champagne was flowing. The night was going well. Rik was out with Lita, of course. Rik didn't travel far. Lita didn't let him. Amin and Zafa were there. Charlie and Forty were standing in a corner talking to Jamal and some girls. Rik couldn't help himself; he had to walk over. There were girls there.

The Muslim brothers arrived like the mob, in long coats and brim hats, surrounding Amin as if they were his bodyguards. Brother Ramzidin, Brother Ramier, and Brother Muhammad were all there. Winston and Blair were over at the bar.

Tracey had called Gena to see if she was coming to the Christmas Eve party, but she and Qua had decided to spend the evening at home.

Tracey, being as single as she was, couldn't have stayed away from that party if she wanted to. Everybody was there, even the city's football and basketball players. Radio personalities were transmitting live from the party. Andrea, Veronica, Bridgette, and Kim were standing together at the open champagne bar, trying to get with somebody else's man. Tracey knew Lita couldn't stand none of them, especially Veronica.

As the evening went on, everybody danced and had a good time.

Lita mingled while keeping a real close eye on Rik, never losing sight of him for more than a few seconds. Amin and Zafa sat at their table. Occasionally, Amin would talk to a girl, but it must have not been anything, 'cause his wife was sitting right next to him.

Kim was dancing with Jamal. *Lord*, Tracey thought. *Gena really needs to be here.* Jamal was all over Kim, and vice versa. Some girls acted like they didn't care if guys felt all over their bodies when they danced, but Tracey didn't think it was right. When she was dancing, she wouldn't let any stranger touch her like that. When she was slow dragging and felt their dick getting hard, she would walk off the dance floor. She hated that, especially when it was some broke-ass nigga trying to get his groove on. *Men, they're so desperate.*

"Guess who?" a man said from behind her, covering her eyes.

"I don't know."

"Who do you want it to be?"

"Dr. Dre."

"Oh, you straight played yourself with that one, sis," Quinny Day said, uncovering her eyes.

"No, baby. You know I was joking," she said, really wishing it was Dr. Dre.

"No, you wasn't, but it's cool." Quinny Day was standing there in front of her, looking too good.

"I'm joking, Quinny Day. You know who I'm trying to see," Tracey said. "You, boy. You, you, you."

"Don't be playing games, Tracey."

"Quinny, please. You know I take you personal."

"Hi, Quinny Day."

Tracey heard a girl's voice and turned to see Bridgette. She looked horrible. Her outfit was cheap. Her makeup looked worn, and she had bags under her eyes. After Quinny brushed her off, he and Tracey looked at each other.

"Damn, she needs to find another fool, like Black had to be to fuck with her trick ass, 'cause sis is going down," Quinny said, looking at Tracey real serious.

"I heard the money ain't been right since Black got killed," Tracey said.

"Her simple, retarded ass should have something."

"Like he had a will? He didn't bequeath nothing to her."

"Huh?"

"I said, he didn't leave her anything."

"So, why did he have to leave her anything? She should've saved something for a rainy day. Come on. You females aren't slow, just stupid. Yo, would Gena be messed up?" Quinny Day asked.

"No, of course not."

"Okay, then. Besides, even if Black didn't leave her nothing, she got herself. If I was a woman, there wouldn't be no way my Black ass would ever be broke."

Rik was on the dance floor with some girl. He was getting drunk, but he hadn't lost his mind yet. Of course, Lita was walking around looking for him. Veronica, a true-blue slut with a capital *S* on her chest, danced with another guy over to the right of him. She always thought she was playing somebody, but the truth of the matter was, she wasn't playing nobody but herself.

Rik took a closer look, and damn if it wasn't Forty dancing with her. "Hey, Forty!" he called out.

Veronica didn't look, 'cause she had already spotted Rik and knew how he was. They were straight up playin' on the dance floor. Rik couldn't help but watch them. Most people couldn't do anything but watch them. Veronica and Forty were doing some serious grinding out there, and the thing about it was, while she was dancing with him, another guy on the dance floor came and danced behind her, even pushed up next to her while she was already pressed up onto Forty.

Girls couldn't stand Veronica, and guys were always in her face but talked about her behind her back like she was nothing. Trying to tell Veronica about herself was a waste of energy. She liked getting attention so much that you could tell that's really what she was after—someone to look at her—and that's exactly what the guys did. Look at her, play mind games on her, and always give her attention. The kind of attention she really didn't need.

Forty was all over her. Rasun thought he was getting ready to pull her skirt up and start fucking her. He'd already flashed her tit to everybody on the dance floor. The girl was drunk, and she needed somebody to get her ass home. Andrea and Bridgette, the "friends" she came with, knew she was drunk 'cause she was at the bar drinking up Forty's champagne like she'd never had it before.

"Forty, I got to go outside. I need some air." Veronica was hot and felt like she was going to faint.

"Well, come on." He helped her fix herself and got her outside. "Come on, here. My jeep is parked right over there. Come on."

Veronica tried to get herself together, but she felt so light, so out of touch, she couldn't walk without holding on to him. Forty's jeep was parked way in the back of the club.

"Damn, Forty, I thought you said it was right outside."

He took her to his jeep. Once he helped her inside, he rolled the window down. "If you start to feel sick, open the door." He didn't want her to throw up in his jeep. "Here, let me move this seat back for you," he said, playing with the control panel on the far side.

Suddenly, Veronica was prone, but she hadn't felt a thing. She assumed it was part of the head spin she wished would go away. Everything felt dizzy, and when she closed her eyes, it was worse.

She didn't feel Forty's fingers running along her inner thigh, and by the time she noticed anything, he was already pushing her legs apart, getting her skirt out of the way, moving into place with a big, fat, juicy dick sticking into the air. It was too late. Forty had his shit out, her panties down, his condom on, and he was ready to go to work.

Veronica was too far gone to put up a fight. Just to raise her arm and utter no took too much effort. Forty kept his head up to make sure he didn't get caught doing what he was doing. Veronica wasn't really moving, but she was breathing, eyelids opening and closing in slow motion, only the whites showing.

Forty couldn't believe how easy it was. He was used to having to buy a big-ass pair of gold earrings or something, but this was too fucking easy. Veronica was too weak to hold her arm up, couldn't tell him to stop, couldn't hold him off her. He was pounding her little ass half to death.

When he was done, he took a rag from the back seat and wiped himself. He tried to get Veronica to get up, but she only moaned. He checked his Rolex. There wasn't much time left. He pulled her underwear up off the floor, pulled her skirt down enough to cover her panties, and went back to the party. Nobody seemed to really miss him.

"Where's Veronica, Forty?" Andrea asked.

"She's out in the car. She didn't feel good. Hey, I can't take the girl home, so don't leave her."

"Forty, you ain't shit!" Andrea said as she headed for the lobby.

"Mm-hmm, whatever. Your girlfriend's gonna be ass out if you leave her. Think I'm playin'?" he hollered back.

Jerrell walked out into the lobby, where Ran was talking to some girl.

"Yo, what up? You ready or what?"

"Man, chill. I got this shit under control. There's a car waiting outside."

"All right, I'm out."

"What's the matter?" Andrea asked, sensing something was going on.

"Nothing. He's ready to go, that's all," Ran answered. "So, we gonna get together or what?"

"Yeah," Andrea replied.

"Well, write down your number so I can call you."

"Can't we go get some breakfast? This is almost over."

Everybody was pairing off for the night, but it looked like Andrea would have to look for a meal somewhere else.

"I can't, baby. I got shit to do. I wish I could, but I can't. I'll make it up to you. We'll go get a nice lobster dinner, okay?" He slipped her number into his pocket. "I'll see you later. Don't give nobody none, either."

She seemed confused. "Who?"

"That nigga you gonna get to take you to breakfast." There wasn't anything slow about Ran. "Damn," he said, thinking about the pussy he could've gotten instead of having to take care of shit for Jerrell.

Forty caught up with Andrea and Bridgette and walked them over to his jeep to get Veronica. She was out cold. Her skirt was on the floor and she was completely exposed from the waist down.

"What you do to her?" Bridgette asked.

"I didn't do that! That's not how I left her," he said.

"This don't make no sense." Andrea got her friend up and out of the drunken sleep she was in.

Veronica didn't know what the fuck was going on. Andrea pulled her skirt up and put her panties in her pocketbook. Bridgette came around with the car, and Andrea helped Veronica get into the back seat. Forty stood a few feet away talking with some girl as if nothing had happened.

Quadir and Gena were lying together in the living room with the fireplace glowing, listening to Sade, sipping on some Alizé, languid from their lovemaking, appreciating the fireplace for more than its glow.

Much to Gena's surprise, Quadir had a gift for her. Over in the corner sat a lidded box, covered in shiny red paper with a silver bow on top. "What is that?"

"Look and see."

He placed the box on the floor next to her, and she removed the lid and looked inside.

"Qua! She's adorable!"

"It's a he."

"Oh, he's so adorable."

She gently gathered up the tiny furball, cuddling it.

"I saw him and I thought he was cute."

Gena inspected the diamond-and-gold tag. "Gucci?"

"I named him Gucci," he said, grinning. "You know, he's a Persian. He's gonna have a lot of hair."

"Qua, I figured that," she said with a hint of sarcasm. "I don't believe you. This is so sweet." She paused. "I got something for you, too."

"Really, is that so?"

"It is," she said, standing up completely in the raw. "But you have to catch it," she said, running up the stairwell butt naked as he ran after her.

The black Pathfinder pulled into the back of the parking lot of the West Point Motel, under a tree and out of the light, where it sat and waited.

Ran was impatient. "Man, what the fuck is the bitch doing?"

"Don't ask me. She's your people. I don't know nothing; don't even know why I'm here. All I know is that sis would want to bring her ass on," Sam said, picking some dirt from under his fingernail.

Ran grabbed his pager out of his pocket. No number. He already knew that. He checked it for sound and sat it on the seat.

"Give her some time," Ran said.

"I'll give her some time, all right."

"Who knows? They might be up there getting their freak on," Sam suggested.

"Man, I don't give a fuck if he up there eatin' her ass, I want the bitch to come on."

The scream of the beeper violated their contrived composure, scaring them half to death. They threw themselves against each other in an effort to shut it off.

"Anticipation is a motherfucker, ain't it?" Ran stated.

"Man, is it her?"

"No!"

"Damn, I'm tired. Jerrell got me out here kidnapping mother-fuckers in the middle of the night. And what's up with your people?"

"I don't know! I'm gonna wring her neck if she fucks up." His pager went off again. "Why do girls got to keep calling my pager over and over again? I'm saying, when you can get to a phone, you'll call a bitch back, right? Why must they do that?" Ran was irritated.

"Who is it?" Sam asked.

"Jennifer. I swear she calls me over and over and over again all motherfucking night. I went to sleep, the girl was paging me. I woke up, she was paging me. You'd think the girl would've figured the shit out by now."

Sam sat there listening to another one of Ran's stories, as usual.

"Man," Ran continued, "don't you know she dialed the pager so much I had to buy batteries every other day. I swear to God, the bitch has to be fucking possessed to page me like that." Ran's pager went off again. "Damn, I been trying to see this girl right here." Ran showed the number to Sam. "She all that."

"Is she?" Sam quickly memorized the number for himself. "What's her name?"

"Tia. She got a beauty salon, Rippin' It, up in Germantown. Now this girl is bad, with her pretty ass. You gots to see it to believe it."

I plan to, Sam thought.

Ran's pager went off again. "If this ain't her, I'm gonna smack her silly."

"Yeah, I'm gonna slap her ass around some, too, for making me sit out here like this."

"Yo, this is it," Ran said. "Look at the time. Three twelve. She said she needs twenty minutes, and then she'll be ready."

Kidnapped

Inside the hotel room, Simone and Forty were preparing to go at it. Simone had no problem putting herself at ease with Forty. He was nice-looking, and Ran was right. He played right into her hands. Ran had come to her with that old, "I need you, baby, you got to help a brother out" talk. Time after time, Simone was always doing something morally wrong for Ran. But the twenty thousand he offered her for her trouble was worth it, and she jumped at it like she was an Olympic contender. Now here she was in a hotel room with some stranger she'd met at a nightclub.

Slowly, Simone eased herself from the double bed and tiptoed over to the door. Carefully, she unlocked it. Then she picked up the phone. Just as she placed the hook on the receiver, Forty opened the door to the bathroom.

"Damn, you're big. You look deformed." Staring, she didn't want him fucking her.

"Think you can handle it?"

"Do you think *you* can handle it?" she asked him.

"Talk now, cry later."

Forty stood at the foot of the bed. Meticulously, he picked up his pants and carefully laid them on the back of a chair. He then placed a gun and a condom on the table. He lay on the bed, picked up the remote, turned on the television, and then clicked off the light. Not watching the television, he concentrated on Simone. Within a matter of minutes, he had Simones's mouth wrapped around his private part. He had a thing about his penis in a woman's mouth. He had to have it, and within minutes, he was giving it to her.

While he concentrated on neutralizing his high, Simone was surreptitiously reaching for the gun he'd so cavalierly placed nearby on the nightstand. Finally making contact with the cold piece of steel, she was able to slip the gun from the table and nudge it beneath the pillow while still simulating enjoyment of Forty's superior anatomy. Not that she could, but he was high and she was on a mission. Forty was the man you'd want to get snowed in with on a cold winter's day. It would never be in this lifetime, and particularly not tonight.

"Roll over," he whispered in her ear, thinking of some sexual innovation, but he was interrupted by an out-of-place sound that disconcerted him.

"Can I join in?" a voice that was neither his nor Simone's asked.

Forty reached for his piece, which was also out of place. He felt a setup as a hand reached around his throat and pulled him off the bed. "What the fuck is going on?"

"Nigga, shut the fuck up." The voice emphasized his instructions with a gun against Forty's jawbone. "You want to live, don't you? I know you do, especially since you're laying up here in all this pussy."

Forty didn't say anything, and he wasn't going to. They ducttaped his hands behind his back and then tied him to a chair, naked and blindfolded, while Simone got dressed in the bathroom.

Ran searched Forty's pants and jacket pockets. When he was done, Ran had the car keys, money, pager, and cell phone.

"The gun's under the pillow," Simone whispered to Ran as she came out of the bathroom.

Ran grabbed the gun, and the two of them left in Forty's jeep while Sam stayed with Forty.

"Damn, I wish this nigga had tinted windows," Ran said.

"I know, right."

"Yeah." He handed her a bag. "Here's your money."

"Thanks, Ran. Mm, twenty thousand. I don't know what I'm gonna do with all this money."

"Simone, so help me God, if you say anything, I swear. If you say one little word, if I even have a reason to think you told someone where you got this money from, I *will* kill you. You hear me?"

"Ran, I'm not sayin' nothin', straight up. You not gonna have to worry about me, okay?"

"I hope so." Ran parked the jeep on a deserted side street. "Damn, we need something to wipe the jeep down."

"Here." She pulled a pair of panties out of her pocketbook.

Ran glared at her. "Man, don't give me your drawers."

"They cool. I haven't worn them or nothing." She pressed them up to his face. "See?"

"Yo, Simone! Are you out your mind? You need to get some motherfucking help."

"Yeah, don't we all?"

While she got out, Ran took the panties and wiped Forty's jeep down. Then he got out and locked the doors.

"Remember what I said," he told her as he led her up the block.

"I swear, Ran, you don't have to worry about me."

"I hope you didn't catch no feelings for the nigga or nothing while he was runnin' up in you."

"Ran, come on, it takes more than a fuck, you know what I mean?" she said, looking up at him.

"Yo, keep your mouth shut and everything will be cool."

"Ran, I don't know shit. I don't know a damn thing."

"All right, baby."

Ran whistled at a cab, but it kept going. Another cab was turning the corner.

"Here, wait a minute."

Simone stepped out into the street and hailed the cab down. Ran got the next cab back to the hotel and let himself into the room. Sam had put Forty in the corner facing a wall.

"Why you put him like that?" Ran asked.

"I don't know. Seem like he not here, right?"

"Man, come on. Why didn't you get him dressed?"

"What, and untie him?"

"No," Ran said. "Dress his ass tied up."

"Man, he's butt naked, man. I don't want to dress him."

Ran looked at Sam, with his one and only look he gave to people when they were getting on his nerves. "Dress him, I said."

"How I'm supposed to dress him all tied up, man? Huh?"

"Never mind, okay? Never mind. Hand me his clothes."

Ran pulled the ski mask over his face and ordered Sam to do the same. He uncovered Forty's eyes.

The swirling blackness and specks of light faded into one, and finally there was vision. Forty looked around. He couldn't believe this was happening. After Ran untied him, he threw his clothes at Forty and told him to get dressed, while Sam had the gun pointed at him, in case he tried anything.

Forty picked up his clothes off the floor and put them on. He couldn't see his assailants' faces because of the ski masks. He didn't say anything; he stayed calm and played along with what was going on. He wanted to go home to his wife, Sharon, and their three sons: Christopher Jr., Brandon, and Andrew.

She'd told him to stay in with her, cried about it 'cause it was Christmas Eve, but he had to be out there. Christmas didn't matter. He had to be out there. And now look at what was happening to him. He wasn't even sure what was happening. He thought about asking but decided not to. He thought about how, in a few more hours, his sons would wake up and run downstairs to the living room and start opening their presents with or without Mom and Dad, and then how they'd run into Mommy and Daddy's room to wake them up. Only Daddy wouldn't be there.

When Forty finished dressing, Sam tied him to the chair and blindfolded him again. There was some movement about the room, and Forty could tell things were being shifted. Suddenly, his arm stung, like a bee got him, and in less than ten seconds, he was slumped over in the chair.

"Let's clean this place up."

"Why? We got gloves on."

"Well, wipe everything off anyway," Ran insisted. "No finger-prints, no body, no weapons, no case."

"Yeah, except Simone. We should've killed the bitch."

"Why? She been helping out for years."

"Man, I would take her out. She knows too much."

"Yeah, yeah, but we don't have to worry about her right now. All we got to worry about is taking care of this."

They carried Forty downstairs and put him in the back of the truck; then Ran went back upstairs and took another fifteen minutes to wipe down the room one last time. Placing the room key on the table, he closed the door behind him. He drove out to West Philly, where they put Forty in the basement of an abandoned house. They tied him to a chair, went home, and spent Christmas with their families.

Gena took her time opening the tiny box wrapped in gold paper with a blue velvet bow. "Quadir!" she gasped. "They're beautiful! You don't think they're too big?"

"No, not at all," Quadir said.

"They're beautiful, baby. I love them, I really do."

"They're pear-shaped."

"I don't care if they're shaped like kumquats. I love them. I wanted a pair of diamond earrings. I was tired of these little dots. Quadir, I'm gonna get robbed with all this jewelry."

"No, you're not. When you're this large, you don't get robbed. People just stare."

"Here," she said as she turned the tree lights on. "I have something for you."

Quadir didn't know what he was doing, but it felt good. Since he was Muslim, he realized it was wrong to have the tree and gifts, but it still felt good. Gena was a madwoman when it came to money and a mall. She'd spent thousands shopping for all the gifts under the tree. She handed Quadir a big box.

"What is it?" Qua opened the box. His eyes glowed when he pulled out the black leather jacket customized by Dapper Dan. "I'm scared to ask how much it cost."

"Then don't. Here," she said, handing him another box.

Inside was a Cartier watch. Qua put his watch on, his eyes sparkling like the diamonds surrounding the bezel.

"I like it."

"I knew you would. Here." She had more. One box contained more than twenty different colognes. "I didn't know which one you'd like, so I got them all."

He stared at her. She'd gone mad. In another box, there was a week's worth of Armani ensembles. Quadir was really getting into it, opening his gifts and throwing the paper to the side. Gena stood there, watching, knowing he'd never celebrated Christmas.

"No. Open that one." Gena knew what was in each box. This one had Genesis cartridges for his Sega.

"Did you get me boxing?"

"Yeah, I got it." Gena had purchased records, tapes, and CDs.

Gena lingered over a little box she'd spotted earlier. Quadir saw her looking at it. "Here."

"What is it?" She smiled.

"I love you. Open your box."

It was a diamond ring, a cluster of twenty-five-point diamonds totaling seven carats in weight.

"Good Lord, but it can't top this. Here, I got you one more thing."

She felt under the torn paper next to the tree, trying to find the tiny box for him. "Here it is."

She handed Qua the box and watched as he tore at the wrapping paper. He opened the box and picked out a key chain sporting a diamond Q.

"Check you out," he said. "Real diamonds. I like this."

"It's a key chain," she said, like he wouldn't know.

"Baby, it's the best key chain I've ever had."

"You like it?"

"I love it."

For twenty-five thousand, you ought to, she thought.

"I'm really scared to ask you how much this cost. So I'm gonna skip that."

Has he been saying that a lot tonight or is it just me? Gena asked herself as she sat there organizing the stuff under the tree like Gah Git always did. She'd never had this much stuff under a tree. It was like someone else's life, someone else's man.

Life had never been easy, and the majority of the time it was hard. But no matter how hard it got, there was always a lot of love. Gena remembered Christmas with her family. One gift, two if you were lucky. Today, she had everything she wanted. Gah Git always said to have everything and no love was to have nothing at all. But to have love was to have everything. For the first time, Gena understood that when she looked up and saw her man staring at her. It wasn't the gifts that meant anything. It was only the love she had for him and all the love he gave her.

Gena leaned over, got down on her knees, wrapped her arms

around him, gave him a real strong hug, kissed him, and told him that she loved him. Then she went back to organizing the gifts.

He gazed at her and thought of how much he loved her, how much he needed her, and how, for the first time, he was happy. If he didn't have anything else, merely having her would be okay. "Do you know what I want from you?"

"No. What?"

"I want a son. I want you to give me a son."

"That's all you want?" she asked with a sexy grin on her face.

"That's all I want," he said, lying on top of her as he held her in his arms.

"Then a son you shall have," she whispered.

Then he kissed her.

A Million's Worth

Forty was dazed and had lost track of how many hours had passed. Yet, he was still aware he had been kidnapped while fucking a girl he could barely remember in a hotel. *Where's some help? There should be a goddamn superhero saving the day by now*, he thought. However, Forty realized he wasn't getting any help. *That bitch, fucking trick-ass bitch, got me set the fuck up.* Forty swore on his life that her ass would see no more sunshine if he got the fuck out on the streets. He would hunt her down to the ends of the earth if necessary.

As he sat in the dark, listening to his stomach growling, wondering what the fuck was going on, Forty thought about what was going to happen next. His mind scrambled as he tried to remember specific details. His heart raced as he thought of his wife, Sharon. Any other time, she'd call the police on him. Now was the time. Where was Rik? Where were his people with the army brigade, ready to battle and get him out of there? It was like that when you hustled for a nigga like Rik.

The door opened, and a tall, skinny guy wearing a ski mask walked down the stairs and threw Forty a bag with a sandwich and soda in it. When Forty was finished, the man tied him back up and left the basement.

Forty was hurting. He couldn't believe he'd been kidnapped. Deep down inside, he had a feeling he wasn't going to make it.

***

Forty's wife was crying. She'd been crying since he'd left the house and her ass at home with the kids like he always did. Their three sons didn't enjoy Christmas Day at all without their daddy there. Forty's mother had called the police, but they couldn't take a missing person's report for forty-eight hours. However, the officers made an exception because of Christmas and told his mother twenty-four hours.

"Damn, you call 911 and they tell you to call back," Forty's mom said with disgust, slamming down the phone.

Sharon called everybody she could think of. Everybody said the same thing. He was at a party last night, but no one knew where he was. Sharon had called the police, the Roundhouse, and all the hospitals. It was as if Forty had dropped off the planet. All the times his Black ass didn't come home, all the times he lied about where he was, and still there was nothing Sharon wouldn't give to see him walk through the door. She'd be so glad he was home, she wouldn't even be mad; that's how badly she wanted her man back.

His mother and father, on the other hand, knew something was wrong. Mom knew her son. There was no way her son wouldn't show up on Christmas Day. No way at all. The following day, the police came out to the house and took a missing person's report.

Forty was hurting, physically and mentally. His body was numb from sitting for such a long time. If he could have a stretch—that's all he wanted, to stretch. Suddenly, he had company.

"Yo, nigga, you up?" a familiar voice asked.

Forty couldn't place the voice, but he recognized it.

"You ready to go?" the ski mask asked, but Forty didn't answer.

The blow to his midsection got his attention, giving him time to focus on his options as he got his wind back.

"Let's try this shit again, motherfucker. You ready to go?"

Forty considered. Why didn't he see the shit before? How did he let it happen? He'd slipped up and let the motherfuckers catch his ass out there. How stupid could he be?

"I'm ready to go."

"Bitch-ass nigga, shut the fuck up." The masked man gave him a swift, forceful smack to his head. "You ready to go when I say so."

Forty sat there seriously trying to figure who the fuck was talking to him.

"I want a million dollars, and then I'll let you go. You only get one phone call. You get that person to take the money to the Springdale Mall tomorrow morning at nine. All they got to do is put the money in the yellow school bus in the parking lot. If they don't, then it's your time to die, nigga. You're not confused about none of this, are you?"

"No, man. I'm not confused."

"What's the number?" Still tied up, with the phone held to his ear, Forty asked for Charlie when a girl answered the phone.

"Yo, man, your girl called and said you didn't come home."

"Listen, I need a million dollars put on a yellow school bus in the Springdale parking lot at nine o'clock tomorrow morning," Forty said.

"Beware of the man in the checkered suit. The iguana has landed on you, too, motherfucker," Charlie joked.

"I'm serious. I've been kidnapped. You got to help me," Forty said seriously.

"What?" Charlie said, realizing his buddy wasn't playing.

"Man, you only got till nine o'clock in the morning tomorrow. Put the million dollars on the yellow school bus at the Springdale Mall," Forty said as the man hung up the phone.

"Hello? Forty!" Charlie said frantically as the dial tone rang in his ear. He hung up the phone, thought for a moment, and turned to his companion for the evening. "Come on, you gotta go."

She protested a little, so he dragged her by the arm. "Get dressed, you got to go. Come on."

"Fuck you, Charlie! Where's my money?"

"Bitch, you get nothing. I'm having a crisis, and I need you to get away from me so I can solve it."

He gave her fifty dollars, and she was pissed. "*No, you didn't. No, you didn't play me* for no paper and be so small about it, with your little-dick self," she hollered, expecting to get her usual $350.

"Bitch, you are a flea. Here, here you go; another fifty. Didn't you hear me say I'm having a crisis?" he asked angrily, pushing her out the door before slamming it in her face.

Charlie got on the phone and immediately called Rik. Rik couldn't believe it. He realized who had Forty and he understood why. Ever since Quadir stopped serving the city, Jerrell had been coming at him instead of Quadir. Quadir never took care of serious business. Quadir let Jerrell push him out of the game by killing all the people who bought hundreds of kilos a month from him. But Rik wasn't giving up anything. He was coming the fuck up in a major way and had just started to come into some serious paper, like Quadir. He wasn't going out like no sucker.

He sat back and listened carefully as Charlie told him about the phone call from Forty. Rik already knew something was going on when Sharon paged him, talking 'bout, "Where is my man? I know he fucking some bitch with you, Rik."

Rik had done everything but hang up on her. He sent Charlie over to Sharon's to explain what was happening.

Rik hung up the phone. There was no problem putting together a million. Forty was worth a million, so paying the money wasn't a problem. Within minutes, a dozen phones were ringing off the hook and the city's ghetto gazette flashed the news headline that Forty had been kidnapped by the Junior Mafia. Rik called Quadir and told him what was happening.

"How much?" Quadir asked.

"A million."

Quadir was prepared to put up the paper. "You got it?"

"Yeah, of course. It's just that there's no guarantee in a situation like this."

Rik and Charlie drove toward the Springdale Mall with a duffel bag placed on the back seat containing the million requested for Forty. All the while, Rik warned Charlie that if it was a set-up to take no prisoners. Entering the Springdale Mall parking lot, Rik could see the yellow school bus parked in a corner off in the distance. He sped in its direction. Reaching the bus, he circled the entire area. There were a few cars parked in the lot off in the distance, but the bus stood alone.

Rik pulled up on the side of the bus. Charlie emerged from the car with the duffel bag of money in one hand and his hammer in the other. The double doors of the bus were slightly open. There was enough space for Charlie to push open the doors. Taking his first step up onto the bus, he pointed his hammer in the direction of the seats. He was ready to lay anybody down who popped out at him. He placed the duffel bag on the floor of the bus. Then he carefully pushed it with his foot down the aisle, past the first row of seats. He exited the bus, pulling the doors back to how he'd found them.

With the task complete, everyone sat back and waited for the phone to ring with the news Forty was home.

The following morning, a yellow school bus pulled up on the 1300 block of Conestoga Street and parked down the block. Ran stepped from the bus with a million dollars in a duffel bag. He went inside.

"The nice thing about this is that everyone got what they wanted. I got the money and you get to go home. I say it's time to celebrate, don't you?"

Forty couldn't see him 'cause he was still wearing the ski mask. Jerrell directed Sam to untie Forty from the chair but to leave his hands tied. Forty was barely able to stand, he'd been tied up so long. It sure felt good to get out of that chair. Once he felt a little bit of strength coming back into his body, he assumed he would be all right. Then he welcomed his anger. Looking like an old man with arthritis, Forty turned on Sam and, with all his strength, threw his tied hands around Sam's head and yanked the ski mask off.

"Sam?" he said as he watched Jerrell remove his ski mask before Ran did the same.

Forty was livid. "You fucked up when you kidnapped me. You not getting away with kidnapping me and taking my million dollars."

"Nigga, I already did."

"You think you did. This shit ain't never gonna be over, so go ahead. Kill me, motherfucker," Forty said, already knowing they were going to do that.

"Pussy, take that!" Jerrell shot him in the right leg. "I already did get away with taking your million dollars. I got it right here."

The bullet ripped through Forty's flesh as his body dropped to the floor.

"I wish I'd known you were the one behind this 'cause you woulda never seen no paper from me!"

"Man, fuck you!"

"Nigga, fuck you, too."

Another explosion tore into Forty's other leg. The pain was agonizing and he screamed.

Jerrell shot him again, getting his arm. "You would'na paid if you knew it was me."

Pow! went the gun as Jerrell shot him again in the other arm.

"See, baby, I'm running this shit and you or nobody else can stop me," Jerrell said as he circled Forty's body.

"Fuck you," Forty rasped as he lay on the basement floor.

Insane with anger now, Jerrell shot again, getting him in the chest. *Pow! Pow!* Then he stood over Forty. "Say your prayers, nigga," he said, and put the gun right between his eyes and squeezed the trigger as Forty tried to duck. The bullet fired and grazed the side of his head, taking him out.

Realizing Forty was dead, Jerrell jumped back into the reality of having a million dollars.

Ran said, "Let's get the fuck out of here. We'll come back tonight and take care of the body."

"Yeah, we can dump that nigga right in the Schuylkill River," Jerrell sneered. "Come on. Let's go."

After going about their regular business for a few hours, hitting their regular customers, Ran and Sam pulled onto Conestoga Street at two in the morning. Yellow police tape was everywhere. "Stay here," Ran said.

He got out of the truck and went up on the porch. Blood was everywhere. He pushed open the unlocked door and went inside and there was more. It looked like a paint roller had made a trail from the basement.

"I don't fucking believe this," he panted, running out and pulling the door shut behind him. "I don't fucking believe it. Get Jerrell on the phone."

They would find out later that a neighbor had looked out his window, thinking he'd heard shots, but didn't call the police. When Forty dragged himself onto the porch and the man saw his bloody body, he then called the police. Forty lay alone on the porch until they arrived. No one came to his assistance, even to put a blanket over him. Forty lay there, dying in the winter cold, all alone, until the ambulance arrived to take him to a nearby hospital.

The police had searched the house, dusted it for fingerprints, and left about forty minutes before Ran and Sam arrived to take Forty's body away.

"Shit. Jerrell is gonna be mad as shit. We got to call him," Ran said in a panic. "We got to call him."

Sam found a payphone and pulled the Cherokee over so Ran could call Jerrell. The phone rang. A few seconds later a girl answered. "Yo!"

"Hello," the girl said.

"Who dis?" Ran asked.

"This is Val, Jerrell's sister."

"This is Ran. Where he at?"

"They got him."

"Who?"

"The police. They came and arrested him."

"What for?"

"Attempted murder and kidnapping."

"Oh, shit."

"They said he tried to kill some guy, Christopher Cole. Who's Christopher Cole?"

"That's the boy, Forty," Ran replied. "I got to go," he said, and hung up the phone.

He and Sam would now have to find someplace to stay, since the police were probably looking for them. Ran went straight across the bridge and into New Jersey. He didn't pass Go and he didn't collect two hundred dollars. He went straight to New Jersey.

All Over

1990

Happy New Year! It was 1990. Fireworks exploded through the night sky as people of all races and ages joined in the New Year's celebration in the middle of Penn's Landing.

"Happy New Year!"

Rik found himself being patted on the back by a white man. "Yo! Has he lost his mind?"

"Come on, Rik. Be happy. It's New Year's," Qua told his friend.

"Fuck the New Year," Rik said, jerking his shoulders as if to shrug off the encounter.

"You see him, Lita?" Qua asked.

"Yeah," she said, laughing.

Ready to party, they ended up at Amin and Zafa's New Year's Eve party. Qua and Rik talked all night while Gena and Lita floated around, mingling through the crowd, greeting all their friends. Qua finally got them some nice seats at the bar, and the bartender replenished every bottle of champagne they went through. Both Quadir and Rik bought lots of champagne for everybody. Rik poured a glass and passed it out to all the sisters who'd given him a shot in the past year.

"Damn," Rik said. "You know her?"

"Talia?" Quadir asked.

"The bitch is all that."

"Been there, did that."

"You better watch what you say before Gena creep up behind your ass," Rik joked as they both laughed.

Qua looked over his shoulder. "It's cool."

But there was a face missing from the proceedings, Rik observed. "The shit is fucked up about the boy, Forty."

"They say if he makes it, he not gonna walk again," Qua said.

"Man, fuck that! They better know their days are numbered, dig me?"

"So Ran and Sam still on the run?"

"Yeah, they're on the run from me and the police, and Jerrell's in jail."

"Good."

"I tell you this much. Ran's not gonna make it, and if Jerrell sets foot back out on the street, he's not gonna make it, either, and neither is that pussy-ass Sam. Their future's already been planned by me, and they don't have one."

Qua knew he meant it. Rik was no joke. The boy would take you out if necessary. Quadir had already known about the half million up for grabs for whoever killed Ran and Sam. The word was in the streets.

"Look, there goes Veronica," Qua said, directing Rik to look her way.

"So, you fuck with Forty now?" Rik asked her.

"What are you talking about?" she asked with a serious attitude.

"I'm talking about you and Forty. Remember last week in the parking lot, or was you that fucked up?" Rik asked, laughing at her.

"Why you worried about me? You the one who wanted that homely bitch, so mind your homely-ass business and leave me alone," she said, walking away.

"She's a Reebok ho," Rik said, flagging his hand at her.

"You liked it!" she spat back at him.

"Hated it!" he shouted back.

Qua sat there falling out laughing 'cause he'd heard the parking lot story, especially the part about her clothes not being arranged quite the same way as when Forty left her. Of course, it wasn't right, but who was to say what was wrong?

The night went on, and the party came to an end. Quadir pulled Gena over to the side and kissed her gently.

"Happy New Year, baby," he said, letting her go.

As everyone made their exit, the cold winter air sent a chill right through Gena's sable. As usual, Quadir looked around the entire set. Girls were hopping into rides, and cars were riding back and forth as people scattered about the sidewalks, pairing off for the night.

"Shit," Rik said as he pulled up behind him. "Yo, Quadir, baby," he hollered, seeing Ran's face in the crowd.

"Yo! Go this way," he said, pushing Lita, trying to move them out of Ran's range.

Quadir saw Rik had his gun pulled. Panic struck him, and he grabbed Gena.

"Quadir!" she screamed as she saw a guy pull a gun and aim straight at them. For one brief second, her mind returned to the fast-food parking lot and the jammed gun. The face behind it was his. He'd pointed the gun at her and fired as the seconds elapsed between one another. Gena's heart pounded like waves against the seashore as Quadir threw her body to the ground and got on top of her like a protective shield. The people out celebrating New Year's Eve were caught in the middle of a drug war, and hundreds scattered, screaming and ducking down on the ground.

Quinny Day saw Quadir go down and began firing aimlessly into the air. The sound of the gunfire left Gena alone to a point where no one could touch her as she huddled in Quadir's strong arms.

Rasun spotted Sam and Khyree and began firing at both. He

watched Khyree tumble to the ground as bullets pierced his lower abdomen. Reds took a shot in the arm and fell behind a car parked on the street. Jamal saw everything in front of him. He stopped his car dead in the middle of traffic. He reached under his seat, jumped out of his brand-new Mercedes-Benz, and aimed at anybody he knew Rik wanted dead.

Rik took his time as he aimed carefully. From nowhere, the bullets hit him, crumpling him to the ground. His back burned like fire as the metal ripped through his flesh. With all his weight, Rik turned around and fired the infrared Glock, dropping one of Ran's rookies.

Rik ducked behind a car as red lasers flickered through the air. His bullets met the enemy as the laser fired directly on its target. His pain was unbearable, but Rik held steady until Ran fell dead to the ground.

The deafening silence that followed allowed the remaining Junior Mafia assassins to hear a familiar motor as a black four-door Cherokee slowed down long enough for everyone to hop in before it sped away, leaving a trail of smoke and bodies sprawled in the middle of the street.

The silence of gunfire was like an alarm, alerting everyone that they could come out of their hiding places. People peeked out from behind cars, buildings, and curtains to see if it was over.

"Quadir, come on," Gena said. "They're gone."

She realized something was very wrong. Freeing her body from his, she realized he'd been shot in the chest as she rolled him off her.

She stared at his lifeless body and began to cry. She picked up his head and laid it in her lap, hovering over him to keep him warm, realizing that her girlfriends' nightmare was becoming her own reality.

"Quadir, please get up." She tried to lift him. "Get up, baby. Quadir! Oh, no! Please, baby, get up! Somebody, help me! Somebody, help me, please! I need someone to help me. Please!" Covered in his blood, she continued to plead. "Qua, please, please . . . Baby, don't leave me. Don't leave me now! Boo, talk to me!"

"G," he rasped, scaring her silly.

"Quadir, I love you, baby. Please don't die. You're gonna be all right."

"It hurts, Gena. It's burning!"

Gena's head spun about, looking for help, only to see Lita sprawled on the sidewalk in a pool of blood and Rik lying next to a car. She was all alone; there was no one left. They were all dead.

"No! No! Qua, hold my hand, please." The bleeding was so bad, and she could feel his body tightening in her arms. Gena heard the sirens but saw no ambulance.

A police officer hunkered down next to her, speaking softly. "Miss, is he alive?"

"Yes! Yes, but he needs an ambulance!"

He touched her shoulder and told her, "There's one on the way. It will be right here." He stood and started counting bodies.

"Take . . . take . . ." Quadir whispered.

"What, baby? What?"

"Take it, take . . ." He closed his eyes again, and she began to remove his jewelry. "Key chain . . . take it." He was able to slip her the diamond Q key chain she'd given him.

"Qua, please hold on. The paramedics are on their way."

She stayed as close to him as possible without smothering him. Finally, the ambulance arrived, and the paramedics gently helped her stand before placing Qua on the stretcher. She watched as they went to work on him, never letting go of his hand. The moist drops made their silent way down her cheeks unnoticed.

"Quadir, I love you. Please don't leave me. God, don't take my baby from me."

Quadir looked up at her, squeezed her hand tight, and winked at her the same way he always did.

"Qua, it's gonna be okay," Gena told him, her face awash with tears. "You're gonna be all right, baby. Everything is gonna be fine."

She looked down at his blood-drenched body. The paramedics were still working, trying to save him, but she didn't know Qua was already on his way to everlasting peace. The journey would take him to paradise, and he had to leave Gena. He didn't want to. He wanted to stay with her. She loved him and made him happy. She was the only woman who loved him without the paper. But he just . . . just couldn't. He wanted to fight. He was fighting for every breath, but he was too tired. *It looks nice there.* His energy waned. *But what about Gena?* He wanted the pain to stop. He was hurting so badly. He gazed up at his beautiful Gena one last time and knew they'd be together one day. Then he closed his eyes and exhaled his last breath.

Gena heard a funny sound, something she recognized. *You only hear that on TV, don't you?* The beep of the heart monitor stopped like a never-ending pause, like an unending scream, and she was confused.

"I'm sorry, ma'am. Ma'am? He didn't make it."

She sat there, holding his hand, looking into his beautiful face as the ambulance continued its route to the hospital. She held on to his hand, but he wasn't holding on to hers anymore. The vehicle stopped, and Gena heard someone speaking.

"Ma'am? I'm sorry, ma'am. You're gonna have to let us take him. Ma'am?"

Someone was helping her take a step down, guiding her through a door. She was entering a building. She couldn't feel the floor, but this looked like a place where you could get help. Yes, help. Help for Quadir.

Gena sat in the place they put her, and wondered, *What is it I have to remember? Something happened, I think. Why am I on this chair? Where is Quadir?* She noticed a man in green scrubs. *Oh, okay, a doctor. I'll ask him. He'll know what . . . What will he know?*

"Doctor," she said. "Where is . . . where is Quadir Richards?"

The doctor flagged down a staff member, who escorted Gena to a gray hospital bed and pulled back the sheet. She moved closer. "Qua?" she said. "I'm here, honey. I'm right here. You know I'd never leave you, right?" she said, her voice cracking. *I bet if I kiss him.* She leaned into him and kissed his lips. What her soul knew as fact would not make its way to her conscious mind.

Qua's body was cold when she kissed him. There was moisture tracking down his still cheek that she slowly realized was falling from her own eyes. She felt a vacuum suck the strength from her midsection. She began to shake him as she kissed him, letting all her tears flow onto his ashen skin.

"Oh, God! Please, Qua! Wake up! Don't leave me! You said you'd never leave me! What am I gonna do?" A big hole was opening beneath her and she tried not to fall in. "Why, baby, why?"

Her man, her only man, the only man who loved her in this cruel, angry, vicious world lay lifeless in a gray hospital bed.

"You took care of me. You loved me so much. Don't do it, Qua." *These words should bring him back. He should listen to me.*

"Qua, I can't live without you. I don't want to live without you. God, please take me, too. Please take me with him."

She started crying, loud, startling an orderly. People came in, looked, and then left. She was holding him, kissing him, trying to bring him back to life.

"Miss," someone said. "Miss, you have to leave."

"Who's touching me?" Her arms flew out. "Get your hands off me!"

"Miss, please. He's gone. There was nothing we could do."

Gena shot the orderly a look that could kill. "You motherfuckers can save every-goddamn-body else. Don't touch me! Don't fucking touch me!"

She was reciting, over and over again like a mantra, "Please don't take him. Please don't take him. Please don't take him. God, take me. Oh, my Lord, why?"

The orderly couldn't deal with it and called the nurses station, glad Quadir's parents had arrived. He asked for their assistance. "Sir, his fiancée is distraught. It's a mess in there. She's lying on top of him, she refuses to leave the room, and I don't know what to do."

"Let me talk to her." When he reached the room, Montell Richards's heart broke, seeing the lovely girl desperately clinging to his son's dead body. "Gena? Gena, I'm here." She heard him but said nothing. "Gena, baby, he's gone. Come on. His mama wants to say goodbye. Come on."

The crooning sounds comforted her, and she let herself be lifted from the cold shell that had been her lover into Montell's arms, and she let him surround her with consolation. "He's all I had," Gena told him. "All I had. He was my life. Without him, there's no me. I can't live without that man. I don't want to."

"Yes, you can, Gena. You have to live. You have to be strong. Why do you think my Quadir loved you so much? 'Cause you're so strong. He loved you. Gena, you meant the world to that boy. It was his time," Montell added as tears filled up his eyes and slowly melted down his cheeks.

"No, no, no. It wasn't."

"Yes, it was, baby girl. And you *will* pull through this."

"I can't leave him here. They might not treat him right."

"They're gonna do their job, Gena. Quadir is in good hands. Nothing can ever hurt him again. Do you know if he could look down and see you right now, and see how you're acting, he'd be hurt to see you like this."

"Please let me stay with him tonight. I can't leave him. I got to stay with him. He's so cold. He needs a blanket. Can't they get him a blanket?"

"Gena, the boy doesn't need a blanket. You have to pull yourself together."

"Why'd they take him from me?" she sobbed. "Why did God take my baby from me? Oh, God, why?"

Montell tightened his hold on Gena so that she wouldn't fall to the floor. She leaned over the bed and hugged Quadir's lifeless body and kissed his cheek one last time. "I'll always be with you," she whispered in his ear. Then and only then did she let Quadir's father lead her from the room.

He passed his eyes over his dead son and continued walking, holding the grieving woman, remembering there was another waiting: Quadir's mother.

Montell took Gena home. When she awoke, Gah Git was sitting in a chair by the bed and Gucci was lying on Quadir's pillow. "You okay, baby?"

"Where am I?" She felt like Dorothy and Gucci was Toto and it was all a bad dream.

"You're home. We brought you home last night."

"Who are you?"

"I'm your grandmother, child. What, you done lost your rabid-ass mind?"

Gena's mind had to rewind itself. She wasn't in the projects; she was at her house and that wasn't Gah Git sitting there.

"Who are you?" Gena asked the girl, not having a clue as to who this stranger was sitting in front of her.

"I'm Nitah, Jalil's second wife." The girl spoke as if being someone's second wife was some normal shit. Nitah was so peaceful, though, and so soft-spoken. She was humble, even in her jewels, and looked like a queen. She was fully garbed in a hijab with a beautiful khimar covering her head.

"Where's Montell?" Gena asked.

"He's probably at the hospital with the funeral director and members of the masjid. They're making the funeral arrangements for Quadir."

"I got to go there," Gena said, trying to get out of bed.

"You can't go. There's no one here who can go there. Here, honey, try to relax. I made some tea. Here, drink some. It'll make you feel better."

There isn't a goddamn thing that'll make me feel better. She swallowed the prescribed sedative Nitah handed her, the first of many.

Nitah was a wise woman; only sleep could fix some things. Gena was only nineteen and this kind of trauma could damage her if it wasn't handled right. *Poor thing,* Nitah thought as she stroked Gena's forehead. She stayed by Gena's side until the funeral.

It was the hardest day of Gena's life. She hadn't been outside or seen anyone other than Nitah since Qua had been killed. The funeral was packed. Rik called Gena from his hospital room. He cried for her and for Quadir but most of all for Lita. Gena had never heard a man cry, not even Quadir. She didn't know what to say; she didn't know what to do. She felt his pain, and she began crying with him, especially when he talked of Lita. She had died that night after being shot in the neck. Rik never saw her go down or anything. He wasn't by her side and he never told her goodbye.

Gena could not take in the splendor the funeral director had arranged for the people who loved Quadir Richards. She only knew her legs wouldn't hold her up. She felt her belly sink some more and an aching pain twist her insides as thoughts of him darted through her mind.

"He looks so fine," someone remarked.

No, she thought. *He looks dead.*

"The flowers are so beautiful," someone else said.

The flowers smell like death. Someone was pulling at her, murmuring to her, "Gena, Gena, come on, baby. Sit down. You gonna hurt yourself. Please, come on."

She heard the person pulling at her tell people, "Please, please, she can't handle it. Never mind the condolences. She can't hear you."

All Gena could hear was someone crying loudly, and it hurt. Her body could no longer hold her up, and she dropped to the floor in front of his casket.

Something's holding me. I can't feel nothin', but I'm standin'. How'd they do that? Then she forgot a lot for a time, and then she was outside, still standing but not alone. It was pretty outside. *We in the park. Look, there's birds. What's that noise?*

The whirring sound of the casket being lowered into the ground registered and brought Gena out of her mental closet for a moment. Into that black hole went all of Gena's hopes, her babies, her life, her one true love. The only man who really loved her. And as his casket sunk deeper and deeper into the ground, her body sank into her grandmother's arms. Gah Git knew her baby would never be the same.

The weeks passed, and Gena never once went outside. The day Rik was released from the hospital, he went to see her and stayed in the guest room. Together, they took care of each other and listened to one another's stories about the good old days. Rik knew Gena was not the same. He wished she would come out of her darkness. He tried everything from jokes to reminiscing about his own memories with Quadir, but nothing seemed to work.

And then someone knocked at the back door. "You expecting somebody, Gena?"

"No."

Rik opened the back door to find Quadir's mother and sister, Denise, standing in the freezing cold.

Gena said, "Hi."

"Hi," Denise replied.

His mother, Viola, walked straight into the white living room where no one was allowed. "How you feeling, Gena?"

"I'm feeling better," Gena replied. "Can I get you something?"

"I'm not on a social call."

Gena wondered why the fuck she was there. "Oh. Well, um, what's up?"

Viola didn't beat around the bush with idle talk about the weather. She got right to the point and broke shit down without blinking an eye.

"Listen, Quadir was my son, and I loved him dearly. However, he's gone now, and life must go on." She reached in her pocketbook and pulled out a sheaf of papers, shoving it in Gena's face. "As you can see, this house is in my name. I own this house, dear, and I have plans for this property."

Gena couldn't believe what she was seeing. Not merely the deed to the house, but Viola also had paperwork on the Range Rover and the BMW. "*Everything*," Viola Richards emphasized. "Not Montell. Not Montell and Viola, just Viola."

The only things that weren't in the bitch's name were Gena's furniture, the jewelry, and the Benz. That was it. Gena sat there glaring at Viola.

Rik stepped in. "You should probably leave now, Ms. Viola. It's time for you to go."

"Gena, I'll give you a week. I hope you understand." She stood up and shook it off as if she had said nothing out of the ordinary. "This has all been so difficult for me to deal with."

No one had noticed Gena coming alive. "Difficult for you? It hasn't been that difficult for you to sink your claws into all of Quadir's shit!"

"These assets are in my name. Therefore, that makes them mine."

"And what *exactly* is yours, now that Qua is dead?"

"The house, the furnishings, the cars, and the jewelry. I want it all back."

"Oh, no, bitch. That's where you fucked up. The Mercedes-Benz is in my name. Would you like to see my paperwork? And the furnishings, I bought." By now she was towering over the woman. "Would you like to see my receipts? And the jewelry is mine, too. Everything in this house is mine. All you're gonna get is the walls!"

Denise came to her mother's aid. "Who do you think you talking to?"

Gena slipped into superior gear. "Whom . . . do you think? Let me tell you something." She turned back to Viola. "When your son came into this house and needed something, the motherfucker came to me. When he had a problem, he told me. I'm the one who gave Quadir what he needed. Anything he needed, he came to me!" She was into it now. Her eyes were boring into the coldhearted woman and her violin-string tight-ass chicken-hawk daughter.

"That man, my man, has only been in the ground two weeks and you're already here to claim his shit."

"My brother wanted us to have his things. That's why he put them in our mom's name."

"Bitch, please. He put it in your mother's name, Denise, because he was a drug dealer. Shit don't mean he wanted her to have a motherfucking thing. Did the motherfucker ever invite you over? Hell no. What's this, your third visit?" She redirected her anger to Viola. "I know it, and you know it, and you know who your son bought this house for. He bought it for me. You remember that when you turn the key and unlock the door, you miserable bitch. And you never liked me, so I'm not surprised you got the fucking audacity to come in my house and tell me some bullshit like this."

"Who you calling a bitch?" Denise asked.

"You heard me. I didn't stutter. Your mother is a miserable bitch who goes around trying to make everyone else miserable. Shit, she can't even hold her man. You want me out? Fuck you, both y'all can kiss my ass. I hope you burn in hell!"

Rik was up. He'd been letting Gena get everything off her chest, proud as a peacock and just as happy to see her again among the living, but enough was enough. "You two should go. You really have no place here. Neither of you do, and what you're doing is wrong. Qua wouldn't have wanted anything like this. He wouldn't have wanted this to go on." He stood his ground against the chicken hawks.

"They don't care about Quadir. How could they? How could she? That bitch didn't even raise him, Rik. His grandmother did, and his sister never knew him. Come in here telling me about my goddamn man. Motherfuck you and this motherfucking house!"

"Curse all you want," Viola said. "You can say whatever you want as long as you get your lowlife ass out my house."

"Fuck you, bitch!" Gena spit at Viola, missing her by a blow of the wind as Viola opened the door.

Denise said, "Hey, Gena, don't let me see you in the street, bitch, 'cause your ass is mine."

"Bitch, we can go round for round right here and right now." Gena was ready to fuck both of their asses up. "Let me go, Rik."

Rik continued to hold her back. "Gena, chill the fuck out!"

He ushered the chicken hawks out the door and closed it behind them. They must've caught a cab to the house or had someone drop them off, 'cause they damn sure were taking the Rover and the BMW with them. Gena wanted to stop them, but what the fuck for? She wanted to kill the bitches, but it wasn't worth it.

"The bitch can have it, Rik. She can have it all. Shit, the insurance is up on the BMW. I should blow it up." Looking around, she felt her belly sinking again. But only for a second. "What am I gonna do, Rik?"

"Call a storage company, pay them to come and pack your shit up and store it for you. Then you're gonna figure out where you're gonna stay and you're gonna move. If you want a house, I'll get you one, or you can come and stay with me."

"No, Rik. I'm okay." She finally sat down. "I want to go home." For the first time in her life, she wanted to go home to Gah Git's house.

"You got money?"

"Yeah, there should be some here. Come on." She led him downstairs to the safe and unlocked it.

"Damn. There should be more. There's only two thousand here."

"Two thousand?" Rik was shocked. "Where the fuck is the dough?"

They stood silent for a moment with Gena wondering, *What dough?*

"There should be way more than that in the safe. Qua said he had millions."

"Millions?" Gena asked.

"Yeah, baby. True-motherfucking-blue millions."

"Millions?" Gena asked again.

"Gena, don't get that shit twisted. Quadir made it clear to me that he was a millionaire. Now, I don't know where, but he had millions."

"His mother must have it. She got everything else."

"Damn, that's fucked up. Gena, you don't have no money saved?"

"Yeah, a couple of thousand."

You spend thousands like they're dollars, and you have no major paper saved, Rik surmised. "Gena, you holding at least a half million in jewelry, furniture, and furs, and you have no cash? Go figure. How much do you spend a week? Ten?"

"No, more like fifteen, maybe twenty thousand."

"See? And you have two thousand. When is the Benz coming out of the shop?"

"I don't know. It should've been ready."

"I don't know what to say. And why do you want to go to your grandmother's house? She lives down Richard Allen, right? I mean, damn, if you don't want to stay with me, then at least let me get you a house or an apartment."

"No, Rik. You act like you're my keeper. Quadir was my keeper and he's gone now. I want to go home. I haven't been home since I was seventeen. I miss home, and I'm sorry if the projects scare you, but I grew up there, remember?"

"I can't figure out how you, Quadir's woman, are broke and going back to Richard Allen."

"Rik, what part of that don't you understand?"

"I don't understand why you want to go back to the projects. Motherfuckers want to get out and you trying to go back."

"I want to go home. Don't you understand? The projects isn't my home. My home is where my family is. They're the ones who care about me. They're the ones who'll take care of me."

Rik looked at her. "Gena, you're a big girl. You can take care of yourself. You don't need to be living down in no Richard Allen." He ran Richard Allen. "Man, those niggas down there are crazy."

Gena suppressed a smirk and looked at him, feeling normal again and liking it. "I want to go home for a while. I really need my family. I mean, this big old house is the best shelter from the cruel world, but without Qua, it ain't the same. And now he's gone," she said, walking over to her fireplace. "He gave me everything, Rik. He gave me a purpose and he loved me like nobody has ever loved me in my whole life. He gave me loyalty, Rik. I mean, he cheated on me from time to time. I could tell. But even with the bullshit, he was the most wonderful man. I don't want to leave here, Rik."

"I know you don't." He surveyed all the expensive furnishings. "Look up in here! It's the *Lifestyles of the Rich and Famous.* Qua said he was gonna get you this house. That his children would grow up in this house and the two of you would live in this house together for the rest of your lives."

"He really said that?"

"Yeah, he really did."

"Isn't there anything I can do to stay here?"

"Whose name is on the deed?"

"Hers."

"Then it's her house. If she wants you out, she can get you out. She can get you out through the courts."

"What kind of fucking justice is this? I lose my man, I lose my goddamn house, the bitch straight up took the Rover. Doesn't she know the goddamn store is five miles down the road?"

Rik said, "That shit was cold. I would've never thought Ms. Viola would come at you like that."

"I have nothing. I'm losing everything," Gena said sadly.

"You buy Armani underwear. Look at all this furniture. Not to mention all the goddamn diamonds you wear. You look like someone went straight to Africa. Please, you sitting up here trumped up talking like life is over. You got more than any woman I know, Gena. Shit, you got paid. Bitches don't see a portion of what you got. You better look around. All this is yours. In another apartment, or another house. What you got, five big screens up in here? Three living room sets?"

"Four!"

"Pool table, video games, and all the cases of Dom you could bootleg. I don't want to see you back down the projects. Qua wouldn't want you down there. Stay in a hotel, then find a place. I'll pay for it."

"Rik, I've made up my mind. I'm going home for a while. When I'm ready, you can get me a house."

"Shit, I really wish you'd stop with that shit."

"What is it you don't understand? You don't understand where the money is? I spent all the goddamn money, Rik. You don't know why I want to go back home? 'Cause I'm not scared of no Richard Allen. I don't understand what's so hard to understand. I don't want to leave here, okay?" She was crying again. "I wish Quadir was here, that's all. If he was here, everything would be okay. Now everything's falling apart. Don't you understand?"

Rik had enough. "What the fuck do you think I been going through? Lita's gone, by the hands of some nigga named Ran. Lita isn't ever coming back. Khy is gone with his grandmom. I don't have a family. I don't have the only motherfucker out here I could trust. So all them tears you done shed isn't doing neither one of us no good, and don't start crying again."

He really didn't understand her thinking. Gena was a hustler's wife. She wasn't supposed to be in the projects. There were too many other hustlers out there who would see her straight on the strength of Quadir.

"I don't know, G. What can I tell you, sister, but to find the money. Before you leave this house, you find the money, 'cause there's money here to be found. Millions, Gena. *Millions.* We should be looking for it now."

She stopped crying. "Do you really think there's millions in here?"

"I know there is. Qua got to have it in a safe."

"There was only a couple thousand in the safe."

"Then that ain't the one, baby. Trust me, there's gotta be another one. Qua had his shit stacked. Why else you think he would give up a yield of fifty, sometimes eighty thousand dollars every week? Quadir had his own thing set up, Gena, with plenty of brothers on the payroll. Quadir had all the money. That money is up in here."

"There's no money in here, Rik."

"Yes, there is. You just don't know about it."

"Rik, I live here, okay? I know every nook and cranny of this house. Trust me, there are no millions nowhere in here. If there was, I would know about it. Every week Quadir used to put money in the safe. That was it. That's where he went to get his money. I wasn't allowed to go near the safe until he told me the combination, and that wasn't until after that bitch, Cherelle, called my house. There is no money. Quadir didn't have millions. His father was over here the other night, and he told Quadir that he had to go on a budget."

"Then his pops didn't know about the money, Gena. Quadir was like that. I'm telling you; you can believe me or not. Quadir said he had millions, and when he said millions, he meant millions. Gena, it's like hitting the lotto. Never having to worry about making ends meet, never having to worry about how you're gonna eat, never having to worry about how you gonna get what you want. Millions. Quadir said he had saved millions and was retiring from the drug game. Now, you can believe me or you don't have to, but I'm telling you now, the boy had money coming out his ass and he didn't take it with him, baby. We should search the house."

"You want to search *this house*?"

"Yeah, I do."

"Then you go ahead, 'cause I ain't searching shit. Ain't no money in here, Rik," she said, walking away from him frustrated.

He started with the walls, looking for trap doors, hollow sounds as he went around knocking. He looked behind pictures, tapped on the walls, searched all over the basement—anywhere one could store a hidden safe. After a good forty-five minutes of searching, Rik concluded the money wasn't in the house.

"I told you." Gena went into the kitchen and poured some food for Gucci.

"Even the cat is paid," Rik said, shaking his head. "Diamond-and-gold Gucci tag, and you don't have no idea where the money is."

"Rik, I don't think Qua told you the truth, because there would be no need for us to go on a budget."

"Gena, where's the money? You spend twenty thousand a week. Come on, he wasn't serving the city kilos no more to be givin' you money like that. That's why he wanted you on a budget, just you."

"Well, it looks like I'm on a budget now, since you didn't find all these millions," Gena said.

"Either that or my pockets is getting ready to hurt me."

"You gonna let me hold Lita's Cadillac?" she asked with a smile.

"Yeah, if you want it," he said, not feeling right about someone else driving Lita's car.

"Yeah, I do."

"Well, you want to go get it?"

"That would mean I'd have to go outside," she said.

"Yeah, you'd be going outside to get the car."

"Okay. Let me get dressed."

Gena went upstairs and threw on a pair of jeans, some riding boots, and a leather jacket.

Rik drove straight to the apartment and parked next to Lita's car.

"You know, I'll really miss Lita," Gena said.

"That girl meant the world to me, man. You don't know how bad I feel. I lost her. That girl was my friend, besides being my woman."

"I felt bad when I didn't go to her funeral."

"Hey, G, after what you went through at Quadir's funeral, you was in the zone. But one thing's for sure, Viola Richards brought you back with the dumbass shit, didn't she?" Rik nudged her with a laugh.

"Quadir was my heart, Rik. He was the only thing that mattered to me, you know."

"Remember that Q is up there, G. He's watching everything you do, and he expects you to move on. In time you will, but it's nice to know there's somebody up there watching over you, somebody protecting you. And that's what Qua is doing. He's got his wings, and right about now they're shielding you. So do the right thing, Gena, and don't sweat that house. You came out on top, baby. Fuck the money, fuck the house, fuck the cars. You still a winner. Shit, you was shootin' for the moon with the nigga and now you among the stars, baby. Just remember that." Rik handed her the keys to Lita's car. "Drive safe."

"I will."

Gena kissed Rik on the cheek and got out of the car.

"Gena, don't sweat no paper out here. Call me, understand?"

"Okay. I will, Rik. I will."

She drove Lita's car to Gah Git's and told her grandmother she wanted the room upstairs and she would pay to have all the junk piled in there put in storage. Gah Git understood why Gena wanted to come home, especially after she told her about Quadir's mother coming there and telling her to get her ass out in a week. Her poor baby was losing everything, and Gah Git was scared Gena wouldn't be able to handle all of this.

In the federal building downtown, Agents Fields and Burson sat with the US attorney, Paul Perachetti.

"He's willing to testify, sir, but we need to place him in the Witness Protection Program," Agent Burson said. "Without him, we have nothing."

"If we want these assholes, we need his testimony. The death penalty is riding on his testimony, sir," Agent Fields said.

Perachetti sat back listening to everything they were outlining for him. The men waited in silence as Perachetti considered and finally agreed.

"Our Witness Protection Program in North Dakota would serve best. Its rehabilitation facility is superior, and he'll have access to therapeutic modalities to get him back on his feet, so to speak. What about the wife and kids?"

Burson replied, "They'll want to be with him."

"Fine. Well, then, we've got it all straight. The witness will be transported to North Dakota."

The field agents breathed sighs of relief as the US attorney continued. "We'll want to keep this low-key, you got that? You'll bring him in by helicopter from the hospital. Collect his family now and take them all down together." He continued to give his instructions and opinions as he made arrangements over the phone.

It wasn't difficult for Forty. The agents were glad he'd decided to cooperate. Actually, they were overly delighted. They had the leader of the Junior Mafia behind bars. They had a live witness. Sure, they were going to put him in protective custody, but that was their job. To them, Forty was only worth his testimony, and past that was nothing but a drug dealer in a wheelchair.

Forty was distressed about the entire situation. Sharon was in tears, having to choose between her life in Philadelphia with her family and her world. She thought long and hard about it. She loved her man, and now that he was paralyzed and in a wheelchair, she couldn't turn her back on him. Besides, her sons needed their dad.

All in all, it had been a difficult call. For Forty, it was hard to walk away from the life he had lived for so long. After all, he was leaving friends and family, not to mention having to adapt to life in a wheelchair. Forty couldn't help but sit back and ask himself, *What was it all for?*

Memories

Gena had taken care of everything before she moved. She forwarded the mail to a post office box. She paid a company to pack and store her furnishings and clothes. Rik had given her twenty thousand, and she'd put the majority of it away. What she didn't put up, she used to fix up Gah Git's project housing unit. She got exterminators and even painters in.

Light blue carpet was delivered the same day the handyman in the neighborhood laid down a new kitchen floor. She put the navy blue leather furniture from her family room into Gah Git's living room, along with a big-screen TV and wall unit. She went to a furniture store and purchased a new bedroom and dining room set for her grandmother.

The nosy neighbors knew something was going on. Before it was all over, Gena had a tiny chandelier in the dining room. Gah Git was overwhelmed. Every time she opened the door, she tried to figure out whose house she was stepping into. She never thought her little project housing could look like it did.

Gena took Gucci upstairs, went into her room, and closed the door. She couldn't sleep. She hadn't been able to sleep since Quadir's passing. The entire situation was so overwhelming for her.

She lay in bed thinking about him as she cradled Gucci. There was a lot of noise outside, and she couldn't help but peek out the window. The brothers were on the corner shooting dice. *How can they see in the dark?* Gena wondered.

A huge 4x4 pulled up sounding like it had robbed a discotheque. The music was so loud and the bass rumbled so hard, it shook Gena's bedroom windows. Then she saw a skinny girl in a blue sweater and gray skirt with a pair of pink socks and red slippers walking up the street. She didn't have a coat on, let alone a bra. She went over to a guy who was on the corner, and Gena watched the exchange. The girl turned and proceeded to walk back down the block.

"I miss you, baby. I wish you could come back. I wish you were here." Gena felt tears well up and trickle down her face. "Why'd you leave me this way, Qua? God, You don't know what You took from me when You took him." She couldn't stop the tears or the pain. "Why is it so hard to let go?" She allowed her head to drop to her lap as the tears fell, hoping each teardrop would take a drop of pain with it.

It was 3:47 a.m. exactly when Gena heard people hollering outside. She peeked her head above her headboard and looked out the window to see a man and a woman fighting in the middle of the street.

"Don't make no sense," Gah Git said, appearing in the doorway. "Them fools is probably out there fighting over who drunk the last of the C&C. It's a damn shame. I don't know how they've stayed together. She is forever kicking his ass."

"For real, Gah Git?"

"Yeah, the police will be here by the time it's over. Child, this is every weekend."

"For real?"

"Honey, this is all the time. Now, go on back to sleep," she said as she shut Gena's door and went back in her room.

The next morning, a knock at the door distracted Gah Git from her usual tirade, and she greeted a girl who lived down the street, a smiling, skinny girl with a fat baby in her arms.

"Ms. Scott, can you help me?" she asked, looking hopefully at Gah Git. "I have a test in English class today and I was wondering, could you watch Ayonna for me?"

"Oh, Lord, Brenda, I guess so. Where's your mama?"

The girl looked away for a split second. "She getting high again, and she said no."

"Well, you know I'll help you out."

"Ms. Scott, the house looks real nice," Brenda said, looking all around.

"Well, thank you. You know Gena?"

"No, ma'am."

"That's my oldest grandbaby. She's Bria and Brianna's first cousin."

"Hi," Brenda said. Gena acknowledged her with a look, but she didn't speak to the girl. "Well, here goes her baby bag and everything you'll need."

Gena felt sorry for her. She didn't look any older than sixteen.

"Gah Git, I have to go. I'll see you around dinnertime," Gena said, kissing her grandmother on the cheek.

"Goodbye. You be careful," Gah Git insisted.

"I will," Gena hollered as she brushed past Brenda on her way out the door.

Brenda handed Gah Git the baby. "I'll be right back after school."

"Okay, she'll be fine."

Gena hopped into a cab to travel to the body shop where her car was being fixed. While she sat in the lobby of the Mercedes-Benz dealership, she started scribbling to Quadir.

I Reminisce
I reminisce for you
I reminisce the days

I try to forget
But the feelings never go away.

I reminisce for you
I reminisce the nights
For the things we did
And how it was so right.

I reminisce for the love
For the love that was always there
I reminisce, I reminisce, and I know in my heart
That you really did care.

Even though my mind plays tricks on me
And I can't seem to let you go
I believe it's because you're still loving me
I reminisce, I reminisce
And the memories tell me so.

Gena got in her car and drove straight to the bank. She was seated in a room with a table, where she opened her bag and carefully began to deposit her jewelry: the 10 carat diamond engagement ring, the cluster diamond ring, the charm bracelet, and the diamond initial G that Rik and Lita had given her; two Rolexes, one Ebel, one Omega, and one Cartier, all of which were diamond bezel; two gold Gucci watches; and one stainless steel and 18k Movado. The girl knew what time it was. She kept her plain gold Rolex. Of the five tennis bracelets she owned, she put four in the box and kept only one. She put her 2 carat diamond earrings in the box and kept her quarter carats in her earlobes. Then she placed fifteen pairs of gold earrings in the box, keeping only three pairs, which she put back in her pocket.

She deposited strands of gold chains, diamond pendants, diamond pins, bird pins she never wore, and a total of seventeen gold and diamond bangles. They all went in the box except for two, which she put on her other hand, letting the smallest, 6k tennis bracelet lay over the Rolex, instead of the 12k. Once she was done placing all her things neatly in the safety deposit box, she started on Quadir's.

Time had changed things. The fate that lay in the hands of another altered Gena's future as well as Quadir's. Gena was ready to lock it up, taking the safety deposit box key and adding it to her own key chain, Quadir's diamond Q.

By the time she got home, Bria and Brianna were fussing about homework and teachers and why Gah Git didn't go up there and defend them like the other parents did their kids.

"What's up?" Gena said, coming into the house. "Gah Git, I got the car."

"You got the car?" Brianna exclaimed.

"Let me see," Bria said, like they both had never seen it before.

"Oh, Gena! Can we go for a ride?" Brianna asked, pushing past her to get a glimpse of Gena's 300.

"Yeah, can we?" Bria whined. Bria was too nice these days. What a change.

"Later," Gena responded.

"Good, we gonna be all that," they said, slapping high fives, not thinking anymore about trying to get Gah Git to go curse out their teachers.

Then Gena heard a baby. "That baby still here?"

"Yeah, Brenda not coming back for that baby no time soon, and Gah Git trying to make us take care of it," Brianna said, eating some Georgie Woods potato chips.

"Like we having that," Bria added.

"Y'all are a trip," Gena said, looking at the twins in disbelief.

"Will somebody go get that baby?" Gah Git hollered. "Y'all see me trying to cook!"

Gena looked at the twins. They looked like they were deaf and dumb and weren't moving, so Gena went and got the baby. It was smelly and too small. Gena had no idea what to do with it.

"Qua wanted me to have one of these?" she said, looking at the baby as if it were not a part of the life force here on Earth.

"Here," she said, taking it to Brianna and giving it to her. "We're going for a ride later, remember?"

Brianna took the baby. "Damn, she stinks."

"What just came out your mouth, Brianna?" Gah Git hollered.

"Nothing! Darn, I said darn, this baby stinks."

"That's what I thought I heard you say. You need to go to church. You want to go to the seven o'clock service?"

"No, ma'am."

"Oh. Then watch your devilish tongue. Child do get it honest," Gah Git said, mashing her potatoes. The baby was still crying. "Oh my God, what's that child's name?"

"Ayonna," Bria said.

"No, her mother."

Brianna sighed. "Brenda."

"Where could she be?"

"I don't know, Gah Git. She has English class with me and she wasn't there and we didn't have no English test today," Brianna stated with disgust, laying the baby on the couch.

Bria rolled her eyes. "I don't know why you're always helping people."

"You might need some help one day," Gah Git reminded her.

"That's Brenda's baby, not ours. She somewhere now with a boy or something, 'cause she sure wasn't in school today," Brianna said. "Besides, she shouldn't have had no baby if she wasn't going to take care of it."

Bria backed up her twin. "Gah Git, we're the ones who suffer when you go out your way to help people."

"Girl, hush your mouth." Gah Git was trying to hear what was going on outside.

"You hear that?" Brianna asked.

They got up and went to the window.

"It must be those idiots next door," Bria said.

Gena looked at the helpless infant. "The baby's crying."

"Go get it," Bria said, nudging Brianna.

"No. Ain't my baby," Brianna answered. "Gena, you go get it."

"What I look like? I ain't never had no babies, and I never babysat no brats. You go get her."

The baby was starting to cry louder.

"I wouldn't get that baby if it rolled off the couch and fell on the floor," Bria said.

Gena looked at her cousin's despicable grin. "Damn, that's cold."

"It sure is." Brianna slapped high fives with her twin.

Suddenly, Gary came running in the house with Khaleer behind him. "Grams!" He saw his grandmother picking up a strange baby off the couch. "Aunt Gwendolyn done stabbed up Royce, y'all. The police is arrestin' her and everything."

"Khaleer, come here, baby," she said, handing Ayonna to Brianna.

Brianna took the baby and sat it down on the floor.

"You okay, son? Gah Git's grandbaby okay?" She held her youngest grandson. "Well, what happened?"

"I don't know. She on that shit, Grams, and she out there with her hair all wild, half naked, titties hanging out, fighting the police."

"Oh, Lord," Gah Git said, shaking her head.

Bria and Brianna silently went out the door to get a dose of the commotion.

"That girl is gonna have to learn the hard way. Did you call Paula?"

"No, Zorian and Avanna was out there. They seen everything."

Gena answered the ringing phone. "It's Aunt Paula, Gah Git."

Another knock at the door brought an additional surprise. Gary opened the door thinking it was family, but Ms. Bradley, the social worker, was standing there smiling.

"Yeah? Can I help you?" Gary asked.

"Yes. I'm here for Ms. Scott."

"Oh, Gah Git!" Gary slammed the door in her face. "It's some white lady!"

He left Ms. Bradley outside in the cold and went back into the house.

"Paula, I got to go. I'll call you right back." Gah Git went to the door. "Oh, my goodness! Come on in. You sure do come at the darndest times. Children, this is Ms. Bradley," she said, ushering her in. "Say hello. She's here about Aunt Gwendolyn's baby."

Everyone said hello to her and behaved like they had etiquette for once in their lives. You could tell the white social worker lady had really caught Gah Git off guard.

"Come on in; have a seat," Gah Git said, sitting the lady at the dining room table. "Can I get you something to eat or drink?"

"I'm a little thirsty, if it's not too much trouble. I see you have a houseful."

"Gena, get Ms. Bradley some juice, please." She excused herself for one minute and walked over to Gary.

"Come here," Gah Git said. Calling him into the bedroom, she explained the lady was there about the baby and how important it was no one ran in and out of the house. Especially since her child was down the street making a spectacle of herself.

"Gah Git, it's cold outside."

"Boy, don't you got no long drawers?"

"No."

"Well, you better get some. Now go on, and don't let nobody run in here." She pushed him out of the bedroom. "And don't go across the street with them hoodlums, either."

"They not hoodlums, Grams."

"Yes, they is. You just don't know it. Don't tell me, fool. I been here longer than you. I recognize a hoodlum when I see one, and I see 'em across the street. Now go on."

Gah Git returned to the dining room and explained baby Ayonna. The social worker was very impressed with the lovely redecorating that had been done, and Gah Git explained how Gena had moved in.

"But there's still plenty of room for the new arrival."

"Well, Ms. Scott, you really don't have to explain. I'm sure the baby will be fine with you, and she'll be with her family. I wanted to tell you in person that the state has awarded you custody of Brandi Valon Scott."

"Oh, thank you, Ms. Bradley. Thank you so much. I been so worried about what would happen to that baby. You don't know how happy I am. Thank you so much."

"You're welcome. I figured you'd be glad."

"Oh, I am! I'm gonna have to thank the Lord for all these blessings. I really appreciate everything you've done for me and my family."

"It was easy to see how much you cared, and that you can give Brandi a good home. But I must be going now."

"Thank you for coming by to tell me in person," Gah Git said.

"Bye," said all the grandkids sprawled all over the living room watching Quadir's TV. Bria had Gucci, Ayonna was asleep, and Brianna held Khaleer.

"Take care." Ms. Bradley waved to everyone in the house.

Gary was standing right there by the door as she exited. He scared her half to death.

"That's my other grandson," Gah Git explained. "Boy, what you standing out here in the cold for? Get your butt in the house." She dragged Gary inside, smiling in Ms. Bradley's face, waving goodbye.

Gah Git got back on the phone with Paula, saying "Oh, Lord," over and over again.

"She gonna have us in church tonight," Bria told Brianna.

Brianna folded her arms across her chest. "I hope not."

"Yo, you should have seen Aunt Gwendolyn beat up that lady police officer," Gary said. "She kicked her ass. They had cameras and everything. She prob'ly gonna be on *Cops* or something."

"Nuh-uh," Gena said.

"For real, I think I was on TV."

"Gary, you always bugging. You not gonna be on nobody's TV, okay?" Bria said.

Gena suddenly froze at the sound that meant loss: gunshots. *Bap! Bap! Bap!*

Bria hollered, "Get down, Gah Git!"

Gary ran over to get Gah Git. "Watch out."

Everybody was on the floor. A bullet shattered the living room window and hit the wall, leaving a hole.

"Lord, have mercy on us all. Please, Jesus, save me. Please, Lord, have mercy!" Gah Git was preaching for real. "Pray! Y'all pray!"

Brianna whispered, "Praying isn't gonna do shit!"

"Sure as hell ain't," Bria agreed.

There were no more shots, and it was over. Outside, two men were lying in the street.

Gary went running out the door. It was his boy, Vic, and this other kid named Freddie. Gena also went running out the door, but Gah Git wouldn't let the twins outside. Baby Ayonna was crying from all the commotion.

Gary put his head down. "Damn, he was my boy."

Gena reached for her cousin, hugging him.

By now, Victor's and Freddie's families were outside, losing their minds. Victor's mother fell out into the street. "Lord, please don't take my son!"

"Gary, come on. Let's go back in the house."

Gary didn't argue, because he knew if he stayed out there tonight, it was gonna be trouble.

"You kids come on in here and settle down," Gah Git said from the doorway. "Gary, you okay?"

"Yeah, Grams. He was my boy, though."

"I know, son. It's a shame to see these young children out here killing one another and taking away good lives God put on earth. I don't know what's happened to these young people out here. They's crazy and they don't have no respect. Now, back when I was coming up, none of this mess was going on. There were drugs and people drank, but they had sense about 'em, and not only that, they had respect for one another. It's a sad shame, and what the dagnabbit they done did to my window?"

Gena walked upstairs to her room. She moved about in the dark and sat on the bed holding her kitten. Funny how they ended up the same way, in the street, covered with blood. She remembered the night that her destiny changed. He winked his eye and let go of her hand, making it happen. Gena mustered up her strength and forced the tears back inside.

"Qua," she said to him with her heart, "I miss you." She paused for a moment, then continued on with her normal conversation.

Bria walked by Gena's bedroom door and heard her talking to Quadir. *She really needs a new man.*

Gena got herself ready for bed and let Khaleer sleep with her. In the middle of the night, screeching sounds of a baby in distress woke up the entire house. Gena got up, but Gah Git told her to go back to sleep.

"I can't sleep no way," Gena said, getting a glass of milk.

"Thinking about Quadir, baby?"

"Gah Git, all the time."

"I know," she said, rocking little Ayonna in her arms. "Quadir was a good man. Child, if I'd had a man like Quadir in my day, I'd have to dig deep to find a reason to go on without him, too, so I understand how you feel. Gena, you got to be strong, honey. You got to count your blessings and thank the Lord for being so merciful. You must keep your mind strong. Quadir would want it that way."

Flashbacks illuminated the image of the gunman aiming right at her and Quadir pushing her out the way. She realized he would've done anything for her, 'cause he did everything that he could.

"I'd give anything to be with him again."

"When God's ready, you will be. All things in time, Gena. Be patient. I worry about you girls, I really do. But, Gena, you had something special, baby. You must never forget Quadir. Keep him alive in your heart and in your soul. What you two had was pure and honest. Cherish that love. Keep it in your heart, and let it grow with you."

The next morning, Gena got up to answer the bell and let Brenda in.

Gah Git took over immediately. "I been waiting to curse you out, but I'm not going to." She got up and went into her bedroom.

"Why did you leave your baby here all night?" Gena asked.

"I'm sorry. I went out, and I thought I'd be back before now."

Gah Git came out of the bedroom, and Gena left it alone. Gah Git handed Brenda her daughter. "Take your baby and go wherever you going but think about one thing. That child didn't ask to come into the world and she deserves a lot better from you. You must be crazy to try some shit like this at 2432, but you'll learn, and you, my dear, are gonna learn the hard way."

"I'm sorry," Brenda said.

"No, you not. You not sorry, 'cause if you was, you would've done what you said you was gonna do: go take an English test and come back here and get your baby. You not sorry. You knew you wasn't coming back. But guess what?" Gah Git gathered the baby's things into the diaper bag. "You won't get me to play your fool no more."

"It's not that. My mother was getting high, and she put me out and then I tried to stay with my boyfriend, but his mother said I couldn't stay there."

"Your mother *been* getting high. That don't got nothing to do with you calling. You young girls treat these babies like they something that just came out of you. Baby, they more than that. You need God. You're going down the wrong path, and I tried to help you, but you took my kindness for weakness. In life, you should never bite the hand that feeds you."

"I'm sorry, Ms. Scott. I really am. I appreciate you keeping her for me."

Gah Git handed her the diaper bag and closed the door. Relief filled her. She looked at the time, noting her babies would be home soon. She worried about them out there in the streets on their own, especially little Khaleer. "Lord, show my babies the way."

When It's All Said and Done

Forty had come a long way. He had progressed quite well with the help of therapy. Even though he would never walk, he'd spent every day for the past seven months determined to beat the odds. The FBI's Witness Protection Program had moved him to the mountains in North Dakota to keep him safe. Now it was time to bring him home. Time to testify against Jerrell Jackson.

US Attorney Paul Perachetti had an open-and-shut case that would defy Clarence Darrow. It was ridiculous that Jerrell Jackson, the known leader of the Junior Mafia, hadn't pled guilty. No one knew why he would even want to go to trial. It was totally ludicrous. It didn't matter. Jackson was gonna get the death penalty. Perachetti had him by the balls, and it felt great. Jerrell deserved to die, not only for all he'd done out in the streets, killing and serving the city cocaine, but he deserved to die for being so damn slick and never getting caught. The Junior Mafia was a fucking nuisance, all of them, and getting their leader, Jerrell Jackson, had made headlines in newspapers throughout the country for the past seven months.

It was time for trial, and it would all soon come to an end. Once Christopher Cole testified, it would be over. Perachetti was eating up all the publicity and taking all the credit for making the streets safer by prosecuting the criminals, especially the notorious Jerrell Jackson.

For him it was a dream come true. He was finally getting what he wanted: publicity. It was time to consider running for mayor.

The courtroom was packed; most of the people were Black. A lot of families who had lost a life at the hands of the Junior Mafia were there watching, hoping and praying for justice—justice that hadn't yet been served. The prosecutor was their God. Only he could give them what they wanted. Only he could bring justice for this cruel and wanton behavior that had swept through the streets like Satan himself.

Paul Perachetti came through the double courtroom doors, his trench coat swinging as he made his entrance. He was at an all-time high. Things were looking good. He felt the power of city hall calling him.

"All rise," the bailiff said as the Honorable Eugene Pearlstein entered the courtroom. "You may be seated," he said stiffly after sitting down.

Voir dire had taken three weeks. Perachetti had used his peremptory challenges early on, giving Jerrell's attorney, Billy DeStephano, a slight edge in the jury selection. As far as DeStephano was concerned, he wanted his client to beat the case. Hell, he was defending the so-called leader of the Junior Mafia, but he didn't care. The bottom line was the niggas and their bullshit had made him a millionaire at the age of thirty-six. Why stop now? He could not stand, nor afford, for Jerrell to be sentenced. There was no way he was gonna let his client receive capital punishment, which was exactly what the state was going for.

Voir dire, one of the biggest problems with the justice system, is the method of jury selection in American jurisprudence. It was totally unfair, but DeStephano felt good about the twelve jurors who had been selected.

The judge explained to the jurors exactly what their job was, which was to find guilt beyond a reasonable doubt. Court was adjourned until the following morning.

DeStephano went back to his office. He rehearsed his opening statement repeatedly, preparing himself for the jurors, ready to look them dead in their eyes and tell them why they wouldn't be finding his client guilty. When he was finished, not only would the jury be dazzled, but the verdict would be not guilty. He'd pocketed $175,000 so far, and another $50,000 was due to him for the professional services he'd rendered. The world had gone mad, and he was making money.

His dead presidents fantasy was interrupted by his secretary. "Billy, your wife is on line three," she said over the intercom.

"Thank you," he said, picking up the line.

Finishing with his wife on the phone faster than his record-breaking connubial speed, he hung up and told his secretary to hold all his calls so that he could go over his opening statement one last time. It was short, simple, and to the point. It was as succinct as possible, designed to whet the jurors' appetites, make them anticipate what was to come. He had a promising future right there in the palms of his hands. The publicity alone was phenomenal, not to mention all the incoming calls from potential clients he had not yet had a chance to review. Thanks to the Junior Mafia, he was famous, and he would get Jerrell Jackson off. He had no doubts about it.

"All rise."

Judge Pearlstein seemed to take his sweet time sitting his fat ass in his chair. Jerrell couldn't figure him out. Perachetti made his opening statement. Then DeStephano gave his opening performance. After opening statements were concluded, the prosecutor presented his evidence, then called his first witness, a hotel clerk who claimed he remembered two guys coming into the hotel and walking past him. When asked if either were sitting in the court-room, he pointed at Jerrell.

"Ain't that some shit? Ran and Sam went up in the hotel," he whispered to Billy.

At least he's honest, Billy surmised as he glanced over at his client.

The prosecutor seemed to introduce something new into evidence about every ten minutes. From pictures to diagrams, he introduced everything except a weapon. DeStephano objected to everything, and Pearlstein was getting tired of telling his ass "overruled." A great deal of investigation and preparation had been done by the US attorney, and it was a shame all the work he had done was a waste of time, 'cause DeStephano was going to get his client off. For $225,000, he'd better.

DeStephano did a good job on cross-examination. "At that time of night, it's possible you were tired, and you didn't know who you saw enter the lobby of the hotel. From fifty yards away, how could anyone recognize my client walking in that hotel room?" He asked each question with sincerity, constantly watching the jurors.

"Objection," the prosecutor said, really wanting to say, "Fuck you," as did DeStephano, but the judge overruled him anyway.

"Ha," DeStephano wanted to say, thinking about the five hundred he'd spent feeding Judge Pearlstein dinner last night. "Ha-ha" was more like it. DeStephano took over the courtroom, making liars out of all of Perachetti's witnesses, until Perachetti called his last witness. "Prosecution calls Christopher Cole."

Christopher Cole, a paraplegic. Christopher Cole aka Forty. By the time Forty got off the stand, the jurors were in tears. Mean stares were what they gave DeStephano and his client. Jerrell wanted someone to shoot Forty's ass.

"Can't you do nothing to shut him up?" Jerrell asked while Forty testified.

"What do you want me to do?" Billy said.

"I don't know, object or something." Jerrell was really getting nervous. "For a quarter million, do something! Damn!"

Forty spoke directly to the jurors, telling them everything, from the girl to the kidnapping, to the basement where he was kept until they received the million dollars. He told them how he'd pulled off Sam's mask, and how Randolph and Jerrell Jackson had removed their masks willingly. He told them that Jerrell Jackson was the one who'd pulled the trigger on him, first in his legs, his arms, and then in his chest. He told them that Jerrell had placed the gun to his head and shot him.

DeStephano cross-examined him, unable to break his story or intimidate him into giving the wrong answer, no matter how many ways he asked his questions. That had always been DeStephano's forte, causing people to twist themselves up and make themselves sound like they weren't sure of what they were saying. But it didn't work. Forty realized what he was doing, and he understood why he was there. He wanted justice, he deserved justice, and justice would be his.

In Gena's world the months passed quickly, and with them, so did her savings. It had been six months since Quadir died, and Gena didn't know if she was coming or going. Her brooding was in direct opposition to her financial situation.

The beauty and change that comes with spring didn't come for Gena. Instead, she talked to herself and stayed in the room she shared with Khaleer. Gwendolyn's other baby, Brandi, stayed in Gah Git's room. Gwendolyn was still in jail, because Gah Git wouldn't let Gena put up the bail money. "No need in wasting. God says it's a sin to waste and Gwendolyn ain't right. Hold on to your money in case you need it."

Gena had nothing going on for herself. There were no adventures, no nights out on the town, no trips to A.C. to gamble and spend frivolously, and no romance. She missed the romance of Quadir, the way he would grab her and hold on to her in a rough passion, tasting her, serving her his penis, which was one of a god, thick and fat with the perfect length. The mere thought of him sent chills down her spine. Only Qua could take Gena far beyond what any fantasy ever could. Quadir. She felt him all the time. She talked to him every night. She cried for him in her sleep, twisting and turning, talking in the bunkbed above Khaleer.

Sometimes Khaleer would sleep in the bedroom with Gah Git and his baby sister. There wasn't good sleep for Khaleer with the new baby, either. Normally, Khaleer would be found sleeping on the kitchen floor, in closets and in the bathtub. Gah Git couldn't figure it out. Finally, one night she caught him sleepwalking and called 911.

Gena couldn't believe it: not the fact that 911 woke up the neighborhood at four in the morning, but the fact Gah Git blamed Khaleer's sleepwalking on her because she was always talking to a dead man. "You talk the boy right out of the room, Gena," Gah Git had said.

Things seemed to be going downhill. Even Gucci, the precious Persian kitty, had endured his share of life in the hood. One day while Gena was out, Gary and his friends were in the house rolling poor Gucci up against the wall like dice. Gena was so upset when she witnessed Gucci being tossed like a football, she didn't speak to Gary for two weeks. The poor cat was never the same. He had started climbing up the walls and jumping on people as they walked by. Usually, he would climb on top of the refrigerator and wait for someone to walk in the kitchen, then jump on their heads.

They had worked on Gucci every time Gena left the house. He'd become a mean cat, and now he was evil. Gena couldn't stand him; he had changed so much. He wasn't cute and cuddly anymore. Now Gucci was a mean old tomcat with long, straggly hair. Gucci blamed Gena for the bad meals and torture he was put through and usually would attack her on sight. Gah Git wanted the cat out of her house.

Then there were the twins. Bria and Brianna weren't living in the same world with the rest of the people on the planet. They had boyfriends now. Life was Kewy Kev, and don't tell Bria it wasn't 'cause it would be something if you did. Brianna was blinded by the gold teeth, obviously, of some kid named Dalvin. "He's all that; he's all that. We use condoms. It's my life."

Yes, they were heavily into sex and down for experimentation. What was Gena gonna tell them? *It's 1990; you can catch AIDS!* Like that would lead them in the right direction. *They don't believe; they just don't believe,* Gena thought. So she kept her mouth shut and always said, "Did the condom break? 'Cause if it did, you have six months to see if you'll die."

"No, Gena, it's not like that." Brianna stared at Gena like she was stupid. "Dalvin was a virgin until he met me."

"He told you that?" Gena shook her head in disbelief, recognizing game when she heard it.

"Of course he was a virgin. Are you crazy?" Brianna asked.

This girl was out there. Gena's mental level couldn't deal with the minds of just-turned eighteen-year-olds. They knew they were grown. There was no reasoning with them, and what they wanted to do, they did.

Gah Git kept fussing, and Gena would get tired of the whole routine inside the house, but outside it was worse. The brothers seemed so angry. People were frighteningly frustrated. The inner-city streets were hard and represented hard times. Gena hated it, the way it looked, all scribbled on and wasted.

Gena had become a hermit like Gah Git. She hated going outside at night. It was always something. The brothers weren't taking any shorts in the streets, either. They would rob you in a minute and victimize you for the smallest amount of materials or cash you may have. It was chaos and mass confusion.

She missed Quadir so much. It had been six months, going on

seven, since his murder, and nothing had changed. She still loved and wanted him. She couldn't forget him. She talked to him every day and night.

Nightmares of Qua's death took the place of happily-ever-after dreams, and Gena often woke in the middle of the night in a cold sweat, filled with a fear whose name she knew but wouldn't say: despair. When she lost Quadir, she lost it all, including her spirit.

The summer months were getting hotter, and it only added to her ennui. *Maybe an air conditioner will help.* She called Rik and he said it wasn't a problem. "Two air conditioners?"

"Gena, that's not a problem."

"And five thousand dollars?"

"That's not a problem either, G."

No problem? Now, that's what friends are for. "Thank you, Rik. I'm on my way," she said, hanging up the phone.

She ran into Gah Git's room. "You got some money?"

"No, baby. Not yet." Gah Git was playing with her false teeth. "I will when the mailman gets here, though. Today's the first of July."

Gena wasn't trying to hear it. She walked to the corner store. If she was lucky, she'd see someone who'd loan her the money. She hated having to ask, but five dollars shouldn't be a problem since they were out there selling caps on the corner of her very block. She was wearing a pair of denim shorts with a Chanel T-shirt tucked inside and a fresh pair of Reeboks.

As she walked on the sidewalk, the kids were playing in the street. People were sitting outside, anywhere they could find shade and a cool breeze. The summer heat was unbearable. Gena's Mercedes-Benz sat in the sun sparkling as if it were on a showroom floor.

Gena crossed the street and walked up to the store like she was going in. "How y'all doing?"

Rob winked at her. "Yo, Gena. What's going on, baby?"

"Nothing, just chillin.'"

"Yo, think you could drop me off at my mom's on Twenty-Ninth and Lehigh?" he asked.

"Yeah, I could do that, but you gonna have to get some gas."

"That's no problem. When you gonna take me?"

"I'll take you now."

"Bet. Come on, let's go."

"No, Rob. You got to go get the gas and bring it back here before we can go."

"Girl, is you crazy? The nearest gas station is on Broad Street." Rob looked at his boy Shomby.

"I'll go get the gas," she said. "Give me five dollars."

"Yeah, you gonna have to 'cause it's hotter than a motherfucker out here. Shit, I might fall out or anything."

"How you rolling in a Mercedes-Benz with no gas, Gena?" Shomby asked.

"Look, times are hard, okay?"

"Here, Gena," Rob said as he handed her a five-dollar bill.

"I'll be right back."

"Mm-hmm," he said, nodding as she walked off pocketing his five dollars. "Shit, times must be hard. It wouldn't be no way she walking to the gas station." He shook his head, unable to believe it.

Gena walked six blocks to the nearest gas station and got a gallon of gas, which she carried in a milk container. She was tired from the walk. The hot sun blazed as she walked down the city street. She turned the corner as a black Mercedes-Benz turned the corner and pulled up along beside her. It slowed down, and Gena realized it was about to stop for her.

"Yo, Gena, you okay? You need a ride or anything?" the guy behind the wheel asked.

With the sun blaring in her eyes, she didn't know who it was until she bent down and saw Jamal smiling at her.

"Hi, Jamal," she said with a smile back at him.

It was good seeing him, especially since she was in true-blue need of a ride. It had been a long time. So much had happened. She had changed, and one would hope he had also. Of course, he questioned the gasoline in the milk container before dropping her off in front of her car.

"I'll see you around," he said.

"Thanks, Jamal. I appreciate it."

She solved the gas problem, dropped Rob off, and went straight to Rik's house. He had moved into a nice house off the Main Line. Rik was all that. He was still hustling, of course. But he was so kind to Gena, and she was truly grateful.

"Where's my kiss?" he said to her as she walked through the door.

Gena and Rik sat for a while, talking about how time had changed things for the both of them. Gena, not really wanting to let him know how right he was about moving back home, sort of came out of nowhere and told him she was ready to move. Rik looked at her, not wanting to say, "I told you so," so he didn't question her at all. Just said they could contact a few Realtors and start looking around for her new place tomorrow. Gena was excited and content at hearing that. For the first time in a long time, she thought of all her furnishings in storage.

"Can I come up here with you, Rik?" she asked, knowing his house had to be a couple hundred thousand at least.

"Yeah, there's some houses around here for sale," he said, thinking of the advantages of having Gena close by.

After she left Rik, she went to an appliance shop and bought two air conditioners. A big one for downstairs and a small one for her bedroom. Gena felt good. Rik gave up loot like Quadir always did. There was something about walking around with a couple of thousand in your pocket. Gena had forgotten the feeling.

She dropped the air conditioners off at Gah Git's and went to LeChevue. Everyone was happy to see her. Bev wasn't there; she and Charlie had a baby girl, so some girl named Lisa did her hair. When she was through, she stopped by her post office box to check for mail, something she rarely did. She had gotten a post office box when Quadir's mother, Viola, put her out with her "mine, mine, it's all mine" routine. Gena hadn't checked on the box much. There was never any mail for her, just a lot of junk mail and mail for Quadir. Unlocking the box, she found thirteen envelopes.

Getting back into the safety of the Mercedes-Benz, she opened up each letter and scanned the mail. There were three letters from a Realtor and a Notice to Vacate addressed to Quadir Richards, 234 Green Street.

"Damn, what's this?" Gena whispered to herself. She started the car and went back to the house. She called the number on the notice but got an answering machine. It was a real estate office, but the office was closed. Gena hung up the phone. She sat on the edge of her bed and read the notice over and over to herself. 234 Green Street. She wasn't even sure what part of the city that was located in.

Gah Git had the air conditioners pumping cool air into the hot and stuffy housing project unit. "Keep that door closed," she hollered to Khaleer, who liked running in and out. "Child, here, drink some water," she said to him. "You gonna fall out. It's too hot out there. Sit your ass down and rest yourself some."

"I'm okay, Gah Git," he said, walking toward the door.

"Boy, sit your ass down and rest a minute," she said, rocking Brandi.

Gena came running down the stairs. "Gah Git, I'll be back," she said as she flew out the door with Quadir's diamond Q key chain in her hand. Gena got in the car again and dashed through the projects, not stopping at any stop signs and turning corners like police were chasing after her. People outside watched as her car sped by them.

Gena drove straight to Green Street and followed it down to Second. Nothing looked familiar. Gena grabbed the notice and looked at it: 234 Green Street was an apartment building. Now she remembered. She remembered all too well. One night Quadir went into the same building and left her outside. She looked at Qua's diamond Q key chain.

Parking the car, she went to the front door. After several tries, she finally found the key that fit and unlocked the front door. Gena took the elevator up to the third floor. Apartment 307 was down the hall. She stood there not knowing what to do. *Should I knock? What if it's some bitch, and she can't pay the rent since Quadir is gone?* The thoughts went through her as she desperately fumbled with the key chain. She found the key. She turned it to the left and then to the right, the lock snapped, and the door opened.

The apartment was too fly. It was living the way living used to be. Leather furniture, a pool table, and a bar in the dining room. Vertical blinds on all the windows and track lights throughout, an eighty-inch screen in the living room, and a sixty-inch in the bedroom. On the table sat a picture of Quanda and Quadir when she was first born. She'd never seen that picture before.

Looking around the living room, she noticed the fine layer of dust covering everything. She could tell the place hadn't been occupied. The garbage in the kitchen had an unbearable odor that filled the air. She opened some windows, letting in fresh air. The bathroom light wouldn't go on since there was no Quadir to pay the electric bill. The bedroom walls and ceiling were covered with mirrors. Gena noticed a picture of Cherelle with Quanda sitting on his bureau, causing her heart to sink. There was another picture of Quadir on the dresser with some other girl Gena had never seen before. She found a photo album on a shelf—more girls. Pictures from Jones Beach in New York with every rapper and groupie on the East Coast and the Greek Picnic in Fairmount Park, the Greek in Virginia Beach, pictures at the Rutgers basketball games with the rappers and the ballers, from Kool Moe Dee to Alpo.

There were pictures out in Vegas and Atlantic City at the Mike Tyson fights. Quadir was even on the West Coast in Cali with everyone you could think of, from Ice-T to Ice Cube, on down the line. The nigga was everywhere with everybody and had the pictures to prove it. She kept flipping the pages, scanning every pretty face and slim but voluptuous figure her man was leaning up against.

She put down the photo album and began opening the dressers. All of them were filled and neatly arranged. The walk-in closet was lined with Dapper Dan leathers and a few fur coats. On the other wall was his tailor-made clothing, and down at the bottom were about fifty boxes of shoes he had never bothered to place on his shoe racks. Qua had as many clothes here as he had at the house. The different outfits, the different clothing. The constant switch, never in the same car twice. All the things she saw once but never saw again popped in and out of her mind.

She went around the rest of the apartment, looking in the closets, taking her time, remembering the clothes she'd seen him wear. They were staring at her. She felt good, she felt bad, she felt miserable. She went back over to the closet and fumbled through his clothes, taking items and holding them up to her as if he were in them. Quadir's scent again. How wonderful life was to have the scent of him again.

The apartment was filled with a mysterious aura. It was as if Qua was there, as if someone was watching everything she did. Gena thought she heard something. Her poor heart started pounding as she went out to the living room, but no one was there. She looked in the kitchen and then secured the chain on the door. Gena walked past another closet door; it wouldn't open. She tried every key until she found the one that fit the lock. Suddenly she felt a hand grasp her shoulder and let her free. Her heart pounded. Startled, she dropped the keys.

She turned around as a cold chill went through her body. She looked behind her to see the apartment as it was when she'd first entered. She reached down and grabbed the diamond Q key chain.

Finding the key, she opened the door, and staring in her face was a gray safe. A safe that sat on the floor and towered above her. It looked like something from out of a bank. Gena couldn't believe it. She couldn't believe what she'd found. The safe. Qua's safe. Quadir's money. She dropped to the floor in disbelief.

DeStephano put forth all his evidence. There were cross-examinations, redirect examinations, over and over again. Finally, DeStephano called Sharice Harding to the stand. The prosecutor jumped up.

"I object. That name is not on the list."

Counsel approached the bench. DeStephano explained the relevance of the witness's testimony and that suppressing her testimony would not be fair simply because there were no prior statements made by her concerning the criminal matter. She had recently come forth with crucial information concerning the case. Finally, it was settled. Ms. Harding would be allowed to testify. Court would be adjourned for a brief recess.

Gena paced and continued pacing. Searching the apartment for anything and everything she could find. Startled by the knocking at the door, she looked out the peephole at a short, light-brown-skinned man wearing a pair of glasses that seemed enlarged through the tiny glass hole in the door.

"Who is it?"

"Locksmith. You called?"

Well, it's about time, Gena thought as she opened the door.

"You called about a safe?"

"Yeah. Hi. Thanks for coming."

"No problem."

Gena led him into the apartment.

"Is this your apartment?"

"Yes, it is. Why?" she asked, leading him to the locked closet door where the safe was.

"I was just wondering. It's very nice," he said, noticing it didn't look lived in.

"You sure you can open my safe?" she asked.

"I need to see the safe."

Oh, great, thought Gena. *Just what I need.* "What do you mean, you got to see it?" she asked, unlocking the door.

"Damn, that's a big one. That cost a lot of money right there."

What costs a lot of money that isn't worth having? "You can get it open, right?"

"Yeah, I can get it open."

"How?"

"Well, there's several ways to get into a safe. You can blow it open or you can use a torch."

"Oh, is that what you're going to do?"

"I can. It's a lot quicker; the only thing is when you use those methods you risk damage to what's inside. You can set what's inside on fire."

"Oh, no. We won't be going that route. That's not the way." Gena could see herself now, trying to salvage burning money. "How you gonna get it open?"

The courtroom was packed as people chatted among themselves, finally taking their seats. All were present, waiting on Judge Pearlstein. Finally, everyone rose, then after Pearlstein's journey to his bench, they sat. Counsel for the defendant called his witness. Sharice Harding made the appearance of a lifetime. The bitch wasn't bullshitting. She strutted down the aisle in a pale blue linen suit, clutching a pale blue Chanel bag by her side. Her hair was done and her makeup looked like something from a beauty counter.

"Ms. Harding, do you swear to tell the truth, the whole truth, and nothing but the truth?"

With her hand on the Bible, she answered, "I do."

"You may be seated."

And so the drama began, from "State your full name" to "On the night in question . . . ?" Forty sat there and listened very carefully to the examination conducted by the defense attorney. Sharice Harding was a nurse. She lived in Texas with her husband and their four children. She had the story of life, and sis was not to be fucked with. Forty sat there intensely staring at her. He didn't like where DeStephano's questioning was leading.

"Mrs. Harding, on December 28, 1989, where were you?"

"I was in Dallas, Texas."

"Where were you, say, between the hours of ten p.m. and twelve a.m. on the night in question? Were you alone, Mrs. Harding?"

"No, I wasn't."

"Were you with your husband?"

"Objection, Your Honor," said Perachetti. "This line of questioning is irrelevant. The crime took place in Philadelphia."

"I will allow the questioning, but please get on with it," the judge said, thinking about where to have dinner.

"I'll ask you again, Mrs. Harding, were you with your husband?"

"No, I wasn't with Charles."

"Were you alone?"

"No, I wasn't alone," she said, glancing at the jurors, never once looking at Forty.

"Who were you with?"

"I was with Jerrell Jackson."

The room buzzed, spectators and jurors alike. The jurors were totally confused.

Forty was not hearing this shit. The bitch was lying her ass off. He'd never seen anyone seem so convincing. "She's lying! She's lying, Your Honor!" He started screaming, wanting to run over to her and wring her lying bitch-ass neck, but he could no longer use his legs. "She's lying. There's no way he was in Texas, Your Honor."

"Order, order!" the judge said as he banged his gavel. Once quiet reigned, he told them to proceed.

DeStephano continued. "Your Honor, I would like to present into evidence receipts for tickets purchased on Mrs. Harding's credit card, showing she, indeed, was not alone."

"Your Honor, I object. That doesn't prove anything," Perachetti argued. And little did he know it, but that was exactly what De-Stephano wanted him to do. Make a big deal over the tickets.

After the battle over the tickets was settled and DeStephano had his way and the tickets were turned into an exhibit, he went back to his performance. He questioned Sharice Harding continuously, and she made a good show of breaking down, totally distraught. She was confessing to adultery and could lose her family, but at the same time, she couldn't sit back and let an innocent man go to jail. Forty couldn't believe she was sitting there.

That's when the tears came. "My whole life is ruined," she said as she took the handkerchief from DeStephano's hand. Who could deny such bullshit in the name of justice?

Christ, Forty thought, *why is this shit happening?* He couldn't believe it. He was paralyzed from the waist down, and counsel for the defendant had a sobbing woman on the stand explaining she was married and she didn't want to ruin her marriage or her happy life, but she couldn't let this man go to jail knowing he didn't commit this horrible crime.

The jury seemed to like the soap opera before them and sympathized with this good woman who'd gotten herself mixed up with Jerrell Jackson, who didn't really look like a criminal. Meanwhile, Jerrell was sitting there as if he was being stopped from saving the world because of this silly trial for kidnapping and attempted murder.

"No more questions, Your Honor." DeStephano took his seat.

"Your witness," the judge said to the prosecutor.

Perachetti knew she was lying. He went through a series of questions. The woman was a fine citizen, never had been arrested, no priors or even a parking violation. No drug use, prescription or otherwise. She was a registered nurse and made it perfectly clear she was cognizant of the night in question.

The drama was blinding even Forty. *Maybe Jerrell wasn't there*, he thought. No, he knew it was Jerrell. He didn't regain consciousness for thirty-eight hours after he lost it, but when he came back, it was Jerrell, Sam, Ran, and Simone, and where was Simone? He had no idea, but he knew who did. He remembered pulling off Sam's mask, he remembered that; then they pulled off theirs, and then Jerrell shot him. Yes, it was definitely Jerrell who was the trigger man.

When Mrs. Harding was excused, defense counsel brought Forty back up on the stand, plunging into Forty with determination and consistency. However, Forty repeated his statements, never wavering, telling the jury again that they did, in fact, kidnap him, drug him, hold him for ransom, and then Jerrell Jackson shot him. By the time DeStephano was finished, the story read that "Christopher Cole, aka Forty, known in the street, was a drug dealer who, in fact, was kidnapped, was, in fact, shot, and yes, he would be a paraplegic for the rest of his life. However, Jerrell Jackson was not guilty of these crimes."

DeStephano made his closing statements, stressing the fact that, while Christopher Cole had been starved, kidnapped, and drugged with Thorazine, he probably didn't know who his captors were, and he might have been hallucinating. "He doesn't know who shot him. He doesn't even know who kidnapped him, nor does he know where he collapsed. After saying he collapsed in the basement, he was, in fact, found on the porch. This man doesn't know, and when you get up from your chairs, walk into that room, and deliberate, I ask that you merely ask yourselves, ladies and gentlemen, in light of the evidence and testimony at hand, did Mr. Perachetti prove, beyond a reasonable doubt, that this man did, indeed, commit that crime? All you need is one doubt, because if you have any doubts at all, you *will* be sending an innocent man to jail."

Wiping his head as if he'd saved the unfortunate in Bosnia, Iran, and Somalia, he told the judge, "That's all, Your Honor."

Forty wanted to kill that bitch for lying. He wanted to take her long-ass legs and wrap them around her throat and choke the bitch. He saw the way the shit was going down. Again, the system would fail, and again the shit would fuck up what little faith a brother could have. *This is such bullshit. How could this be happening?*

After closing arguments, counsel submitted their points for charge to the court, the judge deciding what statements of law would be read to the jury and what would not. The jurors then retired to the jury deliberation room to think hard about the matter at hand. Forty-five minutes later, they returned. A foreman was ready to recite the verdict.

Gena couldn't believe it. She was so close, yet so far. "Is there something else we can do?" she asked as if all hope was lost.

"Well, there's the old 'figure out the combination' trick," he said, pulling out a stethoscope.

"What's that for?"

"This is so I can hear."

"Hear what?"

The guy wasn't one for giving any lessons, but he tried to break it down for her the best he could. "Okay. See, near the combination is a chamber. Now, when you're turning this knob, you can actually hear ... well, it's like a pin drop."

"What?"

"There are seven channels set on this combination. The channels are the numbers; you don't know the numbers. So you got to listen for the numbers."

"Oh . . . I understand. So, you think you can do it?"

"I've done it before."

It had been an hour and a half, and he was still trying to open the safe.

"Oh my God. Maybe I should try," she said, getting frustrated.

"What's in here?"

"Why? Why do you want to know that?"

"Because I can tell whatever is in here, you want it bad."

Boy wonder, you're a real genius to figure that one out, aren't you? Gena thought, looking at her Rolex. Gena couldn't believe it. He wasn't getting the job done. She didn't understand. She was ready to take her chances with the torch. This was not the way. Gena looked at him with such dismay and frustration, she wasn't quite sure what to say. Her main concern was whether she had to pay him for this waste of time. Time was money, and wasted time was wasted money.

Court was back in session.

"Ladies and gentlemen of the jury, have you reached a verdict?"

"We have, Your Honor."

Forty sat there. He knew that the crimes charged against the defendant had been committed by the defendant, and he was guilty and whatever punishment he received would be deemed just and fair. As the foreman rose, Forty looked at him. He glanced at Forty and made eye contact for one brief moment; then he did the same to Jerrell, then began to read.

"On the charge of kidnapping, not guilty. On the charge of attempted murder, not guilty."

Forty was stunned. On the charge of this and on the charge of that, not guilty. Jerrell was free as a bird.

Jerrell hugged Billy DeStephano. "You the man! You know that, right?"

"Of course I am," DeStephano replied. "No gun, no witnesses, you'll always go free," he said in a low voice.

The man *was* all that. One hundred and seventy-five thousand plus another fifty thousand, such a small price to pay for freedom. Jerrell had been down for seven months with no bail. He couldn't wait to get back out on the streets and start terrorizing everybody's ass again.

For reasons Forty accepted and understood, even though he was paralyzed, he felt blessed to be alive. His mind scrambled and "not guilty" was ringing in his ears.

Jerrell strolled up to him, making his exit from the courtroom.

Bending down, he whispered in Forty's ear, "See you in traffic, baby."

Once everything died down, including the reporters looking for a Pulitzer and the not-guilty hype, Forty was left in the courtroom, sitting all alone. He might have been able to accept not being able to ever walk again in life if Jerrell had been punished. There was a lump in his throat too big to swallow, a tear in his eye he couldn't hold back. Just thinking about what the rest of his life would be like as the tear rolled down his cheek, he looked up at the seal carved into the American woodwork behind the American judge's chair in the American courtroom, representing American jurisprudence. *The American eagle. The same eagle that's on all the money. The same money that got me here,* he thought as he looked down, holding some in his hand. He wiped the moisture from his face and rolled out into the hallway, where the officers were waiting to take him back to North Dakota. He saw the US attorney approaching him. He wasn't trying to hear any more shit.

"You know, there will be another courtroom and he won't be so lucky the next time. We're gonna get him. Don't worry, we're gonna get him."

Forty kept rolling. They'd never get Jerrell. They'd never stop the Junior Mafia. The boy was too large. He was untouchable.

Gena felt all hope was lost. "It's not going to open." Then she heard the click. It was definitely a click, she heard it, and when his hand reached up and grabbed the handle on the safe door, Gena knew that all was not lost.

"Oh my God, where did all that money come from?" His eyes were totally focused on the inside of the safe.

Gena was about to faint. *Booyah* kept flashing in front of her like a neon light. For one brief moment, Gena thought of this strange-looking locksmith killing her and taking her fortune. Of course, she didn't realize that the locksmith was also getting paranoid, wondering if she might kill him. It was too much money for him not to be suspicious.

"Okay, what's your name?"

"Chris," he answered nervously.

"Chris, here, this should cover you for your troubles." Gena reached into the safe. Taking a large stack of fifties, she handed them to him.

The guy stood there, looking like a plucked bird, unable to accept her generosity. The guy was staring. He couldn't believe it.

Gena rushed him to the door. "Thank you for everything, Chris," she said as she closed the door behind him.

She went into Qua's bedroom and got some pillowcases out of his closet. She started stuffing the money in the pillowcases and sitting them by the door. When all the money was out of the safe, Gena had thirteen pillowcases neatly lined up by the door. It was unbelievable. She couldn't think straight. She was nervous and wanted to leave. She understood how Quadir felt having this money. *Shit, how could he sleep?*

She looked around the apartment and thought of Quadir. She had loved him with all her heart, had been faithful day and night, sacrificed with patience, and even though he had cheated, it didn't matter. She understood why as if he were right there with her explaining everything.

"Qua, I know you're here 'cause your money is here. Come with me. Please come with me."

Gena felt him; she felt him all around her. She knew he heard her. She knew 'cause there was no way anyone could rest with all that money left untouched. Oh, no. Qua was there, he was in the apartment. But now he could rest. She would be okay with that paper. He had hustled for seven years. Five years of hustling and grinding out there in the streets. Five years of dodging jealous enemies. Five years of dope fiends and pipers. Five years of the streets. There was no one he wanted to take care of more than Gena. There was no one but Gena who was entitled to what was in that safe. And she'd finally found it. He had waited on her for a long time, but she got it. She got it all.

Gena took the poster-size picture of them in a platinum-and-gold frame off the wall. She looked at it for a moment, thinking about the times they had shared. "I don't know how I've made it this long without you, baby."

She looked around for a moment as she walked to the empty safe and locked it back up. She quickly loaded the pillowcases into the car, and with her pocketbook strapped over her shoulder and the last pillowcase of money in her hand, she blew a kiss into the air, hoping that in the breeze Quadir could feel her love. She turned and opened the door but felt something pulling at her shoulder. She turned around, but nothing was there.

"I love you, Quadir. I always did, and I always will." Gena closed and locked the door to apartment 307.

She didn't know what to do, where to go, or who to call. For the first time, Gena trusted no one, and on the strength of Quadir, she never would with his paper. Not even Rik. If Qua didn't, why should she? She got in her Mercedes-Benz and sat there trying to collect her thoughts. She wanted to go somewhere, but where? She wasn't going to the projects with thirteen pillowcases filled with money. *No*, she thought to herself.

She picked up her cell phone and called Gah Git. "I'll be staying with Tracey."

"Okay, baby. Thanks for calling me. I was starting to worry about you. You be careful, you hear me?"

"Yeah, tell Khaleer he can sleep on the top bunk."

"Knowing that fool, he'll be in a closet somewhere or in the tub."

Gena could hear Brandi crying in the background. "I got to go; there goes the baby. Call me tomorrow."

"I love you, Gah Git," she said, disconnecting the line. Gena didn't want to tell Gah Git about the money. Gah Git didn't keep any secrets. She would be on the phone calling the ghetto gazette telling Gena's business.

"What to do?" she asked out loud, wanting guidance. Sitting in the car, Gena thanked God for His blessings. He had truly been merciful. But a reality struck her that life was about change. The funny thing about it was that no matter how much you change, memories always stay the same.

Qua was gone, and the money couldn't take his place. It would never take his place. Nothing would ever take his place, and there would never be another love like Quadir's. When she sat back and thought about it all, his life and the time they'd spent together, and how his life had brought her more riches than the contents of those pillowcases, it was incomparable with the money she found in that closet. If she could give the money back in exchange for his life, in exchange for having him back, she would in the wink of an eye.

Gena took the diamond Q key chain and turned the car's ignition. She took a long look at the apartment building before pulling off toward the Ben Franklin Bridge and the New Jersey Turnpike. Her destination: exit 16, the Lincoln Tunnel, New York City.

Just a Little Note

In a world where evil lurks on every street corner and peace within oneself is a hard thing to come by, we must travel beyond mere existence and live our lives to the fullest, the best we can.

Things have been so hard for a race of misused and rejected people that our African American families today are still suffering. The streets can make you and the streets can break you. The way you play the game is up to you.

To those caught in the trap of temporary pleasures, let me tell you this: the root of all evil, which is the love of money and the next man's pain, will surely come back to haunt you. We have a choice. I believe everyone has a heart, and within our hearts is a conscience. And the inner peace we are lacking in ourselves can be found. All the burdens we carry can be lifted. I also know our perseverance, our will to survive.

Love yourselves and love one another. Give yourself time to grow, and open your minds to education, because it is a key to the way out. Whatever you do, make it worth something. All your consequences in life are dependent upon your behavior. If you know what the consequences are, why do you still exhibit detrimental behavior?

Because . . . you're true to the game.

***

When I wake up to travel what is unknown, yet certain for me and for my life, throughout the day and night, I give thanks for all the many, many blessings bestowed upon me.

Forever protect me, forever guide me, and forever love me. You are the most merciful, the most beneficent, the most gracious. I love you.

Acknowledgments

Meow Meow Productions would like to thank the following for all their past support, time, efforts, concern, and moments shared, which have helped MMP in all its endeavors as an independent publishing house:

Phyllis and Corel, the financial institution for MMP, thanks for the dough, Mom! Leon Blue (How did you do so much for me? You are truly that legendary nigga and that's why I fuck with you. One, nigga, always), Sheena Lester (I try to be nice to people, you just are. Thank you for being so nice to me and for being my editor), Brian Murray, Shirley Macintosh, my brothers Chucky and Dexter, Ms. Hughes and Radio One (You are a magnificent lady and a true role model. Thank you for helping me), Queen Latifah and *The Queen Latifah Show* (How can I thank you? Thank you!), Robert Morales and Ayanna Byrd, Leah Rose, Mia X (Your story is next; you are amazing!), Amil (If you need the shirt off my back, nigga, wha? I got you!), Queen Pen, Nelly and Camp QP (for opening up your door and always keeping it real, One), Method Man, Red Man, James Ellis, Shauna Garr (I love you both, and even though it's been a battle this last year, I truly and sincerely appreciate your various efforts on this project. I really do! You two just don't know how much—with or without the deals—thank you for everything), Tariq and Uniquest

Designs (Thank you for everything you do for my website and for me personally; thank you for the past year), Darryl Miller, Esquire (You understand shit I can't even read; you are that nigga. Thank you!), Michael Jackson, Milligan and Company, Anslem Samuels, Carlito, Tone Boots and Lamont Henchman, Branson and Eddie (Thank you for holdin' me down Uptown), *Don Diva Magazine*, Tiffany Maughn and Cavario (fire escape nigga 4th fl.), the *FEDS Magazine*, Dave and Antoine (Smokey) Clark and Monique, Niki Turner, the many individuals locked down and still holding me down, and of course the streets. You held me down; you helped take *True* to a level I wouldn't have been able to by myself. Thank you so much.

I can't go without saying to the various distributors and many bookstores and individuals who sold my book published under my company, MMP, to the people across the country—thank you for giving my book the chance to be read! It is a pleasure doing business with you all. Thank you.

TRUE TO THE GAME II

TERI WOODS

I dedicate this book to my daughter, the most beautiful image of myself there could ever be, and to my baby boys, what a joy in my life, the greatest reinvention of myself. I love you all with everything I am. Always remember who you are.

—Mommy

Ready, Set, Go

The second time Gena saw the black BMW in her rearview mirror, she thought it was a mere coincidence. The third time she saw the Beemer, she thought it was simply another car traveling east among a plethora of other vehicles. And then she saw it a fourth time, and then a fifth. It was deliberately trying to keep its distance, trying not to be noticed, trying to blend in with the other vehicles on the highway. But she noticed it. And now she suspected she was being followed. *Who the fuck is behind me?*

She stomped on the gas, only to see the BMW increase its speed. When she slowed down, it too slowed. And now she was about to conduct the ultimate test. She was about to exit the turnpike and turn back around toward Philly. If the BMW exited the highway and turned around with her, then she would have her answer.

Being followed was a frightening thing any day of the week, but being followed when you had millions of dollars in dope money in the trunk of your car was something else entirely. *Maybe someone saw me. Maybe someone else knows.*

Niggas had killed for less. And niggas had gone hard in the paint to get paid. But this, this would be an easy come up for anybody. She'd taken the treasure out of its safe hiding place, and now someone had painted a great big X on her fucking forehead. It would be so simple for someone to rob her right now. She wondered if they even had instructions on how to do it. *Peel back cap, dump bullets inside, take money. Congratulations! Now go live happily ever after, motherfucker.*

Gena switched on her turn signal, slid over into the exit lane, and left the highway. Her eyes were glued to the rearview mirror. The BMW took the exit. Fear bordering on panic overtook her.

It's not supposed to be like this! Who the fuck is following me? They must know I got the money.

She hadn't asked for this. She didn't deserve to get fucked off because she'd claimed what was rightfully hers. Qua was her man. He was going to marry her, after all, and she was entitled to the money he left behind.

I should've never taken that key chain.

She had put up with a lot of bullshit for this money: bitches calling, bastard children, and hoes sweating her man all the time.

Yes, I shoulda took the keys. Quadir wanted me to have them, so he must've wanted me to have this money.

She'd lost her best friend, she'd lost her man, and she'd lost Lita. She'd earned this fucking dough. Nobody had the right to take it from her. Not jackers, not the Feds, not the Philly PD, nobody.

Fuck this!

Gena turned onto the access road and accelerated as hard as she could. She'd head back to Philly, where she could lose the motherfucker in the tiny, narrow side streets she navigated like the back of her hand. At worst, whoever was behind her wouldn't be stupid enough to risk following her back to Gah Git's house. Niggas weren't trying to run up in Richard Allen and cause no static, especially at Gah Git's house. Gah Git was too well loved by everybody in the hood for that shit to happen. Naw, she would run back to safety and worry about stashing the dough later.

The black BMW accelerated hard, trying to keep Gena in sight.

The driver didn't want to be detected but could tell he had been spotted by the way Gena was driving. "Fuck!"

There was no doubt he'd been spotted and there was no doubt Gena was trying to lose him. The good thing was the mouse was heading back to the mouse hole, and that was exactly where she needed to be. She'd be easier to catch that way. And so would the money.

Gena raced down the access road, trying to get away from her pursuer. She could still see the halogen lights of the BMW in her rearview mirror. And with each passing mile, she became more of a wreck. She had her whole life ahead of her, and she didn't want to die—not like this.

A yellow light blinked on, and a soft chime rang out, causing Gena to look down at her dashboard. It was her fuel light. She had millions of dollars stuffed inside pillowcases in her trunk, and no gasoline in her tank.

Damn, I ain't never got no gas when I need it. What the fuck am I going to do now? Pull over alone on the side of the road with money in the trunk and be robbed, or even worse, murdered. No, that bitch ain't me, Gena thought, shaking her head.

She was going to find a gas station. Maybe the motherfucker wouldn't risk popping her in front of so many witnesses, especially if she found a big gas station. An Exxon, Mobil, Valero, Shell, or even Lukoil; fuck it, Wal-Mart out this bitch! Just somewhere where there was a bunch of people around. She spotted the red, white, and blue Exxon sign down the road, and a smile slowly spread across her face. She was going to make it.

Gena left the access road riding on nothing but fumes and raced into the gas station parking lot. The black BMW exited with her and followed her. Gena pulled up to a pump while the Beemer pulled into a faraway corner and sat idling. The black sedan's dark-tinted windows prevented her from seeing who, or even how many, was inside the car. She climbed out of her Benz, hit her alarm so her trunk would lock, and raced into the store.

"May I help you, ma'am?" the store clerk asked rudely.

Gena rubbed her sweating palms on her pants. "I . . . I . . . I . . . think that . . . I don't know." She stuttered so badly, and her mind raced so fast, she couldn't form a coherent sentence. "I . . . think . . . Help me."

"What's the matter, pretty girl?" a voice asked from behind.

Gena turned in the direction of the voice, swallowed hard, and shook her head.

Jerrell recognized her instantly. Although he didn't know her name, and he couldn't place her face, she looked familiar.

"What's the matter, ma?"

Gena shook her head. "I'm just . . . having a rough day, that's all."

Jerrell smiled at her. "Well, what can I do to make it better?"

Jerrell's smile was infectious. It made Gena crack a slight smile.

"There you go, pretty girl," Jerrell told her. "That's the way I want to see you looking. You feel better already, huh?"

Gena exhaled and peered out the window. "I had somebody following me."

Jerrell frowned as thousands of thoughts raced through his head. *Why would someone follow this broad? She ain't even wearing no jewelry. Let me find out this bitch got a stash.* He would certainly stick around and find out. If not for some dough, then at least she'd be a good fuck.

Jerrell clasped Gena's hand. "Show me who they are, ma. I'll take care of them niggas."

Gena was startled. The nigga was fine as hell, mad cute. But even beneath his good looks, a motherfucker could tell he wasn't to be fucked with. *Thank God, I've been saved. This nigga looks like he can go round for round, and he talks like he might have a little gangsta up in him. Yeah, he can handle this shit,* Gena told herself. And suddenly, she began to relax.

"It's that black car right there," she told him, feeling every bit a snitch.

Jerrell walked out of the store and peered in the direction Gena had pointed. The black BMW was pulling out of the parking lot and turning back in the direction of the turnpike. Jerrell counted to ten and then walked back into the store.

"Did you see it?" Gena asked nervously.

"I took care of them, ma," Jerrell told her. "You don't have to worry about them no more."

"Are you for real?" Gena asked.

Jerrell nodded.

"Thank you so much!" Gena told him. She wrapped her arms around him and gave him a hug. "I'm sorry, I don't even know your name. What's your name?"

"Jay," he told her. "My name's Jay."

Gena shook Jerrell's hand. "I can't repay you for this."

Jerrell nodded. "Yeah, you can."

"How?" Gena asked, lifting an eyebrow.

"Let me pay for your gas and let me walk you to your car and pump it for you," Jerrell told her. "And then let me follow you back to where you're going, so I can make sure you make it home safely."

Tears fell from Gena's eyes and she hugged him again. "I just met you, and you're so nice. I'm telling you, I was really being followed."

"Hey, don't worry about nothing anymore, ma," Jerrell told her. "You're safe with me. I got you, okay?"

Gena nodded.

"Which car is yours?"

"The blue Mercedes."

Hot damn, that's what I'm talking about, Jerrell thought. *Let me find out this broad is rolling. No wonder she thinks she was being followed. Niggas was probably trying to jack the bitch for her ride. Probably a bunch of youngsters trying to make a quick come up. Jack her car, take it to a chop shop, make a few thousand. See, that's what's wrong with young-sters today—no fucking vision. Why yank the bitch from the car and risk catching a carjacking case? All you got to do is finesse these broads out here; stroke 'em, fuck 'em, and milk 'em until they credit card bills look like a New York lottery number. Youngsters these days have no finesse, no G in their game. But I'ma show 'em how it's done, baby. Old-school style.*

Jerrell tossed a twenty-dollar bill onto the counter. "Put it on the blue Benz," he told the cashier.

Jerrell clasped Gena's hand and led her out to her car, where he placed her inside the vehicle and closed the door. Then he pumped her gas.

Inside the Benz, Gena closed her eyes and leaned her head back on the headrest. She felt something she hadn't felt in a long time. She felt like she had someone looking out for her again. She felt like she'd met a really good man, one who wanted to take care of her and keep her safe. *Wouldn't that be something?* She missed that feeling. She missed being able to wrap her arms around a man and feel safe. She missed having the man of life in her life.

Jerrell finished pumping Gena's gas and then walked to the driver's-side window, which she had rolled down.

"Hey, I want to call you tonight," Jerrell told her. "I want to make sure you're okay."

Gena nodded, pulled a pen from her purse, and wrote her number on the corner of an envelope. She tore the number off and handed it to Jerrell.

"I'ma follow you home to make sure you're safe, okay?" Jerrell told her.

Gena smiled. "Thank you so much, Jay. You're the nicest guy I've met in a long time."

"No problem, pretty girl."

Jerrell caressed the side of her face, and then turned and headed for his vehicle, climbed inside, and waited for Gena to pull off. Jerrell pulled off behind her and trailed her as she headed onto the turnpike, back to Gah Git's house, and back to safety.

His fucked-up crew had blown through all his bread while he was locked up, and he'd spent the remainder of his dough fighting that bullshit case. And now he'd been given a beautiful, lonely, scared bitch to fuck. *Ain't life grand? And it'll be even grander if this bitch got a couple of dollars so I can come up again.*

"Woooooeeeee!" Jerrell let out an excited scream as his imagination ran wild. He dreamed of fucking Gena on top of a pile of money and then suffocating her in that same pile of Benjamins afterward. It was obvious she didn't know who he was, and it was obvious she was feeling all the nice, concerned, protective shit he was throwing her way. Which meant she was lonely and didn't have a man to turn to. *Maybe her man's in jail or maybe the nigga's steppin' out on her every night. Either that or the nigga is a weak motherfucker and don't know how to protect his bitch. Either way, I got to find the story out on Ms. Gena.*

Jerrell had made up his mind and decided he'd get to work on that as soon as time permitted. But first, he had major things to attend to, like catching up with all them niggas who fucked up his dough and had nothing but excuses about why he was broke. Yeah, he'd take care of them, and he'd get with his baby girl, too. One thing at a time, though. One thing at a time.

"Don't worry, boo," Jerrell said to Gena's taillights. "Daddy's here! Daddy's gonna spank that monkey really good and give you all the man you need!"

Jerrell settled in for a long drive back to North Philly, dreaming of what he was going to do to Gena and everybody who owed him. *I can't believe them niggas fucked up my money. They must've never thought I was coming back home.* Never once did he realize the treasure he so deeply desired was only fifty feet away from him in the trunk of Gena's car.

Let the Game Begin

ieutenant Mark Ratzinger lifted his bottle of Advil liquid gel caps
and tossed two of them into his mouth. He tossed the bottle back
onto his desk and washed the pills down with a couple of sips from his
coffee mug. He was up to about ten caplets a day. Those little green
caplets, and his gallon of caffeine-laden coffee, were the only things
that seemed to be sustaining him these days. Why, he didn't know.

He was divorced—twice, to be precise. With his last headache
gone, he didn't know why he was so stressed out. Once the ink
was dry on his divorce papers, he shouldn't have suffered from another headache, or at least that's what he thought. Getting rid of
that bitch had been the best moment in his entire life, and to top it
all off, he didn't have to give her a damn thing. She made twice as
much as he did, and they had the good fortune to not have any little
rugrats, so the divorce was quick, clean, and sterile. Kind of like his
ex–psychotic whore, the one he called a wife, was in bed: quick,
clean, and sterile. What kinda sick bitch cleans her pussy with an
alcohol swab after making love to her husband? Yeah, he was glad
to be done with her.

Lieutenant Ratzinger rose from his desk and strolled down the
hall of the busy police station and into a conference room, where
several occupants were waiting impatiently.

Captain Holiday turned to him. "Make your point, Lieutenant. You're late, and some of us are very busy."

Lieutenant Ratzinger placed his stack of files on the table and walked to the blackboard, where he had photos of Philadelphia's various drug crews pinned up. Each group of photos was arranged in the shape of a pyramid, with the leader of the organization at the top. One group of photos, however, had two individual photos at the top of the pyramid. Quadir's photo sat right above one of Tyrik.

"This is our new plan, Captain," Lieutenant Ratzinger explained. "Working with United States Attorney Paul Perachetti, we're initiating a new operation, one that not only targets the drug dealers, but aggressively targets their assets as well. We take away these assholes' money, we take away their ability to hire big-time drug lawyers, and to influence jurors and the outcome of their prosecution. We're going to hit them where it hurts, in their pockets."

"Not to mention, gentlemen, this department will receive fifty percent of the assets seized from these dealers," United States Attorney Perachetti added. "And that, gentlemen, can add up rather quickly."

"And that's why the mayor is behind this thing a hundred percent," the deputy police chief chimed in. "A lot of nice, shiny new equipment can be bought with this money without costing the taxpayers a cent."

"With that said, may I turn your attention to the board, please," Lieutenant Ratzinger said.

The meeting's participants focused their attention on him again.

"Thank you," the lieutenant said. "On these charts are the organizational structures of some of Philly's most notorious drug crews. These pictures are photos of the main operators, or lieutenants, in these organizations. Up top is the captain, or head of the crew."

"Excuse me, Lieutenant," the deputy chief interrupted. "But why does that organization have two?"

The lieutenant turned toward Quadir's and Tyrik's photos. "Oh, because the one on top, Quadir Richards, is deceased. This organization is now headed by the gentleman in the second photo. Although Mr. Richards is no longer with us, his money still is," the lieutenant explained.

"How much are we talking about?" the captain asked.

"Millions, we believe," Lieutenant Ratzinger explained. "Mr. Richards was one of Philadelphia's biggest and most profitable dealers before his untimely demise."

"Who bumped him off?" the deputy chief asked nonchalantly.

"We believe it was the members of a rival drug crew known on the streets as the Junior Mafia," Perachetti explained. "I personally tried to prosecute the leader of the organization, Jerrell Jackson. Needless to say, I was unsuccessful. He walked away a free man. That's why I'm looking forward to overseeing the operation Captain Holiday and Lieutenant Ratzinger are putting together to get these scumbags off the street."

The deputy chief leaned forward in his seat and whispered to Ratzinger. "I want that money for this department and I want those assholes behind bars."

Lieutenant Ratzinger nodded.

"See to it personally, Lieutenant," the deputy chief told him.

Lieutenant Ratzinger lifted a photo of Gena into the air for all to see. "This is a photo of Janel Scott, better known as Gena. She was the live-in concubine of Quadir Richards. We have reason to believe this young lady is in possession of his money. And we're going after her like we're going after the rest of them. We have to send a message to these young girls, letting them know that harboring and laundering drug money is the equivalent of being on the streets and selling the drugs themselves."

The deputy chief nodded. "Good, make an example out of her."

Lieutenant Ratzinger allowed a twisted grin to slowly spread across his face. "Oh, we will, trust me. We're already in the process of targeting Miss Scott."

Khyree unlocked the door to his apartment and stepped inside. He carried with him two bags of groceries he'd bought from the local store to replenish his nearly empty pantry. He strolled into his kitchen and clicked on the light, only to be surprised by an unexpected guest seated at the breakfast table.

"Jerrell!" Khyree said nervously. "What the fuck are you doing here?"

"That's the greeting I get?" Jerrell asked.

Khyree set his bags of groceries down on the kitchen floor. "What's up, man? Good to see you!"

Jerrell stared at him in silence.

"Man, J, I'm so glad to see you outta that muthafuckin' place." Khyree walked to where Jerrell was seated, leaned over, and embraced him. "That shit's for animals, man."

Jerrell sat silently, staring at Khyree coldly.

"Yeah, man, when we heard you'd won that bullshit case, we cele-brated like a muthafucka!"

"Where's my money, Khyree?"

"Money?"

"Yeah, *my money*?" Jerrell said. "I left you with some work when I got caught up, and now that I'm out, I'm here to collect my money."

"Oh, yeah, the money," Khyree repeated. "Yeah, I ain't forgot aboutcha, baby. It's all good, J!"

"Okay, then, where is it?"

"I got to get it for you. I don't keep no major bread like that in the house. I would've had it here if I knew you was coming."

"Where is it?" Jerrell asked.

"It's at my other spot."

"Other spot?" Jerrell lifted an eyebrow. "What other spot you got, Khyree?"

Khyree smiled and exhaled. "Yo, J, why you tripping? This ya boy Khyree! You know me better than that!"

"The only thing I know is I warned you niggas what would happen if you fucked off my dough," Jerrell told him. "What? You muthafuckas didn't think a nigga was ever coming home or something?"

"Naw, J, it's cool," Khyree told him, lifting his palms into the air. "Just calm down. I got ya bread."

"Then give me my fucking money, so I can be on my way."

"Look, I'ma take you to the spot right now, and get you your bread so you can quit tripping," Khyree told him. "I'm going to put this shit up and then we can bounce. I gotta stick this shit in the freezer so it won't melt while we gone."

Khyree lifted some frozen pizzas out of his grocery bag, opened his freezer, and placed them inside. He began to frantically rearrange the contents of his freezer.

"Looking for this?" Jerrell asked, holding up Khyree's still-cold 9mm. "Nigga, I taught your muthafuckin' ass everything you know. You think you can get me with some shit I taught you?"

Khyree shook his head and gave an uneasy smile. "Man, J, it ain't even like that. I wasn't looking for that!"

Jerrell set the gun down on the table and pulled another one from his pocket. "What about this one? What, are you going to sit down on the sofa next? Or go and use the bathroom? All of them are gone, Khyree. I got all of them."

Khyree began to bawl. "Man, J, you my boy! Why you tripping on me like this, man!"

"You muthafuckas fucked off my paper, Khyree!" Jerrell said angrily. "And now I don't have a muthafuckin' thing to my name! Nigga, I'm scratching to get by."

"J, I can give you some money!" Khyree told him. "Let me give you some money to get by with. Give me a couple of days to make some moves and everything will be all gravy, baby! I'll have the rest of what I owe you and then some!"

"You talking about the money in that shoebox, nigga?" Jerrell asked, nodding toward a blue Nike shoebox under the table near his feet.

Khyree stared at the shoebox. "J, just take it. Take it all, man. I'll get you the rest later. Just give me a couple of days."

"A couple of days?" Jerrell asked.

"That's it," Khyree told him. "All I need is a couple of days."

"I got a better idea," Jerrell told him. "How about I take this money, and we call it even?"

Khyree nodded. "Whatever you want to do, J. But I swear, I can get the rest of the money."

Jerrell rose from the breakfast table. "Nah, let's just call it even."

Jerrell lifted the black Glock and fired several times, striking a screaming Khyree in his chest.

Jerrell gathered up the shoebox and headed out of the apartment, stepping over Khyree's body on the way. "Now we even, muthafucka!"

Money Ain't a Thang

Gena rolled over, clutching her pillow, as she opened her eyes to the sounds of Gah Git.

"Boy, if you don't come on here and put these pants on."

"No!" Khaleer took off running and sideswiped Gena as she was approaching the bathroom door.

"Boy," Gena said as Khaleer pushed by her and slammed the bathroom door behind him. "Open the door." Gena tried the handle but it wouldn't turn. "Gah Git, Khaleer done locked himself in the bathroom."

"Gena, get me a belt. I'm gonna whoop the simple off his little Black ass if he don't stop making me chase him."

"I'm gonna whoop the simple off his little Black ass if he makes me stand out here and pee on myself. Gah Git, I got to pee."

"Me too." Bria was trying to sleep but had been awakened by Khaleer's escapade and was peeking out of her room.

"Get me a credit card so I can open this door without breaking it down," Gah Git said.

"I know that's right, Gah Git." Bria smiled at her grandmother. "Let me find out you be burglarizing the hood with secret credit card entries."

"Go somewhere, gypsy child," Gah Git responded as she began to bang on the bathroom door.

Bang, bang, bang. "Come on, baby, open up the door for Gah Git. Gah Git loves you, baby. I ain't gonna hurt you. Now come on, Khaleer."

There was no answer from behind the bathroom door. Gah Git took the credit card Gena handed her and opened the door to find Khaleer huddled in the corner of the tub.

"'Scuse me," Gena said, pushing Gah Git to the left as she hopped onto the toilet seat.

"When you gotta go, you gotta go," Khaleer said, showing a bright smile.

"Fool, you 'bout to go to ass-whoopin' land; that's where I'm fittin' to send you." Gah Git grabbed him by the arm and swung him out of the tub. "Now come on here and get dressed for school."

Gena pulled on the toilet tissue roll. "Gah Git, don't be mean."

"Don't be mean? Gena, I been trying to get this boy dressed all morning. I'm tired and my day ain't even got started."

"Khaleer, why you won't get dressed?" Gena asked.

"Everybody teases me and calls me 'too-short pants' and they say the flood, it's a flood, and I'm not wearing them anymore."

"Boy, you gonna wear them. They clean clothes and you gonna be glad you got them to wear. Ain't nothing wrong with these pants; they ain't even high waters."

"Yes, they is, Gah Git. I be wondering why you be putting them pants on him anyway," Bria said, teasing her grandmother.

"Didn't I already tell you to go somewhere, gypsy child?" she asked Bria before turning her attention back to Khaleer. "Now, let's go, dammit! That's what's wrong with y'all now. Always worried about clothes and somebody else's name. Shit, Black folks don't even know they own name but they know that Versace shit. Don't you know it's not what's on the outside, it's what's on the inside, Khaleer? You understand?"

"No, please. Gah Git, please don't make me wear them clothes," he begged before he started to cry as Gah Git dressed him in his high waters anyway.

Gena sat on the toilet seat feeling bad for Khaleer. She remembered her school days and all the taunting and teasing she'd endured. *Don't worry, cousin, I got you covered. I'll get you some new clothes today and won't nobody be teasing you when I'm done.*

Yes, Gena had big plans for herself today. After finding a hidden treasure and safely hiding it, Gena had real big plans. She thought, for a moment, about what she had done last night. *The money is safe; I don't have to worry about that.*

Gena had it all figured out. Last night, after she met Jerrell at the Exxon station, she let him follow her back to the city, but instead of going back to Richard Allen, she made a detour and went to Thirtieth Street Station. It cost little to nothing and was a brilliant plan. Inside the train station she purchased several travel bags. She went back out to the car and divided up the money in the pillowcases, placed it in the various duffel bags, then placed the duffel bags in different lockers. By the time she was done, she had eight locker keys. The nice thing was, she could pick the money up any time, day or night, move it elsewhere if she needed it, or keep it right there. No one would ever know what was in the lockers and no one would ever know she'd found Quadir's money.

I got to get dressed. I got a lot going on. I wonder what I should wear.

Gena looked at her closet. She didn't have much of a wardrobe to pick from. Actually, she didn't have anything. It had been like that for months. Gena sort of had no zest in her life, she had no romance, she had nothing going on that was exciting or adventurous, and for the past six months, she had done little to nothing except mourn the loss of Quadir. She didn't want any clothes because she had nowhere to go, but all that had changed. Everything had changed after she found that money.

And what was even nicer was that guy she'd met. *Thank God for him.* If it hadn't been for him, she might not have been able to elude the BMW that had been following her. Because of Jay, she'd been able to stash her cash in her secret hiding place without being followed.

She'd kept only two of the pillowcases filled with money and had them in the closet, buried under her clothes, which were piled in even larger trash bags. *I hope Gah Git don't be snoopin' around in my room and find all this money. God, what would I do then? I can hear her now, boy, oh boy, and I don't want to hear her at all.*

Gena carefully mapped out her day as she slipped into her clothes. "I sure do miss you," she said as she stared at a small picture of Quadir she kept on her nightstand. "Thank you so much for giving me the keys. I'm going shopping now, but I'll be back later. I love you." She kissed Quadir's picture and placed it back down on her nightstand. She grabbed her diamond Q key chain and headed downstairs.

"Gah Git, I'm gone, but I'll be back."

"Okay, baby, be safe out there. All these people with guns and stuff . . . they going crazy. Don't make sense. Watch yourself, Gena."

"Okay, bye."

Gena closed the door and looked down the street at her baby blue Mercedes. It was sparkling in the sunlight like a star in the twinkling sky.

"Yo, Gena, what's up?" the guy from the corner store called.

"Hey, whatchoo up to this early in the morning?"

"Nothing, you know me. Got to get a fresh start with this hustle shit I got going on."

"Well, just be careful."

"I'm good; I'm on it. Tell Bria I'm trying to holler at her."

"Child, please, you better tell her yourself," Gena said as she closed her car door. *I got to get going. I got a lot of money and I got a lot of spending to do with it. I don't have time to be talking to you about your make-believe love affair with my cousin.*

Her mind raced as she tried to figure out where to go first. She needed new clothes and new shoes and—there it was. Sure as daylight was shining, there it was, the black BMW.

"Aww, hell no, not this following-me shit again."

She turned on Thirteenth Street, then made a left on Wallace. *I can't believe this shit.* Yes, the BMW was tailing her again, merely three cars behind her. *What the fuck should I do?*

For thirty minutes Gena drove aimlessly, all the while being followed. She wasn't sure what to do or where to go. She wondered if she parked the car and walked, would she still be followed? Probably. She pulled into the Gallery Mall parking lot on Eleventh Street in Center City. It didn't seem as though the BMW had followed her inside the parking lot, though. She kept driving up the ramp and then back down and then back up, and she didn't see the BMW anywhere.

I wonder where it went? she thought, still looking all around the parking lot.

She parked her 300 CE and paced herself as she walked into the mall, desperate to elude whoever was following her, but now that she was out of the car and in the mall, it seemed as if no one was behind her. If someone was, it would be hard to keep up with her. The mass of people shopping in the Gallery was her haven, a much-needed comfort zone.

She walked through the lower level of the mall until she got to the Eighth Street exit, convinced she was getting away from her follower. She crossed Market and made her way over to Jewelers' Row, all the while making sure no one was following her and there was no black BMW in sight.

She walked down Jewelers' Row, looking at all the window displays until she came across a shop called Barsky. She couldn't help herself, she just couldn't. When she found Quadir's safe, all she thought of was clothes, shoes, and jewelry. She wanted a necklace, some diamond earrings, and a bracelet, and the window display had the look she was searching for.

"How much for that?" Gena asked, pointing at a particularly brilliant platinum-and-diamond ring sitting in the display case.

"That one is thirty-two thousand dollars," said the jeweler, Ray Feldman, across the countertop between them.

Gena nodded and continued to browse the items in the glass case. "What about this one?"

Ray lifted the ring into the air and quickly examined the tag attached to the shank. "This one is . . . twenty-five thousand dollars."

"Can I see it?" Gena asked.

"Give me your hand," Ray said.

Gena extended her hand over the counter, and Ray placed the ring on her finger. Gena held her hand in front of one of the mirrors sitting on top of the counter and examined it.

"That one is my favorite," he told Gena. "I made that myself."

"Really, it is very nice," Gena said. She wiggled her finger, and the ring slid right off. "It's a little big, though."

"I can size anything to fit you perfectly," Ray said.

Gena handed the ring back to Ray, who wiped it clean and placed it back inside the display case. Gena pointed to another ring in the display.

"Wow, you certainly have good taste," he said with a smile. "I see that you dream big, just like me."

"I'm shopping, not dreaming."

Ray Feldman removed the ring from the display case and handed it to Gena.

"Well, then, you're my kind of customer. Sixteen thousand dollars."

Gena placed the ring on her finger. It fit perfectly, no sizing necessary. It was the one. If there was ever such a thing as "the ring of life," this was it. It was a white gold ring with diamonds embedded around the band and a 3-carat solitaire mounted on top. It shone in the light like a sparkler on the Fourth of July.

"I'll take it," Gena told him.

Ray choked on his saliva. "And how will you be paying for that?"

"Cash. Good old cash," Gena told him.

"That would certainly do, now, won't it?"

Gena went into the bathroom and counted out sixteen thousand dollars. She handed the money to Ray and watched while he wrote up a receipt and an appraisal for her records. She walked out of the store feeling icy as she headed into another jewelry boutique.

"Can I see that watch right there?" Gena asked, pointing at a diamond bezel Cartier panther.

The salesman spied the ring on Gena's finger and immediately snapped to attention. "Yes, ma'am."

The display case flew open, and the salesman was snapping the watch around Gena's wrist before she knew it. The gold-and-diamond watch matched her ring to a T. The only problem was the watch and ring would both be on the same hand, leaving her other hand bare. She spied a nice diamond tennis bracelet that would help solve her dilemma. "How much for that tennis bracelet?"

"Oh, that would look so lovely on you," the salesman gushed.

Gena caught the lisp in his words. He was as sweet as apple juice.

"Let me put that on your wrist, honey!"

Gena smiled and held out her wrist.

The salesman clasped the bracelet around Gena's wrist and maneuvered a large mirror in front of her. "You look simply divine."

She had to admit it; she was working those jewels. The only thing missing was something to go around her bare neck. She looked up to ask the salesman what he thought only to find him rushing toward her with a necklace and charm. The boy could coordinate jewelry like a motherfucker. Yup, he was gay.

"By the way, my name is Carlos," the salesman told her.

"My name is Gena."

"Well, Miss Gena," he whispered into her ear, "Mr. Carlos has something here that will knock your socks off. Close your eyes."

Gena closed her eyes. She could feel the necklace going around her neck and the charm resting on her chest. It felt heavy. Carlos turned her around in the direction of the mirror.

"Open your eyes, Miss Gena," Carlos told her.

Gena opened her eyes and gasped. Carlos had placed a diamond chain around her neck with a large, heart-shaped diamond pendant. The whole thing was breathtaking, and it left her speechless.

"You can wear it out," Carlos told her. "'Cause, girl, I know you'll fight me if I try to take it off."

Gena laughed. This fool had to be the store's top salesperson. Her suspicions were confirmed when two fifty-something, super-rich-looking white women strolled into the store.

"Miss Jennifer and Miss Emily, I'll be with you two young ladies in a moment," Carlos told them. "You're rocking that new hairdo, Miss Emily. You go, girl!"

The white women couldn't stop smiling, blushing, and gushing at Carlos.

"Now, Miss Gena, how will we be paying today? Amex, Visa, Discover?"

Again, Gena smiled. Even if she hadn't originally planned on purchasing this many items, Carlos had sold her on them. His service and salesmanship were excellent, and he made her want to give him her money. She opened her purse.

"It'll be cash, Carlos," she told him. "I'm paying in cash."

"Girl, what is the secret!" Carlos blurted out. "I sell this beautiful jewelry to beautiful ladies like you all day long, and I can't figure out for the life of me what I'm doing wrong! Carlos wants to shop here, too!"

Gena laughed, pulled out her money, and counted out the number displayed on the register. She had managed to spend $130,000 in thirty minutes. She felt damned good.

And now it was time to go back to the car. Gena drove a few blocks, observing that no one was behind her. *About time,* she thought to herself. *Or better yet, maybe it's about time that I get the fuck out of this 300 CE and into something a little faster. Yeah, something new, something nobody will recognize, something fast as hell.* She headed out of the mall and to the Porsche dealership.

"Hello, is someone already helping you?" a saleswoman asked.

Gena shook her head.

"Okay, well then." The saleswoman extended her hand. "My name is Candace."

"Gena," she said, shaking the saleswoman's hand.

"What can I help you find today, Gena?" Candace asked.

"I need a car," Gena told her. "A really fast one."

Candace laughed. "Well, you've certainly come to the right place. Is that your 300 CE out there?"

Gena nodded.

"How much do you owe on it?"

Gena shook her head. "Nothing, but I'm not trading it in. It was a gift from someone special."

"Oh, well then, my next question is, have you ever driven a Porsche before?"

Gena shook her head again. "No."

"We have several different models and several different styles," Candace explained. "Are you looking for a convertible, a hardtop, or something in between?"

Gena lifted an eyebrow. "Something in between?"

"Yeah, like this," Candace said, pointing to a nearby car. "It's called a Targa. It has a removable roof panel so that you can enjoy the open air. Not as much as in a convertible, but still, it's more than just having a sunroof."

Gena pointed across the showroom floor. "What about that one?"

"That one?" Candace laughed at her. "You want that one? That's a lot of car, sweetie."

"Is it fast?" Gena asked, not realizing the joke was on her.

"It's the fastest thing on the streets right now," Candace said in all seriousness.

A wide smile slowly spread across Gena's face. "I like it. That's the one that I want."

Candace placed her hand on her hip and shifted her weight to one side. "You want that car right there?"

Gena nodded, walked across the showroom, and climbed into the car. Inside, she caressed the diamond-stitched black leather seating. Yeah, this was her shit.

"Gena, this is a convertible Porsche Gemballa," Candace explained. "It's a convertible 911 turbo. It's really a convertible race car, disguised as a street car. We're talking twin turbochargers, dry sump oil lubrication, Brembo Carbon fiber brakes. I mean . . . the works."

And it's black, too, Gena thought to herself. A rich, deep, shiny dark black convertible Porsche. It could outrace any car on the streets. And it even looked the part. The fenders were flared so wide, she could easily stand on them. And the massive whale tail and side intakes told everyone this motherfucker could move, so get the fuck out of the way. Gena honked the horn, causing the other people in the showroom to jump. *Outta the way! Mad bitch in a Porsche coming through!*

Candace peered down at Gena. "Girl, what's on your mind?"

Gena smiled and shifted her glance toward Candace. "Can't nothing on the street catch it?"

Candace shook her head. "Nothing."

Gena glanced down at the speedometer, which stopped at 250 miles per hour. "Yeah."

"Yeah, what?" Candace asked.

"I'll take it," Gena told her.

Take That

Paula opened the door to Gah Git's house using her key. She peeked into the family room. "Ma, it's me, Paula."

Gah Git peeked out of the kitchen. "I'm here. Come on in."

Paula hurried into the house, closing the door behind her. She looked around at the junky mess. *Why don't Mama make these kids clean up around here?*

That was part of the problem; no one had to do anything. Gah Git did all the work, all the time. Paula was Gah Git's oldest daughter and was the most together sister in the family. She had traveled most of the world, had graduated from college, and had a master's in business. She worked for AT&T as a district field manager, which was how she was able to travel and see most of the world. Paula had worked hard to get to where she was and besides herself and Michael, her younger brother, no one else in the family had achieved as much success.

"Hi, Ma," she said, hugging her mother.

"Shh, I got Malcolm on the phone."

"Who?"

"Malcolm."

"Malcolm?"

"Yeah, shh," Gah Git said as she finished listening to her first-born son.

Paula turned her back on her mother when she heard who she was on the phone talking to. *Malcolm, Malcolm, Malcolm, what does he want now?*

The mention of Malcolm brought back a lot of pain, too much pain. Even though fifteen years had passed since he was sentenced, time hadn't changed the past for Paula. It seemed like only yesterday. But it wasn't for Malcolm; it was fifteen hard years served in a maximum-security state facility called Greene in Pennsylvania.

"Okay, so September twelfth? Okay, I hope it works, baby. I'm gonna keep you in my prayers, Malcolm, you hear me?"

Paula looked over at her mother.

"Okay, I love you, too, son. Bye-bye." Gah Git hung up the phone.

"So, what's going on September twelfth, Mom?"

"Malcolm says he goes in front of the parole board again. They might let him out this time." Gah Git started washing the dishes in the sink. "That sure would be something to see: my son, free, after all these years."

Yes, it would be something, hot damn. Please, God, they've had me locked up too long. Even Maria forgives me. Sweet Maria, I'm sorry, baby. You know that, you know I am. I didn't mean to kill you, baby. I love you, Maria, to this day and all this time later, I'll never love no one but you. That's how sorry I am—I just won't. I never meant to hurt you. I never meant to hurt you. God, let me out of here, please.

"Scott!" shouted a corrections officer on the block. "Scott!"

Malcolm was so preoccupied, he hadn't even realized he was standing in the middle of a hallway.

"Let's go. Keep it moving. Time for count," the corrections officer shouted at him.

Look at this guy, he thinks he's so in charge. Despite being locked up, Malcolm had found a way to keep his mind free. But all those years were now gone from his life and he'd never get them back. He'd never get Maria back. He'd never get the time back. There was a funny saying: *It's not what they give you, it's can you give it back*, and that is so much easier said than done.

People don't understand what time can do to you, and then, when you're under the thumbs of crazy crackers and their bullshit, it can't get no worse. And escape—is you crazy? You not escaping, and even if you did, where would you go? In the middle of Redneckville? With nothing but mountains surrounding you and cascading along a never-ending skyline, where you going? And it seemed like the whole town in its entirety worked in the motherfucker. Shit was crazy. You'd have cousins, fathers, sons, and uncles all working in the same facility, all correctional officers.

That's how all the prisons were in Pennsylvania. They were set up in those kinds of towns, with a bunch of rednecks, who now all had day jobs and benefits, and they couldn't spell *cat* to win a spelling bee. Can you imagine being nowhere, cut off from the world, cut off from everyone and everything that was your life? It had been the hardest fifteen years anyone could imagine, and to think of having to do another ten was pure turmoil. *No, they gonna let me go. They gonna let me outta here this time. I just know it—I just do.* That's what got Malcolm through the day. The belief that one day he would be able to go home.

"Come on, let's go, in your cell, boy, get on."

Malcolm was already at his cell when the CO ordered him inside it. He looked at the man, who was much younger than him. *You really don't want none of this, cracker.* Malcolm wanted so badly to check Mullinberry, but he didn't. Instead, he walked into his cell and faced Mullinberry as his cell door closed.

Let's see if you can count today, asshole, Malcolm thought as he lay on his bed and daydreamed about the upcoming hearing. *I know they're gonna let me go this time. I just know they're gonna let me go.* The thoughts consumed him.

***

"Mr. Scott, the board has approved your parole. You're free, Mr. Scott."

He couldn't believe it. He heard the words echoing through him as he looked around his cell.

"Are you ready, Mr. Scott?" CO Mullinberry asked with a kind smile on his face.

Malcolm picked up a photo he kept inside a Bible his mother had given him. It was a picture of his daughter, Gena, when she was only three.

"I'm ready."

He got his belongings, signed out of the facility, and was on his way back home, back to the way things were, just like they were.

He got off the bus on Broad Street. Three blocks were nothing to walk. He pepped up his step as he passed by a small corner store.

"How much for those flowers?"

"Five dollars," the older lady, of Asian descent, replied.

Malcolm walked out with flowers in his hand and made his way down the street. He walked into the high-rise tower and caught the elevator to the twenty-third floor. He unlocked the door and called out, but no one answered him. He heard a noise coming from down the hall. He set his flowers on a side table next to the sofa.

"Gena? Maria?" he called out.

He walked backward, constantly looking all around him, keeping his eyes on the long, narrow hallway in front of him. As he reached the top of a dining hutch, his hand felt the small metal .22, and his fingers gripped it. The .22 was a little something he kept in the house for that "just in case" moment in life, and he was starting to think this was it. He moved down the hallway to his bedroom door. He pushed the door open slightly and peered into the candlelit room. It was Maria, his wife, his beautiful wife, her long hair, her long legs, her beautiful Spanish cocoa-colored skin, her voice.

"Ooh, papi," she breathed. "Yeah, papi, ooh," she said to her lover, who was holding her ankles up in the air.

It was then that, out of the corner of his eye, her lover saw the tall, dark figure standing by the door. "Oh, damn!" he said, letting her ankles go and breaking their rhythm.

"How could you?" Malcolm screamed as he attacked Maria's lover.

"Malcolm, stop!" Maria screamed as she stood on the bed while both men wrestled beneath her feet. "Malcolm, please, no, I can explain."

Pooooow!

The one shot from the gun seemed to echo throughout the room, and Malcolm looked at Maria's naked body as fear came over her face.

"What have you done? What have you done? Malcolm, look at what you've done."

He looked down at the bed, and with all the shock he had digested, his brother's face took him over the edge.

"You fucking my brother, my little brother?"

"Please, Malcolm, I can explain, I can explain," Maria said, pleading with him.

"I love you! Why would you do this to me?" He violently punched the wall.

"Malcolm, I love you, too . . . It's just . . . we . . . I . . . Malcolm, please, I love you . . . I love you . . . too. I . . ."

Malcolm grabbed his wife around her neck. He threw her up against the wall. With one hand around her neck, he used his other hand to undo his zipper.

"Open your legs."

"Malcolm, no, Malcolm . . . please," Maria said, knowing this was not Malcolm, this was an enraged man, and he wasn't thinking. His brother was lying dead and covered in blood on their bed.

"Malcolm, no, please," Maria pleaded as Malcolm mechanically forced her against the wall, plunged into her, and began fucking her.

"Oh, God, Malcolm, no, please."

The more Maria fought him, the more he forced her.

"You're a whore! You fuck my brother, right? You don't want to fuck me? Maria, you're gonna get fucked real good, you understand? You fuck me like him, you hear? I loved you! I *love* you and what do you do? You shame me."

With each and every word, his grip on her neck became tighter. By the time he ejaculated inside her, she was already dead. He'd crushed her windpipe and suffocated her.

"Daddy!" Gena was holding the bouquet of flowers in her hand. "I have a picture for you, Daddy." Gena reached out her hand. "See."

Malcolm quickly pulled up his pants and walked over to his daughter. He closed the door behind him and knelt down to Gena.

"Here."

Gena passed him a picture, the same picture that now hung on the wall in his cell.

"Here." Malcolm's cellmate woke him. "Here's your mail, man."

Malcolm opened his eyes and looked at his cellmate. *Thank God he woke me,* he thought to himself, taking his mail. Malcolm hated that dream. It wasn't a dream; it was more of a flashback, so real, so like yesterday, and so complicated. His life had never been the same after that. It certainly wasn't the same for his brother, Michael. Thank God he survived the gunshot, but Maria, sweet Maria, died that day.

Malcolm was charged with murder and sentenced to twenty-five years in prison. The only thing that saved him from a life sentence was the fact he'd acted in rage and the crime wasn't premeditated. In that regard he'd caught a break. But everything would change once he had this new parole hearing. His break would come. He felt it.

Jordan's condo was located on the third floor of his building, overlooking a nearby state park. The views from his pad were some of the most beautiful and most breathtaking in the entire state. The condo cost him a few hundred thousand, which he had his lawyer move for him so that eyebrows wouldn't be raised and questions wouldn't be asked.

He'd furnished the luxurious bachelor pad with some of the most ultramodern furniture that could be found this side of the Atlantic. His caramel-colored round sectional had been imported from Sweden, while his metal entertainment center, metal coffee table, and metal end tables were shipped from Morocco. A stainless-steel Martin Bauer pool table sat in the middle of the room beneath an intricately designed stainless-steel chandelier with Swarovski crystals from Jay Strongwater.

Soft cream-colored recliners sat in front of a massive marble fireplace, while authentic paintings by Jacob Lawrence, Charles Bibbs, Sharon Wilson, and William Tolliver graced the condo's snow-white walls. A massive stainless-steel and glass dining room table with overstuffed cream-colored leather chairs sat on the opposite side of the room. Beyond the dining room table was the ultramodern kitchen, where stainless-steel Wolf and Sub-Zero appliances and cream-colored granite countertops could be seen. The glass and stone sculptures throughout the condo screamed money, and lots of it. The game had clearly been good.

Jordan turned the knob and removed his key from the lock. He'd been out shopping all day and was dead tired. He needed a shower and rest, and then he would hit the streets and pick up his money. He had plenty of that to pick up. Business had been good.

The first time he heard the faint sounds of moving water, he dismissed the thought as being ridiculous. Now that he heard it again, he realized his ears weren't deceiving him. There was another person in his house.

He reached inside his gym bag and pulled out his 9mm Beretta. He pulled back the slide, chambering a round, and then quickly ejected his clip and checked it. Yeah, it was full. He quickly slid the magazine back into his weapon and crept over his marble floors into his bedroom. He couldn't believe someone had the nerve to break into his crib. Of all the cribs in Philly, some stupid motherfucker had chosen his. Well, the same stupid motherfucker was about to die.

The splashing sound of water told him the asshole was in his bathroom. *You got to be kiddin' me.* That was when he noticed the soft hum of the jets from his Jacuzzi whirring. *What the fuck! Somebody's bathing in my tub?* He couldn't figure it out.

Jordan crept to his bathroom, shoved open the double doors, and quickly lifted his weapon.

"Jerrell!" Jordan cried out. His heart raced like a NASCAR driver around the Charlotte Speedway. "What the fuck? Man, what the fuck are you doing here? I almost did you!"

Jerrell laughed and waved his arm, dismissing Jordan. Bubbles from the tub flew through the air. "Nigga, quit being paranoid."

"What the fuck are you doing in my crib?" Jordan asked. "What the fuck are you doing in my tub? How did you get in here?"

"Damn, thanks for all the love, partner," Jerrell told him. "I figured that since we was homies and shit, you wouldn't mind if a dirty nigga like me washed a little bit of jail filth off my skin. I mean, seeing as how you got this great big old Jacuzzi tub and all."

"Yeah, well, my girl got a promotion," Jordan told him.

Jerrell smiled and nodded. "They moved her up from fries to milkshakes, huh?"

"Something like that."

"Well, why don't you join me in a toast, then." Jerrell lifted the bottle of Dom Perignon he had next to the tub. "Go and get you a glass."

"I'm not thirsty," Jordan told him.

Jerrell shook his head. "Humph, that's sad. Not going to toast to your girl's newfound success. What kind of a relationship you got?"

"We've already celebrated."

Jerrell nodded. "I'm sure you have, baby boy. I'm sure you have."

Jerrell lifted his hand to his lips and blew some of the suds in the air. "You, Khyree, Mont, Ran, all y'all did a whole lot of celebrating while I was gone, huh?"

"It's not what you think," Jordan told him.

"Oh, it's not?" Jerrell asked. "Tell me, then, how much money did you send me while I was locked up?"

Jordan shook his head and looked away.

"Exactly," Jerrell told him. "You niggas was out here living large, buying new condos and shit. Everybody got new cars, new clothes, new jewelry, just everything brand fucking new. But me, poor old Jerrell, I got to hustle in jail to make a commissary on Tuesdays. What if I would've been desperate, J? What if I had to sell ass for cigarettes, or some shit like that?"

"C'mon, J, it ain't even like that," Jordan protested. "If you would've asked me, I would've looked out for you."

"Ask you? You had my connect, my spot, my runners, my car, my guns, my ideas, my everything, and yet, I had to ask you?" Jerrell slid down farther into the Jacuzzi, closed his eyes, and relaxed. "Okay, so I'm asking you now. Where's my money?"

"Is that what all of this is about?" Jordan asked. "Some money? You gonna break into my crib, jump up into my tub, drink up my champagne, and trip with me because of some money? Whatever happened to Junior Mafia? Whatever happened to us being family? What was all that shit about us being family? What was all that shit about us being brothers?"

"Are you your brother's keeper, Jordan?" Jerrell asked with a smile.

"You muthafuckin' right I am!" Jordan said forcefully.

"Then go and get the money you kept for your brother," Jerrell told him.

"It's at the safe house, where I keep all the dough," Jordan reassured him.

Jerrell laughed. "All you niggas got the dough somewhere else. The dough ain't never nowhere around; it's always a muthafuckin' drive away. You got fucking priceless-ass paintings and shit in this bitch, but no fucking dough. What, a thief will steal my hundred Gs but not your hundred-thousand-dollar painting? You got a muthafuckin' original Paul Goodnight over your fucking fireplace. That bitch had to cost a couple of meal tickets, but you're afraid to hold my chump change in this bitch?"

"So, what are you saying, J?" Jordan asked.

"I'm saying you muthafuckas are full of shit, that's what I'm saying!" Jerrell shouted. "The only reason I'm still in this muthafucka is to kill you."

Jordan smiled and lifted his pistol in the air, showing it to Jerrell. "I think you forgot something."

"What's that?" Jerrell asked.

"I'm the muthafucka holding the pistol," Jordan told him.

"Glocks can shoot underwater," Jerrell told him, squeezing the trigger of his 10mm Glock semiautomatic.

The bullet struck Jordan between his eyes, causing soap suds to mix with the blood that ran slowly down his nose as he fell silently to the ground. Jerrell climbed out of the Jacuzzi, wrapped a towel around his waist, and walked to the closet, where he had Jordan's girl tied up. He opened the closet door.

"I promised you that if you opened the safe and cooperated, I'd let you live," Jerrell told her. "Well, the only problem is, I lied."

Tears flowed from Nina's eyes as she shook her head.

"I'll give you another chance to earn your life back," Jerrell told her. "You want to do that?"

Nina nodded her head frantically.

"Let me wax that fat Latino ass of yours, and then we'll take a bath. After that, we'll leave together. Comprende?"

Nina nodded.

Jerrell helped her out of the closet, led her over to the bed, and threw her down. He ripped off the buttons on her blue-jean skirt, yanked the skirt off her, and threw it to the floor. Next came her panties, which he quickly ripped off and discarded. He climbed on top of her and plunged into her, causing Nina to cry out.

Jerrell hadn't been with a woman since he'd gotten out of jail, and he took all his frustrations out on Nina. She bore the brunt of his anger with the Junior Mafia, his anger over losing his money, and his anger over having been locked up in the first place. He pummeled and twisted and gyrated and thrust like a demon possessed. He hammered at her as fast and as furiously and as deep as he could, causing her to scream and shout at the top of her lungs.

He threw her legs over his shoulders and pounded as hard as he could. He had to get it out of him—all the frustration, the anger, and the fury. He had to exorcize the emotional demons that had become so pent up inside. He stroked forcefully, furiously, fanatically, until his release came. Nina could feel it shooting up into her stomach. She screamed while he let out a deep, guttural growl.

Sweating heavily, Jerrell climbed off his victim, pulled her up by her wrist, and pushed her into the bathroom. She stepped over her boyfriend's dead body and began crying heavily.

Jerrell pointed toward the toilet. "Sit down and piss."

Nina sat on the toilet seat and urinated. Blood, semen, and urine poured out of her sore and aching vagina.

Jerrell pointed toward the bathtub. "Now go and get in the tub and wash yourself good."

Nina rose from the toilet, pulled off all her remaining clothing, and climbed into the tub. Jerrell flushed the commode and tossed Nina a bar of soap and a face towel.

Nina began crying as she cleaned herself. "You're not going to let me live."

Jerrell smiled. "I have your money. I have your jewelry. I'm going to take all your paintings and other valuable shit. I've fucked,

I've eaten, and I've killed the nigga that I came here to kill. What else is left for me, ma? Why would I let you live?"

"I won't tell anyone," Nina said with tears pouring down her cheeks. "I'll leave town. I promise. I'll go back to Puerto Rico, even! I give you my word, I won't tell! I won't tell a soul!"

Before she could speak another word, Jerrell silenced her as he lifted his Glock.

"No, please, no!"

Those were her last three words before Jerrell fired one shot at Nina's head. The bullet penetrated her raised hand and entered her nose. She slid down into the bathwater with her eyes still open.

"I know you won't tell," Jerrell whispered. He turned and left the blood-filled bathroom.

Hear No Evil, Speak No Evil

Reds wiped the sweat from his brow and slid down off the hood of his silver S 500 Benz. It was hot on the block today, in more ways than one. The sun was beaming down on the curb, and the exhaust from the passing traffic only made things worse. But he had to be out there. His boys were grinding hard, and their packs were moving fast. He needed to be around to keep track of everything and to manage his young horses out beating the pavement. Today had been a good day so far, and it was only twelve thirty. He still had the rest of the day left to get his weight up. His crew had moved half of the packs he'd brought to the trap, and the way things were moving, he'd have to shoot to the crib and re-up soon.

"Damn, baby," Rasun said, wiping the sweat from his forehead. "Shit is rolling today!"

"I know," Reds agreed. "It's like the fiends all hit the lottery or something. It's fucked up to say, but crack is the best thing that ever happened to my life. I swear, thank You, God, thank You," he said, kissing a handful of money and holding it up to the sky.

Rasun walked to his candy orange '69 Dodge Charger, opened the door, and turned on his stereo system. The thunderous boom of the deep bass notes resounded throughout the area. Rasun had hooked the system up with eight eighteen-inch subwoofers, ten midrange speakers, and ten tweeters. A total of ten amplifiers helped to push out the system's awesome power. Rasun had the most powerful and best-known system in all of Philly.

"Pass me a beer," Reds shouted.

Rasun reached into his passenger seat, pulled a beer from the cooler, and tossed it to Reds. Reds caught the beer, popped the top, and turned it up, consuming fizz and all.

"Yo, you hear about that boy Khyree?" Rasun asked.

Reds nodded. "Yo, that shit was ill. The boy got popped in his own joint."

"You think Rik had something to do with that shit?" Rasun asked.

Again, Reds shrugged. "Who gives a fuck? He doing his thing, we doing ours."

"Damn, shit ain't been the same since Qua's been gone," Rasun said, shaking his head.

Neither of them, nor their crew members, noticed the two black vans making their way down the street. Reds looked up, only to peep the scene too late. *Fuck, I know that ain't Ola.*

The Drug Enforcement Task Force leaped out from the vans and raced toward Rasun and Reds. Other members of the task force leaped out of the delivery vans that had been parked across the street, while still others raced from unmarked cars that had been in traffic. It had been a well-planned, well-coordinated raid.

The task force had shown up in large numbers, and they were all over the place before anyone realized what was going on. The task force moved like cockroaches when you turned the lights on. Everybody ran for cover like Olympic contenders. You never seen no niggas run so fast in your life. All of Reds's and Rasun's runners were gathered up within seconds.

Reds turned the corner, with Rasun following close behind. Reds hopped three steps onto a front porch and started banging on the door of a girl who lived on the block. She peeked out of the second-floor window.

"Why is you banging on my door like you crazy?"

"Let me in," Reds screamed.

"Boy, wait, *The Young and the Restless* is on," the girl shouted out the window.

"Bitch, open the door."

Just then Rasun peeped the task force rounding the corner and took off haul-assin', leaving Reds standing on the porch.

"Fuck," Reds uttered as he saw the uniformed enemy and took off behind Rasun. They made it no more than five hundred feet down the block before they were both thrown to the ground and hand-cuffed without being read their Miranda rights, as with most cases in the hood.

"Well, well, well, if it isn't Reds and Rasun," Lieutenant Ratzinger said. "Ms. Clair is going to be really disappointed in you boys."

"Fuck outta here, muthafucka, talkin' 'bout my mom!" Rasun shouted.

"I just raided your mother's house. Guess what I found, Rasun?" Lieutenant Ratzinger asked.

"You ain't find nothing," Rasun said, knowing his mom's house was clean. He began to twist and turn and try to get up. One of the officers put a foot on his back and shoved him down onto the ground.

"That's right," Lieutenant Ratzinger told him. "We had your mother face down on the ground in handcuffs, just like we got you. But she offered to give us some pussy if we let her go."

"You muthafuckas!" Rasun shouted. He tried to spit on the lieutenant, but it fell short.

"I went first," Ratzinger told him.

Rasun was foaming at the mouth. "I'll kill you, pig!"

"You can't threaten an officer," Lieutenant Ratzinger told him. "Especially one who's going to be your daddy."

"You muthafuckas make me sick. If I wasn't handcuffed, I'd choke the fucking life out you muthafuckas!" Reds shouted.

The other officers piled the packs they'd found onto the ground in front of Reds and Rasun. They'd even managed to find Reds's stash spot behind the dumpster on the side of the cleaners they were standing in front of, and Rasun's stash spot inside a box of laundry soap inside the cleaners.

"Do you know how much time the Feds are going to give you for all this crack?" the lieutenant asked.

"What crack?" Reds asked. "I don't know nothing about no crack. I was doing laundry, pig."

"Oh, a wise guy?" Ratzinger asked. He placed his shoe on the back of Reds's neck. "Let's see how smart you are when you're sittin' in court, in front of an all-white jury, and I get up there and tell them how you said you wanted to sell drugs to all of the white kids you can find."

"Fuck you, pig. This the hood; ain't no fuckin' white kids around here!" Rasun told him.

Lieutenant Ratzinger turned toward Rasun. "Tough words from a guy who just got his mom a federal sentence. Like it fucking matters; all that matters is what the fuck I say."

"Leave my moms outta this shit! Ain't even nothing in my mom's house," Rasun shouted, speaking the truth.

Ratzinger turned to the other officers. "Get these two losers out of here."

The masked officers lifted Reds and Rasun off the ground, walked them to one of the windowless black vans, and threw them both into the back of it. About twenty minutes later, Reds and Rasun felt the van moving, and within another hour, they were at the precinct and had been fingerprinted, photographed, and thrown into separate holding cells.

It seemed like days, even though it had only been a matter of hours, before two uniformed officers unlocked Reds's holding cell and escorted him to an interrogation room. Reds entered the room and quickly noticed the large mirror hanging on the wall. He held up his right hand and gave the mirror his middle finger, knowing there were detectives behind the glass watching his every move.

"Hey, listen, we're here to help," an officer said. "So you don't have to be so negative."

"Fucking help? You not here to help." Reds wanted to spit in the officer's face. "You muthafuckas never are."

"So, there's nothing I can get you?" the officer asked, again showing Reds pretend concern.

"How about a suitcase full of money from out the evidence room?"

"I can't do that. How 'bout something else?"

"How about you roll out the blue carpet for me so I can Crip Walk my Black ass up outta here?" Reds asked, as if that would do the trick. "Oh, yeah, a Dutch and some chronic, too, while you at it."

"Hey, Bryant, let's get him something to drink," Officer Friedling said.

"Man, look, y'all ain't gotta bullshit me. I don't want nothing from you muthafuckas—nothing. So don't try doing me no favors. Unless y'all gonna give me my phone call so I can call my lawyer, I don't want shit." Reds sounded extremely confident in his choice of words.

"You haven't been given your phone call?" Officer Friedling asked, as if he couldn't believe it.

"Man, y'all muthafuckas ain't even read me my Miranda rights. I still don't know what the fuck you even got me in here for."

"No one read you your rights? Hey, Bryant, you hear this? No one read this guy his rights."

"Fucking read 'em for what? Fuckin' niggas don't have any rights anyway. Waste my fuckin' time reading you your fuckin' rights? Fuck outta here," Officer Bryant replied with a thick, northern New Jersey accent, laughing at Reds.

"Man, fuck you!"

"That's exactly what they'll be doing to you where you're going, hotcakes. Come on, let's get the fuck out of here," Officer Bryant said to his partner.

"Sorry, I tried to help," Friedling said, following behind Bryant.

Reds looked over at the mirror hanging on the wall. "Y'all mutha-fuckas gonna have to do better than that. Fuck outta here wit' your good cop, bad cop routine. Shit ain't gonna work here, crackers. Shit ain't gonna work. Fuck fuckin' Five-O! I hate you!"

Reds continued to sit there and grouse at the mirror, cursing, sometimes shouting, sometimes simply talking, but saying nothing at all that the plainclothes detectives wanted to hear.

Rasun peered around the windowless room nervously. He kept looking over at the mirror hanging on the wall. He was being watched. He could feel the eyeballs on his Black ass as he sat there wondering when all this would be over. He wished this day had never happened. He sat still, thinking of all the things that could've kept him from being arrested today.

Damn, I should've gone over to my aunt's house with my mom like she asked me to. Then he remembered what Lieutenant Ratzinger had told him earlier. *Ain't no way they ran up in my mom's house. They must be bullshitting. Yeah, they're actually lying.*

His leg shook uncontrollably while sweat poured from his palms. His shirt was wet with perspiration around the underarms, and he fiddled with his fingers like there was no tomorrow. He knew the saying "never let them see you sweat," but he couldn't help it.

The detectives watched from behind the mirrored glass as Rasun looked as though he was about to explode.

Ratzinger was clocking Rasun's every move. "We can crack this cookie. Look at him."

Lieutenant Ratzinger walked into the room, closing the door behind himself.

"I don't want to talk to you," Rasun told him.

"Good, 'cause I don't want to talk to you, either," Ratzinger told him as he took a seat. "The captain made me come in here to see if you wanted to work a deal."

"I ain't cutting no deal with you, so you might as well stop wasting your time," Rasun said.

"You know what? You're right."

Lieutenant Ratzinger picked himself up from the table he had been sitting at across from Rasun and walked out of the room. *We'll see how you feel after twenty-four hours of sitting in that room with no food and nothing to drink.*

He walked into the room where a still-handcuffed Reds was sitting with Friedling.

"They still got the handcuffs on you, buddy."

Reds looked at Ratzinger like he was crazy. *Man, this dude is out of his fucking mind. Who the fuck is he calling buddy?*

Reds had decided he would have nothing else to say to anyone. They could send the president in this motherfucker—he wasn't saying shit.

"You know, that's a lot of crack we found today, Reds. You guys really seem to have a very organized and profitable operation out there in those streets. I bet you make a lot of money. Hey, I understand. I know exactly how you feel. If I were in your shoes, I'd probably be doing the same thing. I mean, come on, let's keep it real. Isn't that what you guys say, keep it real? Well, I don't blame you, son. I just want you to know, I think it's a damn shame you're even here. You should be home right now. Hey, as a matter of fact, you should be hustling on your block getting money right now, and you know what, Reds? I'm here to let you go do that. I only need you to answer a few questions for me."

"Hey, buddy, let me keep it real with you," Reds said, leaning toward the lieutenant.

Ratzinger's heart skipped a beat and he leaned forward to hear what Reds had to say. "Yeah, let's keep it real," Ratzinger agreed.

"Suck my dick."

"Your choice, kid. You're going to jail."

He punched Reds so hard in his mouth that Reds fell backward in the chair and rolled onto the floor.

"Suck that, you piece of shit," Ratzinger said before walking out the door behind Friedling.

Two days had passed, and they were still in the interrogation rooms. Unfortunately, Reds was requesting only food and blunts, and a television to watch BET. He would be a tough cookie to crack, and he wasn't cooperating at all.

Rasun, on the other hand, wasn't doing that good. He wasn't as slick as Reds and wasn't as sophisticated in his answering techniques. He ended up holding conversations, and that was his first mistake. The police had him handcuffed with his feet shackled. They escorted him down a long hall and into the back room of the processing unit. The police set up the stage for Rasun to see his mother being fingerprinted. The tears were dried on her face, but you could see her eyes were swollen and her heart was broken.

Ratzinger seated himself on the empty table in front of Rasun.

"Here's the deal, Rasun. Your mother's going to be charged for the drugs we found inside her house, and you're going to be charged with the drugs we found at the cleaners. Things are going to get pretty bad for your family. Your mother's facing a very long sentence. She could end up serving a forty-year sentence at a women's federal prison. And let me tell you something about these women's facilities. The lesbians outnumber the straight women ten to one. And most of those bitches are built like linebackers from the Eagles. Your mother could end up doing some very rough time."

Rasun shook his head, because he'd completely forgotten there was a quarter key of crack in the garage. He remembered hiding it there a couple of days before he was arrested because he didn't want to leave it outside in the car, in case the car got broken into. He was supposed to relocate the cocaine, but he was moving so fast, he never took it to the stash house to have it broken down and vialed up. Not to mention, he was moving so fast, handling so much product, he forgot he'd left that shit at his mom's altogether.

"Look, it doesn't have to be this way," Ratzinger told him. "There's a way to get your mom out of going to prison without you having to take her time."

Rasun looked up.

Lieutenant Ratzinger nodded. "And the best part about it is that you won't have to go to jail, either. Your mom will be released, her arrest record will be cleared, and you'll be able to go free."

"How is that?" Rasun asked.

"Well, the way things work around here is that I look out for you, and you look out for me. We keep everything on the DL. It'll be between us. You're not a bad guy, Rasun, but what I need for you to do is help me get the bad guys off the streets. You got a little brother, right?"

Rasun nodded.

"I want the streets to be safe for him," Ratzinger told him. "I want the streets to be safe for your mother, and your father, and your grandmother. We want them to be able to sit outside on their porch at night and not have to worry about some goddamn drug-related drive-by."

Rasun shook his head. "Man, I ain't down for no snitching."

"I ain't asking you to testify against anybody," Ratzinger assured him. "All I need is a little bit of information. Your man Rik, he's up right now. He took over the crew after Quadir Richards got killed, right?"

Rasun looked down.

"C'mon, Ra." Ratzinger smiled. "That is what they call you, isn't it? Ra? We already know most of this shit. We simply want to confirm the shit we already know. You ain't giving us nothing new."

Rasun shook his head.

"See, it's like this," Ratzinger continued. "Either you play ball, or we go all the way. We press full charges against your mom. And then we seize your car, your mom's car, and your family's house. You know we can do that, don't you? Since we found the drugs inside the house, that gives us the right to seize your parents' house. You want your mom in prison, and your dad and brother out on the street, all because you don't want to help us confirm some shit we already know? Are you that stupid? Do you think Rik would choose you over his mom? Do you think Rik would let his mom go to prison for forty years to save your Black ass? Rik's going to prison anyway. We're already onto him. We already have his number. Might as well save your ass, and your mother's ass, before we pick his ass up and this once-in-a-lifetime chance goes away."

Rasun shook his head.

Ratzinger patted Rasun on his back. "I'll tell your mom that you said fuck her. Rik's more important."

Ratzinger rose from the table.

"Man, this is some bullshit!" Rasun said.

"I'm walking out this fucking door," Ratzinger told him. "And when I do, the offer is off the table. If I walk out this door, that's it. Your mom *is* going to prison, you *are* going to prison, and your mom's house *is* getting taken away. Every fucking thing your parents worked for is gone! Gone! Do you fucking hear me, Ra? It's gone! All because you want to adhere to some bullshit street code no one else adheres to anymore. There's no more code of omertà! There's no more code of silence! Even the goddamn mobsters sing like fucking opera singers once we get them behind bars. Well, you stick to your fucking code of the streets, and I hope you feel like a real big man, and a wonderful fucking son, kid! Your mother . . . Aw, fuck this!"

Ratzinger turned to walk out of the room.

"Okay!" Rasun told him. "Okay, I'll do it."

Ratzinger turned and smiled. He'd figured it would take more than one session to crack this cookie. These so-called street hustlers were getting weaker with each passing year. He turned back to Rasun.

"You made the right choice, kid. If it were my mother, I would've done the same thing. Fuck Rik. Your mother raised you. She's more important than that sorry, lowlife motherfucker."

"You'll drop the charges against my mother?" Rasun asked.

Ratzinger placed his hand on Rasun's shoulder. "Kid, I'm a man of my word. Not only am I going to not press charges against your mother, but I'm not going to file the papers to seize her house. And I'm also going to suspend our case against you for right now. You do right by us, and your case will never go before a grand jury. You made the right choice, Ra. You chose freedom."

Ra looked down. He felt relieved. He didn't really fuck with Rik like that anymore, anyway. Fuck that nigga! He had to do what he had to do—that's all there was to it.

"I'm going to take care of the paperwork, and I'll be back in here to talk to you in a minute," Ratzinger told him. "I'll need you to sign some papers for me, and then I'm going to turn you loose."

"And Reds?"

"He ain't going to know shit," Ratzinger told him. "We'll run him before the magistrate, let him post bond, and then turn him loose, too. That way you'll both be back out on the street and nobody will suspect anything. Trust me, we've been doing this for a very long time."

Rasun nodded. He had jumped in bed with the devil.

Say Cheese

Gena rounded the corner in her brand-new Porsche Gemballa and hit the brakes. The black BMW was sitting parked in front of her. She couldn't see who was inside, and really, she didn't want to. She wanted to get away from there immediately. And she did.

Gena mashed her foot down on the accelerator, and the Porsche propelled itself forward like a fighter jet scrambling down a runway. The car's rapid acceleration thrust her back into the driver's seat and pinned her against it. She'd never experienced power like that before, and she was glad to have it. The black BMW was nowhere to be seen.

Jerrell peered down at his brand-new Rollie and wondered where in the hell his date was. She was supposed to meet him at the park at six, and it was now five after. He wondered if she'd stood him up, hoping desperately she hadn't. He really wanted to tap that. Baby girl had an ass you could set a cup on.

Gena rounded the corner in her new car and spotted Jay standing next to the park bench. He looked fly, real fly. She could tell the nigga had been shopping. Along with his fresh haircut, he had brand-new everything on. The sun was reflecting off his white Air Force 1s so brightly, they had to be fresh out of the box. The watch on his wrist and the piece hanging off his chain were putting out enough light to land a plane. She was glad she'd given him her number and even happier he'd called. She pulled up next to him.

Jerrell rested his hand on the passenger door of the black convertible. "What in the hell are you doing with this?"

"You like it?" Gena asked, smiling from ear to ear. "It's my new ride."

"You mean your man's new ride?"

Gena shook her head. "No, baby, this is all me."

"Yeah, right!" Jerrell laughed. "What happened to the Benz?"

"Nothing," Gena told him. "I wanted to park it for a while."

"Damn, so you balling like that, huh?" he asked with a smile.

Gena shook her head. "Not really. But I *am* starving. No, I'm famished."

"I was going to tell you to park your car and roll with me, but fuck that. I'm rollin' with you."

Jerrell opened the door and climbed into the passenger seat.

"So, where are we headed?" Gena asked, pulling off into traffic.

"Any place you want to go, ma," he said with a wide grin. "Tonight is your night."

"Oh, really?" Gena asked, lifting an eyebrow. "So, you going to spoil me tonight, huh?"

"The world is yours, ma," Jerrell told her. "The world is yours."

Jerrell turned and peered out the window. She'd bought a custom Porsche, easily worth over a hundred grand, and yet she claimed she didn't have a man. *What is wrong with this picture?* Jerrell wondered. Her wrists, neck, and fingers were blinging more than his. He sat in the passenger seat adding up her wrist and fingers. *She holdin' more than me. Who the fuck is this broad?* He needed more information. Hell, he needed a picture. And he knew how to get one.

"Hey, I got a taste for something Italian, baby," he told her. "Let's go to the Spaghetti Warehouse."

Gena nodded. Spaghetti Warehouse was all right. Not too expensive, but pretty good. She shifted gears, turned the corner, and headed in the direction of Spring Garden Street. *Could he be my new man of life? One never knows, does one?* she pondered as she smiled over at him.

"So, what do you do for a living?" Jerrell asked her.

"I'm kinda in between jobs right now," Gena told him.

Jerrell nodded. "Oh."

Maybe she sells real estate or maybe she's one of them hoes that sell cosmetics and shit. Naw, that shit don't pay. She don't look like a salesperson, and besides, the only kind of job she might have, driving some shit like this, is a lawyer or a doctor and she ain't neither.

"So, what do you do when you're not in between jobs?" Jerrell asked.

Gena shook her head. "I want to relax tonight. I don't want to talk about work."

Jerrell nodded.

Mm-hmm, she don't want to talk about work. I bet she don't. She can't be in the game. I know all the majors in this town. So, who the fuck is she? A police bitch, maybe? Naw, she was too scared about being followed. Maybe she was pretending or maybe she's fucking a real live nigga. Either way, it can only be one of the two. It's got to be one or the other. And I'm going to find out.

Jerrell crossed his arms, leaned back into the seat, and kicked the question of Gena's identity around in his head until they arrived at their destination.

The Spaghetti Warehouse was a quiet, romantic Italian restaurant nestled in downtown Philly. It was a casual place, with a bar to the left as you walked through the doors. Imported Italian travertine marble covered the floors. The restaurant resembled an old Tuscan village, with hand-plastered walls, Etruscan vases, stone columns, and wrought-iron artwork throughout. There was even an old-time trolley car in the middle of the dining room floor. Dim wall lighting was augmented by soft paper-covered candles on the dining tables. Modern Impressionist artwork graced the beige plaster-covered walls, while white-jacketed waiters and sommeliers fanned out throughout the restaurant, providing the guests with impeccable service.

Gena and Jerrell were seated in the rear corner of the establishment, where they were ensured their privacy.

"What may I get you to drink?" the waiter asked.

"A bottle of Pinot Grigio," Jerrell said.

"Very good, sir," the waiter told him while writing down his order.

Gena closed her menu. "I already know what I want."

"Oh, then I guess we're ready to order," Jerrell told the waiter.

The waiter opened his tiny notepad again. "Very good. And what will you be having tonight, madam?"

"I want the chicken parmesan with a side order of fettucine alfredo and I'll start with a Caesar salad," Gena told him.

"And I'll take the same," Jerrell told him.

"Very well." The waiter bowed slightly and headed off toward the kitchen.

"So, what do you do when you're not saving girls who are being followed?" Gena asked.

Jerrell smiled. "I thought we weren't gonna talk about work. I was kinda looking forward to enjoying a stress-free, work-free evening with a beautiful woman."

Gena blushed. "So what do you know about my restaurant?"

"What?" Jerrell asked. "You mean the Spaghetti Warehouse?"

Gena nodded.

"I eat here all the time," Jerrell told her. "The calzones are the bomb!"

Gena nodded emphatically. "I know! They stuff theirs with pepperoni and at least four different kinds of cheese! I love those things!"

Jerrell leaned back in his seat. "Wow! A woman who appreciates good food! You're a woman after my heart, ma!"

Gena laughed. "I love good food! Especially Italian!"

"So, tell me this, Ms. Gena," Jerrell said. "How is it that a fine-ass woman like you don't have a man?"

Gena lowered her head for a moment and thought of Quadir. It still hurt deeply. She peered back up at Jerrell. "I don't know why. I guess I just don't."

Jerrell reached out and clasped her hand. He turned it over and examined her ring by the light of the candle. "That's some rock, ma. Big enough to choke a damn horse."

Gena laughed. She nodded toward the diamond-filled charm hanging at the end of his diamond-filled chain. "You're not doing too bad yourself."

Jerrell smiled. He peered up in time to see the restaurant girl with the camera passing nearby. He raised his hand and snapped his fingers loudly.

The camera girl turned in his direction.

"Yo, can we get our picture taken over here?" Jerrell asked.

The camera girl smiled and headed toward him.

"You want to get closer," she ordered, holding up her camera.

Jerrell scooted his chair next to Gena's and put his arm around her.

"Say cheese, baby girl," he told her.

Gena smiled for the camera, and the flash erupted.

"Another one," Jerrell ordered. He rose and walked to the other side of Gena, where he knelt next to her. "Get my good side this time."

Gena laughed, and the camera girl snapped the second photo.

The camera was a Polaroid, and the photos were instant. The camera girl set the pictures on the table, and Jerrell handed her a twenty-dollar bill.

"Keep the change," Jerrell told her. The camera girl smiled and headed for another table. Jerrell lifted the photos off the table and examined them. He now had two clear pictures of Gena, from two different angles. It was the best twenty dollars he'd ever spent.

If Gena wanted to play Miss Mysterious, that would be fine with him. He had other ways of finding out what he wanted to know. He would pass the photos on to his man on the streets and have this bitch's entire history within a day. He would know every nigga she'd fucked, all the way back to kindergarten, if she was giving it up back then. He would have birthdays, parents' names, brothers, sisters, cousins, and practically the entire family's history. He was Jerrell Motherfucking Jackson, and he didn't get where he was by not knowing how to dig up shit. This simple bitch was way out of her league if she was thinking otherwise.

Jerrell lifted the bottle of Pinot from the table and poured some into each of their wineglasses. He handed Gena her glass and lifted his own into the air.

"To new friends, and to making new memories," he told her.

Gena clinked her glass against his. "To new memories."

New memories were something she could desperately use. All her old ones were too painful to bear. She had loved Quadir with all her heart. She had made that man her life. And now that he was gone, she knew, despite the pain in her heart, she had to move on. She had found another gentleman—another kind, sweet, protective gentleman—who was promising her a second chance. She couldn't believe it, but it was as if God was giving her a second man of life, because He had to take the first one away. She wanted this to work out. She wanted to be in love again. She wanted to share all she had with someone again. She was convinced Jay was the one to do it with.

Gena drank up, then lifted her glass into the air again. "To happiness, and laughter, and smiles. May they forever be a part of our lives."

"Hear, hear," Jerrell told her. "I couldn't have said it better myself."

Jerrell poured more wine into Gena's glass. He wanted her to drink up. He wanted her tongue to become loose. He wanted her to slip and say things she normally wouldn't say when she was sober.

And even if that didn't happen, he really couldn't care less. He'd find out who she was soon enough. He'd find out what she did for a living, where she was from, who her people were, and every damn thing else.

Jerrell placed the photos beneath the candlelight once more and examined them briefly before tucking them safely away in his pocket. He didn't want to forget them, and he damn sure didn't want to lose them. They could be his tickets to a brand-new life. They could be his tickets to the jack of the century. They could be his winning lottery tickets.

Wired

The van was disguised as a FedEx delivery truck, with all the corporation's authentic logos. An officer disguised as a FedEx deliveryman even climbed out every once in a while and made actual FedEx deliveries to the businesses located on the block. The Philadelphia Police Department had spent millions of dollars on this super-high-tech observation post on wheels.

Detective Letoya Ellington sat at the communications console with her headphones on, listening as the van's digital recording equipment captured everything their wired confidential informant transmitted back to the van. They were getting some great information and had already gathered enough evidence to round up several of the smaller players engaged in the city's nefarious drug trade. But now they were gathering information on a big fish.

"So, what price did that nigga Rik say we can have them thangs for next week?" Rasun asked.

"The nigga said he was going to give us a good deal," Reds answered. "If not, I hollered at that boy Blair the other day. That nigga got a new connect, and he says he can help spread the wealth."

Inside the van, Detective Ellington took notes furiously. She was writing down all the names Reds and Rasun were mentioning. The more Rasun talked, the more people they'd be able to target for investigation. The more people they were able to target, the more people they'd be able to gather evidence on. The more people they were able to gather evidence on, the more people they'd be able to present to the grand jury for the issuance of indictments, and the more people they indicted, the greater the chances of convicting a larger number of scumbags. The more people they convicted, the better her chances were of making lieutenant. It was all a numbers game.

So far, Rasun had given them information on twenty-three people, and through his conversations with others, they now had the names of more than seventy-three drug dealers. They knew stash spots, meeting places, distribution locations, and even the names of some of the East Coast's biggest suppliers. They had names the DEA only wished they knew about. Names they would give the DEA to earn brownie points, under the guise of interagency cooperation. Rasun had been a gold mine.

"So, where's all the shit we copped yesterday?" Rasun asked.

"Man, all that shit is at the spot," Reds answered. He was becoming annoyed with Rasun's constant questioning. "We gonna do this shit like we do it every week. I already called Ms. Shoog, and she said she can cook shit up for us tomorrow."

Rasun laughed and shook his head. "Old Ms. Shoog! She's gangsta, ain't she? Damn, how long has Shoog been cooking this shit up for us?"

Reds laughed. "Yeah, Ms. Shoog is something. That old lady think she got mad game, don't she?"

"She probably cook for half the niggas in Philly," Rasun said.

"That old lady probably been doing this shit her whole life. I know that she done cooked up more than a thousand keys for you. And probably about ten thousand keys for my nigga Qua!" Reds added.

Detective Ellington wrote down Ms. Shoog's name and typed it into her computer. A name, an address, and a criminal record popped up instantly. Ms. Shoog would have a nice, fat indictment once this was all over.

"Sorry, grandma." Detective Ellington exhaled. "But they got a place just for you. It's called a federal penitentiary."

This conspiracy case they were building was going to be picked up by the Feds. And if Ms. Shoog had cooked as much cocaine as had been alleged in the wire communications, she was going to go away for a real long time. So long, she'd probably spend the rest of her life in prison.

Rasun tossed Reds a beer and walked to his Benz, where he turned up the stereo system. He cut it up just enough to hear the music, but not enough for it to interfere with the wire he had taped to his chest. He walked back to Reds's BMW and seated himself on the hood.

"So, Reds, on the real. What do you think the boy Rik is moving now?" Rasun asked.

Reds shrugged his shoulders. "Probably more than Qua was. Remember, that nigga got his own shit, plus he got all of Quadir's shit."

"And that nigga don't even break bread with us like that. Nigga balling like that, you'd think we could get some better prices out of his tight ass."

Reds shrugged again. "Rik's ass is tighter than a KKK hanging rope. Just be happy he ain't asked us about our side hustle we got going on. I'm surprised that nigga ain't figure our shit out by now. I guess since that nigga's getting all that money, he must be preoc-cupied."

Rasun sipped at his beer, then peered over at Reds. "You think he know?"

Reds smacked his lips. "The nigga ain't stupid. He know we done came up. He see the cars and shit."

Rasun nodded. "What you think that nigga Amin doing?"

Reds lifted an eyebrow. "Doing? Doing like what?"

"You think that nigga pushing more than us?" Rasun asked.

Reds shrugged. "How the fuck would I know? And why would I give a shit?"

Rasun nodded and sipped at his beer. "Anybody talked to Kenny?"

"Amar and Wiz went and visited that nigga the other day," Reds answered. "They got Kenny up CFCF still waiting on his trial. Man, they say that nigga's twisted in that joint."

"That's fucked up. You think he'll be all right?" Rasun asked.

"Kenny's not really the type of nigga who can do time. He ain't built for that shit, you know?" he said, looking at Rasun, wondering if Rasun realized he wasn't that type of nigga, either.

"Yeah, I know what you mean. You think he needs some bread or something?"

"What nigga don't? But if the nigga done lost his fucking marbles like they saying, I wouldn't send too much at one time. Just enough to hold that nigga down for a quick commissary minute. I told y'all that nigga wasn't wrapped too tight. He never was."

"Damn, that shit's fucked up," Rasun said again, lowering his head.

"I hope that that nigga don't start talking," Reds told him.

"Talking?" Rasun quickly shifted his gaze to Reds. "What do you mean?"

"I hope that fool don't start snitching and shit!" Reds told him.

"You think he would?" Rasun asked nervously.

Reds shook his head. "Man, you never know these days. Hell, the nigga right next to you could be in bed with them folks."

Rasun swallowed hard and took a long swig from his beer bottle.

Detective Dick Davis climbed into the back of the FedEx truck and removed his FedEx baseball cap.

"Whew, it's hotter than a witch's tit out there!" he declared.

Detective Ellington laughed and removed her headphones. She turned toward her colleague. "And you think it's better in here?"

"Hey, you don't have to carry packages up and down the street, sweetie," Detective Davis protested. "Any time you want to switch, let me know."

"Dick..."

"What?"

"Stop complaining like a little bitch," Detective Ellington told him.

The two detectives shared a laugh.

"So, are we getting anything good?" Detective Davis asked.

"Are you kidding me?" Detective Ellington replied with a smile. She lifted her notepad filled with names, dates, amounts, and various other information. "This kid's a gold mine! Christ, where the hell did we get him from?"

Detective Davis took the long, yellow notepad and examined it. He smiled. "The kid's telling on everybody but his mother."

"Give him time," Detective Ellington replied. "He'll probably give her up, too."

Again, the detectives shared a laugh.

"So, how are we looking?" Detective Davis asked. "I mean, as far as the grand jury is concerned?"

Detective Ellington shook her head. "Rock fucking solid. I talked to the lieutenant. We're processing this shit tonight and getting as much as we can over to the grand jury tomorrow."

Detective Davis whistled. "Damn, that fast?"

"Baby, we're trying to have the indictments out by tomorrow evening," Detective Ellington told him.

Detective Davis lifted an eyebrow. "Tomorrow evening?"

Detective Ellington nodded. "Tomorrow evening. It's going down tomorrow. So you can get ready for some overtime tomorrow night, baby."

Detective Davis tossed the notepad back onto the console. "The big roundup."

Detective Ellington nodded and placed the earphones back over her ears. "We're going to try to hit as many as we can at once."

Detective Davis whistled. "A lot of manpower."

Detective Ellington nodded again. "We're going in with the Feds, the county, and just about everybody else. The Feds have some of the local guard on standby, in case we need more manpower. I think they're army."

Detective Davis wiped his sweaty brow and rose from his seat. He placed his FedEx baseball cap back on his head and grabbed some packages from the floor of the truck.

"Guess I better get back out there," he said, smiling at his fellow detective.

"Just another hour," Detective Ellington told him. "John and Rick are coming on duty posing as a utility repair crew. They'll be taking over surveillance then."

Detective Davis nodded. "I'll be glad when this shit is over with."

Detective Ellington smiled and waved goodbye to her male partner. "Tomorrow, baby. Tomorrow, we'll be handing out indictments like Halloween candy."

"Trick or treat, motherfuckers!" Detective Davis said, laughing. He climbed out of the back of the FedEx truck and slammed the door behind him.

Tomorrow would be the big roundup. Tomorrow they'd be taking a big chunk of Philadelphia's midlevel dealers off the streets. Tomorrow night, the jails would be full, and so would their evidence lockers, and the price of cocaine on the streets would be sky-fucking-high. But the best thing of all was that tomorrow they'd be getting hundreds of dope-dealing sons of bitches off the streets.

Gena's Sake

Gena seated herself at the breakfast table and unfolded the newspaper.

"Any good sales in there?" Gah Git asked. She washed her coffee cup out and placed it in the dishwasher. "Child, I sure do appreciate this new dishwasher you bought me. I ain't never had nothing like this, all new and fancy. I can't believe this thing really cleans dishes."

Gena smiled and shook her head. "I'm glad you like it. I got some more stuff for you, too."

"What?"

"Yeah, just wait, you'll see. I'm gonna take good care of you, don't you worry."

Gah Git exhaled, wiped her hands on her apron, and turned toward Gena. "Now, don't you go starting on me about no moving again. Girl, I done told you; I've lived here damn near my whole life. Ain't nothing wrong with living here. People just need to take care of they kids and work out they problems and be a family to one another. A few ass whoopings and this place would be back to the way it was."

Gena laughed at her grandmother. "Gah Git, a few ass whoopings ain't gonna solve nothing. Richard Allen is the worst project in Philly. At least let me get you a nice apartment in a decent neighborhood, since you won't let me buy you a house."

"Buy me a house?" Gah Git asked, placing her hand on her hip. "With what, Gena? Baby, you save your money. You done bought me enough already. A new refrigerator, a new stove, a new dishwasher, and all those fancy new clothes I ain't gonna never get to wear!"

"Yes, you will. We got places to go and things to do. And for the life of me, why do you want us to have to live in these godforsaken projects? Gah Git, it's not safe. They always shooting at each other, and they killing people over here. I don't like it here no more. I used to feel safe. but now it's changing. Ask Gary—he's in the streets. He'll tell you the same thing," Gena said, trying to convince her grandmother of the truth.

"Look, Gena, I'm used to it. I done lived here all my life. I don't want to go, that's all. Now leave me alone."

"Man, Gah Git, I don't even sleep with all the sirens and guns poppin' off, and I'm scared to walk to the store. See, you always sending us. But that's not right. You go on out there and see if you like walking down the street. Shoot, I bet you'll be ready to move then."

"Now, Gena, you can't be scared of your own people, baby," Gah Git told her. "You can't never do that, you hear me? That's what got us into this predicament in the first place. Black folks not trusting other Black folks and we separated. You hear me?"

"Gah Git, Black folks can't trust Black folks 'cause white folks got all the money. If Black folks had all the money like white folks, there wouldn't be no issues and Black folks would be all right."

"This may be true, but the white man ain't giving up nothing, so Black folks need to stick together. You youngins sure got a long hard road to travel."

"Yes, ma'am, that road is mighty rough, too," Gena joked. "But still, why we got to be in Rich—"

"Ain't no but still," Gah Git said, dismissing her with a wave of her hand. "I'm gon' stay right here, right here where I'm at. I don't even know why I'm wastin' time talking this long. This is where I raised all my kids, Gena, and all my grandkids. It's what I know. Shoot, I done raised a whole lot of other folks' kids. Gah Git is just fine right where she is."

Gena exhaled and shook her head.

Gah Git turned back toward where her dishwasher was waiting for her. "Gena, don't you go and get no big head now, just 'cause you done got a good job and all."

"I'm not, Gah Git," Gena protested. "It's just that I'm worried about you."

"What are you worried about me for?" Gah Git asked. "You thinking about getting outta here and moving in with that new boyfriend of yours? Don'tcha do it. Don't you even think about it. Every time you date a man, you got to go live with 'em. I don't understand it."

"No, no, I'm not ever doing that no more. Besides, I don't want to live with Jay. Dag, I remember when Jamal threw me out and had my clothes all in the street. Gah Git, it was a mess. You don't know what I go through, and then Quadir, with that house we had . . ." She stopped and looked off to the side. "But I am thinking about getting something somewhere nice. I wish you'd come with me."

"All right now, sugar pie. That's what I'm talking about, girl. God bless the child who's got his own," Gah Git said, scrubbing dishes and placing them into the dishwasher. "Didn't I tell you a man will never buy the cow if he can get the milk for free?"

"Uh, yeah, I think you have." Gena laughed at Gah Git, who was as serious as serious could be. Gah Git had told her that line a million times now. "Hey, Gah Git, ain't no milking going on here."

"'Bout time, 'cause I sure do hope so. Them gypsy-ass cousins of yours is gone." Gah Git turned toward her. "You should talk to 'em."

Gena lifted an eyebrow. "Who? Brianna and Bria? You think they're sexually active, Gah Git?"

"Sexually active?" Gah Git placed the bowl she was washing into the dishwasher and then placed her hand on her hip. "Girl, *sexually active* ain't the word. Them girls is passing out tail like it's government cheese."

Gena spat out her milk. "Gah Git!"

"What? You think I don't know what's going on around here?" Gah Git asked.

Wow, Gena couldn't help but think to herself. She really wasn't minding them like that, dealing with the loss of Quadir and moving back home. Gena shook her head. "No, I know you know everything that's going on within a fifty-block radius. But still . . ."

"But still, nothing, you should try to talk to them about it. They keep telling me I'm too old and I don't understand. Brianna told me, 'Oh, Gah Git, it's just sex.' They not giving me no heart attack. So, I done told them girls not to be messing around and if that's what they gonna do, then God help 'em and use a condom and protect theyself. They said I'm too old to know. I know more than them."

Gah Git turned back toward her dishes. She didn't want to talk about them anymore. Bria and Brianna had hurt her feelings, but more importantly, the young girls had shut her out because she was older, not knowing Gah Git had answers to help guide them. But Gah Git couldn't talk to them, just couldn't reach them.

"So, what's the deal with this new man, and when can I meet him?" she asked Gena.

"Meet him?" Gena replied, surprised. "You want to meet him?"

"I want to meet the man who got you out of your frumpy, frowning ways," Gah Git told her. "Baby, it's good to see you smiling again. It's so good to see you living again," she said gently, holding Gena's cheeks in her hands. "You loved Quadir, but he's gone now. And he'd want you to be happy."

Gena smiled and lowered her head. She didn't know if she was ready to have this conversation with Gah Git. She still wasn't sure if she was ready to begin letting go.

"We still here, baby," Gah Git continued. "And we got to keep on living and keep on loving. We got to live life for those we love. We got to do things they can't do no more. We got to live life for them, too."

Gah Git wiped her hands on her apron, stopped what she was doing, and sat down at the table with Gena. "I need to talk to you about something."

"Why you looking so serious?" Gena asked, smiling at her grandmother.

Gah Git didn't know where to begin. She didn't know where to start. How do you tell somebody that her father might not be her father? She picked up a napkin and began ruffling it through her fingers. Just when she was about to begin, Bria stormed into the house, letting Gena's cat, Gucci, in with her.

Gah Git quickly stood up from the table. "Mm-hmm, I'm not sure what to say out my mouth. If it ain't Miss Five O'Clock in the Morning! You came up in this house at five o'clock in the morning and somehow you got out of here before I could get a hold of you this morning. You know damn well you supposed to have your butt in this house by ten o'clock! Where was you at?"

"Please, Gah Git, please don't ask me questions like that. I was over Dalvin's house and I fell asleep. What's the big deal?" Bria responded as she waved her hand in the air at her grandmother.

"Who you think you talking to like that?" Gah Git wiped her hands on her apron, ready to smack the shit out of Bria. "Young lady, we have rules in this house. And you *will* obey those rules."

"Fuck rules," Bria whispered under her breath as she huffed herself upstairs.

"Excuse me?" Gena asked. "What did you say?"

"I wasn't even talking to you," Bria told her. "So mind your business."

"You're so disrespectful. It's my business if you disrespecting Gah Git!" Gena snapped back.

"No, it ain't none of yo' business, if I'm not talking to you!" Bria shouted, shaking her head. "You ain't my mama, Gena! And you need to stop acting like it!"

"I know I ain't your mama. Your mama is on crack right now. That's why you live here. So, you need to show some respect."

"Whatever! Your mama's dead 'cause your daddy killed her! Now!"

Bria rolled her eyes at Gena and continued upstairs.

"Bria!" Gah Git yelled. "What the hell is wrong with you? Come back down here! Come back down here right now, 'cause if I got to come up them steps to get you, so help me God, I might hurt you, girl!"

As she walked back down the stairs, Bria thought about what she had said, and in her heart of hearts, she knew she had crossed the line. Even if she and Gena never did get along, that was still no reason for her to say what she had said. She didn't realize it, but Bria had unleashed the biggest family secret, and Gah Git had reached her boiling point. She slapped Bria across the face harder than she'd ever hit anything in her life, spinning Bria around and knocking her into the wall before she fell to the floor.

Bria looked up at her grandmother and then over to Gena, who seemed to not have heard her.

"What did you say?" Gena asked, looking confused.

"Nothing, baby, she ain't say nothing. Bria, go upstairs in your room and you stay there until I tell you different, you hear me?" Gah Git told her, squeezing her arm.

"Mm-hmm."

Gah Git squeezed her arm harder. "I can't hear you. What you say?"

"Yes, ma'am."

"That's what I thought you said." Gah Git was still squeezing her arm as she led Bria over to the staircase. "I wasn't sure. I had to make sure I was hearing you. I'll deal with you later. You hear me? I'ma deal with you, though. You got some nerve, honey, some nerve. But I *will* deal with you. If it kills me, you gonna learn to respect me and this house."

Just then Brianna flung open the door and walked in from school. "Dag, what's going on in here?"

Gah Git didn't know what to say. She looked at Gena, who seemed confused and unsure of what she'd heard.

"Gena, you all right?" Brianna asked before hugging her grandmother.

"Yeah, she all right. Go on upstairs and give me a few minutes with your cousin."

Gah Git pushed Brianna over to the staircase.

"Okay, wait . . . hold up." Brianna was trying to avoid being pushed away. "Gah Git, can I get some juice?"

"No! Juice ain't no good for you; it's loaded with sugar. Go on upstairs like I said . . . now."

"Dag, okay. Let me get my book bag, Gah Git."

Gah Git continued to push Brianna.

"Gah Git, okay, I'm going on upstairs. You squeezing my arm, Gah Git. I didn't even do nothing." Brianna struggled to get free. "Dag, Gah Git, why you hurting me? I didn't do nothing," she protested, not wanting to go upstairs but running out of reasons to procrastinate.

Brianna folded her arms and smacked her lips at Gah Git. "Okay, I'll see y'all later, since I'm being forced to go upstairs."

"Bye! Good riddance! Go!" Gah Git turned and walked over to Gena, not sure what to say. "Hey, see, I was trying to talk to you, but Bria came in and I forgot what I was about to say."

Gena looked like she'd been hit in the back of her head with a softball. "I got to go."

She ran upstairs to her room and began to pack a carry-on bag.

Gah Git followed Gena through the house, landing in her doorway. "Go where?"

"I don't know, Gah Git, just away from here. Just to myself. Please let me be."

"Aww, baby, don't be that way. I love you."

"Love has nothing to do with my mother not being here."

Gena looked at her grandmother with eyes of ice. Gah Git said no more after she gave her that look, and silence grew thick in the air as she stood back and watched Gena rush past her and down the stairs. She heard the front door slam closed. She should've told Gena the truth a long time ago. She'd raised Gena to live a lie. Even though it was a lie to protect her, all in all, it was still a lie.

She walked into her room and sat on the edge of her bed. Gah Git looked over to her tabletop at the various pictures of her children and her husband. So many memories. Some were good and some were bad. She picked up the phone and dialed her youngest son, Michael. It was time to tell the truth and time for Michael to come back home. She would have him come home right away—if for nothing else, for the sake of Gena.

Another Day in the Trenches

Mont rode his Suzuki GSX 1300R Hayabusa to his brother's bike shop. The bike was brand-new to the market, and not many of them were out on the streets yet. It was the latest toy, his pride and joy, and he had already spent more than fifteen thousand dollars in modifications on it.

The Hayabusa had been painted money green, with hundred-dollar bills painted all over the bike. The frame had been chromed, as had all the bike's other metal parts. The bike had been modified with a rear extended swing arm that had been chromed out, along with a rear fat-boy rim and tire. The bike's engine had been juiced up with a newly installed power commander, a Garrett turbocharger, and a nitrous system. It was, without a doubt, the fastest street bike in all of Philly. And because of its custom paint job and custom hand-painted graphics and artwork, it was also the nicest.

Mont pulled the bike up to the garage door and climbed off it. He strode over to the garage, bent, and unlocked the massive steel sliding doors. He was fortunate to have an older brother with his own garage. It had been him and his brother who did all the bike's conversions and modifications. Today, there was some tweaking he had to do before heading to the racetrack to embarrass all of them fools on their Ninjas and Yamahas.

Mont climbed back onto his motorcycle and pulled into the garage. The door closed behind him.

Mont turned back toward the door and quickly climbed off his bike. A dark figure emerged from the shadows. "What the fuck? Jerrell!"

Jerrell smiled. "Who'd you think it was? The tooth fairy?"

"What the fuck are you doing here?" Mont asked, surprised. "How in the fuck did you get into the garage?"

"Ancient Chinese secret," Jerrell told him.

Mont's eyes shifted toward the object Jerrell held in his hand. "Damn, homie! What's up with the pistol?"

"This?" Jerrell held the black Glock up and examined it. "This is for you."

"For me?" Mont asked nervously. "Why for me? Why you drawin', homie?"

"This is a present for you," Jerrell told him. "I want to show you how much I appreciate everything you did for me while I was locked up."

Mont swallowed hard. "What . . . what are you talking about?"

"Here." Jerrell tossed Mont the gun.

Mont caught the pistol. "Man, what are you doing?"

Jerrell pulled his shirt over his head. "Here, you want my shirt? You can have the shirt off my back, Mont." He tossed the shirt to Mont.

Mont caught Jerrell's shirt and held it up. "J, man . . . what are you doing? What are you tripping on?"

"I'm not tripping," Jerrell explained. "I'm showing you how much love I have for you. I'm showing how down I am for my niggas."

"We down for you too, J. Junior Mafia forever," Mont replied.

"Oh, yeah?" Jerrell asked. He slowly walked around a metal oil drum with a wrench sitting on top. "Y'all down for me, huh?"

Mont nodded. "Yeah."

"So where's my fucking money, then, Mont?" Jerrell shouted. He lifted the wrench off the drum and threw it at Mont.

"J!" Mont shouted, dodging the wrench. "What the fuck, man?"

"Where's my fucking money, nigga!" Jerrell asked again.

Mont lifted his hands in a calming motion. "J, I got you! Just calm down! I gotcha, baby!"

Jerrell seated himself on the oil drum. "Then where is it?"

"I got it close by," Mont explained. "We can go and get it before I go to the track."

"You sure about that?" Jerrell asked with a smile. He waved his hand around the garage. "Are you sure you didn't spend it helping your brother get all this?"

Mont swallowed hard and nodded. "Okay. I did go in with my brother on this shop, Jerrell. But I still got some of your money. I didn't use it all. I needed to borrow some of it to get this place started. But I can give you what I got, and then I can make payments on the rest. This shop thing is sweet, J! We gonna be making big bucks in here soon."

"So I gotta wait for my money 'cause you wanna open up a motor-cycle shop?" Jerrell asked. "I gotta wait for my dreams so you can take my money and follow yours?"

Mont shifted his gaze to the ground.

Jerrell rose from the rusty old oil drum. "What were the rules, Mont? What were the rules about my money?"

Mont lifted his hands again. "J, I . . ."

"I get mines first, and then you can go and spend your shit on whatever you want to!" Jerrell shouted. "You don't go shopping with my shit! You don't buy nothing without paying me first!"

"J, you were locked up!" Mont shouted. "I figured I could hit this quick lick, pay you back, and then we would both be cool."

"Why didn't you ask me if you could do that?" Jerrell asked. "Oh, that's right. You couldn't ask me because you never came to see me. How much money did you say you sent me when I was locked up?"

Mont shook his head.

"And yet you want to borrow my money without asking and use it to come up?" Jerrell shook his head. "That's a violation of the rules, Mont."

"I'm sorry, J." Mont lifted his shoulders and turned his hands up. "What do you want me to say?"

Jerrell shook his head. "There's nothing left for us to say."

"Just calm down, Jay," Mont said nervously, realizing how shit was about to go down.

Jerrell began walking toward Mont.

"Go on with that bullshit, Jerrell," Mont told him nervously. He lifted the weapon Jerrell had tossed him. "Stay back, nigga!"

Jerrell laughed and continued his slow walk toward Mont. Mont squeezed the trigger on the Glock, and the weapon clicked. He quickly pulled back the slide, released it, and then pulled the trigger again. Nothing happened.

"Nigga, I gave you that gun," Jerrell told him. "Do you think I'm going to give you a loaded gun to kill me with? Nigga, even I ain't that crazy."

"Man, J, quit tripping!" Mont told him.

"Quit tripping? Nigga, you just tried to do me in!" Jerrell told him. He pulled another weapon from the small of his back and aimed carefully at Mont's right knee.

"No!" Mont shouted.

Jerrell squeezed the trigger, and his weapon popped. Mont fell to the ground, screaming and holding his knee. Jerrell climbed on top of Mont's motorcycle, turned the ignition, and started the bike up.

"What the fuck are you doing, man?" Mont screamed.

Jerrell carefully maneuvered the bike around the garage until he was in front of Mont. He raced the engine and propelled the bike forward, riding it over his victim.

"*Aaaaargh!*" Mont screamed like a wounded animal.

Jerrell positioned the rear tire of the motorcycle on top of Mont's chest, and then revved the engine as high as it could possibly go. Once he had the rims on the ramps and the motor at nine thousand, he released the clutch, allowing the bike to catch first gear. The rear tire spun with the ferocity of a Category 5 hurricane, shredding skin, tearing flesh, and sending blood and tissue flying through the garage. Mont was dead before the 440-pound bike peeled the meat off his face.

Detective Letoya Ellington stood in the rain, waiting for her charge to show up. He was late, and it pissed her off more than anything else in the world would, for a lowlife drug dealer to keep her waiting. As if what they did was so much more important than what she did. Who the fuck were they to keep her waiting? She could see the asshole making his way toward her now.

Rasun approached the detective with a smile on his face. It would be the first time they'd met alone. He was glad she'd been put in charge of his case. For one, she was a sister. And two, she was fine as hell. The thought of getting into Detective Ellington's panties had crossed his mind more than once. He wondered how tight police pussy would be, with their uptight asses.

"What the fuck are you smiling at?" Detective Ellington asked.

"You," Rasun told her.

"Maybe you got things twisted," Detective Ellington told him. She kicked Rasun in his nuts, causing him to grab his genitals and buckle. She then slammed him against a nearby brick wall. "Let me make this shit clear to you. You're a lowlife fucking drug dealer. And even worse, you're a lowlife snitching bitch. You couldn't even stand up and do the time for the crime. So you're lower than low. You're lower than maggot shit, so don't you ever keep me waiting again. You hear me?"

Rasun nodded.

"Good. Now that we got that shit straight, we can get down to business," Detective Ellington told him. "We need to get Reds on the scene with the drugs. And we need to get him on tape turning the cocaine into crack."

Rasun turned toward the detective. "You want me to wear another wire?"

"*We* want you to wear another wire," Detective Ellington confirmed. "You got a problem with that? I mean, if it's a problem, we can let the prosecutors know you don't want to cooperate with us, and you want to go ahead and go to prison for a long fucking time!"

Rasun shook his head. The deal was getting worse and worse each time he saw them. They were supposed to be cops, but they rolled like the mob.

"When is Reds going to Ms. Shoog's to cook up his stuff?" Detective Ellington asked.

"Tomorrow," Rasun told her. "Damn, did you have to kick me in the nuts?"

"I started to shoot you in them, so be happy," Detective Ellington told him. "So, he's cooking tomorrow. Damn, that means I have to stop the raids tonight. Shit!"

"Can I go now?" Rasun asked, still rubbing his sore privates.

"Yeah. Meet us at the deli again in the morning. The same place we wired you up before. And don't be late. The other detective won't be as friendly as me."

Rasun nodded. "Good to know."

He turned and headed out of the alley and down the block. The rain began to pour even harder. He had betrayed his friends and allowed the man to get his hooks inside him. As part of the deal, he had to give a confession of guilt, on tape, and then sign it in front of a notary. They had him. And if he tried to run, they'd catch him and give him thirty years. Or even worse, they'd go after his moms again.

He was trapped in a cage filled with lying, cheating, lowlife hyenas with badges. And they were slowly draining the life out of him with each of their sinister bites. But what was killing him even more was his betrayal of his friends. Tomorrow, he was going to wear a wire. And that wire was not only going to entrap Ms. Shoog, but was also going to help the cops solidify their case against his best friend. Tomorrow, he was going to betray someone he considered a brother. He was going to betray Reds.

Watch Sayin'

asun walked to the window and peered out. He seemed visibly nervous, but no one paid him any mind. He wondered if the police were going to raid the cooking house while they were inside it. *Would Reds shoot? Would he run? Would Ms. Shoog survive a drug raid? What about a hefty prison sentence? Could Ms. Shoog do time? And what about the cops? How would they come in? Would they run in with guns blazing? Would they toss in a stun grenade, blowing out everyone's eardrums?*

"Goddamn. Shoog, what the fuck is that smell?" Reds asked.

Ms. Shoog shook her head sadly. "Child, my washing machine is gone out, baby."

"Damn!" Pookey said, waving his hands around. "That shit smells foul!"

"Can we get a window open in here?" Dontae asked.

"Yeah, why not open up all the doors, too!" Amar said sarcastically. "We ain't doing nothing but cooking up some coke!"

Ms. Shoog shuffled across the floor to her laundry room and opened the door, allowing the smell of spoiled clothing to waft into the room. Amar, Reds, Rasun, Dontae, and Pookey all raced for the closest windows.

"Sorry, but y'all better get used to the smell," Ms. Shoog told them. "Maybe if y'all pay me this time, I can go ahead and get a new one."

Reds took his shirt off and tied it around his mouth. "Goddamn, Shoog! Okay, a nigga will handle that shit!"

"For real!" Amar told her. He reached into his pocket, peeled off a couple hundred-dollar bills, and handed them to her.

"Here!" Rasun handed her two hundred-dollar bills as well.

Reds reached into his pocket and pulled out a thick wad of money. He pulled off three hundred-dollar bills and handed them to her. "Here, get that shit taken care of with the quickness."

Shoog turned toward Pookey and stared at him sadly. "Washing machines is just so damn expensive these days."

Pookey shook his head and pulled out a fat wad. He pulled off three bills and handed them to Ms. Shoog. Just when they thought she was cool, that's when she really hit their asses up.

"But it's that dryer that's broke down," Ms. Shoog told them. "I can't dry no clothes, and that's how they get so spoiled."

Dontae shook his head and smiled. "Here, old woman! You sure got a lot of game."

Ms. Shoog took Dontae's three hundred dollars and added it to her collection. She closed the laundry room and tucked her money away in her bra. "Thank you, babies! Now Ms. Shoog can have it all nice and sweet-smelling in here for y'all."

Reds and Rasun exchanged knowing smiles.

"Okay, okay, can we get down to business?" Reds asked.

Ms. Shoog shuffled over to her stove and turned on two of the burners. "You know Ms. Shoog is still the best at this shit, don'tcha?"

Amar turned away from the window. "Yo, here come that nigga Rik!"

Pookey unlatched the door and opened it. Rik walked through it and tossed his gym bag onto the coffee table.

"Shoog, what's the line look like?" Rik shouted into the kitchen.

"I'm hooking up Reds and Ra, and then Pookey, and then Amar, and then Dontae, and then you're next, baby," Shoog told him.

Rik seated himself on the couch, leaned forward, and unzipped his gym bag. He pulled out kilo after kilo from the extra-large bag and set them down on the table.

"Damn, you niggas need to get ya own damn cook!" Rik told them with a smile. "Y'all monopolizing my shit. Ain't that right, Shoog?"

"That's right, baby!" Shoog shouted from the kitchen.

"Then you should've paid for her damn new washing machine and dryer," Reds told him.

Rik laughed. "Word? She hit you niggas up like that?"

"Hell yeah," Amar said, smacking his lips.

Rik shook his head and laughed. "Damn, that old woman got game! What story she sell y'all this time?"

"Her fucking washing machine and dryer broke down," Amar told him.

"And that's why it's funky as a muthafucka in here," Dontae added.

Rik laughed and clapped his hands together. "Damn! The washer and dryer broke at the same time? Shoog, you's a bad muthafucka, yo!"

"Hell, I bought 'em at the same time, so they broke down at the same time!" Shoog shouted back from the kitchen.

Rasun strolled into the kitchen, where Ms. Shoog was preparing her materials.

"Rasun, hand me that big Pyrex dish on the table, baby," Ms. Shoog told him.

Rasun handed Shoog the dish. She busted open one of the kilos of cocaine and poured it into the dish, then set the dish on the stove.

"Ms. Shoog don't use none of that microwave shit, baby," she told him. "I don't need you to tell me what to do, fool. I got this. I do this shit the old-fashioned way!"

Ms. Shoog added a cup of lukewarm water to the cocaine, then lifted a large spatula she had next to the stove and began to stir the mixture. The fire from the stove began to melt the drugs, turning the substance into a thick, oily, yellowish gook. Ms. Shoog stirred the oily concoction, adding a second cup of water and then an unusually large amount of baking soda. The yellowish gook quickly turned into a thick white substance with the consistency of finely blended cake mix.

Ms. Shoog turned toward Rasun and smiled. "This is how you want it, baby."

Rasun examined the pasty substance and nodded.

Ms. Shoog pointed to a stack of glass dishes on the side of the counter. "Hand me another one of those dishes, baby."

Rasun handed Ms. Shoog another glass Pyrex dish. Ms. Shoog took the dish, busted open another kilo, and poured it into the container. She set the dish on the stove and poured in a large cup of water.

"How long you been cooking coke, Ms. Shoog? 'Cause you sure do know what you're doing," Rasun asked, stroking her ego so she would answer.

"Baby, Ms. Shoog been cooking for a long time," she told him, slowly turning her mixture. She poured in a second cup of water and added a large amount of baking soda. "Probably before you was born."

Rasun felt the wire taped to his chest. He knew what he had to do, and he hated every second of it. But it was either Shoog or his mother. "So, Shoog, how much shit you gotta cook up for these niggas today?"

"Hell, Reds, Rik, Amar brought six, Dante brought four with his broke ass." Ms. Shoog pulled the second dish off the burner and set it to the side, next to the first dish. She then reached for a third. "Pookey, with his po' self, want me to cook up four."

"Shit, that ain't nothing compared to the damage Quadir used to do. Shoot, if he was here, you'd be here all day cooking," Rasun said with a smile.

Ms. Shoog laughed. "Oh, that boy would have me busy for two days cooking all his shit! I'll never forget that time Quadir brought me two hundred keys and wanted it all cooked in two days! Hell, I felt like Sara Lee up in this bitch!"

Rasun laughed. He had enough information from Ms. Shoog. It was now time to concentrate on Rik. He turned and headed into the living room to find his next victim.

"So, the bitch stuck her head under the covers trying to fade a nigga, but I couldn't hold that shit any longer!" Dontae said, laughing. "She came up mad as a muthafucka, choking and gasping for air and shit!"

The guys gathered around the living room burst into laughter.

"Man, how could you mess that up?" Pookey asked. "That bitch is finer than a muthafucka! Nigga, I been trying to knock that since day one, and you fuck it off by gassing the bitch!"

Rik threw his head back in laughter.

Rasun walked to the table where Rik had his kilos stacked up. He lifted one of the bricks. "Damn, nigga. How much dope is this?"

"Twenty birds, nigga," Rik told him. "I got thirty more in the ride. I need to have this shit ready for the first of the month."

"It's the first of the month," Pookey said, singing. "It's the first of the month."

"What the fuck you cooking up all that shit for at once?" Rasun asked.

"Because, nigga, I got customers," Rik explained. "I'm expanding into some very lucrative territory. Them Junior Mafia niggas have been dropping like flies in the wintertime, and all their peeps have been calling me trying to get something. Nigga, this shit won't last me four days the way my phone ringing off the hook!"

"You willing to risk a war with them crazy Junior Mafia dudes?

That Jerrell Jackson is a fucking nutcase. I heard that nigga knocking everybody right now over his money that got fucked up while he was locked up," Reds said.

"Ain't gonna be no war," Rik told him. "Them niggas is so paranoid right now, they're all running scared, hiding like some little bitches. Them niggas don't know who's reaching out and touching they ass, so they ain't trying to do nothing to nobody right now."

Rasun nodded. He was finished with his questions for now. He was sure he'd given his slave master more than enough. Now he wanted this shit to be over. He wanted this to be the last time he had to do this shit; it was making him sick to his stomach. And the wire-wearing shit had to cease. That shit made him nervous. What if a nigga hugged him too tight or something? He stayed nervous the whole time he had the damn thing on.

This morning, he had to pull over to the side of the road and jump out of the car. His stomach wouldn't hold his breakfast down, that's how nervous he was. Not to mention, ever since he'd gotten locked up and started fucking with the clown-ass task force, his hair was falling out, he was constantly throwing up, and some days he'd have diarrhea. If that wasn't bad enough, he was literally starting to feel like he was coming down with the flu—just plain old physically sick. Snitching was like a corrosive poison that was eating him up from the inside like a deadly, malignant cancer. If it ended up killing him, he wouldn't complain about that, either.

Crawling under a rock and dying was something he truly felt like doing. He'd betrayed his friends, his boys, his crew. These were the niggas he'd grown up with. The niggas he'd come up in the game with, his boys who'd had his back since kindergarten, and now he was about to fuck them all over.

Rasun could feel himself growing nauseated once again. Sweat started pouring down his face, his mouth became moist, and his head began swirling. He raced for Ms. Shoog's bathroom.

"What the fuck's wrong with that nigga?" Pookey asked.

"Probably that fucked-up smell still getting to him," Amar said.

In the van down the street, Detective Ellington stacked her papers together and removed her headphones. She'd heard enough. Rasun had given them more than enough. This case was a wrap. Everyone in that room would be arrested and indicted within twenty-four hours.

Don't Stop, Get It, Get It

Gena lifted her head from her steering wheel. She was parked in the neighborhood Pathmark parking lot, sitting quiet and still. She watched people pass by—cars, kids, and shopping carts—and she simply tried to digest what she'd heard her cousin say. *That's why your father killed your mother.* Gena couldn't imagine the thought. *That's why Daddy's in jail. Why the fuck they say he tried to rob a bank for? Why didn't they tell me the truth?* Yes, the truth would've been better; it always is. Truth is a hard thing, but maybe harder is sometimes better than betrayal. And right now, Gena felt so betrayed by her family that she was questioning her entire existence. *I bet everybody knows, too.* Gena picked up her phone and tried to call her cousin Gary, but again she got voice mail.

"Dag, don't nobody answer their phones when you need them."

She didn't want to call the house. *What if Aunt Paula answers the phone?* She tried Gary's cell phone once more, avoiding the confrontation with Gary's mother, but there was still no answer. She needed someone to talk to, someone to tell that her whole life was a lie, her mother's death and her father's imprisonment were one and the same, and that her entire family knew and she had not one clue. *There's something extremely wrong with this and with my family for doing that to me.* She felt so betrayed. *I wish you were here, Quadir, I really do.*

Just then her phone rang. She looked at the number. It was Jay. She'd forgotten they had an early dinner date. She answered the phone and confirmed she was on her way. His call had come with perfect timing. Gena needed company, and the truth was Quadir wasn't there. *Jay don't seem that bad. He could be Mr. Replacement.*

She revved her engine and exited the parking lot to meet Jay for dinner. He'd turned out to be everything she'd ever wanted in a man. He was kind, sensitive, handsome, and polite. He listened to her when she talked. He opened doors for her when they went out. He'd call her to say good night, or to tell her how beautiful she was.

She didn't care about his money, but he did appear to have some change. That nice baby blue Range Rover he was pushing wasn't cheap. Plus, he was jeweled out. His apartment was in a swanky part of town and even had a doorman. Jay had an expensively decorated home with fine furnishings and lavish silk tapestries. He had it all. And when they went out, he never, ever let her pay for anything. He always paid for dinner, and the little gifts he gave her were always nice. But he wasn't holding like Quadir. His paper was way short compared to Quadir's. It wasn't fair to Jay to even try to compare ballin' status. But it didn't matter; she had plenty of money. She liked him because he was nice and attentive. Jay was smart, too. He had a nice vocabulary, and he used words the average fella on the street didn't. And he was also a bit mysterious, and even dangerous. She couldn't resist.

The looks they got when they were out on the street told her that she had a real man. The other guys on the street deferred to him when they walked along the sidewalk or into a restaurant. He was a natural leader. He kept himself well-groomed and smelled nice. And he could kiss like there was no tomorrow. She'd become lost inside his strong lips. When they kissed, it often felt as if she were standing on a cliff peering over it, with only him to keep her from falling.

She reached the corner and held her breath. It was here where the black BMW always waited for her. Each time she turned this corner, she held her breath as fear gripped her. Fortunately, today wasn't one of those days. The black Beemer was nowhere to be found.

Gena rounded the corner and headed out of the neighborhood. She was so happy she hadn't seen the black Beemer waiting to follow her today that she completely missed the magenta Jaguar that pulled out behind her. She turned up the stereo and blissfully became lost in her Mariah Carey CD, unaware she had picked up a tail.

Champagne exited her red Alfa Romeo Spider and strutted to where her meeting was to take place. She could see him waiting impatiently near the park bench. He looked good to her still, but she wasn't going to let all his looks, his smile, or his charm overtake her. She'd fallen for those things too many times in the past. And each time, she found herself being hurt. Perhaps that was why she now had a heart as hard as steel.

"What took you so long?" Jerrell demanded.

He eyed Champagne closely. She still looked like she could be on the cover of a beauty magazine, or on a stage twirling down a pole in Atlanta. She had a natural beauty about her, but it was a beauty that could switch from wholesome to seductive with the addition of a little makeup and a change in hairstyle. Champagne had been the girl of his dreams at one time. She was one of the few women he'd ever trusted.

Their relationship had lasted less than six months, but their friendship had developed over time. He had known Champagne for about fifteen years, and she was a trooper, a true soldier, and one of the few people he could still turn to. Had life been fair, she'd still be his woman. But life was far from fair. And unfortunately, she had too much water under the bridge to ever be anyone's wife.

"I got here when I got here," Champagne said gruffly. "What do you want now? What is it this time? More guns to hide? An alibi for some detective? What?"

Jerrell smiled and shook his head. "Damn, why does it always have to be like that?"

"Because with you, it has to be," Champagne told him. "With you, there's always some bullshit involved. With you, there's always a motive."

"Was I really that bad?" Jerrell asked. "You acting like a brother be straight wilding out—like I only call you when I need something foul."

Champagne put her hands on her hips.

Jerrell smiled again. "Glad to know all the love is still there."

"What the fuck do you want, Jerrell?" she asked.

Jerrell exhaled, reached into his pocket, and pulled out the photos of Gena he'd had taken at the restaurant. "You know her?"

"What the fuck do I look like, information or something?"

"You know everybody," Jerrell told her. "I figured you might've screwed the same baller once or twice. You hoes move in small circles."

"Fuck you, Black bitch," Champagne told him. "I know one asshole I wish I'd never screwed."

"Don't get your dirty little panties all in a bunch, ma," Jerrell told her. "Do you know the bitch or not?"

Champagne crossed her arms and squinted at Jerrell. "And if I did know her, what of it?"

"I want some information, that's all."

Champagne snatched the pictures away from Jerrell and examined them.

"Well?" Jerrell asked impatiently.

Champagne shook her head. "She looks familiar. Yeah, I've seen her around."

"Around?" Jerrell grew more animated. "Where?"

Champagne shrugged. "Just around. Clubs, parties, the mall, who the fuck knows? I've seen the bitch. What's it to you?"

"I need you to concentrate," Jerrell told her. "I need you to focus. Where have you seen her, and with who?"

"What is she, a new piece of pussy?" Champagne asked. "Some bitch who's got you all twisted up, and now you think she's stepping out on you?"

Jerrell shook his head. "That shit doesn't matter. I need you to do what you do. Find out everything you can about this bitch and get back to me. I want to know every fucking thing you can dig up. If she lost a fucking tooth in third grade, I want to know about it. I want to know where she lives, where she went to school, and who she fucks with or has fucked with."

Champagne smirked and tucked the pictures into her bra. "This is going to cost you."

"The usual?"

Champagne shook her head. "Uh-un. Something tells me this one is a lot more valuable to you. I want a thousand for this one."

"A thousand dollars!" Jerrell shouted. "Bitch, you must be crazy! A thousand dollars? Have you lost your muthafuckin' mind?"

"Take it or leave it, bitch," Champagne told him. "I would've charged you less, but you don't know how to shut the fuck up. That dirty panty comment is gonna cost, nigga."

Jerrell frowned and pursed his lips. "Okay. You got that. You get me what I want, and I'll give you what you want."

"Don't call me, I'll call you," Champagne told him. She turned and strutted across the street to her waiting Alfa Romeo.

Gena pulled up to the park and spied the voluptuous woman strutting away from her man. She frowned as she thought of the possibilities. *Who the fuck is she? What the fuck is he out here doing?*

She rushed toward Jerrell with a fierce scowl on her face. "Who was that?"

"Nobody."

"Nobody?" Gena turned toward Champagne, who was driving past them. "She didn't seem like a nobody. You were all up in her ass while she was walking away!"

"Gena, that was my cousin!" Jerrell shouted.

"Bullshit!"

"She was!" Jerrell shouted. "She saw me standing here waiting on you, and she pulled over, got out of the car, and came over and said what's up to me."

Gena crossed her arms and shook her head. "Jay, you're so full of shit. I don't even know why I allowed myself to fall for you. I should've known you were like all the rest!"

"Gena, I swear to you!" Jerrell said forcefully. "Why would I meet another woman here, knowing you were on your way? Think about that shit, will you? Why would I do that?" he asked, even though that was exactly what he'd done.

Gena shifted her weight to one side and exhaled.

"Gena, if I was going to creep on you, do you honestly think I'd do it here, in the middle of a park you're coming to, in broad daylight? Think about that!"

Gena lowered her head and nodded. He was making sense. And she hadn't caught him doing anything out of line.

"You know what, Jay?" Gena told him. "That bitch better be at your next family reunion or Christmas party or Thanksgiving dinner or I'm fucking you and your mans up! You hear me?" she said, grabbing his dick.

Jerrell smiled and nodded. "I hear you, baby. Damn, you threatening a nigga's johnson and shit, acting like you own the muthafucka."

"I do own that muthafucka." Gena smiled. "That bitch belongs to me, and don't you forget it."

"Damn, baby," Jerrell said, pulling her close. "I've been waiting for you to claim ownership. You can take possession of this mutha-fucka wherever you want to."

Gena nodded. "I just might do that. I just might do that."

Jerrell plunged into Gena with the force of a high diver hitting the pool. And like the diver, he plunged inside her, swimming inside her, causing her to gasp for air. Gena opened her legs wider, trying to ease the pain. It made him go deeper into her, causing her to cry out.

Jerrell had waited for this day since meeting her at the gas station, and for the past weeks, he'd waited patiently, cunningly plotting how he'd get her to fall for him. He played a role like the Hollywood hustler he was, all because he wanted to tap this fat, caramel-colored ass so bad he could taste it. He let her know how bad he wanted her with every punishing stroke he delivered. He made her regret she'd made him wait so long. Week after week—shit, damn near two months since they'd first met.

Gena placed her hands beneath his stomach as he stroked, in an effort to defuse some of the pain. He was hitting it and hitting it hard. *Wow, it's been so long! He's so big; shit's incredible.* She grabbed the sheets, then the pillow, and finally his waist. She dug her fingernails into his sides, trying to take the pain he was dishing out. She hadn't been with a man since Quadir, and now she was paying dearly for it.

Jerrell kept pounding relentlessly with what seemed to be a much bigger penis than she was used to, trying to go deeper and deeper with each stroke. He could feel every inch of her depth with each of his movements. She was tight as a balled-up fist, and she pulled and tugged at his manhood with each of his strokes. He could feel her tight walls wrapped around him, and he didn't know how much lon-ger he'd be able to take it.

Damn, she got some good pussy, Jerrell couldn't help thinking to himself.

Gena wrapped her legs around Jerrell and pulled him down on

top of her. No sooner had she done it than she realized her mistake. At least when he was pounding her, he was pulling it out a little. Now that pounding had turned into a deep, gut-churning grind. She exploded and cried out in his ear. She could feel him all the way inside her stomach.

Gena's fingernails dug deep into Jerrell's back while her teeth found their way to his sweating neck. He'd been grinding relentlessly for the last ten minutes, and her insides felt like they were on fire. The pounding he'd given her the first fifteen minutes had made her cervix sore, but the deep-ass punishment he was putting on her now felt like it was twisting her guts into a knot. Besides, she'd come six times, and she was beginning to get a headache.

Gena could feel goose bumps beginning to appear on Jerrell's back, and if they meant the same thing on him that they had meant on Quadir, then that meant he was about to get his. And sure enough, he did. Jerrell exploded inside Gena like a volcano erupting. His warm white lava flew deep up inside her, causing her to cry out and come again herself. She could feel his massive member vibrating inside her as it released its load.

Jerrell remained stiff on top of her for one more minute, until the throbbing from his penis stopped, and then his entire body went limp. He relaxed on top of her, and she felt some relief inside her vagina as his manhood shrunk to a decent size.

Gena caressed Jerrell's shoulder and smiled. She wondered if she'd be able to take this kind of punishment every night if they moved in together. The tingling sensation in her body gave her the answer. *Hell yeah!*

Jerrell rolled over and lay on the bed beside her. She was glad, because she was tired. He'd given her ass more than a workout. He'd done something a man hadn't done in a long while. He'd fucked her to sleep. She rolled over, wrapping the blankets around her body, and fell fast asleep.

She'll Be Comin' 'Round the Mountain

United States Attorney Paul Perachetti paced in front of a room filled to the brim with various law enforcement agents, officers, and deputies.

Captain Holiday of the Philadelphia Police Department cleared his throat. "I want to thank all our fellow agencies, departments, and bureaus for coming today and helping us out. Gentlemen, zero hour is almost on us. I'll keep my remarks brief for now. At this time, for those of you who don't know him, I'd like to bring up United States Attorney for the Western District of Pennsylvania, Mr. Paul Perachetti."

"Gentlemen, and ladies, I want to thank you for being here today, and I want to thank you for the enormous amount of effort and sacrifice you've put forward over the preceding months," Perachetti told the gathered crowd. "Some of you have worked this case for more than a year. You've sacrificed much to uphold the laws of our country, and to make the streets safe once again. Over the past year, there have been many missed dinners, missed birthdays, missed plays and school recitals, and a lot of strained families. Your deeds will *not* go unrewarded.

"Today, we have a really big day ahead of us," Mr. Perachetti continued. "Today, we'll be executing some fifty search warrants simultaneously. This will be the biggest drug sting in the history of the state of Pennsylvania. I wanted to thank all the participating agencies. Captain Holiday and the Philadelphia Police Department deserve a round of applause for doing the warrants and managing the confidential informants. These guys really, really are who made today possible."

The officers and agents gathered around the room broke into applause.

"I'd like to thank Special Agent in Charge Rudy Galvani of the FBI," Perachetti continued. "I want to thank Agent Stacey Wynn of the Drug Enforcement Administration, and I want to thank Colonel Whitfield of the Pennsylvania National Guard."

The law enforcement officers gathered around the room applauded their colleagues.

"Colonel Whitfield contacted the governor's office and assisted us in obtaining permission to use his National Guard troops to help conduct the search and seizure, and we also have their full assistance in rounding up the perpetrators," Perachetti informed them. "Without the guard, we wouldn't have enough manpower to raid all fifty of the facilities simultaneously. So they certainly have our deepest appreciation."

Again, the officers and agents applauded.

"I want to thank the sheriff's department, and the Pennsylvania State Police, as well as the United States Border Patrol, and the United States Customs Service, for loaning us their narcotics canines," Perachetti continued. "I'll turn it back over to Captain Holiday so he can wrap things up. I wanted to thank everyone who made today possible. Be careful out there, gentlemen and ladies."

Perachetti left the podium, and Captain Holiday stepped up to the microphone. The officers inside the room gave another loud round of applause of gratitude and then grew silent.

"Gentlemen, what we're doing today will have a direct correlation to the amount of drugs that make it onto the streets of Philadelphia this year," Captain Holiday told them. "This operation will net real results and will undoubtedly result in numerous convictions of some of Philadelphia's most notorious drug dealers. Those of you who know me understand I'm not prone to emotional speeches. So I'll keep it short and sweet. Go out there and kick some ass, guys. Be careful, watch each other's backs, and everyone go home to your families tonight. I'll give up the stage now to the detectives who put this thing together, and who are coordinating today's operation, Detectives Ellington and Ratzinger."

Lieutenant Ratzinger stood behind the podium, allowing Detective Ellington to have the microphone. Whistles shot through the room.

"All right, all right, wise guys." Detective Ellington waved them off. "Keep it down before I tell your wives."

The officers laughed.

"Listen up, guys, we're doing fifty houses all at the same time. That means fifty teams. We're dividing the operations into sections. There will be five section leaders, each with ten teams. Each team will consist of ten to fifteen officers, agents, deputies, and guardsmen. We've already organized the teams, and we'll be passing out team lists, so everyone will know what team they belong to. We'll have time to do some run-throughs over at the academy and at the National Guard Training Center. We'll cycle the teams through, so everyone will have the opportunity to run an operation and get to know their team members. These are search warrants and arrest warrants. I want everyone to make sure these suspects get their Miranda rights read to them as soon as the premises are secure. I don't want anything thrown out because of a Miranda violation. Gentlemen and ladies, this operation is a go. Get your teams together and to the training sites so we can prep for the operation. That's about it. Good luck."

"We're operating on channel five, people," Lieutenant Ratzinger shouted. "Make sure your radios are on secure link five!"

The officers and agents broke up and headed off to their gathering points.

"Hey, what do you think you're doing?" Gena playfully asked as Jay sat next to her with a bottle of massage oil in his hands.

"Smelling your feet?" He picked up her big toe with his thumb and pointer finger and held her foot up in the air like it was a dirty diaper. "I can't be handling fungus, you feel me?"

"Fungus . . . Boy, you see these toes?" She held her feet up to his face. "Look at 'em. Tell the truth—aren't these the most perfect feet you've ever seen in your life?"

Truthfully, they really were tiny, small, perfect feet and toes, and they turned him on. Everything about Gena turned him on. She had a lot going on with her family, and when she asked if she could stay with him, just for a while, until she found her own place, he thought he would mind. He said yes, but at the time he didn't really mean it, and further, he really didn't want her that close to him. But because of the family situation, he said okay, thinking she'd be there for a few days. But a few days had turned into a few weeks. And he liked it. He didn't think he would, but he did, and he wasn't looking forward to her leaving.

Gena would wake up in the mornings and be out the door before 8:30 a.m. to run her own errands and take care of her own business. He didn't give her a key, but he accommodated her comings and goings. There were times when he'd even come home to unlock the door for her and then go back out to whatever he was doing. He gave her little amounts of shopping money, even though he'd already figured out she was holding the bread and the butter. They'd wake, shower, eat, and roll out, and at night, they'd watch movies or play spades, which had become Jerrell's favorite pastime while he was incarcerated waiting for his trial.

"Want to play cards?" he asked after rubbing her feet.

"Again?"

"Yeah, come on."

She'd never played cards as much as she had since she'd met him. And the thing was, it was bad enough that she didn't want to play, but then he'd make her gamble and take her money if she lost.

Gena watched Jerrell throw the cards down and swipe a hundred dollars off the table. "You realize you giving that back, right?"

"Shit, my ass. You snooze, you lose, babe."

"Whatever, Jay, whatever," she said, watching as he counted his winnings.

For the most part, it was a little vacation from the reality of Richard Allen, but Gena wouldn't stay long. No, after Jamal threw her out, then Viola threw her out, Gena had decided that shit wouldn't be happening ever again. As comfortable as she was in Jay's house, she couldn't stay and didn't want to wear out her welcome, either. So, for the past couple of weeks, she'd been apartment hunting and looking at several condos in the Old City section of Philadelphia near South Street.

Jerrell had gotten quite used to her womanly touch. Truthfully, while he didn't want her there in the beginning, he now couldn't imagine her not around. Plus, he liked being able to keep track of his newfound investment. In the end, putting his time in with her would be worth his while. He simply didn't know how worth his while she'd turn out to be.

Rasun woke up sweating in the dark. He could feel bile rising from his stomach to his throat. He swallowed hard to keep it down but found it didn't work. Once again, he found himself racing to the bathroom and kneeling in front of the toilet.

"Fasten my chinstrap for me?" SWAT team leader Johnny Wang asked Detective Ellington.

Letoya Ellington shook her head. "Johnny, I'll bet your mommy still dresses you in the morning, doesn't she?"

"She wouldn't have to if you'd let me move in with your fine ass," Lieutenant Wang said with a smile.

"Johnny, you couldn't handle this pussy if I tied both hands behind my back," Detective Ellington told him.

The SWAT team members gathered around them broke into laughter. Detective Ellington checked the magazine in her weapon, then cocked it, chambering a round. She checked her black Kevlar vest, her tactical utility belt, and her communications radio. Like all the other officers and agents participating in the predawn raids, she was dressed in all-black paramilitary gear with a black mask over her face, black gloves on her hands, and black knee and elbow pads.

Detective Ellington lifted her black Kevlar helmet and strapped it onto her head. "Okay, listen up, everyone, comm link check! Team leader, check your communications. Remember, we're operating on secure link five!"

Detective Ellington lifted the microphone attached to the shoulder strap on her bulletproof vest. "Section leaders, this is Command One. Have your team leaders acknowledge."

Letoya turned to Lieutenant Ratzinger. "Hey, Mark. When they report in, make sure they all did their comm check. And synchronize with me. We are go in T-minus four minutes."

Lieutenant Ratzinger nodded. "Roger that, sweet lady. Make sure you keep your head down in there. Let SWAT go in first."

Detective Ellington caressed Mark's cheek. "Aw, you worry about me too much, old man. I've done this too many times to play the hero."

"My team's all loaded up and ready to rock 'n' roll," Johnny Wang told her.

Detective Ellington nodded. "Well, let's load up and get rolling."

Letoya Ellington adjusted her helmet and climbed into the back of the SWAT truck, behind Lieutenant Wang. She checked her watch.

"Two minutes to showtime," Johnny Wang said.

Detective Ellington clicked the button on her walkie-talkie. "Section leaders, this is Command. We're two minutes to showtime. All sections, we're a go. You have tactical command at this time. I repeat, all section leaders have tactical command at this time. You may begin operations."

Johnny Wang turned toward his driver. "Move out. Get us to the door, Bobby!"

The SWAT van pulled out of the parking lot and rounded the corner. It was 3:00 a.m., and the entire neighborhood seemed deserted. The target's house was down the street, and they'd be there in less than twenty seconds.

"Target looks quiet, sir," a voice declared over Lieutenant Wang's communications link. "Looks like we've achieved tactical surprise," he said, loving every minute of his job.

Lieutenant Wang nodded and keyed his walkie-talkie twice, acknowledging the last transmission. He rose from his seat and threw open the doors of the SWAT van. His men poured out of the van and raced to the front door. One of the team members raced to the left side of the house, while another raced to the right side. They wanted to make sure no one escaped out the sides of the house. Three of the team members raced to the backyard to secure the rear. The others gathered on either side of the front door while the team member holding the steel battering ram smashed it open. SWAT team members poured into the house like ants.

Rik bolted from sleep when he heard the door being smashed open. He jumped out of bed as the first SWAT team member entered his bedroom. The masked, black-clad agent was standing behind a large, black bulletproof shield that had SWAT painted on it in big white letters. Rik could see the officer's black Sig Sauer semiautomatic handgun sticking out of the gun slit in the center of the shield.

"Police department!" the officer shouted. "We have a search warrant! Get down on the floor now!"

Rik lifted his hands into the air.

"Get down on the floor now!" the officer shouted again.

Slowly, Rik dropped to his knees and lay face down on the floor. He could feel himself being handcuffed.

Detective Ellington strolled into the room as two SWAT team members were lifting a handcuffed Rik off the floor.

"Good morning, Tyrik!" Detective Ellington said with a smile. "You look sleepy. Did we disturb you?"

Ms. Shoog was sound asleep when the explosion woke her. Then smoke billowed into her bedroom.

"What the fuck is going on?" Shoog shouted.

She searched her nightstand for her glasses. Once she finally located them, put them on, and turned toward her bedroom door, she found she was no longer alone. Her room was filled with men wearing camouflage uniforms, all pointing M16 rifles at her.

"I was gonna pay my taxes. I was just a little late with the money, that's all," Shoog told them.

Detective Dick Davis strolled into Shoog's bedroom holding a pair of handcuffs up in the air. "This isn't about your taxes, ma'am. This is about you being the Betty Crocker of the hood for all the local dope dealers."

"Oh, no, son, you got the wrong lady!" Shoog shook her head. "Mm-mmm, that ain't me, no, sir."

If he didn't know better, he would've believed her.

"Are you kidding me? You're the right person, Alvetta Clark." He motioned to another officer. "Get her downstairs into the truck."

"All right now, if I got to be going somewhere, do you think I could get dressed? Come on, now, y'all step outta here and let an old woman get dressed," she said, smiling and pretending, her usual.

Detective Davis smiled. "We figured you might say something like that, Ms. Clark or Ms. Shoog, whoever you are. I want you to meet my friend, Irma. She's from the Pennsylvania National Guard, and she's going to do a body search for us."

A massive, stocky, six-foot-two-inch woman wearing camouflage makeup on her face stomped through the crowd of soldiers and smiled at Shoog. Irma was missing two front teeth.

Ohmigod, look at this mountain bitch I got to deal with. Damn, damn, damn, Ms. Shoog thought as the mountain bitch frisked her ass, handcuffed her, and hauled her ass away into the back of a paddy wagon.

Do I Do

LeChevue was the place everybody seemed to pile into. Everybody knew everybody at LeChevue, and the ballers' wives would socialize and get their hair and nails done. It was the place where the wives and girlfriends of the NFL's Eagles or NBA's 76ers went to flaunt their hundred-thousand-dollar cars and multicarat rings. It was the shop of the young, Black, and elite. It was where Gena had been going for years.

Gena and Markita, her old neighbor from Chancellor Street, walked into the shop, and to her surprise, she found many of her old friends inside. They immediately went into shouting, howling, and wailing mode.

"Gena!" Bridgette shouted. "*Girrrrrl*, where have you been?"

Gena raced to the seat where Pam was waiting, leaned forward, and hugged her.

"Girl, I can't believe it!" Beverly wailed. "Ms. Gena's back in the house! Girl, what you been doing to your hair? Gena, you let somebody else do your hair or something, 'cause this ain't my work."

"No, nut, I been doing it myself," she said, hugging Beverly. "How's you and Quinny Day?"

"Aw, we good, we good. What about you, though? Man, it's been months. You stopped coming around."

"I needed some time, that's all. I'm good, though."

"Well, your hair ain't. You did this?"

Gena laughed and shook her head. "Girl, I don't let nobody up in this mess but you. I've been trying to keep it up."

Gena wasn't going to tell them that she'd been trying to lie low for a while, after she found Qua's money. These gossiping whores would have her business all over the East Coast.

"Hey, baby!" Veronica rose, waddled to where Gena was, and hugged her.

Gena placed her hand on Veronica's stomach. "Girl, let me find out?"

"That nigga Rik got me all fucked up, girl. I can't wait till this baby pops out so I can get back to my life. Shit, I can't go to no clubs like this."

"Clubs? Honey, you don't even look like you can make it out the front door, and you worried about the clubs?" Gena joked.

The girls around the shop broke into laughter.

"Hey, y'all, this is my friend Markita. She used to be my neighbor out west." Gena introduced Markita while clasping her arm. "Kita, this is Veronica, and that's Bridgette, and that's Beverly, that's big-head Val over there, and that's Tracey."

Markita waved at everyone and seated herself in the waiting area. Gena made her way around the shop, exchanging hugs with everybody.

"Gena, what the hell is that you're driving?" Tracey asked, peering out the shop's front windows.

"Girl, that's the *Catch Me If You Can* Porsche out there." Gena smiled, patting her hair coquettishly.

"Uh-un, girl!" Beverly said. "No, you didn't go and knock off one of them!"

"Girl, that car is too fly!" Veronica shouted as she and Tina high-fived each other.

"Girl, what's his name?" Tina asked. "And does he have a brother?"

Gena threw her head back in laughter. "Girl, please!"

"What's his name, Gena?" Beverly asked.

"What?" Gena smiled uncontrollably.

Beverly squinted at Gena for several moments. "Umm-mmm-hmmm. Girl, I've known you for too long. What's his name? All of a sudden you outside and you ballin'? Bitch, I know better. Either Quadir is back from the dead or you done stumbled upon a winning lottery ticket."

Gena laughed and turned her palms up toward the ceiling. "What are you talking about?"

Tina rose and walked over to Gena and began to sniff her. "Uh-un, girl. I smell dick on you, too."

The women all laughed.

Gena shoved Tina away. "Bitch, get yo' ass away from me."

"What's his name, Gena!" Pam shouted. "Don't change the subject."

"Girl, your face is clear, you can't stop smiling, you got a new car, and you ain't been coming around," Val told her. "Girl, you getting some dick. And it must be some good dick!"

Again, the ladies around the beauty shop broke into laughter.

Gena nodded. "Okay, I see what this is. This is clown Gena day, huh?"

"All you have to do is tell us 'bout Mr. Put a Smile on Your Face," Beverly told her.

Gena shook her head. "Jay. His name is Jay, okay?"

"Ooh, Jay!" Tina said, pronouncing his name dramatically.

"Where's this nigga from?" Beverly asked bluntly.

The ladies in the shop broke into laughter again.

"He's from Philly," Gena told them bashfully.

"Is he a baller?" Pam asked.

"Something like that," Gena told them. "He don't need no money, I can tell you that."

"Well, all I want to know is whether he's good in bed?" Veronica asked. "Shoot, can the nigga fuck? 'Cause God knows they not worth nothing else."

Gena turned toward Veronica. "Bitch, that's why you like that now. Close ya legs and stop thinking about dick."

"What else is there to think about?" Veronica asked, looking at her like she was crazy. She high-fived Tina. "Dick and money, money and dick. Those are the only things niggas are good for."

Val called for Markita to sit at her station. It was her first time at the shop, so she didn't have a regular beautician yet. Beverly waved for Gena to come over and sit down in her chair.

"So, what do you want to do to this stuff today?" Beverly asked.

"You seen Halle Berry's hair?" Gena asked. "Girl, take it all off. I need a new look."

Beverly shrugged and grabbed her scissors.

"So, where's the Mercedes at, Gena?" Pam asked. "Did you trade it in?"

"No, I still have it," Gena told them.

"Ooh, girl," Tina wailed. "Mm," she hummed, looking at the others in the room.

Gena smiled. It was none of their business who bought her car. And if she told them she bought it herself, too many questions would arise. So she let them believe what they wanted to believe, and they wanted to believe a nigga had bought the car, so let them.

"Girl, I'm so happy to see you doing good," Tracey declared.

Gena exhaled. "Girl, I feel so happy. Jay is a good man."

"You need to bring him to Chances so we can meet him," Pam told her.

"Girl, he won't go to no club," Gena told her.

"Why, he think he too good or something?" Beverly asked.

"No, he just don't do clubs," Gena told her. "Hell, I really don't do them no more, either."

"Oh, you too good to fuck with ya girls now?" Tina asked with a smile.

"Girl, we know you from Richard Allen," Veronica added. "Get your project-chick ass out the house and come and kick it with ya girls!"

"If Sahirah was here, she'd have your ass out the house," Beverly told her. "Girl, we miss her, too. And we miss Qua and Black."

"Yeah, I know, me too." Gena thought about how she and Sahirah used to be in every nightclub every other night of the week.

"Tell that Jay guy to take you to the club, girl," Val told her.

"We'll see," Gena told them. "So, is that why all of you hoes is up in here today? Getting ready for the club?"

"Girl, please," Veronica said, waving her off. "The bond hearing is tomorrow."

Gena recoiled. "The bond hearing?"

"Yeah, Rik and everybody's bond hearing is tomorrow," Pam told her.

"Okay, I'm missing something," Gena told them. "What the fuck are y'all talking 'bout?"

"Girl, Rik, Quinny, Reds, Rasun, Pookey, Amar, Winston, everybody—I mean everybody you can name that we know—got busted," Veronica explained.

"Got busted?" Gena leaned forward in her chair. She was in shock. "Where? How?"

"Girl, the Feds raided all of they asses at the same time, early in the morning," Beverly told her.

"Get the fuck outta here!" Gena shouted.

Veronica nodded sadly.

"What happened?" Gena asked.

"Girl, they got raided by the Feds," Veronica explained. "They all had indictments. They didn't find anything, but they said they'd been watching them for a while, and they all had indictments."

Gena shook her head. "Girl, I'm sorry. You should've called."

"Gena, nobody has your number anymore," Bridgette told her. "Girl, we knew you was doing bad after Qua died, and you needed some space."

"I'm sorry. I still want to keep in touch, though," Gena told them. "I've been trying to get myself back together. I'm going to give y'all my number before I leave. And, Veronica, I want you to give it to Rik and tell him to call me collect. When are you going to talk to him again?"

"Girl, he's supposed to call me tonight," Veronica told her.

"Give him my number and tell him to put me on his visitation list," Gena told her. "I need to go see him."

Veronica nodded. "I'll tell him tonight."

Gena leaned back in the chair and allowed Beverly to finish up her hair.

"Gena, if that man of yours is doing anything illegal, tell him to get out of the game right now," Bridgette told her. "This shit *is not* worth it."

Veronica shook her head and wiped the tears out of her eyes. "Yeah, this shit right here is crazy. Everybody's locked up."

Pam handed Veronica a tissue and added, "I don't understand how they locked up like forty or fifty niggas at one time. That shit is what's crazy to me."

"The problem is too many dudes be snitches!" Beverly said angrily. "Bitch-ass niggas wanna do the crime but don't wanna do the time."

"That's right!" Tina shouted, high-fiving Val. "These snitching-ass niggas want to run and get everybody else caught up. Hell, we need to make a new rule. No pussy for snitching-ass niggas!"

"That's right!" Beverly chimed in. "Hell, these niggas don't want to go and do they time, 'cause they want to stay out here and get some pussy and eat McDonald's and ride around on rims, bumping they systems. Girl, no pussy for the snitches. I don't want no crying, telling-ass nigga up in my shit anyway!"

Veronica wiped her tears again and started smiling. "Thanks, y'all. Y'all trying to make me feel better, and I appreciate it."

"We are, but, girl, we serious, too," Beverly told her. "Girl, we putting out a new rule. No pussy if you're a snitch. Show us your transcripts, your presentence report, your affidavit, and give us three witnesses!"

Laughter shot around the beauty shop.

"Girl, and if they got arrested and ain't never went to trial, that's automatically a bar on the pussy!" Tina added.

"For real!" Beverly wailed. "Nigga, how in the fuck you get busted last year with ten ounces, a machine gun, and two scales in your trunk, and you ain't went to so much as a muthafuckin' evidence hearing, let alone a trial!"

Tina pointed to a blank spot on the wall. "Right there is where we need to hang our No Pussy board! Put the board up and start putting these niggas' names on it. I betcha they'll cut that bullshit out then."

Beverly handed Gena a hand mirror. "All done, mommy."

Gena rose from the chair and turned and stared into the big mirror on the wall. She used the small mirror to check the back of her hair. Beverly had hooked her shit up. She was ready to be in a hair magazine. Gena reached into her purse, pulled out a hundred-dollar bill, and handed it to Beverly along with her phone number wrapped around the money.

"Keep the change," Gena whispered.

Beverly glanced at the hundred-dollar bill and tucked it away inside the pouch on her apron. Gena walked to Val, who did Markita's hair, and handed her a hundred-dollar bill as well.

"You ready?" Markita asked her.

Gena nodded, gathered her purse, and headed for the exit. At the door she turned back toward her friends.

"It was good seeing y'all again," Gena told them. "Veronica, tell Rik to put me on his list."

"Bye, girl," Tina and Veronica said at the same time.

"See ya, Gena." Bridgette waved.

"Bye, y'all. Hey, Tracey, I'll call you later." Gena waved and headed out the door.

Outside, Gena and Markita climbed into her Porsche and pulled away. Again, she didn't notice the black Range Rover pulling into traffic behind her.

Skip to My Lou, My Darling

Skip unlocked the door to his flat and walked inside. He set his bags of groceries down on the counter and pressed the button on his answering machine to check his messages. No one had called him, and he loved it. He loved his privacy, and his anonymity. It was for those reasons he'd chosen his flat on the industrial side of town, away from the majority of Philadelphia's other denizens. He was surrounded by nothing but a few other flats, numerous industrial buildings, and railroad trucks. His neighbors minded their own business, and no one really cared about what went on in his neighborhood. In fact, nothing really ever did go on in his neighborhood. And even if something did, it was unlikely anyone would be able to hear it. The constant passing of trains blocked out most noises.

Skip walked to his stove and turned on the front burner. He then walked to his cabinets, opened a door, and pulled out a steel pot. He was hungry, and he had a taste for some oatmeal. Apple-cinnamon-flavored oatmeal, to be exact. He walked to the sink, turned on the faucet, and filled the pot halfway. He then returned to his stove and placed the pot on the lit burner.

Skip was tired. His feet hurt, his bones ached, and he felt fatigue tugging at his entire body. A nice big bowl of oatmeal would certainly seal the deal for him and give him the full stomach that would put him into a deep, all-consuming sleep. It was sleep he desperately needed. He couldn't wait to hit the sack.

Skip peered around his flat, seeing what needed to be done. He was a borderline neat freak, so very little was out of place. In fact, if one didn't know better, one would've thought a woman lived there and kept the place clean. The only thing that needed to be done was to take out the trash. He'd do that before he ate, but after he took his medicine.

Skip walked to his refrigerator and opened it. He removed a tiny vial of insulin and an injection needle. He closed the door and made his way over to his dinette set. Skip seated himself at his dining room table, leaned forward, and rolled up his pants leg. He tapped his tiny insulin bottle, shaking up the medication, and stuck his needle into the vial. He pulled back the stopper on his syringe until he'd drawn in the correct amount of insulin and then removed the needle and examined the contents. Once he was certain he had the right amount inside his syringe, he carefully stuck the needle into his thigh and injected the insulin.

His diabetes was something he'd hidden from outsiders for most of his life. He'd become a Type 2 diabetic at the age of ten. His body simply failed to produce enough insulin. This insulin deficiency slowly worsened until diet and exercise were no longer enough. And after a few years, even pills were no longer enough. He now found himself a slave to insulin injections, which the doctors said he would need for the rest of his life. To him, the good news was his diabetes was well under control. The bad news was he could never let another member of Junior Mafia find out about it.

That Junior Mafia killing him if they ever found out was a foregone conclusion. They hated weakness. And to them, he would personify weakness. If he couldn't fight off a sugar cube, how could they trust him to fight off some niggas rolling in on their turf? If word of his condition ever got out, he'd be a target not only for Junior Mafia, but also for every other dealer in the city who wanted his territory.

They'd all come after him, thinking him sick and weak. He would have a big fucking *M* on his forehead, for *mark*. Easy mark. So he definitely had to keep his condition to himself.

Skip rose from the table, walked to his kitchen trash can, and pulled the bag of trash out. He set the trash bag on the floor, tied it closed, lifted it, and headed for the door. His water was close to boiling, and he would soon be ready to pour it into a bowl filled with oatmeal and enjoy one of his favorite dishes. His affinity for oatmeal was a product of his youth. He'd been raised in the projects on fried bologna sandwiches and big bowls of Frosted Flakes, and equally big bowls of oatmeal had been a staple in his household. If it hadn't been for fried bologna, grits, and Kool-Aid, lunch would've been practically nonexistent. And if it hadn't been for cold cereal and oatmeal, breakfast would've been a dream. He still loved all those things to this day.

Skip lifted the trash bag and headed out the door and around the corner of his apartment to where his larger trash cans were kept. He lifted the lid off his sixty-gallon trash can and tossed his white kitchen trash bag inside. He replaced the lid and made sure it was on tight so that the cats wouldn't be able to knock the trash can over and cause the lid to fly off. When this was done, he turned to head back into his house. When he turned, however, he found an unexpected guest.

"Jerrell!" Skip said, surprised. "My nigga! What's happening?"

Skip peered down and saw the black semiautomatic in Jerrell's hand. It was pointed at his stomach.

"Yo, J!" Skip said. "What the fuck's up with the pistol, B?"

Jerrell nodded toward Skip's apartment. "Why don't we go inside and talk about this?"

"Yo, this shit is foul, my nigga," Skip told him. "What the fuck kinda shit you playing, yo?"

Skip headed back into his flat with Jerrell following right behind him. Jerrell locked the door. Skip turned and faced him.

"Okay, now, you wanna tell me what the meaning of this bullshit is?" Skip demanded.

"It's about my money, Skip," Jerrell told him. "All of you niggas fucked off my money!"

"I ain't fucked off shit, nigga!" Skip shouted. "What the fuck are you talking about?"

"Okay, then, where's my money for the shit I fronted you before I got locked up?" Jerrell asked.

"I got your money, nigga!" Skip told him.

Jerrell exhaled. "Don't tell me—you got it, but it's not here. We got to go and get it, right?"

"I got your money right here, nigga," Skip told him.

"Okay, where is it?" Jerrell asked.

"It's inside that old broke-ass stereo," Skip told him, nodding at an ancient, circa 1980s console stereo. "The speaker cover pops off, and the money is inside."

Jerrell peered at the stereo and then back at Skip. "Get it for me. And no funny business, either. Don't try no tricks, no reaching for no pistols, no bullshit, Skip."

Skip walked to the stereo and kneeled. He popped the cover off the right speaker, reached inside, and pulled out a bundle of money wrapped in plastic. He tossed the bundle onto a chair next to where Jerrell was standing.

Jerrell lifted the money and examined it. There was a light cover of dust on it, telling him the money had been wrapped up and waiting for him for a good little while. He shifted his gaze to Skip.

"How much is this?" he asked.

"All of it," Skip told him. "Every red cent I owe you."

Jerrell's mind was fucked up now. He should've known Skip would have his money. Skip wasn't like the rest of them niggas. Skip was old-school. He didn't live lavishly, he didn't try to be flashy, he didn't wear jewelry or drive a fancy car. Skip lived in an old flat next to a train track and drove a banged-up Jeep Cherokee. Skip had never, not once, come up short with his money. He'd always done what he was supposed to do, when he was supposed to do it. He was the most loyal nigga in Junior Mafia. Skip took it seriously. And now Jerrell had shown up at Skip's pad with a pistol and forced him at gunpoint to give him something he was going to give him anyway.

"Why didn't you come to any of my hearings, or to my trial, Skip?" Jerrell asked. "Why didn't you show me some love? Why wasn't you there for me when I needed you?"

"What?" Skip asked, surprised. "Nigga, have you bumped your muthafuckin' head or something?"

Jerrell frowned.

"Is that what this bullshit is about?" Skip asked. "You felt like niggas wasn't down for you? You felt like your Mafia family abandoned you? Nigga, I ordered everybody to stay away from all that shit. Are you crazy?"

"You ordered them to?" Jerrell asked.

"Jerrell! You were facing a conspiracy charge!" Skip shouted. "They wanted you for being the head of Junior Mafia. If you would've had a bunch of Junior Mafia niggas show up to your trial, those jurors would've hung your Black ass! We stayed away so you'd have a chance of getting out of that shit! We didn't want to go and visit you in jail 'cause we wanted your Black ass out of jail! We stayed away so you could be free, nigga!"

Jerrell closed his eyes. It was too much for him, and he didn't know what to do. Skip was right. And Skip had done the right thing. He was truly a soldier. He had every dime of Jerrell's money and had been waiting for him to come home to give it to him. He'd done everything right and had shown Jerrell nothing but loyalty. But Skip's loyalty was to the Junior Mafia, not him, and that brotherhood was dead to Jerrell. All those niggas were a bunch of snakes. They'd fucked him over, turned their backs on him, and not one of them tried to slide him a dime when he stepped out.

"You killed them, didn't you?" Skip asked. "You killed our brothers because of this bullshit, didn't you?"

"You don't know what the fuck you're talking about," Jerrell told him, wishing he'd stop and not say anything else.

"I do know what the fuck I'm talking about!" Skip yelled. "You killed them, you fucking snake! How could you do that? How could you betray your brothers over something as trivial as money? It's just money, Jerrell. We're your brothers!"

"Brothers!" Jerrell shouted. "Brothers? What kind of brothers spend all their brother's money? What kind of brothers don't give money to their brother's lawyers, or let their brother's family go without? How many of you niggas went to my mom's house and dropped off some bread? How many of you took any money to any of my kids? How hard would it have been to find a dope fiend, give him a twenty, and have him cut my mama's grass for her? You niggas are snakes! You're a bunch of users, riders, muthafuckin' passengers! Well, the free fucking ride is over! It's time to get the fuck off the Jerrell Express! No more muthafuckin' gravy trains here, nigga!"

"Fuck you!" Skip shouted. "When we started this shit, we was all supposed to be equals. You're the one who made yourself into a god. You the one who set yourself up to be the leader over everybody! You did! You stopped being our brother and tried to be our daddy! You did that shit, nigga! You can't force people to love you like a brother; you have to be a brother. You can't force someone to be loyal; you have to win a nigga's loyalty! I can't believe you killed them."

Jerrell thought quietly for a moment. Skip was correct and everything he was saying was right. Skip made perfect sense, and Jerrell was doing everything he could to not waver in his decisions. *Do I have to kill Skip? He's been so loyal, but he knows I killed everybody else. He knows I came here to kill him. I can never trust this nigga again. And he'll never trust me, ever. Fuck, Skip, why'd you have to have my money?*

Why'd you have to be right? Damn, I wish I didn't have to, but this nigga knows too much.

"Fuck that shit!" Jerrell shouted. "I gave you niggas everything! I took care of y'all. I put you niggas on top! I organized Junior Mafia, I planned the campaigns and the hits to seize those spots, I set up the distribution, I got us the contacts! I took care of everything, and you niggas benefited from it! I showed love, and I got nothing back! I got nothing!"

Skip fell back onto the couch and shook his head. Sweat began to bead on his forehead. "You demanded our loyalty, J. You can't demand a person's loyalty. You wanted to take care of us by handing shit out to us, like it all belonged to you. We all worked hard for that shit. We got out there in those streets, and we killed niggas, and took the risks, took the bullets from taking over those spots. We did it, and we did it together."

Jerrell stood quietly and examined Skip for several moments. "What the fuck's wrong with you, nigga?"

Skip swallowed hard and shook his head. "I need to eat something, that's all."

"You need to eat something?" Jerrell shifted his gaze toward the kitchen table, where he spied Skip's insulin and syringe. He walked to the table, lifted the bottle, and read the contents. He turned back toward Skip. "Why, you lying, conniving, sick muthafucka, you!"

Skip leaned back into the couch, growing weaker by the moment. His head was pounding and sweat was pouring down his face. "I need something to eat. Some . . . fruit . . . anything. Please . . ."

Jerrell nodded. "I'll give you something, all right. My brother."

Jerrell stuck the needle back into the insulin bottle and pulled the stopper all the way to the top, filling the syringe. He walked to where Skip was now lying on the couch, yanked Skip's shirt up, and stuck the needle into Skip's stomach. He injected the full syringe of insulin into Skip.

"No!" Skip knocked the empty syringe away and tried to get up. He found himself tumbling onto the floor. "Help . . . me . . ."

"Fuck you," Jerrell told him. He stepped over Skip and walked to the stereo, where he pulled the rest of Skip's money out of the speaker.

"Please, you can have all the money," Skip pleaded weakly. "Just help me. Orange, in the icebox."

Jerrell walked to Skip's other speaker and yanked off the cover. This speaker was packed with blocks of money wrapped in plastic. It had to be millions. He'd hit the fucking jackpot.

Skip began convulsing, and foam and slobber began leaking from his mouth.

"So, which one is it, Skip?" Jerrell asked as he removed the money from Skip's speaker. "Are you having a diabetic stroke, a diabetic heart attack, or is it just a really bad reaction? You look pretty bad, Skip. You'll probably have been in a coma for way too long before anyone finds you. And that means, even if you survive, you'll most likely be a vegetable. Sorry, B. But shit happens."

Jerrell rose, stepped over Skip's motionless body, and headed into the kitchen, where he grabbed a trash bag to carry out all his newfound wealth. By the time he finished loading his car, he realized Skip had saved every single penny he'd gained from hustling. And it was a damn pretty penny. Skip had been over five million strong. Skip's money, combined with the money Jerrell had taken from all the others, now made him over ten million strong. He was back on top again. Almost as rich as the old Jerrell.

Jerrell loaded the last bag of money into his Range Rover, peered around the quiet, nearly pitch-black neighborhood, and lit up a fat Cuban cigar. He wasn't a daily smoker; in fact, he only lit up on special occasions. Tonight was a special occasion. Jerrell exhaled, blew the smoke into the cool Philly breeze, and allowed himself a big, wide grin. It felt fucking good to be the king again.

Visiting Hours

The county jail was a massive concrete structure with long, narrow, gun-slit-style windows covered over with a thick steel wire mesh. The imposing facade gave the entire complex an air of foreboding. That, and the sharp, thick strands of concertina wire that surrounded the entire establishment caused goose bumps to appear on Gena's arms.

Gena made her way into the building and located the visitation desk. A heavyset guard seated behind the reception desk peered up at her over his glasses.

"May I help you, miss?" the guard asked.

"Yes, I'm here for visitation," Gena told him.

"Inmate's name?" the guard asked.

"Smith," Gena told him. "His name is Tyrik Smith."

The guard looked up the name on his list and lifted the telephone.

"Visitation for Smith, Tyrik, inmate number one-zero-nine-two-five-two." The guard peered back up at Gena. "You have your driver's license, miss?"

Gena lifted her Chanel bag onto the counter and pulled out her wallet. She opened her billfold, pulled out her driver's license, and handed it to the guard. The guard took the license and typed Gena's information into his computer. When he finished typing her information, he handed the license back to her and nodded toward the hall.

"Visitation room's around the corner," he told her. "You know how to get there?"

Gena nodded. "I know where it is."

"If you get turned around, follow the signs posted on the walls," the guard said.

Gena nodded again and headed off toward the visitation room. She'd been there before to visit two of her ex-boyfriends and even a couple of her cousins. She knew her way to the room by heart.

"Who are you here to see?" another guard asked as soon as she walked through the door into the visitation room.

"Tyrik Smith," Gena told him.

The guard nodded as he checked his list. "All right, in here. You're gonna need a locker and you'll have to remove all your jewelry. Your pockets need to be empty, no gum, and any money you want to carry inside needs to be contained in a plastic see-through bag. Carry nothing on you through security except your key to your locker. Do you understand?"

He talked so fast, had she been a new jack at the whole process, she would've been ass out. She nodded and took the key from the guard. When she finished signing in, she waited in the sign-in area until the number the guard had given her was called for a search. Nothing major: a walk through the metal detector, mouth check, and hand scan.

"Take booth number six."

Gena nodded and headed into the visitation room. As she passed the other booths, she could hear babies crying, women shedding tears, other women talking dirty, while others were cursing and shouting at the person they'd come to visit. She found her booth, seated herself on the tiny bench seat, and waited.

Tyrik walked into the room wearing a county-issued bright

orange jumpsuit. His hair was still neatly trimmed, as was his goatee. He smiled uncontrollably when he saw Gena. He grabbed the phone and seated himself in the booth opposite.

"Hey, baby girl!" Rik told her.

"Hey, Rik!" Gena said enthusiastically. "Man, I didn't even know you were locked up. You all right?"

"I'm good," Rik told her. "How about you? How have you been?"

"I'm doing good," Gena told him. "Just getting everything back on track."

Rik nodded. "I heard that. I can't tell you how good it feels to see you again."

"It feels good to see you, too," Gena told him. "So, what are they saying?"

Rik shook his head. "They not saying anything good, mama, that's for damn sure. They hitting us with the whole enchilada. Conspiracy to distribute crack cocaine, and conspiracy to carry out a continuing criminal enterprise. They hittin' us with a conspiracy to manufacture crack cocaine, too. They tryin' to roof a nigga in this muthafucka. They got a confidential informant and they got tapes, supposed to be a lot of tapes. They ain't saying what they got on the tapes, though, or at least not yet."

Gena lowered her head and leaned her cheek on the palm of her hand. "So what is the lawyer saying?"

"He's saying it looks pretty bad. What the fuck can he say, Gena? Shit, only thing I know right now is that we might find out something at the discovery hearing. He thinks we might be able to figure out who the informant is after discovery. I wish I knew who the snake muthafucka was . . ."

"So, what happens then?" Gena asked. "Even if you find out who it is, will that help you?"

Will that help? Will that help? Is she nuts? I'll dead that nigga before anyone can blink or even think of a trial. Will that help? But of course Rik didn't respond like that; he knew the mice were listening in the walls.

"Well, we can discredit the witness, and shit like that," Rik explained. "But other than that, who knows . . ."

Gena shook her head and wiped her eyes as she pretended to be tired. She didn't want Rik to see her upset at his misfortune.

"Don't you be tripping over me. You be happy, Gena. I'll handle this. You just worry about Gena, you hear me?"

Gena nodded.

"So, what's this I hear about you having a new man?" Rik asked with a smile.

Gena nodded.

"That's good," Rik told her. "I was so happy to hear that. I'm glad you're finding happiness again, Gena. You deserve to be happy. Quadir would want you to be happy."

"Who told you? Veronica?"

"Yeah, she claims she having my baby."

"Oh yeah, congratulations, big papa."

"Man, don't congratulate me till the blood test comes back. Shit, I don't know, Gena, I don't know."

"I don't know neither, Rik." Gena looked up and peered into Tyrik's eyes. "I just don't . . ."

"Hey, I know Qua, he was my nigga, for real, all day strong," Rik told her. "That boy loved you more than anyone else in this world. He loved you with everything he had. You were his whole world, and making you happy was something he wanted to always do for you. Trust me, he'd want you to be happy."

"Sometimes it's so hard to go on. I miss him so much, Rik. I still lie in my bed and cry for him. We were supposed to be together forever. It's so hard to live life without him."

"Gena, listen to me. You have to keep on going. It's your love for Quadir that keeps him alive. You have to live life for both of you now.

Your happiness is his happiness, your joy is his joy. Qua is a part of you from now on, and you carry him with you wherever you go. Be happy, baby; live life to the fullest for both of you. The world can be a cruel place, full of trickery. It took away the person you were supposed to spend the rest of your life with. Life tricked you, so I understand how you must still feel and I don't blame you. But you must find a little bit of happiness out here, take whatever good this life allows you to have, and run with it. So, you run with it, Gena. Take whatever's given. Make a new life for yourself and be happy."

"I'll try, Rik, I'll try. What about you? What about bail?"

"Man, that fuckin' judge said two-million-dollar bail and I thought I'd die. I knew then I'd sit for a minute."

"Why? I don't understand why you don't post it."

"'Cause the Feds ain't like the state. In the state, if you get a two-million-dollar bond, you have to get a bail bondsman to get you out, and they'll charge you about two hundred grand. In the Feds, you put up the bond money, and you get it back when you show up for trial and stuff."

"Oh!" Gena said, surprised. "Well, do you have it to put up?"

Rik shook his head, not answering that question over the phone.

"Do you want it?" Gena asked.

Rik peered into Gena's eyes. "What do you mean, Gena?"

"Don't answer a question with a question, Rik," Gena said nervously. "Do you want the money so you can get out on bond?"

"Two million dollars?" Rik asked. "Gena, how are you going to get two million dollars?"

"Do you want the money, Rik?" Gena asked again.

"And this new boyfriend of yours is going to give you two million dollars to give to my lawyers so I can get out on bond?"

"Do you want the money?" Gena asked him again.

Rik thought about what Gena was asking. *Do I want the money? What the fuck would that shit look like if she walks up to my lawyers with two million dollars? It'd be a mess and the Feds would be all over my ass if I made that bail. I definitely don't want that.*

So far, they'd left his baby mama and his houses alone. He really wanted to keep it that way. He wanted them knowing as little as possible about his money, about his family life, about his business. He had to think seriously before he took her up on her offer and, now, for the second part of her question.

Rik leaned back against the glass booth and contemplated Gena's offer. *I do want out of here, bad, but where she even getting this money from? Her new boyfriend? Nah, I ain't buyin' that.* Niggas with that kind of bread to throw around were rare, and he'd know the nigga. The only one he knew personally had been his nigga Quadir. Qua had the paper to do shit like that . . .

Rik dropped his telephone when the thought hit him.

"Rik, are you all right?" Gena asked.

Rik nodded. He was still in shock. *Gena done found Quadir's stash. That explains it all: the new car, the clothes, the jewelry, everything. Why didn't I see that! How could I have been so stupid! Gena's sitting on the most incredible meal ticket and keeping that shit on the low-low.*

"Rik, what's the matter?" Gena asked.

Rik shook his head. "No, nothing, I'm okay."

"So, what's up, baby?" Gena asked. "Do you want to get out on bond or what?"

"Gena, I appreciate the offer, I really do," Rik told her. "But it's a lot more complicated than that. I have to think about what these people will think if I plunk down a two-million-dollar bond."

"It's not your money, so why would they trip with you?" Gena asked.

"Yeah, but they'd think it was my money," Rik explained. "Who'd put up two million dollars for someone else? And if they didn't think it was my money, they'd want to know whose money it was, and where they got it from. Do you really want them asking those kinds of questions, Gena? Think about it."

Gena lowered her head and nodded. He was right.

"I don't want to pull you into this mess, Gena," Rik told her. "I care about you and I'd never want you to do anything for me that could hurt you. I want you to stay as far away from this mess as possible. I don't want them looking at you in any way possible, understand?"

Gena nodded. She certainly didn't want that kind of heat. Too many questions would be asked, and they were questions she wouldn't be able to answer. *Naw, fuck that, Rik is right.*

"Rik," Gena said as she rose from the bench, "you can call me whenever you want, okay?"

Rik nodded and smiled goodbye to her.

Gena placed the phone down on the counter, turned, and walked out of the visitation room with eyes watching her from inside the walls. Something told her that she'd made one of the biggest mistakes of her life. She felt like she should never have come to this place.

Bugged Out

Detective Ellington hit the rewind button on the tape and once again replayed the conversation between Gena and Rik.

"She's offering him the two million dollars." Detective Dick Davis nodded.

Detective Barrientes nodded. "I agree. It's an offer."

"So we're all in agreement that little Miss Gena has her dead man's money?" Lieutenant Ratzinger asked.

The detectives arrayed around the room all nodded in agreement.

"So, what's our next move?" Detective Barrientes asked.

"We can't grab her, because, technically, she didn't say she had the money," Lieutenant Ratzinger told them.

"You think we should squeeze her?" Dick Davis asked.

"Or how about we put twenty-four-hour surveillance on her until she leads us to the money?" Detective Barrientes offered.

"Maybe we should do both," Lieutenant Ratzinger suggested.

"I have another idea," Detective Ellington told them.

"What's that?" Ratzinger asked.

Letoya Ellington walked to the window and peered out across the downtown skyline. She folded her arms as her thoughts began to formulate. "I say we use our CI on her. They know each other well. Let's get her to confide in him on tape, saying she has the money, and then we can really squeeze her. We bring her in, I play the big sister role, Davis plays the hammer, and one of us will get it out of her."

Lieutenant Ratzinger nodded. He liked the idea. Besides, getting her on tape was something they could take to a grand jury if necessary. They might do that if she refused to give up the money. They could charge her with money laundering or profiting from an illicit trade. He'd have someone from the US attorney's office look it up. Living off drug money was illegal, even if you weren't the one who sold the drugs. He was certain they could find plenty of things to charge her with and find plenty of statutes under which to seize that money. Again, he nodded his consent.

"Let's run with it, Letoya," Lieutenant Ratzinger told her. "Get your informant up to speed. See what he knows about the money, and about this Gena girl. And then tell him what we need."

Letoya nodded. "He's in the next room. I'll see what I can get out of him."

"Need some help?" Dick Davis asked.

Detective Ellington paused and thought about the offer for several moments. She'd already established herself as a hard-ass with the CI. Maybe she could bring in Dickie Davis to play the good cop.

"Yeah, Dick, maybe I could use a little help," she told him. "Feel up to playing the nice, sympathetic cop today?"

"Why do I always have to play the good guy?" Dick asked, following Letoya out of the room.

"Maybe because you look all nice and sweet and young," Letoya told him. She turned and squeezed Detective Davis's cheek. "And you look seventeen, Dickie. Who's going to be intimidated by someone who looks like the kid who carries their groceries to the car?"

Detective Ellington strolled into the room where Rasun was seated and waiting for her. Dickie Davis closed the door behind them.

"Rasun, this is Detective Davis, my partner," Letoya told her informant. "Detective Davis, this is the young man who's been helping us out with the investigation."

Detective Davis and Rasun exchanged handshakes.

"So, Rasun, the reason I had them bring you over today is I have a few questions for you," Detective Ellington told him.

"I don't think I want to answer any more of your questions," Rasun told her.

"And why is that?" Detective Ellington asked.

"Because you people are all snakes!" Rasun said venomously.

Detective Ellington laughed at him.

"Why do you say that?" Dickie Davis asked.

"I'm still in jail, ain't I?" Rasun asked. "What the fuck did I do all of this shit for if I was gonna go to jail anyway!"

"Rasun, we did it to protect you," Detective Ellington explained. "If we'd left you on the streets and rounded up everyone else, they would've figured out you've been helping us."

"And what about now?" Rasun asked. "Why am I still in there? Why didn't the judge give me bond?"

"You are bonded out, Rasun," Detective Ellington told him. "You've been released into our custody. We're waiting for the right time to kick you back out on the street. We're trying to be careful and make sure you're safe."

Rasun shook his head. "Man, I don't want to be locked up anymore."

"Okay," Detective Ellington told him. "Some of the others we arrested are starting to make bond. We'll kick you out with some of them. We'll say your attorney got the judge to reduce your bond, and then he posted it and had you released into his custody."

"Will that work, Rasun?" Dickie Davis asked.

Rasun looked down and nodded.

"I have some questions for you, Rasun," Dickie Davis told him. "But before I ask them, I need to know you're still part of the team.

Detective Ellington tells me you've been a real asset to her investigation, and they're thinking about going before the United States attorney and getting you a sweet deal so you won't have to go to jail and so your mother's house won't be touched. Are you still down for that deal, Rasun?"

Rasun rolled his eyes and nodded as he sat uncomfortably in his chair.

"Good, good man," Dickie Davis said with a pat on the shoulder.

"Did you know Quadir Richards?" Detective Ellington asked him.

Rasun nodded. "Of course."

"How well did you know him?" Dickie Davis asked.

"He was my homie," Rasun admitted.

"How did he die?" Detective Davis asked.

"He was killed in a drive-by outside of a club on New Year's Eve," Rasun told them. "Y'all the police. You should be telling me. Damn, don't y'all know how the fuck he died?"

Letoya nodded. "Okay, we won't insult your intelligence. Was your boy a baller?"

Rasun nodded.

"A big-time baller?" Dickie Davis asked with a smile.

"Is there any other kind?" Rasun asked, looking at Detective Davis like he was stupid.

"So Qua was a baller, huh?" Detective Ellington repeated. "That's what the homies called him, wasn't it? Qua?"

Rasun nodded.

"So Qua must've had some major chips stacked up, then?" Detective Davis asked.

Rasun shrugged.

Detective Ellington slapped Rasun's hat off his head. "Did he have some fucking paper or didn't he?"

Rasun jumped and gave Detective Ellington a look that said he wanted to kill her.

"Did he?" Detective Ellington asked again.

"Yeah." Rasun rubbed his head where she had struck him. "They say Qua was papered up."

"Who is *they*?" Detective Davis asked.

Rasun shrugged. "Just people, the people on the streets. Qua was known to be papered up. It was the word on the streets."

"Do you know Gena Scott?" Detective Ellington asked.

Rasun nodded.

"How well do you know her?" Detective Davis asked.

"We all right," Rasun said. "I talked to her girlfriend Sahirah for a minute and I used to see her around and shit."

"Would you consider yourselves friends?" Detective Davis asked.

Rasun nodded. "We cool."

"How much does she trust you?" Detective Davis asked.

Rasun shrugged. "I don't know."

"Would she confide in you?" Detective Ellington asked.

Rasun shrugged again. "She was closer to Rik than she was with anybody else. She would confide in him first."

Detectives Davis and Ellington shared a glance and made a mental note. Gena had, after all, offered Tyrik two million dollars.

"When's the last time you saw her?" Detective Ellington asked.

"Not since Qua's funeral," Rasun told them.

"So you don't know how she's doing now?" Detective Davis asked.

Rasun shook his head.

"What kind of girl is she?" Detective Davis asked. "I mean, how did she grow up? Was she rich? Was she poor? Tell me about her."

Rasun shrugged. "I don't really know nothing about her. She was Qua's girl. I think she grew up over in Richard Allen. I don't think she was papered up or nothing."

"What if I told you that she was rolling in a two-hundred-thousand-dollar Porsche?" Detective Ellington asked.

Rasun shrugged once more. "Then I would say she doing damn good. Better than I am."

"She kept all of Quadir's money?" Detective Davis asked, leaning in and whispering like he was asking a secret.

Rasun lifted an eyebrow. Damn, it was something he hadn't thought about. He'd thought she was broke.

"You're quiet all of a sudden," Detective Ellington said. "What's the deal, Rasun? Does she have Quadir's money?"

Rasun shook his head. "I don't know. I mean, the last I heard, old girl was doing bad. Rik was helping her out and shit. Qua's mom pulled a gangster move on her for the house and the cars and shit, booted old girl out on the street with nothing. Everybody thought the mom and pop had Qua's loochie."

Again, the detectives exchanged glances. This was new information for them. They both tried desperately to make a detailed mental note so they could later write it all down.

"So Quadir's mother has his money?" Detective Davis asked.

Rasun nodded. "That's what everybody always thought, because Gena went back to the projects, broke, sad, and all fucked up like the rest of us."

Detective Davis rubbed the lower half of his face and turned away in shock. "So where would she be getting all of her dough from now?"

Rasun shrugged. "Maybe another baller or something. I wouldn't know. I ain't heard nothing about her since after the funeral. Last I heard, she was doing bad, living back at home with her peeps up in the projects."

Detective Ellington opened the door to the interrogation room and nodded for Detective Davis to step outside. Once her colleague joined her in the hall, she closed the door so Rasun couldn't hear them talking.

"What the fuck is going on, Letoya?" Detective Davis asked.

"Sounds like we've been attacking this thing from the wrong angle," Detective Ellington told him. "We need to be following the mother, Viola Richards, for that money, and we need to be following Miss Scott so we can open up an investigation on her new boyfriend. Sounds like Miss Gena was accustomed to living a certain way, so she ran out and got her another baller."

Detective Davis laughed. "I still say we see what kind of information he can get out of her. Maybe he can find out who she's messing with, and we can get some good information by putting them two together."

Letoya nodded. "Hell yeah, I still say we wire his ass up and set up a meeting between the two. See what we come up with."

"You take care of the Gena angle, and once we get a name on the boyfriend, I'll start watching him and seeing who he scores from and see if we can put together another major bust."

Detective Ellington lifted her hand into the air, and Detective Davis slapped it.

"Lieutenants by next May!" she declared excitedly.

"Lieutenants by next May!" Detective Davis smiled.

"I'm going to get the paperwork done so I can cut our bait loose," Detective Ellington said.

"I'll give him the good news and arrange for his transportation back to county in the meantime," Detective Davis told her, opening the door to the interrogation room.

"Rasun, I got some good news for you!" Detective Davis said excitedly. "You'll be outta this place in a couple of hours, back on your block, hustling your rock like the good old days. Now, for the bad news, we need to wire you up again."

Rasun leaned over and began to vomit.

Payback's a Bitch

Champagne leaped out of her brand-new black S Class 600 wearing a black leather catsuit with matching black leather knee-high boots. The suit looked like it had been painted onto her body. It was backless, with only her long, burnt-orange hair covering her milky yellow skin. She wore an oversize pair of dark Chanel sunglasses and walked like she was gliding across a catwalk in Paris or Milan. Every man on the street within a two-block radius stopped and stared. Her body was the stuff of every man's fantasy, and she knew it.

Champagne looked to cross the street, and cars came to a screeching halt, the mostly male drivers all wanting to let her pass so they could garner a better look at her unrealistic-looking ass. It stuck out so far and was so round it looked like you could set a table on top of it.

Jerrell sat on a park bench shaking his head.

"So this is what you call clandestine?" he asked. "And in case you don't know what that means, it means secret."

"Fuck you. I know what it means, asshole," Champagne told him.

"You're looking mighty tasty today," Jerrell told her.

Champagne placed her hand on her hip and shifted her weight to one side. "Don't even think about it."

Jerrell smiled. "Not even for old times' sake?"

"Not for all the tea in China, dear heart."

Jerrell pulled out a massive wad of money and tossed it to her. "How about for all of that? Can I hit it for all of that?"

Champagne examined the massive wad of hundreds. "How much is this?"

"See, look at your trick ass!" Jerrell teased. "A minute ago, a nigga couldn't hit for all the tea in China. Now you see cash money and you open like a Chinese takeout spot in the middle of the night, huh?"

"Cream, baby. Gotta get it," Champagne told him.

Jerrell shook his head and snatched his money out of her hand. "I wouldn't stick my dick in you if you gave all this money to me. I might as well go over there and stick my dick in that trash can. It'd be a whole lot cleaner."

Champagne turned and began to walk away. Jerrell leaped up from the bench and clasped her elbow. "Champagne, wait."

Champagne wiped the tears from her eyes. "What? Let go of me, you sorry son of a bitch!"

"I'm sorry," Jerrell told her.

"I know you sorry." Champagne nodded. "You sorry as hell and I'm tired of your shit. You didn't want me when you had me, so what the fuck you want me to do? Stop living?"

"Champagne, it's just that I still have feelings for you," Jerrell said softly. "And when you said you wouldn't sleep with me for all the tea in China . . ."

"You have a funny way of showing you have feelings for someone," she told him.

Jerrell removed her hands from her face and turned her around. "I do. When someone says something to hurt me, the only way to protect myself is to hit back." Jerrell wrapped his arms around her waist and pulled her close. "What did you find out for me?"

Champagne exhaled. "I found out a lot."

"Oh, really?" Jerrell lifted an eyebrow. "And tell me what exactly *a lot* is that you found out."

"What do you want to know?" Champagne asked. She unwrapped his arms from around her waist and took a step back from him.

"Does she have a man?" Jerrell asked.

Champagne nodded. "Yeah, you."

A slight smile made its way across Jerrell's face. "Who was her man before me?"

"You mean who was she about to marry," Champagne corrected. "Who was going to be her husband."

"She was in a relationship like that?" Jerrell recoiled slightly at the information.

Champagne nodded. "She was two steps away from marrying Quadir Richards, aka Qua."

"Get the fuck outta here!" Jerrell was in shock. His archrival, the nigga whose ground he hated to see himself have to walk on. *Get the fuck outta here. I got Quadir's wife. See, nigga, that's what you get for not getting down with the M.* Damn. Irony was a motherfucker.

Champagne nodded. "Yeah, you fucking Quadir's girl. Quadir, the nigga you and your boys killed. Ain't that nothing?" she asked, looking at him out of the corner of her eye like Terry McMillan as she used her fingernail to pick at her teeth.

Jerrell shifted his glance to Champagne. *I can't stand this crazy bitch. Now I know why we didn't make it and why we never will.* Say what you want, but Champagne was quick, and she knew way too much for her own good.

"Is she in the game?" Jerrell asked, getting frustrated.

Champagne shook her head. "The only game she's in is the shopping game. That's all this bitch does is shop and hang out."

"Is she fucking with another baller?" Jerrell asked.

"Besides you?" Champagne asked, lifting an eyebrow. "No."

"And her paper?"

"Where do you think it comes from?" Champagne asked rhetorically. "Um, let's see, her boyfriend was like one of the biggest dope boys in Philly. They say Quadir was sitting on millions. And that money disappeared the moment they lowered him into the ground. My guess would be it's drug money Quadir left behind. Oops, right answer, Johnny, I win!"

Jerrell turned away from Champagne and thought about what he'd been told. That nigga, Quadir, had millions. Word on the street was the nigga was something like twenty million strong. And if this bitch got his money . . .

"Goddammit!" Jerrell shouted. "How could I miss this shit? How could I be so stupid!"

"What?" Champagne joked, sounding like Amil. "You had a gold mine right beneath your nose all this time, huh? And to think you needed me to figure this shit out for you. I'm not surprised, though."

Jerrell closed his eyes to gather his thoughts. Champagne knew him too well. That left him with one of two options. He could either kill the bitch or make her his wife. And being she was much more useful to him alive than dead, he certainly didn't want to kill her. No, he'd leave that fate for Ms. Gena. He needed to come up with a plan to get that money from her and get the hell outta town. Maybe he and Champagne could take all the money and relocate to the South. A nice crib in Atlanta or Charlotte or Miami sounded real nice right about now. Yeah, Miami, or better yet, Palm Beach. He could fuck the shit outta Champagne all night and lay up on the beach all day sipping on exotic-ass drinks—a whole new life. Yeah, he needed new keys.

Jerrell turned toward Champagne. "Thanks for the info, sweetie. I might have an offer for you later."

Champagne lifted an eyebrow. "Oh, really?"

Jerrell smiled and nodded. He leaned forward and kissed her on her cheek. "Yeah. But right now, I got a lot of planning to do."

"I bet you do." Champagne smiled.

Jerrell and Champagne shared a knowing laugh. They both knew what he had on his mind. They both knew he was about to go and sit down somewhere and make preparations to rob a bitch. Oh, what fate lay ahead was unknown, but one thing was for certain, ol' Mr. Jerrell would be planning to come out on top.

Bria lifted Gah Git's coffee cup off the table, walked to the coffeepot, and refilled it. "Gah Git, you want some milk in here?"

Gah Git nodded. "Yeah, baby. And put a little sugar in there for me, too."

Brianna walked through the kitchen with a load of laundry in her arms, heading for the utility room, where the washing machine was kept.

Bria placed Gah Git's coffee on the table, grabbed the trash bag from the garbage can, and headed out the back door.

"Gena still ain't called?"

"No, ma'am," Brianna replied.

"It's been over a week, and she ain't even called me."

"She all right, Gah Git. My girlfriend's sister works at the hair-dresser and she was in there getting her hair done. Don't worry, she just mad at us right now. She'll be back."

"I sure do hope she okay out there in them streets. Mad or not, she could call and talk to me, let me know she's okay."

Just then they heard the doorbell, and seconds later, as Bria opened the door, Gah Git and the twins heard Khaleer shouting. "It's Uncle Michael. Uncle Michael's here," he said as he ran back into the kitchen to tell Gah Git.

Gah Git jumped up and almost pushed Bria down trying to get past her to the door.

"Michael," she said, flinging the door open to see her baby boy standing there.

"Ma," he said, before falling into her arms like he used to do when he was a baby.

Bria whispered, "Dag, Uncle Michael look good."

"He sure do. He lucky he's our uncle," Brianna agreed.

Gena rolled over and looked at the alarm clock on the nightstand on the other side of the bed, where Jay was still sleeping. She rolled back over and lay in the bed thinking about the past couple of weeks. She'd finally found an apartment, off City Line Avenue on the Philadelphia side. A nice apartment right behind Friday's restaurant. She had a security gate, so no one could get into her complex, and she had an alarm system inside her apartment, so she felt safe there. She was assigned two parking spaces for her cars and she was allowed to have dogs and cats for an additional security deposit. The kitchen was small, but had an eat-in. The apartment had a dining room, family room, master bedroom, master bath, and a half bath. It was honestly all she needed for herself.

She had central air, wall-to-wall carpeting, washer, dryer, garbage disposal, white cabinets with green granite countertops, and she had the nerve to have imported tile set in the floors and half of the walls in the master bath. It was quite charming and affordable. Gena was scheduled to pick up the keys next week. She'd been to every furniture store in the city, from the ones up on the boulevard down to the ones in South Philly, and had furnishings paid for and ready to be delivered. She was excited, to say the least. This would really be her own apartment. The apartment she once had was in a three-story row house her uncle Michael owned in West Philly on Chancellor Street next door to her girlfriend Markita. She thought the whole time she was there he'd paid her rent, but the truth was there wasn't any rent, because he owned the building.

She looked over at Jay sleeping. He had been nice about letting her stay with him. She could tell he didn't really want to in the beginning and he certainly never gave her a key, so her stay with him was temporary. Jay was very domesticated. He cooked, he cleaned, he ironed, he pretty much did it all, even grocery shopping, and seemed to know the grocery store like the back of his hand, locating everything from soap to paper towels with ease. He certainly didn't need a woman to keep it together for him. He was meticulous, neat, and kept his apartment in tip-top shape. While he had a cleaning service come in once a week to do the major cleaning, he did a fine job keeping his place tidy.

Every morning when they got up, he'd cook breakfast. Sometimes he'd even cook dinner. And he didn't make simple dishes, either. He made stuff she didn't know how to cook, like grilled salmon with curry mango chutney and green beans with a wild mushroom casserole. And one night, he even made pot roast so tender the meat fell off the fork. She was quite impressed with him and had no idea he was so independent. But Jay had learned early in his life to never depend on a woman for anything, and that's how he sustained himself so well, being single. All he pretty much needed a female for was pussy; other than that, he needed women for nothing at all.

Jerrell rolled over and saw Gena lying in the bed staring up at the ceiling.

"Whatcha doing?" he asked as he pulled her closer to him and snuggled with her.

"Nothing really, just thinking."

"About what?"

"My new place."

"Oh, you ready to roll out, huh?"

"Don't even try it. You're ready for me to go," Gena said, tickling his underarm.

Naw, bitch, I don't want you to go nowhere with all that paper you holding. You got this shit twisted. If you holdin' like I think you are, you can stay here as long as you want.

"Man, you must be crazy. I don't want to stop you from doing you, but you more than welcome here, ma. Please believe it."

"As good as you cook, it's gonna be hard to go."

"Sure it don't have nothing to do with Big Daddy Candy Cane here?" he said, motioning toward his penis.

"Um, now that I think about it, I might not be able to ever leave your side."

"See, now you saying something."

"Whatever. You gonna make breakfast?" she asked, accustomed to his breakfast-in-bed routine.

"Yeah, what you want?"

"Waffles and turkey bacon, scrambled eggs with cheese, and some fresh-squeezed orange juice, please."

"Look, you putting me to work as it is."

"You'll be all right."

Jerrell cooked breakfast and cleaned up his kitchen before Gena had finished showering and getting dressed. The two ate together and then discussed their day and evening plans. Jerrell read the paper while Gena watched *Family Matters*.

"Do you believe these people?"

"I believe anything. There's nothing that surprises me, Gena."

Gena thought about surprises and her family secret that everyone seemed to know except her. She felt bad because she hadn't called Gah Git since she ran out, and Gah Git was probably worried to death about her. *Maybe I'll go see her today,* Gena thought, wondering if that was a good idea.

She got up from the table and started grabbing her essentials to get out the door: sunglasses, pocketbook, and cell phone.

"Hey, Jay, you seen my car keys?"

"Yeah, on the counter in the glass dish," he said, pointing at them.

"Damn, what would I do without you?"

"Be all fucked up," he said. *No, the question is where will I be with that money you holding once I get it?*

Gena grabbed her keys, bent over, and kissed Jerrell goodbye, never having a clue that his saving her back at the gas station would turn into a ploy to follow her closely. His whole objective was to find where she was keeping her money and then rob her ass. But she had yet to lead him to her hiding place. *I hate to see you go, but I'll be following you. Don't you worry.*

"Have a good day," he hollered as she closed the door, waving goodbye.

Gena drove up Broad Street. She was headed to meet her cousin Gary, who had finally returned her call. She turned off Broad and drove a few blocks over to Camac Street. Gary was outside, as he said he would be, sitting on his front porch. Gena parked her car and made her way over.

"Hey, hey, hey!" He motioned to her.

"Hey to you, too," Gena said, giving him a hug.

"Hey, cuz!" Gary said, spinning her around. "How have you been?"

"Going crazy without you!" Gena told him. "Boy, you don't know how to call nobody!"

Gary shook his head and smiled. "Man, you don't know how busy I've been. Plus, I lost my phone, so I got your messages but you didn't leave me no number and I didn't have it 'cause it wasn't in my phone. By the time I seen Gah Git, damn near a month had gone by. I'm sorry."

Gena grabbed Gary's hand and led him away from the front porch. "You can tell me all about it while we walk and talk."

Gary shrugged as Gena led him down the street. "Really nothing to tell. Just working."

"And how is domestic life?" Gena asked. "Living with that new girlfriend of yours. Are you two getting along?"

Gary laughed and nodded. "About fifty percent of the time, which is pretty good, I hear. We argue over the most trivial shit you can imagine, though. But other than that, it's all right. And how about you? I hear you got a new man?"

Gena smiled and shrugged. "He's all right. He's good to me, treats me nice."

"Do you love him?" Gary asked.

Gena crinkled up her nose as she contemplated that question. She'd never really sat down and thought about it. She'd never looked at herself in the mirror and seriously asked that question. *Do I love Jay?*

"I don't know. I don't know."

Gena really didn't know if she could even see herself living with the man. Strangely, her mind drew a blank on the answer to that question. It was then she realized how little she knew about her new man of life. How could she be prepared to spend the rest of her life with a man she knew so little about? She hadn't met any of his family, she knew none of his friends, and she didn't know anything about his past. *Maybe I need to put Mr. Jay under investigation.*

"Your silence answered my question," Gary told her.

"I was thinking really hard about it," Gena told him.

"If it takes you that long to think about it, the answer is obviously no." Gary stopped in the middle of the street and turned to her. "Hey, cuz. There's no rush. Don't think you're in a race, or you have to run out there and find somebody to replace Quadir, because you don't. Take your time, and love will come. It'll come when you least expect it."

"Enough about love. All I really want to know is, why you ain't tell me?" she asked him, not wanting to believe he knew, too.

"Tell you what, about your moms? Come on, man, you charging

me? Gena, my moms ain't having it. That shit is old news, like back when it all went down."

"What went down?"

Gary looked at his cousin, and honestly, he didn't know what to do. If he went against what his mom said, he could have a true family crisis to deal with.

Stay out of it. Gena's father needs to explain; he needs to tell her what happened to her mother. That was Paula's voice and opinion he heard in his head. So he'd never spoken about it, and he didn't want to now.

"You know I love you, right? So when I tell you this, don't get mad and don't say I told you, okay?"

"Gary, come on, I'm not going to tell nothing, and I'd never put your name in nothing. You realize that," she said, pleading to know what seemed like the biggest secret in the world.

"Okay, check this out, right, your mom and Uncle Malcolm was together for like a real long time, right? But all the while . . ."

"All the while what?" Gena asked, upset he'd stopped in the middle of a sentence. "Come on, tell me. What?"

"All the while she was married to Uncle Malcolm, she was sleeping with Uncle Michael, and one day your dad came home and caught them together . . . and he . . . shot up Uncle Michael and strangled your mother."

"My dad killed my mother?"

"Yeah, true story, and Uncle Michael lived. Even though he didn't testify, Uncle Malcolm still went to prison for killing your mother. They say you witnessed it, but you was little, like three or four or something."

Gary knew there was more to the secret, much more, but this was where he drew the line, and this was all he was going to tell her. They headed back to the porch and sat down.

"Please, Gena, you can't say I told you this, all right? I swear, I don't want to hear my mother's mouth."

Gena sat there staring into the thin fall air, not really looking at anything in particular. There was a breeze blowing up on Gary's porch, and the two of them sat there for the next hour and seventeen minutes without saying one word. The sounds of the city and cries of the streets filled the air, but Gena blocked it all out. She took in every word Gary had spoken. *How could they keep something like that a secret all this time? My father killed my mother and I watched him do it. I don't remember that. I don't remember that at all.*

Gena pierced the inner depths of her brain, trying to recollect, but she couldn't find one iota of a thought that brought back any memory of that fateful day. She'd always wished she had her mother, always wished for her in her life. She'd needed her mother, and to find out why she couldn't have her was heartbreaking. She didn't know what or how to feel about her father. She'd always wanted him, too. All her life she'd wished he wasn't locked away so they could've been together, but now she was older. She had her own life going on and she rarely even thought of him. But she would now.

The breeze that quietly blew seemed to blow a little. And the smooth breeze that once blew across her face now seemed to turn to wind that whipped across her cheeks—stinging, violent, dangerous, even. They were wild winds, winds of uncertainty. She was playing her life by ear at the moment, with no certainty of anything, and that was becoming more and more uncomfortable to her. Her family and everything she knew her life to be had been suddenly unbalanced, and she felt somewhat unsure and inadequate and very vulnerable.

Then there was Jay, and she honestly didn't know what the relationship they were sharing was all about. She didn't know enough about him to make any solid decisions. Yes, the breeze was a strong wind, and it smacked her in the face. She needed a plan, she needed stability, she needed to know where she and Jay really stood and what her feelings toward him really were. And now a man who'd been a stranger to her seemed to be the most familiar of all. All the dilemmas of her life had seemed to fall in her lap at once. She felt sick, almost ready to vomit, and as she sat and thought about what Gary had said, the sick feeling seemed to increase. She reached down and rubbed her belly, hoping to soothe her stomach. Unknown to her, her sickness had nothing to do with Gary, her father, or her mother. Her upset stomach was from the small life she was carrying, the small life that would change her entire world.

Schemesters

O'Hara's was an old, smoke-filled establishment located in the city's old section. The Irish-themed bar played host primarily to the city's working-class plebes. Construction workers, firefighters, emergency medical services technicians, and policemen all congregated within the four walls of the dimly lit establishment. Conversations ranging from the blood and gore of patching up bullet wounds to the proper techniques for putting out smoldering brush could be heard throughout. Off-duty police officers bragged about their marksmanship skills, while others simply drowned their troubles silently in glass after glass of scotch. Gathered around one of the old wooden circular tables was a group of Philly's finest who had celebrated themselves into inebriated states.

Lieutenant Ratzinger lifted his glass in a toast. "To Letoya Ellington, one of the best damn detectives it's been my sorry misfortune to meet!"

"Hear, hear!" Dickie Davis shouted, lifting his glass into the air.

"To Letoya Ellington, the most meticulous, the most crawl-up-your-ass, leave-no-stone-unturned detective a guy has ever met!" Detective Cornell Cleaver added.

The detectives around the table broke into laughter.

"You deserved that promotion, Toya," Lieutenant Ratzinger told her. "You did a stand-up job on that investigation. You handled that CI perfectly, you coordinated the raids, and you managed the entire operation with perfection. I wish we had a dozen more like you on the force."

Detective Ellington lifted her glass into the air. "Thanks, guys. You guys are absolutely the best. A girl couldn't ask for a better partner, a better ex-partner, and a better boss. You guys are the best."

"We're the best!" Detective Cornell Cleaver shouted.

"To Philly's finest!" Dickie Davis shouted.

Dozens of firemen and police officers began cheering.

Detective Davis rose from the table, swaying back and forth in a drunken stupor. "Ladies and gentlemen, may I have your attention, please! May I have everyone's attention?"

Slowly, the bar grew silent, and all eyes shifted their focus to the detective.

"I have an announcement to make," Detective Davis continued. "I have with me one of Philadelphia's finest detectives. She is a phenomenal woman, and the best partner a guy could ask for. She's the best woman I know with a Glock, and she can drink and piss fire with the best of them."

Laughter shot through the bar.

"Today, my partner was promoted to the rank of sergeant, a promotion that was long overdue," Dickie Davis slurred. "She's saved my ass so many times I've lost count. She lays it on the line every day to make the streets safe for all of us. And if she wasn't such a mean-ass motherfucker, and if I wasn't scared of her, I would marry her."

Laughter shot through the bar again.

"Ladies and gentlemen, my partner, the newly promoted Sergeant Letoya Ellington!"

Cheers rang throughout the establishment while everyone stood and clapped, giving Letoya Ellington a standing ovation. Letoya stood and lifted her glass in acknowledgment.

"A round on the house for Letoya," the bartender shouted. "But one round only, you lousy meatheads. I catch anybody trying to double back, I'm busting chops!"

The officers really began shouting and cheering. This was truly their establishment as the bartender, Stuckey, was one of their own. Stuckey had retired from the force as a captain and opened the bar several years ago. He'd made it a home away from home for Philadelphia's law enforcement personnel. The bar was filled with plaques and citations he'd been awarded, as well as lots of other police and firefighter memorabilia. It also had decommissioned weapons hanging on the walls, as well as lots of Texas Ranger memorabilia. Stuckey had a deep affection for the legendary Rangers, as well as for other well-known lawmen of the Old West. Old Western badges and wanted posters and pictures hung throughout the bar. It was truly a law enforcement officer's haven.

Dickie Davis seated himself and turned toward his partner. "Congratulations, Toya. I'm so proud of you."

"Thanks, Dick," Letoya told him.

"Hey, pull it out," Dickie told her. "Let me take a look at that thing!"

Letoya smiled, reached into her purse, pulled out her shiny new gold-colored sergeant's badge, and showed it to her partner.

Lieutenant Ratzinger took the badge and examined it. "I remember the day I made sergeant. It was one of the proudest moments in my life. I think it was three days after that when I got my divorce papers, which was an even happier moment."

The detectives arrayed around the table broke into laughter.

"How it always is," Detective Cleaver told them. "We work our butts off, and we pay the price for it at home."

"We miss the school plays, the anniversaries, the PTA meetings, the birthday parties . . ." Dickie Davis continued.

"And we get served with the divorce papers while they keep on getting richer," Ratzinger added.

"Straight bullshit!" Sergeant Ellington declared.

"I busted a punk the other day who had twenty thousand dollars on him," Detective Cleaver told them. "Right in his front pockets! The kid had twenty thousand dollars in pocket change, half my fucking annual salary, right inside his pockets."

"I busted a kid last week who had a Range Rover for every day of the week," Ratzinger told them. "A fucking different-colored Range Rover for each day of the week. And the kid's house looked like one of those houses on the cover of *Rich and Famous* magazine! The kid had fucking marble floors all throughout the place. Marble! And not the bullshit you find just anywhere. No, this was the good shit."

"They ride around like they won the lottery while we're risking our lives living paycheck to paycheck," Dickie Davis said, shaking his head. "I drive a Toyota; they drive Porsches and Mercedes."

"Sometimes it kinda makes you feel like you're on the wrong team," Ratzinger told them.

"Yeah, because the law protects them more than it does us," Cleaver said. "And we're the good guys. Shouldn't the good guys be the ones not having to scrape by?"

"They should." Ratzinger nodded. "They really should. The playing field sucks."

"Well, maybe it's time the playing field was equalized, dammit!" Detective Cleaver declared.

"What do you mean?" Dickie Davis asked.

"Maybe it's time the good guys take what they deserve!" Cleaver told them.

"How?" Sergeant Ellington asked. "Busting up some drug ring, so the Feds can come in and seize all of the assets and then pass us the leftovers?"

"Who says we need the Feds!" Ratzinger declared. "I'm tired of their bullshit anyway."

"You mean start keeping the funds for the department?" Sergeant Ellington shook her head. "Feds won't go for that one!"

"Who said the Feds even have to know?" Ratzinger asked them. "Hell, who said the department even has to know?"

"What are you suggesting, Lieutenant?" Dickie Davis asked.

"I'm saying there is about fifteen million dollars in unaccounted drug money belonging to a dead drug dealer that's waiting to be found," Ratzinger told them. "Nobody knows about it; nobody is going to miss it. And I for one would rather see that money in the hands of some hardworking police officers who lay their lives on the line every day than see it in the hands of some young bimbo whose only claim to it is letting some fucking lowlife scum-bucket drug dealer fuck her in the ass."

"So, let me get this straight," Detective Davis said. "Are you saying we keep this money if we find it?"

Detective Cleaver placed his arm around Dickie's shoulders. "That's exactly what he's saying, my boy. We'd be setting up our own little private retirement fund."

"We do all of the work, and we track down that money and find it, why shouldn't we keep it?" Ratzinger asked.

The officers around the table nodded in agreement.

"Are we all in?" Detective Cleaver asked.

"I'm in," Ratzinger announced.

Dickie Davis nodded. "I'm in."

"Sergeant?" Detective Cleaver asked.

Sergeant Ellington stared off into space and thought about the consequences of her answer. These were her fellow officers. Guys she trusted, guys who trusted her. They had her back, unquestionably, and now they were asking her to do something that wasn't fully legal.

Letoya leaned back in her seat and thought about what they

were asking of her. The money was illegal proceeds from the sale of narcotics. And it did belong to a dead drug dealer. And nobody would really miss it, because nobody even knew it existed. Nobody except for this drug dealer's mother, or his girlfriend, and neither one deserved to keep that money. They couldn't go to the police and say, hey, the police stole my illegal drug money. And she and her brother officers did lay it on the line every day for nothing. Hell, her lights came close to getting cut off last month! They could take that money and pay off their bills and use the rest of it to help get things done. They could use it as flash money, or buy money, without having to go to the department and fill out ten thousand request forms. That money could be used for some good.

"Letoya, are you in?" Dickie Davis asked.

Letoya Ellington looked at her partner's face and realized how badly he wanted her to be down with him. Dickie desperately needed that money. He was the only child of a pair of rapidly aging parents who had little money and escalating medical expenses. She couldn't let her partner down.

"Of course I'm with you guys," she declared.

The group leaned in closer around the table and began to speak in hushed tones.

"This doesn't leave this table, agreed?" Ratzinger declared.

"Agreed," Detective Cleaver said.

"Agreed." Dickie Davis nodded.

"Affirmative," Letoya said.

"We lean on the broad, and on the mother, and we find that cash," Ratzinger whispered. "We get the cash, we threaten whoever had it with prosecution and a long jail term, and we hush them up. We split the cash four ways, and we never speak of it again. And remember, nobody puts the cash in a bank, and nobody splurges on anything crazy. We don't need Internal Affairs all over our asses. Is that clear?"

"Clear." Dickie Davis nodded.

"I'm Internal Affairs," Detective Cleaver told them. "I'll cover our asses from that end and keep my eyes and ears open."

"Agreed," Letoya told them.

"One question," Dickie Davis said.

"What's that?" Lieutenant Ratzinger asked.

"What if the mother or the girlfriend or whoever doesn't want to keep silent after we snatch the money?" Dickie asked.

"Then we silence them," Cleaver told them. "Are we all in agreement on that? We do this, we go all the way if necessary. Is that clear? We are all in, all the way!"

Detective Davis nodded. He'd never shot anyone before. In fact, he'd never fired his gun in the line of duty. And now they were potentially talking about murdering someone for money. He wondered if he'd gotten in over his head.

"All in," Letoya declared.

Lieutenant Ratzinger nodded. "We go all the way, guys. We have to lay somebody down, we do it. No turning back. It's payday for the good guys."

"Payday for the good guys," Dickie Davis repeated, lifting his glass into the air.

"Payday," Letoya said, lifting her glass.

"It's about fucking time," Detective Cleaver declared, lifting his glass. He would kill for thousands. For millions, he would bury every fucking nigger in Richard Allen and then bulldoze that motherfucker personally.

Home, Sweet Home

Gena stepped into the freshly painted apartment and inhaled deeply. She loved the smell of new construction. She didn't know whether it was the smell of new carpet, the smell of fresh paint, or the smell of fresh lumber hiding behind the walls. Whatever it was, it was a smell she adored.

Gena walked farther into the apartment and spun around, taking in the apartment's many features. The small brass chandelier over the dining area, the massive brick fireplace in the corner of the family room, the nice, light eucalyptus-colored wood cabinets in the large kitchen, the sparkling granite countertops, the white-painted crown molding and baseboards, and the view of downtown—her mind was trying to rapidly absorb all these things. Yes, this was definitely it. After days and days of morning sickness and thinking she merely had some type of stomach virus, Gena discovered she was pregnant. She was excited, or happy, or rather scared and unsure of what to do. She decided to get a three-bedroom instead of a one-bedroom, so, if she needed extra space, she'd be prepared.

"The apartment has twenty-two hundred square feet. The master bedroom and the two secondary bedrooms are all upstairs," the leasing agent told her. "The master has its own bathroom, and the two secondary bedrooms share a bathroom. There is also a half bathroom here on the first floor. The apartment comes with all stainless-steel appliances, including a built-in dishwasher and refrigerator. Of course you have your fireplace, and your bar, and you also have your own utility room."

"Gena, girl, this place is banging," Tracey told her.

"You have a nice dining area, and plenty of built-in shelves as well as closet space," the leasing agent continued. "And security here is first-rate. The complex is completely gated, and there is a guard at the entrance, so everyone checks in before being allowed to enter the premises—but you know all that already from your tour of the one-bedrooms."

"Oh, girl, they got security at the gate!" Tracey laughed. "That'll keep all the bustas out."

"There is an on-site indoor gym, an indoor and an outdoor swimming pool, two basketball courts, a playground for children, a sand volleyball court, covered parking spaces for the residents, and a residents' clubhouse, complete with seating, a big-screen television, video games, card tables, an air hockey table, pool tables, and the works," the leasing agent told them. "And there is residents' night on Fridays, when the residents of the complex get together and watch newly released movies in the gathering center."

"*Girl*, sounds like we done died and gone to heaven! I wish I could live here." Tracey laughed again.

Gena continued to examine the apartment. She thought about the furnishings she was ready to have delivered and how nice they'd look in the space.

"Girl, what are you thinking?" Tracey asked.

"About where to put my aquarium filled with sharks." Gena smiled.

"An aquarium? Filled with sharks?" Tracey asked.

The leasing agent laughed.

"Sharks?" Tracey asked again.

Gena nodded. "The small ones. The ones that don't get really big."

"Let's go look upstairs, girl!" Tracey said excitedly. "Some damn sharks! Girl, you crazy!"

Gena turned and followed her friend up the stairs into the landing area.

"This area is really large," the leasing agent pointed out. "It would make a wonderful upstairs game room. You could put a nice-size television against that wall, and a sofa and love seat over here. You could make this room really functional. And there's a phone outlet up here, and a cable outlet as well."

Tracey made her way into the master bedroom. She screamed.

"Girl, what's the matter?" Gena asked, rushing to see what the deal was.

"Girl, this damn bedroom is bigger than my whole damn apartment!" Tracey told her.

"Bitch, you scared the shit out of me!" Gena told her.

Tracey opened the master closet. "Girl, this is my bedroom right here. Your closet is my bedroom."

Gena peeked into the closet. She was going to have a lot of fun filling that closet up with shoes and clothes.

Tracey rushed to the master bathroom and threw open the double doors. "Girl, there's a Jacuzzi in here big enough for two people!"

Gena smiled. Thoughts of her and Jay snuggling up in the tub made her feel warm inside. She could imagine herself riding him in the tub, until she thought of her new passenger and a big, round, protruding stomach, and the thought of riding Jay somehow seemed to disappear.

"Girl, I don't know," Tracey told her. "This place might be a little too big for you all by yourself!"

"Not really," Gena told her.

"Girl, what are you going to do with all this room?" Tracey asked.

"You can turn one of the bedrooms into a study," the leasing agent suggested.

"I don't know. It seems so big for you, Gena. You sure you need all this space? It's just you living by yourself, remember. Girl, I'd be scared up in this chumpy all by myself."

"This is nothing compared to the house I lived in with Quadir. Girl, this is a little small for me."

"You won't be scared?"

"Mm-mmm."

"Lonely?"

"Mm-mmm."

"All right, then go ahead and do the damn thing, but this place sure is big."

"Tracey, wouldn't this room look really nice in pink?" Gena asked.

Slowly, Tracey peered around the room. "I guess so . . ."

"I could put the crib on that wall and a dresser here and a changing table over there. What do you think?"

Tracey looked at her friend sideways. "Gena, you pregnant?"

"Am I?"

Tracey gasped. Once the initial shock wore off, she grabbed Gena and began screaming. "You! Oh my God! Why didn't you tell me? Oh my God, Gena, you're pregnant! We're going to have a baby!"

Tracey screamed at the top of her lungs. Gena laughed and kept pushing her off.

"Congratulations," the leasing agent said with a wide smile. She left the room to give them some privacy.

"No wonder you need this great big old place!" Tracey said. "What did Jay say when he found out?"

"He doesn't know yet," Gena confessed.

"He doesn't know!" Tracey shouted. "Oh my God, Gena! Why haven't you told him?"

"I just found out myself," Gena lied, not sure why she hadn't said a word. "Besides, I'm not really sure. I took the test, and it came out really light. And then the second one said I was pregnant. And then the third one said I was pregnant."

"Then, bitch, you pregnant!" Tracey told her. "Girl, get your ass to the doctor!"

"I'ma go. I got an appointment with a Dr. Afriye Amerson," Gena told her.

"You want me to go with you?" Tracey asked.

"You can if you want to," Gena said.

"So, when are you going to tell Jay?"

Gena shrugged. "Girl, I don't know. I guess when I feel like the time is right."

"He gonna be trying to move up in here with you and the baby," Tracey told her. "See, I didn't know you was pregnant. That changes everything."

"Maybe, maybe not," Gena declared.

"How many months are you?" Tracey asked.

"Girl, I'm weeks, only a few weeks at that. I *just* missed my period. But I can feel it already."

"Then how do you know it's a girl?" Tracey asked. "You getting me all excited and you don't even know for sure!"

"Girl, I can feel it," Gena told her. "I think it's a girl."

Tracey put her hands on her hips and eyeballed Gena. She couldn't believe it.

"So, what do you think?" the leasing agent asked as she strolled back into the room.

Gena peered around the apartment and nodded. "I like it."

"How are the schools around here?" Tracey asked.

The leasing agent laughed. "Well, she won't be worried about that for a while. But just to let you know, the school system in this neighborhood is the best. My own son goes to school in this district."

Tracey seemed satisfied with that response.

"How far are you going to be commuting for work?" the agent asked Gena.

Gena shook her head. "I won't have to commute. I'm self-employed. I'll be working out of the apartment basically."

"Oh, really?" The agent smiled. "What do you do?"

"I'm a talent agent," Gena lied.

"Oh, how interesting!" the agent declared. "Do you represent anyone I know?"

"Probably." Gena smiled and quickly changed the conversation. "So, what's the next step here?"

"Well, your credit application was already approved for the one-bedroom, so I'll just need an additional security deposit and your signature on the lease. We can take care of that right now, if you like."

"Okay, then, let's do it," Gena said, ready to sign her name on the dotted line. Her phone began to ring. She scrambled through her bag and spoke into the receiver. "Hello?"

"Hey, Gena, what's going down?" Rasun asked.

"Who is this?" Gena asked, not certain who the voice on the other end of the phone belonged to. It sounded familiar, really familiar, but she couldn't make it out.

"It's me, Rasun."

"Hey!" Gena said, becoming animated. "What have you been up to! Wow, it's been a long time!"

"Yeah, I know," Rasun told her. "Hey, I really need to talk to you."

"Oh, yeah?" Gena asked. "What's up?"

"I don't want to talk about it over the phone," Rasun told her. "Is there any way I can meet you somewhere?"

"Yeah, sure," Gena answered. "When?"

"How about tomorrow?" Rasun asked. "Hey, meet me at that spot where we used to count dough."

Gena thought about it for several moments until she remembered. It was a motel on the edge of town. Qua had taken her there before when he had gone to count up some money with the boys.

"What time?" Gena asked him.

"How about seven?" Rasun asked.

"See you tomorrow at seven," Gena told him. She disconnected the call. Thoughts ran through her head about the strange conversation. She wondered what he wanted.

Rasun hung up the telephone and leaned his head against it. He didn't want to do this. He felt like he was betraying a friend. Quadir had been there for him when no one else had, and he hated having to set up his girl. But it was his freedom, his mother's freedom, and his mother's house on the line. Quadir would have to understand, and if not, then fuck him.

Rasun lifted his head, turned, and headed for his car. He climbed inside, cranked up the stereo, and pulled off. He didn't pay attention to the black BMW pulling off behind him.

Sneaky, Sneaky

Jerrell walked through the hardware store like a kid in a candy store. He turned his basket down the first aisle and grabbed a long cord of thick, yellow rope. He tugged at the plastic rope, testing its strength. Once he was satisfied it would hold, he placed it inside his basket and headed for the next item on his list.

Jerrell turned onto the aisle with the duct tape and tossed a couple of rolls into his shopping cart. He headed over to the aisle where the chains were kept. He reeled off about ten feet of thick, stainless-steel chain and had one of the store's customer service personnel cut it for him. The chain was heavy, exactly what was needed for the job he had in store for it.

In the home and garden section, Jerrell selected two large metal buckets and two bags of quick-dry cement. He loaded his wares into the cart and headed over to the checkout counter.

"Somebody's doing some home improvement," the salesgirl joked as she gave him a flirtatious smile.

"You don't know how much this project is going to pay off," Jerrell answered.

"They say the best way to increase value is by sprucing up the kitchen and bathrooms!" the salesgirl advised him.

Jerrell nodded and smiled. "Oh, yeah, this is going to increase my net worth significantly."

"Oh, well, that's wonderful!" the salesgirl told him. She rang up his merchandise. "That'll be eighty-seven dollars and fifty-three cents."

Jerrell peeled off ninety dollars in cash and handed it to her. "Keep the change."

"Oh, sir," she said nervously. "I can't."

Jerrell spied a container on the counter asking for charitable donations. "Then give it to Jerry's Kids."

Jerrell turned and walked out of the store with his merchandise.

Gena pulled up to the motel and spied Rasun standing outside one of the rooms. She parked, climbed out of her vehicle, and made her way over to him. Rasun wrapped his arms around her and hugged her tightly, as if he were a true-blue friend.

"It's so good to see you," Gena told him.

"You're looking good," Rasun replied.

"You are, too," Gena told him.

Rasun shook his head. "Not me. I'm going bald so fast, I'll look like a bowling ball in a few more weeks."

Gena laughed.

"Come on in, let's talk," Rasun told her. He turned and walked into the motel room, and Gena followed close behind.

"So, what's going on, Rasun?" Gena asked. She seated herself in one of the motel room's accent chairs.

Rasun seated himself on the bed. "How are you doing, Gena?"

Gena nodded. "I'm good. I'm really good."

"Do you think about him a lot?" Rasun asked.

The question made Gena frown. She found it peculiar. "I do. We're talking about Quadir, right?"

Rasun nodded. "I think about my nigga a lot. I miss him."

"I do, too," Gena said softly. "Rasun, what's the matter?"

Rasun shook his head, allowing a tear to roll down his cheek. "I'm in trouble, Gena, a whole lot of trouble."

"What is it?" Gena asked, full of concern, leaning forward in her seat.

"This bust was a bad one, Gena," he explained. "They got a lot of stuff on us. It looks really bad."

Gena shook her head sadly. "Rasun, I'm so sorry."

"I got this lawyer, but he's full of shit!" Rasun explained. "He ain't doing shit to help me. I went to some other lawyers and I showed the paperwork I have, the indictment and everything, and they all want an arm and a leg to defend me. I don't have that kind of bread, Gena. I don't . . ."

"Have you talked to Rik?" Gena asked.

"Rik don't got it like that, either," Rasun told her. "They seized everything."

Gena nodded.

"Gena, I don't want to get in your business or nothing, but my man Qua was papered up. I know he left you papered up. You think you could spot a brother until I work this shit out and get back up on my feet?"

Gena recoiled. She hadn't been expecting this, and instead of saying, "I don't got it, I can't help you," she said the entirely wrong thing. "How much are you talking, Rasun?"

"The lawyers are all asking for about two hundred and fifty to three hundred grand to fight this thing," he told her. "It's a pretty big fucking conspiracy case."

Gena shook her head. "Damn, that's a lot of dough, man. I mean, what happens if you pay them and they can't beat the case? What happens if you go to prison?"

"I'll have to pay you when I get out," Rasun told her.

"When you get out?" Gena sat back in her seat. "Damn, baby!

You lose this case, you getting a *Star Wars* date! You looking at getting out sometime in the next century. A fucking 2032 out date or some shit."

Rasun laughed. His laughter made Gena laugh. The truth was so fucked up they couldn't do anything but laugh.

"Gena, I hated to have to come to you like this, but you the only one who can stand to shoot me that kinda paper," Rasun told her. "Qua had millions put away."

Gena's face remained passive.

Rasun sat up and leaned in toward her. "Gena, you did get Quadir's shit, didn't you? Mrs. Richards didn't fuck you out of it, did she?"

Damn, this nigga comin' at me hard. What the fuck he worried about what Qua left me or even what his mother got, for that matter? Something here smells very fishy, Gena thought to herself. She suddenly wished she hadn't come to meet Rasun. *I don't want to help him, either.*

"I don't want to talk about Quadir right now," Gena told him.

"No, I was just wondering if you were all right," Rasun told her. "I wanted to know if you were able to help a brother out. I really need it for these lawyers, Gena. I don't want to go to jail."

Gena stood. "Let me think about this, Rasun. I don't really have that kind of paper, but I might be able to help with something."

"That would be great, Gena, really," Rasun told her.

He rose and followed her to the door.

"I'll call you tomorrow, okay?" Gena told him.

Rasun nodded. Gena leaned forward and kissed him on his cheek before turning and walking away.

The door leading to the adjoining suite opened as Rasun was closing the motel room door.

"You almost had her," Sergeant Ellington told him. "You did a good job."

"Does that mean I'm finished?" Rasun asked.

"Almost," Sergeant Ellington told him. "We need for you to meet with her tomorrow and see what she says about the money. We need her to admit to having the money."

"And if I get her to admit it, then I'm finished?" Rasun asked. "Am I free once I do this?"

"Rasun, you'll be free," Sergeant Ellington told him. "Free to keep your ass where we can find you when we need you. Until all your little friends are sleeping in federal prisons, you're on a short leash. Is that understood?"

Rasun unbuttoned his shirt and unhooked the tape recorder he had strapped to his waist. He handed the mini recorder to her.

Sergeant Ellington waved him away. "You keep it. You'll need it for tomorrow."

Rasun turned and stormed out of the hotel room, slamming the door behind him. Sergeant Ellington turned and headed back into the adjoining suite to collect her gear.

Huffing and cursing under his breath, Rasun made his way across the motel parking lot. He didn't notice the black BMW pulling up alongside him.

The black-tinted window of the BMW slid down slowly, and Rasun peered into the vehicle. He jumped, and his heart stopped.

"Give me the fucking tape," the driver told him.

"What the fuck!" Rasun exclaimed. "How?"

"Shut the fuck up and give me the tape," the driver told him.

Rasun immediately tossed the recorder to the driver.

"You fucking snitch. I can't fucking believe you, nigga," the driver sneered. He lifted his weapon and fired ten shots into Rasun before peeling off into the night.

Sergeant Ellington and Detective Davis heard the shots from their motel room. They ran out into the parking lot with their weapons drawn.

"Over here!" Dickie Davis shouted.

He raced to where Rasun was lying on the ground, shaking. Letoya raced to her confidential informant and dropped to her knees beside him.

"What happened?" she shouted.

"Who did this?" Dickie Davis asked. He lifted Rasun's head off the ground.

Rasun began convulsing violently.

"We're losing him!" Dickie shouted. He lifted his walkie-talkie. "I need an EMS unit at the motel on Chestnut!" He shouted the address. "I repeat, officer requesting a medical unit to the motel on Chestnut! Gunshot victim going into shock!"

Dickie Davis laid Rasun's head down, ripped open his shirt, and began beating on Rasun's chest. Sergeant Ellington began breathing into Rasun's mouth.

"One, two, three, four!" Detective Davis counted as he pumped Rasun's chest.

Sergeant Ellington desperately tried to breathe into Rasun's mouth.

Rasun's eyes rolled back, and his body went limp. They could hear the sirens of the EMS unit growing closer with each second. Time was of the essence, and they realized they were losing him.

The M Is Dead

Mark crept through the front door of Skip's dark apartment, peering around the eerie living room. Everything inside told him to leave immediately, and that nothing good would come from this trip, but still, he had to see why he'd been summoned to this place. Mark pulled out his pistol, pulled back the slide, and chambered a round. He was going to shoot at the first shadow he saw moving.

Mark's eyes slowly began adapting to the darkness of the apartment, and he was able to make out shapes. One of the first was that of a lamp. He walked to the end table and leaned forward to turn the lamp on. He froze when he felt the pressure of cold steel placed behind his ear.

"Don't move, and don't try anything stupid," Jerrell told him. "Put the gun down."

Mark opened his hand, allowing the gun to fall to the floor.

"Good," Jerrell said quietly. "Now turn on the lamp."

Mark twisted the knob, turning on the light and brightening the room, bringing clarity to all the objects inside.

"What's going on, Jerrell?" Mark asked. "Where's Skip?"

Jerrell shoved Mark down onto the couch. "I'm asking the questions, nigga, not you!"

Mark's head struck the back of the couch, causing him to check his forehead for blood. He turned toward Jerrell and sat down.

"What the fuck's going on, J?" Mark asked.

"Collection time," Jerrell told him. "Where the fuck's my money?"

"Your money?" Mark looked off to the side and smacked his lips. "Man, is that all you can think about? Somebody's out here killing off our brothers, and you're worried about your money?"

Jerrell looked at Mark like he was stupid. He couldn't believe his dumb ass still hadn't figured shit out.

"This was supposed to be a Junior Mafia meeting," Mark shouted. "Where's everybody else?"

Jerrell smiled and lifted his arms into the air. "This is everybody! We're it, just me and you, baby!"

Mark frowned. He didn't find Jerrell's humor funny.

"I hereby call this meeting to order," Jerrell told him. "Well, I guess the first order of business is to read the minutes from the last meeting. Any volunteers? You, sir, over there on the couch, how about you?"

Mark sat on the couch, sour-faced.

"Okay, well, I move that we skip the reading of the minutes and get down to business," Jerrell continued. "Today's meeting is about money. It's time to pay your dues!"

"Where's Skip?" Mark asked.

Jerrell peered down at the floor. Mark's eyes followed Jerrell's, and he noticed for the first time that there was tape on the carpet. Mark's eyes followed the circuit of tape, and he quickly came to realize the tape was an outline for a body. He jumped.

"Whoa!" Jerrell told him. He pointed his weapon at Mark. "Have a seat, nigga, and hold your horses."

Mark sat back down on the couch. "What the fuck's going on?"

"You asked where Skip was," Jerrell told him. "Just answering your question."

Mark shook his head. "You killed him?"

"Where's my money?" Jerrell asked.

Mark shook his head. "Man, I don't have any money! I had to get the fuck outta town with the quickness, remember? I've been on the run! I didn't have no time to hustle!"

"Oh, so you still have all the dope I fronted you, then?" Jerrell asked.

Mark shifted his gaze to the ground.

"That's what I thought," Jerrell told him. "You had time to hustle my dope, but no time to put my money away."

"I needed some ends to get out of town, and to lay low," Mark tried to explain. "That's what I used the money for. Hell, it wasn't like I fucked it off! I can hustle and make it back."

Jerrell pulled out a pair of handcuffs and tossed them to Mark. "Put these on."

Mark caught the cuffs and peered up at Jerrell. "Why should I? If you gonna kill me, then do it here."

"I ain't gonna kill you, nigga," Jerrell told him. "Not unless you make me. Now put the damn cuffs on!"

Mark placed the cuffs around his wrists and snapped them closed, handcuffing himself in front of his body. Jerrell walked to the couch and pulled him up off it. He shoved Mark across the living room and out the door of the apartment. Mark headed for the cars parked out front, but Jerrell tugged him away from the cars and shoved him straight ahead. He soon found himself heading toward what appeared to be a train yard—not Amtrak and not SEPTA, but train tracks that ran through town.

"Right here," Jerrell told him.

Mark felt Jerrell place a cuff around his ankle and lock it. He peered down in time to see Jerrell lock the other side of the cuff to a railroad track. He watched as Jerrell repeated the procedure with his other leg. He was now shackled to the railroad tracks.

Jerrell lifted his pistol, turned it around, and struck Mark with the grip of his handgun. Mark fell to the ground as blood poured from his head. Jerrell knelt, removed Mark's handcuffs, and then handcuffed his right hand to one side of the track.

"What the fuck are you doing?" Mark asked. His head was spinning, and he was dazed. He could feel Jerrell cuffing his other hand to the other side of the railroad track. He didn't realize the full implications of Jerrell's actions until he felt a slight vibration in the tracks. The vibrations were growing stronger.

"Okay, Jerrell," Mark told him. "I get your point. I'll give you all the money I have left. It's almost enough to pay you back. It's like forty-five thousand dollars. You can have it, it's yours."

Jerrell stood over Mark and shook his head. "Now you want to pay me back. It took me handcuffing you to a railroad track to pay me back."

Mark tugged at the handcuffs, trying to free himself. "Look, I'll pay you back! You can have the money, and I'll get the rest of it to you within a week. Now, please, uncuff me."

The light from a freight train could be seen in the distance.

"Man, come on, this shit ain't funny no more!" Mark told him. "Come on, I'll take you to get your fucking money!"

Jerrell stepped off the track, peered down at Mark, and smiled.

Mark felt the vibrations of the train nearing. They were getting stronger and stronger as each second passed.

"I'll give you all your shit tonight! I'll get the rest of that shit from my pops! I'll give you everything I owe you tonight! Uncuff me!"

Mark pulled at the cuffs desperately.

"Jerrell! This is some bullshit! We're brothers, nigga! We're Junior Mafia for life!"

"If we're Junior Mafia for life, then you got about thirty seconds before you're not Junior Mafia anymore," Jerrell told him. He turned and began to walk away.

"Jerrell! Jerrell! You can't do this, homie!" Mark shouted. He could hear the train's horn blaring nonstop and felt the tracks vibrating violently. "Jerrell! I'll give you more than what I owe you! I'll give you a hundred grand! A hundred thousand dollars tonight!"

The freight train was loaded to the hilt with grain. It felt like a strong gust of wind blowing by Jerrell when it ran over Mark. Jerrell heard the brief scream, a squashing sound, and then nothing else. There was nothing else. Mark had disappeared from the face of the earth. He was now bits and pieces of blood and tissue beneath a freight train.

"Have a safe trip," Jerrell joked as he walked back to his car.

Gena opened the door to Gah Git's house and crept inside. It was early in the morning, and the entire house was still sleeping. Gena crept up the steps and slowly down the hall to Gah Git's door. She peeked inside to see her grandmother sleeping. Quietly, she tiptoed over to the side of Gah Git's bed and leaned down. She stroked her grandmother's forehead, and Gah Git's eyes widened.

"Where you been?" Gah Git asked.

"Nowhere. I needed some time, that's all," Gena said, still stroking her grandmother's forehead.

"You couldn't call me and let me know you was all right? I got to get bits and pieces from everybody else." Gah Git grabbed Gena's hand and looked at her. "You all right?"

"Mm-hmm, I'm okay. It's all okay. I'm not mad anymore, and I'm sorry I didn't call you."

Gena hugged her grandmother. Gah Git returned the embrace, happy to see Gena safe and sound.

"Life always has a way of dishin' out what's least expected at the most least expecting time. The test is really in how gracious we can respond to it all, and you handled the situation like an adult woman, and I'm so proud of you."

"I really don't know how to handle it all, though. I mean, what am I supposed to do?"

"Take one day at a time." Gah Git patted her on the back. "One day at a time."

Captain Holiday chucked the thick manila folder at the gathered officers, striking the wall beside Letoya Ellington's head. Loose papers flew everywhere.

"What in the fuck were you thinking!" Captain Holiday shouted. "Oh, change that! You weren't thinking! You couldn't have been thinking! You don't have a fucking brain to think! Not pulling the kinda shit you pulled!"

"Captain, I'm sorry," Letoya told him.

"Sorry!" the captain shouted. "You're sorry? A man is dead because of you! I just left a meeting with the chief and the goddamned city councilman, and both chewed my ass out! Do you understand the kind of shitstorm you've got this department facing?"

"Sir—" Dickie Davis tried to intervene.

"Shut the fuck up!" the captain bellowed. He looked like he was about to pop a blood vessel in his forehead. "I didn't ask you to fucking speak. Detective Davis, when I want your goddamned opinion, I'll let you know!"

Captain Holiday turned and lit up a fat Cuban cigar. He scowled at Detective Davis with disdain. "Fucking numb nuts!"

"Sir, we had the situation controlled," Ratzinger told him. "The CI was killed while he was leaving the scene. He was no longer under Sergeant Ellington's control."

"Bullshit!" Captain Holliday shouted. "That CI is under your control until you safely tuck his ass into bed at night! You know that, I know that, everybody knows that! If the media gets ahold of this shit, it's our asses! Do you hear me, it's our asses! And the mayor has already made it clear that if this thing blows up, heads will roll!

Somebody's going to have to fall on their goddamned sword, and it sure as hell ain't gonna be me! You got that, Lieutenant? Badges! I'm collecting fucking badges—gold ones, green ones, and silver ones included!"

"Sir—"

"Shit rolls downhill, Sergeant!" Captain Holiday shouted at Letoya Ellington. "Now, does someone want to tell me what the fuck you had a CI doing out at that time of the night, on an operation not sanctioned by me? Seeing as how you all work for me, I should know about the little operations you have going on, don't you think?"

Letoya nodded. "Yes, sir!"

"Well, let's hear it, Sergeant," the captain said to her. "What the fuck was going on?"

"Sir, Detective Davis and I, during the course of questioning the confidential informant, learned there may be another large drug ring operating in the city," she explained. "Perhaps as large as the one we recently took down."

Captain Holiday leaned back in his overstuffed leather chair. "And exactly how did you come to this conclusion?"

"The girlfriend of one Quadir Richards, the previous leader of the group we took down, has a new boyfriend providing her with quite a lavish lifestyle," Ellington explained. "We believe this boyfriend is part of the other drug ring. We wanted to target him, branch out, and track all the members of his organization, and even roll up his supply chain."

"And his name, Sergeant?" Captain Holiday asked.

"We were trying to ascertain that information on the night the CI was killed, sir," she explained. "He was meeting with Gena Scott, Quadir Richards's former love interest, to acquire the name of her new boyfriend."

"And then he was killed?" the captain asked. "Any idea who did this?"

Dickie Davis shook his head. "None, sir."

"Why in the hell did you two try to play Starsky and Hutch and go at it alone?" the captain asked angrily. "Why didn't you go through the proper channels and set up a proper operation, so you could have enough officers to back you up? What? Do you two think you're Don Johnson and Philip Michael Thomas now?"

"We were under time constraints, sir," Sergeant Ellington told him.

"Bullshit!" Captain Holiday said. "This had the makings of a long-term operation. You just told me you wanted to roll up the entire organization, Sergeant!"

"Yes, but the window for meeting with the girlfriend and obtaining this information was narrowing, sir," Davis put in. "We used the CI's arrest as an excuse for the meeting. He was asking her for money and talking to her about moving on after the death of her boyfriend, trying to gain her sympathy and trust, sir."

Captain Holiday shook his head. "I'm too old a cat to be fooled by a bunch of kittens; this thing stinks. The whole damn thing stinks to high heaven. Let me tell you all something, and listen up good. I've got a pissed-off mayor, a super-hot city councilman, and a furious chief chewing on my ass. I've got Internal Affairs looking into this entire incident. One thing looks suspect, and I'm collecting your badges and having your asses thrown in jail. Is that clear?"

Lieutenant Ratzinger, Detective Davis, and Sergeant Ellington all nodded.

"If the press gets wind this was a police operation, and this guy was killed while working undercover for the department, your careers are effectively over," Captain Holiday told them. "I'm going to hand them your asses and they're going to crucify you . . . or what's left of you. The department is going to run for cover and let them know this was an unauthorized operation."

Captain Holiday leaned back in his chair and examined the three officers standing before him. Something was fishy. He couldn't put his finger on it, but the entire damn affair stank. He blew a giant circle of cigar smoke into the air toward them and frowned.

"Get the hell out of my office," Holiday told them.

The Verdict's Out

Jerrell wrapped his arms around Gena and pulled her close. She rested her head against his shoulders and closed her eyes. The wind blowing on her face felt good to her. It felt relaxing, purifying almost. She was happier than she'd been in a long time. She had her a good man, a new apartment, two cars, plenty of money, and a baby on the way. Life couldn't have been better for her.

Jerrell turned her face toward his and kissed her deeply, passionately. She felt his kiss work its way from her lips, through her body, and all the way down to her toes. She became lost in it.

The park was empty today, with only one or two others milling about. Most of the usual parkgoers were at work at this time. They pretty much had the park and all its greenery to themselves. It was the benefit of not having a regular nine-to-five. They were free to do as they pleased, whenever they pleased.

"Want some more cake?" Gena asked.

Jerrell waved his hand, turning down her offer. "No thanks, baby. I'm pretty full."

"What?" Gena asked with a smile. "You didn't like my cake? I made it just for you."

"No, I loved it," Jerrell told her. "I loved the whole meal, baby. I ate like a pig, don't you think?"

Gena's eyes narrowed. "Uh-huh."

"What? Are you trying to get me fat or something?" Jerrell asked playfully. "What are you going to do when I try to climb on top of you all fat and greasy and stuff? Are you still going to give me some loving?"

Jerrell tickled her side, and Gena tried to knock his hands away.

"Are you still going to let me work that thang?" he asked, still tickling her.

"Maybe," Gena said, laughing and fighting his hands off.

Gena grabbed a slice of cake and smeared it onto Jerrell's lips. She leaped up from the picnic blanket and took off into the park. Jerrell leaped to his feet and chased her.

Gena cut through the playground area and stopped on the other side of a large, colorful slide. Jerrell chased after her, and she quickly raced to the other side of the slide.

"You aren't going to catch me," Gena told him.

"That's only because you got me full," Jerrell told her while breathing heavily. "I have another idea."

"And what's that?"

Jerrell turned and raced back toward their picnic basket. On the way, he turned and shouted in her direction. "I'm going to drink up all of the Moët!"

Gena took off running toward the picnic basket. She arrived just after he did and dove on top of him. Jerrell dropped the bottle and grabbed her. Together they rolled around on the blanket until he found himself on top of her, staring into her eyes. Slowly, he leaned down and kissed her passionately.

It was as if they were kissing for the first time, Gena felt. She'd become turned out on him more than anything else. His sex was good, really good, and like a magnet. She kept wanting more and more of him, all of him that she could get. And it wasn't solely the sex she was falling for; he was a protector. He'd vowed to protect her and kept telling her he'd keep her safe and he'd never let anyone cause her any harm. She loved hearing how she'd be protected, and more than merely being lost in his arms, she found herself lost in him. She couldn't believe she could feel this way again, but she had a deep, caring love for Jerrell. It wasn't driven by passion, but it was driven by a yearning to simply be loved.

She could see herself spending the rest of her life with this man. She could see herself waking up in his arms, cooking his meals, and having his children. For the first time in a long time, she could honestly say she was genuinely happy.

United States Attorney Paul Perachetti strolled into the room wearing one of his usual three-thousand-dollar Armani suits. He was tanned and toned, with graying sideburns and an always fresh haircut. He looked more like an expensive Mafia lawyer than a US attorney. His Rolex watches, dark Italian suits, and the Cadillac Seville he drove certainly made it seem like he was mob-affiliated, not to mention the fact he was Sicilian through and through.

The gathered officers, detectives, and agents all spoke in hushed whispers, wondering why they'd been summoned to the federal building today. Many guessed it was another major operation the Feds wanted them to take part in. The fact that there were several assistant United States attorneys whispering in the ear of the Perachetti made them all nervous. And the fact there was a United States district judge and a United States magistrate in on the whispering made the entire affair seem even more ominous. Even the FBI agents were nervous.

"What do you think it is?" Detective Davis asked his partner.

Letoya shook her head. "I don't know. Whatever it is, it can't be good."

"All these damn Feds in one room makes me nervous," Dickie said.

"We're all law enforcement officers," Sergeant Ellington told him. "Besides, the Feds look like they're nervous, too."

There were about fifteen United States marshals inside the room already; another fifteen to twenty walked into the room and stood at the rear like they were guarding the door.

"What the fuck's going on in here, Sergeant?" DEA agent Stacey Wynn asked Letoya.

She shook her head. "Hell, you're a Fed. You should know more about this than I do."

Up front, the US attorney finished speaking with one of the deputy attorneys, the federal district court judge, and the federal district court magistrate. There were lots of whispers and nods exchanged. The US attorney turned toward the room full of law enforcement officers and cleared his throat. Instantly, the room grew deathly silent.

"Gentlemen and ladies, as most of you know, my name is Paul Perachetti, and I am the United States attorney for this district. I know some of you, and some of you I've seen your face a time or two but haven't had the pleasure of getting to know you. I asked you all to come here today so I can look you in the eyes and give you my deepest and most sincere apology and express to each of you my personal regret."

Murmurs echoed throughout the room as the gathered law enforcement personnel wondered what the US attorney was talking about.

"Recently, we conducted a multiagency operation in this city that resulted in numerous arrests," Perachetti continued. "We seized hundreds of weapons, millions of dollars in vehicles, jewelry, and other personal property, and were able to remove hundreds of drug dealers from the street."

The gathered law enforcement agents broke into applause.

Perachetti held up his hand to silence them. "During the course of this event, we gathered numerous pieces of evidence, the primary evidence being electronic PIN gathering, telephone monitoring, video surveillance, and wire recordings gathered by a confidential informant. This evidence was in the hands of a federal agency and has unfortunately been mishandled. I apologize to all of you who worked so hard and made so many sacrifices to gather this evidence. I take full responsibility for everything that has happened, as I should have shown more diligence in safeguarding this material, instead of delegating that duty. I am the United States attorney, and the buck stops here. So I want to personally apologize to all of you."

Agent Wynn raised her hand.

Paul Perachetti pointed toward her. "Yes, Agent Wynn?"

"What are you saying?" Agent Wynn asked. "Are you saying all the electronic surveillance evidence is missing? Is it lost, misplaced, or what?"

Paul Perachetti cleared his throat. "What I'm saying is the evidence was mishandled, and all of the recordings have been destroyed."

"Destroyed?" another agent asked.

"I'm sorry, I don't know all of you, and I regret that fact," Perachetti told them. "So I would ask everyone to state their names and the agency they work for when they ask a question. That way I know who I'm talking to, and I can get to learn your name, and be able to put a face with your name in the future."

"Matthew Sauls, FBI," the agent stated. "So, when you say destroyed, do you mean literally destroyed, like it's been smashed or something?"

"Good question," Perachetti told him. "When I say destroyed, I mean the evidence is no longer usable. The disks have been somehow magnetically wiped clean."

Letoya lifted her hand.

"Yes?" Perachetti asked, pointing at her.

"Sergeant Letoya Ellington, Philadelphia Narcotics Division," she told him. "Wiped clean? All of them? And how did this happen?"

"The disks were stored in a metal cool-storage unit, and on the other side of the room, federal security police were using a large X-ray screening device for security purposes," Perachetti explained. "Apparently, the device emitted some sort of magnetic current that found its way into the storage container in the next room and cleared all the disks. That's all I know."

Another agent raised his hand.

"Yes?" Perachetti asked, calling on the gentleman.

"Anthony Hopkins, Alcohol, Tobacco, and Firearms. Sir, how the hell did this happen?"

The United States marshals in the rear of the room stirred uneasily. That was when Sergeant Ellington realized why they were there. They were there for the protection of the US attorney.

"No one ever thought the placement of this new cool-storage locker would be affected by the magnetic radiation being emitted by the scanning device on the other side of the wall," Perachetti explained. "This is a new storage device, recently purchased and installed by the DEA, and this had never happened before. It was one of those things no one could have foreseen."

"Sir, what does all of this mean?"

"I'm sorry," Perachetti told him. "Your name and agency, please?"

"Oh, sorry," the agent said sheepishly. "Cody Coil, DEA. Sir, what does all this mean in layman's terms?"

"It means we've lost all of our evidence," Perachetti said matter-of-factly.

"Agent Nick Best, FBI, sir. Have we tried some deep data recovery on the disks, sir?"

Perachetti nodded. "The disks were sent over to the NSA, so their technicians could work some of their magic on them. The NSA couldn't get it done. We sent the disks over to the navy. They couldn't recover any data, so we sent them over to NASA, and still no luck. We've pretty much exhausted all resources. We even had a guy over at the CIA write a special recovery program, and that fell through. The data is irrecoverable."

"Joseph Cannon, FBI, sir. So, what does all this mean?"

"I'm glad you asked that question, Agent Cannon," Perachetti told him. "The bottom line is, we have no evidence to try the accused with."

Murmurs shot through the room.

"Sir, Nick Best again. Are you saying they're going to walk?"

Agent Cannon raised his hand.

Perachetti called on him.

"Sir, we still have the confidential informant," Agent Cannon said. "His testimony before the jury, as well as any new evidence he could gather from new communications intercepts . . ."

Perachetti looked down and shook his head. "Gentlemen, I regret to inform you that the confidential informant utilized to gather most of the evidence in this case was killed a few nights ago in what appeared to be a random homicide."

"This is bullshit!" Agent Anthony Hopkins shouted. "We busted our asses, risked our lives, and now you're telling us these scumbags are going to walk!"

"Gentlemen, you all have my sincerest apologies," Perachetti told them. "I know the amount of energy, the amount of sacrifice, and the dedication you all put into the case. I want to assure you that my office will do all it can to salvage this case. I wanted to let you know where we stood, and to apologize to you personally."

"Fucking DEA!" several agents shouted.

"Hey, fuck you!" a DEA agent shouted back.

"Gentlemen, please!" the judge yelled. He'd heard enough. He had an evidence hearing coming up, and many of the defendants' attorneys would be pressing him to proceed and pressuring the US attorney's office to share the evidence they had against their clients. Pages and pages of blank transcripts wouldn't do the trick. He faced the unpleasant prospect of having to rule in the defendants' favor based on the lack of evidence. He'd have to kick all of them back out onto the streets.

A dead confidential informant, the judge thought. *How convenient. How fucking convenient.* He wondered if the officers and attorneys working this case could screw things up any worse than they already had. *Clusterfuck* was the term that entered into his mind.

You Lose to Win

Gena was seated on the floor of her new apartment, pulling out the home décor accessories she'd purchased from Neiman Marcus, Crate & Barrel, and Fortunoff. Packaging paper used to wrap the various porcelain, crystal, and ceramic items was scattered throughout her living room. She couldn't believe she was finally at this point in her life.

Markita stepped over several of the valuable items as she made her way into Gena's kitchen for another glass of soda. Tracey was seated at the glass breakfast table unwrapping more of Gena's little odds and ends and wiping them clean with a slightly damp cloth.

"Girl, you want something to drink?" Markita asked, holding up a bottle of Sprite.

"My doctor said sodas are the worst. Dr. Amerson said to only drink water," Gena told her.

"What about juice?" Tracey suggested.

"Only in the morning with breakfast. She'd rather me eat fruit instead of drinking juice because of all the sugar."

"Oh Lord, here we go, and you ain't even out the first trimester yet. I can see this is gonna be a long nine months. I'll be glad when my little godbaby gets here," Markita told her.

"Our little goddaughter!" Tracey corrected her.

"What if I'm wrong? What if it's a boy?" Gena asked.

"How did he have your legs up when you got pregnant? That will tell you right there," Markita said in all seriousness.

Gena and Tracey broke into laughter.

"What the fuck are you talking about now?" Gena asked.

"Girl, if the nigga had ya legs straight up in the air and he was digging up in that shit deeper than a muthafucka, then it's a girl," Markita explained. "If you was riding him or if he had you doggy style when he nutted, then it's a boy."

"How in the fuck do you figure that?" Tracey shouted. She and Gena were laughing their asses off.

"Kita, where do you get this shit from?" Gena asked.

Markita nodded. "All right, just watch, you'll see. Y'all hoes think Markita don't know what the fuck I'm talking about, but I do, and when I try to tell you something, you don't wanna listen."

"Whatever," Tracey joked.

"Look, Gena, do you want some juice or what?"

"Yeah, dag!" Gena told her.

Markita grabbed a glass from the counter and poured Gena some orange juice. She placed the container back inside the refrigerator and turned toward Tracey. "Do you want something to drink while I'm over here?"

Still laughing, Tracey shook her head. "No, I'm good."

"Y'all hoes gonna learn to pay attention when I'm trying to tell y'all something," she told them both, pointing her finger at them while taking the glass of orange juice to Gena.

Gena and Tracey continued laughing. Finally, Gena held her arms out toward Markita.

"Aw, my baby is mad," Gena said in a teasing tone. "Come and give sister a hug. Come on over here, Tracey. We gonna give Kita a group hug."

Tracey rose from the table and joined Gena on the floor. She opened her arms toward a pouting Markita.

"Fuck y'all, you know that?" Markita told them as she walked to where they were and fell into their arms. "I hate y'all bitches."

Gena, Markita, and Tracey hugged, and then broke into laughter.

Markita rubbed Gena's stomach. "So, what did Jay say when you told him about the baby?"

Gena shook her head. "I haven't told him yet."

"What?" Tracey shouted. "Why haven't you told him?"

"I'm waiting for the right moment," Gena said.

"The right moment?" Markita repeated. "Bitch, when is that, during delivery?"

Tracey and Markita laughed.

"Are you afraid to tell him or something?" Tracey asked.

Gena shook her head. "Of course not. Girl, it's just that once I tell him, the shit will become real."

"Girl, the shit is already real!" Tracey told her. "What are you talking about?"

Gena shrugged. "I don't know. It seems like it'll become a lot more real once I tell him. I don't know. I guess I figure that once I tell him, all the bullshit will start."

"Is he a sorry-ass nigga?" Tracey asked.

Gena shook her head.

"Is he a deadbeat muthafucka?" Markita asked.

"No, he's not like that at all," Gena told them.

"Then, girl, why are you tripping?" Tracey asked. "You say he's not like that."

"I know, but I don't want him to become like that," Gena told them. "Babies have a way of complicating things. Besides, we've never talked about babies, or family, or any of those things."

"Gena, what are you thinking?" Tracey asked. "Are you thinking you can go nine months without telling him, and then pop up with a baby one day?"

"Your stomach is gon' get big, you do know that?" Markita said.

Gena nodded and pulled her legs close. She wrapped her arms around her legs and rested her chin on her knees. "I don't want things to change between us."

"Girl, you're going to have a baby," Markita told her. "Sorry to burst your bubble, but everything's gonna change."

Gena nodded and peered off into space. *They're right, my life is going to change.*

The heavy steel door slowly opened, and Rik walked through it with his big bundle of paperwork. He had motion after motion and brief after brief tucked beneath his arm. His attorney had been busy. He had to remember that for future reference. It was rare to find a drug attorney who actually did some work for his clients. He would definitely use this guy again, if it ever came to it.

Rik waited at the elevator door for the guard to arrive and take him downstairs to process out to freedom. He'd prayed every single night to be delivered from the clutches of the powers that be, and someone upstairs had heard his prayers.

His lawyer said the case had been dismissed for lack of evidence. How that could be was beyond him. When they were first arrested, the lawyers said the DEA had tapes on top of tapes of recorded conversations from phone taps, wired informants, and pager interceptions. They had enough shit on him to make the transcriptions of his recordings thicker than a New York phone book. And now, apparently, it was all gone.

Poof. Rik smiled as he stepped onto the elevator. Just like that, from a mountain of evidence to none at all. He wasn't quite sure what had happened, and neither was his attorney, but apparently there had been a problem with the tapes. *Beautiful! Fucking beautiful.* He really didn't care what had happened to those tapes as long as something had happened to them. He wasn't down for spending the rest of his life in some underground fucking federal prison in Colorado, or some fucking US pen in bubble-fuck God knows where with the KKK pretending to be fucking correctional officers.

"What the fuck are you smiling about, asshole?" the deputy working the elevator asked him.

"America," Rik told him. "America, the land of the free. I love this country!"

The guard frowned. He knew about the big kick out, and like all the other pigs, he wasn't exactly happy about it. They'd have to give back all the shit that had been seized as well. He probably had his fucking eye on one of his partners' Rolexes or something, and was mad 'cause he couldn't steal it at the police auction for a hundred bucks now. Fuck him. He chose his profession, like everyone else chose theirs. If he wanted to wear chuck jewelry and roll in a Range, a Benz, or a BMW, then he should've chosen a different profession. He was a hater like all the rest. Mad because he had to get up early in the morning, put on a tight uniform, and fight traffic. *They couldn't pay me enough to watch dicks all fucking day,* Rik thought. And that brought him to his second line of thought.

In order to get his shit back, he'd have to prove he'd had the income to purchase it. He would have to show receipts, tax returns, check stubs, and all that other bullshit. He had none of those things. And he damn sure couldn't claim the millions of dollars those fucking pigs seized from his stash house, which meant all his hard-earned savings were wiped out. The DEA would certainly be on their asses again, waiting for them to so much as jaywalk. He wouldn't be able to spit on a sidewalk without the Feds swooping down on him, especially in Philly. He had to take his show on the road and find a new city to live in. And he had to do it quietly, so the Feds wouldn't know where he relocated to.

The problem with finding a new spot for Rik was he was worried about not knowing the town, the players, or how the niggas got down. Not to mention the way guys were snitching on each other these days; it wasn't good. But Rik needed bread, like yesterday. He had overhead, not to mention he needed some new wheels and another crib. He needed to come up, and he needed to come up fast. He needed a jack move. He needed to play stickup kid one last time to get some score fair. The problem with that was most of the niggas he knew had got caught up in the bust, and everybody was sort of in the same predicament he was, waiting for the next couple months to get back the shit that had been seized. Hell, they were probably all thinking the same thing he was thinking at this very moment. *Who the fuck can I rob out here to hold me over until I get my shit back from the government, if I ever do?*

Rik laughed at the thought of that. A bunch of broke-ass ballers, sticking each other up for peanuts. *I rob this nigga one night, and another nigga comes through the window and gets me the following night.* Naw, he needed to get away from them fools and to catch a come up nobody else knew about. He needed a mark he could keep to himself and hit all by himself. Only one target like that came to mind.

Clair opened her door to find a box sitting on her front porch. She peered around, wondering who had rung her doorbell at this time of the night, but could see only the red taillights of a big black sedan driving away. It looked like a BMW or a Mercedes, or some other type of expensive car. *Why are people ringing my bell and then driving off like that? Crazy asses,* she thought. But then, this had been a crazy week for her. It was as if the entire world had gone mad.

The only reason she'd even opened her door was she thought it was probably some old friends of her son's wanting to pay their respects. Rasun had many friends, and many of them had come by already. More and more were showing up with each passing day, now that their cases had been dropped and they were filtering out of the jails. But none of them could offer her the help she so desperately needed, because they were all dealing with their own issues. It was something she understood.

She didn't have any life insurance on Rasun. She hadn't had any since he was a small child. She and her husband hadn't been able to afford it. Times had been tough while he was growing up, and even tougher in recent years. She knew that he was out there hustling, and understood the consequences that lifestyle held, but life insurance was something she simply couldn't afford, not unless she wanted to skip something called eating. So she found herself in her present dilemma, not having enough money to bury her child.

She set the large black box on top of her kitchen table and pulled the ribbon off it. She carefully lifted the lid and peered inside. To her astonishment, she found wads of money and a note. Clair grabbed the note, placed her hand on her chest, and sat down. In a shocked, monotonous clip, she read the note aloud.

"Dear Clair: Please accept this money as a token of my love for your son and as a sign of our friendship. There is enough money inside of the box to pay the cost of his burial and to help you with all your bills. I'll do what I can from time to time."

Clair crumpled the note in her hand and broke down in tears, happy, sad, and confused about who would give her all this money.

On and Poppin'

love you so much!" Gena said as she opened her legs wider, allowing him full access to her most private possessions.

"I love you, too, baby," Jerrell lied. He went into her deeply, feeling her viselike clamp around him. It was torture . . . almost. Torture because it felt so good, and torture that he had to waste some of the best pussy that had ever been put on the planet. But for now, he was going to make the most of it.

Gena wrapped her arms around his back and kissed her man passionately. Tonight, she wanted him to have all of her. She was going to throw it back at him and take all the pain she knew was coming. She wanted to fully become his, to mold herself to his body. She was going to share with him the news of the life they had created together. She was going to share with him her plans for their future.

Jerrell kissed her passionately. He had never felt her like this before. He was inside her, working her, trying to savor her tight canal. It felt like she was gripping his manhood with a tight fist. She was working him nearly as much as he was working her. He swallowed hard, trying not to cry out. It felt good to him. It felt like something he'd never felt before, like a level of lovemaking he didn't know existed.

"Oh my God!" Gena cried out. She bit down on his shoulder.

She could feel him really getting into it now. It seemed like he'd grown even bigger inside her. "Oh, Jay!"

"Gena!" Jerrell grunted. Never before had a woman made him call out her name. Whatever secret she had inside her, he wished he could bottle it up and keep it.

"Oh, Jay!" Gena cried out even louder. "It . . . it . . . it . . ."

It had begun to hurt. Jerrell was touching her in places where no one and nothing else had ever touched her before. He was reaching deep inside her, stretching her out, hammering at things clearly not meant to be hammered. She came once and then immediately again. She thought about how she must feel to him, being deep inside her, gutting her, stretching out her interior walls. The thought of his pleasure made her come again. She could feel water flowing inside her as if she had turned on some secret faucet.

"Gena . . ." he cried out again. Jerrell could feel himself tightening up. He wanted to explode inside her. Never before in his life had he not been able to control his orgasms. Never before in his life had he been reduced to being a fifteen-minute man. No, he had hour power at least. He had the ability to make passionate love for hours on end, and sometimes even into the wee hours of the morning. But this, this was something completely different, something completely new to him. How could she do this to him?

Jerrell exploded inside her, shooting his fluids even deeper into her body. She arched her back and cried out. She gasped for air and held on to him tightly. She could feel his entire body shaking. She had never felt him come like that before.

"You okay, baby?" Gena asked, rubbing his sweating back. "You're still shaking."

Embarrassed, Jerrell rolled off her and lay next to her in bed. He was tired. He'd been up the previous night, planning tonight's events. He'd been on his feet all that day, wrapping up all the loose ends, and now he was feeling it.

Gena placed her arm beneath his head and caressed his sweating chest with her index finger. "There's something I want to talk to you about."

"What?" he asked softly.

"It's nothing, really," she told him. "It's a little surprise I want to share with you."

Jerrell yawned, closed his eyes, and quickly dozed off. Gena stared at the snoring body before her, not believing that when she finally had the courage to tell him, he'd fallen asleep on her.

She slid her arm from beneath his head and carefully got out of the bed. She could still feel the pressure on her stomach, and it felt like she had to use the restroom. She hoped the room had toilet paper in it. It would be a real bitch to have to get dressed and walk all the way to the office for some toilet paper.

Why Jay had chosen to take her to a motel room tonight puzzled her deeply. He had an apartment, and she'd told him that she now had her own apartment. They could've gone back to either of their places after dinner, so why he chose a motel so far on the outskirts of town was beyond her. The thought that he had another woman at home, or nearby, crossed her mind.

Gena made her way across the motel room to the bathroom. She opened the door and walked inside to find buckets, chains, and bags of cement. She also found handcuffs and rope.

"What the fuck?" she said softly.

Gena closed the bathroom door and turned the lock on the knob. She didn't want to wake him, and she didn't want him walking in on her while she snooped around. She opened the shower curtain and peered in the bathtub. There was a bucket labeled ACID sitting inside it. The hair on the back of her neck quickly stood at attention.

Gena sat down on the toilet and peed. It flowed out of her rapidly, as her pregnancy, combined with her nervousness, wreaked havoc on her bladder. She quickly located a roll of toilet paper, wiped herself, and then began to snoop around some more. She found a large duffel bag beneath the bathroom counter.

Gena opened the large green Army-issue duffel bag and, to her surprise, found herself staring at millions of dollars in cash. Her mind began to race. Why the bag full of money? Why the acid, the cement, the buckets, the handcuffs, the chains? He was going to get rid of a body and get out of town. And being she was the only body around, it was clear what Jay had in mind. *But why?*

Gena sat back down on the toilet and began to think. *What the fuck is he doing with acid and all this money and why the fuck does he got me in this hotel room when I could be home in my own bed? This shit ain't right. I better get the hell outta here.* Her mind formulated questions faster than she could even begin to process them. But there was one thing she did know for sure. She was getting the hell out of that room. Thank God she hadn't told him where her new apartment was.

Gena rose and opened the door. Jerrell was standing in the doorway.

Gena screamed and tried to close the bathroom door. Jerrell bum-rushed his way inside.

"What the fuck are you doing?" Gena screamed. "What the fuck is all this shit?"

Jerrell punched Gena in her face, grabbed her by her hair, and dragged her into the bedroom.

"You nosy bitch!" Jerrell shouted.

Gena reached up and dug her nails into Jerrell's face, scratching him deeply. "Let me go! Let me go!"

"Aaaaarrgh!" Jerrell shouted. He knocked her hands away and slapped her with the back of his hand. Gena flew onto the bed.

"Let me out of here!" Gena leaped up off the bed and jumped at

Jerrell, trying to claw his eyes out. He was going to kill her, but she wasn't going out like no crying, docile bitch! This nigga was going to have to fight for his kill.

Jerrell protected his face, pushed Gena back, and then kicked her in her stomach. Gena dropped onto the floor. Jerrell kicked her in the face, causing blood to shoot across the room. Gena raced to the nightstand, grabbed the lamp from it, and swung it at him. The lamp struck Jerrell on the side of his head, and blood ran down into his eye, temporarily blinding him. Gena raced for the door.

"Come here, bitch!" Jerrell shouted. He grabbed Gena as she was opening the motel room door.

Gena kicked and screamed. She bit down on Jerrell's forearm, causing him to drop her. Again, she raced for the door. Jerrell threw a fierce punch at her before she could open the door all the way. The punch caught her in the back of her head, causing her to go dizzy. She fell backward, still clutching the doorknob. The door to the motel room swung open as she hit the floor. She could barely make out the shadow standing in the doorway.

"What the fuck?" Jerrell asked. "Nigga, mind your own mutha-fuckin' business! Don't try to be no Captain Save a Ho!"

"This is my business," he told Jerrell.

"Oh, really?" Jerrell asked.

Jerrell started for the bed, where he had his gun beneath the pillow. He heard the click of another weapon.

"Go for it," the shadowy figure told him.

"Who the fuck are you?" Jerrell shouted.

The shadow stepped into the light of the motel room. Jerrell's eyes grew wider than grapefruits.

"You! This is bullshit! This can't be!" Jerrell dove for his gun. "You're supposed to be dead, nigga!"

Gunfire lit up the motel room as bullets struck Jerrell in his neck, his chest, his side, his arm, his back, and his thigh. Blood and smoke poured from his body as he lay on top of the motel room bed.

Gena felt herself being lifted off the floor. She felt herself in familiar arms, smelling a familiar smell. She was dizzy; her eyes had been beaten almost shut. But she was barely able to make out the face of the man who was carrying her across the parking lot to the black BMW that had been stalking her every move. She was tired, bruised, bleeding, and growing weaker by the moment.

She stared into his face and smiled. "Quadir."

Then she passed out in his arms.

TRUE
TO THE
GAME III
TERI WOODS

This book is dedicated to Leon Blue.

Prologue

February 18, 1991

Gena slowly tried to open her eyes, feeling pain beyond belief throughout her entire body. She was bruised from her head to her toes. She looked around the room, not quite realizing where she was. At first, she thought she was in a hospital, lying in a bed. But as time passed, she realized she wasn't. The room's décor was unlike any hospital room she'd ever seen. Her head, left arm, rib cage, and left thigh were all bandaged. She could barely open her bruised and blackened eyes. She couldn't pull herself out of the bed without feeling agonizing pain. Her body felt sore, and she needed rest. Her only assurance she was safe was she was being taken care of by a nurse and a doctor. She felt the nurse near her bedside constantly and could overhear the nurse talking to the doctor in the distance. The nurse sang to her, she read to her, and she talked to her. The kind and loving nurse fed Gena and gave her pain medication and sleeping pills. She closed her eyes again.

Gena rested her body and mustered her strength as the weeks passed. Early one morning, Gena awoke to a ruckus outside her bedroom door. The sound of voices filled the tiny hallway. Startled but not afraid, Gena looked around the room. It was intricately designed, with a touch of sophistication. Gena did not recognize anything.

Where am I? she couldn't help but wonder. She decided to make finding the answer to that question her life's mission. Ready to move around, Gena rose from the king-size bed she'd been lying on. There was a breeze blowing through an open window, she noticed, as the soft silk panels were billowing gently with the air. She could smell the sweet fragrance of flowers wafting through the window. She mustered up as much strength as she could, desperately wanting to know where she was.

Gena clasped one of the bedposts and made her way to the bottom of the four-poster bed. From there she threw her wobbly legs forward and grabbed hold of a nearby accent chair. She braced herself using the arms of the chair, and then carefully made her way around it until she was able to grab onto a nearby dresser. Using the dresser as support, she slowly made her way to the open window, where she was finally able to peer outside and get a glimpse of her surroundings.

She was on the second floor of what appeared to be a home. She could see very large homes all around her. Steeply pitched slate- and granite-tiled roofs and well-manicured backyards with massive swimming pools and tennis courts filled her view. She peered down into the backyard below her and found an equally large swimming pool and adjacent tennis court, along with the fragrant garden that had attracted her attention initially. The azaleas, roses, Russian sage, gardenias, and other flora spread throughout the landscape painted it in rich hues of blue, red, white, yellow, green, and purple. *Where the hell am I?*

Gena turned toward the dresser and pulled open the first drawer only to find it empty. She moved on to the second drawer and found it in the same state. The third, fourth, fifth, and sixth dresser drawers were also empty. She was in a guest bedroom, and there were no secrets kept there. She turned and spied two doors on the opposite side of the room. One she surmised to be a closet, while the other would have to be the guest bathroom. Hoping the closet or the medicine cabinet would reveal something, she made her way across the room toward them. She had regained her equilibrium and was doing quite well moving around the room.

Gena opened the first door to find a row of plastic clothes hangers facing her. There was nothing on the shelves, nothing stored at the bottom of the closet, nothing period. Disappointed, she turned her attention to the next door. She had been correct in her assumptions as the second door led to the guest bathroom. Gena braced herself on the door handle and stumbled inside. She held on to the bathroom sink and yanked open the medicine cabinet. Nothing.

"Dammit!" Gena cursed. She was growing frustrated with each passing moment. She was in a luxurious prison, all alone and wounded. She couldn't run away if she tried. Her entire body was one big ache and pain. *Think, Gena,* she told herself. *Think. What do you remember? What do you remember?*

Gena thought long and hard as she slowly made her way back to the massive four-poster bed, where she lay down again. *Where am I and who brought me here?* She started to think back and remembered Jay. *We were in a motel.* It was then she remembered going into the bathroom and looking in the duffel bag Jay had under the sink. She remembered the duffel bag full of money, and the rope, the bucket of acid, bags of cement, the handcuffs, and the chains. Jay had taken her to a motel room, where he had tried to kill her. She remembered fighting him. *Yes, I remember, but then what? What happened? Did I trip or fall or something? No, I was running for the door when he grabbed me, and then . . . ?* At first, Gena could not recall. Then she slowly began to remember. *The gun. Someone shot Jay and saved me, or was it Jay who fired the gun?*

Who had done the shooting and who got shot? Did Jay shoot someone? *He was trying to kill me and now he must have me here, holding me hostage. What the hell does he think he's doing? It doesn't even make sense. If he was going to kill me, why didn't he go ahead and do it? Someone else must have saved me, but who? None of this makes any sense at all.*

Nothing added up. She was bandaged but had no idea who had rescued her. She was somewhere but didn't have a clue where, and she was definitely in someone's house but again had no idea whose. She had been in and out of consciousness but had no idea for how long. Someone had expended a lot of money and effort to heal her and care for her. *But who?*

Gena leaned back and closed her eyes, and her tears began to fall. Her mind had granted her an additional memory from that night, one she knew couldn't be true. She had dreamed Quadir was alive. She had been barely conscious, but it all seemed so real at the time. Her Quadir had rescued her from that monster and carried her off to safety. *If only it could be true.*

Gena clutched her stomach and curled into a ball on the bed. It was then she remembered the visit with her ob-gyn.

"Congratulations, you're going to have a baby," Dr. Amerson had said joyfully, smiling from ear to ear.

A baby, my baby. She couldn't help but think of the unborn child she was carrying as she rubbed her belly. She was in a dire predicament. *That's right, I was going to tell him about the baby,* she thought to herself, remembering how nervous she was and how she couldn't wait to hear what he'd say. She'd been hoping Jay would be pleased with her and happy for the both of them. She was so ready to be with him and be a family.

How could I have been so dumb? He didn't love me; he didn't even care about me. He was trying to kill me.

Gena couldn't believe it. She was carrying the child of a man who had tried to kill her, fantasizing about a man who had been dead now for more than a year.

I can't believe Jay has me here. It's only a matter of time before he comes back to finish me off. My only chance will be to try to escape, go get my money, and get out of town. That's what Jay wanted: Quadir's money. He never wanted to be with me. He could not have cared less.

That reality brought tears to Gena's eyes, and she realized Jay had only pretended to love and care about her.

How was I so stupid that I didn't see him for what he really was? I can't believe he was after my money.

Gena sat on the edge of the bed thinking about everything that had happened, unable to justify anything and unwilling to believe it was all happening to her.

I wonder where he is. Shit, where the hell am I? And how long have I been here?

She needed to get in touch with Gah Git. She needed to talk to her grandmother and tell her where she was and let her know she was all right. Gah Git would be worried half to death.

Poor Gah Git. I hope she's okay.

Gena had already looked around the room, and there was no phone.

Someone has to help me. I need to be rescued. But rescued from who? Whoever it is that bandaged my wounds, fed me, and took care of me? Yes, I need to be rescued, especially if that person is Jay.

The door to the room cracked open, and Gena expected the worst. Instead, she was greeted by a plump and friendly housekeeper.

"Oh my God! Señorita, you're awake!" the housekeeper said. "Oh, they will be so pleased! Mr. Smith is about to have breakfast on the lanai. I can bring your breakfast out there so you can eat with him. He will be so pleased, señorita! It is so good to see you're awake now!"

"Who are you? And who is Mr. Smith?" Gena asked.

"My name is Consuela, and Mr. Smith is Señorita Hopkins's boyfriend," the housekeeper explained. "Señor Smith is the one who rescued you and brought you here."

"Rescued me?" Gena was confused. She shook her head to rid herself of the cobwebs inside.

Who is Mr. Smith?

Gena needed to see this Mr. Smith. She needed to talk to him, and she needed him to fill in all the blanks from that night. What had happened? Where was Jay? Why did Mr. Smith bring her here? She had a million and one questions that needed answering.

Gena began to rise. Consuela rushed to her and helped her stand.

"No, wait here," Consuela told her. "Señorita Hopkins brought something for you, for when this day would come."

Consuela hurried out of the room and returned seconds later with a metal walker. She placed the walker in front of Gena and then clasped her arm.

"I'll help you to the elevator and then to the porch. I'll bring your breakfast out to the garden."

"Thank you so much, but I can walk," Gena told her.

"Are you sure?" Consuela asked, as if it were a miracle.

"Yes, yes, of course. You are very kind, though. Thank you, but I'm fine. I can walk."

"Ven, I will help you."

Consuela helped Gena to the elevator, and they rode it down to the first floor. The doors opened to reveal a massive two-story family room. The dimensions made Gena gasp.

The room was forty by sixty feet, with a ten-foot diameter, wrought-iron chandelier. Antique furnishings and expensive décor filled the room. The art and tapestries hung on the wall were all originals, while the tables appeared to be hand-carved with great care and detail.

"Who lives here?" Gena asked.

"Señorita Hopkins," Consuela told her. "She is at work right now. Señor Smith is out on the lanai."

Gena followed as Consuela led her across the family room, out the large double patio doors, and onto the lanai. A gentleman was seated across the lanai, facing away from them, looking over the swimming pool. She could see he was dressed all in white and reading a newspaper. A table with a pitcher of orange juice was next to him, and she could see he had already poured himself a glass.

"Señor Smith," Consuela called out to him. "Look who has awakened."

Gena watched as the stranger rose from the chair and turned to her. Consuela had to catch her.

"Señorita, are you all right?" Consuela asked.

It can't be. It can't be. Gena shook her head.

"I'll take it from here," he told Consuela.

"No. No. It's not possible. I don't understand. You're dead!" Gena said, staring at a ghost.

He guided her to the table and poured her a glass of water.

"You're alive," Gena said softly. She gently caressed his face, reassuring herself she wasn't dreaming. "You're alive!"

Tears streamed from her eyes as she covered her face.

Quadir sat next to her and gently placed his arm around her. "Gena, it's okay. I'm here now."

He kissed her face, took her hand in his, and rubbed it gently against his face. He was alive. Her Qua was here with her, and he was alive! *But how?* was the only thing she could think. She looked over at him; sure as day, he was there. *How could this miracle be possible? I saw him dead at the hospital. I was at his funeral.*

Gena sat still in silence. Neither of them said a word. Quadir didn't want to interrupt her thoughts, knowing his presence was as heavy as his death. He'd done what he had to do and what was best for him at that time, but he'd never meant to hurt her.

Confused, Gena didn't know what to say next. "I don't understand."

She looked him in the eyes for a split second and wondered if he had any idea what he had put her through. Out of nowhere, she slapped his face. His expression remained blank. She started to slap him again, but he caught her hand and held it in his.

"Why you beatin' on me?" he asked with a smile.

"Why are you alive? You're supposed to be dead."

She shoved him away, and a frown shot across her face. "Where have you been? How could you do that to me? How could you be alive? I don't understand. I saw you; you were dead."

Quadir nodded. "I know, Gena, I know. I have a lot of explaining to do."

"You're goddamned right you do! How could you let me think you were dead? How could you up and leave me like that without telling me anything? Do you understand the hell I've been through since you died? Do you?"

Gena tried to slap him again, and again he caught her wrist and prevented her from hitting him.

"You bastard! You're an asshole! You sorry, inconsiderate son of a bitch!"

"Gena, wait!" Quadir held her arm down. "Calm down! You're going to bust your stitches. You have to take it easy until you've fully recovered. I'll explain everything. I promise. Give me a chance."

"What possible explanation could you have for what you've done to me? To us? Why would you put me through all of that?"

"I had to. I had no choice. I had people trying to kill me and the police about to indict me. I needed to start over. And I needed it to look real."

"So you had someone kill you? I was there that night. I saw you die."

"No, that part *was* real," Quadir explained. "I had nothing to do with them sorry-ass Junior Mafia motherfuckers shooting at us. Are you crazy? They really tried to kill me. In fact, they did. All of that was real, baby. But once I got to the hospital, I was resuscitated. I can't explain it; I wouldn't let go. There was something inside of me like a light that refused to go out. That light was my love for you, Gena. My love for you wouldn't let me die," he said, hoping kind and submissive words would soothe her.

"Nigga, are you crazy? You were dead. I saw you; you were dead." Gena crossed her arms and lifted a questioning eyebrow. "If you weren't dead, why didn't you call me, Quadir? Why didn't anyone call me and let me know you were alive? Do you realize how crazy you sound right now?"

"Because, baby, everyone thought I was dead. That was the only way my plan would work. It was my only chance to get away from the police and from the Junior Mafia. I was going to go down South, Gena. I was going to get everything set up, and then I was going to come for you."

"And why couldn't I be a part of the plan? Why couldn't you have let me know what was going on?"

"Because I needed my death to be real, and you were the biggest key to everyone believing I was gone. I needed to let everything die down first, and I needed you to convince everyone that I was dead and buried."

"Who did I bury?"

Quadir exhaled. He settled in for the long story he was about to tell her. "You may want to eat a little something before I get started."

"Quadir, I will die of starvation before I let either of us leave this lanai and I still be in the dark," Gena told him. "I hope this little explanation of yours is a good one. If it's not, I'm going to kill you myself. And this time, there won't be no coming back."

Quadir smiled and leaned back in his chair. "It's like this . . ."

Heaven Can Wait

Hahnemann University Hospital
January 1, 1990

The orderly strolled into the room to collect his cadaver. He had been at the job for a little more than a year now, and he loved it. Working in the hospital morgue paid well and afforded him the peace and quiet he needed to study for his premed courses. The job suited him more than most, as his goal was to become a surgeon. He was now in his final year of premed, one semester away from actual medical school, where he'd be cutting open bodies and not merely transporting them from one floor to another.

The body he was picking up now was fresh. The gunshot victim's time of death had been called, and his family had recently walked out of the room.

The orderly lifted the cadaver's hanging hand to lay it on the bed. The hand felt weird. Stranger than any other dead guy's hand he had ever touched. The damn thing was warm, really warm. And more than that, it had a fucking pulse.

"Oh, shit!" The orderly rushed into the hall to find a nurse, a doctor, anyone who looked like they could do something. "Excuse me, ma'am. I have an emergency."

Dr. Hopkins stopped and read the orderly's name tag. "Stan, what can I do for you?"

"Doc, I got a dead guy in there who ain't dead," Stan told her.

"What?" Dr. Hopkins rushed into the emergency operating room. She clasped Quadir's pulse. Sure as shit, he had one. She rushed to the wall and pressed the intercom button.

"Emergency room personnel to the OR stat. This is Dr. Amelia Hopkins. Emergency room surgical personnel to the OR immediately!"

Masked emergency room personnel ran into the operating room, some of them still covered with Quadir's blood from minutes ago.

"We got a live one here, people!" Dr. Hopkins shouted. She rushed to a corner of the room to scrub up before several nurses dressed her in surgical garb. Two more surgeons, Dr. Benjamin Brant and Dr. William Hartley, rushed into the room. "Ben, he's still alive."

"Hot damn!" Dr. Brant rushed to Quadir and immediately began working on him.

Dr. Hartley began issuing orders as he scrubbed up and the nurses dressed him in surgical garb.

"You're a tough son of a bitch, aren't you?" Dr. Brant said, smiling at Quadir. "Fight, son. That's right, fight."

"Set up a pint of plasma for him," Hopkins ordered one of the nurses. "Get him hooked back up so we can monitor his blood pressure. What's the deal, Benny?"

"Couldn't find that last fucking bullet. It hid behind his heart. He flatlined and we couldn't get him back. We called him."

"You need a woman's touch in here," Hopkins told him. "My hands are a lot smaller than yours. Let me see if I can work my way around in there and get that little booger."

Dr. Brant moved out of the way and allowed Dr. Hopkins to

become the primary surgeon. Within seconds, she was smiling at him beneath her surgical mask.

"Was this the pesky little thing you were looking for?" she asked, holding up a small, bloody lead ball. She placed the bullet into a small dish and then proceeded to repair the internal damage it had caused.

"Ben and I repaired most of the damage already," Hartley told her.

"I see—you guys did a fantastic job," she told him, massaging their egos. Dr. Hopkins reconnected a severed artery, suctioned the blood from the wound, and monitored her patient for several moments before turning to a nurse. "What's he looking like?"

"Blood pressure has climbed to 112 over 70 and is holding steady. Everything looks good."

"Close him up for me, get him into ICU, and page me in an hour with his vitals," Hopkins told them. She lifted the chart from the bottom of the bed. *Deceased* had been scrawled across it. "Get him a new chart. The patient's name is John Smith. Everybody clear on that?"

Dr. Brant peered over at his colleague.

"I'll alert the authorities and his family," Dr. Hopkins told them. "Until I or the authorities say otherwise, Mr. Richards is deceased. Mr. Smith, however, is alive and doing quite well."

"I signed the death certificate," Hartley told her.

"I'll take care of that, too," Hopkins said. She turned to the orderly, who had watched the whole thing from the corner of the operating room. "Come with me."

Amelia Hopkins led Stan out into the hallway and led him into a corner. "Stan, what I'm about to say to you is very important. I need your undivided attention. Do I have that, Stan? Do I have your undivided attention?"

Stan nodded. "Yes, ma'am."

"Good. Stan, I have a patient in there who had a whole lot of bullet holes inside of him. Somebody doesn't like Mr. Richards and thought it best he not remain with us in this life. My job, as a doctor, is to see to it that he does. But in order to do that, I'm going to need your help. Can I count on you to help me?"

Stan nodded again.

"Good. Now, how many John Does do you have down there in the morgue?"

"Right now about four or five, but the weekend is coming up. We should have a shitload of 'em coming in."

Amelia Hopkins nodded. "Any of the ones we have fit the description of Mr. Richards in there?"

Stan smiled and scratched his chin. "One, maybe. A buddy of mine works over in the morgue at the county hospital. I'm sure I could get you a John Doe close enough to match."

It was Dr. Hopkins's turn to smile. "You do that. You get me a John Doe to match, and you put this chart on him. Make sure John Doe becomes Quadir Richards. And you let no one in to see it. He's already been identified by his family, and you tell them the authorities aren't allowing anyone else to see the body at this time. You got that?"

Stan nodded once more. "Dr. Hopkins, in a few years, I'll need a surgeon to intern under."

Amelia shoved the chart into his hand. "You want to be a surgeon, I'll get you there. But you better have the grades and the stamina to keep up with me."

Stan smiled. "Deal."

Dr. Hopkins walked to the nurses station. "That patient in the OR. I need you to get me his family's address and telephone number."

The nurse nodded and lifted a large telephone book from beneath the nurses station.

Dr. Hopkins knew one thing was for certain: a mother would do anything to keep her child alive. A wife or girlfriend could be after an insurance policy, or her jealous lover could've been the gunman. But a mother, she'd kill or die to protect her offspring. She needed the mother's address.

The nurses and a couple of ICU orderlies wheeled Quadir out of the operating room, heading for the elevator.

"What's he look like?" Hopkins asked.

"Vitals are stable. Blood pressure is 118 over 80."

"Good job, Amelia," Dr. Brant told her, exiting the operating room.

"Thanks, Benny."

"I'm heading over to the cafeteria. Want to join me?" Dr. Brant asked.

Amelia nodded. She could use something to eat. Besides, she wanted to run a few things by Dr. Brant. He was her mentor, and she trusted him completely. It had been Dr. Brant who had trained her and helped her to hone her surgical skills to what they were today. Benny Brant was probably one of the top surgeons in the country. And for him, a wealthy Jewish surgeon from New York, to have taken a poor Black girl from the Alabama countryside under his wing was unfathomable. He had dozens of doctors from some of the finest families all over the country trying to intern under him, some of whom were the sons and daughters of his colleagues. The fact that he'd pulled her under his wing was something she'd forever be grateful for.

The two of them headed for the elevator.

Game Plan

Amelia moved through the parking garage with the ferocity of a cheetah on the prowl. Her determined steps took her rapidly through the parking structure to the secluded corner where her meeting was to take place. The person she was to meet was already there.

"Viola Richards?" she asked.

Viola nodded. "What's going on? Why did you ask me to meet you here?"

Amelia peered around the parking garage to make sure they were alone. Still, she thought it was best they move to the even more secluded second level. She clasped Viola's arm and led her off.

As they walked, Amelia said, "I wanted to meet you here because I had some questions about your son. I operated on him in the emergency room."

Viola sniffled. "Do the police have any suspects or leads in the case?" she asked, shaking her head. "My son was a young Black man whose occupation was questionable. In situations like these, they don't care about finding the killers. They chalk him up as another statistic."

Amelia nodded. She understood exactly what Viola Richards was talking about. Young Black men, drug dealers or no drug dealers, were all statistics. The police would lump their deaths into one of two categories: drug-related or gang-related.

"I take it you don't have great faith in our police department," Amelia observed.

"Could as well been them that killed my baby," Viola told her.

Amelia nodded. Good. Viola was no fan of the police department, which meant, in all probability, she'd cooperate with her request. "Any idea who did this to your son?"

Viola shook her head. "No, it could've been anybody. You know how things are; nobody wants to be a snitch. It could be your best friend, your mama, even your own child. That's the way it is."

"Take care of it in the streets, huh?"

Mrs. Richards nodded. "But the only problem is it's more kids getting killed."

Amelia nodded. "I believe in taking care of our own."

Amelia led Viola to the upper level of the parking garage and stopped in front of a black Mercedes S Class. "Are you a religious woman, Mrs. Richards?"

"Of course. I go to church every Sunday."

"Sometimes God has a plan for each of us. And sometimes we don't understand what His plan is. Sometimes He works in ways so mysterious, even we doctors can't explain it."

"Amen! I know that's right."

"Sometimes when we doctors have exhausted all medical means possible, God steps in with His hand and touches a person. Even when we have given up, sometimes God says, 'I ain't done using this person yet.'"

Viola smiled. "My Quadir is with the Lord. God still has a plan for him, and for each of us." She clasped Amelia's hand and shook it. "I want to thank you for all you did to try to save my son."

Amelia smiled. "Don't thank me yet. You may want to lean up against this car right here."

Viola leaned back against the Mercedes and stared at Amelia. She was truly puzzled.

"After the surgeon worked on your son, he thought he'd lost him. He declared your son deceased. A short time later, an orderly went into the room and discovered your son wasn't dead."

Viola clasped her hands against her chest, and her knees buckled. Amelia caught her and held her up.

"I rushed into the operating room, and I began to operate on your son. I found the bullet the first surgeon couldn't retrieve, and I was able to repair the damage to your son."

Viola stared at her in bewilderment.

Amelia smiled and nodded. "Quadir is alive," she whispered.

Viola gasped and began to slide to the ground again. Amelia could not hold her up this time. Tears flowed from Viola's eyes, and she began to kiss Amelia's hands. "Thank you, thank you, thank you! Oh, dear Lord, thank you! My baby is alive! Thank you!"

Amelia knelt beside her. "We don't know who tried to kill Quadir. We have to be very, very careful. I want to keep him alive. I don't want to tell *anyone* that he's alive, understand?"

Viola nodded.

"I don't know who I can trust. Does he have a wife?"

Viola frowned at the thought of Gena. She never had liked the girl, but that was her son's choice, not hers. "He has a girlfriend and they were engaged, but they hadn't tied the knot. Even still, though, I don't want to tell anybody! *Nobody!* Don't call nobody else, Doc."

Amelia nodded. "I haven't informed the police."

"Good! Don't tell them neither!"

"Quadir is in stable but critical condition. These next few days are going to be crucial for him."

"Can I see him, Doctor?"

"Eventually, yes. But right now, to have you coming up to the hospital . . ."

She nodded. "I understand. Do whatever it is you're doing. Keep doing your thing, baby!"

Viola wrapped her arms around Amelia and hugged her as tight as she could.

"I love you." Viola began crying heavily. "I don't know you, but I love you, baby. I love you so much. You brought my baby back to me."

Amelia rose and helped Viola to her feet. "We're going to have to be smart on this one."

"Whatever you need, baby, you tell me."

"We can't let anyone catch on, especially the fiancée. We can't let her snoop around. I've taken care of the autopsy report. The death certificate has already been signed by another doctor. I have a body from the morgue with Quadir's chart on it."

"A body!"

"He was a John Doe. No one has claimed him for some time. He was young, about Quadir's age, decent shape. Probably homeless, maybe even a drug addict. He probably has no family, so to speak, and his looks are perfect to allow him to pass for Quadir."

Mrs. Richardson nodded solemnly.

"So, tomorrow you can have the undertaker pick him up, okay?" Amelia suggested, hoping Quadir's mother was following her line. "And you'll take care of the fiancée, right? Make sure she doesn't make trouble for us."

"Oh, I can handle that. I can keep her from getting into things. Once I get into his house, I can control everything." *The first thing will be to put her ass out. Once I get rid of Gena, everything will work itself out,* Viola couldn't help but think to herself. "Mm-hmm, I can get in there, control things. Keep her from his papers, his money, and all the things she can use to mess things up for us."

Amelia nodded.

Viola bounced up and down slightly. "I can't believe my baby is alive!"

Amelia nodded.

"When can I see him?"

"I'll call you and let you know. Once he's fully conscious, and feeling a lot better, I'll get you into the hospital."

"Was there any permanent damage to anything? I mean, don't get me wrong. I'll take him as a vegetable, as long as he's alive."

"I understand. It's a perfectly normal question. Right now, only time will tell. I don't believe there will be any permanent damage, but again, time will let us know. He *will* need therapy, lots of reha-bilitation, and a good diet of soft foods at first."

"Are you going to see it through?"

"Huh?"

"I know how things go. You're a doctor; you have other patients. I don't want you to pass him on down the line to a bunch of other doc-tors and therapists and who knows who else. I want you to look after my baby."

Amelia nodded. "I'll see him through, Mrs. Richards. I'll see him through."

Viola hugged Amelia once again. "What church do you go to?"

"I go to First Baptist in Germantown," Amelia replied.

"Come to church with me this Sunday. Please."

Amelia hesitated for several seconds and then relented. "Okay, I'll go."

"Thank you so much." Viola kissed the doctor on her cheek. "Your parents must be so proud of you! I'm so proud of you, and I just met you! Where are you from?"

"Alabama."

"Alabama! Wow, you sure are far away from home. Do you have any family in these parts?"

Amelia shook her head. "No, only my colleagues and patients."

"You poor, sweet thing. I want you to come to dinner at our house on Sunday after church! You can call your folks in Alabama and tell them you got stolen by a crazy lady in Philadelphia! I'm adopting your butt! I'm sure you like soul food!"

Amelia nodded. "Raised on it."

"Girl, my collard greens will make you wanna slap your mama!"

Amelia threw her head back and laughed. She liked Viola. She knew then and there she'd found a foster family in her new city.

Dr. Do Good

melia rushed into Quadir's hospital room, closing the door behind her.

"Your name is John Smith. Do you understand me?"

"What?"

"I said your name is John Smith."

"Why do you keep telling me that?" Quadir asked.

"I'm telling you again today, in case you didn't understand me the other day. You were still a little out of it. But understand me, this is extremely important."

"Why?"

"Because someone tried to kill you and because I sent Quadir Richards's body to a funeral home where they held a funeral service for it and buried it almost two weeks ago. Quadir Richards is dead. John Smith, someone no one wants dead, is alive and well in the hospital. Understand?"

Quadir nodded. "Why?"

"Why what?"

"Why are you trying to help me?"

"I promised someone that I'd see things through."

There was a knock at the door.

"Come in," Amelia shouted.

The door opened, and two gentlemen in scrubs walked in.

"How's he doing today?" one of them asked.

Amelia nodded. "Cranky, but alive."

"That's a good sign." He extended his hand to Quadir. "Hello, young man. My name is Dr. Benjamin Brant. How are you feeling today?"

Quadir shook his hand. "Doing pretty well, Doc."

"Well, that's good to hear. Any pain anywhere?"

"No."

"That's good. You feel any discomfort, you let the nurses know, and they'll give you something for the pain. We want you to be as comfortable as possible."

"Thank you, Doc."

"Don't thank me. Thank Dr. Hopkins over there. She's the one who saved your life. You're a very lucky young man. You're fortunate she was here that day."

Quadir turned and stared at her. She was young, Black, and country as all backwoods. He'd assumed she was a nurse or something. But the doctor was now telling him that she was a doctor, too. A surgeon! In fact, the surgeon who'd saved his life. *Ain't this a bitch?*

Amelia lifted Quadir's chart. "I want you to go easy on the pain medication. I've written up orders to start your therapy today."

Amelia turned and waved her hand toward the second gentleman in the room. "This is Neal Ryan, your physical therapist. Neal's the best we have here at Hahnemann Hospital, and probably the best in Philly. He's going to get you back up and running in no time."

Neal extended his hand to Quadir. "Pleasure to meet you, Mr. Smith."

Quadir clasped Neal's hand and shook it.

"We're going to have you back up to a hundred percent before you know it," Neal told him. "Can you move your leg for me?"

"Well, I'll leave you guys alone. I have some more patients to peek in on," Dr. Brant told them. He patted Quadir's arm. "You get better, young man. I'll see you tomorrow."

"Thank you, Doc," Quadir said.

Brant exited the room, leaving Quadir, Neal, and Amelia alone.

"Okay, try to move your leg for me," Neal said.

Quadir stared down at his legs, but neither of them moved. "I can't move them! I can't move my legs!"

"Relax, it takes time," Neal assured him.

"Relax? What the fuck do you mean, relax? I can't move my fucking legs!"

"Okay, calm down," Neal told him.

"I can't move my legs!" Quadir cried out.

Neal turned toward Amelia.

Amelia shook her head. "He's not paralyzed. There may be some internal scarring we didn't know about. I'll order some X-rays."

Neal placed his hand beneath Quadir's leg and bent it. "I can feel your nerves jumping and your muscles contracting. Try to force your leg straight."

Quadir's face contorted as he tried to force his leg straight.

Neal turned to Amelia and shook his head. Nothing.

Amelia examined Quadir's chart. She made several notations on it.

"I'm modifying your diet. Right now, I have you on liquids and soft foods. I'm going to slowly adjust it to include more solids. I want to increase your proteins and lean foods. Also, I'm ordering a dietary supplement to be given twice a day."

"I'm going to add the pool to his therapy regimen also," Neal told her. "Starting him off slow with some water resistance would be good." He faced Quadir. "From what I can tell, your muscles have been used to doing nothing for the past few weeks. We're going to have to whip them back into shape. I want to get you down there into our therapeutic pool and get you started today. It's a heated pool, really warm water, and it should feel good on your body. It may also cause the internal swelling to go down a bit. How's that sound?"

"Like a bunch of medical bullshit!" Quadir told him.

Neal smiled. "I'm going to run and get the pool ready, take care of some paperwork, and I'll be back with a wheelchair."

Neal turned and exited the room. Amelia replaced Quadir's chart.

"I'm paralyzed," Quadir said flatly, unable to believe it and at that very moment wishing he was dead.

"You are not."

"Bullshit! I can't move my legs!"

"I'm the doctor here, and I'm telling you that you're not paralyzed! You're lazy."

"Oh, like I wanna be stuck in this fucking bed!"

"Why is it that when Dr. Brant or one of the white doctors come around, it's *yes, sir, no, sir, thank you, Doctor.* But with me, it's *fuck, bullshit,* and every other curse word you can think of?"

"What?"

"Is it because I'm young, Black, or a woman? What is it? Whatever happened to manners?"

"No, it's because I can't move my legs and I'd rather be dead than paralyzed."

Amelia couldn't help but smile. He was an asshole. "You're a bitch, you know that?"

"I'm a bitch? I didn't know doctors called their patients bitches nowadays."

"This one calls them like she sees them. You're more than a bitch; you're a *punk* bitch. You bow down and suck up to the white man, but you treat me like shit."

"What?"

"You're one of them house niggas, aren't you? You'll pick up a gun, and you'll aim it at another Black man, but you'll throw that bitch down and put your hands up when the white man comes around."

"Fuck you! You don't know me! You don't know shit about me or who I am!"

Amelia nodded. "I know your type. Big, bad, brave man, tough with a gun. Quick with your mouth. But when it really comes down to it, you ain't shit. You ain't a real built-to-last nigga. You're a quitter and a coward."

Quadir tried to sit up. "Bitch, you don't know me! I ain't nobody's fucking coward!"

"Coward!"

Quadir sat up, clasped the bedrail, took his free hand, and swung his legs off the side of the bed.

"You want to know something, Quadir?"

"What?" Quadir snapped.

"A paralyzed man wouldn't be able to sit up in bed."

Quadir looked down and examined himself. He caught on to what she had done.

"You're not a coward. You're a fighter. The way you were going to come after me, that's the same determination you have to use to regain all your abilities. You have to fight for your life again. Fight to get it back! If you're counting on some medicine or some magic potion or formula to give it back to you, it ain't going to happen. Sorry, brother, but nothing like that has been invented yet. You're going to have to fight."

"You should be a motivational speaker," he said sarcastically.

"You should sell shit to mushroom farms 'cause you're really an asshole."

Quadir laughed. She was sharp. He had tried to push her buttons, disrespected her, doubted her, even. But it was now obvious she was the real deal.

"Do you want to walk again?" Amelia asked.

Quadir shrugged his shoulders. "I don't know."

She'd heard that answer before. She'd done volunteer work the previous summer in Chad. Many soldiers had given her the same answer. Walk again for what? To go back out there and face a world that would still be just as hard, just as hostile to them? She knew where his answer was coming from.

"You don't know, because what would change, huh? What would be different in the world if you went back out there again? Everything would be the same. All the bullshit would be exactly the same. Am I right?"

Quadir shifted his gaze toward her.

"One thing would be different. You. You'd know that you took what the world threw at you, and you handled it. You get up, go back out there, and you smile at that fucked-up world, and you let it know it didn't defeat you. Let them know they may have knocked you down, but you got right back up. Let them know you are a real soldier, a warrior for your people! You may encounter defeats, but you must not be defeated!"

"You're quoting Maya Angelou now."

Amelia startled slightly. She had been taken by surprise. "How did you know that?"

"I can read."

"I'm shocked."

"That I can read?"

"That you would know Maya. Most guys your age . . ."

"I guess we both made the mistake of prejudging each other."

"I guess we did."

Neal walked into the room pushing a wheelchair. "Wow, look at you sitting up!" He parked the chair next to Quadir's bed and then helped him into it. "Be back in a while, Doc."

Amelia nodded.

Quadir stopped the chair right before they were about to exit the room and turned back toward her. "No more prejudging each other?"

"No more prejudging each other."

Neal looked at them strangely.

Quadir smiled and shook his head. "You're a pain in the ass, Doc. And that's no prejudgment."

Amelia threw her head back and laughed. "And you are an asshole, Mr. Smith. A bona fide asshole who's full of shit."

Quadir wheeled himself out of the room, smiling.

The Good Foot

Amelia strolled into the physical therapy room and spied Quadir in a nearby corner with Neal. Neal had Quadir lying on his back on a mat, while Neal was pushing his leg, shouting for Quadir to push back against him. He had been in therapy for only a few days now, and results had been slow in coming. Quadir was not physically disabled. He was simply indifferent to trying. He acted like he simply wanted to give up.

She approached and stood over him. "Lying on your ass again, huh?"

"Now is not the time for humor," Quadir told her.

"Any time is a good time for humor. How's he coming along, Neal?"

"If he'd put as much effort into his therapy as he did into resisting it, he'd be ready to run a marathon right now."

Amelia nodded. "So, what's the deal, John?"

"Ain't no deal."

"Push," Neal ordered.

"I am pushing. Can't you tell?"

"You're not pushing. You've got more in you than this. Hey, if you don't want to walk, that's your problem. I can't make you walk."

"Then why don't you leave me alone? I was fine lying in my bed watching TV. You came and got me, remember?"

"A regular wiseass," Neal said, peering up at Amelia.

"I already know."

"Aren't you like a surgeon or something?" Quadir asked. "Shouldn't you be somewhere cutting somebody open and charging them an arm and a leg for it?"

"Neal, let me take over for a little while," Amelia told him.

Neal nodded. He was happy to be rid of John Smith, if only for today. "Be my guest!"

"Hang close. I'm going to need you to help me get him into his chair."

"I'll be right across the room if you need me," Neal said.

Amelia turned to Quadir. "I thought we had this conversation already."

"And what conversation is that?"

"The conversation about you being a quitter."

"We didn't converse. You talked; I listened."

"Funny. So, are you going to be a coward and give up?"

"I thought you said I wasn't a coward?"

"All quitters are cowards."

"Kenny Rogers said you got to know when to fold 'em."

"So your life is a game of cards now?"

"Life has always been nothing but one big gamble."

"So you fold, huh? Gonna go back to your room, cash in all your chips, and call it quits? I wish I would've known you were a quitter before. I wouldn't have wasted my time."

"Why did you?"

"I saw a man who wouldn't quit! I saw a man who refused to give up, a man who refused to die! I thought you were a fighter."

"It's easy to stand there and judge somebody! You haven't been through what I've been through!"

"Oh, you poor baby! You got shot. So the fuck what! What are you going to do now? Are you going to get back on the goddamned bike, or what?"

"What?"

"You heard me! What are you going to do, John? When little kids get a boo-boo, they get up, dust themselves off, get back out there, and keep going. What are you going to do, little boy? 'Cause frankly, just about everybody in here is tired of your whiny attitude. It's time to either shit or get off the pot!"

Quadir went for his wheelchair. He pulled it close, put the brakes on, and then pulled himself up into it. The therapists in the room clapped when he was finished. Quadir looked at Amelia like he wanted to kill her.

"I don't need your fucking help! Yours or nobody else's!"

"You owe these people in here more than that! You owe them more than your scorn. You owe a whole lot of people some god-damned effort!"

"Everyone keeps telling me what I owe. Everyone keeps telling me how grateful I should be, how good of a goddamned doctor you are, but you know what? I can't see it! All I see is a fucking pain in the ass!"

"You fucking quitter. If you don't believe you owe these people who've spent all their time taking care of you, trying to get you better, then maybe I can take you to somebody you do think you owe something to!"

Amelia grabbed Quadir's chair, turned him around, and pushed him out of the room. She headed down the hall, out of the therapy ward, around a few corners, and into the chapel.

"What do you think you're doing?" Quadir asked.

"When's the last time you sat and prayed?"

"I prayed the other night."

"You should pray every day."

"Don't tell me what I need to do. What are you, a priest *and* a doctor?"

"If I were a priest, I would drown your ass in some holy water." Quadir smiled.

"Someone wants to see you. Since you don't feel like you owe any of us any effort, maybe you'll try to get better for her."

Amelia pushed him all the way into the chapel. A woman rose from her knees, turned, and smiled at him.

"Mom!" Quadir's eyes flew open wide with amazement and surprise.

Viola's tears flowed as she rushed to him.

"Baby!" She leaned forward and embraced her son tightly. "You really are alive. Thank you, Lord! Thank you!"

She pulled Amelia close and hugged her. "Thank you so much! Thank you for saving my baby!"

"Now we have to get your baby to want to save himself," Amelia told her.

"What do you mean?" Viola asked.

"Tell her, Quadir."

"Tell me what?" Viola said as she looked back and forth between the two of them. "What's going on, Quadir?"

Quadir smacked his lips. "Nothing. She's crazy, that's all."

"Quadir, Amelia has been over to my house many times since we've met."

"What?" Quadir recoiled.

Amelia smiled at him.

"And she may be many things, but one thing she is not is crazy. What's going on?"

"Do you want to tell her, or should I?" Amelia asked, looking at Quadir.

"Do what you want. You've been doing it anyhow."

Viola could see her son's attitude and placed her hand on her hip as she looked down at him.

"Quadir here has given up," Amelia told her.

"What?"

"Yep, he's thrown in the towel. Doesn't want to try in therapy, wants to sit back and eat Jell-O and watch television."

"No, that's not my son. My son isn't a quitter. My baby's a fighter!"

The two women stared at Quadir in silence. He could feel their eyes on him.

"Quadir . . ." Viola started.

"Okay, okay!"

"Okay what?" Amelia asked. "Okay, you admit to your mother you're a quitter, or okay, you're not going to let her down and be a quitter?"

Quadir peered up at Amelia and rolled his eyes. She was the most nerve-racking woman he'd ever met.

"Baby, I want you to walk out of this hospital on your own two feet," Viola told him. "I want you to hurry up and get well and get outta this place."

Quadir nodded.

"His gunshot wounds are healing rather well," Amelia explained. "He has one I left open because of infection. We pack it twice a day, and we've been giving him antibiotics for it. I want it to close up on its own. It'll leave only a slightly larger scar than if we'd sewn it up. But he's coming along rather nicely."

Viola caressed Quadir's head and nodded.

"We need for him to give us some effort, so we can get him walking."

"I'm sore and it hurts like hell!" Quadir told her.

"Try, baby. Do it for me. Promise me you'll try," Viola pleaded.

Quadir nodded. "Okay, I'll do it."

"Good." Amelia smiled. "Well, I'll leave you two alone so you can catch up. I'll be back in, say . . . thirty minutes?"

"Thank you so much, Amelia." Mrs. Richards leaned forward and kissed her on her cheek.

Amelia turned and left the chapel.

"How's Gena doing?" Quadir asked.

"She's doing good. She's fine."

"Where is she? Why didn't she come here with you?"

"Baby, after this happened to you, I didn't trust nobody. I decided it'd be best to let her think you were dead."

"What? That's Gena! Why would you do that?"

"Baby, I know. But it was for your own safety."

"My safety? She didn't shoot me!"

"Listen, I didn't even tell your father, and no, I didn't tell her. Do you know what could happen if Gena finds out you're alive? Do you understand that Amelia put her entire medical career on the line to help protect you? If Gena knew you were alive, the entire city would know. There's no way she could keep this kind of secret. Please trust us, trust *me*, and trust Dr. Hopkins. Don't worry about Gena. You go ahead and get well. I want you to walk out of this place, then go get your precious Gena and get the hell outta Philly."

"Get outta Philly? Where's Rik? Where's everybody else?"

"Baby, you can worry about them after you get better! But, son, you got to understand, you're a ghost to these people. To them, you don't exist."

Quadir nodded. "I want to see Gena."

"I know you do. I know, son, but she's fine. She's tough and she can handle herself until you get yourself together and figure out where to go from here with your life."

Quadir thought about his money. He'd been out of it for weeks. Rent needed to be paid, mortgages needed to be paid, and all his other bills had to be taken care of. "I need you to take care of a few things for me."

"What?"

"I need you to pay some bills for me."

"I already took care of all that, Quadir."

"All of them?"

Viola nodded. She thought she had in fact taken care of all her son's bills, not knowing he had many others she knew nothing about—one important one in particular.

"Quadir, I've taken care of everything. You relax, do your therapy, son, and get better. Okay, baby?"

Quadir nodded. He'd do as she said. He'd focus, and he'd hurry up and get the hell out of that hospital. Either that or he was going to catch a case for killing Dr. Hopkins.

Viola maneuvered herself behind her son's wheelchair and began to push. "I want you to come up to the front of the chapel with me so we can pray together, okay?"

Quadir looked blankly ahead. He didn't know what she expected of him, but he didn't have any prayers left. He had prayed more than anyone would ever know. Every time he tried to use his legs to hold him up, he prayed. And every time he tried to take a step, he prayed. *Don't she know all I been doing is praying?* He knew his mother, and he knew that even if he didn't want to, Viola wouldn't take no for an answer.

"Okay."

Can't Get Right

Six Weeks Later

Dr. Hopkins strolled into her patient's room pushing a wheelchair.

"Up and at 'em, sleepyhead."

Quadir was lying in his bed, staring out the window. He turned to face her.

"You are a pest. You should get an award for being the peskiest doctor in the world. Why won't you stop?"

"Because, Mr. Smith, you are a fighter. You fought for your life on that operating table, and now it's time to fight to get back into the game of life. So up, up, up."

Amelia lowered the bedrail and clasped Quadir's arm. He snatched it away from her.

"You're not even my doctor anymore. And you're not my therapist. I don't feel like it today!"

"Look, Mr. Smith, I didn't save your ass to see you sit here and wither away. Now stop acting like a little bitch and get your fucking ass in the wheelchair."

Quadir frowned at her, trying to figure out why she was constantly calling him Mr. Smith. *Damn, she won't stop. She just won't stop.*

"You're like the Energizer Bunny. You should wear a bunny outfit and get some rollerblades," he said, laughing at her. "Look, you could roll down the hall and shit, in and out of all your patients' rooms, constantly being a disturbance. You know how you do," he said, looking at her with his eyebrows raised, waiting for her to agree with his jokes.

"You really are an asshole."

"And you're really a pain in my ass. You know what, Doc? That's all the fuck I do feel—the pain in my ass from your constant bullshit."

"Get the fuck up and get in the goddamn chair," she hollered as she took his vitals chart and held it like a weapon, ready to attack him.

"Please, you can't hit me. You're a doctor and I'm a sick patient."

"Get your ass up and get in the chair! I'm not leaving until we're done."

"Fuck, man, come on," he said, huffing and puffing, but he did it, because he knew she had to win and she wouldn't stop. She meant every word she said. He sulked his way off the bed and into the wheelchair.

She pushed him to the elevator, and they made the short trip to the rehabilitation center.

"Can I just pay you for your services?" Quadir asked.

"Are you serious?" She stopped the chair and walked around in front of him. "You could never repay me. Do you understand, Mr. Smith?" she said, looking like Bette Davis.

"Yo, you ever see that movie *What Ever Happened to Baby Jane?* That's you." He started laughing at her again.

This Black man must be out of his mind, she thought.

"I got your Baby Jane. Shut up before I really show you how Bette I can get," she said, slapping the back of his head.

"I'm going to file a report against you if you keep hitting me."

"Listen, Mr. Smith, I'm tired of your shit. You can do this. I'm positive you can. If you could come back and cheat death the way you did, you can make a full recovery. Gosh, if you believed in yourself as much as I do, you'd have walked out of here by now. So come on, it's showtime."

She hit a button on the wall, and the double doors to the rehab center in the west wing of the hospital opened. She wheeled him up to a set of walking bars.

"Okay, here we go. God, do you believe all that energy? You are so draining, Mr. Smith, I mean, really," she said as she unbuckled him, raised the foot bars, and gently set his feet on the floor.

She pulled him out of the chair. Quadir gripped the bars tightly, holding on for dear life. Amelia stood behind him and placed her hands on his waist.

"How many times are you going to bring me down here to do this?" Quadir said, gritting his teeth. "I can't do it yet!"

"You can do anything you put your mind to. You can do this, Quadir. You're stronger than you even know. I watched a soldier who refused to give in, who stared death in the face and told it to go to hell. You can do this. One step, Quadir. It only takes one step."

Quadir closed his eyes and gritted his teeth again. He wanted this pesky, silly bitch gone and out of his life. He wanted to be alone, and if he had to be around someone, he wanted it to be someone who would understand what he was going through. He wanted Gena.

"Only a coward gives up, Quadir."

A coward? Is she calling me a fucking coward?

"What? You heard me. You're not even trying. A fucking coward. I can't believe this shit," she huffed under her breath, loud enough for him to hear.

Bitch, please. He couldn't help it. She must be crazy to offer such an analysis. Quadir had been through more than Amelia Hopkins could ever dream about. He was a soldier, a warrior, and a gangster to the fullest. He ate niggas for breakfast, and bitches like her were nothing but a midmorning snack.

"You going to let a bar beat you?" Amelia asked.

"Shut up!" Quadir exploded. "Will you shut the fuck up!"

"That's right! Get angry! But what are you going to do with all that anger? Are you going to yell at me and sit back down and quit? Or are you going to get angry at the people who tried to take life away from you, the people who put you in this wheelchair? Are you going to let them win? Are you going to let them beat you, John?"

Quadir breathed in heavily and gripped the bars tightly. He lifted himself up as much as he could, staring at his right foot.

Move, dammit, move, he commanded.

And it did.

The left foot slowly followed, and then the right one. He walked to the end of the track and turned around, gasping for air. He was exhausted.

"Oh my God. No, no, stay there. Oh my God. John, oh my God. That's good for one day. Stay right there. I'll bring the chair to you," Amelia said in amazement and disbelief.

"No, leave the chair where it's at," Quadir told her. He stared at his feet again and willed them to move.

Amelia cupped her hands over her mouth as tears began to stream down her face. These were the moments she lived and breathed for. These were the moments that made every sacrifice in her life worthwhile. Quadir took four tiny steps before collapsing into her arms.

"Yes! Yes! I knew you could do it!" She hugged him as if he were her child taking his first baby steps in life.

Quadir held on to her, hugging her and fighting back his own tears. He wanted to cry, he wanted to cry so badly, but Baby Jane wouldn't have that on him. He had shown her; he had walked. He couldn't believe he had walked. He hugged Amelia tightly and kissed her cheek, and he felt her kiss his cheek back. And out of all the hugging and kissing, their lips met, and she kissed him back, a long and passionate kiss. Amelia completely forgot her position and role as a doctor. She didn't even realize the road they'd started down in that one kiss.

The next day, after her rounds, Amelia entered Quadir's room with her trusty wheelchair and was met with a happy face. "I take it you're ready."

"Might as well be. I don't have any choice."

"Well, today, I have a surprise for you," she said, helping him into the chair as she placed his feet on the footrests. She pushed him down the hall and onto the elevator as usual, but this time, when the doors opened, she made a left instead of a right.

"Where we going?"

"I told you, I have a surprise for you today."

Amelia took her patient for a stroll through the hospital's gardens, hoping some fresh air would do him good. He'd accomplished so much in such a short period of time. His recovery bordered on miraculous.

She stopped his wheelchair next to a bench in front of a statue commemorating the hospital's founder. She took a seat on the bench close to him.

"Are we about to have *the* conversation?" Quadir asked.

"And which conversation is that? We have a couple of them we need to have."

Quadir laughed. "I guess you're right. But I figured you were strolling me out here so we could talk about why I'm here and why someone would try to kill me. You know, *that* conversation."

"Those things have crossed my mind a few times."

"Well, you know my name, and I'm pretty sure you know my date of birth." Quadir peered off into the distance. "It's hard to know where to start. I mean, you already know all my personal information. Not to mention, you operated on me and saved my life."

Amelia nodded and laughed. "Yeah, I guess I know a few things. I'll admit that."

Quadir shrugged. "I really don't know where to start."

"Would you rather I ask you?"

"I guess that probably would be better."

"Do you have a nickname?"

"Yeah, sort of. Qua, sometimes Q."

"Is that what all your friends called you? Qua?"

Quadir nodded.

"Are you originally from Philly?"

"Yeah, I was born at Pennsylvania Hospital downtown. I grew up in North Philly my entire life. Where are you from?"

Amelia exhaled and peered off into the distance. "I'm a country girl, straight off the farm in Alabama."

"How did you wind up in Philly?"

"I wanted more. I couldn't see myself working on my parents' farm for the rest of my life or marrying some drugstore clerk in the nearest town and cranking out babies for the next twenty years. Not much out there in the country. So after high school I got accepted to Temple University and then took up my residence at Temple University Hospital. After completing my residency, I got offered a job here at Hahnemann, so I decided to stay in Philadelphia and see how things worked out. I've been here at Hahnemann now for five years."

"That's good, really good. You stayed focused. Sometimes I wish I'd stuck it out and stayed in school."

"Why, you dropped out of high school?" Amelia asked.

"No, I graduated with honors from high school. And I went on to college at the University of Delaware."

"Did you graduate?"

"Yeah."

"Really?" Amelia had never presumed for one second that Quadir had a formal education.

"I got my bachelor's, and after that, I wanted to become a dentist. I got sidetracked."

"What do you mean by that?"

"I struggled to get through school. It wasn't like I came from money. My pops hustled in the streets. He did the numbers game and had speakeasies in the city, and while we weren't poor, we weren't rich, either. I guess, after I graduated and I came back home to Philly, I saw everybody hustling, getting fast money, and I wanted a piece of it. I always said I'd go back to school and become a dentist and open my own office someday. I got sidetracked and one thing led to another."

"I see it led you right here to my operating table."

"Yeah, I always thought I was invincible. I never saw myself shot up and in a wheelchair. I have a friend, Christopher Cole, who we all called Forty, and he was kidnapped last year and held for a million-dollar ransom. Even though I paid his ransom, his kidnappers still shot him up and left him for dead. I remember going to visit him in the hospital. His body looked weak and frail and he was all beat up and bandaged up and the doctors said he'd never walk again. To this day, he's still in a wheelchair. I'll never forget the day I went to see him after he'd been shot up, and I knew then I didn't want this life. I didn't want to end up like that."

"So what did you do?"

"I stopped. I gave up the life, and I stopped selling drugs."

"Really?"

"Yeah, and the true irony is that I ended up shot and in a wheelchair anyway."

"Well, we're gonna work on that, right?"

"Hey, I'm surprised you let me outside."

Amelia couldn't help but laugh. "Yeah, you're lucky, real lucky."

"In more ways than you could ever know."

"I don't understand why you would choose to sell drugs. Of all the things you could do to make your life better, you chose that."

"Don't do that."

"Don't do what?"

"Don't judge me. I hate that. People always think of drug dealers being these lowlife scum buckets, and for the most part, that is never the case."

"I'm not attempting to judge you. I'm only trying to understand."

"That's just it. It's something you can never understand. The life I live, and the life these brothers are out here living in these streets, can't be explained or understood. Not from sitting on a park bench beneath an oak tree on a nice side of town."

"I guess I deserved that. I can never understand the world you come from, but I can learn more about it."

"Why would you want to?"

"Why do you live it? All bullshit aside, you're smarter than that. You're a very intelligent man who could do so many things with his life. Really, that's what I don't get. You're smart, you're fearless, you're young and handsome. The world would lie down for you, if you asked it to. Why not go out and do bigger things?"

Quadir leaned back in his chair. He was at a loss for words. He didn't know how to feel about Amelia. She was drop-dead gorgeous, a dime to say the least. And she was one hell of a surgeon. The fact he was still breathing testified to that. She was smart and dedicated, and she was straight up. She didn't act all high and mighty like some bourgeois bitches after they finished college. And what was really tripping him out was she truly seemed to care about him. Not solely about getting him back up and walking again, but about his life and his future. She was challenging him physically, mentally, and emotionally. He'd never had a woman do that before.

"C'mon, let's get you back inside before those bitches in the recovery ward start tripping."

Quadir threw his head back in laughter. "I have never heard a doctor like you before."

"I'm the new generation of doctors. We kick ass. We heal it, but we kick it, too." Amelia rose from the bench and began to push Quadir back into the hospital. "Don't make me have to fuck you up behind your therapy, either, 'cause I will."

"And you said you're the new generation, huh?"

"And don't get it twisted."

Fully Loaded

Amelia tossed Quadir a towel so that he could wipe the sweat from his brow. He quickened his pace on the treadmill to a rapid jog.

"Okay, Jesse Owens, let's not overdo it," she told him.

"Relax, Doc. I'm one hundred percent. Plus, I had a pretty good therapist who whipped me back into shape."

Amelia tilted her head and smiled. "Good try, but flattery will get you nowhere." She climbed onto a nearby stair stepper and began exercising. "I'm going to check and make sure your wounds are healing okay. I don't want them to reopen from the inside. That could be the worst."

"Will you stop worrying? Doc, you did your thing. The Q is back!"

"All right, Qua. Let's hope he's here to stay. It'd be a shame to have to take you back to the hospital because your gigantic ego burst open your stitches."

Quadir laughed. He flipped the off switch on the treadmill and walked to the stair stepper, where he lifted the doc into the air.

"Boy, what are you doing?" she shouted. "You can't lift me; I'm too heavy. You'll rip your insides for sure."

"Heavy? What do you weigh, a buck fifteen at the most? And

that's probably with all your clothes on and soaking wet." Quadir set her down.

"Watch your wounds, please," Amelia said in all seriousness as she turned to face him.

"Why? I got the best doctor in the land."

"I know that's right. See, I realized you were a smart man."

"What made you want to become a doctor?" Quadir asked.

"It was all I could think of being when I was a little girl. My first little plastic stethoscope had me hooked."

"Man, that's a lot of schooling, though. How'd you stay focused?"

"I don't know; I just did," Amelia said.

"I'm sure your family is proud."

"Oh, God, yes. You should see my father. He has an entire photo collection of me in his wallet. He's my biggest fan."

Quadir sat down on a weight bench, grabbed the towel again, and wiped the sweat from his brow.

"This is a really nice gym you got here."

"Thanks! I figured since I don't have any children, no roommates, and no pets, I'd turn the spare room into my own fitness center. Why pay for a gym?"

Quadir looked at Amelia as she lay on her back doing crunches, moving her upper body off the floor and then back down again. She was quite amazing. She was not only beautiful, but also smart, practical, financially independent, and full of determination. After Quadir's extended stay in the inpatient rehabilitation center of Hahnemann, he was upgraded to outpatient status. It was then Amelia brought him home with her, where she and her housekeeper could nurse him back to health.

"Doctors must make a lot of money."

"We do pretty good. The industry is suffering with insurance and HMOs and all that, but yeah, we make an honest living."

"Well, if this is an honest living, I've been wasting my time in them streets."

"Why do you say that?"

"Yo, this is a mansion. Your house is amazing. You sure you're just a doctor?"

"Of course. Don't be silly."

"Damn, I'm in the wrong profession. If motherfuckers in the hood could see this shit here, they'd all be signing up for medical school."

"Really?"

"Really," Quadir responded, looking around the weight room.

Outside the door near where he sat was a sauna, a steam room, and an indoor swimming pool with a retractable glass top, making it an outdoor swimming pool on sunny summer days.

"Why me, though?"

"What do you mean, why you?"

"What I said. Everything you've done for me. Saving my life, fighting to make me walk again—against my own will—and bringing me to your home. You didn't have to do half the stuff you've done for me. So I'm a little curious as to why you're helping me."

Amelia looked Quadir in the eyes and realized she didn't really have an answer.

"I don't know. I guess maybe because you needed someone to help you. I wanted to help, that's all," she said as she gently caressed the side of his face. "Is that okay with you?"

"Yeah, it's just that where I come from, most people ain't into putting themselves out there to help anyone. Help is the last thing you're gonna get."

"Well, for me, being a doctor, I guess it's in my blood."

"Thank you. Thank you for everything."

"You don't have to say that, but you're welcome."

They both sat in silence as Amelia wrapped up her crunches and Quadir thought about his life. All he had done and been through could make a bestselling novel. *I should write a book.*

Amelia finished her last crunch, hopped up from the floor, and stood over Quadir.

"Hey, I got to hurry up and get to the hospital, make my rounds, and check out for the day. Is there anything you'd like me to get you while I'm out?"

"No, I'm fine. But I do have a favor to ask of you."

"Sure, what is it?" she asked.

"I was wondering if I could borrow your car."

"Ready to rock and roll, huh?"

"No, no, not like that. Get out and move around a little."

"I understand, but, Quadir, you do understand you cannot afford for anyone to see you. You're *Mr. Smith*, and until you have some minor plastic surgery, you really need to stay inside and out of sight."

"I'll stay low. Trust me."

Amelia stared straight through him as her mind wandered.

"Well, I guess it's okay," she said, coming back to reality. "But take my black BMW. It has tinted windows, so that way I don't have to worry about you being spotted. Geez, Quadir, don't you realize the chances you're taking?"

"Listen, I got this. Trust me. I'm not crazy. I'm not going to let anyone see me."

"Well, what about the beard and mustache I got for you?"

"Are you serious? That's a Santa Claus outfit. The only thing that's missing is the red suit."

"It is not. Santa's hair is white; this is like dark brown."

"He's a young Santa, then."

"Well, you're wearing it."

"No, seriously, I'm not."

"Quadir, do you understand the trouble I can get into? You're wearing the Santa face."

"Okay, I'll wear the Santa face," Quadir agreed, not wanting to bring her any trouble. In a way, she was right. If he were to be spotted alive, she'd wind up in a heap of trouble.

"You'll look great."

"No, I'll look like Santa, only younger and Black."

"Well, at least no one will recognize you. Come on, let's go. I got to get a quick shower and get dressed for my rounds," Amelia said as she grabbed her water bottle and threw her hand towel around her neck.

"Amelia."

"Yeah," she said, turning to face him.

"I wanted to say thank you. Really. Thank you for everything."

"You don't have to keep saying that."

"No, I do. I really do. I want you to know I'm going to repay you, Amelia, for *everything*. I'm going to give you back all the money you've spent helping me."

"Quadir, you don't have to. I don't want your money. I have plenty of money. Really, you don't owe me anything."

"I owe you my life, and I will repay you, Amelia, if it's the last thing I do on this earth." Quadir thought about his hideout spot and all the millions he had stashed away in his safe. "You're not the only one with money."

"Money means very little to me, Quadir. There are far more important things in my world than money. Remember, my job is to save people's lives. Money becomes rather unimportant when you're staring at death every day."

Well, it means everything to me. Shit, I hustled too hard and got way too much paper stashed. I need to check everything out and make sure everything's safe and sound.

Eye Spy

Quadir parked the black BMW near the corner of Second and Green. He could see the door to his building. Large numbers were mounted above the door: 234. *Two-thirty-four Green Street,* he thought. *My old secret hideout.* Still in his car, he reached into a plastic bag and took out the Davy Crockett hairpieces Amelia had suggested he wear. He carefully put them on, pressing the sticky backs to his skin. He checked his mustache and beard in the rear-view mirror, making sure they were on straight, and reached into the back seat for a baseball cap to put on his head. Feeling safe and undetectable, he got out of the car and walked to the front entrance of the apartment building. *I need my keys.* He wished he had his diamond Q key chain.

A locksmith carrying a small duffel bag and a locked metal box brushed past him. Quadir couldn't help but notice the man's smile.

"Excuse me, I'm locked out of my house and I was wo—"

"Sorry, pal, I can't help you right now. I'm, um . . . I'm off!"

Quadir watched as the man got into a van and pulled away from the block. "Thanks a lot!"

It turned out the locksmith was the same one Gena had called to open the safe. The duffel bag the locksmith was holding had his money in it, and the reason the locksmith couldn't help him was he was in a rush to get home and share his good fortune with his wife and kids.

Quadir walked around the side of the apartment building and looked up at his old bedroom window. *That's what I'll do. I'll call the management office and have them come down here and let me in. Oh, damn, I can't do that with this Davy Crockett getup. They won't recognize me. Shit, maybe I should call another locksmith.* Quadir had to see his apartment, and he desperately needed to know all its contents were safe and sound, especially his money.

He got back into the BMW and started the engine. No sooner had he put the car in park than he saw her. It was Gena. She was right there in front of him, fewer than two hundred feet away, carrying a large, gold-framed photo of them that had hung on the wall of his apartment. She placed it in her car.

Wow! She found my hideout spot, he thought to himself. He watched her as she placed two pillowcases inside the car. *Is that my money in those pillowcases? What should I do?*

His first thought was to jump out of the car and run over to her. That he didn't would be the biggest mistake he'd ever make. That one opportunity, that one chance was right there, but instead, he stalled, and those few moments cost him dearly. Before he knew it, the lights of the baby blue Mercedes reflected off the car in front of it and the driver maneuvered her way out of the parking space. Quadir stepped on the gas, following the car down the street.

Where the hell is she going? he wondered as Gena made her way out of the city and onto the New Jersey Turnpike heading north. He sped up, not wanting to lose her in the sea of red brake lights. Catching him off guard, she quickly exited the turnpike. He cut off a car in the next lane, almost causing a rear-end collision, and made the exit ramp in the nick of time.

He paid the toll and followed Gena's baby blue Mercedes into an Exxon station off the highway. He watched as Gena hopped out of the car and ran into the gas station. His gut instinct was to jump out of the car, run over to her, and tell her that he was alive and that everything would be okay. *Yeah, that's what I'll do; I'll tell her. I'll tell her right now.* As he was about to get out of his car, he saw the door to the gas station open, and Jerrell Jackson, his archenemy, stood in the doorway, staring straight at the BMW.

He turned on the car's engine and watched as Jerrell walked across the gas station lot, heading toward him. He quickly turned the car around and sped away.

What the fuck is she doing talking to him? Quadir's mind wandered in all directions, searching for possible explanations, but nothing made sense. *Isn't he supposed to be in jail? Forty testified and they still found that nigga not guilty?*

He couldn't believe it—nothing was making sense, and worst of all was his money. It was no longer in its safe hiding place.

What is she thinking? What the hell is she thinking? She was in on this with him? She got my money for him?

Quadir didn't know what to do. He'd lost her trail and couldn't follow her anymore. He didn't want to return to Amelia's house, at least not yet. What he really wanted to do was visit his old neighborhood. Ride down the streets he'd built an empire hustling on. The streets he once owned. The streets that made him "that nigga." The streets he hadn't seen since the attempt on his life. That's what he wanted to do and that's what he was going to do. *No one can recognize me anyway.* He couldn't help it. He saw her with the pillowcases and the picture and knew she had found his money. He drove through the streets of Philly, hoping no one would notice him. He realized he was asking for trouble, coming to this side of town.

I hope the police don't pull me over. Boy, oh boy, he couldn't let that happen. *No way, Jose,* he thought.

He drove down North Philly across Twenty-Ninth Street over to Lehigh Avenue. Then he went down Lehigh to Seventeenth Street and took Seventeenth Street all the way up to Erie Avenue, then Erie over to Broad and back down. The streets were so familiar, it all seemed like yesterday. But it wasn't yesterday and things had somehow changed over the last six months. He thought of Gena and wondered where she was. Still on Broad, he took it down to Girard and crossed over to Thirteenth and took it down to Wallace, entering Richard Allen. He had hoped to see Gena's Mercedes parked in front of her grandmother's house, but it wasn't. He rode around the block a few times, but he didn't see the car. He looked down at the clock display in the BMW.

It was getting late. Quadir decided it was time to go back to Amelia's house. *I'll be back first thing in the morning. We'll see what you're up to then.*

The next morning, Quadir was again waiting outside Gena's grandmother's house. He followed her to a mall, maneuvered the BMW into a parking space across the street from a Porsche dealership, and sat quietly and watched. Gena had started her day rather early. Had he gotten to Richard Allen a minute later, he would've missed her. As soon as the mall opened, she was the first one through the doorway. Quadir watched her as she loaded up the Mercedes with shopping bag after shopping bag. Then she went down Jewelers' Row.

No telling how much damage she did at the jewelry store. She looks happy, though. She don't look like she misses me at all.

Watching Gena, he couldn't help but wonder what in the world she was thinking. She was like a madwoman with money, and she was spending it big. He looked across the street at an unmarked police car and watched the detectives inside. It seemed Gena's start wasn't that early; she had more company. Quadir watched as the detectives snacked on bagels and their morning coffee. He wished he could get out of the car and go to her. He wanted so badly to rush to her, to embrace her, and to tell her that he was alive and kicking. But to do that would've been too dangerous. Those extra eyes watching her would then be watching him, and he didn't want that.

Instead, Quadir lay low and stayed out of sight. He had no time for the Philly PD or whoever those guys were. *Maybe they're following her, hoping she'll lead them to me.* That was his first thought, but then he thought again. *Maybe they know about the money and they're hoping she'll lead them to it.* It could be anything, but one thing was for sure: she was under surveillance. He'd have to keep his distance if his plan was to have any chance of success. He couldn't even get close enough to Gena to warn her.

The fact Gena had found his money certainly complicated things. Now she was being watched. *How the hell am I gonna follow her if Ola is on her ass? How the hell will I ever get my money back?*

His plan was simple: Follow Gena until she led him to his pot of gold. But now they had company, and Gena was moving around a lot. She was all over the place. He couldn't afford to let the Philly PD catch him following her. Not those jokers; that would be a nightmare. *I bet it's a hefty sentence for faking your death.* Not to mention Quadir certainly hadn't come this far to end up behind bars. The plan was the Bahamas, not the pen. He'd have to shadow Gena carefully and do his best to keep her safe from a distance. *But how?*

Gena exited the Porsche dealership and stood patiently by the front door. Soon, it became evident what she was waiting for. A saleswoman pulled up in a black Gemballa 911 convertible.

"Holy shit, she's fuckin' nuts!" Quadir exclaimed. "Don't do it, Gena. They're watching you! Don't do it!"

He watched from across the street as the Philly PD pulled out surveillance cameras. Gena finished with the saleswoman, shook her hand, then pulled out of the dealership parking lot. She'd blown over three hundred thousand dollars of his money, and it wasn't even lunchtime.

***

Several weeks later, Quadir sat on the sofa silently and pictured himself flipping over the coffee table and the stacks of medical journals lying on it.

"Dammit!" he muttered as he moved away from the table before he could trash it.

"What? What's the matter with you?" Amelia calmly asked.

Quadir looked at her, not even wanting to explain. "I can't talk about it right now."

"Talk about what?"

"Nothing. Please, not right now, Amelia."

He witnessed her smile slowly fade. He had hurt her feelings. Her entire mission in life was to help, to save, to be a hero. He completely understood that, but there was no way in the world she could help him. No one could.

"Why don't you sit down, Quadir? Take it easy and get your thoughts together."

"Gena is seeing someone," he said.

"Gena? Your Gena? No way." Amelia seemed surprised by his accusation.

"Not only is she seeing someone else, she's seeing the guy who tried to kill me. His name is Jerrell Jackson."

"Oh my God, Quadir! Are you sure? That doesn't make sense. Does she know he tried to kill you?"

"I don't know what she knows, but even still, the streets are always talking and everybody knows Jerrell was behind my murder. Everybody! What the fuck is wrong with her?"

That's when Quadir's vision came to life. Amelia sat calmly by as her coffee table was flipped over and knocked to the floor and her medical journals landed all over her living room.

"Are you done? Because tearing my things up isn't going to fix the problem, and it certainly won't help."

Amelia righted her coffee table, positioning it perfectly back in place. Quadir began to pace back and forth.

"Yo, don't you hear me? This bitch is sleeping with the mother-fucker who tried to kill me. And that's only half of it. Gena found my money, so she's got it, all of it, and I can't figure out how to get it back. I can't even figure out where she's got it."

"Maybe she doesn't know Jerrell shot you. And obviously she has your money because it was made available for her to get," Amelia said as she gathered her journals off the floor and began stacking them back neatly on the coffee table.

"She might not know who he is, but trust me, he knows who she is, and if he thinks for one minute she's got my money, he'll kill her for it. I know him, how he thinks. Every nigga I know and trusted would bring me harm if they could get their hands on that kind of money. I never let anyone know about the money I had saved. No one knew."

"Quadir, it's only money."

"You always say that, Amelia, because you come from a well-to-do family, but twenty million ain't nothing to sneeze at."

"Twenty million? You've got twenty million?"

"Do I? Well, I did. Now Gena has twenty million, or better yet, my archenemy, Jerrell Jackson, has twenty million."

"Oh, Quadir, twenty million?"

"Well, technically, a little over seventeen million, Amelia. And she's spending it like water running out of a faucet."

"Well, what are you going to do? Quadir, twenty million is a lot of money."

Quadir scratched his head, trying to figure out his next move. "Amelia, please, you're making my head hurt."

"What makes you think if you can't figure out where the money is, Jerrell will? I'm sure Gena's not that gullible. I'm sure she's smart enough to hide the money in a safe place."

"Amelia, Jerrell is the grimiest dirtbag I know. If he thinks Gena has something, he'll torture her to death to take it. This shit is crazy. It's getting more and more complicated as time goes by. Now I have to babysit this nigga."

"Listen, I have money. I can give you a loan. I can help you get a new start out here, if that's what you want. I don't have twenty million dollars, and that's a lot of money, but, Quadir, it's not worth your life. It's not worth prison. You understand what I'm saying?" Amelia said, hoping he was smarter than she thought.

"Amelia, a loan? Are you nuts? We're talking about *my* twenty million, Amelia. My twenty million dollars, and I *will* get my money back. I have to get it back!"

"No, we're talking about Gena's twenty million, and we're talking about you risking your life!" she shouted, hoping to penetrate his brain with common sense.

Quadir stared at her blankly, not wanting to hear her logic. "That's my twenty million. Mine. I busted my ass for that. I damn near lost my life for that. I want my money. I want it back!"

"Well, what do you want me to do to help? What about hiring a private investigator to help track the money down?"

"No, that would be one more nose up in the mix. Shit, he'd probably find out where the money is and take it himself."

"Quadir!"

"What? I would," he said, eyes wide.

"Can I ask you a question?"

"Yeah, what?" he asked, stopping his pacing for a split second to hear her out.

"Are you mad at Gena for having your money or are you mad at her for being with Jerrell?"

Quadir thought about her question and honestly didn't know the answer. His pride was hurt, of course. Any man's pride would be. That was only the tip of the iceberg. The truth was his archenemy had his girl *and* access to his dough. Nothing could be worse.

"Right now, I want my money back," he said, brokenhearted.

Amelia tried to reason with him. "She thinks you're dead."

"I know, but he's the enemy."

"She probably has no idea who she's dealing with."

Quadir shook his head. The situation was way out of control. *Why didn't I stop her at the apartment? Why didn't I stop her then, before she had a chance to get into the car? What was I thinking?*

"Damn, I want my money."

Amelia said nothing. She let him pace around, scratching his head, hoping he'd figure out something without harming himself or, worse, her medical career. Of course, he realized doing something foolish would be plain stupid. He had everything going for him: a new life, a fresh start, and twenty million dollars somewhere out there. And he'd figure out where. He'd come too far not to. He'd have his money. He might not have Gena, but he'd get that money back, one way or the other.

What are you doing, Gena? Of all the dudes out here, why him?

Gena had committed the perfect betrayal. If Quadir didn't know any better, he'd swear she was in cahoots with Jerrell. *No, she loved me, didn't she?*

"Are you okay?" Amelia asked, lightly touching Quadir's shoulder.

"No, I'm really not."

"Seriously, let me hire someone to help you get your money back."

"Not yet—not right now. She already has Philly PD on her, and if you hire a PI then it'll look like a damn caravan going down the street. I need to change up my tactics and I need to switch cars, too."

"You can use the jeep, if you want." Amelia was hoping to be helpful. "Be careful."

"I will. Don't worry."

"Quadir, don't you worry. She'll be back."

Quadir thought for a moment, and the truth was, after he saw Gena and Jerrell together, he didn't know if he wanted her back.

She'll be back? Maybe she should stay where she's at. Maybe she doesn't need to come back.

Amelia strolled out of the room while Quadir contemplated his next move. He'd switch cars and push the Range, and he'd change up his hours. She was hiding the money somewhere, and sooner or later, she'd lead him to it. Either that or Jerrell would, but one way or another he was going to watch her like a hawk. And watch out for those snooping detective motherfuckers, too! *I wonder if they're FBI.*

"Doc!" he hollered as she walked out of the living room and into the dining room.

"Yeah, what's up?" she asked, leaning backward through the doorway.

"Thanks!"

"Don't thank me. I'm waiting to see these twenty million dollars. Maybe I *will* let you pay me back," she said, laughing.

"I thought you said money could never repay what you've done for me," Quadir said, trying to match his tone to hers.

"Are you nuts? Twenty million . . . I'm ready to go and follow Gena around myself. She's lucky I've got rounds to make or I'd be out there with you. Now, you said you needed the jeep, right?"

Sparkles

That night when Quadir returned to Amelia's, he found her in the kitchen preparing what appeared to be a homemade gourmet meal.

"Wow, I didn't know you knew how to cook."

"Yup, it's true. You learn something new about a person every day. See, you never know, right?"

"I know I'm hungry."

"Yeah, well, be patient. This is very serious food I'm preparing. So, how did it go tonight, private eye?"

"Well, it went. From what I could see, she's fallen for Jerrell, that's for sure. She went back to his place. I stayed outside until . . ."

"Until what?"

"Until they turned the lights off."

"Quadir, I'm so sorry," Amelia said as she stopped draining linguini long enough to see the hurt in his face.

"Hey, I guess that's life. Sometimes you win and sometimes you lose."

"Yeah, but sometimes you lose and you also win, you know?"

"No, I don't."

"Well, like right now, you feel like you lost, but, Quadir, you're on top. You're alive, you have the upper hand, and most of all, you realize what's going on around you. Gena might not know, but you do."

"How will I get my money back?"

"Now that, I don't know. Have you ever thought of simply asking her for it?"

"Yeah, but now that she's with Jerrell, I don't want her to see me. I'd rather her think I'm dead."

Amelia looked at Quadir as he lowered his head. She understood how he felt and wanted to do whatever she could to make him feel better. But the truth was, there was nothing anyone could do that would make him feel better.

"Hey, want to play cards?"

"I don't much feel like playing cards."

"Well, let's eat. Dinner's ready."

After dinner, Amelia cleaned up the kitchen and loaded the dirty dishes into the dishwasher. Quadir retired to the living room, where he turned on the news. He sat on the sofa and fell asleep.

Right then, Gena knocked at the door. Amelia entered the living room and let Quadir know she was there.

"Let her in."

Gena walked into the living room where Quadir was. Their eyes met, and Quadir took her hands into his. "I love you."

"I love you, too, Quadir. I'm so glad you're okay. Now we can be together."

Quadir took her into his arms and caressed the back of her neck, cradling her head in the palm of his hand. He kissed her mouth ever so gently. Their lips locked as they had so long ago. At that moment Quadir realized it was Amelia he was holding and not Gena.

"I want you, Quadir. I want to be with you."

"Amelia, there's no turning back. You understand? No turning back."

"I understand."

In her heart, she understood exactly what he was saying. There was no turning back. There was only the forward motion of them together.

Their lips locked tightly as Quadir moved, swiftly covering her body with his. His hands pulled up her shirt, and his fingers caressed her breasts. With each breath he took, she breathed in unison, and she could feel his hard penis through his clothing pressing against her mound. He moved his hand down to her pants and unbuttoned them, pulling them down, freeing one leg at a time. How he had gotten his clothes off was beyond her. All Amelia knew was she was ready. Ready to be with him, ready to make love to him, and ready to be loved by him. There was nothing she wouldn't do for him, *nothing*. She'd already proven that by saving his life and risking her career by faking his death.

They made love for hours, and when they were done, it was as if the memory of Gena had been completely erased. The only thing on his mind was how he was going to get his money back.

Maybe Amelia is right. Maybe I should ask her for it.

Rik hurried into the restaurant, closing his umbrella at the door. The weather outside was beyond dreadful. Rain fell from the sky like a monsoon. Rik took off his raincoat, folded it over his arm, and walked to the hostess stand.

"Table for one, sir?" she asked.

"No, I'm with the Santero party."

"Oh, he's already here. I showed him in a minute ago."

The hostess turned and started for the table. "Follow me, please, and I'll show you to your table."

She led Rik to the table where his dinner guest was waiting.

"Rik, what's happening, my man?" Tony rose and embraced him tightly. "Here, have a seat."

Rik took the seat across from Tony.

"Have the waitress bring us a bottle of your finest wine, please," Tony told the hostess. He waited until she departed and then took his seat again. "Rik, my man, how are you?"

Rik shook his head. "Not good, Tony. Not too good."

Tony waved him off. "We'll make it all better, my man."

"I don't know."

"Don't worry. Wait until you hear the proposal we have for you."

The waitress arrived with the wine and two glasses. "Are you ready to order, sir?"

"What would you like to eat, Rik?" Tony asked.

Rik shrugged. "Um, let me do the filet, medium well, butterfly cut, with the creamed spinach and mashed potatoes. And, also, let me get a Caesar salad to start."

"And for you, sir?" the waitress asked Tony.

"I'll have the filet well done, butterfly cut, but Oscar that with a side of the sweet potato casserole, please. And I'll take a Caesar salad also."

"Very well, sir." The waitress nodded, removed the menus from the table, and disappeared.

"Here is what we have in mind," Tony continued. "Twenty keys a week. We front you half, you pay for the other half up front. You don't have to pay for the front until the following week when we drop you off another ten."

"Damn. That's sweet."

Tony smiled. "I told you we'd take good care of you."

"Good, because I'ma need a little help."

Tony lifted an eyebrow. "What kinda help?"

"I'ma need an extension on what I owe you."

Tony recoiled. "An extension? What kinda extension?"

"Well, really, I was hoping you could spot me some dope and let me work off what I owe you."

"Work off what you owe us? Are you telling me that you don't have the money, Rik?"

"I got busted, Tony. You already know this. The cops hit my stash house and found the shit."

Tony looked down and shook his head gravely. "That's not our problem, Rik. You know how we operate."

"Man, that shit was beyond my control. I got busted. Man, c'mon."

"Rik, I understand the way my uncle thinks. His first question is going to be, if the cops found the dope, then why are you out on the streets? That's a question you don't want him to ask. He's not going to understand all the legal technicalities involved. The first thing that's going to come to his mind is that you've rolled over. And that would be very bad for you."

"I didn't roll over. I'd never do anything like that. They threw the case out because the snitch turned up dead."

"But you're saying they found the dope."

"Yeah, in a house rented under a fake name. They couldn't trace it back to me. They found out me and the homeboys met there sometimes. That's what got the house raided. But they couldn't put the dope on any specific individual."

Tony smiled. "Rik, my uncle's old-school. He ain't gonna understand all that legal mumbo jumbo bullshit. He's gonna want his money, or he's gonna want you in prison because of that dope, or he's gonna want you dead."

"Man, I'm not trying to fuck over anybody. I need more time, and some more work to get it all back to you."

"Do you hear yourself? You're asking for more work without paying us for the work we've already given you. After you tell us you got busted with previous work, but you're still out on the streets. Do you hear this shit?"

"You know it's true."

"Rik, we're men, aren't we? Let's talk like men. You speak much truth, and I believe you, Rik. If I didn't, we wouldn't be sitting here. But this is the problem, Rik. Quadir fronted you a lot of product before he was killed. Do you remember that?"

Rik thought quietly for a moment, knowing exactly where Tony was going with this.

"And from what I know, Quadir passed you at least two hundred keys, my friend. At least that much, maybe more. And you paid little to nothing back. Quadir died and you walked with all that coke and all that money. Rik, now you have nothing. Wow, my friend, you had it all. You had it all."

Tony exhaled and shook his head.

"Here's what I'm going to do. I'm going to pretend like we never had this conversation. I'm going to pretend like I haven't gotten around to picking up the money you owe us. I'm going to stall and try to buy you a little time. In the meantime, I suggest you do whatever the hell it is you need to do to come up with that money. My uncle is *not* going to understand. If I can't collect from you after a certain period of time, he's going to send a fucking hit squad over to wipe the streets up with your ass. It's nothing personal, only business. Get the money."

Tony rose, pulled out a wad of money, and threw several hundred-dollar bills onto the table. "Enjoy the meal. Then go home and get some rest. You look like shit."

Rik lowered his head into his palms as Tony disappeared. He had to come up with the money. Tony was serious about what his uncle would do if he didn't. He needed time. A little bit of time, and a little bit of dope to work. He could hit the streets and make miracles happen, if only he had a little bit to work with.

Rik scratched his head. Truth be told, he didn't know how much time he had. *I wonder how long Tony can stall his uncle. Even if I had some coke, I might not have the time I need to flip it. No, I definitely need to pay Tony. But how? I need some major coins to build my stash back up and get the Santeros off my ass.* Rik knew he'd have to dust off his pistol and jack someone. *Damn, who's holding these days that I might stick?*

Most ballers had an entourage and bodyguards. And none of them would let him borrow that kind of dough. *Hold up—wait a minute.* A light suddenly went off in his head. He did know someone who'd let him borrow that kind of dough. She'd offered it to him once before. There was no doubt she'd offer it again.

Gena—she's holdin' all Quadir's loot. She's the one, the missing piece to my puzzle.

Rik sat back and smiled as the waitress delivered his meal. Everything was going to be all right. He knew exactly where to get the money to get those fucking Barranquilla Colombians off his back. The only question was how he'd get it. *Should I ask her or should I jack her?*

Resurrected

Gena listened as Quadir finished his story. Still dazed and unable to believe Quadir was alive, Gena couldn't help but think about the series of unfortunate events that had led her here. Meeting Jerrell at that gas station was the worst thing that could've happened. What was worse was that he was Quadir's enemy, the one behind killing her beloved Quadir. He was nothing more than a monster. *How could I have been so stupid?* Gena couldn't help but blame herself. She thought of the baby she was carrying—Jerrell's baby. *Quadir must not ever know I'm pregnant. What will I do?*

"So, you've been staying here, getting well?"

"Yes. Amelia brought me here after I was released from the inpatient rehabilitation center at the hospital. Now I have physical therapy here and I go to outpatient treatment."

"And Amelia, where is she?"

"She's at work. She's always at the hospital."

"So you said you and her became involved after you saw me and Jerrell together."

"Gena, listen . . ."

"No, Quadir, please, answer me. You *are* involved with her, right?"

Quadir was silent, trying to figure out her angle. He honestly didn't understand her line of questioning, but the look on her face told it all. Her entire world had crashed down around her the night he died. Now it would crash again when she learned he was not only alive but also in love with someone else.

"Answer me, please. Please tell me the truth, please."

"Yes, Gena, yes. I love her."

"You love her?" Gena asked as tears began to stream down her face. She broke down, seating herself gently on the end of an ottoman next to a chair. "I don't understand. Why, Quadir, why? Why'd you do this to me? Why? I thought you loved me. Please, I would've never been with Jerrell. I didn't know who he was. Please, Quadir. I don't know what to say," Gena said, trying with all her might to hold back the tears that seemed to flow nonstop down her cheeks.

She wanted to be strong, she wanted to have an ounce of pride, but she had none. The man she adored and loved more than life itself was standing there confessing he was in love with someone else.

"I mean, what is there really left to say? You and Jerrell were together, or at least you were with him," Quadir stated, full of frustration.

"Oh my God, I can't believe what you're saying. It can't be this way. It's not supposed to be this way, no," she said, freaking out, shaking her hands in the air, trying to find the reason for everything that was happening.

"Gena, please calm down . . ."

"No, don't tell me to calm down. You were dead, Quadir, gone. Why would your mother throw me out like that if . . . Did she know?"

Quadir sat still, knowing what his mother had done. "Listen, Gena, my moms did what she had to do. She was only trying to protect me."

"Protect you? Protect you? Are you serious? That's your answer? You let her throw me out like that, with nothing. You left me with nothing. You died, and now you're back, but you're back and you don't want me anymore because of Jerrell, and I can understand that. I can understand it all. I see it all real clear. Fuck me, right? Fuck me, right, Quadir?" she yelled at the top of her lungs, ready to break something.

"Gena, please, it's not like that. It's not like that, really."

"Then what could it possibly be like?"

"You don't understand. You're too emotional to understand right now."

"Please, Quadir, please leave me alone."

They both stood in silence as Amelia's BMW pulled into the driveway. The garage door opened, and then they heard it close.

"I guess that's her. Amelia, the most fabulous doctor in the world. The doctor who brings people back from the dead. Wow, she must be something, really something. Not only does she save her patients, but she also fucks them," Gena said as she began to make her way back to her room.

"Gena, wait, listen . . . Please, Gena, there's something I need to tell you. Please listen to me, it's important."

Quadir followed her. She slammed the guest bedroom door in his face.

"Tell it to yourself!" Gena screamed, opening the door. "No, better yet, tell Amelia," she said, slamming the door in his face again.

Gena searched the room quickly for her clothes. She dressed, quietly crept down the stairs, and climbed out an open window in the library. She snuck away before Quadir and Amelia realized she was gone.

Terrell walked briskly through the park, trying to make it to his meeting place and wrap things up before the rain started coming down again. He hated the weather this time of year, especially when it got locked in a rainy cycle. It was one of the reasons he'd left the city. He hated the rain, and even more so, he despised the cold. The weather in his new city was as different from this shit as night and day. He'd relocated to beautiful, sunny South Florida, and he loved it. He'd vowed never to set foot in the City of Brotherly Love again, but now business had forced him to come back. He'd flown in to avenge his brother.

Champagne pulled up to the park in her black S 600 and backed into a parking space. She hated meeting Terrell; he was worse than his twin brother. At least Jerrell had a little bit of sense about him, even a little bit of class, compared with Terrell. They were both cold, heartless men, but Terrell was a straight-up animal. He was a brute with no sense of social grace, no understanding, no limitations, no nothing. He followed his most basic instincts, as if he were a hyena or lion or some other wild-ass animal. The bad part about Terrell was his attitude. The penal system ate him up a long time ago, and even though he had not been locked up for more than fifteen years, he still had an institutionalized mentality. He didn't give a fuck and he didn't care. He never would, like most men who served time.

Champagne could see him in the distance, standing and waiting for her. Goose bumps covered her body, and she felt creepy, crawling creatures up and down her spine. It was a feeling she got whenever she was around Terrell. She hated the way he looked at her, the way he stared at her body. He really was the worst. Champagne knew if he ever got the chance to sex her, he would. And she had no doubt he would be as brutal as possible while doing it.

Jerrell had told her plenty of stories about his brother. Terrell liked to take pussy. Jerrell never understood why the women didn't press charges. Some would end up with black eyes and bruised bodies. But no one *ever* pressed charges. Jerrell figured the women were too scared. Either that or they had such scandalous pasts, the charges would never stick and they would end up looking like the whores they truly were.

Champagne looked at the sick, twisted grin spread across Terrell's face. She could picture him beating the shit out of her, raping her, and then sadistically burning her body inside some giant cathedral or something. He was a fucking weird, deranged, serial killer type, waiting to be set off—probably from the simplest of things, such as saying the wrong word, like "bananas."

Champagne walked to the center of the park where Terrell was standing and waiting. He pulled her close and hugged her. She could feel his hand sliding down to her ass as his fingers reached between her legs.

"Hey, motherfucker, slow down!" Champagne shoved him away.

"I'm grieving and distraught, and this is how you treat me?" Terrell asked.

"Not distraught enough where you can't grip a handful of ass, though, huh?"

Terrell smiled. "People grieve in different ways."

"Don't put your filthy hands on me again," Champagne ordered him.

Terrell raised his hands in surrender.

Champagne stared at him in silence for several moments before exhaling. "So, you all right?"

"Fuck no, my brother's dead."

"I'm sorry for your family."

Terrell shrugged her emotions away. "What do you have for me?" he asked as he let his eyes roam down her body and stare between her legs.

Champagne shook her head. "Never that. Don't ever even think about that!"

Terrell smiled again and looked up at her.

Champagne opened her Louis Vuitton handbag and pulled out a photo. "This is the chick he was fucking with. He had me check up on her before he got shot up. I have no doubt he was with her when it happened. Her name is Gena Scott."

"She set him up?"

Champagne shrugged. "Only he or she could tell you that. I wasn't there. But one thing's for certain, she ain't no innocent bitch. She's down for fucking with a baller, so she could've set J up."

"Tell me everything you discovered about this bitch."

"She's from Richard Allen. She lives with her grandmother, some old bitch they call Gah Git. She was fucking with the boy, Quadir, real strong until he got killed. Rumor has it your brother was behind his murder, so it's very well possible Gena sought revenge against Jerrell for Quadir, or at least that's what some people are saying. Who knows what makes people tick?"

"So, she could've been setting my brother up all along to get revenge for her nigga, Quadir?"

Champagne shrugged. "I don't know, but it does make a lot of sense. But only she could tell you that."

Terrell took the picture and examined it carefully. "I can find this bitch in Richard Allen?"

"Richard Allen wouldn't be a bad place to start. That's where she's from and it's where her family lives. As far as I know, she's still living with her grandmother. That's the word."

Terrell examined Gena's picture. Blood rushed to his face as it became twisted in a dark mask of pure evil. He was staring at the bitch who had set his brother up. *This the bitch that was playing you, bro, misleading you, smiling in your face and shit? Don't worry, I got you. She probably gave you the pussy to throw you off, all so she could get even for her man. Mm-hmm, I see you, bitch.*

He couldn't help thinking of all the things he planned to do to Gena. He decided right then and there he was going to fuck her. He was going to tie her up and torture her and fuck her in places she never knew she could be fucked. He was going to make her beg him to kill her. She'd plead with him to end her pain, end her life, end her miserable suffering. He was going to do things to her that he'd never done to anyone else before. And he'd done so much to so many people in his lifetime. But this one was going to be special.

Champagne saw the look on Terrell's face and began to panic. His face was set in a deep scowl, and his eyes had become red and glazed over. The nigga looked like he was about to explode.

Champagne backed away from him. "You can keep the picture."

Terrell seemed to not even notice her leaving. He was too deep in thought about all the things he planned to do to seek his revenge against Gena.

Once Champagne was a safe distance away, she turned and hurried to her car. *Bitch, ain't you glad you didn't say "bananas"!*

Lieutenant Mark Ratzinger lifted his hand, calling for a round of beer. The bartender nodded, and Mark turned back to his associates.

"Where are we at on this?" Ratzinger asked.

"We're tracking her," Dick Davis told him. "She's made some big purchases, but she hasn't led us to the money yet."

Letoya Ellington shrugged. "She's smarter than we thought. She must've kept an extremely large sum out to spend. The rest she must've hidden. And besides the car and some jewelry, she hasn't really spent big."

"She might not touch that stash for months," Dick added. "Hell, maybe even years."

Ratzinger shook his head. "Well, it's getter harder and harder to justify the money and man hours we're spending tracking her. Pretty soon, somebody is gonna wanna know why we're on her, and why we haven't produced anything."

Cornell Cleaver nodded. "He's right, guys. This thing can't go on too much longer. We're going to have to come up with something, and soon."

"Like what?" Ellington asked.

Ratzinger shrugged. "Is she dirty in any kinda way? Can we swoop on her and press her?"

The drinks arrived at the table. The detectives sat in silence as the waitress passed their beers around. The conversation resumed as soon as she left.

"As far as we can tell?" Ellington shook her head. "Other than spending drug money, no. She's clean."

"Can we plant something on her, bring her in, and then pressure her?" Cleaver asked.

Ratzinger shook his head. "That means we'd have to bring in a black and white."

"So? There's enough money to go around," Cleaver replied.

"The fewer people we have involved in this, the better," Ratzinger told him.

"I'm Internal Affairs. I can get us a couple of dirty patrolmen to pull her ass over and plant the shit. That's nothing. We do it every day," Cleaver told them.

"I can break her in the confession room," Ellington added.

"Break her? She hasn't committed a crime. Police 101, guys— remember your first day at the academy. An innocent person isn't going to confess," Ratzinger pointed out.

Cleaver leaned forward. "I say we get her in the room, let her know how much time she's facing, and we get her to trade her freedom for the goddamn money."

"And if she doesn't confess?" Ratzinger asked. "What if she doesn't break? What if she requests an attorney? What if some hotshot lawyer walks her ass out of the station and is on the phone with Internal Affairs the next day? What happens then? Anybody thought about that shit? Jesus Christ, guys! Think! We can do better than that shit!"

Davis leaned back in his chair. "What about a boyfriend? You think she'd give it up to a lover?"

Ellington smiled. "I don't think you're her type, Dickie."

"Not me, asshole. I'm talking about bringing in a young detective friend of mine to seduce her ass."

"And you think he looks hot enough to seduce her?" Ellington laughed. "Dickie, I'm going to have to watch you."

"Fuck you, Toya!" Davies groped himself. "This is all dick, and it loves nothing but pussy."

"Okay, at least you guys are thinking," Ratzinger told them.

"Hey, what about the big fish you caught? What was that guy's name, um, Rick or Rik?" Cleaver said. "What about him?"

Ellington shrugged. "What about him?"

"She offered to help him once, didn't she? Maybe she'd be willing to offer it to him again."

Ellington nodded. "Maybe."

"We have to make him need it." Davis smiled.

"We'll bust his ass as soon as he jaywalks," Cleaver added. "We can plant some shit on him, juice things up for the judge so his bond is through the roof, and put the word out on the street."

"How can we guarantee she'll get the word, or even give a shit?" Davis asked. "And how can we be sure she'll even make the offer again, or that he'll accept it?"

"Look, we need to come up with a way to get her to lead us to wherever she's got it stashed," Ratzinger told them. "What about the grandmother? Any medical bills? Any creditors? Anybody close to her she'd loan a large sum of money to? That's what we need to start looking for. See who she's close to. Start tracking friends and family. See who she hangs out with and calls all the time. Real police work, ladies and gentlemen. Time to show why each of you made detective."

Ellington lifted her beer into the air. "To making detective."

"Detective!" The others lifted their glasses to toast.

"Let's hurry up and put this bitch in the poorhouse," Cleaver added.

The others around the table laughed.

Manhunt

Terrell walked to the door and pounded on it forcefully. He hated being in Richard Allen, especially on a day like today, when he had business to take care of. There were always some stupid-ass niggas wanting to stare you down or eyeball you like they were hard. And when you played the game with them, it almost always led to a gunfight. He had no time for that kind of bullshit today. No, today he was on a mission. He needed to handle his business and keep it moving.

Gah Git opened the front door. "May I help you?" she asked.

"I'm looking for her." Terrell held up the photo he had of Gena.

"Her?" Gah Git eyed him suspiciously. "I don't know who that is."

"Your granddaughter."

"I don't have my glasses on. You got a name?"

Terrell smiled. "Gena. I'm looking for Gena."

"Oh, well, Gena don't live here no more. What's your name? If she calls, I'll tell her you came by. If you want, you can leave your phone number for her."

"I heard she *does* live here."

"Well, you heard wrong, son."

"You wouldn't be trying to play games with me, would you?" Terrell asked. "She's not inside hiding or anything like that, right?"

"Who the hell do you think you're talking to? Now, I said she ain't here and she don't live here, and don't you come back here no more," Gah Git said, trying to slam the door in his face, but Terrell stuck his foot in the door.

"What the hell are you doing?" Gah Git shouted. "Gary! Gary!"

Terrell shoved the door open, knocking Gah Git onto the floor. He stepped inside and closed the door behind him.

"Get the hell outta my house!" Gah Git shouted. "Gary!"

Gary ran down the stairs. "What the fuck is going on?" He leaned forward and helped his grandmother up. "Who the fuck are you?"

"Where's Gena?" Terrell demanded. "Is she here?"

"Nigga, you better get the fuck outta here!" Gary told him.

Terrell shoved Gary out of the way and walked into the kitchen.

"Nigga, I said get the fuck outta my grandmom's house!" Gary shouted. He charged Terrell.

Terrell backhanded Gary and then clasped his hand around Gary's throat. Gary gripped Terrell's hand and struggled to free himself. Terrell tossed Gary aside like a rag doll, sending him flying over the coffee table.

"Oh my God, Gary! Gary, you okay?" Gah Git rushed to her grandson's side. "Get the hell outta here!" she shouted as Terrell.

Gary rose and charged Terrell again. Terrell punched Gary in his stomach, dropping him to the floor. He kicked Gary in his stomach and then pulled out his pistol.

"I'm tired of this bullshit! Where the fuck is she?"

"Oh my God, no, please! Oh, God, please don't kill him! Don't kill him!" Gah Git pleaded.

Terrell turned the pistol backward and struck Gah Git across her jaw. "Where the fuck is she?"

Gah Git fell to the floor.

"Where the fuck is she?" Terrell asked, striking Gah Git with the pistol once again.

Gary tried to rise. "Leave her alone!"

Terrell struck Gah Git across her face again and then kicked her in her stomach. Gary braced himself and stood back up to charge Terrell, but before he could, Terrell turned around with the pistol in his hand and fired a shot into Gary's stomach. "Lay down, bitch!"

Gary flew back into the end table, knocking over a lamp.

Terrell turned his attention back to a crying Gah Git. "Where is she, old woman?"

"I don't know!"

Terrell gripped Gah Git's hair and pulled her face up toward his. "How do you get in touch with her?"

"She comes by!" Gah Git shouted.

Terrell struck her with the handle of his pistol several times, causing blood to pour from her head, her nose, and her mouth. "Wrong answer, old woman!"

Terrell continued to beat Gah Git with the pistol until she was unconscious. He then began to search the apartment. Terrell tore through the place, ransacking it in the process. He searched drawers for an address or a telephone number that would lead him to Gena. He found none. By the time he returned downstairs, Gah Git was awake and dragging her bloody, beaten, and bruised body into the kitchen, where the phone hung on the wall.

"Well, well, well." Terrell smiled. "Where are we going?"

"No, please," Gah Git begged. "Just go. My grandbaby needs an ambulance. Please . . ."

"Call her," Terrell said sternly.

"What?"

"Pick up the goddamned telephone and call Gena!"

"I don't have her number! I swear to the good Lord, I don't have no number for that child!"

Terrell grabbed Gah Git by her hair and bent her over the kitchen table. "When you see her, I want you to give her a message for me."

"Okay."

"Tell her I said this." Terrell lifted Gah Git's housecoat in the back and ripped off her underwear.

Gah Git screamed like a wild animal, but Terrell covered her mouth as he forced himself inside her. He ravaged her violently, though what seemed to last a lifetime lasted only four minutes. Gah Git had found herself at some low times in her life, but somehow she'd always made it through. She'd always found strength in her God.

Once her assailant left the apartment, Gah Git crawled up to the telephone and dialed 911. She then crawled into the living room, lifted Gary's head into her bloody lap, and talked to him to keep him from going into shock.

The entire time she waited, she couldn't help but call to God. *You gonna have to carry me through this, carry me on. Why, God, why? Please don't let my grandbaby die in here today. Take me, Lord, take me, but don't take my grandbaby. Don't take him.*

Gonna Getcha

Joshua Harbinger had been in the Federal Bureau of Investigation for the last eight years of his life. He'd graduated from Harvard at the top of his class at the age of nineteen and been recruited by the Bureau straight out of college. His plan had been to go to Harvard Law, but after talking to the Bureau's recruiter midway through his senior year, he caught the FBI bug.

Josh, as he was called, had, for the most part, lived a very sheltered life. His father was the United States ambassador to Australia, and his mother was a former United States attorney, and she was also a former White House counsel. Josh grew up around privilege and power. He also grew up around money, lots of it. His maternal grandfather was a former international commodities trader who later became a United States senator, while his father's father was the founder of a very successful Wall Street brokerage firm. Josh was the product of Andover prep school and had been groomed to go to Harvard Law so that he could take over the family business. However, he craved excitement and danger.

His first years in the Bureau were spent chasing low-level counterfeiters and investigating missing children's cases. Eventually, after plenty of wild and loose but lucky stunts, he'd worked his way up the ladder and built a reputation as a maverick who would get the job done. His reputation won him a transfer to New York to work on the high-profile organized crime leaders and the New York Mafia families. Once they had been pretty much broken up, he was transferred to Philadelphia, where he was biding his time until he made Deputy Special Agent in Charge. He wouldn't be content until he was in charge of his own major field office. He'd been told his promotion was in the works. The actual words were more along the lines of "It's basically a done deal." All he had to do was sit tight. He, on the other hand, had other plans.

Josh knocked on the door of his boss's office, none other than Special Agent in Charge Rudy Galvani. Galvani was a no-nonsense FBI agent through and through. Born in the Bensonhurst neighborhood of Brooklyn, Galvani had been raised on the mean streets of New York. He'd watched his older brother, two uncles, and several of his cousins fall victim to gang and drug violence. It was after the funeral of his cousin Manuel that he'd promised his mother he'd keep his shit clean, and he had.

As a youngster, Galvani stuck his nose into his books and, for extracurricular activities, played football and basketball and ran track. He was something of a high school football star. He'd led his traditionally horrid football team to a ten and three season, losing in the playoffs after meeting what was destined to be the state's high school football champions that year. So the team held its head up high, and Galvani, the star running back, was the pride of his community.

Academics took Galvani to Harvard on a scholarship. He was the first person in his family to go to college, and he did it in a major way. Harvard Law followed graduation, and then a clerkship with a Supreme Court Justice. A short stint with the Justice Department and a change of administration found him transferring over to the Bureau. That was fifteen years ago, and now he oversaw his own major field office. He was known in law enforcement circles as "the

Hammer." He'd bust his own mother if he found her doing something illegal. His reputation for being an asshole was something he was proud of. He gave no quarter, and he expected none in return. That was why his relationship with Josh was a curious one. Josh was Mr. Cut Corners, while Galvani was Mr. Straight and Narrow. How they even got along was a mystery to everyone in the Bureau. Agents in the office had taken to calling them oil and water. They simply did not mix.

"In!" Galvani shouted.

Josh pushed open the door and stepped inside. "Hey, boss man!"

Galvani nodded toward the chair in front of his desk. "Have a seat."

Josh sat down and started digging through the jar of candy on his boss's desk.

"I got your report, Josh," Galvani told him. "Do you really want to open this can of worms? It's going to cause a shitstorm."

Josh shrugged. "I don't care. This Cleaver guy is dirtier than a prostitute's panties on a busy Saturday night."

Galvani nodded.

"He's the cancer," Josh continued. "He's rotten at the core. He's spreading his corruption throughout the department."

"You can't go after this guy with nothing more than a hunch."

"I have more than a hunch, sir. He's dirty, sir. Also, I had a peek into his file."

Galvani leaned back in his chair. "You investigated his file? How did you get access to an Internal Affairs detective's file?"

"I have this friend who works for—"

Galvani lifted his hand, silencing him. He didn't want to know. That way, if the shit hit the fan, he could say he didn't know and at least that would be the truth.

"Sir, something's off. Hear me out. Cornell Cleaver's been reassigned, investigated, reprimanded, and transferred more than any officer in the history of the department. Someone keeps sweeping his shit under the rug. That tells me he's probably got someone higher up looking out for him, probably just as corrupt."

Galvani shook his head. "Keep it focused, Josh. Don't worry about any higher-ups. We'll keep them out of the loop on this one. So, how do you plan on pursuing this?"

"I don't think going undercover is necessary."

"You want me to get you assigned to a case with this guy?"

Josh nodded. "That would be great, sir. If you could do that, I could bring this asshole down. But in the meantime, I want to do a little snooping around. I noticed he associates only with certain officers and only one from Internal Affairs. The others are from various other departments and precincts."

"And?"

"Well, it's weird, sir. These Internal Affairs guys are pariahs. No one wants to hang with the guy charged with investigating them and possibly getting them fired or sent to prison. Yet, there's a whole clique he's rumored to be tight with, and they're mostly detectives."

"Be careful on this one, Josh. No wild and loose stunts."

Josh smiled. "I wouldn't think of it."

"I want to be kept in the loop and know what you're up to at all times."

Josh nodded. "Will do. I'm going to do a little snooping around and see what I can come up with."

Galvani nodded. "Good luck and happy hunting."

Josh rose. "I'm going to bag this crooked bastard and bring everybody down with him. You can bet your ass on this."

Galvani nodded, and Josh exited the room.

It must have taken Gena three hours before she caught a cab. She realized she was in the suburbs. The neighborhood was nothing but grass, trees, and monstrous million-dollar homes. *I'll never get a cab out here.* Tired, hungry, and still not a hundred percent, she felt weak and faint standing on her feet. Every few minutes she'd stop and rest by sitting on the curb or leaning against parked cars. Finally, she saw a cab heading up the street toward her. Thank God it stopped.

"Where to, lady?"

For a few seconds, Gena didn't know where she was going. She thought quickly and then gave the cabbie instructions. Gena had the cab drop her off at the corner of her old block, at Fifty-Second and Chancellor Street. She wished she still had her old apartment, but wishing would get her nowhere. Had she not moved in with Quadir, her uncle Michael would still be providing the place for her. She walked down the block unnoticed and up the steps to Markita's door. She rang the bell and waited.

"Who?"

"It's me, Gena."

"Gena, girl, everybody and they mama been calling here looking for you. Where the hell have you been? Something happened to your grandma. They said some man attacked her and shot Gary up and he's in critical condition."

"What?" Gena asked, confused.

"Girl, it's bad! It's been on the news and everything. The police are looking for the man. They got a bulletin out with his picture. You know how they do the drawings? You better call somebody. You better call home."

Gena picked up the receiver of Markita's phone and dialed her cousin Bria's cell phone. There was no answer, so Gena hung up and dialed again. On the second ring, Bria answered the phone.

"Bria, it's me, Gena. What's going on?"

"Gena, some man came up in Gah Git's house looking for you. But Gah Git told him she ain't know where you was and he beat her and Gary tried to stop him, but he beat Gary, then shot him in the stomach and then he . . ." Her voice faded out and Gena couldn't hear her.

"And then what . . . what happened?"

"Then he raped Gah Git."

Gena began to unravel. "What? Oh my God!"

"She's in the hospital at Temple and Gary's there, too. Gena, it's bad. Aunt Paula, Uncle Michael, and Aunt Gwendolyn are all at the hospital, and they saying Gary's not gonna make it." Bria started crying. "He's on life support, Gena."

"Okay, okay, I'm on my way. I'm on my way!" Gena said before placing the phone in its cradle.

"What happened?" Markita asked.

"It's like you said. Gah Git and Gary are in the hospital. Some man went to Gah Git's house looking for me. He beat Gary and shot him and beat Gah Git and raped her."

"Oh my God, Gena, no!"

"That's only the half of it." Gena thought of Quadir.

She wished she could tell her friend but realized that would only make matters worse. Instead, she decided to keep the news of Quadir to herself. She bent her head and began to cry. Her entire world was falling apart, and there was nothing she could do to make it better.

Markita placed her hand on Gena's head and tried to comfort her friend. "Come on, it's gonna be okay. Come on, I'll go with you to the hospital."

Monkey See, Monkey Do

Gena stood outside the hospital-room door, afraid to open it, afraid to step inside, afraid to see her grandmother. She blamed herself for what had happened to Gah Git. *If only I had been there, then maybe none of this would've happened. Oh, Gah Git, I'm so sorry.* Gena couldn't help but think that all this had something to do with Quadir's money. Since she'd taken the money from Quadir's hidden apartment, her entire world had begun to go downhill. Nothing was right anymore. *I wish I'd never found that apartment or that money.* Even though the attacker didn't ask for money, and only asked for her, it didn't matter. Gena had heard the saying "money is the root of all evil," and she was beginning to take the saying seriously. *What kind of monster would rape an old woman? Who is he? What does he want with me?* Nothing good, that's for sure. *He probably would've done the same to me or worse.* Gena started to think about everything that had happened. Like a bolt of lightning, it hit her. *Quadir, oh my God. He wants his money! He sent that guy to find me, and look at what he did.* She reached down and felt her stomach. *Why would that guy do that to Gah Git?* She had so many unanswered questions; nothing made sense. But here she was today, standing outside a hospital room, scared to see her grandmother.

Gena slowly pushed open the door and stepped inside. Gah Git was lying in bed with tubes protruding from various parts of her body. She was bandaged and bruised all over. Because of her age, the doctors were uncertain about the full extent of her recovery or if she'd ever fully recover at all. As a result of being beaten and raped, Gah Git had required four separate surgeries to stop her internal bleeding. Gah Git's heart was sturdy; that was the good news. She had suffered several skull fractures from being struck with the handgun, and her bones were brittle because of her age. Healing was a coin toss. But they were going to do everything in their power to get the job done.

The doctors and the police had done the best they could to keep the incident out of the media, to no avail. An assault on an old woman would draw unbelievable media coverage and, perhaps, cause even more deaths. These types of crimes often sparked a chain reaction. Copycats sometimes came out of the woodwork on cases such as those. However, the efforts were worthless. The news spread through the city like wildfire. Other elderly people barricaded themselves indoors behind locks and chains, some refusing to go out even to get medical attention. Crimes like this would reverberate across the community for months. Even though the detectives were upset about how the case was being handled in the media, they refused to comment. Their main reason was clear. They all had grandmothers and mothers, and something like this was inconceivable, inhuman even. A crime like this was done out of pure evil. Brutally beating and raping an old woman. No, they were going to lay this sick bastard to rest. When they caught him, his judge, his jury, and his sentence would be given to him inside a holding cell in a precinct house.

Gena approached her grandmother. She looked like she'd aged ten years since the last time Gena had seen her. Gena bent down, kissed her forehead, and began to caress her arm softly, causing Gah Git to open her eyes.

She smiled at Gena.

"Hey, Gah Git," Gena said, barely audible. "How you feeling?"

Gah Git lifted an eyebrow, telling Gena how stupid her question was.

Tears fell from Gena's eyes. "Gah Git, I'm so sorry! I don't know why someone would do something like this. I'm so, so sorry. Please don't be mad at me."

Barely able to speak, Gah Git whispered, "I'm not mad at you," then reached up to wipe Gena's tears away. She placed her hand on top of Gena's gently, too weak to do much else. She looked into Gena's eyes and silently said everything would be okay without saying a word.

Gena wiped her tears and smiled and held Gah Git's hand. She leaned forward and buried her head in her grandmother's chest. Gah Git was so strong. *Only you, Gah Git, only you.* Gena didn't know what it was but there was something about her grandmother that, no matter what, she was able to see a bigger, better, brighter picture, even when the world was dark and gray and hopeless. For Gena, it seemed the older generation simply had that way about them. No matter what, it was still okay, and somehow, the Lord would give whatever strength was needed. Maybe it was some damn magic potion they drank when they were younger or something. Gena thought of all the stories her grandmother had told her about Gah Git's mother and father not being able to go to school and having to work the fields in the South, picking cotton all day in the hot sun. And she remembered Gah Git's stories of the sixties and seventies and the Black Panthers and the civil rights movement and Martin Luther King Jr., and Malcolm X. *Maybe that's why she's so much stronger than me.* Gena would never have thought of marching or boycotting and would never have imagined Gah Git out there, either.

Yes, her grandmother Gah Git was one of the last few out there who had endured the water hoses, the dogs, the police batons, the beatings, the jails, and everything else, and still she held up her head and kept going. Gena never understood how her grandmother managed to always take nothing and turn it into something. She'd take in her grandbabies and accept the responsibility and all that came with them. She made sure they had food to eat and clean clothes on their backs. She helped each one of them with their school lessons and preached day in and day out about staying out of trouble. This was her Gah Git, and for Gena to know she'd caused her grandmother pain broke her heart in two.

Gah Git caressed Gena's head, and Gena could hear her grandmother trying to speak. "Huh, Gah Git, what did you say?"

"Don't cry, baby," she whispered, taking in small breaths.

Gena smiled at Gah Git and watched her close her eyes. She was on heavy sedation for the pain, and just like that, she was asleep.

"My life is so messed up right now and I have no one, Gah Git, no one. I don't know what to do and I don't know where to begin. I'm pregnant, Gah Git. I'm going to have a baby." She looked at her grandmother. Not even a flinch. Gah Git was definitely sleeping. "I thought the guy that I was seeing really cared about me. And when I went to tell him I was pregnant, he tried to kill me. He was after Quadir's money and he tried to kill me, but Quadir rescued me and then I found out that all this time, Gah Git, he wasn't dead. Quadir didn't die. He's been alive all this time.

"A doctor saved him and she helped him recuperate. And he never came for me. He let me keep thinking he was dead and the guy I was seeing—oh, Gah Git, it's such a mess—is the guy who tried to kill Quadir, so Quadir hates me. He thinks I was in cahoots to bring him harm. And I love him, Gah Git. I love him so much. It's just that he doesn't love me anymore. He thinks I'm his enemy and all he wants now is his money. And I'm starting to think it was Quadir who sent that man to the house looking for me because I ran away. I snuck out of the window and I left him. But the only reason I left is because he told me about him and the doctor.

"You should've heard the way he was talking. You could tell he really loves her. He doesn't love me no more, Gah Git, and I wish he did. I wish he did."

Gena laid her head back down on her grandmother's chest. Gah Git had listened to every word Gena said. *Oh, Lord, what a mess, Gena. What a mess you've made with your life.* Gah Git wanted to speak so badly, but she didn't. She lay still and pretended to be asleep. She simply listened to what was going on with her grandbaby. Truth was, she knew if she opened her eyes, Gena would stop talking. So she lay there listening to Gena talk about her sordid life.

When she was done spilling out her heart and soul, Gena walked out of the room and found Markita sitting among her family in the hospital's hallway.

Out of nowhere, like a saber-tooth tiger, Gwendolyn jumped up and went over to Gena, who hadn't even had a chance to get the door closed.

"You lucky I don't fuck you up in here. See, see, see, all that shit with them gangster-ass niggas of yours got my mother all fucked up." Gwendolyn was getting ready to swing on Gena.

"Fight, fight, fight." Bria smacked high fives with her twin, Brianna, as they stood on the sidelines as if watching a boxing match episode.

Michael grabbed his sister's arm and held her back. "Calm down, calm down."

"No, Michael, let me go. She needs her ass kicked. That little bitch wouldn't even help me get out of jail."

"Gah Git told me not to get you out," Gena cried. "And I don't know what's going on. Bria told me what happened. I swear, I don't know who's looking for me."

"Well, take your ass on somewhere until you figure it out," Gwendolyn said.

"Stop, Gwendolyn. Knock it off in this hospital, making all this commotion," Paula said, who would've rather seen the family quarrel in the privacy of their home.

"Don't nobody want to hear that shit, Paula. Michael, let me go."

"You know what, Aunt Gwendolyn? You got so much to say about me, what about you? You broke Gah Git's heart, running around Richard Allen like a wild crack monkey." Gena was ready to go toe-to-toe. "You really got some nerve."

"Bitch, I'll whoop your little ass. Who you think you talking to? I'm your elder."

"Whatever, Aunt Gwendolyn. You're nothing but a crack monkey," Gena yelled as she was being pushed to the elevator by Paula and Bria. Michael and Gwendolyn's boyfriend, Royce, held Gwendolyn back.

"Come on, Gena. Leave her alone. Come on." Bria pushed the buttons on the elevator panel, trying to close the door behind them.

"Aunt Gwendolyn is crazy, ain't she?" Bria asked.

"Yeah, she crazy all right. But she's telling the truth, though."

"Gena, it's not your fault. You can't blame yourself or let nobody else put the blame on you. Regardless of whether or not some mad, crazed lunatic is looking for you and raped our old-ass grandmother and done damn near killed Gah—"

"Bria, please, I get the point. It's just that, truth is, she's right."

"Well, what are you gonna do? 'Cause everybody is really scared for you, Gena. If that man would do that to Gah Git, Lord only knows what he'll do to you once he finds you."

She's right; there's no telling what he'll do. There's no telling what Quadir has told him to do. I better get out of town quickly. But where will I go?

"You okay? You look like you're staring out into space."

"No, no, I'm fine. I'm okay."

"So, what you gonna do, Gena? You better get out of town while this crazy man is looking for you."

"Yeah, I know. I can't believe he'd do something like this."

"Who?"

"Nobody, nothing."

Gena hugged her cousin.

"You gonna be okay?"

"Yeah, yeah, I'll be fine."

"Where you gonna go?"

"I have no idea."

It's probably better you keep your whereabouts to yourself, especially since you got crazy rapists and murderers hunting you down, mm-hmm, thought Bria as she watched the elevator doors close, with her cousin on the other side of them.

Mommy Dearest

Quadir strolled through the back door of his home, nearly scaring his mother to death.

"Quadir!" She rushed to him and embraced him tightly. "What are you doing here? You shouldn't be here! If someone sees you . . ."

"It's okay, Mama." Quadir nodded. "I wanted to drop by and see you."

"Quadir, if you needed to see me, you could've left the code, and I would've met you at the meeting place."

"I wanted to see you right now. I didn't feel like waiting."

Mrs. Richards exhaled. "Qua, boy, what's the matter?"

Quadir shook his head.

"This better not be about that damn money."

"Not really."

"Not really?" She placed her hands on her hips. "What does that mean?"

"It's about Gena."

Mrs. Richards turned back to her dirty dishes. "What about Gena?"

"She woke up."

Mrs. Richards froze. "And?"

"She knows it was me who rescued her."

She turned toward her son. "She knows you're alive?"

Quadir nodded.

"And so, what's next?"

Quadir shrugged. "That's the problem. I can't answer that question."

"Well, I can't answer it for you. So if it's those kinds of answers you're looking for, you've come to the wrong place. There's a mirror behind you. Turn around and ask away, because that's the only person who can give you the answers you're looking for."

Quadir smiled. She was as blunt as always. And just as truthful. But like all her truths, this one was also filled with many other truths. He'd come there to find an answer, and she had the key to unlock the code keeping him from finding peace.

"Amelia says hi," Quadir said.

"Nice girl." Mrs. Richards faced her son. "I really like her. Nice, polite, honest, straightforward, smart. And a doctor, making her own money. What's not to like?" She turned back to her dishes and continued washing them.

Quadir nodded. "She does have everything going for her."

"Nice girl."

"You said that already."

"Did I?"

"You did."

"Hmm."

"Another *hmm*."

"Are you two getting serious?"

"I don't know."

"Why don't you know?"

"I don't know that, either."

"Are you sure you don't know?" Viola asked with a knowing smile.

"A lot of loose ends to wrap up, I guess. I want to make sure one door is closed before I open a new one."

"Wise to always do."

Quadir seated himself at the table and lowered his head onto his arms.

"Sometimes doors are hard to close, son," she told him. "Sometimes, there's so much behind those doors our heart won't let us close them."

"What if it has to be closed?"

"It's hard to say goodbye to the ones we love."

Quadir remained silent.

"You do love her, don't you?"

Quadir lifted his head and looked at her.

"I mean, it takes a lot for someone, especially my son, to hang up his playboy hat and settle down. She must've really been something special for you to have done that. I used to wonder what was so special about Gena that could make you do that."

Quadir remained silent.

"Do you remember, son?"

"Remember what?"

"What was so special about her that made you want to settle down and be with her?"

Quadir lowered his head. His mother had sucker-punched him in his heart. He did remember. He remembered her smile, her innocence, that killer body. She was his G, and he was her Qua. She was from the projects. He was trying to make a dollar out of fifteen cents. He was balling, trying to shine so that they could have things they'd never dreamed of having. He remembered the day he promised himself that he'd always take care of her. He remembered when they went to the Bahamas and stayed over at the Valiant Hotel. He remembered the first time they made love, on the beach. It was as if the drink was named for them. He remembered everything about her. *Why did she have to fuck with Jerrell. Why?* Things would be so much easier if she hadn't fucked with him.

"Ah, so you do remember," Viola said. His silence and daydreaming had answered her question.

"She met somebody else."

Mrs. Richards nodded. "She's young, the man she loved was murdered, and in her mind, you were never coming back. I'm sure enough time passed by. I'm sure she mourned her loss and then moved on. Come on, what do you expect? You were dead, and you were never coming back." She turned to him. "I remember being met by those doctors in the hospital and being told you were dead. I broke down right there and fell into that doctor's arms. The first thing I thought was, my poor baby. And then I thought about how I was never going to see you alive again, how I was never going to get to see that smile of yours, how I was never going to get to hold any grandchildren from you. My Quadir was dead, and he was never coming back.

"I was preparing for a funeral in my head and preparing for a life without my baby. Right up until Amelia called and had me meet her in that damn parking garage across from the hospital. I got down on my knees and prayed so hard to God that night, thanking Him for giving my baby back, I couldn't walk for two days. I had the privilege of knowing you were alive. She didn't have that. Your death to her was as sure as the sun sets in the evening time. She had to move on. She had to live."

"You don't understand. She was fucking with Jerrell, Mom. And he's the one who tried to kill me."

Viola finished her last dish and turned to her son. "It hurts like hell, and you feel betrayed by that. Quadir, I put that girl on the streets, so I could hide the fact you were alive and look for that damn money. Put her on the streets! That was the worst thing I've ever done in my entire life. She had nothing and nowhere to go when I did that. We can't blame her for moving forward with life. She's strong, Quadir. She wasn't going to curl up in a ball and die. I raised you to be a man.

To stand up and be a man. No one is at fault here. You got shot, we had to protect you to keep you alive, she thought you were dead, and life happened. It's life's fault. So now you have a choice. You can go on and always wonder what if, or you can put those questions to rest."

"How?"

"Do you love her?"

Quadir went silent.

"Do you still love her?" Viola asked more forcefully.

"I love her."

"Then that's all that matters."

"And Amelia?"

"What about her?"

"I love her, too."

"You love her for everything she did for you? Or are you in love with her?"

Quadir shook his head. "That's just it, I don't know. She means everything to me. She's everything I've never had in a woman. She's independent, she's smart, she's fun to be around, she's strong. She puts my ass in check when I need it. I've never met anybody like her."

"Well, that's because she's independent and not no project chickenhead like you're used to."

Quadir laughed. "Mom!"

"You were dating these hoochies looking for some tennis shoes and something to eat, and maybe get an outfit and their hair and nails done. Let's keep it real." She kissed Quadir on top of his head. "And for the first time in my baby's life, he's met a real Black woman. A strong sister who tells him to keep his money in his pocket, she's got this. She doesn't need anything from you, Quadir. She only wants your love."

"And I want to give it to her. She deserves it."

"Don't give it to her because you think you owe it to her, baby. One thing about women like Amelia, they always land on their feet.

No matter what decision you make, even if your decision is to make none at all, she's going to be all right."

Quadir exhaled. "You got a quarter?"

"A quarter? What for?"

"Hell, for the coin toss. I don't know what the hell I'm gonna do."

Viola threw her head back in laughter. Quadir joined in.

"Follow your heart, Quadir."

"My heart is pulling me in two different directions."

She shook her head solemnly. "No, it's not. It's pulling you in one direction, but your pride and sense of duty are pulling you in another. You don't owe anyone anything. You don't owe Amelia anything for saving your life. She's a doctor; it's her job. You don't owe those niggas on the street no explanation. You don't owe Gena, and who cares what she did in the midst of your absence? Listen, son, you make your decisions in life based on what will make you happy. You were given a second chance to live. Take it. Don't let nothing stop you from living your life to the fullest and being happy."

Quadir nodded. "I thought you liked Amelia better."

"What mother wouldn't want their child to marry a doctor? But hell, I'm from the hood, so I'll always root for the underdog. Listen, it's not that I don't like Gena or that I like Amelia better. You're the one that gots to lay up with the broad. Shoot, not me. I want you to make whatever decision will make you happy. I'm your mother. I love you. That's what mothers do."

Sneaky, Sneaky

Rik pulled up to the shopping center in his black Range Rover and found a parking space up front. Today was a good day for shopping. He had a little change left over, and he might as well get some new kicks. Even if he wasn't balling out of control like before, there was no sense in looking like shit. He lived by the mantra "never let 'em see you sweat." So even though times were desperate, he was still going to look like he was the fucking king of Philly.

The clothing store he chose today was one of his favorites. It was a small Italian clothier that sold fine Italian suits. They could hand-make you a suit or tailor something off the rack to fit you right. They also carried the latest in street gear in another section of the store. Today, he was there to do a little bit of shopping for both.

Rik stepped into the shop and waved to the owner's son, Anthony. Anthony was a typical young Italian. He wore the flyest tailored suits out there but fucked them up by wearing too much jewelry. He had a Rolex on one wrist, a Rolex bracelet on the other, three rings on his left hand, and four rings on his right hand . . . Way too much.

Rik headed for the suits. He was going to find something on the rack and have it tailored to his specifications. Charcoal was the color he needed, something in a dark gray color, not too close to black, but none of that light gray shit, either. Something that looked fly. He already had shoes and a tie that would go perfectly with what he had in mind.

"Well, hello, Tyrik!" Sergeant Ellington greeted him from behind.

"Spending a little bit of that dope money today, are we?" Detective Davis asked, stepping to the other side of Rik.

Rik realized the detectives had him boxed in. "Man, what y'all want?"

"We're putting together a greatest hits mixtape," Ellington told him. "We got your soundtrack from the dope deals you made."

"And your conversations with your cellmate while you were in jail," Davis added.

"And, of course, the best one of all, your conversation with Miss Scott," Ellington told him.

"The one where she offered you the money to make a two-million-dollar bond," Davis added, placing his arm around Rik.

Instantly Rik became nervous. *How the fuck do they know that?*

"I don't know what y'all are talking about," Rik told them.

"Ah, ah, ah, ah. Let's not play stupid, Tyrik," Davis said. "Don't make me pull out my little tape recorder and play it back for you."

Ellington shook her head and whispered into Rik's ear. "You really don't want him to pull out the tape recorder. It really pisses him off when he has to do that. Besides, if we listen to all those tapes of you discussing drug deals and drug money, we might find reason to indict you once again."

"Okay." Rik lifted his hands in surrender. "What do you want from me?"

"The offer your little friend made to you. Do you think you can get her to make it again?" Ellington asked.

"What, the offer to post my bond?" Rik asked. "Why would she do that? I'm not in jail."

Davis produced a pair of handcuffs. "That's not a problem. I can make that happen."

"I haven't done shit!" Rik protested.

"You think that means something to me?" Davis asked with a crooked smile.

"Let's just say, we have an arrangement to make with you," Ellington told him.

"And that would be?" Rik asked, lifting an eyebrow.

"We want you to borrow some money from her," Ellington told him.

"For what?"

"To keep your Black ass out of prison!" Ellington snapped. "However much you want, so long as it's an emergency and she'll loan it to you. She offered it to you once, right?"

"What, you want to get her on tape offering me some money?" Rik asked. "I ain't wearing no wire!"

"No, dipshit, we already have her on tape offering you the money!" Davis told him. "Can you get her to loan you the money or what?"

"Maybe," Rik said, looking at the pair of oink-oinks standing in front of him. "What's in it for me?"

Davis and Ellington exchanged glances. "Um, like besides staying out of jail, you get to keep whatever you can get her to loan you," Ellington replied.

"Bullshit!" Rik said, looking at Letoya like she was out of her mind. "This is a setup."

Davis shoved Rik up against a clothing rack. "This ain't no bullshit, boy! You either cooperate with us, or we'll make your life a living hell. You got that?"

Rik nodded.

"Good." Ellington stuffed one of her cards into Rik's pocket. "If she agrees, you contact me ASAP. You got that?"

Rik nodded.

Ellington and Davis turned and exited the store. Davis turned to his partner. "There ain't no way in hell we're letting him keep that money."

Ellington nodded. "I know, but it sounded good, right?"

Davis laughed and climbed into the car.

Inside, Rik straightened out his clothing. *What the fuck is wrong with the police? Those two must be out their minds. If they think for one second they're getting in on my meal ticket, they can forget it.* There was no way he was calling them or doing anything else for them or with them. He pulled the detective's card from his pocket, tore it up, and tossed it over his shoulder. He was there to enjoy himself, relax, and shop, and that was exactly what he planned to do.

The Clam Tavern and Pat's King of Steaks in South Philly were where everyone hung out on the weekend, especially after the clubs closed down at two in the morning. Grabbing something to eat and hanging out on the smaller streets of South Philly was a long-standing Saturday-night ritual for Philly's young hip-hop partygoers. Showing off their new clothes or skimpy outfits and their souped-up cars with shiny rims was the thing to do.

And if you were a female, being with a hot boy was also the thing to do. Kewy Kev's 5.0 Mustang Convertible GT made him a hot boy, and that was one of the reasons Bria made him her boyfriend. Kewy Kev's 5.0 was burgundy, with a ground-effects kit and a massive whale tail in the back. It was sitting on seventeen-inch all-gold Daytons that matched the car's peanut-butter interior and gold trim. And Kewy Kev's stereo system was off the chain as well. Without a doubt, Kewy Kev had the cleanest ride on the scene every weekend. Bria loved to be seen inside that car, especially when the top was down and the system was booming. They would joyride for hours, driving around the city aimlessly.

Tonight, Kewy Kev had the top down, and everybody was out

and about. The weather had finally cleared, and for the first time in a long time, the stars were visible.

"What do you want outta here?" Kewy Kev asked.

"Get me a cheesesteak with fried onions, mayonnaise, ketchup, and salt and pepper. And get some cheese fries and a Pepsi," Bria told him.

Kewy Kev climbed out of the car, and Bria caressed his behind. She loved herself some Kewy Kev. And so did a lot of other girls she knew. She had already gotten into four fights over him, but that was okay, because he was worth fighting for. Kewy Kev had the dreamiest brownish-green eyes a girl could ever imagine. She loved it when he sat between her legs while she cornrowed his long hair, and he'd stare up at her with those damn emeralds he called eyes. And those lips of his were the sexiest lips she'd ever come across. She loved to suck on them. They felt like orange slices in her mouth. She was getting wet from thinking about how fine and how cute he was.

"Hey, Bria!"

She turned to see who was calling her. A car filled with football players from her high school pulled into the parking lot next to her.

"What's up, baby?" one of them, a guy named Tommy, asked her. "When you gonna drop that half-breed zero and get with this hero?"

"When that hero gets his own car and stops riding in the back seat of somebody else's."

"Oh, it's like that, huh?" Troy asked.

"Troy, you not even riding shotgun yet. You still back seat, right passenger-side window."

The rest of the guys in the car started clowning Troy.

"Bria, you fine as hell," the driver told her.

"Marcus, don't even start, 'cause you know me and Stephanie is friends. I'll tell her everything you say to me."

"Girl, why you tripping?" Marcus asked.

"Where's Brianna's fine ass?" J-Roc asked.

Bria shrugged. "I don't know. What I look like, her keeper or something?"

"Here comes your busted-ass nigga!" Troy told her. "You need to come and get some of this pure Black Mandingo and leave those Vienna sausages alone!"

The boys cranked up their car and pulled away laughing. Kewy Kev returned and passed Bria her food. "What the hell they talking about?"

Bria shrugged. "Nothing, as usual."

Kewy Kev climbed into his car and closed the door. Bria opened her food and began eating.

"Bria, right?"

Bria peered up from her sandwich. She'd never seen his face before. And he was way too old to be in high school. "Do I know you?"

"No, but you know the person I'm looking for," Terrell told her.

"Do I look like the Yellow Pages to you?" Bria asked, craning her neck.

"Cute." Terrell smiled. "Real cute." He pulled out the picture of Gena and held it up. "Where's your cousin?"

Bria's eyes flew open wide. Instantly, she realized this was the man who'd hurt her grandmother. "I don't know where she is!"

"Say, man! Go on with all that bullshit!" Kewy Kev said forcefully. "Can't you see we eating?"

"I wasn't talking to you," Terrell told him.

"Yeah, well, I was talking to you!" Kewy Kev opened his door and started to climb out of the car.

Terrell pulled out a handgun and shot Kewy Kev in the groin. The sound of gunfire caused pandemonium, and people began to flee.

Terrell grabbed a screaming Bria by her hair and pulled her face closer to Gena's picture. "Where is she?"

"I don't know!" Bria shouted. "I haven't seen her but once since she moved out!"

"Where did she move to?"

"I don't know! I think she moved in with her friend!"

"What friend? Give me a name."

"Markita!" Bria shouted. "Her friend Markita!"

Terrell let go of her hair. "Are you lying to me?" He pointed his weapon at a squirming, crying Kewy Kev.

Bria leaned over and shielded her man from the gun. "No! I'm not lying! She moved in with her friend!"

Terrell nodded and tucked his gun away. He could hear the faint sound of sirens in the distance. "If you're lying to me, I'll find you, and next time, it'll be you I bend over and fuck like there's no tomorrow. You understand me?"

Bria nodded, scared as all back doors as she looked into the eyes of a madman.

Terrell leaned over and stuck his tongue into her mouth for several seconds before rushing to his car and peeling away.

Gena rose to her feet and looked around the hotel suite she'd been staying in now for the past several weeks. After her visit to the hospital to see Gah Git, Gena had decided it was best not to go anywhere near her family or anyone else she cared about. She walked into the bathroom and turned on the sink. She looked at herself in the mirror. *Today is the big day, no turning back,* she thought as she splashed some water across her face and reached for a washrag.

Gena showered and dressed, packed up a small bag, and left the room. A continental breakfast was being served in the hotel's lobby, but Gena would have to pass on that. *I wish I could have something to drink. My mouth is so dry,* she thought, knowing food and water were out of the question.

Gena made her way out to the parking lot where she'd parked the Mazda rental. She got into the car, exited the lot, and drove over to Thirty-Eighth and Lancaster. Across the street from a bar was a women's health clinic. She looked at her watch. It was 8:42 in the morning; her appointment was scheduled for nine. *Are you ready?* She couldn't help but ask herself this question. Her mind roamed constantly as she parked the car and walked into the clinic.

"Hi. Your name?" the receptionist behind the counter inquired.

"Gena Scott. I have a nine o'clock appointment," Gena said.

"Okay, here you go. Have a seat and fill these papers out. Make sure you sign the bottom of each form where indicated."

After Gena completed the forms and gave them to the receptionist, she went back to her seat. Minutes later her name was called, and she followed a woman to the second floor of the clinic.

"Have you eaten or had anything to drink since midnight last night?" the woman asked.

"No," Gena responded.

She put Gena in an examination room and took her weight, blood pressure, and temperature. She asked her one hundred and one questions and finally told her to undress and put on a hospital gown. She said the doctor would be in shortly, and then she left the room.

Gena lay on the table and rubbed her belly. She thought of having a baby, and the thought alone scared her half to death. Then she thought of her grandmother. Gah Git would cry a hundred and one tears if she knew Gena was having an abortion. She thought of Jerrell and the times they did have sex. She thought of the night he tried to kill her and realized she'd been tricked by a horrible monster. Then she thought of Quadir.

If I have Jerrell's baby, there's no chance, no chance at all, he'll ever be with me again. He'd only hate me even more.

Gena realized that if she had a baby by Jerrell Jackson, she could kiss Quadir Richards goodbye. *He's mad enough at the fact that I was messing with Jerrell—to have his baby, no way.* No, Gena knew she was doing the right thing. She only wished it was over.

Dr. Amerson entered the room and sat down at the end of the

table Gena was lying on. Quickly, she went through a series of questions, basically the same questions Gena had already answered. Then she asked her if she was ready.

"Yes, yes, I am."

Dr. Amerson explained the procedure and attempted to make her feel comfortable with the knowledge of what would be happening. Once the procedure was completed, she'd be moved into a room and placed on a recliner, where she'd have to stay for at least two hours before she'd be permitted to leave. The anesthetic would make her drowsy, and the rule was she'd have to call a cab to come and get her. Her intention was to have the cab take her around the block and right back across the street to her car. She had to be careful driving, but she wasn't going far. Her plan was to have the abortion and then go check into the Sheraton Hotel on Thirty-Eighth and Chestnut, a few blocks away. She could make it there.

A nurse entered the room with a needle and a small bottle. Dr. Amerson explained they were going to mildly sedate her. She wouldn't be asleep during the procedure, but she wouldn't feel anything. Gena turned her head away, not wanting to watch as the nurse injected the sedative into her bloodstream.

Gena began to feel light, as if lying on a cloud. She looked around the room, and it was like an angel had appeared right in front of her.

"Sahirah?"

And like that, the angel was gone.

"Okay, I'm going to lift your feet and place them in the stirrups. I'm going to insert my fingers. Okay, Gena? I want to examine your uterus before we get started." She could hear Dr. Amerson's voice.

"Dr. Amerson, I don't know if I should go through with it."

"Gena, give me one minute."

"Is everything okay?"

"Well, everything seems to be okay, but . . . Nurse, please hand me her chart and prep the sonogram machine."

"What, what's the matter?" Gena was in a state of semiconsciousness.

"Gena, your uterus feels normal. Let me finish examining you, okay? Now, let me see. You were here three weeks ago, right? Yes, and you were six weeks pregnant. Let me count and make sure. Yes, you were here and you were definitely pregnant." Dr. Amerson turned on the monitor of the sonogram machine, only to find Gena's uterus was intact. She wasn't pregnant.

"Gena, I'm so sorry. You've obviously suffered a miscarriage."

Gena heard what Dr. Amerson said, and the strangest feeling of relief came over her. She didn't feel sad. She had no remorse. She was ready to celebrate. All she could think about was the possibility of winning Quadir back.

Using all her strength, Gena tried to lift herself up, but she was too groggy.

"Here, here, it's okay. I got you." Dr. Amerson helped her off the table. "Let's see if we can't get you into recovery, and you can wait there for the anesthetic to wear off."

"Do you believe this? Isn't this the most wonderful news?" Gena started crying. "You don't know what this means for me."

This was probably the only thing Gena knew for sure. Maybe, just maybe anyone else's, but Jerrell's child—for Quadir to have to look after that baby was the last thing on this earth that would ever have happened, and Gena knew it.

"It means you don't have to have an abortion," the nurse answered. "Come on, we have crackers and juice. Surely you're hungry. Come on, hold on to me and I'll get you situated."

Gena held on to the nurse and followed her into recovery. She lay on a recliner and was given a blanket. Within minutes, Gena nodded off to sleep.

Wires

Dick Davis rushed through the halls of the police department like a schoolboy who'd received his first kiss. His smile was uncontrollable, and he pushed aside police officer after police officer, making his way back to his partner's desk. His excitement was electric.

"What?" Sergeant Ellington asked, peering up from her desk. Her partner's smile made her smile. It was infectious.

Davis held up a cassette tape. "Hot off the presses! I just came from the recording room. Guess what our wiretaps intercepted?"

"What?"

"She's leaving!" Davis told her giddily. "She blowing town! Which means?"

"She's got to get the money." Ellington stood and grabbed her purse. "How soon do you think she's leaving?"

"Who knows. You figure she's probably got to tie up a few loose ends, but trust me, she won't leave that money behind. If she's got it, then it *will* be going with her."

"Call Cornell and fill him in," Ellington told him. "Do we have anybody tailing her right now?"

Davis shook his head. "Nah, not that I'm aware of."

"We need someone on her twenty-four seven from now on." Ellington threw her purse onto her shoulder. "I'm going to see Mark and let him know."

"You want me to have narcotics put a tail on her?"

Ellington shook her head. "Those guys are idiots. They all think they're on *Miami Vice* or something. She'll spot them a million miles away. We'll all have to take turns tailing her."

Davis nodded and lifted the telephone. Ellington strutted down the hall to see her boss, Lieutenant Mark Ratzinger. She knocked on his door.

"In!" Ratzinger shouted.

Ellington pranced into his office and plopped down in the chair opposite his desk.

"What's up, Toya?"

"We got her."

Ratzinger lifted his head from his paperwork. "Her? As in *her*?"

Ellington nodded. "Miss Money Bags. She's trying to skip town."

Ratzinger lifted his telephone without saying another word to Ellington. "Hey, Sammy, this is Mark over in Narcotics. I need you to put a tail on a suspect for me." Ratzinger lifted a paper from his desk. "Gena Scott. License plate Sierra, Charlie, Alpha, six, five, six. Keep the tail loose; this is a priority suspect. And if you can, give me details of all her stops. Thanks, Sammy."

"You really want those guys in on this?" Ellington asked.

Ratzinger shrugged. "They're only going to follow her. Every time she stops, they'll call me, and I'll call you. Get out in the streets and be ready for my call."

Ellington nodded.

"Anybody call Cleaver yet?"

"Dickie's doing it now."

Ratzinger shook his head. "I don't trust that guy. I realize he's your ex-partner, but there's something about him."

Ellington nodded. "He's one to be watched closely."

"I want this one controlled. No coming back on us."

Ellington nodded.

"I want you to handle it. Handle *everything*, you understand?" Ratzinger asked, wondering if Ellington had gotten his point.

"I'll put a hole in the little cunt's forehead myself."

Ratzinger nodded. "Good." *She got my point*, he thought.

Ellington rose and hurried out of the room.

Ratzinger sipped from his cup of warm coffee, then rubbed his tired eyes. He couldn't believe things were finally coming together. He shifted through the papers on his desk until he found his boating magazine. He turned to the classified pages in the back and stared at the boat he'd been dreaming about since the current issue came out. He could see himself retired, sailing off the shores of Cape Cod in the four-hundred-thousand-dollar beauty. He was one or two days away from having the money to leave this shit behind, one or two days away from having the money for his dream boat. He couldn't wait.

Ellington rushed out of the police station and climbed into her car. Davis was right on her heels. As soon as he hopped inside, they were on their way. Neither paid any attention to the gray van parked in the corner of the police station parking lot.

"I can't believe you!" Agent Phil Covington shouted, tossing his headset onto the console. "We're dead! We are so dead! Galvani is going to fire us and then kill us!"

"He's not going to fire us," Agent Josh Harbinger replied. "Lavon, tell him."

"He's not going to fire you," Agent Lavon Stokes said flatly without peering up from her computer.

"Yeah, right! He's going to fire us all, and then he's going to shoot us, and then he's going to throw us in jail!"

"He's not going to throw us in jail," Josh told him with a smile.

"He didn't authorize this! There's no way you can get me to believe Galvani authorized this!" Phil said hysterically.

"Authorized what?" Josh smiled.

"Josh! You bugged a police station! Jesus! You bugged a lieutenant's office! A lieutenant who happens to oversee the Vice squad!"

"A dirty lieutenant, I remind you," Josh retorted.

"We wouldn't have known unless we bugged him!" Phil threw himself back in his chair. "Josh, we're in so much trouble. We've broken so many statutes, it isn't funny! And you brought me along! How could you have done this to me!"

Josh patted Phil on the shoulder. "Relax, Phil. You're going to be a hero. Tell him, Lavon."

"You're going to be a hero," Lavon said flatly, again without peering up from her computer.

"See, Lavon sees the big picture," Josh told him. "We've got them on conspiracy to commit extortion, murder, robbery, and about a half dozen other criminal statutes."

"Oh, God, what am I going to tell my mother when I get fired?" Phil lamented.

"You're not getting fired," Josh told him; then he added, "Lavon."

"You're not getting fired," she said as flatly as she had before, still focused on her computer screen.

"Do you think they get care packages in Terre Haute federal prison?" Phil asked.

"Yes, but you're not going to Terre Haute," Josh told him. "We're sending *those* assholes to federal prison. We need backup. Lavon, you get that license plate number?"

"Sure did."

"Call Rich and tell him to tail her. No, change that. Tell him to tail *them*. We want to catch them when they're making their move. If they see a tail on her, they may back off. Let him know that it's cops he's tailing, so hang back and be on his p's and q's."

"I can't believe you bugged the police department," Phil whined.

"Phil, we're going to save this girl and put away a bunch of crooked cops. See, I told you that bastard Cleaver was dirty!"

Lavon nodded. "You did say that."

"Did you at least get a judge to sign off on the wiretaps?" Phil asked.

Josh smiled deviously, looking like Brad Pitt's twin. "I did."

Phil shook his head. "No, no you didn't. Josh, please tell me you didn't."

Josh nodded. "I did."

"You got my father to sign off on the warrant?" Phil asked incredulously.

Josh nodded and smiled. "I did. Your father is a federal magistrate."

"This whole thing is bordering on illegal. Christ, I'm going to spend the rest of my life in a federal penitentiary," Phil whined.

"Improper, not illegal," Josh corrected. "Lavon, we need to get this tape in front of a grand jury pronto. Who's the best deputy United States district attorney to get this to?"

"Watts, I'd say, seeing as how this thing was so fast and loose."

"Can you get this over to Watts for me?"

Lavon exhaled. "Why did I know you were going to say that?"

Josh kissed her on her cheek. "I got to go and smooth things out with Galvani. Get him on board."

Phil shook his head. "Galvani's going to kill you."

"We're heroes, Phil. Relax."

"What am I supposed to do in the meantime?"

"Check with the guys in the van over at Philly PD's headquarters."

"Another van? You got another van? You brought more guys in on this thing? Who'd you bug over there, the chief of police?"

Josh smiled. "Cleaver's office."

"You bugged Internal Affairs?" Phil exhaled. "We're dead."

"We're FBI agents, and we're going to put those crooked sons a bitches away for good!" Josh reassured him. He fixed his collar and climbed out of the surveillance van. "Phil."

"What?"

"Smile."

Hold Me Down

H ello?"

"Hey, Gena, this is Rik. What's up?"

"Hey, Rik! How ya doing?"

"Trying to make it, but it's hard, lil' mama."

"Shit, you telling me. My whole life has been turned upside down this last month. Really, since Qua—"

"I miss that nigga, too. Qua was my boy."

Silence fell for several seconds as Gena thought of yesteryears and Rik thought of what to say next.

"Hey, Gena. I need to talk to you about something."

"What's up?"

"When I was locked up, you offered to hook your boy up with a little something-something."

"Yeah."

"When I got knocked, they found everything. And everything wasn't mine. I owed some people. And the people I owe aren't a very understanding bunch. They came to see me, and they let me know what was going to happen if they don't get they bread."

"Damn. I'm sorry to hear that. Rik, I'm here for you."

"I was hoping you'd say that. I need to get these guys off my back and then come up. Gena, it won't take long for me to get back on my feet."

"I realize you're a hustler, boy."

"Can you do something for me?"

"What you talking?"

"A half a ticket, no more. I can get it all back to you in a couple months. Say four months at the latest."

"That's a lot of bread, Rik. Besides, I wasn't planning on being around here four months from now."

Damn, bitch, a month ago you had two mil to get me out of jail. Now a half is a problem? Rik couldn't help his greed, but he didn't want it to show. "Gena, this is your boy. I'm good for it. And even if you ain't around here, planes fly. I'll take it to wherever you at."

"Damn, why now?" *How the hell am I going to get the money and get it to him and do everything else I need to do before I fly the chicken coop?*

"Gena, you're the only person I can turn to. They gonna kill me and my whole family if I don't pay them."

"All right. I'll get it to you. But you gonna have to meet me today."

"No problem. Tell me when and where."

"Urn, let me think." Gena thought of all she had to do and the places she had to go. "Okay, I'll call you when I'm ready."

"Cool. Thanks, baby."

"Talk to you later."

"Bye."

"Later."

Quadir strolled across the patio and seated himself on a recliner near the pool. The maid had set him a tall glass of ice-cold lemonade out by the pool, and he wanted to take in the sunset and relax. He had a lot on his mind, a lot of things he had to make sense of.

He couldn't help replaying his last conversation with Gena before she snuck out to only God knew where. In a way, it was his fault. Maybe if he'd stopped her when he first had the chance at the apartment building that night, she would never have gotten onto the highway, never have stopped at that gas station, and never have met Jerrell. *Damn, he was really going to kill her.*

She'd gotten caught up in something completely beyond her control. He thought back to New Year's Eve and the night he was gunned down, the night he almost died. He remembered how scared she looked, how broken she was, how her tears and screams for him flew freely out of her. He could hear her voice begging him not to leave her, begging him to hold on, begging him not to die. She hadn't asked for him to be shot, and she hadn't asked for him to die before her eyes. It wasn't her fault she was forced out onto the street, forced to survive without him, without anything, and forced to make something out of nothing. She was playing the cards she was dealt. And now it seemed like she'd been dealt the losing hand.

"Hey, you okay? You always seem like you're miles away," Amelia said as she bent and kissed Quadir on the side of his face.

"Yeah, I'm fine. What are you doing here? Aren't you supposed to be at the hospital?"

"Would you believe I have the afternoon off? Go figure. There was a mix-up with the schedules. So I have an entire day to play house with you," she said, unable to control her smile as she sat on his lap, straddling him like a pony.

"Wow," Quadir said, never once taking his mind off Gena's situation. He pulled Amelia closer to him and kissed her lips.

"Oh, and did you hear what happened?"

"No, what?"

"Haven't you heard the news?"

"Yeah . . ."

"I overheard my colleagues talking about an elderly woman who'd been beaten and raped. She underwent surgery and was placed in ICU. They asked me to look at her chart and check on her. Which I did. I looked in on her, and it turned out the elderly woman is Gena's grandmother."

"Really?" Quadir gave her his full attention. He'd had absolutely no idea the family on the news was Gena's.

Amelia shrugged. "She suffered some pretty traumatic injuries. She's having a lot of complications."

Quadir gently pushed Amelia off him so that he could stand up. "What type of injuries?"

Amelia shook her head and looked down. "She was raped, Quadir, brutally raped and brutally beaten. She has all kinds of injuries, from internal bleeding to a concussion."

"I didn't hear all that on the news. She was raped?"

"Yes, and beaten."

"Damn, I can't believe it," he said as he began to pace up and down the patio.

"I thought you heard the news."

"Yeah, but I wasn't paying attention."

How can you pay attention to anything when all you do is daydream about Gena and your hidden treasure?

"Do the police know anything? Did they get the bastard who did it?"

Amelia shook her head. "No suspects, from what I hear."

"Raped. That's crazy, right?"

"Sick, really sick," Amelia agreed.

Quadir shook his head. "She's an old woman. Who in the fuck would do that to an old woman?"

"A sick and crazy man," Amelia whispered. "There was also the grandson, Gary Scott. He's the one who tried to protect her, but the rapist shot him in the stomach. So I checked in on him also."

"How's he doing?"

"He'll live, but he's going to need multiple surgeries. He was shot in the stomach; his lower intestine is useless for now. He'll probably wear a bag for the rest of his life unless surgery can correct it."

"A shit bag?"

"Um, yeah, if that's what you want to call it. Then there's another granddaughter, Bria Scott, who was assaulted by this same guy. The police brought the girl into the ER. I saw her, but I didn't treat her."

"Well, what happened?"

"Apparently this rapist guy felt her up and kissed her on the mouth after shooting her date, who was also brought into the ER, but he died on the operating table. I think his name was Kevin Coffield. Police had the medics swab the girlfriend's tongue for DNA at the crime scene. I guess they checked it against the DNA taken from the grandmother and got a match."

"Damn, that's crazy." Quadir was thinking things over. "No wonder I can't find Gena. I bet she's scared to death."

"Yeah, she probably thinks it's you coming after your money. I'm sure she's avoiding you like the plague."

"Why would you say something like that?" Quadir asked, taking offense.

"Gosh, I'm saying, she was here, realized you were alive, and not only have you moved on, but you want your money back. She leaves out the window and never returns. She hasn't come back or made any contact. She has your money and I'm sure she realizes you want it. Meanwhile, someone attacks her grandmother and her cousins, allegedly looking for her. In her mind, who else would be looking for her except you? Technically, that's correct, since you do that very thing every single day and night."

Quadir completely ignored her sarcasm. "So it's not random?"

Amelia shook her head. "Some animal is fucking with them." Amelia nodded solemnly. "And he's after Gena."

"Maybe he's not after Gena. Maybe you just think that." Quadir hoped Amelia didn't know what she was talking about.

"Well, after I heard my colleagues talking about the family of patients they'd treated, I spoke to a friend of mine who is a detective at the Thirty-First Precinct. She told me that, in both incidents, the rapist was looking for Gena."

"Somebody's after Gena? What the fuck for?"

Amelia lifted an eyebrow as if stating the obvious. Quadir nodded once his mind caught up.

"They want my money!"

"Bingo!"

"Jesus, that fucking money! Talk about more money, more problems. Somebody's after my money!"

"Your money and God only knows what else," Amelia said as she rubbed Quadir's arm. "She's in danger."

Amelia lifted her shirt over the top of her head to reveal a stunning two-piece.

"And the police are probably trailing her ass four cars deep trying to catch this guy."

"They don't know where she is, Qua. She's disappeared, gone underground."

Quadir sat down and leaned back on the sofa. His mind was trying to process all the information.

"The police can't find her, but I bet if there's one person who could find her, it's you," Amelia said softly before kissing his cheek, then jumping into the swimming pool for a couple of laps.

I can't believe someone hurt her grandmother. That's some sick shit. Not only was her grandmother attacked, but her cousin Gary had also been shot. Not to mention the attack on Bria's boyfriend, and the police had said they were all related. They hadn't released the motive and claimed they had no clues as to who the assailant was.

Quadir remembered the reporter also indicated the family had refused to cooperate with the police, giving them very little information to go on. There was a lot going on, too much going on. *I wonder if Gah Git is going to be okay.* Quadir knew how much Gena loved her grandmother. Gah Git was all Gena had for most of her life. Their recent conversation had been a good one at first; he'd learned so much about what she felt, about what she'd gone through. She still loved him and that gave him added comfort even though they weren't together.

"Why are you still sitting here? It's getting dark," Amelia said as she emerged from the pool. She tied a towel around her narrow waist and ventured toward him. Quadir watched her the entire way.

Amelia's body was banging. She had the perfect frame, the perfect ass, the perfect-size breasts, and perfect-size legs, but her feet were the most beautiful feet Quadir had ever seen in his life. Amelia was toned and firm, the product of a dedicated diet and exercise routine. Not to mention she was beautiful, even more so than Gena, and Gena had been his dream. Amelia had the most beautiful face he'd ever seen, along with a head full of brains. She was a winner in anybody's book, a twenty on a scale of one to ten. And yet, he found himself torn between his feelings for her and his feelings for Gena.

"What's the matter?" Amelia asked, sliding onto the sofa with him.

Quadir shook his head. "You know what's the matter."

"Money, police, Gena, crazy rapists on the loose. What else?"

What else is there? he couldn't help thinking but didn't say a word.

Amelia rose from the sofa. "My offer still stands, Qua. You can forget about the money. We can take my money, and I'll move with you wherever you want me to. You can go back to school, you can open a business, you can do whatever the fuck you want to."

"I have to love you."

"That's all I'll ever ask. Love me, baby. I don't need anything else."

That's it! Leave the money, leave everything, and go with Amelia. The offer was tempting, and it wasn't the first time Amelia had thrown it out there. But Quadir couldn't accept it. He couldn't accept abandoning his fortune, with the thought of Gena having his money for God knows who to spend it. It didn't sit right with him. Fair was fair, and while she might have found it, he hadn't given it to her. She took it. And he was determined to get it back.

Amelia turned to leave him deep in his money schemes and thoughts of Gena, but Quadir wouldn't let her get away that easily. He yanked the towel from around her waist and examined her voluptuous curves. The sight of her slim waist, full hips, and perfectly round ass gave him an instant erection. He quickly leaped up and clasped her wrist.

"You don't need nothing else?" Quadir gestured, pulling her close to him so she could feel the bulge in his shorts.

"Well, I do need one more thing, daddy . . . please," Amelia said in a sexy, whispering, moaning sort of way as she leaned into his ear. Amelia shoved Quadir back onto the couch and yanked his shorts down to his ankles. "Hmm. Somebody is excited."

Quadir grabbed his meat and stroked it a few times.

"Gimme that," she said as she moved her string bikini to the side and climbed on top of him. *I bet you ain't thinking about her now.* Quadir wanted to explode as soon as he felt her insides wrap around his dick, pulling at it with each stroke. He leaned back, gripped her ass, spread her cheeks apart, and held on for the ride.

Big Pimpin'

Gena had planned her day very carefully. It took much planning, and a little help from her family, to make things work. She hoped Brianna had planted the car in the right spot and that Bria had handled her part. If they had, things would go smoothly, or at least that's what she was praying for.

Gena parked her car and strolled into the mall, hoping that, whoever her pursuers were, they would see her and wait in the parking lot for her to come out. Her plan depended on it.

Gena rushed through the shopping mall and into the department store where Bria worked. She made her way through the store to the junior miss department, her cousin's department. Gena spied Bria behind the counter helping a customer. She made eye contact and then stopped and pretended to be browsing through some dresses. Gena tried her darndest but couldn't tell one way or the other if she'd been followed into the Gallery.

Bria finished up with her customer, then grabbed a dress and some shoes she had held behind the counter. She also grabbed a large straw sun hat, a large handbag, and some sunglasses, and headed for the women's changing area. Gena continued to browse through the department's offerings until Bria returned to her counter and gave her a nod. Gena turned and headed for the dressing area.

Inside the dressing area, Gena walked from stall to stall, opening each door until she found the clothing Bria had left for her. Once she found the right stall, she stepped inside, locked the door, and changed clothes.

The clothing change took less than four minutes. She turned and examined herself in the mirror. She looked completely different. It was perfect. Now she needed the last touch. She headed out of the dressing room, through the department store, and out into the mall. Bria had removed all the security tags for her, so she made it safely through the store's theft detectors.

Inside the mall, Gena headed to her second stop, a large wig and beauty supply store. She knew exactly which wig she was looking for. It was the one with long braids.

Gena paid for the wig, walked to the mirror, placed it on her head, and adjusted it until it was right. Once she was satisfied, she placed her large straw hat on her head and adjusted that too. Next came the sunglasses. Her entire getup was perfect. No one could possibly recognize her. *Shit, I can't even recognize myself.*

Gena headed for a mall exit opposite the entrance she'd come in. She strolled through the parking lot to a designated parking spot. The car was there, exactly as they'd planned. Brianna was on her job. A beige Ford Taurus Brianna had rented the day before was sitting in the parking space with the doors unlocked. Gena climbed inside, lifted the floor mat, and found the key. She stuck the key in the ignition and started the car.

"You muthafuckas ain't the only ones who can pull some double-oh-seven shit!" Gena said with a smile. "Shit, fuckin' dead-ass Quadir following me around, like he's fucking crazy. We'll see who's crazy, though. We'll see."

She backed the car out of the parking space and headed for her first destination, checking her rearview mirror the entire way. Her plan had worked perfectly; no one had followed her.

Gena's first stop was the Sovereign Bank on Twentieth and Market Streets in downtown Center City. This was where she'd rented the safety deposit box and stashed half a million in jewelry. She waited patiently for about twenty minutes before a representative was able to help her. Finally, she was led in through a doorway to the back of the bank. She was seated in a tiny room, where her safety deposit box was waiting for her.

"You have your key?" asked the woman who had assisted her.

"Oh, yeah, it's right here."

Gena waited for the lady to close the door before she slowly unlocked and opened the safety deposit box. It was all there: the 10 carat diamond engagement ring Quadir had proposed to her with; the cluster diamond ring; the birthday charm bracelet Quadir had given her on the night he threw her party; her diamond initial G pin that Rik and Lita had given her; two Rolexes; one Ebel; one Omega; one Cartier; two gold Gucci watches; one stainless steel and 18k gold Movado; four tennis bracelets; 2 carat diamond earrings; fifteen pairs of gold earrings; and a slew of gold necklaces and bracelets. She removed all her jewelry and carefully placed each piece side by side as she examined it all carefully. Out of everything in the safety deposit box, there was only one thing she wanted: her 10 carat diamond engagement ring. She slipped the ring on her finger and placed everything else back in the safety deposit box. She closed the lid and locked it.

Her next stop was Thirtieth Street Station. She pulled up in front of the train station, parking her car at the Market Street side entrance. She took out two suitcases from her trunk and walked through the doors of the station. She took the escalator down to a lower level where the lockers were located. She looked around and peered back up the escalator to be sure no one was following her. The coast was clear.

Gena strolled down the row of lockers until she came to hers—

405. She inserted the key, opened the door, and looked inside. Her small bundle was sitting as she had left it. She opened the suitcase, pulled the bag from the locker, and neatly placed it in the suitcase. Lockers 405, 406, 407, 408 all held her secret stash, which totaled a little under $17 million. Once she was done removing the money from each of the lockers and placing it in the suitcases, she walked back down the hall, back up the escalator, and out the side door, carrying with her some $17 million in cold, hard cash.

"Whew, that was crazy," she said once she was in the safety of her car. She looked around as she pulled out of her parking space, careful that she wasn't being followed. This was the most dangerous part of all. For the first time since she'd found it, the money was all going to be in one place again.

Her destination was 4-U Self Storage, where she could safely count the money she needed for Rik and the money she needed for her great escape, then tuck the rest away in a secure hiding place. She pulled up in front of the storage unit and used her key to open the lock. Inside were the contents of her house, which she had placed in storage after Viola threw her out into the street. She looked around at all her old furnishings and thought of the life she'd once shared with Quadir. She went outside to the car and got the suitcases out of the trunk. She brought them inside the storage unit and closed the door behind her. She looked at the bags of money staring at her and thought of all the trouble the money had caused. *It's not worth it; you're not worth it.*

She quickly counted out the money she needed, the five hundred thousand she planned on giving to Rik. Then she counted out the money she'd take with her. *This is my new-start-at-life money.* Her plan was simple: she'd take only what she'd need to relocate herself. She'd decided the rest of the money would be safer there, tucked away in the storage unit, than with her.

C.R.E.A.M.

Detective Cleaver stormed up to the table. "How the fuck could you lose her?"

Dick Davis peered up at him. "What?"

"Rosco P. Coltrane couldn't have fucked this one up! My one-eyed, one-legged grandmother could've kept up with her! She was at a fucking shopping mall!"

Davis rose from the table. Ellington grabbed him.

"You don't know what the fuck you're talking about, asshole!" Davis told Cleaver. "You don't fucking know me! You don't know shit about me!"

"Inspector Clouseau could've done a better job of keeping up with that bimbo!" Cleaver shot back.

"He wasn't on her," Ratzinger told him.

"What?"

"None of my people were on her," Ratzinger repeated. "I had Narcotics trailing her."

"What?" Cleaver shouted. "You had those bumbling idiots shadowing her? They couldn't keep up with their dicks if they weren't attached to their fucking bodies!"

"We needed their manpower and resources," Ratzinger told him.

"Dammit, Ratzinger! I thought we were all in agreement on this. No mistakes, and we keep this as tight as possible!"

"Narcs don't know shit. All they were told was to trail her, and to call me at each stop."

"And she happened to lose you at her first stop." Cleaver shook his head. "Brilliant, fucking brilliant. She turned into James fucking Bond and made you look like Gomer fucking Pyle."

"Watch yourself, Detective," Ratzinger said sternly.

"Our money disappeared, Lieutenant."

"Guys, can we put away some of the testosterone here?" Ellington remarked. "This bickering is getting us nowhere. The broad pulled a fast one on us. She thinks she's fucking Harry Houdini, so now we gotta be who we are. We're detectives, so now it's time to hit the street and act like detectives. We find this bitch, and this time we make sure she doesn't get away from us, that's all."

"We watch her twenty-four seven," Davis added.

Ellington shook her head. "Naw, we're putting cuffs on this bitch when we find her this time."

"What are we going to charge her with?" Davis asked.

"How about naming her as a suspect in the shooting of her little boyfriend?" Ellington smiled.

"What?" Cleaver was shocked. "What the hell are you talking about, Toya?"

"Her little boyfriend, Jerrell Jackson, was blasted in a motel about a month ago," Ellington explained. "The room was trashed like there had been a struggle and Miss Scott's prints were all over the place."

"How come nobody said anything about this before?" Cleaver asked.

"Why hasn't Homicide swooped on her?" Ratzinger asked.

"I dug this up only recently. A friend of mine over in Homicide confirmed everything for me this morning," Ellington told them.

"They haven't swooped on her yet because they can't find her. Oh, by the way, she's not a suspect. She's a person of high interest."

"She's not a suspect?" Davis asked incredulously.

Ellington shook her head. "Apparently Homicide is of the opinion that if by some miracle she did do him, it was self-defense. Her blood was all over the room. Her skin was beneath his fingernails, and the victim had bite marks and scratch marks everywhere. And the kicker is, he or she—and they are guessing he—had rope, cement, acid, chains, and all kinds of macabre shit tucked away in the bathroom."

"Jesus!" Cleaver leaned back and tossed down a drink.

"Evidence suggests he was going to torture her, kill her, and dispose of her body," Ellington told them.

"Torture her? Why torture her?" Davis asked.

"Information," Ratzinger said.

"Information?" Davis lifted an eyebrow.

"He was going to torture her and get her to give up the location of the money," Cleaver said. "Jesus. How many others are after this damn money? This thing's becoming a fucking race to the finish. Like a damn hunt for buried treasure or something."

"We can't put out an all-points bulletin on her; that's Homicide's job," Ratzinger explained. "People will wonder why Vice is putting out an APB for a homicide. It'll raise too many eyebrows. I'll be getting all kinds of calls from Homicide, from the captain, from everywhere."

Cleaver nodded. "I agree. And we can't alert patrol because they'll want to know why she's wanted. We have to get out in the streets ourselves."

"We could try to smoke her out," Ratzinger suggested.

"How?" Davis asked.

"Press her grandmother."

"She's in the hospital," Ellington said.

"What for?" Ratzinger asked.

Ellington shook her head. "Another surprise. A gentleman showed up at her door looking for Gena. When they wouldn't, or couldn't, tell him where she was, he shot a cousin, beat the grandmother and then raped her."

Cleaver leaned forward. "Raped her?"

Ellington nodded.

Cleaver threw down another drink. "Jesus!"

"Someone else looking for the money?" Ratzinger questioned.

"You think?"

"You don't rape an old woman for kicks," Ratzinger said. "He did it to send a message. He did it to smoke her out."

"How many other people are searching for this girl and this god-damn money?" Cleaver asked. "It'll be like a damn madhouse when someone does find her. Hell, it'll probably be the biggest shootout since D-Day!"

"Sounds like Miss Gena's days are numbered," Ellington observed.

At the Philadelphia federal building on Sixth and Market Streets in Center City, Agents Phil Covington and Josh Harbinger stood at attention in front of the desk of Special Agent in Charge Rudy Galvani. The SAIC leafed through a small stack of papers with a deep scowl embedded in his face. Finally, he peered up at his agents.

"You bugged the office of a Vice lieutenant, two detectives, and an Internal Affairs detective, and you did it without my authorization?" Galvani asked.

"Sir, I thought I had your consent."

"And what exactly made you think you had my consent, Agent Harbinger?"

"You gave me permission to see what I could dig up, sir."

"Do you know what professional courtesy is, Agent Harbinger? When we conduct an operation of this nature, it's professional courtesy to notify the chief of police, and perhaps the local district attorney."

"Sir, the primary target of the operation is a detective in the Philadelphia Police Department's Office of Internal Affairs. I didn't know how many others were involved; in fact, I still don't. Sir, what we've uncovered so far involves murder—"

Galvani held up his hand, silencing his agent. "I can read. The problem I have with this operation, *Josh*, is that I signed off on none of it. You pulled in other field agents, redirected Bureau resources, retasked Bureau assets, and ran roughshod over standard operational procedures. Those procedures are in place for a reason, Agent Harbinger."

"Please consider all the evidence. They're dirty, sir, and they're planning on killing an innocent girl for money."

SAIC Galvani sat and stared at his young agent for several moments before leaning back in his seat and waving his hand toward the chairs in front of him. "Okay, numb nuts, let's hear it."

A smile spread across Josh's face as he seated himself. Phil wiped away the beads of sweat on his forehead and quickly plopped down into his seat.

"We've got them, sir," Josh said excitedly. "We have recordings of a couple of different conversations. And we've narrowed it down to this small cabal: the Vice sergeant, Cleaver, and the two Vice detectives."

"And you knew Cleaver was dirty?"

"Yes, sir."

"All this time, you've had an itch in your pants for this guy. Why?"

"Sir, when I went undercover as a police detective, he approached me several times to join him in some very questionable activities."

Galvani lifted an eyebrow. "Questionable?"

"Illegal."

Galvani lifted the file and flipped through it again. "Well, it appears you were right about him."

Josh swallowed hard and nodded.

Galvani handed the file back to Harbinger. "If you fart without permission, I'll have you reassigned to the US embassy in Sri Lanka. Do you understand me?"

Josh smiled and nodded.

"Good work, Agent Harbinger. Next time, remember who's the SAIC of this field office."

Josh rose and nodded. "Yes, sir."

Phil also rose.

Galvani lifted his phone and pressed a button. "Sylvia, get me the US attorney on the telephone, please." He turned to his agents. "You get out, and make sure you get these crooked sons a bitches off the street. You need anything, you call me. You got that?"

Josh nodded. "Yes, sir."

The speakerphone came alive. "Sir, I have United States Attorney Paul Perachetti on the line."

Galvani lifted the receiver. "Paul, how's it going? You're not going to believe what I have for you today." Galvani covered the receiver. "You two misfits, get the hell outta my office."

Josh and Phil turned and headed for the door.

"Gentlemen, one last thing," Galvani said.

They stopped and turned back to their boss.

"Don't let them kill her."

Josh nodded and headed out of the office with Phil following close behind.

"I told you he wasn't going to kill us." Josh smiled.

"So, what's next?" Phil asked.

"We make those assholes our new best friends."

"What?"

Josh stopped and turned to his partner. "They're after this money. With a couple of FBI agents hanging around, they're going to get anxious about trying to get it. They're going to be desperate to make their move, and they're going to do something careless. And when they screw up, we're going to nail their asses to the wall."

"And the girl?"

"They can't touch her with us around."

"How are we going to pull this one off?" Phil asked. "They aren't going to open their arms and allow us to hang out with them."

"We become part of the new federal Vice task force."

Phil laughed. "There's no such task force."

"That's never stopped us before. Besides, we know that, but they don't know that. Wherever they are, we will be. I want that bastard Cleaver to make his move."

G

Quadir strolled into the living room and plopped down on the couch. He'd completed an intense workout session in the gym, and yet, he still found himself stressed out. Usually working out relaxed him, but today, no matter what he tried, Gena was on his mind.

He'd always been there for her when they were together. And he always did whatever was within his power, not only for her, but also for everybody around him. Back then, he could throw money at the problem, he could send some of his boys to fix it, or he could take a quick trip out of town to unwind and relax. None of those things were within his power to do now.

Gah Git was on Gena's mind. She'd always occupied a special place in Gena's heart. Whatever was happening there would be key to making Gena's troubles go away or, at least, easing them. And Bria—whatever was going on there would probably work itself out. Teenage drama usually faded with age. And last but not least, the money. Gena had the money, and she was using it. Whatever problems she had involving money, she was certain to have fixed those by now. The only issue she could be stressing over with the money was whether to give it back. She was probably wondering what she'd do if she gave it back.

Quadir leaned back on the couch and began to massage his temples. *I wonder how Cherelle and Quanda are doing.* He'd sent his mother to Cherelle to make sure they were okay. Believe it or not, Viola was without a doubt, absolutely one hundred percent convinced Quanda was her granddaughter. And she was nothing but a skeptic, especially when it came to her son.

"Quadir, you can't really believe that girl's baby is yours," she had said when he first told her about Cherelle's baby. "She's looking for a handout. Forget about these chickenheads out there and stay focused, son."

For months and months, Viola had preached the same old sermon, until one day she decided to go off on her own and pay Cherelle a visit.

"Can I help you?" Cherelle asked, standing at the door with Quanda at her side.

"Are you Cherelle Byrd?"

"Who wants to know?" Cherelle wasn't volunteering any information.

"I'm Viola Richards, Quadir's mother. I'm looking for Cherelle Byrd."

"Oh my God. Come in, please. I'm so sorry. I didn't know who you were."

Cherelle opened the screen door for Viola and welcomed her into her first-floor row home apartment. She only had one bedroom for her and Quanda to share, but her apartment was clean, Quanda was clean, and it was clear Cherelle did the best she could do for herself and her daughter. She had a sofa and a chair and one floor lamp facing a twenty-eight-inch television sitting on a stand, a small kitchen, an even smaller dinette set, a bathroom, and a bedroom.

"I found your name and address among Quadir's personal things. I tried calling but the number was disconnected."

"I'm glad you came by here." Cherelle was all smiles, feeling a sense of acceptance for herself and her daughter from Viola. She'd yearned to be accepted ever since the birth of her daughter, not only by Quadir, but by his family as well.

"Look, Quanda. Look who's here to see you." Cherelle introduced Quanda to her grandmother.

"Hi, baby, let me take a good look at you." Viola meant that shit in every sense of the word.

Cherelle said, "This is your grandmom."

Viola stared piercingly at Cherelle, not appreciating one bit being introduced as the child's grandmother. *That fact remains to be proven.* But the more she examined the child, the more she envisioned her own son when he was a toddler.

"I'm not Grandmom, I'm Granny. You call me Granny, okay?" she said, embracing the little girl as she picked her up and placed her on her lap. "Granny is going to take you shopping and buy you all kinds of toys and clothes, and you and I are going to go to church. How's that?"

Viola looked up and saw a big smile on Cherelle's face. From that point on, there was a bond and a relationship between the two women. Cherelle got exactly what she'd always hoped for—Quadir's family's acceptance for her daughter—and Viola got what she wasn't expecting, a granddaughter. By the time Viola was done, she'd made up her mind that her grandbaby would never want for anything. From that day on, if Cherelle needed something, the Richards family had her back.

Quadir smiled as he thought of his mother, Cherelle, and his daughter spending Sunday mornings at church together. He thought of Gena, and the happy smile on his face slowly faded. He could see her now, absolutely disgusted. He could hear her, too.

Are you crazy? You let your mother throw me to the fucking wolves while she does everything in her power to make sure Cherelle and your baby are hunky-fucking-dory?

Yup, that's about how it would sound. He'd decided he'd also have to take care of Cherelle once he got his money back. And, of course, Amelia. Gena and Cherelle would both be fine, if they didn't try to live like rap stars. A million dollars was enough to buy a decent house and car. They'd have enough to pay their bills, and Gena could even finish school. She could make a nice life for herself. With a million dollars, Gena could even look out for her grandmother and the rest of her family. God knows, she wouldn't have to work. And to show how decent he was, he'd put up a million, in case she needed more later. Maybe ten or twenty years from now, he'd shoot her a second mil ticket. That should definitely hold her.

Amelia breezed through the front door.

"Hey."

"Hey yourself," she said, tossing her keys onto a Bombay chest in the foyer. She sat her briefcase down next to it, strolled into the living room, and kissed Quadir on his cheek. "Whatcha doing?"

Quadir shook his head.

"Why so glum?" she asked.

"Doing some thinking."

"About?"

"Money, Gena, all of that stuff."

"You seem to never stop thinking about her. It seems like she's the only thing you ever do think of."

Quadir peered up. "How do you figure?"

"Oh, Quadir, please. It's true."

Quadir looked away. He wasn't quite sure what he was supposed to say. In a way, Amelia was right. Gena was all he thought of, her and his money. He often wondered whether, if she didn't have his money, he would ever have thoughts of her.

"I didn't tell you this, but remember the night you brought Gena here? Well, when I examined her, I realized she'd suffered a miscarriage."

"She was . . . pregnant."

"Yeah, she lost the baby, though. I guess Jerrell beat her so bad, she lost it."

Silence fell and a look of despair came upon Quadir's face.

"Are you okay?" Amelia asked.

The last thing he wanted to hear was that Gena had been pregnant by Jerrell.

"I said, are you okay?" Amelia asked again, realizing for the first time how deep his concentration was set in Gena mode.

He still loves her. Amelia realized the truth of the matter. She'd never thought in a million years that hearing Gena had a miscarriage would even remotely affect him. Honestly, she assumed that piece of information would drive him further away from her, and he'd let it go, let her go, even let the money go. However, his reaction indicated he wasn't about to let anything go.

"Quadir, I can't do this anymore," Amelia said in a hushed tone.

"Can't do what?"

"I can't pretend. Maybe you can, but I can't."

"Amelia, what are you talking about?"

"I'm talking about you, me, you and me. It's nothing, it's make-believe. You pretend to have feelings for me that you don't have, and I sit here and pretend like maybe, *just maybe*, you'll forget about her and love me. But the truth is you won't, and I'm tired of pretending that maybe you will."

"Are you saying that I'm in love with Gena?"

"I don't have to say it. Why does anyone have to say it? I mean, my God, it's written all over your face. She needs you, Quadir."

"Doc, I don't understand."

"That's your problem, Quadir. You always want to try to figure things out, you always want to try to dissect, to label, to understand and rationalize. Some things are not meant to be understood. Some things are because they simply are. You love her, she loves you, and right now, she needs you more than ever."

"And what about us?"

"What about us?" Amelia asked with a smile on her face. "Maybe we're meant to be together. Maybe we aren't. Maybe it's simply bad timing. Maybe in another life. I don't know. But I know this: you need to help her. You're the only one who can."

"Yeah, but—"

"But nothing, Quadir. I'm here, you know, and besides, you don't stop loving someone, Quadir. In fact, if it's true love, it never really ends. It changes, it grows deeper, more profound, it morphs into different manifestations, but it's always there. True love lasts through time and space and distance." Amelia paused for a moment, hearing her own words as tears welled up in her eyes. "She loved you, even when you were on the other side. You think I'll stop loving you because you're across the country?"

"I thought we were going to go across the country together."

"Sometimes people are meant to travel this life together for great distances, sometimes short ones."

"And you and me?"

"Who said our journey together is over? Who knows what the future holds for us, Quadir? But right now, what we do know is Gena needs you."

"And you don't need me?" Quadir looked down.

"No, I don't need you," Amelia said, knowing deep, deep down inside that she wished, dreamed, and even prayed for Quadir to be for her. However, no matter how much she prayed and wished on one hundred four-leaf clovers, he wasn't. And she knew in her heart she deserved better. She deserved someone for her, someone who would be only for her.

Of course I need you, and of course I want you. And I have been blessed to have you in my life. But I need one hundred percent of you, not half of you because the other half is still somewhere in the past. Amelia caressed the side of his face. Maybe she should've spoken those words, but she didn't, and she wasn't going to. She'd rather he thought the opposite than know she was truly and deeply brokenhearted.

"I really think you need to go to her. You need to work everything out with her, and then, if you're sure, sure your heart is free and you're sure you want to be with me, then I'll be here. But not like this. Not with all this hanging over your head."

"I love you," he said as he leaned forward and kissed her on her cheek. "I owe you my life. I owe you more than words can express."

"You owe me nothing, Quadir. The only person you owe is yourself. We get one shot at this game called life. One shot. And we have to take that one chance and live it to the fullest. Enjoy every fucking waking moment of it. Never let a sunrise go by without appreciating it and being thankful for a new day. Never walk by a pot of food without tasting it and never walk by a flower without stopping to smell it."

Quadir smiled and rose.

"You go and save Gena, you hear me? It's the right thing to do."

Quadir nodded.

"Wait a minute, before you go."

Amelia rose and rushed down the hall to her bedroom. She was gone for several moments before she returned. She handed Quadir a black .40-caliber Glock pistol and several loaded clips. "I know, I know. I'm a doctor. What the hell am I doing with that? Well, I'm also a single Black woman living alone."

Quadir shook his head and smiled. "Doc, I've never in life met anyone like you."

Amelia nodded and smiled. "My daddy says I'm crazy, but I get it from his side of the family. Hey, you go and find that girl. You find her, and you two get the hell outta this place. I don't want to hear from you again until you're safe. You understand?"

Quadir nodded.

"Unless, of course, you need me, and if you ever need me, you know where to find me. That Glock has a twin right in my closet, and

I'll bust a muthafucka's ass if I have to. I'll have to try to save the son of a bitch after I shoot him, but that won't stop me from pulling the trigger!"

Quadir laughed, leaned forward, and kissed her on her cheek again before turning and heading for the front door.

"One game," Amelia shouted. "The only game that matters—the game of life. Be true to that game, Qua. Be true to the game!"

Goose Chase

W ho is it?" Markita shouted.

"It's me!"

"Me who?"

"Me!"

Markita opened her front door to find a stranger standing before her. "May I help you?"

Terrell smiled. "Hey, baby, why you look so disappointed?"

Markita smiled but wasn't for the bullshit. If it wasn't for the fact the nigga was tall, dark, and handsome, she would've slammed the door in his face. *I ain't hardly disappointed,* Markita thought, wondering who he was and what he wanted.

"Were you expecting someone else?" Terrell asked.

"No." Markita was still smiling. "I'm not expecting anybody, but you gonna have to come on 'cause *The Young and the Restless* is on."

"Damn, it's like that?"

"Like what? What do you want?"

"Well, I'm a friend of Gena's, and she told me she was staying here. I wanted to drop by and see how she was doing and check on her, see if she needed anything."

Immediately, Markita let her guard down, not realizing the

handsome stranger standing in front of her was the enemy who'd been hunting Gena, not the friend he was pretending to be.

"Oh, Gena, she's not here right now. You want me to tell her you stopped by?"

"Yeah, that would be great. Do you think you can take my number down and have her call me?" Terrell asked.

"Yeah, sure. Let me get a pen."

And that was it right there. Markita turned from the doorway, took two steps, grabbed a pen off the coffee table, and turned around to find Terrell standing right behind her, her front door closed.

"What are you doing? I didn't invite you in."

"I invited myself."

Terrell began to unzip his pants and fondle himself in front of Markita.

"Oh my God! Help!" Markita screamed as she tried to run.

She made a dash for her bedroom and slammed the door shut, locking it simultaneously. She picked up the telephone receiver and dialed 911. But as the phone rang, Terrell busted through her bedroom door, saw her with the phone in her hand, and snatched it away, disconnecting the call as he slapped Markita so hard she fell back on the bed and onto the floor. Desperately, she began to crawl across her bedroom floor, but Terrell was on top of her as she reached the doorway.

"Where you going? The party's about to begin."

"*Heeellpppp!*" Markita screamed.

"Shut the fuck up." Terrell punched her head, grabbed her by her throat, and yanked her off the floor. "If you fucking scream, I'll kill you. Do you understand me? Do you understand?" he hollered like a maniac in her ear.

"Yes, yes, I understand. Please don't hurt me."

"You do what I say, everything I say, and I might let you live."

"Okay, okay," Markita said as she felt him letting go of her neck.

"Take your clothes off."

Markita didn't know what to do. She was standing there desperately trying to think of something to do or something to say that would get her out of the situation she was in.

"What the fuck is you standing there for?"

Terrell savagely attacked her, pushing her onto the bed and ripping at her clothes.

Markita attempted to fight him. She tried to use her strength, but Terrell was physically stronger, and he hit Markita again, this time on her face, immediately swelling her eye. It was then Markita stopped fighting. She let him have his way. As he pulled at her clothes and ripped off her pants, she simply lay there imagining it was a bad dream.

Terrell raped Markita repeatedly, pinning her down, holding the back of her neck as she lay on her stomach. Then he pulled out of Markita and quickly reinserted himself into her other hole. Markita almost leaped from the bed, but Terrell grabbed her arms and held her tightly. She screamed at the top of her lungs.

"Oh, God, please, no, stop, please, no!" she screamed as Terrell ripped into her. She could feel a wetness and suspected she was bleeding. The only sound besides her cries was Terrell's grunting. He sounded like a wild animal.

"Stop it!" Markita screamed. "Please, help! Please, stop!"

Terrell held her arms in place and continued to brutalize her anus.

"Stop it, please!"

More grunting.

"Help me, please!" she screamed louder.

Grunting.

"Help me!"

Grunting.

"Somebody help me, please!"

More grunting, followed by a wild cry of carnal pleasure as Terrell exploded inside her asshole. His thrusting and throbbing caused her to let out a bloodcurdling cry.

"Shut up! Shut up! You fucking whore, you know you like it." Terrell continued to breathe heavily, trying to regain his expended energy. "*Markita.*"

It was then she realized he knew her name, and she'd never told him.

"I have a question for you. And I need for you to be really honest with me."

"What?"

"I need you to call Gena for me and I need you to tell her to come over here."

"What?" Markita tried to force her way out from under Terrell. He gripped her arms tightly.

"You heard me. I need you to call Gena and tell her to come over here. You probably will have to make it sound like an emergency or something."

"How the fuck am I supposed to do that? I don't even know where she is. I don't even know how to reach her."

"Tell me where I can find her."

"I don't know!"

"Where can I find her?"

"I don't know!"

"Don't lie to me, Markita," Terrell said. "I know she lives here."

"Gena don't live here!" Markita struggled to break free. "I don't know where you got your information from, but they telling you wrong! Gena used to live in the apartment next door a long time ago!"

"Her cousin said you two live together."

"Her cousin lied!"

"Why would she lie to me?"

"Who the fuck knows! Get off me!"

"Tell me where I can find Gena."

"I don't know. I swear I don't know, and if I did, I wouldn't fucking tell you anyway," Markita screamed at the top of her lungs.

Terrell scooped her up and wrapped his massive arms around Markita's neck. He kissed the back of her neck and licked around to the right side of her ear, and then twisted in one quick, forceful motion. Her neck sounded like a dry twig when it snapped.

Terrell remained on top of her as her body spasmed and convulsed. Once he was finished, he climbed off her and began to search her apartment for evidence of Gena's whereabouts. Gena had lots of clothing in Markita's apartment, some of which she'd worn recently. It was in an older pair of pants where Terrell found what he was looking for: a business card for 4-U Self Storage.

Finders Keepers

Gena knocked on the door more forcefully the second time. Still no answer. Markita was known for hopping into the shower or getting lost in a damn soap opera and simply tuning out the rest of the world. *Oh, come on, Kita, I got to use the bathroom, girl.*

Gena knocked once again and twisted the doorknob to see if the door was unlocked. The knob turned. The door was open all along. She pushed open the front door and crept into the apartment.

"Markita."

No answer.

The television was on, as were most of the lights. The apartment looked to be even messier than usual, which wasn't saying a lot, because Markita's house was always junky. Gena made her way into the bedroom. It was dark, the bedroom shades and curtains were drawn, and sure enough, Markita was lying in bed.

"Girl, get your ass up. What are you still doing in bed? We got things to do. Come on, I need your help."

Gena tapped on her girlfriend's shoulder. Markita felt cold. "Markita?"

No answer.

Gena pushed her friend more forcefully, causing the blankets to move. The dried bloodstain over Markita's butt became visible. Gena covered her mouth.

"Markita!" Gena shook her friend. "Markita. Oh my God!" Gena pushed Markita over to find herself looking into her friend's open but lifeless eyes.

"Markita!" Gena grabbed her friend's wrist and felt for a pulse. There was none. "Oh my God! Oh my God!" Gena backed against a wall, then slid down to the floor and burst into tears. She knew what had happened. Whoever had hurt Gah Git had now killed her closest friend. *He must have been looking for me.* Yes, the crazy man had gone there looking for her, and Markita had paid the price. He'd done to her what he'd done to Gah Git, but even worse. Gah Git still had some life left in her after he'd gone, whereas Markita had none.

Gena wiped away the tears pouring down her face. She'd lost another best friend, another friend to bullshit. It was the city. The city was taking life away from her, slowly but steadily. It was closing in on her. It was out to get her. She had to get away, she had to run for her life. If not, she'd also be dead soon. She could feel it coming. Death was around the corner, creeping toward her. Slowly but surely, death was tracking her down.

Gena willed herself to rise. She kissed Markita's dead, cold, lifeless cheek. She was out of there. *Fuck Philly, fuck Richard Allen, fuck Quadir, fuck my entire life.* Gena was done; she was ready to go and never, ever look back. Philly had taken her parents, it had taken Sahirah, it had taken Quadir, it had taken Markita, it had almost taken Gah Git and Gary, and it was about to take Bria and herself if she didn't do something about it.

Gena moved away from Markita's corpse and made her way out to the living room. *Should I call the police? Just to get someone here? God, she'll be lying here all alone for days if I don't call. I have to do something. But what should I do?* Before leaving, Gena called 911 and reported the discovery of a dead body. She remained anonymous and imme-diately hung up the phone after giving the operator Markita's address.

Gena headed down the steps and climbed into her rental. She had to get out of town, and she had to go tonight. She'd meet with Rik, square him away, stash her cash, and then leave for good. She was heading south, maybe Norfolk, maybe Charleston, maybe Charlotte, maybe even Atlanta. She'd know once she got there. The only thing she knew for certain was she was going tonight. Her life depended on it.

Cornell Cleaver stepped under the yellow police tape and made his way into the apartment. He flashed his badge at the uniformed police officer guarding the door and was allowed to pass.

"What the fuck is IAD doing here?" Detective Smith shouted from across the room. "Nobody's fucked shit up yet."

"Curtis Miles!" Cleaver smiled. He walked to where the Homicide detectives were standing and shook his friend's hand. "It's been a long time."

"What's your ugly face doing here?" Miles asked.

"Just passing through," Cleaver told him.

"Passing through, huh?" Miles asked suspiciously. "Bullshit. Whose balls are you trying to break? IAD doesn't crawl out of its little cubicle unless it's trying to bust balls."

Cleaver lifted his hands and shrugged. "I'm just passing through, Curtis. Honest to goodness."

Miles waved to the gentleman standing next to him. "This is Detective Harmon Brittingham. He's one of my best detectives, and he's going to be the lead detective on this case. Harm, this here is Cleaver; he's IAD. Used to work for me in Homicide, used to work for me in Vice before that, used to work Narcotics before that. He used to be a real cop once, and now he's a ball buster."

"You flatter me with your kind words, Lieutenant," Cleaver told him.

"You come here to fuck with my guys, you let me know," Miles told him with a "don't fuck with me, either" look on his face. "Those are the rules of the game. You don't fuck with my guys without me knowing about it, you got that?"

Cleaver nodded. "Where's the victim?"

"She's in the bedroom." Miles peered up at the door. "Holy fuck, what the fuck we got going on here, a convention? This is a Homicide investigation, not a goddamn policemen's ball! What do you two numb nuts want here?"

Cleaver turned and spied Ellington and Davis making their way toward them.

"What the fuck is Vice doing here?" Miles asked.

"We heard she was connected," Ellington told him.

"I haven't heard that," Miles shot back.

"You're Homicide, not Vice, so you wouldn't have heard that, now would you?" Ellington asked in an aloof tone.

"Letoya, you're looking mighty tasty as usual."

"And you're still looking desperate, Lieutenant."

"How's your mother?"

"Good, since she's never met you."

Lieutenant Miles threw back his head in laughter. "I see your tongue is still sharp."

"And I see your belly's getting rounder. Picking up some weight, are we?" Ellington placed her hand over Miles's stomach and giggled at his belly.

"Watch it. Moves like that make it turn hard."

"How would you know?" Ellington smiled. "You haven't seen that shriveled little piece of meat since Nixon was in the White House."

The detectives and officers around the room laughed heartily.

"What we got here?" Davis asked, peeking through the bedroom door.

"Female, Black, early twenties, death by strangulation, looks like.

Coroner's on his way. We'll know more then," Harmon Brittingham explained. "You wanna see some weird shit?"

The detectives followed Brittingham into the bedroom. He pulled back the covers, displaying Markita's naked body. "She got fucked in the ass, probably right before her death."

"Or perhaps even during," Ellington suggested.

"Sick bastard," Cleaver chimed in.

"Judging from the amount of blood, it wasn't something she did on a regular basis," Brittingham advised.

"Raped?" Davis asked.

"She knew the perp," Cleaver added.

Brittingham shrugged. "I mean, from what I can tell, she let the guy in, but something went wrong. No telling what made it turn bad."

"The apartment looks like it's been ransacked," Ellington observed.

"Talked to the neighbors, and apparently the victim kept a pretty messy apartment," Brittingham explained.

"Any leads?" Cleaver asked.

"Forensics are on their way. We got semen, tissue maybe, definitely skin cells, sweat, perhaps some hair. All the usual trace elements from sexual intercourse," Brittingham advised.

"Whoever did this doesn't give a fuck if he's caught," Davis observed.

"He's probably not planning on being in town long enough to give a shit about any evidence," Ellington said.

"All right, spill it!" Miles ordered, watching Ellington and Davis summarize a case, although he had no clue what they were summarizing.

"What?" Ellington asked.

"What the fuck are you working on that made you show up here today? And how did you conclude this son of a bitch is planning to skip town? I want to know what you know, Detectives, and I want to know now!" Miles said forcefully.

"Remember the assault on the old lady that happened last month sometime?" Ellington asked. "The really brutal one?"

Miles scratched his head as he tried to remember. "I think I do. The old woman from the projects. She was raped."

"Jesus!" Brittingham whistled. "Same fucking MO. You think they're related?"

Ellington nodded. "I know they are. The girl he was looking for when he attacked the old lady was her best friend." Ellington pointed to Markita's naked dead body.

"Why in the fuck didn't you say so when you first walked in?" Miles shouted. "What is this, a fucking poker game or something? We holding our cards close, Sergeant?"

"What the fuck does Vice have to do with any of this?" Brittingham asked.

"The girl's fiancé was a major dealer who got popped. He was a Vice target. She was also a Vice target. Her new boyfriend popped her lover. He was a major dealer, and a Vice target, and then he got popped," Ellington explained.

"Who'd he get popped by, her third boyfriend?" Miles proclaimed. "Talk about some bad-luck pussy."

"So, who are we after here?" Brittingham asked, wanting his job to be as simple as possible.

Ellington shrugged. "I wish we knew. The only thing we do know is this guy is a fucking nutcase."

"I want the file on this one," Miles told her. "I want to know everything and I want to know it yesterday. I'm getting this son of a bitch off the streets."

Two dark-suited men stepped into the bedroom. They were young, clean-shaven, and well-dressed. They screamed Feds.

"And you two are?" Miles asked, not playing any more games with his crime scene.

"I'm Agent Harbinger, and this is my colleague, Agent Covington. We're from the Federal Bureau of Investigation."

"FBI?" Miles huffed. "What's your jurisdiction here?"

"Excuse me?" Josh asked.

"Well, we got Homicide, Internal Affairs, and now FBI. I guess DEA and Customs will show up next, telling me she was smuggling for the cartel. This whole thing stinks to high heaven. Why are so many noses interested in a young, dead Black woman with no criminal record, no known boyfriends, vices, or any other red flags in her history? Why is the FBI here, at a homicide scene? Don't tell me: she was kidnapped at the age of four? You heard me. Why are you here?"

Josh smiled. "Was she a victim of an abduction?"

"Don't get cute with me, son!" Miles bellowed. "What's the FBI's business here? I'm trying to conduct a homicide investigation."

"We're conducting a highly classified federal investigation," Josh told him. "We're going to look around, if you don't mind. By the way, why did you say you had Vice detectives here?"

"I didn't."

"Why are they here?" Phil asked Josh. He removed a notepad and pen from his pocket.

"And why is Internal Affairs here?" Josh added.

"Just leaving," Cleaver told them. He stormed from the room angrily. Fucking FBI. *I needed a chance to search the damn place and these assholes show up. Fuck! I'll have to come back later when the circus is over.*

Ellington and Davis headed for the exit.

"I'll get those files to you, Lieutenant," Ellington told Miles as she left the apartment.

Phil and Josh turned to each other and smiled.

"You wanna tell me what's going on here?" Miles asked, looking at Harbinger and Covington as the room cleared out.

"Hey, we wanted to jump-start the marathon," Josh joked as he patted Covington on the back.

"Yeah, get 'em up and runnin.'"

Let's Call It a Comeback

Michael pulled up his Lincoln Navigator in front of Gah Git's house. His mother looked somewhat tired.

"You okay?" he asked as he placed his hand on top of hers.

"Yes, son, yes, I'm fine. You gonna have to help me out this big truck you got," Gah Git said.

Bria hopped out and opened the door for her grandmother. "I'll help you, Gah Git."

Michael pushed Bria out of the way to assist his mother. "Here, I got her."

"Dag, Uncle Michael, just push me down the next time," Bria joked.

"Come on, Mama. Don't pay her no mind."

Gah Git agreed with her son. "That crazy child right there, is you kiddin' me?"

"Whatever! Say what you want. You know who be in here taking care of you, Gah Git. Uncle Michael's a visitor. I'm the one who's gonna take care of you."

"Lord, have mercy, I'll be all tore up in here with you and your crazy sister."

Gah Git looked at her granddaughter and thought of Irene, the twins' mother, who had died while giving birth. Gah Git thought of her daughter every day. Everybody did, but no one talked of the twins' mother. No one ever said Irene's name, ever. That's how Gah Git had ended up with the twins.

Gah Git brought them home from the hospital and went over to the funeral home the next day and buried her daughter. Gwendolyn's crazy ass was too busy doing other things, like getting high, to take care of Khaleer, so Gah Git demanded the youngster stay with her. And when Gwendolyn had Brandi, addicted to crack cocaine at birth, Gah Git stepped in and took her from Social Services. Ms. Bradley, the social worker assigned to Brandi's case, still came by from time to time to visit Gah Git. She'd been trying to get Gah Git to foster some abandoned children in the system, but Gah Git had her hands full.

Paula was the only child of hers who seemed to have it together. She worked at the bank as an assistant branch manager, she dated on and off, took her yearly vacations to the Caribbean, and was raising Zorian and Avanna on her own.

Michael swung open the front door as Bria held the screen door for Gah Git. Out of nowhere, the darkened living room lit up and all the family popped out of nowhere.

"Surprise!"

Everyone yelled in unison as Gah Git stepped through the doorway. Gah Git looked around the room at her family and thought her eyes were playing tricks on her. There were WELCOME HOME balloons and banners, and flowers from neighbors and well-wishers filled the tiny living room. Paula had cooked for two days and two nights, and if you didn't know better, you would've thought it was Thanksgiving.

"Malcolm? Malcolm, is that you?"

"Yeah, Mama, they done let a Black man be free."

"Malcolm, oh, son. I can't believe it." Gah Git used every bit of strength she had in her and embraced her son. It had been so long since she'd seen him. Tears rolled down her cheeks.

"I been praying, son, praying you'd come home. I'm so glad you're here. You just don't know," she said, still cradling her firstborn son in her arms.

"Yes, Malcolm, that's all she's been talking about: you coming home. We're glad to see you." Paula gave her older brother a hug as Gah Git finally passed him over.

Gah Git's heart lit up like the Christmas tree in Rockefeller Plaza as all her grandbabies ran over to her.

Gah Git joked with Khaleer. "You been sleeping in that bathtub, boy."

"No." He laughed at her, knowing darn well he had been.

"Yeah, brother, good to see you," Gwendolyn said, looking like she'd partied like a rock star all night long as she gave her brother a long embrace.

Royce extended his hand. "Yeah, man, congratulations on coming home."

It didn't take a rocket scientist to figure out his sister and Royce had a habit, a bad habit. Maybe he'd talk to her about it later. Let her know that no matter what, he had her back.

"Come on, Mama," he said, helping Michael get Gah Git over to the couch.

"Look who's here, your grandbaby Gary," Michael said as he moved Gary's wheelchair over to his grandmother.

"You can't walk, Gary?" Gah Git noticed the wheelchair and was about to get upset no one had told her.

"Of course he can walk, Gah Git. We stole that chair from the hospital and brought it home for you. So this way we can roll you around," Brianna said, bending over and kissing Gah Git on the face.

"Mm-hmm, roll me around, all right. I can see you rolling me right down a flight of stairs."

"Gah Git, nuh-uh, we love you," Bria said, standing next to her sister.

Michael patted his older brother on the back. "Hey, brother, we got to talk. I got some big things planned out for you."

"Yeah?" Malcolm replied.

"Hell yeah! Don't worry, big brother, you gonna be fine. Fine and dandy."

Malcolm looked around the room at all his family. Their smiling faces and warm embraces and love filled him with joy. He didn't know what to say. Everyone acted like nothing had happened. Michael had visited him many, many times. His brother had forgiven him a long, long time ago. He thought of all the time he'd missed, all the time that had passed him by. He was glad to be home.

At first, he'd been scared, but when he saw his little brother waiting for him outside those prison gates, he realized everything would be okay. He'd be all right. He looked at his family, laughing, joking, eating, and sharing one another's company. Just about everyone was there, everyone except Gena.

Gena pulled up to the motel room and extinguished her headlights. She saw Rik peeking out through blinds as she parked her car. It made her smile, and she waved to him. She looked around the parking lot. Rik's car was parked out in front where she could easily see it. Unknown to her, Rik and Quadir used to meet at this same motel back in the day when they did business. Rik had chosen the motel for sentimental reasons.

Gena turned off the ignition, climbed out, and headed for the motel room with the plastic bag of money in her hand. She imagined what it must've been like to do a dope deal. All the sneaking around, the intrigue, the secret locations, the peeking out of windows. They acted like they were James Bond or something.

Rik opened the motel room door and embraced her tightly. "Hey, baby girl!"

"Hey, Rik." Gena hugged him.

"How have you been?"

Gena shook her head and burst into tears. "It's too much. I'm going through it. You have no idea what I'm going through."

"What's the matter?" Rik asked.

"Markita, my friend, something bad happened to her."

"What's going on?"

"She's dead. I found her body," Gena blurted out. Her tears fell more rapidly.

Rik wrapped his arms around her. "I'm so sorry to hear that."

Gena wrapped her arms around Rik and began bawling. "And Gah Git, my grandmom, someone beat her and raped her, Rik. She's still in the hospital. And my cousin Gary tried to save her, and the guy shot Gary, and Bria's boyfriend."

"Who?"

Gena shook her head. "I don't know. He's trying to kill me. They all said the same thing, that this guy is looking for me."

Rik pulled her close and walked her into the motel room. He shut the door and locked it. "Gena, what's going on? Why would someone be trying to kill you?"

Again, she shook her head. "I don't know."

"You have no idea?"

Gena shook her head. "I don't even know what he looks like. He showed up one day asking where I was and started attacking people."

"But why you? Why now? Why all of a sudden? What do you have he would want?"

Gena pulled away. "I don't know, Rik! Why are you questioning me like this?"

"Gena, you offered me a lot of money when I was in jail."

"So?"

"Is he after the money?"

Gena shook her head. "I don't know."

"Where did you get that kinda money?" Rik asked. "And be honest with me, Gena."

"What does it matter where the money comes from? What difference does it make?" Gena lifted the plastic bag and tossed it to Rik. "Here's the money you asked me for."

She turned and headed for the door. Rik grabbed her.

"Gena, did you find Qua's money?"

"Rik, let go of me!" Gena yanked her arm away and unlocked the door. Rik pulled her back.

"Gena, do you have Quadir's money?" Rik asked more forcefully.

"Rik, let me go! What the hell is wrong with you?"

Rik slung Gena back onto the bed. Gena fell onto the bed and rolled off onto the floor. *This shit can't be happening again. Not again—not Rik!*

She rose and charged at Rik, digging her nails into his eyes. Rik howled, pulled her hands out of his face, and backhanded her. Gena stumbled back a few steps, then raced for the door. This time, she was able to get it open before he grabbed her.

"Help me!" Gena screamed. "Somebody help me!"

"Shut up and tell me where the rest of the money is," Rik shouted. He slung Gena onto the bed and tried to kick the motel room's door closed. The door flew back open. Rik turned to see what was blocking the door. Quadir was standing in the doorway.

Rik's eyes bulged from their sockets, and he backed up into the room.

Gena jumped onto Rik's back. He flipped her off him onto the floor.

"Son of a bitch!" Gena shouted. She spat at Rik, missing him by a couple of inches.

"Now, now, Rik. Is that any way to treat a lady?" Quadir asked. He leaned forward and helped Gena up. "Especially your best friend's girl?"

Rik reached for his weapon, but Quadir already had his drawn.

"Uh-uh, don't even think about it," Quadir told him, pointing his Glock at his friend.

"You sorry muthafucka!" Gena tried to go at Rik again, but Quadir held her back.

"Quadir, what the fuck is going on here?" Rik asked nervously. "What the fuck's going on? This ain't right, man. This shit ain't right."

"What's not right is trying to rob Gena for my dough, nigga. Now, that ain't right," Quadir told him.

"Qua, man, this is some twisted shit. I saw you, Ock. I went to your funeral. I was a pallbearer. This ain't no real shit."

Quadir nodded. "Oh, yeah, I'm real all right, which is a whole lot more than I can say about you, Ock."

Rik shook his head. "Man, you not understanding. I'm doing bad, Qua. Them Santero motherfuckers is going to kill me, man. If I don't give them they bread by yesterday, I'm a dead man."

Gena tried to spit on Rik again. "I was going to give you the money, you son of a bitch!"

"This ain't enough, Gena!"

"I woulda given you anything you asked for!" Gena shouted.

"So, you were going to do Gena in?" Quadir asked. "Instead of being a brother to her, and protecting her, and helping her, you were going to kill her and take the money I left for her? Damn, nigga, that's some fucked-up shit. I can't believe you."

Tears fell from Rik's eyes. "Quadir, you were dead! And she'd already moved on! She moved right on to the next dope boy. She wasn't coming around us no more; she wasn't being part of the family! She started fucking with the same nigga that did you! What the fuck, Qua? She wasn't family no more, and she betrayed you with them Junior Mafia muthafuckas!"

"Regardless, you ready to kill her, Rik?" Quadir asked.

"She betrayed you, Ock! For all we know, she set you up for them niggas! She could've been setting you up the whole time! Qua, she's brand-new to the game! But me and you, we go back to the sandbox, homie! It was us who used to be breakdancing up in my yard on cardboard boxes. It was us who got our first piece together! It's me, black."

The three of them turned toward the window when they saw the flashing red-and-blue lights outside. Gena raced to the window and peered outside. The patrolman was walking into the motel room office.

"It's one car," Gena told him. "Somebody probably called about the disturbance."

"I got a plan, Quadir," Rik told him. "I got a connect who's willing to send us so much snow, it'll be like January the whole year around. All I need is the money to square up what I owe. After that, they cut on the faucet, and the dope runs like water. We set up another crew and rake in the bread."

Quadir clasped Gena's hand and shook his head. "Thanks, but no thanks."

"Quadir, what is you doing? I need that money!" Rik shouted.

Gena lifted the bag of money off the floor.

"Don't tell me you not down, Quadir. I know you, nigga. I know how you get down for that paper, homie. Come on, baby boy, ride with me. I'm your brother, Ock. You gonna let me die, Qua? What part of the game is that?" Rik asked, not realizing Quadir was going to murder him himself.

"Qua, we gotta go," Gena said softly. She pulled him toward the door.

"Whatever happened to being true to that game?" Rik shouted.

Gena opened the motel room door.

"I need that money, Qua!"

"Rik, don't."

"I need that money!"

"Rik, don't!"

"I need that fucking money!" Rik reached for his weapon.

Quadir squeezed the trigger of his weapon several times, sending Rik flying back onto the bed. Just as the gunshots rang through the silent night air, the officer ran out of the motel office. Gena yanked Quadir out of the motel room, and they raced through the parking lot toward her car. The officer spotted them, Gena with a bag of drug money and Quadir with a loaded weapon in his hand.

"No, we'll never make it past that cop!" Quadir shouted. He yanked her in the opposite direction. "My car is parked around back!"

"Freeze!" yelled the officer. Without hesitation, he began shooting at his runaway targets. *What the fuck? This guy is trying to kill me, not capture me,* Quadir thought as a bullet skimmed right by him. He could feel the bullets in the air zooming by him as he made his escape. As they made their way through the dark parking lot, they wove and ducked as the officer aimed directly at them.

Quadir and Gena raced around the rear of the motel, disappearing as the police officer ran over to his squad car and yelled through the radio for backup.

The race was now on. They both had to get out of town, and they had to do it tonight—Gena because she had a killer lurking somewhere in the city desperate to find her, and Quadir because he'd murdered his best friend in a motel room.

Gena climbed inside Quadir's black Range Rover, and they raced down the street. She peered out the window, thinking about how many other lives would be lost because of the fucking money. She wished it would all burn to ashes.

"I loved him like a brother," Quadir said softly.

"I know," Gena told him. She placed her hand on top of his. "I did, too. I never thought he'd hurt me, though."

For the first time in a long time, she and her man were together once again, helping each other, comforting each other, and being down for each other. For the first time in a long time, the old Quadir and Gena were back.

Crime Scene 101

Davis strolled into the motel room, followed by Ellington. Lieutenant Miles rose from his knee and gave them a cynical smile.

"Well, well, well, here we go again. A regular fucking family reunion we're having. You two keep showing up at my crime scenes, I'm going to have you reassigned to Homicide. So, what gives this time?"

Ellington and Davis exchanged glances.

"Don't tell me. He was the other victim's long-lost uncle, who also happened to be a coke dealer you were investigating."

"He was our CI," Davis told him.

"He was a confidential informant for Vice. Well, isn't that convenient. Could that be the reason he's no longer with us? I wonder. I mean, working for a couple of numb nuts like you two could get somebody killed."

"Lieutenant, may we take a look around?" Ellington asked.

"Don't disturb anything; don't touch anything. Forensics has started their work."

Ellington nodded. "Anybody check his pockets?"

Miles shook his head. "Forensics will handle it. He was DOA when the first officer arrived on the scene. Seems there was a disturbance call about the room. So a patrolman was already at the motel office when the shooting went down."

"Do we have anyone in custody?" Ellington asked excitedly.

Miles shook his head. "The police officer ran out of the front office when he heard gunshots. He exchanged gunfire with the assailant before the assailant fled the scene. The police officer called for backup, then ran in here to the motel room, found the victim, tried CPR, and had someone call the paramedics. The police officer says he couldn't resuscitate the victim, so he immediately secured the room."

"Which was rented to?" Davis asked.

"The victim."

"What kinda commotion?" Ellington asked.

"A huge brawl. Thumping, crashing, banging, screaming, shouting."

"Screaming? Like a woman screaming?"

Miles nodded. "You got it."

"Any eyewitnesses?" Ellington asked.

"We're running down leads right now, but besides the officer, none," Miles told them. "And since you two are so interested in this case, why don't you make yourselves useful and go and help interview some of the motel guests and see if anyone saw or heard anything?"

Ellington and Davis exchanged glances.

"And I want to know everything you find out," Miles hollered.

Agents Covington, Harbinger, and Stokes strolled into the motel room.

"Well, well, well . . ." Miles shook his head and smiled. "Last time I checked, Philadelphia wasn't part of the District of Columbia, so murders here are within the jurisdiction of the state."

"Right you are about that, Lieutenant." Harbinger smiled.

"Then why in the hell do you keep showing up at my homicide scenes?" Miles asked angrily. "They say the perpetrator always returns to the scene of the crime."

"Are you accusing me of something, Lieutenant?" Josh asked.

"If I was, you'd be in handcuffs," Miles barked back.

"The day you try to slap handcuffs on me is the day you decide you want to spend a long time in a maximum-security federal penitentiary," Josh warned.

"Sir, we have something," an officer informed the lieutenant.

"What is it?"

"We have a witness who saw a man and a woman fleeing around the back of the motel."

"A man and a woman?" Miles asked.

"Any descriptions?" Ellington chimed in.

The officer shook his head. "No, too dark."

"Any description of a vehicle?" Ellington asked.

Again, the officer shook his head.

"She has a man with her?" Ellington asked.

"We don't even know if it's her," Davis said.

"It's her. But who in the hell is with her?"

"I don't know, but we're running out of time."

"Where would you go if you left a murder scene?" Ellington asked. "Where would she go that was safe?"

"I don't know, but if I was her, I know where I wouldn't be going. I wouldn't be going to Grandma's, or to her friend Markita's. Remember, she's still got some asshole out searching for her."

"If she's smart, she's on her way out of town. She's got to be. There's nowhere left for her to go. Especially knowing a maniac is after her," Ellington said. "She's getting out of town tonight."

"Who is this *she*?" Miles asked.

"It's in the report," Ellington told him. She and Davis raced out of the motel room and headed for their car. "She's going for the money!"

"Yeah, but where?" Davis asked, climbing into the vehicle.

"Where in the hell would you keep that kinda cash?" Ellington asked. "And remember, wherever it is, it's got to be accessible to her tonight. That pretty much rules out all the banks."

"So, where else do you store money?" Davis asked. He and Ellington stared at each other. The answer hit them both at the same time. "At a fucking storage unit!"

"Call Cleaver!" Ellington told him. "And the lieutenant!" She peeled out of the parking lot.

Neither of them saw the FBI agents in the Chevrolet Impala pull off behind them. And neither was aware a tracking device had been planted beneath their car.

"What are we doing?" Gena asked, peering out the window.

"What do you mean?" Quadir asked.

"I mean, this, all of this. What are we doing?"

"We're running. What does it look like?"

"I can see we're running. I'm trying to figure out where we're going from here."

"Safe, we're going somewhere safe."

"Safe, did you say safe? That's a fucking joke but, then again, I guess I would be safe with you, huh? Now you can call your wolves off, right?"

"Wolves? What are you talking about?"

"Quadir, because of you, my grandmother was brutally raped, Gary is all fucked up and needs more corrective surgery, and Markita is dead. She was raped and then killed."

"Hold on, Gena, I didn't have anything to do with what happened to Gah Git or Gary or Markita. Ever since you left, I've been looking for you. I'm putting myself out there rescuing you and all you can do is point the finger at me like I've done something. I saved you from Jerrell, remember? And if I hadn't come when I had, Rik would've had your ass tied up and buried six feet under."

"I thought . . ."

"You thought wrong. I don't know who's behind the attacks on your family. I figured whoever it is, he's after my money. Come to think of it, where is my money, Gena? Because I really want it back. I want my money back."

Gena sat and listened to every word he spoke with her eyes wide open. He was telling the truth. He didn't have anything to do with the attacks. *Then who the hell is after me if it's not him?*

"You haven't been after me to get your money back?"

"After you for what? Gena, you're going to give me my money back. I don't have to harm you or anyone else. You're going to give me my money back."

He spoke as if he had a crystal ball foreseeing the future. *Why does he think I'll give him anything? Is he crazy? Does he really think I'd give him all that money so he can go run off with his Doctor Dolittle bitch and have a merry life, while I have nothing? He must be mad. I won't do it.*

Quadir pulled the car over to the side of the road, put it in park, and took his foot off the brake. Raindrops began to drizzle, hitting the windshield with every breath he took.

"What?" Gena asked as she kept her eyes glued to the window, unwilling to face him.

"Gena, I want my money. Had I died, you'd certainly be the rightful owner of my hidden treasure. But you aren't, and I need you to do the right thing. I really, really, really need you to do the right thing."

"Or what, Quadir?"

He looked at her strangely. "What do you mean, or what?"

"What I said. Or what? If I don't give you back your money and do the right thing, then what?"

Quadir thought for a moment. Ever since they'd been together, he'd done nothing but provide for Gena, take care of Gena, and love Gena. To this day, he still did. He couldn't believe she was so selfish and greedy that she wouldn't willingly give him back his paper.

"Then this is where we say goodbye. You go your way and I go mine."

"Just like that, you'd let me go? You'd let me walk away with your money?"

"Gena, if I had to hurt you, or do anything outside my character to make you return my money, then I wouldn't want it. I want my money—yes, I do. I hustled for that shit, I died for that dough, so of course I want my money. But you have it now and I can't make you give it to me. It's not a pawn, it's not an option, and it's not a deal. There are no deals here, Gena.

"You want to give me my money back, fine. You don't want to give me my money back, then all that shows me is I was completely wrong about you. And if I'm wrong, then I don't want to be right. You take it, have it all, if that's what you want, but I swear to God, you'll never, ever have to worry about seeing me again. Ever."

He spoke with true conviction in his voice. He wanted to be as forceful as possible without hurting her. He didn't know if she believed him, but every word he spoke was the God's honest truth. If she didn't tell him where his money was, he had every intention of leaving her standing on the side of the road. He had every intention of moving on, even if it meant moving on without her.

She watched as the rain fell and listened to every word. Deep down, she realized he was right. Once she gave him the money, she'd probably never see him again. The money was his, all his. It wasn't hers. And the right thing to do was to let him have it. If that's what he wanted, she'd oblige him and give it back.

"It's at 4-U Self Storage," she whispered as she kept her head turned away from him. The last thing she wanted him to see were her tears. The little bit of pride she had was swallowed up by his demands and the reality that she'd be left with nothing, not even him.

A Deadly Ringer

"Excuse me, may I help you?" the storage night watchman asked.

"Yes, I'm looking for a storage unit," Terrell replied in all seriousness.

"Oh, we have plenty. What size unit do you need?"

"No, you've already rented the unit I want."

"I'm sorry, come again? I don't understand."

"I'm looking for a storage unit in the name of Gena Scott," Terrell said, hoping and praying this guy was smart enough to give him the storage unit number.

"I'm not following you." The guy brushed his blond hair back from his forehead.

Terrell noticed a Range Rover pulling into the storage unit. He watched the truck park and noticed the girl and the guy immediately.

"Never mind, thank you."

"I'm sorry. Excuse me, you can't go out that doo—"

Terrell silenced the night watchman with a gunshot to the head. He slumped down like a cartoon character. Terrell stuffed his body under a desk, placed a sign on the counter that read BE BACK IN 15 MINUTES, and walked out the door the night watchman had told him he couldn't use.

Quadir pulled up to the storage facility and parked around the back. He peered around the nearly empty parking lot and thought twice about where he was parked. He backed the Range Rover deep into a wooded area next to the storage facility, parked, and then followed Gena past various units until she came upon hers.

She used her key to unlock the lock, opened the door, and showed him the two suitcases filled with his cash. Quadir rushed over to the suitcases, opened them, and breathed a sigh of relief. His money was there.

"Let's hurry," he told her.

Quadir lifted the suitcases as they both headed for the door, only to find a stranger waiting for them.

"Going somewhere?"

I thought he was dead. Oh my God, nobody dies anymore? What's he doing here? Gena thought to herself, amazed at the dead man in front of her.

"Jerrell," Quadir said, unsure, and knowing Jerrell had died during their altercation in the motel room.

"Naw, nigga, don't look so amazed. You act like you don't remember me. Nigga, we grew up together."

Quadir realized it wasn't Jerrell at all but his brother, his twin brother. "Terrell?"

"That's right, you do remember me. I used to fuck you up at the playground, nigga. You couldn't hide, either, remember? I'd find you and whoop your little ass and take your fucking lunch money."

Gena still wasn't connecting the dots. "Who is he?"

"He's Jerrell's twin brother, the one that's been after you. He must've thought you killed Jerrell." Quadir added that line with mad sarcasm, hoping to catch Terrell's attention. "Truth is, you should've been after me, Terrell. I'm the one who killed your brother, not her. And all that talk about the playground, just know it's a new day, nigga, and I'll murk your ass like I buried your brother."

Ice-cold blood ran through Terrell's veins at Quadir's confession.

He stood toe-to-toe with Quadir. Their eyes met, and Terrell saw no remorse. Quadir's face was emotionless. He had no sympathy and no regard for what he'd done, and to top it all off, he had the nerve to admit it was him who'd murdered his brother.

Who do this nigga think he is? Him and this bird-ass broad? I'm going to fuck her while he watches. We'll see how cocky this motherfucker is then.

Quadir saw the gun first, and he reacted. He slung one of the suitcases toward Terrell, distracting him. Terrell caught the bag as Quadir dove into him, knocking the gun away and sending it sliding down the hall. The two of them fell to the floor and began to struggle. Gena realized it was him. This had to be the man who'd brutally violated her grandmother, the man who'd shot Gary, the man who'd shot Bria's boyfriend, the man who'd killed Markita. And now she understood why. He looked exactly like his fucking brother. He'd been stalking her to avenge his brother's death.

Terrell and Quadir grappled with each other, rolling around on the floor, jockeying for position while trying to free their hands. Each was occupied with not allowing the other's hands to become free. Both men understood they were in a life-and-death struggle.

Terrell landed a punch squarely on Quadir's jaw that stunned him and allowed Terrell to throw Quadir off him. He immediately began to crawl for his weapon. Quadir grabbed Terrell's leg and yanked him back. He punched Terrell on his back and side and crawled back on top of him. Terrell elbowed Quadir in his stomach and rolled over, again knocking Quadir off him. Quadir threw a wild punch, striking Terrell in his chin. He followed with a left cross that struck Terrell's nose.

Terrell swung and landed a solid blow on the side of Quadir's head. This blow was followed by one that landed on Quadir's ear. Quadir wrapped his hands around Terrell's throat, determined to squeeze the life out of him. Terrell broke Quadir's grasp by kneeing him in his testicles. Pain shot through Quadir's body, causing him to cry out.

Quadir's wounds had closed, but they had not fully healed. His tissue began to pull apart from the inside, causing a searing pain throughout his body. He wasn't going to last much longer, not going blow for blow with the monster he was battling. But then again, he couldn't lose. His life and Gena's life were on the line. Not to mention, if he ended up at another crime scene, Amelia's life also would be affected, and he didn't want that. If his body were found, there would be some serious consequences behind it. Amelia would lose her license and probably even go to jail. Gena would lose her life, and that would send her grandmother to an early grave. So many people depended on him at that moment. So many people were counting on him to be the man they always believed him to be. Was he truly gangsta? Was he really built to last? Were they all wrong for looking up to him, admiring him, wanting to be like him?

Quadir summoned every piece of strength he had left in his body and swung at Terrell. The blow sounded like it could be heard clear across the city. He followed it with another blow, and then another. He wanted to put this nigga to sleep. But Terrell had other plans.

Terrell growled and head-butted Quadir, opening a gash between Quadir's eyes, right above his nose. Terrell realized Quadir was built to last. He wasn't going out like no sucker. He wrapped his hands around Quadir's throat.

Gena could hear Quadir gasping for air. She raced down the dark hallway searching for Terrell's gun. Desperate, she dropped to her knees and scoured the floor until she found it. Quadir needed her. And despite what she'd said before, she didn't want him to die. She loved him. She wanted him to live. She needed him to live. No matter what happened between them, no matter what was going to happen between them in the future, she wanted him to live, even if that meant he'd be with someone else.

Gena raced back to where Quadir and Terrell were struggling and pointed the gun. She was scared to pull the trigger. Scared of hitting Quadir instead of Terrell. Scared of having to kill another human being.

Quadir's eyes rolled to the back of his head, and he leaned forward slowly. Terrell smiled, knowing he was squeezing the life out of Quadir. There was nothing like killing a person with one's bare hands. Quadir leaned forward until his and Terrell's faces were nearly touching. And then he smiled. He was a built-to-last nigga.

Quadir opened his mouth and clamped down on Terrell's nose with the ferocity of a hungry pit bull. He shifted his last bit of energy to his jaw muscles and bit until his teeth met. Blood ran down his chin as he rose and spat Terrell's nose down the hallway. Terrell covered the bloody hole where his nose used to be and rolled around on the floor, screaming in pain.

Quadir kicked Terrell in the head, then stomped his head down into the ground so the back of it hit the concrete floor hard. He stomped again, and again, and then again. After the fourth stomp, blood oozed from the back of Terrell's head, and he stopped moving completely. Quadir turned to Gena, who rushed into his arms.

Quadir was barely able to stand. His old wounds felt like someone was sticking a red-hot poker into his flesh. He was out of breath, tired, and sore all at once. "Help me pick up all of the money," he said weakly. "We got to get out of here."

Dick Davis hung up his cell phone and turned to his partner. "Ratzinger said this thing's getting out of hand. He wants us to tighten things up."

Ellington peered over at her partner. He looked pale.

"Dickie, what's the matter?"

"He wants us to kill her," Davis whispered. "He wants us to kill her and whoever's with her. No witnesses."

Ellington nodded. She'd known what the deal was from the beginning. Gena's death warrant had been signed the moment they'd all agreed to go after that money. Davis was green. "Dickie, are you okay on this?"

Davis nodded. He hadn't bargained on having to kill anyone. He thought it would be a matter of taking drug money away from some undeserving little dope dealer's woman and distributing it among police officers who truly deserved it. But murdering people over it was something else entirely. Would that make them worse than the drug dealers?

"What did Cleaver say?" Ellington asked.

"He said there's only one self-storage place along this highway open this late. That's 4-U Self Storage."

"He give you an address?"

"Yeah."

"Well, let's go and get our fucking money," Ellington said excitedly.

"Josh, it's Steve over in technical," Lavon Stokes said.

"Hi, Steve!" Josh shouted toward the receiver.

"Josh says hi, Steve," Lavon told him. She turned back to Josh. "Steve says they intercepted a call from Ratzinger, giving the order to kill the girl."

"Holy shit! They got it on tape?"

Lavon nodded. "He says he's already played the tape for Galvani, who had it played for the US attorney and one of the federal magistrates. The judge is heading into his office to sign the arrest warrants as we speak."

"Yes!"

"The US attorney is going before the grand jury first thing in the morning with evidence," Lavon told him.

Phil patted Josh on his shoulder. "Good work."

"Ask Steve where those assholes are right now. I want to slap the cuffs on them as soon as the warrants are signed," Josh said.

"Steve, you got a location on the suspects' vehicles?" Lavon asked.

She turned back to Josh. "Cleaver's vehicle is headed this way. Ellington's car is right up ahead. Ratzinger is still at the station."

"Good work, Steve!" Josh shouted toward the handset. Then he said to Lavon: "Get rid of Steve, and call Tony, Mike, and Dan. Have Tony and Mike round up Ratzinger and tell Dan to meet up with us as soon as we give him a location. We can take down Cleaver, Ellington, and Davis all at once. Get some more agents out here. We're going to get these sons of bitches tonight!"

The Getaway

Ellington pulled up about the time Cleaver arrived.

"Are you sure this is the place?" Cleaver asked. "I hope I don't look like an asshole."

"What's with the patrol cars?" Ellington whispered.

Cleaver shook his head. "I called them. That little bitch isn't giving us the slip this time. There's a fire escape around the back of the building. I'm going to send the officers in through the front while we cover the back, which is probably how they intend to escape."

Davis nodded. "Good thinking."

"Ready to get paid?" Cleaver asked with a smile.

A gun went off inside the building, causing several of the gathered officers to duck and scatter for cover.

Several black Suburbans raced into the parking lot. Josh, Phil, and Lavon leaped out of the lead SUV and rushed up to Ellington, Davis, and Cleaver.

"Nice night for an arrest, isn't it?" Cleaver smiled.

Josh smiled and shook his head. "You took the words right outta my mouth, you sack of shit."

"Turn around and place your hands on your heads!" Lavon shouted.

"What?" Ellington asked.

"We're fucking cops, you assholes!" Cleaver protested.

Phil and several other agents had their weapons drawn.

"I said turn around and put your hands on your heads!" Lavon shouted again.

"This is bullshit!" Ellington said. She turned and placed her hands on her head. Davis did the same.

"Turn around and place your hands on your head!" Josh told Cleaver.

"Will you wait a goddamned minute!" Cleaver shouted. "I'm Internal Affairs, and you're interfering in some serious police business!"

"I'm FBI, and I say you have no business being a police officer!" Josh told him. "Now stop resisting before I have Phil shoot you!"

"We have suspects inside!" Cleaver shouted. "And a damn gun went off."

"The real cops will take care of it!" Josh told him. "Now turn around!"

"You fucking asshole! They're escaping around the back!" Cleaver shouted.

Josh drew his weapon.

"You're going to let them fucking escape!" Cleaver shouted. He pulled away from Josh and began running.

Josh holstered his pistol and chased Cleaver, tackling him by the side of the building. The other agents quickly came to Josh's assistance. They manhandled Cleaver into submission and handcuffed him.

"They're getting away!" Cleaver shouted. "Agent, let me talk to you in private! I have an irresistible deal for you!"

Josh turned to Phil. "Go and listen to his deal and then add attempting to bribe a federal agent to his charges."

Phil laughed and headed off to an SUV where the other agents were shoving Cleaver inside. Lavon walked up to Josh.

"And what are we going to do about them?" she asked, nodding toward the storage facility.

Josh shrugged. "Not our business, Lavon. Not our business. We're here to bust some crooked cops."

Lavon lifted an eyebrow. "Somebody's getting away with a lot of money in there."

"It's her money, and judging from the things that have happened to her, she deserves it. Hey, Lavon, I get my jollies fucking over the big guy, not the little ones." Josh walked to the front of the building and stared up at it. "You better run, girl. And you better take that money, and you better do something with it. Do something good with it."

A patrolman walked out of the building.

"Find anything?" Josh asked.

"Two bodies. The night clerk and an unidentified Black man," the officer told him.

"Anybody else?"

The officer shook his head. "No, sir."

"Call Lieutenant Curtis Miles from Homicide," Josh told the officer. "Tell him that, in all probability, I've got the murder suspect he's been searching for lying dead in there."

The officer nodded and headed for his patrol car.

"Wow, we saved the day, huh?" Lavon asked.

"We sure did. Good work, agent," Josh told her. He pulled her close and wrapped his arm around her. "C'mon, let's get outta here. Buy you a hot cup of coffee."

"And a doughnut?" Lavon asked, as if the coffee wasn't enough.

"Sprinkles?"

"Yeah, sprinkles."

One Year Later

The water was absolutely postcard perfect. It looked like someone had clicked a button on a computer and chosen the perfect color blue for a brochure ad. Royal blue faded into aquamarine see-through water, breathtaking, simply beautiful, a few shades darker than the cloudless baby blue sky sitting above it. Gena couldn't believe she was back where it all started: the Valiant Hotel on Paradise Island in the Grand Bahamas.

Palm trees swayed gently in the soft breeze, moderating the temperate Caribbean climate even more. The weather was a perfect seventy-seven degrees, while beneath the white silk canopies it felt like it was no higher than seventy.

All the guests were dressed in white. The women wore white cotton beach gowns while the gentlemen all wore white cotton shirts and pants. All the guests wore sandals, since the ceremony was being held on the white sand beach. White gardenia floral arrangements were arrayed around the canopy and the tables and chairs beneath it. Eighteen white doves that had been imported from Europe sat in cages around the beach, waiting to be released at the conclusion of the nuptials.

Gena sat alone in a small dressing room. Everything was perfect. There was no detail left unfinished, nothing more to do. The day had dawned with a perfect, sunny, cloudless sky, and who could ask for more? Gena thought back to the night she'd met Quadir in Harlem on 125th Street. Who could've known? Who could've guessed? They'd been through the fire together without getting burned.

A gentle knock at the door brought Gena out of her reverie.

"Come in," she said as she watched a tall, handsome man, wearing a tuxedo and looking like a million bucks, stick his head around the door. "Daddy, come here." Gena reached out for the father she'd never known.

"You look like a princess," Malcolm said, his eyes beginning to water. "I don't know if I can do this, Gena. All those people out there and all."

"Daddy, you'll be fine. I'm going to hold your hand and we're going to walk together like we did last night at rehearsal." Gena smiled at him reassuringly.

"I wish your mama could see you," Malcolm said, envisioning his wife in his daughter's smile.

"I know, Dad, I know. Listen . . ." Gena took her father's hands into her own and stared up into his big, strong brown eyes. "We can't change the past, but we can change where we go from here, from now on. It's okay. My mother's not here. The only thing that matters to me is that you are. You're here. And I'm so, so grateful for this day."

"Baby girl, you think you're grateful. Them white folks had me locked up so long, I don't know if I'm coming or going, and I don't have much . . ." Malcolm stopped for a minute to clear his throat. "But I'd give my life for you, Gena. I'd give my right arm for you to have this day."

"Oh, Daddy, I love you," she said, embracing her father.

"I love you, too, baby girl. I love you, too."

"Hey, whatch'all doin' in here?" Michael asked, peeking through the partially open door. "Wow, Gena, look at you. You must be the most beautiful bride I ever laid my two eyes on."

"She sure is," Malcolm agreed.

Gena rushed over to her uncle. "Uncle Michael!"

"It's been a rough couple of years, but you weathered the storm. You and Quadir have nothing but smooth seas ahead," he said with his hands firmly on Gena's shoulders. "I pray God blesses your union today and for the rest of your lives," Michael added, congratulating her.

"Oh, Uncle Michael, you're going to make me cry, too." Gena made her way over to the mirror for one last glance. "Look, my makeup, y'all."

Michael gripped his older brother's hand and hugged him. "You okay, brother man?"

"Yeah, I'm here. I don't know what I'm doing, but I'm here."

"Hey, don't worry. I got you, man."

"Seriously, though, I need to take you up on that offer. I can't walk her down this aisle, man."

Michael looked at his brother and then down at his watch. "Okay, guys, let's go. Let's make time."

Holding a bouquet of white roses in her hands, Gena stepped out into the hallway and found her wedding party all lined up, waiting and ready to make the walk.

Everybody was there; not one person had been left out.

Viola walked over to Gena and kissed the side of her face. "I don't think I've ever seen a more beautiful bride."

"Thank you, Viola, for everything."

Viola took another look at the wedding party, nodded with approval toward Gena, and gave the cue for the music to begin. The groomsmen and the bridesmaids took their places at the altar. The flower girls and the tiny ring bearer walked down the red carpet next. Viola took her seat next to Montell and her daughter, Denise, as the bride appeared at the doorway.

"Aww" was all that could be heard as everyone turned around to see Malcolm standing tall and proud on her left and Michael standing tall and proud on her right. Everyone there knew about the situation between the two brothers, the death of Gena's mother, the reasons of it all, and even Gena's questionable paternity, but on this day, none of that mattered. The only thing that mattered was they were all there together. For Gah Git to see both her boys standing side by side after being separated for so, so long brought tears to her eyes. No matter how hard she tried she couldn't stop crying.

"Gah Git, you okay?" Paula asked.

"She all right. She's crying at the sight of Malcolm and Michael holding Gena," Gwendolyn said, grabbing a tissue out of a crying Royce's hand and handing it to Paula to pass to Gah Git.

"Give me my tissue back, woman," Royce demanded.

"Fool, don't start wit' me on this goddamn island out here in the middle of nowhere," Gwendolyn whispered harshly at him as she passed the tissue to her sister.

Paula frowned. "It's been used."

"So, it ain't gonna kill her." Gwendolyn shoved the tissue back at Paula.

Gena, her father, and her uncle made their way down the aisle.

"Dag, Uncle Malcolm looks good, right?" Brianna whispered.

"Mm-hmm, *real* good. He looks better than Uncle Michael," Bria whispered back to her twin.

"I see why Gena's mom was letting them both dick her down."

"Mm-hmm, she sure was," Bria added as Gena's two bridesmaids snickered to each other throughout the entire ceremony.

Gena looked like she belonged in a Walt Disney World parade. She glowed like a fairy-tale princess wearing Cinderella's gown, about to finally kiss her Prince Charming.

A Caribbean band played the traditional wedding march as Gena made her way to the floral altar. Only the minister was wearing black. When they finally reached the end of their walk, her uncle Michael reached down and kissed her cheek before stepping to the side. It was Malcolm who then placed his daughter's hand into Quadir's. He looked at her father, and the two men nodded at each other with approval. Holding hands, Quadir and Gena faced each other.

"Dearly beloved, we are gathered here today to join together these two young people in holy matrimony."

But the moment of all moments was when a tiny Quanda stepped forward and handed Quadir a red-and-gold Cartier box containing their wedding bands. It was probably the sweetest gesture of the ceremony.

Quadir bent down and took the box out of Quanda's hands. "Thanks, baby girl."

"I now pronounce you husband and wife. You may kiss the bride."

Acknowledgments

Mom, Corel, Jessica, Chuck, Dexter, Carl, Brenda, Lucas, Brandon, and my girlfriend, Kashan.

Oh yeah, my secretary, Tracy.

Thanks.

About the Author

New York Times bestselling author Teri Woods began selling hand-made books out of the trunk of her car in 1998. To date, she has authored, coauthored, and self-published over twenty-one titles. She has sold millions of books worldwide; she jump-started the entire urban fiction genre and helped create millions of dollars in revenue for Black independent authors and major book publishing companies. Her book series, *True to the Game* and *Dutch*, have been successfully turned into major motion pictures and that can be viewed on multiple streaming platforms. Teri Woods has also written eight children's books. She is currently working on several projects, including a sequel, *True to the Game 4*.

To transcend decade after decade, never saying a word, simply being read . . . is truly one of God's greatest gifts.